## WHEN THE SNEAKSOULS CAME…
The story of those who wore the Chi Rho

by

Susan Fielden

*This tale is not fantasy but a future possibility,
for who can say what is in the future may not seem fantasy to us today.*

*THE YEAR IS 3533 CE …*

Copyright © 2021 Susan Fielden
All Rights Reserved.
No part of this book may be used or reproduced by any means, graphic, electronic, or mechanical, including photocopying, recording, taping, or by any information storage retrieval system without the written permission of the publisher except in the case of brief quotations embodied in critical articles and reviews.
Published by edfbooks

# PART ONE

## STOLEN SOUL ...

Slicer smelled blood, live blood, pumping through veins and arteries, setting his razor teeth clacking.

Crouched in gorse bushes beneath the pillar-like cliffs they call Donkey Crags, his gaze was fixed on the narrow path winding up from the valley.

Peggy, his ganglefowl was hunkered beside him, gangly legs tucked beneath her plumped-up feathers. Nearby lay an old dog-wolf, not long dead, and Slicer had to keep an eye on Peggy, as now and then her long neck snaked towards the carcass, hoping for a peck of fresh meat.

Two figures drew near his hiding place: the first – his boss – he let pass, then he pounced, crushing the second in his steel and muscle arms. Throwing the body to the ground, he plunged. Slicing twice across the throat with his razor teeth, warm blood swirled around his tongue, filling his mouth with a fishy savour he'd never tasted before, sending ecstasy trembling through his orange pelted body.

Slicer is a Frit, an android killing machine of flesh and metal. His speciality is his famous slicing action, which is how he got his name.

Frits ride the ganglefowl: a specially bred bird, with long gangling legs, flesh-tearing clawed feet, and rump feathers which, when they contact warm flesh, inflict a sting so painful it sends the victim crazy.

Slicer wondered what species it was, that tasted so good. Shutting his camera lens eyes, he booted up his database. Clicking on Species Recognition, he scrolled down the list to click on Bipeds. A choice came up: Humanoid, Gaiakin, Others. He clicked Humanoid. There was another choice: hairy, naked. He selected naked. A sub-list came up: skin colour: yellow, black, brown, pink. He flicked his eyelids open and studied the body's face and hands: the skin had a shade of green. He returned to Bipeds and clicked Others. There were three choices: Skwids, Boskies, and Rarities. He found what he was looking for in Rarities: a biped with pale green skin. Attached were the following records:

*Extract from The Polychronicon of Zagzagel.*
*DELPHINS.*

*Simian species. Mesozoic era. Returned to oceans and intermingled with dolphin species. Returned to land as a Plesiadapiform. Hid in remote places, evolving into humanoids.*
*Short in stature. Hardy: did not succumb to the Great Dying of 2100. Skin: green-hued. Small eyes, slanting eyebrows, wide mouths, more teeth than homo sapiens. Flaps of skin behind ears, indicating ancient blood line. Speaks Common Language but has preserved ancient language of clicks and whistles. Some show trait of syndactylism: two or more digits growing fused together.*

*CONTAGION FRIT FACTORY RECORD:*

*Threat: weak. Intelligence: no information. Religion: worshippers of Phul. Eating Qualities and Availability: This species is a luxury delicacy.*

Slicer's eyes snapped open. Drooling, he smacked his rubber lips: he'd never eaten Delphin; his usual fare was tough old ganglefowl. About to take a bite, a stinging pain shot up his arm. Squealing, he cringed away.

His boss was standing over him, dagger in hand, the long blade dripping Frit oil.

'Keep yer thieving claws off,' snarled the harsh voice from inside the Delphin called Roach Dandrum. 'No eating 'til I've searched the body!'

A shiver fizzled through Slicer's electric wiring. In the depths of Roach's eyes glimmered a sinister green light. Roach might look like a runty Delphin on the outside, but inside lurked the dark presence of a demon. This demon was called Raaum, a servant of Lord Gressil. Known as Phraggs, they invade living bodies, sucking out their souls, becoming Sneaksouls.

Raaum was on a mission: to search for a certain Delphin named Marlin Dandrum who owned a treasure Lord Gressil greatly desired. It was Marlin, recently invested as Head of the Delphins, who lay dead at Slicer's feet.

Raaum had come upon Roach, Marlin's younger brother, full of fire-whisky after their father's funeral, wandering in a drunken haze along the borders of Withered Wood. Sneaking into Roach's body and sucking out his soul, he'd sent it to the Land of Contagion, for the feeding of Maabella, Lord Gressil's Queen. So, Raaum the Phragg now looked out of Roach Dandrum's eyes: Roach's soul no longer inhabited his body.

Scuttling back into the gorse, he snuggled into the comfort of Peggy's soft feathers and licked his arm where his boss's knife had cut deep into his orange fur, exposing fleshy muscle and a network of copper wires.

He watched Raaum searching the corpse with Roach's stubby fingers, gingerly avoiding the gaping throat wound. Inside Marlin's leather jerkin he found a gold medallion on a leather cord. Ripping it off and studying it closely, he threw it away with an irritated snort. Opening the shirt front wide, he gave a throaty gasp: the Delphin's chest had a deep raw wound. The wound was strangely shaped; in the style of an X overlaid by a P, about the size of a man's palm, the outline so clear it could have been cut with a branding iron.

Overcome by curiosity, Slicer sidled out from the safety of Peggy's feathers.

'Boss, how come Lord Gressil's t'rested in this povvy carrion? I don't see no jools!' His mechanical voice box had taken on a wheedling whine.

Raaum spun around and glared suspiciously. 'If you've found something, you'd better hand it over!' he snarled.

Terrified, Slicer cringed away. 'I ain't pinched nothing!'

Impatiently pushing the lifeless body over, Raaum searched down the back of the shirt, and finding nothing, Roach's brow puckered in a distracted frown.

'Fetch that wolf's body over here,' he growled, 'then make yourself scarce whilst I play the distraught brother and blow an alarm on his hunting horn.'

Dragging the carcass next to Marlin's body, Slicer carefully laid it out as if it had just dropped dead. Taking an arrow from Marlin's quiver lying nearby, he thrust it deep into the wolf's side, releasing a whiff of guts and giving his smell sensors a pleasing tickle.

'Nice 'n juicy: I'll be back for that wolf when it's safe,' he silently promised himself.

Seeing his boss occupied fumbling for the silver hunting horn at Roach's waist, he snatched up the gold medallion from the ground. Tearing off the leather cord and shoving the disc into his grubby loin cloth, he clambered onto Peggy's back. Heaving on the reins he brought her to a standing position. Digging his metal heels into her flanks, they scrabbled up a rocky path between the crags, heading to the high moors and the border of Withered Wood.

Meanwhile Raaum, lifting the horn to Roach's lips, blew a long-drawn-out blast, sending a silvery note ringing across the valley...

# 1
# SUSPICION OF MURDER

Lark Annunder heard the horn. Striding on the path beside the river, he looked up towards Donkey Crags: had they caught the wolf?

Early that morning, instead of going on the hunt as he had hoped, his Uncle Hollin had ordered him to deal with the rabbits infesting the woods bordering the lower meadows.

'Take yer jill ferret and her new kits; the warren's ripe for harvesting, and the kits need training up.'

Seething with resentment, Lark had watched the hunting party preparing to set off. Armed with crossbows and spears, hounds milling around their legs, the males of Dandrum Den had gathered by the courtyard gates: Marlin, his brother Roach and Roach's son, Kelp, accompanied by their ghillie, Lark's uncle Hollin.

Fin, Marlin's son, was not with them.

The castle-like home of the Dandrums, rising out of rocky cliffs, was known as Dandrum Den. On the right stood the imposing Great Hall, its tall windows covered with thin horn to keep out the weather. On the other side stood the farm buildings: kitchen and brew house, cow shed, kennels, with living quarters above for the farm workers and ghillies. A narrow passage led to the kitchen gardens, the pigsty, and slaughterhouse. A high stone wall made up the fourth side, with wide wooden gates, at present standing open, allowing a view of the farmland beyond, and a road winding down through fields, orchards, and meadows to where the river Brightwater flowed through Brightdale valley, marking the end of Dandrum lands.

The road crossed the river over a stone bridge, and on the far side, the way divided into three. To the left, a footpath followed the river north-westward towards the forests and high fells of Annunder Territory. To the right, a well-trodden highway ran east alongside the river for some fifteen miles, through the lower Dale and on to the borders of Brightdale. The track ahead led past outlying cottages, to the market town of Watersmeet, with the Spinner lands beyond, bordered by wild forest and heather moorland above.

Yesterday, Hollin and Lark had come to Dandrum Den to report the slaughter of six lambs on the lower slopes of the fell. The Dandrum males were sat by the courtyard wall drinking beer in the warm Saprise sunshine; they had escaped the depressing atmosphere in the Great Hall where their women folk, sobbing into their handkerchiefs, were still mourning the death of Old Fin Dandrum, the much-loved Head of the clan.

'I reckon t'were a lone dog-wolf hiding up in the caves below the Donkey Crags that took the lambs,' Hollin had said, gesticulating vaguely towards the north-west.

Roach lowered his mug and gazed around challengingly. "I'm good for a hunt – females' weeping and wailing's giving me belly gyp. How about it lads?" His voice sounded unusually harsh for a Delphin, as if he had a bad sore throat.

'I could try out my new crossbow!' his son, Kelp said eagerly.

Roach turned to Marlin: 'How about it brother – bring back our young days?'

Marlin gazed speculatively in the direction of Donkey Crags, his cold sea-green eyes troubled. 'It seems a lifetime since I went hunting, Roach.'

'Aye, too long!' Roach growled, taking a gulp of beer, and belching noisily.

Grimacing at the foul smell, Marlin put down his mug, and stood up to go. 'Right, I'm off now, down to Watersmeet. Promised to meet the Sheriff at the Meeting Barn. Now father's gone, and I'm Head, I need to go through the Statute Books with him.' He frowned in thought for a moment. 'Perhaps I'll call in at the Bookshop, to see if Fin would like to come on the hunt.'

Kelp gave a snort of scorn. 'Wouldn't hold out any hope, Uncle Marlin! Fin hates hunting – ever since last Leafturn when he nearly got us all killed by that great boar, fumbling with his spear, and tripping me up, just as I was aiming with my crossbow.'

Marlin sighed. 'Aye, you're right, Kelp. Fin's better off learning his letters with old Mossy.' He headed for the courtyard gates, shoulders bowed.

Watching him go, a baleful green light flickered for a second in Roach's sinister eyes: as his brother had put down his mug, he'd spotted a metallic glint inside his open shirt.

Seeing Hollin and Kelp were deep in discussion of hunting tactics, he cautiously followed his brother. Sidling out through the gates, ducking into the shadows by the outside wall, he watched Marlin's slender figure as he made his way down the Watersmeet road, passing the fields, newly green with shoots of young barley and wheat, and dipping out of sight when he came to the orchards, resplendent with creamy white and pink Saprise blossom.

From deep inside his chest Raaum's voice rasped: 'What's that shiny thing around your neck, Delphin? Make sure you're back by dawn: you and I have an appointment.'

After the hunters had gone, Lark had collected his equipment from the ghillies' shed, depositing Silky, his jill ferret with her two kits, into their carrying box. Whistling to Mick his terrier, he'd set off for the warren. He hoped to take at least two pairs of rabbits for the Dandrum kitchen, useful food in the lean time of Saprise.

Setting up his nets over the dark rabbit burrows pock-marking a sandy bank, he took the ferrets from their box, and tying a long cord to Silky's collar, sent her with her kits down one of the holes. Hunkering down in a bed of last year's dead bracken, he gazed across a dell of lemony primroses to the warren and watched for signs of activity. Mick crouched by his head, his warm body so close, Lark could feel his little heart thumping.

It was a hidden place where Lark and Mick lurked: an ancient forest of oak, ash, beech, and alder with an underwood of hazel, birch, crab apple and willow, the buds on their branches ripe for bursting into yellow and emerald leaves. Lark inhaled the scents of new growth: Saprise was under way at last. Ahead lay Highsun, with the promise of warm days and velvet nights.

This Highsun's Rout he would finally find the courage to ask Thetis Dandrum to come Skinny Dipping; then they could get married. That is the Brightdale tradition: a moonlight Skinny Dip down by Aidan's Shrine, where the Brightwater ran slow and deep by a sandy river beach, and marriage arranged next day. But before then, he had to get Silky's kits up to scratch. Impatient at the lack of activity, he tugged on the cord snaking across the dell, disappearing down the net-covered hole: it remained slack.

Lark's thoughts turned again to Highsun, and his plans for him and Tissy. He wondered what Roach would think of his ambition to marry his youngest daughter. Her family didn't treat her right he thought angrily; she let them boss her, but she was cleverer than any of them. She was nifty too with her fingers; at present she was embroidering dolphins on the Dandrum Ceremonial Cloak, choosing just the right coloured threads, silvers mixed with blues and greens. He pictured her deft fingers working magic, transforming the silver twine he'd given her into foamy waves where embroidered dolphins leaped and dived against a sky of blue velvet. Aye, the silver thread made a grand present for her birthday. She'd kissed his cheek in thanks!

'Glad I spotted that shiny thread on the Rom stall at the Market,' he whispered to Mick, patting the terrier on his smooth head. Mick wriggled impatiently, staring unblinking at the netted holes. Old Dinah, Lark's ancient terrier, had died last year and one-year old Mick, her son, was being "trained up". Lark still mourned Dinah: she'd been his close companion since he was fifteen, when he had come to live and work at Dandrum Den.

Lark gazed dreamily into the undergrowth, thinking of his beloved Tissy's eyes. You could swim forever in their lavender and green ocean and never drown of boredom. Some say her beauty is marred by her hare lip, but they must be blind; her puckered lip makes her special. His Grammer Nutmeg had told him how Mr Mossy had sewn up her lip when she was newborn, leaving just a small scar. Brave baby Tissy never let out a whimper, Grammer had said.

'Goes to show, Mr Mossy isn't all that dangerous,' he whispered to Mick. 'Mind you, if you got on the wrong side of the great black giant, you'd find out his power right enough.'

Mr Mossy wasn't Delphin. He'd arrived in Brightdale one day and set up his bookshop in Market Place, so long ago that there is no one living who can remember when. The story goes that when he first arrived, his great height and black skin caused much consternation, and some Delphins were for telling him to move on. Gradually he was accepted, not least because the Dandrum Head at that time befriended him. He got the name Mossy, because of his hair: the curly silver mass reminded folk of the moss festooning the trees in the deep forest. His real name no Delphin knew, other than his friend Marlin Dandrum.

Listening to his master's chatter, Mick whined softly, allowing himself a swift glance up at the face of his god, before whipping his gaze back to the warren: he'd picked up the scent of frightened rabbit.

Mick knew his skills were just as important as the female ferret's. His body a ball of muscle, his reaction lighting quick, his bite deadly. He was an essential part of the team of Delphin, terrier and ferret: yes, ferrets came last, being brainless, bloodthirsty creatures. Ferrets who ate the kill were not tolerated: their job was to flush out. Ferrets were no good with rats: that was his job. He was a deadly rat-killing weapon – with brains. He looked up in irritation at a branch above their heads where a thrush, its speckled chest swollen out, had decided to start a long and complicated aria. Above the racket, his keen hearing picked up a shriek of fear, the pitch so high, he knew his master couldn't hear it. So, he alerted him, sitting tall, his muscles taut in readiness to spring.

Lark felt a strong tug on the cord as a wild eyed, furry face appeared behind the net covering one of the holes. In a trice, Mick was across the dell and on the hole. Hardly had he killed the rabbit when two more appeared at other holes, caught in the nets. His master was there, only seconds slower, catching one, whilst Mick dealt with another.

A few moments of frantic action saw two more dead before Lark concluded that Silky had flushed out all the rabbits in that warren. They'd taken six. As only one of Silky's two kits had reappeared, he would have to dig out the other. Firstly, he dealt with the catch: gutting and trussing with practised skill, throwing the entrails to Silky and her kit. Half an hour's hot digging later, he found the other kit, earth covered and angry. Slinging his spade over one shoulder, the rabbit bodies strung by the back legs from the shaft, and the ferret carrying box over the other, he set off home.

As he loped along, Mick trotting ahead, he thought about the call from the hunting horn. Had they killed the wolf? How he wished he were with them!

His thoughts turned to Fin. Before setting off for the hunt, they had waited a while for him to appear, but he didn't show up. Lark had agreed with Kelp, who'd said it was a good thing the lanky half-breed hadn't joined them.

In Lark's opinion, Fin was too indulged by Grammer Nutmeg and Tissy: all that 'lovely handsome Fin', 'poor motherless lad', stuff was over the top. He, Lark, was also motherless, but his mum was dead: she hadn't run off like Fin's crazy ma had done. But what do you expect from a Rom woman? Fin's half Rom too, and it shows, what with his long legs and dark hair. He was already taller than is natural for a Delphin. And then there were his disconcertingly different coloured eyes: his right iris nut brown, inherited from his mother's dark Gypsy eyes, and his left iris, cold sea green, inherited from his father. He could be weird too: look at the strange day when Master Marlin reappeared after being gone, nearly nine years, searching for Fin's ma. As if Fin somehow knew his father was coming back, sitting all day on the frosty ground by the courtyard gate, saying he must be ready, his dad was coming home.

'As for him being friends with those Spinner twins!' Lark seethed, his resentment growing. 'Mick lad, don't you think it's about time the two lasses settled down, instead of tom-boying about the Dale with Fin? Other Delphin females of their age have been Skinny Dipping and are married, some even starting a brood.'

It had been a mistake sending Fin for learning with Mr Mossy at the Bookshop. He should have been made to learn proper skills – how to use a crossbow and spear, how to track deer and such. Scribbling in books is not natural for a Delphin lad. He'll be Head one day, and he won't know a thing about running the farm and keeping an eye on the encroaching forest.

As for the Evil that lurks over to the West beyond Withered Wood – an ever-present threat – would he be any use leading the Delphins in driving them off? He didn't think so! If it were to happen that Master Marlin passed on, perhaps it would be better if Master Roach took over as Head. Lady Ramora, Marlin's and Roach's mother, would like that.

Lark pictured Roach as Head. 'Not a good idea,' he exclaimed loudly, causing Mick to stop and look back, his ears pricked enquiringly. 'Now don't you be telling anyone, Mick, but I've my suspicions about Master Roach – Grammer Nutmeg reckons he's been taken!'

Nutmeg had got that idea into her head when Roach had wandered off after Old Master Fin's funeral, and nobody could find him. The family reckoned he'd gone to drown his sorrows with wine and women in Rascal town with its population of criminals and outlawed Delphins. But Nutmeg believed he'd wandered too near the Withered Wood and his soul had been taken by a Sneaksoul. He'd returned after a few days, pale and sullen, his few spoken words strangely harsh, his clothes in a mess, but seemingly unharmed; he wouldn't say where he had been.

Mick trotted ahead, ignoring his master's muttering.

Hearing another blast of the hunting horn, Lark stopped and frowned: it had in it a note of distress. Suddenly anxious, he started to run, taking a detour towards Donkey Crags.

As he drew near, he saw Master Marlin lying on the ground. Master Roach was crouched beside him, his hand resting on Marlin's chest. Nearby lay the body of a wolf. Recognising the distinctive red feather fletching of the arrow in the wolf's flank, Lark thought the animal must have attacked when Marlin shot it. But when he came close, seeing the gaping wound in Marlin's throat, his blood chilled – no wolf could have done such an injury.

'Teg's knackers!' he gasped, flinging down his rabbit-festooned spade and box of squeaking ferrets.

'Mind your language lad, near the dead!' snarled his uncle Hollin, his face a sickly grey, the hounds huddled around his legs. Nearby, Kelp was being noisily sick into the gorse bushes.

Roach shot Lark a momentary glare before making a show of weeping. But Lark hadn't missed the sinister sickly green gleam in his eyes. Had he imagined seeing him searching inside Marlin's open jerkin? Something was very wrong with Master Roach; the face was the same, it was his eyes, they weren't Master Roach's washed-out grey eyes. Was Grammer Nutmeg right, had Master Roach been taken?

'Was it that wolf?' he asked Hollin, indicating the now stiffening carcass.

Hollin frowned and nodded, uncertainty in his voice. 'Aye seems it must have been. Best get on now: there's now't more we can do here. We must take Master home – fetch our spears, Lark; we'll make a stretcher with master's cloak.'

Staring at the wolf's death snarl, Lark wasn't listening. He couldn't see any trace of blood on the teeth.

'Get a move on lad!' Hollin shouted.

Stumbling over Mick, Lark ran to fetch the spears. Tying Marlin's cloak to the shafts, slinging the straps of his box of ferrets over his shoulder, he and Hollin lifted the body on to the makeshift bier, and carrying it between them, they set off. Kelp, helping his weeping father to his feet, followed.

Trudging down the path back to Dandrum Den, none of them noticed the tall figure looking down from one of the pinnacles of Donkey Crags, the drapes of his long ink-blue robe stirring in the breeze, the slender form of his lurcher dog close by his side.

Mossy gazed down on the little procession, his beautiful ebony-skinned face puckered with sorrow. 'Farewell, Cross Bearer! Marlin, my friend – may your soul dive with the dolphins and may Phul be there to greet you in the tropical sea!'

A sob from his chest made his hound look up, fear in her brown eyes. Taking her by the collar, Mossy pulled her away from the pinnacle's edge. 'Come Lass, we must return home – to bring the evil news to young Fin!'

On the other side of the valley Fin Dandrum, stretched out on a grassy bank also heard the call of Roach's hunting horn. A skylark trilled high above as it soared and dipped in the golden dawn. He'd been sent here by Mossy, to search for the rare blue gentian, and had found a small clump by a sheltering rock, hidden among the other alpine flowers, primroses, violets, spangling the dewed grass in hues from pale purple violet to sky pink. As he leaned closer to study the array of petals, the purple blue started to fade turning to a cloudy blue green; he fancied he could smell the salt tang of the sea.

He was sinking through warm salty water. Below him a dark forest of sea kelp swayed, to and fro, to and fro. Suddenly, a swimmer shot out, and darting away, disappeared into the hazy depths. There was something tantalisingly familiar about the way the figure moved. Kicking hard with his heels, Fin tried to swim after him, but the vision drifted away, and he found himself once more in the open air, his face pressed into the patch of blue gentian.

Blinking from the brightness, he sat up and looked about him: nothing had changed, he was still on the fellside, the sun was still just peering over the moorland behind him. The skylark still trilled above. Across the valley, he heard the distant crying of lapwings on the high tops as they fluttered and dived above the roofs of Dandrum Den. Guiltily, he turned away, not wanting to be reminded that he'd broken his promise to his father to go on the wolf hunt.

Yesterday evening his father had visited the Bookshop. For a while they sat drinking nettle tea in Mossy's room above the shop; his father on the sofa beside him, hugging his mug close to his chest, a yearning look in his eyes as every now and then he glanced at his son.

Mossy broke the silence, suggesting they go down to the shop. 'Marlin, come and see Fin's work.'

Reluctant to be there whilst his father looked at his drawings and writing, Fin stayed behind, finishing his tea. Absentmindedly massaging behind Lass's ears as she leant against his leg, he thought about his father: he wished Marlin could have been more like Bird and Bee's dad. Absolem Spinner would roar at the twins sometimes if they'd done something bad, but just like the sun reappearing from behind a passing cloud, they'd soon be taken into his arms for a hug.

His thoughts brightened: this Highsun he and his father were going camping together. It had been his father's suggestion, and had it come as a surprise. 'As you'll be Head one day, you must get to know your territory,' Marlin had said. 'We'll spend a day or two in Rascal town, before going on to the borders, then follow the river through the lowlands to the coast, where you can see how the Scavs earn their living.'

Ever since, Fin had been excitedly planning what equipment he should take. He'd already collected most of what he would need, especially parchment and charcoal for sketching. Mossy had joined in enthusiastically, lending him various items. 'Take my second compass, Fin. And you must have a new flint box, too. Yours is falling to bits. I've a map showing all the various important landmarks along the river, make sure you keep it in your plustic envelope along with your sketches, so they don't get damp.'

His rucksack became so full, he'd had to repack it several times.

His tea finished, he went downstairs, finding Marlin waiting for him by the front door. 'Your handwriting is better than mine, Fin,' his father said. Looking at his son's work seemed to have cheered him. 'Come, walk with me as far as the bridge: I've a favour to ask.'

Wondering what he could do for his aloof father, he eagerly agreed. At the bridge, they stopped to look over the parapet and listen to the river, in full snowmelt rushing in the shadows beneath the arches. A fierce longing filled Fin: to jump in and let the flow carry him along, through the fields of Brightdale, past Rascal town, over the border, through the dense uninhabited lowland forests, to the muddy estuary where the Scav people lived, before flowing out into the wild grey sea. Like all Delphins, Fin had an inbred yearning for the sea: legend has it that they were once sea creatures who evolved, over millions of years, to walk the land.

Fin saw, in the fading light, his father's shadowed face had a troubled look. 'Your Uncle Roach has got up a hunt for tomorrow,' Marlin said. 'He's hoping to clear the fellside of a rogue wolf. He's asked me to go with them. Will you come too? I know you hate hunting but stick close to me— we'll look out for each other.'

Fighting down panic, Fin knew that the hunt could be opportunity to prove he wasn't completely useless with crossbow and spear. 'O.K.,' he said hesitantly, 'I've been target practising and I've hit the bullseye several times.'

Marlin smiled bleakly. 'You needn't get involved in the kill, just back us up.'

'Right, but I ought to check with Mossy first,' Fin muttered lamely.

But back at the Bookshop, Mossy, keen for him to find a specimen of the rare blue gentian flower before their petals closed in the bright sunlight, made plans for an early rise the following morning.

As Fin settled down to sleep on the sofa, Mossy called from his bed in the corner: there was a chuckle in his voice. 'I challenge you to find the right colour mix that will come anywhere near the amazing blue of the gentians.'

Inwardly guilt-stricken about his promise to his father, Fin had called back. 'I bet you'll cheat – using magic to conjure up a new paint out of the air!'

Drifting off into sleep, he'd soothed his conscience with the thought that he would only be in the way on the hunt, and they'd get on better without him. He loathed hunting: getting out from under warm sheepskins when it was still dark, bare feet freezing on the privy's stone floor, then out into the icy dawn without breakfast. Stumbling across the courtyard to the ghillies' shed, trying to find a suitable spear for his height. Then the vile business of the actual hunt: tracking down a quarry, his insides churning at the sound of a boar grunting in the undergrowth. Finally, the terrifying violence of the kill, with the sudden sharp stink of blood and viscera.

That was last night. This morning, his conscience still raw, as they ate breakfast Fin became aware that something was troubling Mossy. Finishing their porridge, they had wandered into Mossy's back garden, and sat on the bench encircling the old apple tree, waiting for the light to show in the sky above the cottage roof. Fin noticed Mossy glancing anxiously across the river in the direction of the Dandrum lands. Finally, Mossy had jumped to his feet and began distractedly pacing the path between the vegetable beds. Bending to pluck at a clump of dandelions, he crushed a golden bud between his brown fingers.

'What is it Mossy?' Fin asked, looking at the mangled flower lying on the path; Mossy usually had a deep tenderness for anything growing.

Mossy started, as if he'd forgotten Fin was there. He forced a bleak smile. 'It's nothing – just being fanciful! But I think I'd better go and....' his voice trailed off as he frowned again towards Dandrum Den. He turned to Fin. 'It's light enough now lad. Get your collecting box and go to find the gentian. Take the path past Spinner Hall and on towards the tops.' He pointed to the east.

Fin had followed Mossy's directions to the heathland. Mossy referred to it as an area of sugar-limestone, where he would find an interesting plant community. 'A relic from the last ice age,' Mossy had explained, in what Fin thought of as his teaching voice, 'there could be sheep's fescue, dog's violet, eyebright, bird's eye primrose. Among them will be the gentian, which only flowers for a very short period. Pick samples only where it grows in good numbers.'

Now he'd found the flower, Fin felt a strange reluctance to leave this peaceful place. But he knew he should be getting back; he wanted to start his painting before Mossy returned from his mysterious errand. Carefully picking a spray from the clump of plants, he laid it gently in his collecting box. As he did so, he heard the horn again. This time it had a strident, urgent note: they must have caught a wolf. He knew he should have been there, but it was too late now. Shading his eyes against the sunlight flashing on the river, he stared across the Dale. He spotted two distant figures, Mossy and Lass, making their way over the open moor towards Donkey Crags. Hearing a low humming, he spied a Drone Bird flying low across the horizon. He shivered: Drone Birds were a rare sight in Brightdale. Was it an omen for good or bad? Gathering up his equipment, he set off down the path back to Watersmeet.

# 2
# HALF-BREED

Hurrying back to Watersmeet, Fin passed Spinner Hall, home of his friends, Bee and Bird. Hoping they might be around, he listened at a crack in the tall gates; from the other side, Wolfie, their deerhound, snuffled and growled. About to pull the bell rope, he changed his mind: this early in the morning the twins would still be asleep in bed.

Thinking about Bird asleep, he imagined her tousled hair, the colour of green-gold wheat, spread over her pillow. He'd never dared tell her how he longed to kiss her. If he had, she would probably have had a fit of giggles, like the time Sparrow Chippen had tried to steal a kiss from her when they were dancing at the Harvest Hop.

He stood for a moment listening to the Whippetwater tumbling towards the Brightwater, the air full of the strong smell of garlic from the ramsons growing beneath the trees along its bank. An ancient oak loomed by the path; the tree house still sat in its twisted branches.

The twins' father, Absolem, had built it when they were small. Fin and his cousin, Tissy often used to play there with the twins whilst Grammer Nutmeg gossiped with their Grammer Magette in the Spinner Hall kitchen. Sometimes Fin, being the best reader, would read from story books borrowed from Grammer Nutmeg. When he'd read all of Nutmeg's limited collection, Tissy suggested that as Mossy had a shop full of books, they should borrow some of his. He and the twins had shuddered at the idea. Tissy had surprised them by announcing that once she'd plucked up courage to go into Mossy's shop. He'd left her to wander about, studying the books on the shelves, whilst he carried on writing, scratching with an ink laden quill on a piece of parchment. But she'd got scared when his dog woke up and squinted at her from under the table – remembering that it was a spirit dog, that it could change into a snake and bite her – and she'd run out.

He remembered in Highsun, when the branches were thick with leaves, if they were very quiet, they could spy on people as they passed below. Once Mossy came by, accompanied by a man as tall as him; a lean giant with red-gold hair, his thin face weary, leather clothes worn and stained, but on his back, encased in a silver sheath, a great sword. Then there was the time a group of Skwids had loped past. Keeping to the undergrowth along the side of the path, the strange creatures were so quiet at first, they didn't spot them. But then, Tissy catching sight of an iridescent flash of scaly green, let out a shriek, making the Skwids' lizard-like skins ripple pink and orange in alarm as they strode away towards the fells. After the Skwids had gone, they hadn't dared to move for ages in case they came back – Skwids had a reputation for eating small tender-fleshed Delphins.

The tree house was old now, the rope ladder rotting, the heather thatching on the sloping roof covered in green moss, and full of holes.

He was startled out of his reverie by the sound of clattering buckets from Spinner's Forge, not far down the path. Sam, the twins' older brother, was drawing water, ready for opening. Fin hurried on.

When he reached Market Place, he found it lively with activity: the townsfolk were preparing for the first market of the new year, when traders of diverse races would come with their wares along the broad river road from the eastern coastal regions.

Gypsy Roms were the most regular visitors to the market, arriving in their brightly painted horse-drawn caravans, bringing salt, sugar, exotic spices, rich silks and velvets, and their much-prized hunting dogs. Over the years, Fin tried to find out more about the Roms. He'd hang around their stalls, hoping to see in the women resemblances to his own non-Delphin features: his straight nose, square jaw, and high cheek bones. He realised that all Roms had brown eyes, like his own right eye. He'd once found the courage to ask a group of Rom women if they remembered a Miryam Smith, but as his mother had been gone over eighteen years, the women hadn't known her.

Then there were the bands of mud-encrusted Scavengers. Commonly called Scavs, their history much like that of the Delphins, some believe their blood lines are related. Small and hardy like the Delphin race, they did not succumb to the Great Dying. Some settled in the northern lands, on the salt marshes around the mouths of three rivers, where they scavenged rubbish which over centuries had drifted in on the tide, accumulating in the mud. Even now, there are useful quantities of pieces of glass, metal and plustic to be found.

(The reader should note that plustic – or plastic as it was known during the 20th and 21st centuries – was once a vital material for manufacturing, highly adaptable and cheap, but unless recycled, all the plastic ever made is, of course, still in existence – plastic bags take over two thousand years to vanish.)

Gathering and selling these fragments is a lucrative trade. The Scavs come backs bowed beneath bulging sacks of their foraging, which they unload and spread out in untidy heaps. Rusted metals in one pile, in another worn down nuggets of coloured glass. The plustic is divided into two distinct heaps: a heap of ragged, parchment-like stuff, faded grey or beige, useful for wind and waterproofing, the other pile different shaped pieces of plustic, in washed-out colours: pale yellows, blues, greens and pinks.

Once Bird bought Fin a small piece for his birthday – it looked like a pale pink leg with tiny neat toes. The Scav she bought it from, eyeing Fin, said it would ward off long legs. Bird's brother, Sam Spinner drilled a hole in the top for Fin to hang it on a cord about his neck. He lost the strange trinket when swimming in the river. He used to believe that was why he'd grown long legs. He knew better now – his legs were long because he was a half-breed.

The most eagerly looked-for visitors to the market were the Tall Folk, mysterious people dressed from head to foot in flowing robes that shimmered like a rainbow dancing about a waterfall. Those who glimpsed a face beneath a deep hood would spy a marvellous beauty. Delphins would empty their savings to purchase their cleverly crafted jewellery, as well as produce from their famed Garden of Florain: bags of fat ripe sunflower seeds (so good to keep you going when working out in the fields) and exotic fruits: tongue-curling lemons and oranges, prickly pineapples, fat bunches of purple grapes, dripping with juice; all grown in their hidden garden where it is always Highsun, somewhere in the north.

Mr Mossy is friendly with these magical folks who occasionally visit his Bookshop. Once a bold Delphin ventured to ask Mr Mossy who his friends were; Mossy called them Gaiakins. The enquirer was left none the wiser.

At the bookshop, Fin saw no sign of Mossy and Lass, so taking the key from under the mat, he let himself in, entering a small lobby from where a passage led to a scullery and the back door. Ahead, a flight of stairs rose to a dark landing, with a water bowl marked 'dog' placed on the first stair, and to the right, from where there came the smell of leather and rabbit skin glue, a curtained archway led into the Bookshop. Drawing back the curtain he entered the shop.

Fin was fifteen when he came to learn at the Bookshop; his father had been home from his wanderings searching for Fin's mother for six years. It was the first time that Fin had come close to Mossy, his eyes meeting a blue-robed chest, before looking up into the lovely black face smiling down at him. Gazing up into his dark eyes, for a fleeting moment he'd fancied he was caught up in the vastness of a universe full of brilliant stars.

He remembered his dismay as he looked at the hundreds of scrolls and books stacked on the shelves around the walls and wondered how many years it would take him to read them all. He'd never been inside the Bookshop before, although he'd sometimes peer in through the dusty window at the big oak table in the centre of the room, covered with a jumble of book related items. Once, when he and Bird were loitering outside licking Berry Banquets, Bird had pressed her nose to the glass, and Mossy's face had loomed into view, so startling her she dropped her Berry Banquet in the dust.

On that first day, Mossy had tested Fin's writing skills, helping him on to a tall stool at the table, and putting before him a sheet of creamy parchment, and a pot of ink by his elbow. Choosing a feather quill from a jar, Mossy sharpened the point with a craft knife. 'Let me see your penmanship, lad. Start by writing your name, age, address etcetera.'

Shakily dipping the nib into the ink, Fin started to write his name, Fin Dandrum. The creamy sheet seemed vast. While he struggled, Mossy busied himself, pouring out rusty-red lumps from a jar among rows of others at the back of the shop, and grinding the lumps to powder in a mortar. After a fraught struggle, and many blots, Fin produced a few spidery words. Mossy considered the result. 'Not too bad – you'll need to practice. Now let me see your drawing. Your Grammer Nutmeg says you have a real talent.'

With fresh parchment and a stick of charcoal, Fin was much happier. Proud of his skill with clouds, he quickly drew geese flying in formation across a wintry sky. Mossy exclaimed in admiration. 'Fin, that is good. Your father also has a talent for drawing.'

The picture was still pinned on the wall, alongside his sketch of Grammer Nutmeg's rough hands lying in the folds of her starched apron, so real looking they could have waved at you.

From that first day, his life changed utterly. Early every morning he would set off down the hill to Watersmeet, glad to get away from his family and the endless criticism from his grandmother, Ramora, and his aunt Brewdy, Roach's sour faced wife. Worst of all, had been the glowering resentment from Old Fin, his grandfather who, never reconciled with his eldest son marrying a Rom woman, unfairly blamed Fin for Marlin going searching for her when she had deserted them, soon after Fin was born. Well, now Old Fin was dead, and Marlin was Head, so he hadn't that problem anymore.

Each day at Mossy's seemed happier than the last. Sometimes writing, sometimes drawing, or sometimes looking through a book or a scroll. If they were in a foreign language, Mossy would translate passages, tracing his long finger over the strange words. 'One day I will teach you these languages Fin,' Mossy said, 'then you will be able to read these books for yourself.'

On warm Highsun days, they would sit in Mossy's back garden, on the bench under the apple tree, talking and reading as the Whippetwater rushed beneath the cliff beyond the lane outside the garden hedge. Across the lane, a privy leaned precariously over the water.

Occasionally Fin would stay the night, sleeping wrapped in a blanket on Mossy's saggy sofa.

On that first day, Mossy had shown Fin a battered, leather-bound book. 'This is your father's book. Tomorrow you will start your own.'

Carefully turning the pages, studying his father's painted pictures illuminating the pages, Fin had never seen such vibrant colours before, and he had eagerly looked forward to learning how to mix and use some of the pigments from the shelves of carefully labelled jars at the back of the shop. At first his father's writing was crude, the pages blotched with ink, but gradually they became cleaner, and the lettering neater. Marlin had skilfully added drawings amid his neat writing: a tall ivy-covered tower, a wicked-eyed bird-like creature, with gangling powerful legs and a sinuous twisting neck. On the last page, he had drawn the head of a dark-haired woman with large sad eyes: she was very beautiful.

'That is your mother,' Mossy said, 'your father sketched her from memory.' Fin had gazed longingly at the face, seeing a wistful smile playing about the corners of the mouth. 'He loved her very much, Fin,' Mossy had said softly.

Fin took down his book, standing next to his father's. The titles on the spines read:

*'The Book of Brightdale, Part One, by Marlin Dandrum.'*
*'The Book of Brightdale, Part Two, by Fin Dandrum.'*

As he turned the pages, the crisp parchment crackled softly. When he'd bound the book, with Mossy's guidance, the oiled calfskin had shone conker brown, the pages creamy clean, but now the cover was dog-eared, and the pages stained with ink and paint. Mossy hadn't let him write in it until his lettering had improved, so there'd been days of writing practice. Used to making quick strokes for sketching, Fin almost despaired of disciplining his wrist and fingers to outline each letter of the alphabet. But the day came when Mossy declared his writing good enough. Leaving space to paint a title picture, as he began to write, he had felt as if he was under a spell; all the everyday worries about hunting and target practice faded, as if they were another person's life. He'd now become so skilled that he'd already filled thirty pages; it wouldn't be long before he'd have to bind in more pages, an idea that pleased him, now he was nearing twenty years old, and adulthood.

He flicked through the pages, scattered with his illustrations: sketches of flowers, grasses, seeds, insects, snails, stones, and rocks, with notes of where found. Finding the next blank page, he dipped his quill in the ink pot. He thought for a moment, and then began to describe the blue gentian, visioning the place where he'd found the plants: the skylark hanging high in the pale dawn sky, the short grass, fragrant with thyme and dotted with bright flowers. As he wrote, a shaft of sunlight coming in through the shop window filled him with wonderful peace.

He decided to mix the paint for the blue gentians, remembering Mossy's challenge to mix the right blue. He studied the plant from his collecting box then went to the shelf of jars containing the pigments: some lumps to be ground, others already powder, ready for mixing with a binder of egg yolk, egg white, vinegar, or linseed oil. Peering at the scratched and stained labels, he found Verona Green; this he would mix with a dash of Paris Green for the leaves and stems. Farther along, his hand fell on the tightly sealed pot labelled Lapis Lazuli, containing small blue stones; to make Ultramarine he would need to grind a small lump into powder and mix it with a dash of slippery mercury. Back at the table, he took out one of the blue stones, dropped it into the pestle to grind with his mortar.

He was just considering what colour he should choose for the background wash when he heard the familiar rattling of the front door, and Mossy's stick tapping on the stone floor of the lobby, followed by Lass's skittering claws.

'You're back too soon,' he called with a grin, 'I've not even ground the lapis…'
His voice trailed away.

In three great strides Mossy was crushing him to his chest. 'Fin! A terrible thing has happened – your father is dead – killed!'

For a moment, the room heaved around him, as if it were on a ship. What had Mossy said? His father killed. He mustn't have understood. He remembered then the wolf hunt, and the urgent note of the hunting horn.

Pushing Mossy away, feeling Lass's rasping tongue frantically licking his hand, he clung to the table edge. He noticed the jar of silver mercury had spilt over his book, staining the space he'd kept for his flower painting: now he would never mix the pigment, never capture that amazing blue. His father hadn't finished his book either.

'Was it a wolf?' he whispered. 'Last night father asked me to go on the hunt with him. He – he said we could watch out for each other. I should have gone with him. But – but I went flower hunting instead!' he wailed.

'Fin – Fin!' Mossy shook him gently. 'It was not your fault – your father's death has nothing to do with hunting wolves – he was murdered!'

Stretching to his full six feet, Mossy stabbed a finger in the direction of Dandrum Den. 'Fin Dandrum, the time has come for you to show your mettle. Ready or not, you are now Head. You must return to Dandrum Den and claim your Birthright!'

He didn't linger, he did as Mossy had commanded: make for home. Stumbling out of the shop, as he ran, Mossy's words echoed in his fevered brain: your father's death has nothing to do with wolves – he was murdered!

Murdered – how? Fin tried to imagine his father lying dead. Had he an arrow through his heart? Or strangled, with a rope tight around his neck? Or had he been stabbed?

Who had done it? Rough types from Rascal town? More likely enemies he'd made when on the search for his mother. He'd probably mixed with some dodgy company – there was the tale of him bringing back treasure. Was someone after it? Where was that treasure now?

When he reached the courtyard, he hesitated, dreading what he might find. The side doors to the Great Hall were flung back. Taking a deep breath, he forced his trembling legs to walk in. His father's body lay on rush mats by the entrance, the family grouped around, their excitedly hissed murmurings echoing in the dark vaulted roof. Apart from Tissy and Nutmeg, they were all there: his grandmother Ramora, leaning on her walking stick, bent over the body, her pointed nose almost pecking it; Kelp staring at it, a sickly leer on his green face, his sister, Alaria, clinging to him, looking as if she were about to faint. Roach and Brewdy were kneeling on the rushes, Brewdy, her tongue darting in and out of her mean little mouth like a snake smelling the air, was watching Roach fiddle with the buttons on the bloodied leather jerkin.

Standing a respectful distance from the family, Hollin Annunder was working his soft leather hunting hat through his trembling fingers. Lark was by his side, shoulders hunched, clutching his little terrier, Mick, to his chest.

Fin frowned: Why was Roach poking around in his father's clothes? Pushing through the group to look closer, he staggered back, almost falling as his feet slipped on the rushes.

'Ah, no, no!' he moaned: where his father's throat should be, was a gaping red gash.

Hollin came and took him by the arm. 'Steady there, lad!' he growled, helping him to a nearby stool, and shoving a mug of beer at him. Distractedly taking a sip, Fin felt Roach's sinister eyes on him: the malevolent gleam turned his stomach. He looked away, only to be confronted by the family's hard stares: their look of hate was too much for him.

Dropping the mug of beer, he stumbled blindly to the back of the hall where a curtained archway led into a lobby with a flight of stairs up to the bedrooms. Bounding up the stone steps two at a time, passing the landing where he shared a bedroom with his cousin Kelp, he continued on, heading for Grammer Nutmeg's attic room. Lifting the latch, he fell in through the door.

Nutmeg was in her rocking chair by the fire, her apron flung up over her face. Tissy stood with an arm around the old Delphin's heaving shoulders, trying to comfort her. The floor around Nutmeg's chair was scattered with stalks of dried lavender. They'd been tying them into bunches when Roach had blundered in, bringing the news of Marlin's death. 'We've laid the body in the Great Hall – but don't come down, Grammer!' he'd commanded. 'He's been nastily mauled, and it will upset my Brewdy to have you in hysterics! Tissy, stay with her, until she calms down!'

'My lovely lad, my lovely Marlin!' wailed Nutmeg. 'My little chick – dead! Murdered!'

Seeing Fin, Tissy's face crumpled into tears. 'Fin, help me – Grammer won't stop crying!'

Fin gently pulled the apron away from Nutmeg's face. 'Hush, hush, Grammer,' he cooed.

Nutmeg peered at him through her tears. 'Is it you Fin?'

'Yes, it's me,' he said softly, dabbing at her eyes with a corner of the apron. 'Don't cry anymore, you'll make yourself ill – just when we need you!'

Nutmeg gave a hiccupping sob. 'Aye, lad. There's no one better than me at laying out – did your granfer proud, last week. Dressing his old, worn out body in the Ceremonial Clothes – not been used in years and smelling strong of fleabane – soaking the winding cloths with rosemary oil – for remembrance, you know.' She let out a moan. 'T'was only last week! Never would I have thought to be doing it all again so soon.'

Tissy went to Nutmeg's dresser and poured some honey coloured liquid from a bottle into a small glass. 'Here, Grammer, a tot of your special poppy water. Take a sip, it'll help you feel stronger!'

Bringing a stool, Fin sat next to Nutmeg, lovingly watching as, sobbing every now and then, she sipped from the glass.

Nutmeg was a familiar figure in Brightdale. Her short round figure, grey hair plaited in a bun on the top of her head, was often to be seen roaming the woods and fields, her herb gathering basket on her arm. She came to Dandrum Den as a young Delphin to be a nursemaid to Marlin and Roach when they were children, then stayed on to nurse Fin and his cousins, Kelp, Alaria and Thetis – known to everyone as Tissy. Nutmeg was also grandmother to Lark Annunder, and sister to Hollin Annunder.

Her attic room looked out over the sloping roofs of Dandrum Den, towards her Annunder childhood home away to the north-west. A place of refuge for Fin, the room breathed comfort, her feather bed in one corner, in another her dresser, crowded with china, jars and pots, and in the middle a round table set with four stools. A wooden bench covered with sheepskins faced the fireplace; he spent a lot of time there with Tissy. When they were very little, he and Tissy would listen with pleasurable dread to Grammer Nutmeg's frightening tales of the black-hearted humans from the Badlands away to the south, or even worse, the evil Skwid people, who'd slit your throat before you could ask the way home.

'Now, if you happened to stray too near to Withered Wood, you'd better watch out!' she would hiss, her plump face flushed with drama. Then she would recount, yet again, of how once she'd gone too close, and been spotted by an imp, it's orange pelt gleaming as it weaved in and out of the tangled thorns, its razor teeth snapping. It would have sliced her throat open if Mr Mossy hadn't suddenly appeared and chased it back into the Wood. 'And I know I was right, when I saw a cloud of fiery fog with red glaring eyes, wumping after it. But Mr Mossy only laughed when I told him, saying I've got an imagination – that's one thing I haven't got!'

Distractedly watching Tissy gather up the scattered lavender, Fin noticed the silly detail that the flecks of greens and blues in her eyes matched the flowers and stalks. Tissy, being more akin to the Dandrum clan, was unlike plump Alaria her older sister, who took after their mother's Cletchen clan. She was slender figured, yellow-green curls softly framing her face, which was pretty, even if marred by a light scar running from her mouth to her nose.

As Nutmeg had become calmer, Fin got up from his stool, and gave her a hug. 'Would you mind, Grammer, if I went now? I'd better see what going on...' His voice trailed away. A desperate desire had come over him, to get away – to escape the Den, where his father's body lay in the Great Hall, with that dreadful wound in his throat.

'Aye, Fin, off you go!' Nutmeg nodded. 'Make sure they're showing proper respect for master's body!'

Downstairs in the lobby, he hesitated, trying to pluck up courage to go through the curtain into the Hall, from where he heard raised voices.

His Aunt Brewdy, Roach's wife, was screeching about him.

'I don't ken the thought of Fin being Head: he's got a nasty streak – inherited from his Ma, along with his brown skin and long legs. And his eyes – it's not natural, one brown, one green – I get shivers every time he looks at me!'

He heard his uncle Roach grunt. 'Aye, he doesn't know anything about being Head! The half-breed causes nothing but trouble – it was a bad day when our Marlin got taken up with a Rom female, letting himself be caught by swaying hips, and dark flashing eyes!'

Sick with misery and grief, Fin lurched from the lobby, out through a side door into the courtyard.

# 3
# FUNERAL RITES

He found himself by the Dandrum Chair, but didn't remember climbing to the plateau above Dandrum Den.

More a bench than a chair, it was made of stone from the crags above Dandrum Den, a slab laid upon two thick rough-hewn legs, polished smooth by generations of Dandrum Heads; their shuffling feet had worn deep grooves into the peaty soil.

This was where his grandfather had sat, yearning for Marlin to come home from searching for his lost wife. When small, Fin had come here too, sitting on the ground near the old Delphin, watching him as he proudly surveyed his Dandrum lands. Peeping up into his face, seeing his grandfather's rheumy old eyes racked by misery, Fin knew he was desperately missing his much-loved son.

Brushing his hand over the smooth stone, Fin wondered if his father, for the too short time he was Head, had sat here. Probably not – it was only a week since Old Fin's death. Had his Uncle Roach been tempted to sit here? If he had, what might have happened to him? Legend had it that if anyone other than the Head sat on The Chair, a bolt of lightning would strike them dead. Once, when Fin was five years old, tempted to see what would happen, he had tried to climb up, but the seat was too high.

Now he was more than tall enough. Taking a deep breath, he sat down. He waited. Nothing happened, no thunder, no lightning. He searched the sky where a few puffy clouds floated on a high breeze. A great bird hung there, a black dot in the blue; it could have been an eagle, or a buzzard, or it might have been the portentous Drone Bird. Scornful laughter bubbled up inside him: how furious the family would be if they knew he'd sat on The Chair.

Looking down on the grey slate roofs of Dandrum Den, he wondered if it had been a glorious Saprise day like today when his ancient ancestor, Grayling Dandrum had first come here, five hundred years ago, and named this dale, Bright. Did he stand on this spot, and decide to put a seat here?

Hearing the pathetic mewing of the lapwings on the fell behind him, he imagined they were weeping for his dead father. As were the bleating lambs huddled against their mothers' wool, little family groups dotted about the brown fell like patches of dirty grey snow. Swivelling to face the east, he looked down on the farmlands below, hearing the distant soft cooing of a collared dove in the apple orchard. Was she too mourning his father? In the fields covered in new green growth, he spied a flock of rooks on their daily raid. Their cawing was surely a paean to the dead. Farther off, where a meadow ran down to the riverbank, the dairy herd stood amongst the golden drifts of celandine and buttercups lowing as if keening for their master.

He climbed on to the stone seat and stretching his five feet as tall as he could, he drew in a deep breath of moorland air and shouted out to them all: the lapwings, the lambs, the dove, the rooks, the cows, and the Delphins of the Dale:

'NO NEED FOR MOURNING! Here is your Head, as it has been for five hundred years: I am here!'

His youthful voice, muffled by the bracken on the fell, made him wonder if they could hear him far down in Watersmeet; he spied two distant, doll-sized figures walking along the riverbank – they didn't look up. Uncertainty overtook him: his voice was too weak, he was too weak, he was not true Delphin, a half-breed, without the steely Dandrum qualities needed to lead the Dalers in peace and safety, as they had done since they first settled in these wild northern lands.

It was Year 3033 when the Dandrums came to this place, naming the river Brightwater; the dale becoming known as Brightdale. They made their home beneath the pillared crags overlooking the river, a river that teemed with salmon and trout and fished by herons and otters, and where in the forest, deer, wild sheep, goats and boar roamed, preyed upon by wolf and bear, as well as tigers, lynx and puma, descendants of the great cats that had escaped from captivity after the Great Dying.

As the years passed, the Dandrums tamed the land: clearing the forest for fields, and for their homes, digging up the dressed stones of the ruined dwellings of the ancient inhabitants, dead a thousand years, who once lived in the dale. More Delphin clans followed: firstly, the Spinners who claimed and cleared the land across the river, then the Annunders, who settled in the wilder upper dale. After them, other Delphins came, and the village of Watersmeet grew into a town. Humans never attempted to settle, so the Delphins were left to themselves, making use of everything this hidden dale had to offer.

Irritated with himself for his maudlin daydreaming, Fin jumped down from The Chair, and glaring down on the Den below, imagined the family, hearing his shouting, looking up, cowed and respectful. Whatever his breeding, he was son to Marlin Dandrum, and they must know it was his right to be Head.

'IT'S MY INHERITANCE – AT THE HOUR OF MY FATHER'S DEATH,' he yelled at the roofs. 'I've sat here now, and have claimed my right, I, Fin Dandrum, born to Marlin Dandrum and Miryam Smith of the Rom people!'

He ran back down the path to keep vigil by his dead father's body.

Slipping quietly into the Great Hall, he saw the body now lay on the carved oak table standing on a dais at the back of the hall. The family had gone, leaving Nutmeg and Lark to prepare his father for dressing in the Dandrum ceremonial regalia, in readiness for the Dalers to pay their last respects.

Standing in the shadows, he watched Grammer Nutmeg, calmer now, washing away the blood smearing the stiff face, using a cloth soaked in vinegar. Lark stood beside her, holding the bowl of strong vinegar, Mick crouched miserably at his feet. Lark's eyes were red with tears and Fin wondered if the tears were from the vinegar fumes, or if he really was weeping – he'd never seen his down-to-earth ghillie cry before.

Nutmeg spotted him. Peering into the dark corners of the Hall, her old voice trembling, she called softly to him: 'Take care, Fin, you'll have enemies now!'

A chill ran through him: did Grammer mean an outside evil, or just to beware of his Uncle Roach? He thought of Roach crouched over Marlin's body. What was he searching for? He forced himself to step closer to watch Nutmeg bathing the wound in his father's throat: no wolf had inflicted that injury.

Nutmeg turned to Lark. 'Get yer knife out, so we can cut away the jerkin from poor master's body.'

Drawing his sharp boning knife from its sheath, leaning over the body, Lark carefully sliced through the leather jerkin. Opening the shirt, he stepped back with a sharp whistle: the chest bore a livid scar, so deep that it showed white bone.

Feeling sick, Fin recalled his father's habit of slipping his hand inside his shirt to massage his chest: he knew now why his father never bared his chest. 'Grammer, did you know about this wound?' he whispered.

She nodded. 'Sometimes when it got very sore, he allowed me to dress it with marigold ointment. Your dad said it was from an accident – that he'd fallen on a piece of hot metal. I didn't like to argue – you know how he was.'

'Strange shaped wound, isn't it?' Lark muttered, 'Like an 'X' over a 'P' – same as a branding iron a farmer uses to mark his cattle. I don't see how Master could have fallen on a hot bit of metal, shaped like that – unless he was full of strong fire whisky!'

Nutmeg frowned at him. 'Whatever happened, Master's at peace now: he can suffer no more pain.'

Fin studied his father's face. Yes, all his pain had gone: Marlin's soul had moved on.

Leaving Nutmeg and Lark to their sad work, he went out into the courtyard. Slumping on a bench, he recalled his strange dream this morning, up on the moor, when looking for the blue gentian. He knew now who the swimmer was: Marlin Dandrum. His spirit was diving with the angel Phul in a far-off warm sea. He had taken the mystery of the wound on his chest with him. Aching with grief, he longed to be able to cry like Lark.

Watching Fin's retreating figure, Lark too felt the need to escape the oppressive atmosphere of the Hall. As his grandmother finished bandaging the wounded throat, he put down his bowl and swiped his sleeve across his watering eyes. 'Grammer, I've a mind to do some investigating – to have another look where the killing happened.'

Nutmeg looked up from her work. 'Aye do that Lark – we owe it to Master, to find the truth of how he was killed. Tissy can help me dress him in the Ceremonial robes.' She peered suspiciously into the shadows. 'But have a care nobody sees where you're going!'

Outside in the courtyard, Lark saw Fin, his eyes shut, on a bench in the sun. He wondered if he should say something; offer his condolences. He decided to leave it for now. Mick close on his heels, he hurried through the gates.

At the scene of Marlin's death, the wolf's body had gone. Lark's rabbits had also disappeared, his spade still lying where he'd dropped it. The churned ground showed traces of footprints, mostly Delphins' boots, but there were others too: small, almost hand-like prints, and others, much larger, more sinister, as if left by a huge bird. Crouching down, he sniffed them, picking up an unpleasant whiff. Following the prints, he came upon a broken leather strip half buried in the bloodstained sandy soil. He recognized the familiar plaited leather cord his Master wore; a heavy gold medallion had hung from it. He searched around for a glint of gold, but finding nothing, he tracked the footprints towards a clump of gorse bushes. The reek here caught his throat. Taking a swig from his water bottle, he spotted a fluffy white object stirring in the breeze. Crawling further into the bushes, he found a downy feather caught on a branch; could it be from the bird with the giant footprints? Warned by its stink and reluctant to touch it, he searched his jerkin pockets for the square of soft suede he used for polishing his arrow heads. Using it as a makeshift glove, he folded it over the feather and put the package in his hunting bag.

Backing out of the gorse, he was startled by a strange sound: an eerie low hissing, coming from the crags somewhere above his head. Just then, Mick tumbled down the rocks, ears flat. Badly spooked, Delphin and dog turned tail and ran, not stopping until they'd reached the refuge of Dandrum Den.

Safely through the gates, Lark collapsed on the nearest seat. Hand shaking, he took great gulps from his water bottle; he was glad to see Fin wasn't there. Reassured by his surroundings, he gradually came to his senses. He pondered on what he had discovered at the killing place. What kind of bird could leave such huge footprints?

'It might have been the Drone Bird,' he told Mick, stroking his little dog's smooth brown and white head. 'Drone Birds are lucky, so there's no need to be afeared! But then again Mick, what about that stinking feather?'

Rummaging in his pack for the leather packet, he let out a yelp. 'It stung me!' he growled indignantly. Cautiously pulling the packet out he saw a bit of white feather poking out. Opening it out on the bench, he bent close and sniffed – the feather still had a strong stink.

'Well, our Mick, I'll know not to touch that whiffy thing again! Whoever heard of stinging feathers? But what to do about it?'

Sucking on his tingling fingertips, he considered. Normally he would have gone to his uncle Hollin, but he had a feeling his stolid uncle would scorn him, telling him to burn the feather and forget about it. Speak with Master Roach? He remembered what he thought he'd seen Roach doing to the master's body. No, he'd have a word with his Grammer Nutmeg.

Carefully wrapping the feather again, and leaving Mick licking his paws in the sunshine, he went into the Hall. Nobody was there. The oak table where his master's body lay had been decked with greenery: ivy, yew, and holly, and decorated with the special silver scallop shells reserved for such an occasion. The body was dressed in the Dandrum ceremonial regalia.

Climbing the steps to the dais, he stood admiring Nutmeg and Tissy's work: his Master looked kingly. Set about the cold brow was a crown of silver dolphins leaping through a pearl sea and encircling the slender waist was a silver belt decorated in fine gold wire depicting more dolphins leaping through foaming crests of silver-wire waves. From it hung the Dandrum sword. Encased in a sheath of richly encrusted pearls, its handle was made of finely forged silver, and Lark knew that the thin steel blade inside, also richly decorated with gold tracery, was for ceremonial purposes only and of no use as a fighting weapon. He also knew that all the precious pieces were very old, brought to Brightdale by Grayling Dandrum, five hundred years ago.

The garments adorning the body were more recent, made over the years by the Dandrum females: a jerkin of mother-of-pearl discs, reminiscent of fish scales, with close fitting kid-leather trousers, embroidered with silver thread depicting yet more dolphins swimming through seaweed tendrils. They fitted Marlin's body as if they had been made for him. Lark noticed with satisfaction that the rich velvet cloak which Tissy was embroidering, had been laid folded at the feet, showing her skill to full advantage. He touched his cheek where Tissy had kissed him, remembering she had done the embroidery with the thread he'd bought her at the Market.

Shaking off his happy daydream, he went in search of his grandmother. First, he tried her Still Room, where Nutmeg prepared her jams, pickles, and special brews. Peering into the cool gloom, he found no one there. He lingered a moment, eyeing the mouth-watering trays of red and purple fruit jellies, set with costly carrageen, gleaming invitingly on the marble slab: they would be served at the funeral feast. The smell of roasting meat drew him along the passageway to the kitchen. Lifting the latch and opening the door a crack, he peeked in. Cooking for the funeral feast was well underway, the hot kitchen bustling with chopping, stirring, mixing, and kneading.

Saprise being the season of scarcity, the food needed careful planning, restricted to what stores were left over from last year's Leafturn. One of the old wemmers had been slaughtered, the roasted mutton to be served with boiled salted pork, confit of duck leg, stuffed goose neck, and a stew of beans and white cabbage. There would be freshly baked rosemary-bread, dishes of sharp tasting sallets – made up of such young shoots as could be found at this time of year, sorrel, ramsons, and bittercress – all gathered by Lupin, the cook. Most special of all would be her fairy-ring mushroom fritters, prepared to her secret recipe. The jellies setting in Nutmeg's still room would complete the feast.

To assist Lupin, helpers had been recruited: Bird and Bee, the Spinner twins, were there as well as Mistress Brewdy, Tissy and her older sister, Alaria. Alaria's friend, Daffodil Akest was there too.

He saw his grandmother, sitting in her special chair by the bread oven, a mug of camomile tea clutched in her worn hands, her head resting back on a cushion. Opening the door wider, he hovered in the entrance, hoping to catch her eye.

Bee Spinner spotted him and grinned. 'Your fav' grandson has come to cadge one of your tasty mutton pasties, Grammer Nutmeg!' she observed cheekily, making Bird, her twin giggle.

The two sisters were at the long table in the middle of the room, rolling out pastry. Alaria stood at the far end chopping cabbage, with Daffodil next to her, kneading bread dough. Seeing Tissy standing at the sink scrubbing potatoes, Lark's heart gave a flutter.

'Keep out, Lark lad,' Nutmeg called, 'we don't need males under our feet whilst we cook for hundreds!'

Basting the sizzling joint of mutton roasting over the open fire, Lupin the cook nodded knowingly. 'It's my opinion, half of 'em aren't coming to mourn our Master but to nose, hoping to see inside Dandrum Den and gawp at the finery! Folk still wonder where them boxes and bags are, that Master Marlin brought back from his wanderings – gone nine years he was and turned up with a laden pony.' She pointed her basting spoon accusingly at Lark, as if it was his fault.

'Old Master Fin should never have allowed Marlin to marry that Miryam Smith, her being a sly wandering Rom,' screeched Brewdy from the cooking range, where she was stirring a pan of frying onions. 'T'was wicked abandoning young Fin, him only a tot – broke Marlin's heart it did! Then Marlin going off, leaving all the work for my Roach.'

A wave of irritation swept over Lark: Mistress Brewdy wouldn't let that tale lie.

'Don't let Fin hear you talk like that about his ma!' Bird called, giving Brewdy a defiant glare. 'He's Head Dandrum now, Mistress Brewdy, and should have respect!' Pink cheeked, she brushed back a strand of corn-green hair, leaving a flour smudge across her black eyebrows.

Bee chipped in; her eyes misty: 'What a looker Fin's turned into – fair makes me wobble at the knees; must've got his handsome looks from his Rom Ma. There's loads of lasses fallen for his strange eyes, one green and one brown. But I've heard tell he has Delphin gills under his dark locks. Is that right, Grammer Nutmeg?'

Lark hoped his grandmother wouldn't answer but come and see what he wanted.

Not noticing her grandson's urgent stare, Nutmeg smiled fondly at Bee. 'When he was a little 'un he'd more of the Delphin about him, a bit of green tinge to his hair too. He's kept his Delphin brows – nice and pointing down, just like you 'n me.'

'Well, I've seen his gills,' Daffodil Akest simpered from the far end of the table. 'I don't have to speculate. I won't be giving too much away to say that Fin and me, are more than just friends. Poor lad, he'll be coming to me for comfort, now his pa's dead.'

Bee and Bird glared scornfully at the plump Delphin: it was a longstanding joke among their friends, that Daffodil had a crush on Fin.

'I don't believe you, Daffy – Fin wouldn't be interested in a fat lump like you!' Bird hissed.

Lark became even more irritated: this way of talking about Fin was daft. He wasn't a patch on Kelp his cousin, when it came to target shooting, let alone hunting.

To his deep annoyance, Brewdy started up again. 'Fin's only half Delphin! Roach and I don't like the thought of such as him ruling the roost.' In her indignation, she'd forgotten her onions, and a smell of burning started to fill the room.

'Watch your pan, Brewdy Cletchen! We don't need your opinion on Dandrum affairs,' Nutmeg spat, 'your Cletchen clan has no cause to be high and mighty, them being the last to come to the Dale – so don't you put on mighty airs, woman!'

'I've more 'titlement 'n you to be involved in Dandrum affairs, Mrs Annunder!' Brewdy shrieked. 'I'm ma to a Dandrum brood, to Kelp and my girls, Alaria and Thetis. Just you wait and see – things 'll be different around here, now Marlin is dead!'

Her pasty-faced daughter, Alaria, dropping her chopping knife, chipped in: 'Pa should be Head, shouldn't he, ma?'

An awkward silence fell: Alaria had let a secret out into the open.

'It's daft, this talk of who should be Head – it's Fin's right!' It was Tissy who spoke from the sink.

Lark gazed across at her adoringly. Trust dear Tissy to stand up for what's right, he thought. Her courage in speaking out made him bold.

'You females shouldn't be gossiping, with – with master's body hardly cold,' he gasped, trying to sound stern, but his wobbly voice letting him down.

The indignant glares were too much: banging the kitchen door shut, he sloped off back to the courtyard. Tissy's remark that it was Fin's right to be Head made him realise that there was no alternative, he would have to show the feather to Fin.

He found Mick sound asleep in the sun. Wondering if Fin could be in his and Kelp's bedroom, he went into the stair lobby. Through the curtains, he heard the rumble of male voices in the Hall. Squinting through a gap he saw Roach, Kelp, and his uncle Hollin, sitting around the empty fireplace, mugs of beer in their hands. Fin wasn't with them.

'I'm not happy to have a half Delphin as Head,' Roach growled. 'Fin will never be accepted by me!' His harsh rasp made Lark shiver; he was rapidly losing respect for Master Roach.

'If any has a right to be Head, it's you pa. You're eldest Dandrum now,' Kelp said.

Anger welled up in Lark. What sort of talk was that? Kelp should know better. He spotted the toe of a boot protruding out of the trailing greenery beneath the oak table on which the master's body lay. He smiled wryly: Fin was there, hiding from the family. Bending double, he slipped between the curtains, and climbing unseen onto the dais, wriggled down in the dust under the table.

'What do you want, Lark?' Fin hissed, shrinking away.

Doubt filled Lark: had he done right, seeking Fin out? Lately he'd found it even harder to get on with Fin, especially as he was now spending nearly all his time at Mr Mossy's bookshop. Tissy had encouraged them to be friends, but Kelp's company was more to Lark's liking. He and Kelp had become good mates, working well together.

Fin sat, stiff and proud, his dark hair brushing the underneath of the table. A wave of pity washed over Lark. The lad had lost his dad – nastily killed too. It's rough on him, alright. He put his hand on Fin's shoulder, and leaning close, whispered in his ear. 'Sorry if I'm intruding, like, but now you're Head, I've a problem—' He hesitated, wondering if Fin would think him daft if he told him about the feather.

Fin glared at him. 'You said I'm Head – you'd better take care; it could be dodgy for you.' He nodded fiercely in the direction of the group gathered around the fireplace. 'If they've anything to do with it, you're assuming too much!' Then he sighed. 'Anyway, what's the problem?'

Awkwardly, Lark indicated his hunting pack. 'I need to show you something strange – something I found up by the Donkey Crags where your dad was killed. I suppose I could have gone to Master Roach, but to my mind he's changed, if you take my meaning?' He gave Fin a significant look.

'So, you've noticed, too?' Fin murmured, adding impatiently: 'Oh, come on, let's get away from here so we don't have to talk in whispers!'

Creeping through the curtains out into the lobby, they tiptoed up the stairs.

Following Fin, Lark studied his long legs; even though not yet twenty years old, Fin was already taller than him, aged twenty-five. Lark reckoned he must be over five feet now; no pure Delphin grows beyond four and half feet. He thought of the Dandrum ceremonial robes and doubted they would fit Fin. Probably wouldn't get to wear them anyhow, the way things were shaping, he thought gloomily as they reached the first landing.

They found the door to the Fin and Kelp's bedroom flung open.

Following Fin inside, Lark gaped: 'Teg's knackers – what's happened here!' he bellowed, forgetting to keep his voice down. Fin's mattress had been tipped off the bed, the sheepskin coverings thrown on the stone floor, the pillow ripped open, feather filling still floating in the air.

Fin rushed to his box of most precious possessions. Someone had dragged it from beneath his bed, and broken it open, with everything tipped out.

'Anything missing, Master?' Lark asked, watching as Fin searched anxiously among his things.

All Delphin children are given their own special box for things important to them. Fin had nothing of great value, except to him: a little wooden horse his father had carved for him when he was born, a rag doll Nutmeg had made for him, gifts from Tissy and the twins, Bird and Bee. Also, bits and pieces that had caught his eye on his rambles in the Dale: oddly shaped stones, interesting pieces of bark, birds' nests. An unusual find was the football-sized egg he'd spotted in the reeds by the river, its hard shell having an unpleasant smell which he couldn't quite get rid of, however hard he polished it.

The one thing of real value was a gold coin he kept in a red leather purse, hidden in a secret compartment at the very bottom of his box.

He was given the coin on his sixth birthday. Grammer Nutmeg had taken him to the spring that trickled out of the hill, outside the courtyard gates, when she produced a leather purse.

'On the day your ma disappeared, she left this gift for you. I found it on my dresser when I woke – she must have crept into my room during the night. Inside the purse is a coin. Now you're nearly growed, I reckon it's time for you to have it.'

Opening the purse, he had reverently laid the crudely forged gold coin on his palm. Scratched on one side was the name Saro, and on the other, the name Saroson.

'Your ma scratched those words when she baptised you,' Nutmeg had told him. 'She left me a letter explaining it's the tradition of Rom mothers to baptise their first born in secret, giving their baby a significant name. She brought you here to this spring, and named you, Saroson. In the letter, she said her own secret name, given to her by her mother, is Saro. So, Fin, your name is also Saroson!'

Every birthday since, he and Grammer Nutmeg carried out a little ritual. They would go to the spring, and laying a posy of primroses there, would say a prayer to Phul for his mother's safe return.

Releasing the catch on the hidden compartment in the bottom of the box, Fin sighed with relief: the coin was there, safe in its purse. Tipping it out on to his palm, he showed it to Lark. 'My mother gave me this when I was born.' Grim faced, he tucked the coin back in its purse and put in an inner pocket of his jerkin. The rest of his things he put back in the box.

'I wonder who did this and what they were looking for?' Lark asked, peering under the bed.

Fin thought of Roach's bloodstained hands poking about in his dead father's clothes. He jumped to his feet. 'Come on Lark, we'd better check my father's room!'

Running along the corridor, they skidded to a halt: here too the door was wide open. Again, they found chaos; clothes strewn about, even the bed had been overturned. Marlin's box, like Fin's, had been broken open, the lid smashed, hanging on bent hinges. Pale with anger, Fin went over and righted the box, returning to it pieces of parchment and other odds and ends.

'Do you know if anything has been taken?' Lark asked.

'Not sure. I don't think my father kept anything precious here. I know he stored the more important stuff in Mossy's attic above the bookshop.'

Putting back the mattress on the bed, they sat on it, puzzled.

Lark thought about the boxes and bags Marlin brought back from his travels. There was a rumour they contained wondrous riches, and that Marlin had hidden them somewhere secret. Suddenly he remembered why he had wanted to find Fin.

'Teg's knackers, I've forgotten the feather!'

Fin looked at him in surprise.

Gingerly, Lark felt inside his pack, cringing as he located the makeshift leather packet. He carefully opened it out on the mattress.

'I wanted to show you this – don't touch it!' he warned as Fin went to take it. 'It stings something dreadful.' He showed Fin his swollen red fingertips. 'I found it caught on a gorse bush near where your dad died. Whoever heard of a feather that can sting?'

Fin bent close and sniffed. 'Yuck, it has the same stink as my giant egg, but much worse!' He thought for a moment, then came to a decision. 'I bet Mossy would know about weird birds that have stinging feathers. Can you keep it a while longer? Then when the funeral's over, we'll take it down to the bookshop to show him.'

Lark nodded, and warily wrapping the feather again, returned it to his rucksack.

Fin pushed his father's box back under the bed. 'I'd better go and get ready for the funeral. I'm going to pack a rucksack too, with the important things from my box – I don't want to leave them here! I'll take them down to Mossy's for him to look after.'

He smiled wanly. 'I'm not looking forward to the next few hours! Can we meet up after the funeral? I'm sorry, but you'll have to miss the feast. Do you mind?'

'No Master Fin – somehow I've lost the taste for feasting, even Lupin's fairy ring fritters! I'll tell Grammer Nutmeg that I'll be taking you back to Mossy's: she'll like that.'

With that Lark left.

Back in his own room, Fin found it difficult to decide what to take. As he'd no intention of returning any time soon, he packed extra clothes, but his rucksack soon became too full. Chucking out some vests and a pair of thick trousers, he made room for some of the more precious things from his box: the little wooden horse, the rag doll, and some of the mementos the twins and Tissy had given him. He left the giant smelly egg sitting on top of the bits and pieces he didn't want – it looked as if a huge bird had crept into the dormitory and had laid her egg there.

Raking a comb through his tangled hair, he heard the familiar creak of floorboards from the room above: it was his grandmother Ramora's bedroom, where she spent her time if she wasn't warming her old bones in front of the fire in the Great Hall. He supposed she must be getting ready for the funeral.

Shouldering his rucksack, he hurried out, slamming the door behind him. Cantering down the stairs, he stamped through the lobby, kicking over the clutter of spears leaning against the wall, making as much racket as possible to warn them in the Hall of his arrival; but he found it empty, his father's body on the oak table left unguarded. He realised the males must've gone down to Watersmeet to announce the funeral.

Mounting the dais and bending down, he brushed his lips against his father's cold brow beneath the silver crown; as he did so his eye was caught by the gleaming silver handle of the sword encased in its pearl scabbard, nestling in the greenery at his father's side.

He recalled the day he'd first seen the Dandrum sword. He'd been very small, long before his father had returned home. He had watched in awe as Nutmeg, lifting the lid of the Dandrum robe chest, had reverently taken out the regalia: the crown, the silver belt, the sword in its pearl scabbard, and the rich ceremonial garments. 'When your dad comes home and becomes the Head after your granfer has passed on, he will wear these,' Nutmeg had said, 'and it will be your turn to wear them when you become Head – so don't grow too tall, Fin!'

He looked at the garments now, the jerkin covering his father's torso, the embroidered trousers: they would be too small for him. On an impulse, he drew the sword from its scabbard. As he did so, he heard a soft sigh. For a second, he fancied his father had drawn breath, but the white face remained stonily expressionless. Running his finger along the keen edge of the sword, he studied the design of interlocking gold circles along thin steel blade. He listened for a moment. The Great Hall was silent. Shoving the bare sword deep inside his rucksack, he jumped down from the dais, and slipped cautiously out into the courtyard.

There was no one about. Sprinting across the cobbles to the wall by the gate, he ran his fingers over the stones, and finding the familiar loose one, pulled it out to reveal a large crevice. He'd just pushed in his rucksack, and heaved the stone back into place when, from the road outside the gates, he heard the rumble of many voices. The Dale folk were coming to pay their last respects. Racing back into the Hall, he stood grinning: he'd just stolen the Dandrum Sword! He strode to the fireplace, and lifting his father's special chair, staggered up the dais steps with it. Placing it at the head of the oak table, he sat down. Spotting a gap in the greenery above the pearl scabbard, he leapt up and rearranged some ivy leaves over the empty space.

As he sat down again, through the tall doors from the courtyard the Dandrum males entered; Roach first, then Kelp, followed by Lark and Hollin Annunder. Outside in the courtyard a large crowd milled about.

Hollin and Lark stood guard by the doors, whilst Roach and Kelp mounted the dais, Kelp standing behind the oak table, and Roach swaggering to Marlin's feet where he placed his hand proprietorially on a large conch shell resting there. Roach shot Fin a challenging look, and understanding his uncle's action, Fin stared back defiantly, but didn't speak. The ancient shell was called the Horn of Passing and was traditionally blown by the new Head to mark the passing on of the mantle of Headship.

At the doors, Lark and Hollin looked across at Roach, waiting for a signal from him, and at his curt nod, they stood back. Solemnly forming a line, the crowd shuffled in. Their muted murmuring echoing softly around the great chamber, they began to process past the dais, each bowing to the body before going out again.

All through the rest of the morning and afternoon, the line grew ever longer as hundreds came from all parts of Brightdale to gaze upon the body of Marlin Dandrum. By late afternoon when the queue finally came to an end, Lark and Hollin closed the doors, and the Dandrum males were released from their posts to prepare themselves for the Funeral.

The mourners gone, screens were placed around the dais, so the Great Hall could be made ready for the feast. Farmhands and ghillies came to lend a hand, even Tom Gotobed the shepherd, from his bothy on the fells. They put up trestle tables, placed benches, and rolled barrels of beer and mead up from the cellars. As soon as these workers had finished, a team from the kitchen carried in check tablecloths, wooden cutlery, plates, platters, and horn mugs. The family's damask tablecloth, silver cutlery, crystal goblets and china plates, would be laid on the oak table when the Master had been borne away.

In the meantime, Nutmeg Annunder had to prepare the body for burning on the funeral pyre: removing the ceremonial garments, and winding oil-soaked linen bands around the body. Outside her still room, she met Bird Spinner carrying a tray of horn mugs.

'Bird lass, leave that, and help me tend to the body. You'll know what to do – didn't you help your Grammer Madgette with the laying out of your Granfer Joshua? Help me fetch the winding cloths and rosemary oil – thank Phul I still have a good supply of oil left over from old Master Fin's funeral!'

They were stripping off the ceremonial regalia, when Nutmeg, unbuckling the silver belt, tottered back with a cry. 'The sword has gone!'

Bird looked in consternation at the empty pearl encrusted scabbard. 'Do you think one of the Dalers has stolen it?' she gasped, searching amongst the discarded greenery on the floor.

She was about to crawl under the table when Nutmeg groaned. 'Dang me, I'm a giddy wemmer! Our Fin will have taken it – to carry in the procession up to Kirion Hill.'

Bird was surprised, but assumed Nutmeg was right.

The garments removed, Nutmeg started wrapping the body in the linen bands, first dipping them in a bowl of spicy scented rosemary oil. Holding the bowl, Bird kept her face averted. She hadn't minded the sight of her old Granfer's wizened body being bound, but Master Marlin's wounds and scars shocked her.

To distract Bird, Nutmeg chattered as she worked. 'Would you like me to teach you the Healing Arts, lass? Your Grammer Magette tells me you might have Healer's hands. I'll have a word with your ma if you like.'

But Bird wasn't listening. She was thinking about Fin – had he seen the dreadful wound in his father's throat? She hoped not. She'd spotted him earlier, striding out through the courtyard gate, and had ran after him, but by the time she'd got outside, he was already halfway up the path to the Dandrum Chair. She'd felt a pang of sadness that he hadn't come to see her – she thought they were close friends. Then she recalled what Daffodil Akest had said in the kitchen: 'Poor lad, he'll be coming to me for comfort, now his pa is dead.'

Jealousy, and memories of missed opportunities engulfed her. Fin holding her close as they whirled around the floor at the Highsun Prance; him pulling waterweed from her hair when they fell from the old pear tree into the duck pond; the first time they had held hands, lingering behind the others on their way home after Harvest Rout. She had a feeling Fin had wanted to kiss her, but shyness overcame her, and she'd run on to the river where Bee, Tissy and some of the lads and lasses were fooling around, splashing each other.

'Bird! Bird! Are you coming?' called a voice.

Coming out of her reverie, Bird looked around: The Hall had emptied, Nutmeg was gone. The body was bound head to foot in the winding cloths.

'Get a move on!' Bee called impatiently from where she stood with Tissy at the entrance to the back lobby. 'We haven't much time to change for the funeral. Didn't you listen to what Grammer Nutmeg said, we can borrow some of her dark green funeral clothes?'

Bird hurried after them as, chattering they clattered up the stairs.

In the attic room, they dragged Grammer Nutmeg's box of mourning clothes from under her bed. Flinging back the lid, filling the room with the strong smell of fleabane, they pulled out the dresses, blouses, and skirts, some made of rich velvet and some of luxuriously soft wool, coloured bottle green, dark olive, and myrtle. To their glee they found beneath these clothes a hidden stash of fancy underwear.

Watching from her rocking chair, Nutmeg's cheeks turned pink. 'Eee! I'd forgotten I had those!'

Giggling, they pulled out lacy petticoats, wispy knickers, stiff-boned satin camisoles, all heavily flounced and frilled, in gaudy orange, mauve and shocking pink, now much too small for old Nutmeg's portly figure.

Bird, her mind still seething with pictures of Daffodil and Fin clasped in each other's arms, soon gave up the fun of trying on the underwear. She took a jumble of leather strips and dark green velvet ribbons lying on Nutmeg's dresser, and sat down on the bench to plait them, intertwining the ribbons and leather with grey feathers, to make hair bands for Bee, Tissy and herself.

Grammer Nutmeg leant forward and peered at her with concern. 'What's up, lass?'

'Nothing, Grammer,' Bird said, fiercely twisting a piece of leather and velvet together and stabbing in a feather. 'Well, if you must know it's that Daffodil Akest.' She spat her enemy's name. 'I'm sick of the way she's always hanging around Dandrum Den, her piggy eyes ogling Fin. Now she says she and Fin have come to an understanding.'

Bee hopped over, a flounced petticoat in frantic pink half-way up her legs and collapsed beside her. 'Hey Bird, what's all this about?' She scrutinized her twin's angrily puckered face. 'You've got it bad for Fin, haven't you?'

Tears flooding her eyes, Bird nodded dumbly.

Tissy, dressed only in a pair of green frilly knickers and a puce camisole, pirouetted over to sit on Bird's other side. 'You mustn't take any notice of what grotty Dilly says! Fin isn't a bit interested in her. You know how he goes off into that misty faraway look – she's probably thought he was giving her the glad-eye.'

Bee nodded in agreement. 'Besides, you're not trying hard enough to attract him. You need to do lots of eyelash fluttering.'

Nutmeg chuckled. 'I've always wanted you and Fin to get together, Bird. But you'll have to work harder to catch him, otherwise you'll miss the boat – there's many a lass in the Dale sighing for our handsome Fin. Even so, I can't ken he'd have his head turned by a silly creature like Daffodil—'

She was interrupted by her door latch clattering as the subject of her observation bounced in, Alaria strutting behind her: both dressed in dark green, shiny satin, their lowcut bodices stretched revealingly over their plump busts.

Alaria stared outraged at her sister. 'Thetis, whatever have you got on?' she screeched, sounding just like her mother. 'You can't wear those horrible things to the funeral. Take them off immediately, or I'll tell Ma.'

'Yes,' Dilly sniffed, her podgy features screwed up in pious disdain. 'It would make me fair blush as I follow the bier by Fin's side, if you're seen with us, dressed like that.'

Tissy glared at her. 'What are you talking about, Dilly? It's only supposed to be family that follows the bier!'

Alaria gave a simpering giggle. 'Ma says as Daffodil is nearly family, what with the understanding between her and Fin, she can process with us. Anyway, there's no time to argue, Ma will be furious if you're late, so get a move on and put on something decent.' With that, she strutted out. Daffodil waddled after her, shooting Bird a look of triumph.

Quickly they searched through Grammer Nutmeg's funeral dresses, each trying to find one that would fit. Her mind full of ways to have her vengeance on the evil Dilly, Bird eventually put on a muddy-green velvet dress, and with shaking hands tied one of the plaited bands she'd made around her soft curls.

As they dressed, they noticed Nutmeg sobbing into a small square of green silk: the ordeal ahead had suddenly dawned on her. She soon became so distressed, Tissy had to help her do up the buttons down the front of her best silk dress.

Finally, with the twins supporting Nutmeg between them, they went downstairs. Leaving Tissy to join the family in the Great Hall, the twins helped Nutmeg across the courtyard and up the path to the funeral ground.

When they reached the clearing in the pine trees the sun had sunk behind the high fell. The evening star sparkled frostily as it peeped down on the scene through the dark circle of pines. The clearing was called Kirion, a fitting place for the funeral of a Head Dandrum, for it was here the passing of kings had been marked since ancient times. Most of the mourners were already there, crowded in a circle around the pyre, their faces ghostly white in the falling dusk. Nutmeg groaned at the sight of the stack of wood topped with straw on which the body was to be placed for burning. As they waited for the funeral procession to arrive, the twins searched the crowd for their family, spotting them across the circle: their parents, Absolem and Sable, brother Sam with Berry his wife and their older sister, Honor.

Bird, shivering in her borrowed dress, couldn't stop thinking of Fin, wrapped in Daffodil's fat arms, his faced pressed into the shiny green satin stretched across her ample bosom. Turning to peer into the looming dark among the pine trees she thought she caught a whiff of burning rubber on the whispering breeze.

The sound of distant chanting drifting up the path from Dandrum Den distracted her. A stir rippled through the crowd. The chanting grew louder. A flickering light appeared through the gap in the trees. Kelp came into view holding a torch aloft, lighting the way for the funeral procession. First came the bier, carried by Fin, Lark, Hollin Annunder and Tom Gotobed. Seeing Fin bending his long legs to make himself same height as the other bearers, Bird's heart went out to him, and she forgot she should be upset with him.

Roach came next, strutting behind the bier, his hand resting on the conch shell. He was followed by Brewdy and Alaria supporting old Ramora between them. The old Delphin's face was heavily veiled and, from the evidence of her heaving shoulders, she was weeping violently. Tissy came next, by herself, dressed in a dark green, floaty gauze concoction that looked two sizes too big for her neat figure. Bouncing a few steps behind Tissy, Daffodil came into view, her snub nose stuck in the air; Bird had to fight down the urge to rush over and scratch the smug face.

Suddenly Nutmeg let out a wail, making Bird start. Grabbing her arm, she only just held her from tottering forwards to the bier. 'Hush Grammer,' she whispered, 'come, lean on me.'

The old Delphin lifted her tear-streaked face to her. 'Ah, lass! It's not easy for me, this funeral. At my time of life females should enjoy a funeral, but this one for my lovely Marlin is fair breaking my heart.' She glowered around the circle of mourners. 'The ache in me won't go away 'til I know the truth of how our Master was taken from us!' she sobbed.

Several heads turned in their direction.

'Hush, Grammer!' Bee begged, 'folk are looking at us.'

Undaunted, Nutmeg turned her attention to the Dandrum family group gathered around the pyre. She scowled at old Ramora. 'That heaving of shoulders is all pretend – you won't be finding any tears flowing under widow Ramora's thick veil!'

Dabbing her nose with her bit of green silk, she hissed: 'Mistress Ramora blamed Marlin for Old Master Fin's early death. She always hoped Master Marlin would never return, so Roach, her favourite, would be Head when Old Fin had passed on!'

She glared challengingly across at Roach. 'I reckon that's the cause of all this trouble: he'd do anything to be Dandrum Head, even murder! I reckon it's because he has more of Ramora's Cuddywif blood in him, than Dandrum.'

'There, there, Grammer, don't upset yourself,' Bird whispered, giving Bee an agonised look over the top of the old Delphin's grey head.

But Nutmeg was still in full flow. 'There he is, the apple of Ramora's eye,' she hissed, 'beloved Roach. Can you see his sly look? There's more than Cuddywif in him now – I've seen the unnatural green glow in his eyes. It makes me shudder the way he looks at young Fin – it'll be him next, on a pyre.'

Roach heard her mutterings and turning, gave her a furious look. Nutmeg ignored him, and nodded towards Fin, standing next to Lark. 'Poor lad, younger than his age in many ways,' she whispered to Bird, 'he's not weeping, but I know that he's fair lost without his dad. Haven't I been there in place of his ma and pa all his growing years, not to know how he feels? There's my grandson, Lark, at his side, which is a comfort: these sad troubles must have brought them closer. Wasn't always so. Lark always got on better with Kelp…'

She stopped her bitter tirade, seeing Roach nod curtly at Kelp who was holding the torch that would light the pyre. The moment had come that she had been dreading. Kelp stepped forward and set the flames to the wood and straw. As he did so, a strange cantillation filled the air: the older mourners were singing a hymn of passing in their ancient Delphin tongue of whistles and creaks. It was a stirring moment, but few were weeping; Bird knew most of the mourners were looking forward to eating and drinking far into the night, down in the Great Hall.

The singing died away as the flames, licking up through the wood and straw, reached the body wrapped in the oil-soaked cloth. With a sudden violent whoosh, the blaze leaped high, soaring above the encircling trees into the evening sky. Then, above the crackling roar, there came the sound of a horn. All heads turned: Roach had blown a blast on the Horn of Passing.

'What's he doing blowing the conch shell!' shrieked Nutmeg. 'That's the right of the next Dandrum Head! Who's decided Roach should be Head?' No voices came to her support. Anger fired her. She shrugged off the twins, and pushed through the crowd into the circle of firelight, her hands fisted, ready to do battle on behalf of Fin.

A tall figure stepped from the shadows and pulled her away: Bird saw it was Mr Mossy. In the light of the flames, she could see Nutmeg's tear stained face looking up at him as he bent to speak in her ear. Mossy beckoned to Bird and Bee. As they approached, he called to them in a low voice. 'Lasses, take Mrs Annunder away from here, she could be in danger!' Then he was gone, vanished into the trees.

But before Bird and Bee could reach Nutmeg, Brewdy stepped forward. 'Come Grammer Nutmeg, let's go down to the feast together!' she said in her high scratchy voice. The twins watched in dismay as Brewdy and Alaria, catching Nutmeg by the arms, marched her off down the hill. As they ran after them, Bird stopped for a few seconds to search the crowd for Fin. He'd disappeared. Daffodil Akest had disappeared too.

She didn't spot the two figures darting furtively down the hill to Dandrum Den; Fin and Lark were hurrying away before the crowd descended for the feasting.

Slipping into the courtyard, Fin took his rucksack from its hiding place in the courtyard wall and re-joining Lark, waiting outside the gate with Mick, they set off down the road to Watersmeet.

As they ran, a dark ragged form followed them, flitting through the shadows beneath the hedge. Every now and then a flash of fire rippled through it, and it stank of burning rubber.

# 4
# INHERITANCE

Trudging down the road towards the comforting lights of Watersmeet, weariness dogged Fin and Lark; even Mick had lost his jaunty bounce. A stomach-turning stink, oiling out of the hedgerow seemed to snatch at their ankles. At the bridge Fin halted. 'What's that smell?' he muttered, peering over the parapet to where from the darkness he could hear the rushes hiss and crackle in the breeze.

'Reckon it's coming from the funeral pyre,' Lark replied, 'Grammer must have soaked the winding cloths in rancid oil.'

Fin looked up to Kirion Hill; above the circle of pines the dying fire cast a red glow into the navy sky. Should he be there, he wondered?

'Get a move on, Master,' urged Lark from the far end of the bridge, 'I don't want to be out here in this creepy dark a moment longer than I have to.'

Fin hesitated. 'Lark, should I have kept vigil until the body was all burned away?'

Lark shook his head impatiently. 'No! You heard what Grammer Nutmeg said, you could be the next on a funeral pyre!'

'That's nonsense. My uncle wouldn't…' Fin let the sentence die, and hurried after Lark, already halfway up the lane to Market Place.

They found the bookshop in darkness. 'I bet he's still at the funeral feast,' Fin groaned, banging loudly on the door with the cross-shaped knocker, causing lights to go on in neighbouring cottages.

As they turned to slink away, bolts rattled, and the door opened a crack. 'At last!' breathed Mossy, pulling them inside before slamming it shut, nearly docking Mick's tail.

Holding his lamp aloft, Mossy led the way upstairs to his living room. Striding across to the window he peered through a gap in the heavy velvet curtains. 'Everything seems quiet, you don't appear to have brought anything nasty with you.' He drew the curtains tighter and hung his lamp from a hook in a ceiling beam. 'Come in lads – Fin, help our guests feel at home!'

Trotting over to where Lass lay on her sheepskin rug in front the cooking range, Mick settled beside her. Her pink belly luxuriously exposed to the logs glowing in the grate, Lass lazily thumped her tail in greeting but didn't say a word, belying the rumour that she was a talking dog.

'Take a seat, Lark,' Fin called to Lark, still hesitating at the door, and waving to the sagging sofa facing the range. Pouring two mugs of acorn coffee from a pot warming in the hearth he handed one to Lark. Then dropping down beside him, rested his head back on the sofa.

Mossy lifted the lid of a saucepan gently bubbling on the stove and stirred the contents, filling the room with a rich aroma of meaty stew. On Lass's rug, Mick's nose twitched.

Gulping a mouthful of sweet coffee, Lark wriggled into the sofa trying to relax, nervously hoping that, in this wizard's room, the shadows dancing around the walls wouldn't come to life. The smell of stew making him very hungry, he saw with relief that plates and cutlery for three were laid on a gingham cloth at one end of the long table in the middle of the room.

A jumble of objects covered the rest of the table: fossils, shells, pinecones, seed heads, dried insect cases, birds' eggs; among them stood a strange brass object, its jointed arms having balls of different sizes attached to the ends. The arms seemed to be moving of their own volition, twisting, and circling, the gleaming metal glittering in the lamp light. Lark didn't know it, but this machine, called an orrery, represented the solar system in miniature.

He gazed around the rest of the room, which extended the length of the cottage. In the farthest corner stood Mossy's six-foot long bed, his distinctive inky blue robes and baggy black trousers hanging on hooks above the wooden bed head. To one side of the cooking range stood Mossy's rocking chair, and on the other a dresser: plates, pots and pans jostled for space with jars of preserves, packets of seeds and dried fruits. Strings of onions and bunches of herbs, hanging from the oak-beamed ceiling, gently turned in the warmth rising from the range.

Pouring himself some coffee, Mossy sat in his rocking chair, shoulders hunched, the only sounds in the room the occasional fizz and crackle of resin from the apple tree logs burning in the grate.

Finally, Fin broke the silence. 'Mossy, there's something we want to show you.' He turned to Lark. 'Get out the feather, Lark.'

Lark took his pack to the table. Laying it well away from crockery and cutlery, fished out the leather packet and unfolding the soft suede, exposed the feather. It looked harmless, its downy lightness gently stirring in the warm air. Mossy came and peered at it.

'Being suspicious, Mr Mossy, sir, I went to have another look at where Master Marlin died,' Lark explained. 'First, I found that leather cord he always wore about his neck – you know, the one with a gold medallion. But although I searched, I couldn't find the medallion. I followed some dodgy-looking footprints to a clump of gorse bushes, and found this feather caught on a twig. I nearly touched it – glad I didn't – it stings!'

Mossy looked up sharply. 'So, you know about these feathers?'

'Well, no. Its stink stayed my hand. It was back at Dandrum Den, when I took it out to have a better look, it stung me! I was wondering if it came from a Drone Bird?'

Mossy cautiously folded the feather back into the leather. 'No, this is a ganglefowl's rump feather and must be burned before anyone gets badly stung.'

Going and throwing the packet on the fire, a yellow flame flared up.

'Whatever's a ganglefowl? Is it bigger than a Drone Bird?' Lark asked, coughing at the smell of rotten egg.

'No, a Drone Bird, as you call it, is something altogether different.' Mossy gave him a wintry smile. 'You may yet have a chance to come up close to one of those: then you'll understand. No, ganglefowl are a creature bred for evil.'

He returned to his chair. 'Fin, it is time you knew the truth about your father. As I have already told you, he was not killed by a wolf, but was murdered.'

Fin shivered at the memory of his father's wound. 'It's pretty obvious it wasn't a wolf bite in his throat. But what creature could have made such a wound?'

'No natural creature! Fin, your father was killed by a Frit – it is they who ride the ganglefowl.'

'Raddled rams, are they real?' exclaimed Lark, 'I thought them one of Grammer Nutmeg's fairy tales, to give us naughty lads a fright.'

Mossy smiled grimly. 'Mrs Annunder has told me the tale of the orange imp she saw lurking on the borders of Withered Wood. I didn't want to worry her, so I said she must have imagined it. But I recognized it as a Frit – slaves of the Sneaksouls.'

Lark shuddered. 'It's fearsome to think of such critters in our Dale!'

Fin frowned into his coffee mug. 'I think there's a Sneaksoul inside uncle Roach, I've seen an eerie green glow in his eyes.'

Looking up, he asked: 'Mossy, why are the Evils interested in our Dale? Are they after something my father owned? He never told me much about his travels in search of my mother, but I'm sure he intended to, when we were on our camping trip. Now I'll never know if he ever found her, and why he never brought her home—' his voice broke into a sob.

Mossy leant forward and laid a comforting hand on his knee. 'Yes, your father died too soon. I know he was going to tell you everything.'

Leaning back, he sighed. 'You both know the tale: when he returned from his wanderings, he was supposed have brought back fabulous riches. Little of that is true. There was a treasure. Just one, which eventually, after a terrible struggle with himself, he gave into my safe keeping. We put it away in a box and hid it in my attic.'

Fin and Lark looked up at the beams, where the bunches of herbs and strings of onions slowly spun in the lamp light.

'The treasure has been with me ever since. We hoped it would be safe here, in Brightdale. Few knew that your father possessed it – at least we thought so, but it seems we were wrong. I dread to think how the demon Lord Gressil found out: I have my suspicions!'

'But before we go up to the attic, we must eat. A full stomach does wonders!' He smiled at Lark. 'Even if you are not hungry, your small terrier is drooling so much, he will forget his manners, and jump on the table.'

Half an hour later, heartened by big helpings of rabbit stew, and leaving the dogs gobbling bowls of leftovers, they went out onto the landing, where Mossy pulled down a ladder from a hatchway in the ceiling. Lamp in hand he led them up into the attic.

Kneeling on the floorboards below the low roof, they made out boxes and crates, some with the lids open, scrolls and books spilling out. Everything was covered in dust; nobody had been up here in a long time. Fin wondered which of the boxes contained his father's mysterious treasure.

A thud on the roof made him start. Looking up to a small square window, he saw starlight twinkling. Suddenly a hideous face filled the square. Shrinking back in horror, two angry red eyes glared down at him. A mouth of long yellow teeth gaped open. As it leered, from behind him a flash of blinding light shot up and hit the glass. With a shriek the face vanished. His heart thumping, Fin swung round to see Mossy's face turned up to the window: a faint glow still flickered in his dark eyes.

'Heck, was that an owl?' Lark exclaimed. 'Fancy an owl giving me the frights, as if I were a silly female!'

Fin looked at him in surprise. In his stress had he imagined that evil face? Mossy's voice coming from a dark corner distracted him.

'Here is the box! It has been hidden away up here for nigh on ten years.' Wiping away the dust with his sleeve, he crawled back and put the box down in the circle of light from his lamp.

Much smaller than the usual Delphin treasure box, it was about the width and depth of a man's large hand, its silver and mother-of-pearl decoration gleaming in the lamplight, far richer than any Delphin box Fin and Lark had ever seen.

'I kept the key for it in the trunk under my bed,' Mossy said, taking a small silver key from his pocket. About to put it to the lock, he changed his mind and handed the key to Fin.

'No, this is now your box Fin, it is for you to open.' He searched the shadows. 'But I advise you to wait until we are in more pleasant surroundings.'

Tucking the key into a pocket in his jerkin, Fin lifted the box, finding it surprisingly heavy for its size. Crawling to the hatch, he climbed down the ladder, Lark behind him.

Mossy didn't follow immediately. Gazing up through the small window, his fathomless eyes roaming vast distances amongst the stars, he spoke softly to himself: 'Old man – what is there to fear, for has not my Universe of Stars been saved?'

If they had heard, Fin and Lark would have been astounded.

In Mossy's room Lark cleared a space on the cluttered table for Fin to set down the box. They stood back for a moment, admiring the rich decoration, before bending close to study the intricate inlay of silver wire tendrils and mother-of-pearl flowers trailing over the dark wood on the sides and lid: the silver had not tarnished, even though the box had been hidden in the dusty attic for years. Set in the very centre of the lid was a silver cross, shaped in the form of an X intersected by the letter P.

'How did my father come to possess such a box?' Fin breathed. 'It's beyond our skills here in Brightdale!' Tracing the lines of the cross, it dawned on him: the shape was the same as the scar on his father's chest.

'The box was made long, long ago, by a Gaiakin.' Mossy said. 'That oddly shaped cross on the lid is called a Chi Rho; in the ancient Greek language, 'X' stands for Chi and 'P' for Rho, representing the name Christos. Open the box and you will understand why the Gaiakin made such an elaborate container.'

Looking up, they were disconcerted to see he had gone to sit by the fire, his face averted.

Taking the silver key from his pocket, Fin fitted it into the keyhole in the side of the box, where it pierced the palm of a small inlaid silver hand. The key turned smoothly. As he lifted the lid, he thought he detected the faint odour of dried blood. Lark moved in closer to see.

The box was lined with rich scarlet velvet, as bright as when first dyed. Resting on the velvet was a bundle of shimmering blue silken cloth.

'Just like a dragonfly's wing in sunlight!' breathed Lark. 'Take the cloth out Fin – let's see what's wrapped inside.'

As Fin lifted it out, a neatly folded piece of parchment fluttered on to the table. He saw his name written on the outside. 'This is my father's writing!' he exclaimed, studying the faded lettering, 'he's written to me!' He started to open it eagerly.

'I suggest you do not read it now, Fin,' Mossy said from his chair, 'wait until daylight, when you will be able to see more clearly.'

Reluctantly tucking away the parchment in his jerkin, Fin turned to the bundle. Unwrapping the blue folds, a long gold chain cascaded out, and then with a clunk, a heavy gold cross landed on the table. Reverently Fin picked it up and laid it on his open hand. Lark leaned in. It had the same shape as the Chi Rho depicted on the lid of the box and was the size of Fin's palm. The gold cross-pieces, decorated with a filigree of twisted silver wires, were fringed along every edge with tiny pearls, and upon the filigree were laid rows of brilliant-cut gems: sapphires, emeralds and rubies. Where the cross-pieces met in the centre, a gold mount held a smooth lozenge-shaped crystal, about the size of a wren's egg. It was as flawlessly clear as spring water; beneath the crystal lay a disc of pale blue enamel. The enamel looked as if it were damaged, with a dark hair-line crack in the centre.

'Fin, look at the back of the cross,' Mossy said, 'there is an inscription there.'

Turning it over, Fin laid it back on the blue cloth. He and Lark bent close and saw, along the vertical of the letter P, a smooth fillet of gold had been welded, upon which a line of tiny letters had been engraved.

Rummaging amongst the bits and pieces on the table, Fin found Mossy's magnifying glass. Peering through it, he saw the words were in Common Language.

Haltingly, he read them out: 'Having slept a short sleep on the tree, the King of all, The Word, who is both God and man, gave the wood virtue.'

They looked across at Mossy, hoping for an explanation.

'The inscription concerns what lies beneath the crystal,' he said, 'perhaps one day you will unravel the conundrum.'

Turning the cross over, in turn they peered through the magnifying glass at the blue enamel beneath the crystal, wondering what the blemish was.

'It might not be a crack,' Fin said, 'it could be a piece of thread.'

'Looks more like a trout bone to me,' Lark said. A sudden irresistible urge to stroke the crystal's smooth surface came over him, and he was about to put his finger on it when Mossy called out sharply. 'No, Lark! Do not touch the crystal!'

Shrinking back, Lark stared at Mossy in surprise.

'Lark, the cross is Fin's burden – it has been left to him to bear.'

'What do you mean,' Fin exclaimed, shocked by Mossy's sudden fierceness. 'What is this cross? Why do you call it my burden?' He remembered again the deep scar etched in his father's dead chest: had he worn this cross? Had it caused his scar?

Mossy motioned the two Delphins to the sofa. 'Put the cross down Fin. The time has come to tell you the story of the Chi Rho.'

Fin laid the cross on its blue cloth, and they settled on the sofa. Lark anticipated what he called 'a good yarn'. Like many Dalers, he enjoyed Mossy's 'preachifying' as it was known among the Delphins when he recounted stories from the life of the Christ.

How long Mossy's weekly Praising Hour on Holydays had been going on, no one remembers. In cold weather, it is held in the Meeting Barn, but on bright Highsun days it is outdoors in Market Place, where he leads the gathering in singing praises to the Creator, of whom he appears to have much knowledge. A lot of what he says is difficult to understand, but they enjoy watching his face, which takes on a shining joy, starting in his eyes, and spreading as a soft light all around him. Some don't approve of this Praising Hour, saying it's not right for Delphins. Had they not got their own traditions? Delphins don't have an official religion but do have a deep reverence for the land and the seasons. They believe powerful spirits are behind everything, to whom they give thanks with festivals at set times of year. Some are not sure if Mr Mossy should be allowed to carry on in such a way. But he continues to hold the Praising Hour, attracting many, who take part with great enthusiasm. Lark couldn't attend very often, but when he did, he enjoyed the stories hugely.

Putting another log on the fire, Mossy began his story. 'It started with a vision – a vision of a cross.'

'Long ago, in a far-off land, so the legend goes, (Lark settled deeper into the sofa – he approved of stories that started that way), there ruled a warrior emperor who was constantly at war, driven by a desire to conquer all the Known World.

One evening, resting in his tent before a battle, he fell into a trance: he was mounted on his war horse at the head of a great army. A strangely shaped cross shone in the sky above him. A loud voice cried: "In Hoc Signo Vinces" – in Common Language that means "In this sign, conquer!"

When the emperor awoke, he ordered a new battle standard to be made, depicting this cross, and the next day, bearing his new standard before him, he won a mighty victory. Eventually all the Known World came under his domination, and all quailed before the Standard, known as the Chi Rho.'

Mossy stopped and smiled at them mischievously. 'But that legend is purely a fairy story for recounting around a fire on a dark night!'

Lark snorted in disgust.

Mossy continued: 'There was an emperor, that is true, whose standard was the Chi Rho; ancient statues show him wearing such a cross. There is proof too, that the emperor's mother commissioned a gold jewel-encrusted Chi Rho as a gift to her son when he adopted her religion.

'But Fin, your Chi Rho has an entirely different history: it was made long ago by a Gaiakin. As you know, the Gaiakins are skilled jewellery makers.'

'But how did my father – a mere Delphin – come to possess it?' Fin snapped, irritated by Mossy's ramblings. 'Was that why he was murdered – because he owned it? Anyway, why is it so special? The Gaiakins make loads of jewellery, and people aren't killed for their bracelets and necklaces!'

'I know your father intended to tell you the strange tale of how he came to possess the Chi Rho: perhaps he explains in his letter. This cross has, shall we say, a reputation. Some believe it has healing powers, even magical powers. There are many who covet it. It is well known that the Lord Gressil greatly desires it. I am not at liberty to tell you the whole the truth about it – that secret belongs to the Gaiakin who made the cross.'

He raised his hand as Fin began to ask another question. 'Fin, allow me to finish the tale! Now, it was when the Gaiakins were living in their faraway tropical garden that this Gaiakin made the Chi Rho. On their borders was a community of holy people, known as the Desert Fathers and it was for these people that he made the cross. The story goes that when he had completed the last delicate piece of welding, he was overcome by a burning desire to lay the beautiful object close to his great Gaiakin heart.

His brother, seeing a shadow in his beautiful golden eyes, quickly came to his aid, gently prising the cross from his tight grip. Wrapping it in a shimmering blue silken cloth, they put it in the box they had made – that box!' Mossy gestured to the box on the table.

"Come," said the Gaiakin's brother, "your work is finished. We can now give this beautiful Cross to the Desert Fathers' Community." They took the cross to the Community, and for centuries nothing more was known of the Chi Rho. It was during the Great Dying, many, many centuries later, that the Chi Rho was found again, hidden in a far-off desert oasis. After journeying through many lands, it came to our northern shores, and into the safe keeping of the Holy Community on Lindisfarne. There it remained, until recent times.'

'Did my father go to this place, Lindisfarne? Is that where he got the cross?' Fin exclaimed. 'Where is Lindisfarne?' He jumped up and clattered downstairs to the shop, returning a few moments later, bringing a much-thumbed atlas. Flicking through the index, he found the page he wanted. 'Here we are, reference 4C, Lindisfarne or Holy Island. It's on the coast, way up north! Did my father get as far as that?'

'No, by the time your father possessed the Chi Rho, it had long gone from Holy Island.'

'What happened to it, Mr Mossy?' Lark asked eagerly, 'was it stolen?'

Mossy nodded. 'It was stolen by a Skwid called Shifter whose clan lived in the forests of the nearby mainland. The story goes, that the Skwid, seeking healing for his young son, wounded by a lynx, went to Holy Island, to ask the Holy Community for help.

Shifter saw how, by using the power of Chi Rho, they saved his child's life, and being of the Skwid's devious nature, he noted the secret place where they kept the cross. So, when the Sneaksouls came north, searching for slaves, Shifter sought to befriend those evil ones: he told them of the magical properties of the Chi Rho, and offered to steal it in exchange for the freedom of his family.

Helped by the amazing ability of Skwid kind to take on the hue of any background, he stole the Chi Rho, and took it to the Sneaksouls to guarantee protection. They in turn, looking for gratitude from Lord Gressil, took it to the land of Contagion, so Gressil could heal the deep wound in Queen Maabella's side.

'But before they got there, the cross mysteriously disappeared; some say that Shifter stole it back; others said the Sneaksoul leader lusted for it. The Chi Rho vanished, until years later, by amazing chance, Crow the Scav found it whilst nosing in the marshes on the border of Contagion.

But what Crow did with it after that and how your father came by it, Fin, is your father's story. Let us hope he will have given you an account in his letter!'

Lark sighed. 'That was a tale and a half, Mr Mossy! And now Master Fin has the Chi Rho. Well, I'll be…!' He turned to Fin. 'Why not have a go at reading the letter from your dad, now?' he asked hopefully.

Fin unfolded the parchment and held it up to the lamplight.

*Dear Fin, my beloved son...* He peered at the close lines of writing, but the ink was so faded, and the light too dim. 'I'll need daylight,' he muttered, quickly returning the letter to his pocket.

Going to cross lying gleaming on the shimmering blue material, he once more stared into the crystal lozenge, at the blemish in the blue enamel.

'Thinking of Gressil, what I want to know is how he came to lurk in those rotting lands beyond the Withered Wood, so near to us in Brightdale?' Lark growled from the sofa. 'The tales my Grammer Nutmeg told when I was still in short trousers, sounded farfetched; I remember she said old Gressil looks like a huge scorpion, and his wife Maabella like a great fat slug, and that they came crawling out of the Grey Sea, causing trouble!'

Looking grim, Mossy said: 'That is a long and terrible tale, Lark. Gressil is what is known as a Manticore. He is a Dark Angel. Aeons ago he became imprisoned in the body of one of the creatures known as eurypterids, large fearsome predators of the Palaeozoic period. He lives in constant torment, plagued by greed and hate, desperate to escape from the hard shell of his scorpion body.'

Mossy leapt to his feet, making them start. Picking up the poker, he stabbed fiercely at the burning logs in the grate. 'One day you may come to know the tale: it would be better if you never did.' Sitting down again, he rubbed his tired eyes, suddenly looking old and weary. 'But come now, before we go to bed, we must decide what to do with the cross.'

Lark sighed with disappointment – tales about monsters and demons were the best.

But Fin was deeply troubled by Mossy's stories. Surely, they were just fantasy? Then recalling how his father had suffered, he realised there was something disturbing about the Chi Rho: that it had great power, for good and evil. He glowered down at it glinting on its bed of blue.

'This thing can't stay in Brightdale,' he said fiercely, 'it has brought enough evil here already, and I suppose it's my job to take it away, as soon as possible! But where? I'm born a Delphin of Brightdale, and never been beyond our borders.' He looked pleadingly at Mossy. 'Should I take it to the Scavs? No? I know, I could throw it in the sea! Gressil would come chasing after it, like a dog after a stick, and return to the ocean, taking his evil with him – the trouble is, I'm scared stiff.' He shivered, avoiding Lark's anxious gaze.

Mossy came over and put an arm around his shoulders. 'Fin, fancy thinking I would let you go off without help!'

Fin looked up at him hopefully. 'You'll come too? I wouldn't feel so afraid if you were with me.'

Mossy shook his head. 'You know I must not leave Brightdale unprotected.'

Fin nodded sadly. 'I wasn't hopeful, what with Contagion being just over the hill...'

'Have courage Fin, I have powerful friends out there.' Mossy waved his hand towards the curtained window. 'There are those who can help and guide you. Indeed, I have already made plans!'

'Besides, you won't be going alone, and that's for sure,' Lark said, standing arms folded, a look of grim determination on his face. 'I'm coming too, and I won't accept a No.'

Fin shook his head. 'Lark, this is not your problem, however courageous your offer.'

'Now, you didn't listen to what I've just said, Master Fin. I won't accept a No. Besides, I need to get to know you better, now you're Dandrum Head and I'm in your employ: there's no better way, than going on this jaunt with you.'

Mossy and Fin couldn't help smiling.

'It's no good Fin,' Mossy laughed, 'you will have Lark as a companion, whether you like it or not. But seriously, Lark, I was hoping that you would volunteer to go with Fin: he will need you to guide him through Annunder Territory to the borders of the Dale. I have already sent word to a friend: his name is Sandy. He will meet you at Ireshope, a trading post on your northern borders. You have been there, have you not?'

Lark nodded eagerly. 'Yes, when I was a little 'un. I'll never forget that adventure with my Granfer Fox: we traded charcoal for metal pieces. I know the way alright.'

'Good,' said Mossy. 'Ireshope lies beside the river Durholm, on the path to Durholm Garrison, where there are those who will advise you Fin, and may even be willing to take the cross into their safe keeping. I have hopes of it being put with the Blessed Cuthbert's reliquaries.

'Sandy has a deep knowledge of the northern forests. He will take you a safe way – you don't want to get tangled in the Withered Wood!'

He turned to Lark. 'Now Lark, off you go home. Come back at first light with your gear.' Mossy shooed him towards the door.

'Thanks Lark,' Fin said, coming over and giving him soft punch on the shoulder. 'Take care – run home quickly!'

'Don't you worry about me, Master Fin,' Lark said, surprised; he was beginning to take to Fin. Whistling to Mick, he clattered off down the stairs.

After bolting the front door behind Lark, Mossy came back up and opening a drawer in his bedside chest, brought out a purse of new calf skin. 'I've made this for you Fin.' Opening the small drawstring bag, he showed inside. 'It will serve to keep the cross safe on your journey – the box is far too bulky.'

Fin saw Mossy had plaited cord for hanging it about his neck. Dropping the cross inside, he slipped the cord over his head and tucked the purse inside his jerkin.

Mossy reverently returned the folded blue cloth to the box, locked the lid, and put the box in his bedside chest. The key he tucked inside his robe.

Fin asked: 'Are there Gaiakins who still make those beautiful boxes?'

'Yes, two brothers who live in the Garden of Florain continue the craft. Maybe one day you will be able to go there and visit their workshop!'

Listening to him, it dawned on Fin that his future could get very interesting.

Meanwhile, up at Dandrum Den, the funeral feast was in full swing, singing and laughter echoing around the Great Hall. The young ones, some with flutes and fiddles, had cleared an area of floor and were energetically dancing.

But Bird wasn't enjoying the feasting or dancing, she was busy searching for Fin. When Tissy, still in Nutmeg's old-fashioned funeral finery, twirled past with her brother Kelp, she grabbed her arm. 'Have you seen Fin or Lark? I can't find them anywhere!' she called above the noise.

Pushing Kelp away, Tissy looked about the hall. She too had been wondering why Lark hadn't come to ask her for a dance. Scanning the tables, crowded with older Delphins enjoying their food and drink, there was no sign of Lark or Fin. Now uneasy, she noticed that Alaria and Daffodil, usually to be found tucking into mounds of food, were also missing. She grabbed Bird's hand. 'We'll ask Bee if she knows anything,' she called, leading her to a nook behind the dais, where she knew Bee was locked in passionate embrace with Jacko Gladden.

Bird shook her twin by the shoulder. 'Bee, have you seen Fin or Lark? We can't find them anywhere!'

'Daffodil and Alaria have disappeared too,' Tissy wailed.

Exasperated, Bee extracted herself from Jacko's arms. 'I expect they're – oh I don't know – in the kitchen, doing the washing up?' she added sarcastically. But seeing their worried faces, she sighed. 'Oh, come on, let's go and find them. I'm sure I saw Alaria earlier, waddling to the kitchen, to filch more jelly.'

'Yep – reckon I saw Fin and Daffy having a cuddle in the larder!' Jacko grinned mischievously.

Bee gave him a simmering look. 'Don't run away lad, I'll be back to deal with you!' Jacko pretended to look scared.

As they passed Nutmeg Annunder's still room, they heard sobbing. Looking in, they found Nutmeg there, slumped on a stool, tears streaming down her crumpled cheeks.

'Grammer what are you doing in here?' Tissy asked, putting her arm around her. 'You should be at the feast, enjoying all that food we worked so hard to cook!'

'No, no! I can't be feasting – I'm too worrit!' Nutmeg moaned, clutching Tissy's hand. 'There's an evil fiend roaming the Dale, and I'm afeared it's going to murder Fin and Lark, just like it did Master Marlin!'

'Now, Grammer,' Bee said firmly, 'you mustn't let your imaginings run away with you!'

'The only hell-hags after Fin and Lark, are Alaria and Daffodil Akest,' Bird muttered venomously, 'I'm sure they've sneaked off together.'

Grammer Nutmeg sniffed, then shook her head vigorously. 'No, no!' she wailed, 'Mr Mossy told me to get a message to the lads – real serious he looked. They were to go to his shop straight way, but I couldn't get to them – that Brewdy waylaid me. An' when I 'scaped and went looking for the lads, I saw them already on their way down to Watersmeet, but they were being followed – never will I forget that loath sight!' Shaking with terror, she would have fallen off her stool if Tissy hadn't supported her. 'Like a pile of burning rags t'was, mothing through the grass by the road. It wasn't even one of those orange imps, t'was worser!'

'There, there, Grammer,' crooned Bee, 'don't you fret – Bird and I will go to Mr Mossy's. I bet we'll find the lads with him, deep in some boring book-type matter.'

'I'm coming with you,' Tissy said determinedly. 'I'm sure I didn't imagine that lingering look between Lark and Alaria in the kitchen this morning – Alaria's pasty cheeks turned all pink.'

So, wondering if Nutmeg's imagination had tricked her or not, making them feel a little scared they might be attacked by something unnatural, the three hurried down to Watersmeet.

Mossy's shop was in darkness, with no light in the shop and the upstairs curtains tightly drawn. 'Mr Mossy must be at the feast,' Tissy whispered in a scared voice.

'Well, I didn't see him there,' Bird hissed, 'we'd better wait and see if he comes back.'

'Don't let's hang about in the open! Can't we hide somewhere to keep watch?' Tissy whispered, looking about her fearfully. The shadows in the deserted square had a menacing air, as if hidden eyes were watching them.

Scurrying like frightened mice across Market Place, they headed for Chippen the wheelwright's yard. Ducking down beneath a cart, they had a clear view of Mossy's shop. Pale clouds scudded across the night sky, now and then obscuring a strangely red moon.

Bird shivered, feeling a chill wind through the thin dress she'd borrowed from Nutmeg: it was a west wind, the Evil Wind, as the Delphins called it, blowing over Withered Wood, from out of the Land of Contagion. She regretted that she'd been too agitated to go back to Grammer Nutmeg's room to change back into her jerkin and trousers before leaving Dandrum Den.

Time passed. There was no sign of Mossy. She began to wonder whether they were making fools of themselves. Nodding towards Mossy's dark shop, she whispered: 'I'm sure there's no one there. I bet the lads have gone to a secret place, to meet up with Daffodil and Alaria – perhaps on the sand by the river down by St. Aidan's shrine.'

Tissy looked at her in dismay. 'Don't say that! I can't forget the way Lark looked at Alaria in the kitchen, especially when Daffodil was going on about skinny dipping with Fin.'

Bee snorted. 'Lark interested in Alaria? Newt's knickers, Tissy, everyone knows he's in love with you!'

Tissy sighed. 'Do you think so? But with my lip, I can't blame him if he looks elsewhere.' She ran her finger over the small puckered scar on her upper lip.

They sat for a while in silence.

Glancing through the gloom at Bee, Bird saw her eyes sparkling; excitement seemed to crackle from her like electricity: she realised her twin was enjoying herself hugely. She was about to say that they must go and knock on Mossy's door or go home, when she noticed something weird beneath the bookshop window. It looked like a bundle of rags lying there. She was sure it hadn't been there when they first came. It was moving, heaving up and down. From it, a rubbery stink oozed across the cobbles towards them. The vague form gave out an eerie light, turning from red to orange to yellow, casting a pulsing glow on the whitewashed stone. A hideous face suddenly appeared, red glowing eyes, a yellow toothed grin. Looking straight at her, it let out a sound that froze her blood: a malevolent wheezing snarl of pure evil. Like a shadowy fog, slowly and furtively, the glowing bundle slid up the shop wall, and reaching the roof, disappeared over the ridge. A moment later the night was rent by a piercing shriek. At the same time from the back of the roof a bright beam of light shot into the sky.

Bee screamed. 'What was that?'

Suddenly their adventure didn't seem so exciting.

'I think I'm going to be sick!' whimpered Tissy, struggling from under the cart.

Bird scrambled out and caught her before she slumped in a faint to the ground. 'Help me Bee, we'll have to get her home to Spinner Hall.'

Sobbing with fright, half carrying, half dragging Tissy, stopping once for her to vomit her feast over a wall, ten long minutes later they reached the safety of Spinner Hall.

Thankfully the small door in the high gate had been left unlocked. Stumbling into the courtyard, they slammed it shut behind them. Their hound Wolfie bounded over, his joyful baying sundering the quiet night. 'Shut it Wolfie!' Bee scolded as she helped Tissy up the steps to the oak door of the Hall. Collapsing on the top step, they sat trembling.

Bee was the first to recover. 'That was a tad nasty,' she giggled shakily as she pushed away Wolfie's wet tongue from her neck. 'What do you reckon we saw?'

'It wasn't Daffodil or Alaria – unless they've changed dramatically,' Bird grinned sheepishly. 'I hope Mossy and the lads weren't in the shop. Do you think we should go back and check if they're O.K.?'

'Oh no! I couldn't face going back,' moaned Tissy, 'I'm sure Mr Mossy wouldn't let any harm come to the lads. Oh dear, I feel so sick!'

Bird felt Tissy's forehead. 'You need to lie down, Tissy. Come on – we'll take you to our room.'

Supporting her between them, the twins helped her upstairs to their bedroom, where she gratefully snuggled down under a soft blanket on Bird's bed.

'You need something hot and sweet,' Bird said, looking worriedly at Tissy's chalk white face. 'I'll go to the kitchen and make some tea – we could all do with a cup!'

A little while later, she came back with three steaming mugs on a tray.

'Anyone ask why we weren't at the feast?' Bee asked.

'The place is empty: even cook's gone!'

Bird had also peeped into the bedroom shared by their older, unmarried sister, Honor and their toddler sister, Abb. Their Grammer Magette was there dozing in an armchair next to sleeping Abb's crib.

Letting the honey-sweetness of the camomile tea soothe their jitters, reassured by the familiar surroundings, Tissy and the twins speculated as to what they'd seen outside Mossy's shop.

'It could have been a bit of loose plustic, blown in on the wind,' Bird said, sounding doubtful.

'Do you think we'd drunk too much mead?' Bee wondered.

Tissy made a face. 'I didn't drink any, but Holly Greenwood made me try a mouthful of his firewater – it was disgusting.'

'I vote we go back,' Bee said.

'Oh, no! I couldn't go out in the dark again,' cried Tissy, clutching the blanket to her chin.

'We'll take Wolfie,' Bee said, 'he's very fierce in dangerous situations!'

'Go on Tissy, we'd be perfectly safe with him to protect us,' Bird said. 'And I bet there'll be loads of people about now, coming home from the feast.'

Despite their reassurances, Tissy became so agitated they feared she would be sick again, so reluctantly they agreed to wait until daylight.

'If I catch that Daffodil Akest pawing Fin and upsetting Bird, she'll have me to deal with,' Bee hissed, slamming the empty mugs on the tray by the door, before slipping into her bed. Blowing out the candle, Bird snuggled down next to her.

Bee quickly fell asleep, but Bird lay awake, listening to her twin's soft breathing close to her ear. Her mind churned with nasty things she would like to see happen to Daffodil: such as being hexed by Mossy's dog, and all her hair falling out.

Until Daffodil had announced her supposed closeness to Fin, Bird hadn't given much thought to herself and Fin settling down together; she'd just taken for granted that one day they would get married. She hadn't realised until today how much she cared for the lanky lad, with his dark Rom looks; the realisation that he might be interested in another female had come as a shock.

In Mossy's room, Fin lay wrapped in a blanket on the sofa, his thoughts wandering over the day behind him. Was it only last night that his father had asked him to go hunting for the wolf? Now he was dead, his body ashes, up on Kirion hill.

Shifting to get more comfortable, his new purse with the cross inside had started to dig into his chest, so he hid it under his pillow, along with his father's unread letter.    As he settled again, he remembered the ceremonial sword he'd taken from his father's body. Flinging back his blanket and tiptoeing across to his rucksack, he woke Lass, who sat up and watched him warily. Feeling the hard metal outline of the sword amongst his clothes, satisfied he returned to the sofa.

Once more beneath his blanket, he thought of the cross his father had left him, hidden all these years in Mossy's attic. How had his father come by such an extraordinary object? Hopefully, his letter would explain. Slipping his hand beneath his pillow, he pulled out the letter and tried to read his name written on the outside, but it was too dark to see. Putting the letter away, his hand brushed against the leather purse. Curling his fingers around the soft suede, feeling the shape and weight of the cross, hidden inside, he plunged into a dream.

*He was kneeling on the ground, on a hill in a strange land, yellow light all about him. Above him, a man hung on a wooden cross, his hands pinioned to the crossbeam, his feet nailed to a pole dug into soil soaked rusty red with blood. A crowd pressed around, some jeering, some weeping. The ground, the air, the people, everywhere smelt of blood.*

*Choking for air, the man was still alive. His tormentors had forced a coronet of tangled thorns about his brow, and the blood was flowing down his face and running into his mouth.*

*Fin became aware of a tall, cloaked figure kneeling beside him, head bowed, his face hidden inside a deep hood. He had a long thin-bladed golden dagger in his hand.*

*The man on the cross, spitting out blood, gave a sudden cry: 'Eloi, Eloi, lama sabachthani?'*

*Even though they weren't in Common Language, Fin understood the words: 'My God, my God, why have you deserted me?'*

*Turning to the hooded figure, he plucked urgently at his sleeve. 'Please, please, help the poor man!' he begged.*

*The figure ignored him. Standing up, using his dagger, he began digging at the blood-soaked wood of the cross. As he prized out a piece, a gobbet of blood from the bowed, thorn-crowned head dripped onto to the back of his hand. The figure staggered back as if he had been burnt. Lifting his hand to lick the blood away, a ruby red jewel flashed on his finger.*

The hill, the people, the tortured man on the cross, all faded away, and he fell into deep dreamless sleep.

# 5
# LEAVING HOME

Next day, at first light, Mossy cooked Fin his favourite breakfast: salt pork with a fried duck egg, wrapping the last of the pork in a parchment parcel, which he tucked into Fin's rucksack. Clearing up, they went into the garden to wait for Lark, sitting on the bench beneath the apple tree, listening to the Whippetwater, at present in full spate, rushing below the cliff path beyond the hedge.

The air smelt clean, the rubbery stink of the night long dispersed. As the sun rose above the cottage and the garden filled with light, Fin could see to read his father's letter. It was the right place, here beneath the old apple tree where his father had loved to sit.

Fin, too, had spent happy hours here, listening to Mossy's accounts of the world outside, a world Fin had no desire to visit. His roots were deep in Brightdale. His mother was from the travelling Rom people, but he was of the Dale, part of its soil, rivers, rocks; its creatures, trees, and grasses; part of its air, its cold winds and balmy breezes; part of the Delphin Dalers, and their lives and deaths.

Now he had to leave. He'd never imagined this destiny for himself; the Burden, as Mossy called the Chi Rho, had been thrust upon him without his consent. Full of resentment, he wished he'd been born just an ordinary Delphin lad, with a long life ahead of him: marrying Bird and raising a brood of young Dandrums.

Could he back out, he wondered? Let someone else dispose of the cross? Who? Mossy? Looking at Mossy beside him, head hidden deep in the cowl of his ink blue robe, Fin's strange dream came back to him: the man hanging on the cross, the hooded figure digging at the wood. Who was the poor, tortured man? Who was that person on whose hand a gobbet of blood had dripped? Were they real, or were they conjured from a dark corner of his mind?

He fished out his father's letter and again read his name, written in his father's spidery writing on the folded square of faded parchment. When was this letter written? Was it soon after his father came home from his wanderings – over ten years ago? Taking a deep breath, he opened the letter.

*Dear Fin, my beloved son...*

Tears blurred his eyes: his father had never called him beloved when he was alive. Swiping his eyes with his sleeve, he continued reading.

*First: I hope that you will never read this. If you are, then I am most certainly dead – killed because of the cross you will find with this letter. I intend soon, to take the cross away from Brightdale – then I will destroy this letter.*

*Beware the cross, it has unpleasant powers. I came to possess it by the oddest of chances. I had been searching for your mother for some years, travelling with a clan of Roms. We were at Jarrow, on the coast. Whilst they bought silks and spices from a newly docked ship, I was occupying the time wandering along the shoreline when I came upon a Scav lying in the mud. I saw the poor creature had a deep wound in his thin chest and going to his aid, I was astonished to discover a golden cross embedded there! Intending to help the pathetic mite, I pulled the cross away, but to my horror, I thought my action had killed him – it was only later that I found out I was mistaken.*

*Wiping off the blood, I studied the cross, amazed by its richness. As I gazed, a fierce desire overcame me: I forgot the Scav, forgot my Rom friends, and worst of all, I forgot my search for your mother. Hanging the cross on its chain about my neck, my only desire was to escape with my new-found treasure: I had succumbed to the terrible power of the Chi Rho.*

*My life became a nightmare, never at peace, forever fearful my precious treasure would be stolen from me. I realised that if I was to be saved, I must return to the safety of Brightdale. I was ill and weary when I finally reached home. By this time, the cross had become embedded in my chest. Knowing Mossy alone could help me I went to him for aid, and after enduring much agony (in mind as well as body), Mossy removed the cross from my flesh. He had in his possession a beautiful box, a fitting repository for the cross, and it is in there that we have put it. I will enclose this letter with it, then we will hide the box in Mossy's attic – until I have the courage to take it out of our Dale.*

*Fin, if you are reading this letter, I will have delayed too long!*

*My son be guided by Mossy. Take care not to be overcome by the cross, as I was. Do not wear it!*

*Farewell Fin. One day, may we swim together with Phul beneath the waves of a tropical sea!*

*This letter was written by Marlin Dandrum of the Delphins, in the year 3523.*

Putting down the letter, Fin gazed unseeing at the pink apple blossoms fallen on the ground at his feet. 'Mossy, it's a weird rambling story my father tells. He said he gave up looking for my mother – he forgot her, all because of a finding a flashy jewelled cross!

'She's probably dead, anyway,' he muttered bitterly, stuffing the letter in a trouser pocket.

Pushing back his cowl, Mossy looked down at him thoughtfully.

'Fin, do you still have the coin your mother left you?'

'Yes!' From inside his jerkin, Fin brought out the red leather purse. 'I didn't want to leave it at Dandrum Den.'

Laying the coin on his palm, he showed it to Mossy.

'That is good,' Mossy said, closing Fin's hand over it. 'The coin is Rom gold and has strong protective properties! Keep it with the Chi Rho in your new purse: it will lessen the pulling power!' Smiling at him, he added: 'Fin Dandrum, you are fortunate indeed to be the child of Miryam Smith!'

Gripping the coin tight, Fin asked fiercely: 'Mossy, do you know what happened to my mother?'

'The wild Rom girl who married your father – and gave birth to you – is no more. Time passes, and humans change, but one day, I promise, you will know what happened to your mother.'

Listening to Mossy, an unlooked-for joy bubbled up in Fin – perhaps he would find his mother! Before him was a journey into darkness, but now he had hope. He laid the cross in the palm of one hand, and the coin in the other. Looking at them both, he pondered his gifts of gold. His mother's gift was a bitter-sweet joy, but what of his father's gift? He put them away together in his new purse.

As he did so, there came a clanking from the path outside, and Lark came through the white picket gate. Fin and Mossy looked at him in awe: on his back was an enormous rucksack. How he could remain upright amazed them. Noting the two bed rolls strapped to the outside along with a cooking pot and a frying pan dangling beneath, Fin wondered what could be inside the rucksack. At their first stop he'd get Lark to empty it: surely, he could take some of the stuff? Having repacked his rucksack, leaving his toy horse, rag doll and other precious odds and ends for Mossy to store in his attic, he had enough room.

Lark announced that Grammer Nutmeg had fed him the king of all breakfasts: 'Black pudding, sausages, beans, and salt pork! Last night, when I got back to the Den, she was still up. I found her in a right state, going on about a monster wumping, as she called it, after us as Fin and I went down the road to Watersmeet. She'd sent Tissy and the twins in search of us, and they hadn't come back. I managed to convince her that the twins were just up to their usual mischief, with Tissy tagging along, and they were probably spending the night at Spinner Hall.'

Mossy frowned when he heard this but said nothing.

'Anyway, I explained to Grammer, that Fin and I were going on a camping trip, which is true, and we hadn't time to go searching for the lasses, and that I would tell you, Mr Mossy. Sir, she's hoping that you'll go and check on them, to put her mind at rest.

'She also gave me something for you, Fin.' Heaving the rucksack off his back, he pulled out the pearl-encrusted sheath of the Dandrum sword. 'She said to give you this, with a parting message: not to wear damp socks.'

Fin choked back a groan. 'I forgot Grammer would be certain to discover the sword was missing. Bless her for understanding!' Delving deep in his own rucksack, he took the sword out and on an impulse, brandished it above his head.

Watching the polished blade flashing in the sunlight, Lark's heart leapt in wonder: it seemed to him as if cold flames were licking about Fin's hand. Lifting his gaze to the hills above Watersmeet, to Mossy and Fin's astonishment, he called out: 'The Dandrum Head has taken up his Sword, and is going on a Quest…' His voice faltered, his face a picture of puzzlement. 'Whatever possessed me!' he muttered, turning red.

'I've a herald, Mossy!' laughed Fin.

Sheathing the sword in its pearl scabbard, he buried them deep amongst his clothes. 'I don't suppose I'll ever have to use it for fighting,' he muttered grimly.

'It fair shocked me that you had taken the Dandrum Sword,' Lark said, 'but thinking on, as you're Head Dandrum, it's fitting you should have it, as you're going amongst strangers. It would show folk out there,' he waved vaguely to the north, 'that we're not just uncouth bumpkins in Brightdale.'

'Indeed, such a sword was not intended for fighting,' Mossy agreed, 'Lark thinks rightly, it will give you status, Fin.

'Hurry now lads, time is passing, and you must be on your way!'

'Yes, get a move on Fin,' Lark said, 'Grammer specially warmed up a couple of mutton pasties for us. We could stop for elevenses when we're a bit away from Watersmeet.'

Ah, Grammer's pasties,' sighed Fin, 'they're to die for.'

'Do not say that!' Mossy said sharply.

Whilst Fin went inside to check he'd not forgotten anything and say goodbye to Lass, Lark, his cheeks colouring, brought out a small box from a pocket. Anxiously, he showed Mossy what was inside.

'I wonder if you could give this ring to Thetis Dandrum, sir. It belonged to my mother. Even though it's buckled, and the green stone cracked, it's all that I have of her after she died in the fire. I wanted to give it to Tissy before leaving, but she wasn't there at Dandrum Den. I was hoping to ask her to marry me this Highsun: I'm worried if I don't get back in time, that someone else will ask her to go Skinny Dipping….'

He looked past the cottages to the fells. 'Do you think we'll get back by Highsun Rout, Mr Mossy?'

Reverently, Mossy took the box and put it inside his robe. 'Rest assured, I will give the ring to Thetis, but you might not be back for a while. You have a job to do first. Have courage Lark! You know in your heart that she will be loyal to you.'

Lark sighed. 'I hope so, sir. Can you take care of Grammer Nutmeg as well as my Tissy? I'm worried they might be in danger at Dandrum Den.'

'Do not fear for them. I will be going to Dandrum Den to deal with the problem there, just as soon as I've seen you and Fin on your way. Now, go with my blessing.' He laid a hand on Lark's thatch of pale green hair.

Wiping his watery eyes, Lark said, 'Well, goodbye Mr Mossy, sir. I'll take care of young Fin, never you fear, and we'll find your friend at Ireshope – Sandy, did you call him?' He'd decided privately he'd be wary of the human; to his mind they could be dodgy, even if this one was known to Mr Mossy.

He saw Fin returning, so he whistled to Mick, at present out on the path busily sniffing at a gap in next door's hedge.

'Come Mick, stop mucking about.' His voice was husky as he slammed on his floppy hat bedecked with a mass of shining fishhooks, shimmering as if infested by a cloud of mayflies.

'Now before you go, I have bound some new sketchbooks for you,' Mossy said to Fin, giving him a bundle of bound parchment, 'I expect a detailed record of all you see. I have made a plustic folder to keep them dry. You have a good supply of charcoal sticks, eraser and your sharpening knife?'

Fin nodded. 'I've put them in an outside pocket of my rucksack in readiness – I'm hoping to be back before I run out of sticks.'

Mossy gripped him by the shoulders. 'Remember Fin, on no account hang the cross about your neck. Keep it hidden inside your new purse with your gold coin.'

Fin shuddered. 'I would have to be pretty desperate to wear it. I'll not forget that deep scar on my father's chest! In his letter, he said the little Scav had a wound too, where the cross had been embedded.'

As he turned to go, he hesitated, and looked up hopefully at Mossy. 'Couldn't you come with us some of the way? It would be great to see a bit of the outside world with you.'

'I would have liked that Fin, but at present, those you leave behind need my protection: as to the future, who can tell?'

With a wan smile, Fin shouldered his rucksack and hurried off to catch up with Lark, already disappearing towards the Brightwater Bridge, his frying pan and cooking pot clanking. He was making for the track along the east bank of the river, heading north-west into Annunder Territory.

Neither of them spotted the two watchers crouched behind the garden hedge next door to Mossy's, where Daffodil's aunty lived.

In the twin's bedroom up at Spinner Hall, seeing the pale morning light peeping in through a crack in the curtains, Bird prodded Bee awake.

'I can't sleep for fretting,' she whispered. 'We must get back to Mossy's, quick. I've remembered something! Daffodil's auntie – you know her – she lives next door to Mossy! She fair dotes on her niece and spoils her rotten! Last night I bet Daffy and Alaria spent the night with her, so they could go for a sneaky dawn skinny dip with Fin and Lark, them being handy next door at Mossy's – Daffy hinted at something yesterday in the kitchen, didn't she?'

Bee looked doubtful. 'I don't reckon Lark would go along with that,' she whispered, 'he's too stick-in-the mud. On the other hand,' she frowned in thought. 'He might have ambitions to marry Alaria and get in with the Dandrums. A skinny dip would put him in a strong position to get permission from Master Roach to marry Alaria.'

Bird nodded. 'Anyway, now it's daylight, it wouldn't do any harm just to do a recce.'

Bee sighed. 'Bird, it's scarcely dawn! I wouldn't mind a bit more shut eye. Anyway, I feel mean disturbing Tissy, she's sleeping so peacefully.'

'We needn't wake her, we'll just go and see if we can find out anything, then come back to report. You can catch up on your beauty sleep tonight!'

So, careful not disturb Tissy, they dressed in hunting clothes, jackets, and trousers, and put on the plaited leather headbands Bird had decorated, to keep their hair out of their faces. Slipping out of their bedroom, all was quiet in Spinner Hall, everyone was sleeping off last night's revelries. Returning to Market Place, they sneaked along the narrow ginnel between the cottages, to the path behind the Bookshop and Daffodil's auntie's cottage.

Peeping over Mistress Akest's thick privet hedge, they saw her curtains were still tightly closed. Dithering on the path, they were startled when they heard a raised voice: they recognised it as Lark's, coming from Mossy's garden. They heard him say something about "a Quest". This was followed by Fin's laughter. Straining their ears, they couldn't hear Daffodil's or Alaria's voices.

The sudden creak of the rusty hinges on Mossy's gate panicked them. Diving through a hole in Mistress Akest's hedge and crouching low, they peered through the foliage. Feeling very foolish they waited, dreading what the lads would think if they found them. Moments later Lark's legs came by, accompanied by a clanking of pots and pans. Shortly after, Fin's long legs loped past. There was no sign of Alaria's or Daffodil's skirted plump ankles.

'I bet Daffodil and Alaria are already waiting for them, down by the river,' Bird hissed, her face white with rage.

'Quick, let's follow and catch 'em at it!' Bee said, scrambling through the hedge on to the path.

'Wait a mo' Bee! We must think this through,' Bird called, wriggling after her, 'I vote we go back home and pack some things, and go skinny dipping ourselves.'

Bee giggled: 'That'll put Daffodil's nose out, especially when she sees how much slimmer your figure is, compared to hers!'

Racing back to Spinner Hall, they found Tissy still sound asleep. Hurriedly packing their rucksacks, they put in lipstick, face powder and a couple of frilly blouses. Guilty at leaving Tissy, Bird scribbled a note explaining their suspicions, and telling Tissy not to worry – they would be back later to report. Pushing it into one of Tissy's shoes, she hurried after Bee. From the pantry, they took a bag of marshmallows and a bottle of berry juice. Passing through the Great Hall, they took their small crossbows and quivers of arrows from by the door where they hung with the other family weaponry.

Wolfie, sensing something was afoot, watched his young mistresses suspiciously; their deerhound was not only their pet, but their protector too, having several times saved them from danger.

'Come Wolfie!' Bee called, strapping her quiver to her belt, and slinging her crossbow over her shoulder. He rose reluctantly, loath to leave his warm rush mat. Stretching his long legs, he gave a wide yawn, showing a jaw full of strong yellow teeth, and with a grumbling growl, loped after them.

Running fast, their light rucksacks bouncing on their backs, Wolfie trotting behind, the twins returned to the path outside Mistress Akest's cottage. Here they commanded Wolfie to 'go seek'. After half-heartedly sniffing about a bit, he set off towards the river. Fizzing with excitement, the twins followed.

'I bet they're going to meet up at Brightforce, the water's deep there this time of year,' Bird said.

Bee stopped and groaned. 'Oh no, we didn't pack towels!'

'We can't go back now, Wolfie's hot on their trail,' Bird said, dragging her sister along by the hand.

And so, unknowingly, Bee and Bird set off on the big adventure they had often talked of. An adventure that would turn out to be far beyond their wildest imaginings, and which would not only bring them both into darkness and horror, but also lead them to find new friendships, and from which one of them would not come home alive.

On the heights above Dandrum Den, where only yesterday Fin had claimed the Head's seat and his rightful inheritance, Mossy shaded his eyes against the rising sun, and looked down on still sleeping Watersmeet. He spotted two distant figures on the far bank of the river: Lark and Fin were marching smartly along the path towards Annunder Territory. Some way behind, followed Bee and Bird, scuttling through the scrub and reeds, attempting to keep out of sight. Ambling openly on the path, their deerhound led the way.

Mossy shook his head in exasperation. 'There will be uproar at Spinner Hall today!' he exclaimed to Lass at his side, 'I shall have to call there, later. But first I must get word to Iskander!'

He groaned: 'Mortals! Is it little wonder Lucifer has such sport with them?'

He smiled down at Lass gazing up at him adoringly. 'You are mortal too, my Lass, and perhaps even your simple innocence could be tempted. Has your species ever desired to be furred gods?' Chuckling at Lass's blank look, he ruffled her brindled head. 'I think not, your race is too full of humble love.' Bending low, he gave her a hug, and in return, received a lick from her rough tongue.

'God be praised for the wonder of your kind!' Mossy exclaimed. 'Come Lass, first we have to call at Dandrum Den, to cast out a demon!'

Trying to be puppy-like, but her stiff joints creaking, Lass lolloped off in front of him down the steep path.

They had not quite reached the gates of Dandrum Den when, hearing from the south-west, a low droning, growing ever louder, they stopped to look up. Mossy smiled in delight as a moment later a flying object came into view. Moving slowly, about a hundred feet above their heads, it could have been a great bird, but of course no bird would make such a noise. Raising both arms, Mossy waved and gesticulated towards the high fell. A pale face wearing goggles looked down at him and gave a hearty thumbs-up. The stubby wings of the machine dipped from side to side in acknowledgement, and banking around, disappeared behind Kirion Hill.

On the path by the river Lark stopped suddenly. 'Well, who would've thought it!'

Fin, walking behind, bumped into him. 'Who would've thought what?' He looked back down the path in alarm.

Lark sighed. 'Here I am – lambing time, Silky's kits not yet trained, keep-nets muddled: all abandoned. I dread to think what my Uncle Hollin's language will be.' He shook his head in wonder, sending the fishhooks on his hat dancing.

For the first few miles, the land along the side of the riverside path was familiar to Fin. On their right lay the Spinners' farmland, the barley and oat shoots still in Saprise green, the stands of coppiced birch and willows beyond, in full bud. To their left, across the river lay the Dandrum meadows, their fields and orchards rising beyond.

Normally Fin's spirits would have lifted, but today he couldn't forget why he was here. He thought about the Frit that had killed his father. Could it still be lurking in the Dale? The reeds fringing the riverbank seemed menacing, making him jittery. What did it feel like to have your throat sliced open? He felt the stiff leather cord of his new purse around his neck. It was kind of Mossy to make the purse, but the cross and his mother's coin were growing heavy. He scowled at Lark's back: all he had to worry about was the state of his keep-nets. Guilt washed over him: Lark was in just as much danger of being murdered – a Frit probably couldn't distinguish between Delphins.     Lengthening his stride, he caught up with Lark. 'I'm sorry Lark. I've been too wrapped up in my own troubles to give a thought to what you're leaving behind. I'd be lost in no time in your wild Annunder country if you weren't there to guide me.'

Lark stopped and turned around. 'No worries, Fin. Just finding it difficult to get it all into my thick skull – give me time, and I'll get there.'

So, having cleared the air between him and Fin, Lark set about enjoying what he hoped would be an exciting jaunt. Besides, he told himself, it's high time I got to know Fin, now he's the boss. And Mr Mossy put him in my care. When I get home again, I'll have to report to him, as well as Grammer Nutmeg.

A while later, they found a sunny flat rock by the river, and settled down to their elevenses, tucking into Mossy's salt bacon sandwiches and Nutmeg's pasties. Licking meaty gravy off their fingers, they threw the scraps to Mick who, eagerly watching them at the river's edge, hadn't noticed his tail was dipped in the water.

Soaking up the rock's warmth, gazing at the river rushing by Fin pondered the journey before them, wondering about Mossy's friend. Very ordinary name: Sandy. He was probably one of the low life types who supplied Mossy with rabbit skin glue and rags to make paper.

Then there was Durholm Garrison where he hoped to be handing over the cross. He'd never heard of the place before. Was it a kind of army camp? It seemed odd that Mossy thought he could leave his cross with a bunch of rough soldiers. Anyway, the place was well east of Withered Wood, which was a relief.

He looked across the river, towards the north-west where wooded fells marched up to the high moors. Out of sight beyond lay Withered Wood and the Land of Contagion where Gressil had his Fortress: two places he was determined never to go.

He recalled what Mossy had told him about Withered Wood.

*'Legend says that the Gaiakins caused the thorn break of Withered Wood to grow up, as a protection for the good folk of Brightdale. Only those who know the secret ways can get through that barrier.*

*First there are ten miles of tangled, knotted thorns, as tough as wire, and armed with finger-long spikes as sharp as eagle talons. After the thorn barrier comes the Withered Wood, a gloomy pine forest, extending for more than thirty miles over high hills and deep dales. Only pine trees survive there, the ground carpeted in a thick layer of parched pine needles that deaden all sound.*

*The forest ends on the borders of the Land of Contagion where not even thorn and pine can grow. Contagion is a dead land, the air foul from the poisons that seep out of the deep fissures in the arid, rock-strewn ground. In this evil place, Lord Gressil has built his fortress, and has made a nest for Maabella, his Queen.'*

'Time to get a move on,' Lark said, startling Fin out of his reverie.

Scrambling to his feet, he brushed the flaky-pastry crumbs off his trousers for Mick to lick up. Then, he insisted they rearranged Lark's rucksack, and share the contents more evenly. Watching Lark spreading his stuff on the rock, he was impressed.

Strapped to the outside, as well as the two bedrolls, cooking pot and frying pan, were a coil of rope, a small axe and spade. From within, Lark produced a set of three pans, stacked neatly inside each other, and wrapped in a water-proof plustic sheet. The sheet, Lark explained could either serve as a groundsheet or bivouac. Diving deeper, he produced a spare. 'This one's for you. Don't suppose you thought of bringing a waterproof?'

Fin shook his head, awed by Lark's practical knowledge.

Next came Lark's supply of dried food: fruit-leathers, sunflower seeds, with a small box of salt. He left, along with the sword, his spare shirt, socks, and underwear in the bottom.

'I keep my special equipment on me all times,' Lark explained, rummaging in the numerous pockets of his jerkin, bringing out flint, tinder, and a candle stub from one pocket, from another a fishing line with weights, and from a third a small fishing net.

Fin wrapped the dried food in the spare plustic sheet and stuffed it into his rucksack, with the coil of rope on top. On the outside, he tied one of the bedrolls and the small spade. Lark firmly refused to let him take more.

'You've got your own heavy Burden,' he said, looking significantly at Fin's chest, where he assumed the Chi Rho hung.

Loads sorted, they resumed their journey north-west, keeping to the path beside the river, which Fin knew would eventually reach Brightforce, a favourite spot with young Delphins to go skinny dipping.

By late morning they came to a low stone bridge over a swift stream. 'Here we are – the Plashywater,' Lark said. 'This is where we turn off. The Plashywater runs from the hills in the east to join the Brightwater.'

'We're not going as far as Brightforce then?' Fin looked disappointedly up the main path – he was hoping for a swim.

'Nope, the quickest way to Ireshope is over the top, above Plashydale. Besides, I want you to meet the family at Hiddenhaven.'

Lark plunged into the undergrowth of holly and trailing ivy where a narrow track ran beside the stream, sunlight flickered through the budding branches, lighting up patches of celandine, violets and primroses. Fin felt uneasy; the holly bushes seemed to harbour secret watchers. He glanced behind, thinking he saw large yellow eyes blinking at him out of a bush, but then realised it was only a beam of sunlight on a dead yellow leaf.

'Do you get big cats in these parts?' he called, quickening his pace.

Lark slowed for him to catch up. 'Not so many as when my granfer was a lad. Having said that, there was a prize sized puma-like cat found dead in a wolf trap last year, but that was up near the borders of Withered Wood.'

Fin shivered at the thought of a puma stalking them for a meal; he'd learnt from one of Mossy's books that even though they weren't native, tigers, pumas and even lions, thrived in these northern climes – descendants of animals which, centuries ago, had escaped from human captivity.

When the Delphins first settled in Brightdale, the Annunders were the only clan to brave the dense forests of northern Brightdale, and even now most other Delphin folk seldom venture into these parts, knowing large predators to be prowling there. The Annunders claimed this land as their territory, clearing very little of the forest, settling in small communities along narrow valleys filled with tumbling waterfalls and noisy streams. Over the centuries, they prospered, becoming famous for their hunting skills and charcoal making.

Plashydale, the valley where Lark's family first settled, was named by Skylark, the Annunder's original ancestor, and the small river became known as the Plashywater.

The Annunders built their homes where the valley widened for half a mile or so. Called Hiddenhaven, the settlement has never grown large: just a row of cottages and farm buildings huddled beneath sheltering cliffs. Alongside the river they grow vegetables, and rear livestock. Over five hundred years, Annunder homes have evolved from crude roundhouses to substantial stone cottages, slate roofed and small windowed to keep in the warmth.

It was at Hiddenhaven that Lark wanted to introduce Fin to his relatives. Then he intended to continue by the Plashywater until they reached a waterfall, from where a path would take them up to the moorland; they would keep walking until sunset, pitching their first night's camp on the north-east border between Brightdale and Durholmdale.

They arrived at lunchtime when most of the family were working in the forest, but Lark's grandfather, Fox Annunder was there, seated on a bench by the river, eating bread, cheese, and pickles. He was surrounded by a motley pack of hunting dogs whose belligerent barking forced Mick to take refuge between his master's legs. The commotion attracted Marigold Annunder, Lark's grandmother, who came out from a cottage beneath the cliff.

Fox's commanding shout called the dogs to order, and Lark introduced Fin to his grandparents.

'How do ye do, sir?' said Fox, doffing his hat respectfully. Marigold dropped a little curtsey. 'Honoured we are to have a Dandrum come visiting,' she said.

Lark explained they were on an errand for Mr Mossy, and hoped to cadge lunch before going on to camp on the borders of Durholmdale. 'Tomorrow we're meeting up with a friend of Mr Mossy's at Ireshope,' he said importantly.

'Mind you keep to the track!' Fox warned, 'and look out for strangers. Rook's eldest lad said he'd seen giant footprints up by Brightforce – from a kind of great bird that could have been as tall as a poplar tree, or so he claimed.'

Lark and Fin exchanged looks but said nothing. After discussing family news, Fox got up. 'Must get on with the rest of the day,' he said, whistling to his dogs. 'Just you be on your guard, young Lark; Master Fin's in your care, and he's an important person now!' With that he disappeared into the trees, the dogs, now in hunting mode, following silently.

Seeing the surprise on Fin's face at Fox's remark, Grammer Marigold said, 'I've heard some at Dandrum Den might not accept you as Head, Master Fin, but us Annunders know your rights.'

'Thank you, Mrs Annunder,' said Fin feeling sad. Would he ever really be Dandrum Head, he wondered?

'Just so long as you know we have concern for you,' Marigold said. 'Now, how about some bread and cheese to fill those long legs?'

After she'd gone to fetch the food, Fin and Lark sat discussing the footprints seen near Brightforce. 'They could belong to that ganglefowl who's lost a feather,' Lark muttered. 'Anyway, Brightforce isn't on our route, so we needn't get in a bother. We're heading north east, well away from the Force and dreaded Withered Wood beyond, where I reckon that ganglefowl came from.'

Marigold soon reappeared with plates of bread and cheese, and pickles on the side.

Lark's eyes gleamed, 'Ah, your pickled onions! Grammer Marigold, can you spare a small pot for our journey?'

Looking pleased, she scurried off to get some ready.

As they ate, Fin studied his surroundings, particularly the row of cottages. He noticed a gap next to Fox and Marigold's cottage, where the cliff face had been blackened by fire.

Lark followed his gaze. 'That was where I lived as a small lad. We've never rebuilt our cottage.' His normally merry eyes misted, and his broad shoulders slumped, reminding Fin of a terrier who'd lost a rat.

'What happened, Lark?' he asked gently. He knew Lark's parents, Larch and Celandine, were dead but did not know how they had died.

Lark began his story. 'I'd just turned eight. We'd spent the day on the moor – my cousin Rowan and me. I looked up to Rowan, he was six years older, and soon to be apprenticed as a ghillie to the Spinners.

'It being Leafturn, nights were drawing in, hearth fires built up. We were contented with our catch: three brace of pheasant. As we wandered home, we smelt smoke – not the welcoming smoke from a homely chimney at dusk, this had the reek of scorched resin from tarred beams.

'Running the last hundred yards, we came on a dreadful sight: our cottage was a ball of fire. I searched the sooty faces around me but couldn't find ma and pa. I started to run towards the flames, when Granfer Fox held me back: "Lad, there's now't can be done!" So, I was left with nothing but the clothes I was standing in, and my precious hunting gear: my pa and ma were dead. Granfer Fox and Grammer Marigold took me in until I was fifteen, and old enough to be assistant ghillie at Dandrum Den.'

Fin gazed dejectedly down at the ground. 'We're both orphans now. Thanks for telling me your story – if I was a better Head, I should have known it.'

'It takes a lot of years to find out what you should or shouldn't know as Head,' Lark said, sounding wise. 'Anyhow, I'm pleased to be ghillie for the Dandrums, that's for sure!'

Fin smiled. 'I hope you don't think me nosey, but I find Annunder family relationships complicated. I've never liked to ask your Grammer Nutmeg why she's called Annunder, when your other Grammer, Marigold is also called Annunder. It seems to me you have too many Annunder grandmothers!'

Lark laughed. 'Grammer Nutmeg is my Granfer Fox's younger sister: so, she's also my great aunt, as well as my grammer.

'As you know, Grammer Nutmeg never married. She was courting with Ged Spinner, brother to old master Joshua Spinner, Bee, and Bird's granfer, but he was killed by a boar. My mother, Celandine, was born after he died.'

Fin sifted this information. 'So, you've Spinner blood, too?'

'Aye, I have. Which makes me just as good as any Spinner or Dandrum.' Lark sat up proud.

His expression turned serious. 'As you're finding out all about me, Fin, I might as well tell you: I feel I'm worthy to be husband to your cousin Tissy. When I get back, I'm going to ask her to marry me, even though some won't approve.'

Fin grinned. 'I promise you Lark, when we get back, as I'll be Head Dandrum, I'll make sure you do marry Tissy! Having you as a family member would be an honour.'

Lark shot Fin a sidelong look. 'Talking of marriage, Fin, you'll have to think who you should marry now you're Head. According to Grammer Nutmeg, both Daffodil Akest and Bird Spinner have hopes. It's been a falling out between them.'

Fin looked agonized. 'I've never thought much about marrying; I've always imagined no Delphin lass would want me, being only half Delphin. Anyway, there are loads of lads after Bird, and I'm dead sure I couldn't spend the rest of my life with Daffodil Akest! Are Bird and Daffodil waiting for me to choose between them? I couldn't cope with that,' he wailed. 'I suppose I'll have to think about it when I get back.' A shadow crossed his face. 'If I get back. Now, let's get going! Despite Frits and ganglefowl, we've to be at Ireshope by tomorrow morning. Lead on, Lark!'

Collecting their jar of pickled onions, they said goodbye to Grammer Marigold, and she insisted on handing Lark something savoury smelling, wrapped in parchment.

Lark, having to whistle twice to Mick busy causing panic amongst the chickens, with a final wave to Marigold, they set off. The sun behind them, they continued along the Plashywater towards the waterfall. Lark explained a path there would take them up out of the valley onto the moorland.

'I know a good camping spot near the borders of Durholmdale. It should be safe from anything unpleasant, but we must make sure to keep well east of Killhope Gate!'

'Whatever is Killhope Gate?' Fin asked in alarm, 'what danger lurks there?'

'They say it's the opening into the main tunnel in and out of Contagion – where the evils come and go on their wicked business.' Lark gave a mischievous leer.

'Knowing how you're into history, you'll find Durholmdale interesting, Fin. There are parts that are as it was in Brightdale, five hundred years ago, before any of us Delphins came and tamed our land. It is said that if a Delphin climbed a tree to spy the way, all he would see are treetops, stretching for miles 'n miles.'

Listening to Lark, Fin thought about a passage he had recently read in one of Mossy's books. Titled 'The Great Human Dying', it detailed the root cause of the Great Dying. He'd learned some of the passage by heart: A mutant virus from pigs tripped over into humans; plague swept throughout Gaia; millions succumbed to sickness and death; the human population plummeted... (For more information, the reader should consult Zagzagel's book for the full text.)

When Fin asked Mossy what a virus was, they had looked at some through Mossy's microscope; it had amazed him that things so minute could cause such enormous devastation.

Mossy had gone on to explain how the world has changed over the last thousand or so years. A lot of what he said was difficult to understand, referring to things like global warming, solar flares, electronic communications, and world banking systems. Mossy had given his half-moon spectacles a vigorous polish. 'That's all advanced technological stuff. You'll have to learn the basics first.'

Fin wondered wistfully whether he would now ever learn "technological stuff".

Realising that Lark and Mick were some way ahead, he ran to catch up.

Coming to a waterfall, they stood watching the silvery curtain of water pouring, twenty or so feet above their heads, over an ivy-covered cliff into a deep dark pool, before spilling out into the river.

'The Plashyforce!' Lark said. 'Not as high as Brightforce but us Annunders like to come skinny dipping here on Highsun morn. I want to bring Tissy here one day, if I ever…' He broke off sadly.

He gestured towards a path zigzagging through boulders up the steep cliff side. 'We leave Plashydale now – that's our way.'

Taking a farewell look at his home territory, he began to climb. Mick and Fin followed.

Ten minutes later, hot and puffed they reached open moorland. A carpet of green and brown heather spread before them, broken by clumps of low growing juniper, willow, and rowan. High above in the gold-pink evening sky, a bird hung on the air; by its silhouette Fin knew it was a mighty golden eagle. Turning about, he searched the horizon. In the distance, a small flock of wild goats plucked at the young buds of a willow, and far to the west, he could just make out in the glare of the setting sun, the shadow of Withered Wood, whilst to the east, he spied the tops of a vast forest. A shiver ran down his spine: this high lonely moor was the borderland between the safety of Brightdale and the unknown beyond.

In single file, Lark leading, they headed north east, following a peaty path through the heather, the only sounds, the wind in the heather, the crying of lapwings, and the distant bleating of goats.

After a while, Lark stopped and looking back, sniffed the air. 'I keep feeling there's something following us,' he muttered, 'there's a smell, not ganglefowl mind! Something new to me.' Mick seemed twitchy too.

They had walked ten miles, and the sun had sunk below the horizon, when Lark stopped by a stunted wind-twisted oak leaning over the path. He sighed with relief. 'Phew, thank goodness! This is our camp tonight: Phul's Hollow.'

He jumped down into a hollow hidden in the heather. Fin followed, glad the march had ended. In the fading light, he saw a shallow cave dug out of the peaty wall. Inside stood a worn stone figure, its lower half buried in the sandy soil.

'Us Annunders set this statue here: it's Phul, our Delphin angel guardian,' Lark said. 'We put him here to ward off evil from the lands beyond our borders.'

'The love of Phul was strong when the Delphins first came to Brightdale,' Fin smiled, 'you've picked a good place to camp. Good old Phul will protect us!' He studied the figure: it was about the height of a Delphin, its face worn away with age, the outstretched wings mere stumps.

Heaving off their rucksacks, they gratefully collapsed onto the soft floor. They'd walked twenty miles that day and were tired.

'I'll have to get used to long hikes carrying a heavy rucksack,' Fin said. 'How much further to Ireshope?'

'Only three miles. We'll start again at first light and soon be there. If memory serves me right, there are places where we can hide to spy out any threat before we make ourselves known to that Sandy fellow.'

'I wonder who Sandy is,' mused Fin, 'surely he must be someone we can trust, if he's a friend of Mossy's?'

'With a name like Sandy, I don't suppose he is as—' Lark hesitated, looking for the right word, 'magical as old Mossy,' he finished lamely. 'Do you think Mr Mossy is able to do magic, Fin?'

'No, he's neither a wizard, nor a magician.'

'Is he one of the mighty Gaiakin, then?'

'No, I don't think so.' Fin frowned in thought, trying to find the right explanation, for himself as well as Lark. 'Do you remember the story he tells of the Christ's rising from his tomb? About two beings in dazzling white robes standing by the entrance?'

'Yes! Mossy's favourite story: the beings told the disciples not to look for the living amongst the dead. Old Ma Gonebatty who looks after Aidan's shrine in Watersmeet, once told me that Mr Mossy could be one of those blokes, but I wasn't sure how she knew.'

'I think she's right,' said Fin. 'I reckon he's a companion of Phul.'

Lark sat amazed. 'Well, I needn't worry about Tissy then. Mr Mossy said he'd look after her – he seems to me, kind of more solid than old Phul here.'

He sighed happily and began to prepare their camp for the night. Sniffing the air, he decided they needn't protect themselves from rain, so he spread his plustic sheet on the ground. Whilst Fin dug a shallow pit for a fire, he went in search of firewood, gathering fallen branches scattered beneath the twisted oak, choosing material that wouldn't make much smoke. Back in the hollow he laid the kindling in Fin's pit. With sparks from his flint, he soon got a small blaze going, and using one of the stronger oak sticks as a prop, hung his cooking pot, filled with water from his drinking bottle, over the flames.

Fin, settling on the groundsheet, discovered his father's letter in his trouser pocket. Smoothing it out and refolding it, he put in his jerkin. He thought again of his father's wanderings with the cross hung about his neck. Where had he gone all those years? He promised himself, one day he would find out; perhaps someone in this mysterious Durholm Garrison would know.

Thinking about the cross, a longing to feel its jewels and to stroke the smooth crystal crept over him. His hand strayed inside his shirt. Feeling the purse's weight, he recalled Mossy's warning: 'Remember: keep the Chi Rho hidden. The safest place is with your mother's coin; the Rom gold will protect you from the influence of the cross that caused your father such pain.'

A low warning growl from Mick broke the spell. He'd stationed himself at the top of the entrance and was peering out through the fringe of heather.

Lark was watching him, looking worried. 'Go search, Mick,' he hissed. Mick bounded off, swiftly and silently.

A moment later there came a clatter of whirring wings, and the strident call of a pheasant shattered the quiet. Mick reappeared; feathers stuck around his muzzle.

Relieved that the alarm was only a silly-headed bird, they settled down to the supper Marigold Annunder had provided: hunks of fresh bread, generously spread with dripping, slabs of cheese, and of course her pickled onions. Their hunger satisfied, they sat in companionable silence, gazing into the dying embers of the fire, sucking fruity squares of berry leather and sipping nettle tea.

Lark broke the silence. 'I've been pondering that owl last night – remember, when we were in the attic. I don't know about you, but I've a feeling that was no owl: I didn't want to worry you last night, you'd had enough troubles! But there was something unnatural there, I thought.'

Fin shivered. 'I reckon whatever it was might've been after the Chi Rho – I hope to get rid of the cross at Durholm Garrison, so the sooner we get there the better! Let's get some sleep now. Even if Phul is supposed to be guarding us, I think we ought to keep a watch tonight. As I need to do some serious thinking, I'll take first turn. Two hours on and two hours off?'

Giving a cavernous yawn, Lark nodded. Wrapping himself in his blanket and covering his face with his fishhook-festooned hat, he was soon snoring. Mick leaned companionably against Fin, searching himself for fleas.

Watching their little fire slowly dying, Fin let his mind roam over the events of the last few days. He had been looking forward to the camping trip with his father this Highsun. Now he was holed up far from home, his father murdered, with the threat that who or what the killer was, they could be after him now. He pushed Mick away and stood to peer out of the hollow. The moon had come up, bathing the heather in silver. A fox barked in the distance. A rustling nearby made him start. Just a fox after a rabbit, he told himself.

Returning to his place next to Lark, he noticed Mick again stationed at the entrance to the hollow, ears pricked as he turned his head sharply from side to side, picking up sounds that only a dog could hear. Lark sighed in his sleep and turning over, muttered indistinctly.

Fin looked down at his sleeping form, tinted grey by the moonlight – a nagging thought surfaced again: Lark's task as guide would be finished when they reached Ireshope, and they'd met up with Sandy. He would miss his companionship, but he knew he must insist Lark should return to Brightdale. Besides, there was a romance to encourage he told himself with a wistful smile. Anyway, as soon as he'd delivered the cross, he too would be able to return home; the thought that he would be able to continue his new friendship with Lark cheered him.

He absent-mindedly put his hand inside his shirt once more. Stroking the leather purse, he felt a pleasant tingling in his fingers. Surely now they were on the borders of Brightdale, he ought to hang the cross around his neck on its gold chain? The dazzling jewels should be seen. People should know that he wasn't an insignificant half-breed Delphin!

He'd started pulling open the purse when something landed with a soft thud in the entrance to the hollow. Hastily tucking the purse away, he crawled up the slope, wondering what Mick was doing, snarling fiercely somewhere nearby. Feeling about, his hand landed on something hard and sticky. Peering in the dim light, he saw it was a rough black stone, its weight and shape reminding him of a piece of clinker from a smelting furnace. Limpet-like, it started to cling to his palm, biting and burning his skin. In panic, he tried to dislodge it, but it wouldn't shift.

He tried to call out to Lark, but no words came. His limbs were turning to lead. As a suffocating fog pressed in, deep lethargy engulphed him, dragging him down. Far, far away, a dog was barking furiously. He hoped he wasn't dying: no warm sunlit sea washed over him, no swimming figure looking out of waving kelp, waiting for him, all was darkness and despair.

# 6
# DOOMSTONE

Lark, jolted awake by frenzied barking, sat up with a curse. His befuddled brain grasped that Mick was in fierce fight with something squealing. Rubbing his bleary eyes, he saw Fin slumped halfway out of the hollow. A figure was crouched over him, pawing his chest, its monkey-like form outlined against the moonlight.

'Where you, pretty cross? Don't hide darlin', don't hide from your Crow,' it croaked softly.

'OI, GET OFF!' yelled Lark, flinging himself at the creature. Snatching at the grubby jerkin hanging off its skinny body, his fingers struck chain mail; the jarring pain made him lose his grip and the creature shot off into the dark; at the same time, a snapping, squealing ball of fur and blood hurtled past Lark's face, landing with a thud in the bottom of the hollow. Mick, bloody but triumphant, stood over the twitching body of a huge rat. Remembering Fin, Lark scrambled to him, and turned him over: in the moonlight, his open eyes stared blankly, his face a mask.

'YOU ADDLED GOOSE EGG,' Lark shouted at himself, 'you shouldn't 'ave gone to sleep and left young Fin in charge! Mick, what am I to do?'

Leaping out of the hollow, brandishing his boning knife, he bawled curses into the night. 'Where are yer, yer slimy string of toad's spawn?' he howled, uselessly slashing at the heather with his blade. 'Come here an' I'll slit your scrawny throat!'

Breath rasping, he stood listening, but all he could hear was the wind rattling the dead leaves of the twisted oak. He jumped back down, and scrabbling for the water bottle on his belt, splashed Fin's face: he didn't stir. Snatching up his blanket, he wrapped it around him, and sitting down held him close, every now and then feeling his icy face and hands.

After a while he felt warmth, and Fin's chest began to rise and fall. Drawing in a deep breath, his blank eyes focused. Lark nearly wept with relief.

'What's going on, Lark?' Fin mumbled, '—your turn to watch. I'm too sleepy to keep awake.' Closing his eyes, he fell into deep slumber.

Lark sat with him the rest of the night. He would have liked to have treated Mick's deep rat bites but had to leave him to lick the wounds without help. He realised the rat wasn't dead, as he'd first thought, but lay twitching. He saw with surprise that it wore a richly jewelled collar.

'Must be that evil creature's pet,' he muttered, watching in disgust as it crawled up the slope and disappeared into the heather, leaving a trail of blood.

The sun rose, promising another bright day. However hard Lark shook Fin, he couldn't wake him; but there was colour in his cheeks, and gently probing about, he couldn't find any injuries. Not liking to, but knowing he must, he carefully put his hand inside Fin's shirt, and felt for the purse holding the cross: it felt heavy and the cord was tightly drawn. He came to a decision: he would have to leave Fin and go alone to Ireshope to find Mossy's friend. He stood and stretched his stiff joints.

'Phul, old mate, I'm leaving Fin in your charge,' he said aloud, glaring challengingly at the statue. 'I'll bring Sandy back here – hopefully, he'll have a bit of common sense and believe that I've come from Master Fin and Mr Mossy.'

Seeing Mick had licked his wounds clean, and lay dozing, he tenderly dressed them with marigold ointment.

'Mick, I'm sorry but I'll have to leave you to guard Fin – not that you'll be much help to him with those nasty bites.'

Putting water where Fin and Mick could reach without getting up, he climbed out onto the path.

Driven on by worry and fear, he walked fast and covered the three miles to Ireshope in just under an hour, jumping from tussock to rock down the steep fell, following a brook he knew fed into the Durholmwater. He was relieved he remembered the way, despite being a child when he'd come here with Granfer Fox. The stunted moorland trees and heather gave way to woodland, fallen branches and thick vegetation hindering his progress: he was entering the forest of Durholmdale. Keeping close to the brook, he came at last to the moss-covered ruins of the ancient settlement of Ireshope.

This remote place, being close to Killhope Gate, is where the more ruffianly Scavs come to trade with Gressil's servants. Occasionally the Annunder Delphins come to exchange metal and plustic for their famous Annunder charcoal, but they only come if they are in urgent need, preferring to barter with the more trustworthy Scavs at Watersmeet market.

As Lark drew near, darting from cover to cover, he slowed his pace. He wanted to spy out Sandy, to decide what kind of person he was; from experience, he found most humans could be dodgy. 'Downright scoundrels,' Granfer Fox would growl when a deal had not gone in his favour.

He found the meeting place he remembered from childhood: an open piece of ground surrounded by ruins, the earth beaten bare by the passage of many feet, patched black by old cooking fires, and scattered with sun-bleached logs used as makeshift seating. The place appeared deserted.

Crouching behind a tumbled wall, listening hard, he wished he had Mick's keen ears. Apart from the nearby rushing river and the soft chirping of a lone chaffinch perched above his head, all seemed quiet. Looking at the logs, he was puzzled by something strange: it looked as if someone had pushed them about, and the ground around them caked with patches of a glistening yellow slime, reminding him of great gobs of snot. He'd no chance to take in more: a hand fell on his shoulder. Springing up he spun to face a tall man, over six foot.

'Delphins used to have sharper ears – living off the fat of the land in peaceful Brightdale seems to have blunted your ancient skills – but never mind, we shall soon hone them again. Do I speak to Fin Dandrum, son of Marlin Dandrum?'

Lark gaped. He'd been expecting a grimy-skinned, smelly, bow-legged human, with close-set eyes. The proud figure before him brought to Lark's mind one of the warriors from Grammer Nutmeg's story books. His eyes were dark blue, as if made of the midnight sky. For a fleeting moment, he wondered if the awesome stranger might be a Gaiakin, but then his down-to-earth Annunder breeding brought him to his senses, and on second glance he saw just a human, his careworn face etched by hardship, his red-gold hair frosted with grey.

Stretching his four and a half feet as tall as he could, he said indignantly: 'I wasn't expecting a giant to come creeping up on me when I'm on lawful business, sir. You're mistaken in my name! I'm Lark Annunder, ghillie to the Dandrums. Now, as I have shown my manners in introducing myself, I hope you will show yours, and tell me your name.'

'Iskander, Warrior, Leader of a Trekker Squad, at your service master Lark,' answered the man, bowing low. 'But my friends call me Sandy.'

All Lark's pent up anxiety flooded out. Tears started to his eyes. 'Oh, Mr Sandy, I'm so glad I've found you! It's Fin – he won't wake up, and I don't know what to do!'

As Lark's story tumbled out, the man's expression became grave. 'You heard the creature call himself Crow? This is bad! Very bad! That devious Scav is dangerous. Come, we must hurry and hope he has not returned whilst you are away.'

Sandy, making no allowance for Lark's short legs, set off fast up the fellside, taking the way Lark had come down. Lark pounded doggedly behind, his gaze never wavering from the long legs in front of him.

As Phul's hollow came into view, Mick valiantly stood guard, barking fiercely. Seeing his master, he forgot his wounds, and with a shriek of joy leapt into Lark's arms.

Fin was still fast asleep but appeared unharmed.

Sandy knelt to feel his brow. 'Good, he has no fever. I wonder why he is sleeping so deeply.' He began probing Fin's head for injury, gently running his long fingers through Fin's dark curls.

Lark studied the man more closely, feeling a little guilty. Common sense should have told him that Mr Mossy's friend would be one of those Trekker warriors, and not some low-life ruffian. He'd occasionally seen troops of Trekkers from a distance, loping swiftly along, awesomely long swords strapped to their backs.

Though obviously fighting fit, Sandy looked as if life had been hard, his thin face lined. He was clean shaven, his long hair, braided into numerous plaits, reaching down to his shoulders. His thick hooded jacket, and leather trousers, in hues of greys and greens, were worn and stained. At his back hung his sword. Richly jewelled around the handle guard and pommel it was set in a silver sheath. Over one shoulder was slung a crossbow, and at his belt a quiver full of arrows.

Prising open Fin's tightly clenched fist, Sandy gasped: lying in his palm was a rough black stone. 'So! This is the cause,' he breathed, 'Crow has used a doomstone on your master.'

'What the heck's a doomstone?' Lark cried, reaching to pull it away.

'No!' Sandy hissed, grabbing his wrist. 'This stone has not only fastened on to Fin's flesh, but onto his mind too; pulling it away would plunge him into suicidal despair.'

'But – but there must be something we can do, Mr Sandy,' groaned Lark.

'Only a Gaiakin can deal with this. We must get Fin to our Stonetree camp with all speed, where I pray Fescue will be waiting for us – he is of the Florain kindred and knows how to deal with doomstones.

'Come, wrap him in that blanket, and help me lift him. You must follow as best you can. I am sorry, but you'll have to run some more miles! Stonetree is six miles beyond Ireshope – I suggest you lighten your rucksack: abandon your pots and pans!'

Cooking equipment stashed behind Phul's statue; Lark found himself once more running behind Sandy. With Mick wriggling agitatedly inside his jerkin, it was a nightmare journey. Jumping and slithering down the fellside, he tumbled several times, picking up some nasty grazes. If Sandy hadn't been slowed by the burden of Fin and Fin's rucksack, Lark doubted whether he could have kept up.

Reaching Ireshope, they halted to spy out the land. Lark pointed out the yellow matter spread around the disturbed logs. 'I don't like the look of that weird stuff, Mr Sandy, sir.'

Sandy grimaced. 'Bugslugs have been sliming there, but from the way the matter is beginning to dry, it must have been some time ago.'

Lark looked at him puzzled.

Sandy shook his head in irritation. 'I see these creatures are a mystery to you! No time to explain now – you can learn about Maabella's Babes later. Come, that is the way!'

He gestured to a worn track by the river. 'Scav traders use this path, so if we hear any approaching, we must hide in the undergrowth – thankfully there is good cover most of the way. I would rather have kept to more secret ways, but with my burden, and your short legs, it would take too long!'

Determined not to fall behind, his eyes fixed on Fin's dark head bumping in the crook of Sandy's arm, Lark forced his legs into a rhythmic stride. Aware of the rushing river to his left, and the deep forest to his right, he dreaded the sluggerbugs, or whatever Sandy had called them, might slime out of the undergrowth, and smother him in their gunge. How long they tramped, he didn't know; he was only conscious that the sun was now high in the sky, and he was very hungry, having had no breakfast.

Eventually they came to a shallow part of the river, where a line of flat stones, set at intervals in the swirling water, led to the north bank.

'Stonetree is on the other side,' called Sandy, leaping from stone to stone.

Lark jumped for the first stone, but his tired legs let him down, and he almost fell into the icy water. Mick let out a howl, alerting Sandy who, already halfway across, came bounding back. He grabbed Lark by his collar, and still holding Fin's limp body in the crook of his other arm, lifted him up by the back of his belt. Dangling him over the rushing torrent, he carried him with Mick howling inside his jerkin, across, dropping them unceremoniously onto the muddy bank. Then without waiting, he set off once more, Fin in his arms. If Lark hadn't been so weary, he would have been furious with himself. Negotiating fast flowing rivers, with far more precarious steppingstones, was part of his everyday work. Slamming his fish-hook hat back in place, he scuttled red faced after Sandy's fast disappearing figure.

Morning turned to noon, and just as Lark's legs began to give final warnings of rebellion, Sandy stopped, ducking into the undergrowth. Dreading that he'd sensed danger, Lark stumbled after him, collapsing onto a patch of soft wild garlic.

'Have courage, Lark, we are nearly there,' Sandy murmured. 'You can rest now whilst I go on ahead to see if all is well at Stonetree.'

Gently laying Fin on the wild garlic, and propping his back against a moss-covered boulder, Sandy disappeared along a track, just discernible, cutting a swathe through the bluebells.

The smell from the garlic plants making his stomach rumble, Lark tried to open Fin's stiff fingers, but they were too tightly clenched around the strange stone. He studied his pale face, anxious that his cheeks seemed to have lost their colour again.

Mick crouched nearby, miserably licking his wounds, which had begun bleeding. Tut tutting, Lark dug out his marigold ointment. 'These are going to take time to heal, Mick,' he muttered, lifting him onto his lap and massaging cream into the deep teeth holes, 'rats have dirty bites.'

Helping the little dog to settle, he rested his head back on the boulder.

It seemed like he'd only shut his eyes for a moment when he was woken from a deep sleep by Sandy gently shaking him. He stared uncomprehendingly up into the lean face, and then groaned. 'Phul forgive me! I was so tired I fell asleep. Is Fin...?' He sat up and found Fin safe beside him, eyes closed, his face still pale.

'I am not surprised you are tired; Iskander tells me you ran all the way from Phul's Hollow on those short legs!' laughed a rich musical voice.

Looking up, Lark found a beautiful face smiling down at him. Lifting Mick off his lap, he staggered to his feet.

The wonderful Being bowed. 'I am Fescue a Gaiakin of Florain.'

Never in his wildest dreams had Lark imagined anyone so awesome; this Being, with eyes like golden sunlight, had spoken to him, Lark Annunder, a humble Delphin lad.

His only knowledge of these perplexing people was from Watersmeet market. Dressed in long floating robes with faces hidden in deep hoods, they brought exotic fruits and rich jewellery. This Gaiakin was dressed like Sandy, in travel-stained leather and woollens but, even so, a faint ethereal inner light seemed to radiate from him. He carried on his back a long sword, jewelled like Sandy's, and at his waist hung a gold long-bladed dagger.

He gazed spellbound as the lithe figure bent over Fin, his sun-gold hair tumbling over Fin's face. Watching the Gaiakin trying without success to prize his fingers from around the black stone, Lark noticed he wore a gold ring set with a large red ruby, the colour of blood. On the back of his hand, a rough red mark marred his translucent skin: it could have been a burn scar, which surprised Lark.

'You'll make Fin better, won't you, Mr Fescue, sir? I couldn't bear it if I lost him.' Lark choked.

A shadow momentarily dimmed the golden eyes. 'Doomstones can be very powerful: I will have to work hard to remove this stone.'

The Gaiakin studied the undergrowth around them. 'The creature who laid it could even now be spying on us, so we must hurry away from this place.' Gathering Fin up into his arms, he strode away into the green gloom.

'Hurry Lark, we must follow Fescue,' Sandy said urgently, 'take heart, we are now very near to Stonetree, where you can rest and have something hot to eat!'

Back on his weary legs, tucking Mick into his jerkin, Lark shouldered his rucksack. Trotting as close as he could to Sandy's heels, he felt there were menacing eyes watching him from the bushes; now and then there came a muffled rumbling from Mick. The sounds of the river faded. Soon, a smell of roasting meat drifted towards him, making his mouth water. A few yards more brought them out into a clearing within a circle of tumbled stone walls and warmed by sunlight filtering through the surrounding trees.

He stumbled to a tree stump and collapsed, bowing his swimming head as weariness drained him; he was too tired even to help Mick as he struggled out from his jerkin. Lifting his head, gradually he took in his surroundings. Fescue had laid Fin on a bed of animal pelts by a ruined wall and struggling to his feet he went and crouched by him. Fescue gave him a reassuring smile as he gently massaged Fin's tightly clenched fist.

Across the clearing, Sandy was talking with a man who was barbecuing small carcasses skewered on sticks over a cooking fire, turning them every now and then to roast evenly. Lark reckoned they might have been either rabbits or squirrels, perhaps both.

The cook was a powerfully built man, broad shouldered, shorter than Sandy by a good foot, and younger looking, his glossy black hair tied back in a ponytail. His tanned complexion had a faint yellow tinge. He wore a Trekker warrior sword at his back, this one in a polished black enamel sheath, and a crossbow hung on his shoulder with a quiver of arrows at his waist. Unlike Sandy and Fescue, his clothes were made of padded cloth, richly embroidered with coloured silk threads, once bright, but now faded.

Noticing Lark watching him, the man grinned a greeting, his narrow beetle-black eyes gleaming beneath hooded lids. Thrusting his sticks of meat into the ground he came over, and bowing low, addressed Lark. 'It's an honour to meet a Delphin at long last. I've heard all about you from Sandy here! My name is Kenji. I'm a warrior in Iskander's Trekker Squad. I'm of the Samurai brotherhood.' He thumped his chest proudly.

Lark's interest was caught by his belt buckle: it looked like a monkey skull, but made of shiny metal, with two green stones set in the eye sockets. His high boots were interesting too, fringed by garishly orange nylon fur. (Later, when Lark got to know Kenji better, and could study these adornments in detail, he learned the skull and fur came from a Frit.)

'Come and eat,' Kenji said, pulling Lark to his feet. Leading him to a tree stump by the fire, he handed him a hot cooked carcass. Mick followed closely, his little face looking pleading up at Kenji who threw him a glistening chunk of raw liver which Mick fell on voraciously.

Sinking his teeth into the succulent meat a wonderful flavour flooded Lark's mouth, recalling the patch of wild garlic he had sat in earlier.

Seeing his delight, Sandy laughed. 'You're eating food cooked by the best chef this side of the Humber! We are much envied for having Kenji in our Squad.'

Lark shot Kenji a look of admiration. 'I'm no mean cook myself – learned from my Grammer! You have my respect, Mr Kenji.'

Kenji grinned. 'Ah, I also have a grandmother: it was she who taught me my cooking skills. Her marinades are famous, secret recipes passed down through generations. She can transform even an old fox into a feast some would believe only a Gaiakin could have prepared, with the fabled herbs from the garden of Florain!'

Sandy groaned. 'Lark, you don't realise what you have unleashed: Kenji can talk of cooking all day.'

Grinning, Kenji crouched down next to Lark, and handed him another skewer of meat. Attacking one himself, between mouthfuls he quizzed Lark on Brightdale food. He listened keenly as Lark explained what was available in Brightdale during the lean time of Saprise, carefully attending to how Lupin the cook prepared her fairy-ring fritters. After picking two carcasses clean, Kenji regretfully returned to his cooking fire.

Revived by the talk, rest and food, Lark settled against a tree stump near Fescue to watch him massage Fin's fist, still clenched tightly around the stone. As he worked, the Gaiakin sung a sweet lilting song; the sound of his deep, melodious voice sent a tingle down Lark's spine. Occasionally Fin stirred and smiled in his sleep. Once he opened his eyes and, looking around unseeing, closed them again.

As he watched, Lark mulled over his limited knowledge of Warrior Trekkers: in Brightdale they had the reputation of being dangerous brigands; he would never have believed that one day he would be eating with them.

Then there were those slugbuggers who had left that goo at Ireshope. Whatever they could be, he just couldn't imagine – what did Sandy call them? Maabella's babes? He hoped he wouldn't have to meet any. Mick settled on his lap, a squirrel leg in his mouth. Lark looked at the little dog's bite wounds: they would soon need more ointment. The sounds around him faded, his chin dropped on to his chest and he fell into an uneasy sleep.

Yesterday, back in Brightdale, Bird and Bee, hampered by the reeds fringing the river as they tracked Fin and Lark, found it increasingly difficult to keep sight of them. At first, the sound of Lark's jangling pans gave them hope that they'd catch up, but the jangling grew more distant and eventually faded away. Wolfie, irritatingly ignoring their sharp commands to 'come hide!', loped along in full view; so abandoning their cover, they joined him on the path. They hadn't gone much further when he came to an abrupt halt. Hackles raised, he stuck his head into the reeds from where a strong stench wafted.

Bird wrinkled her nose. 'Phew, have you let off, Wolfie? Had too much raw rabbit?'

Across the river on the far bank she saw the Dandrum dairy herd at the water's edge peacefully drinking and wondered if the smell came from them. Suddenly something spooked the cows. Snorting, they lumbered off up the muddy bank, udders swaying, to a far corner of their meadow.

'Silly beasts,' she muttered, hurrying to catch up with Bee. 'Sis,' she called, 'that thing we saw last night crawling up Mossy's wall – have you any more thoughts what it might have been?'

Bee turned and frowned. 'Well, for a start, I don't reckon it was plustic blowing in the wind, like I first thought. There's been rumours too, of orange imps being spotted up by the Donkey Crags – do you think they're real? Grammer Nutmeg says she saw one in Withered Wood, but you know how she likes scary stories!'

'She scared herself last night,' Bird said, 'normally I would have thought it was just her imagination, when she said she saw a pile of burning rags mothing, as she called it, after Fin and Lark. That creepy thing we saw last night was rather like a pile of rags – it made such a horrid noise, too!'

Bee shuddered. 'I've heard talk, too, that it wasn't a wolf that killed Master Marlin – Hollin Annunder talked of a dreadful wound in his throat.'

Bird recalled the thick bandage Nutmeg had wound about his neck. Fighting a wave of panic, she quickly changed the subject.

'Bee, are we unbridled?'

'Unbridled? What are you on about?'

'It's what I overheard Mrs Cletchen tell Grammer Magette: "your lasses are unbridled – you should keep 'em on a tighter rein".'

'Sounds like we're a couple of ponies. I'd rather be unbridled; it's what we do, "unbridleness". What's brought up this nonsense? Are you thinking of settling down?'

'Getting married you mean? Not just yet – I'm still feeling too unbridled. But if it meant keeping Fin from that Daffodil, I'd marry him tomorrow. How about you? Sparrow Chippen's not bad looking.'

'Sparrow? Until recently I thought you'd decided to pick him, instead of Fin,' grinned Bee.

'No way! I was only encouraging him, to make Fin jealous – it didn't work.'

Bee sighed. 'I can't see us as married old biddies for ages, but as you're older, you should be the first to take the plunge.'

Bird glared at her twin. 'I don't know why you think being two minutes older, makes me the one to go first.'

'Well, you're prettier,' snapped Bee.

'I'm not – we look just the same,' Bird snapped back.

They stood for a moment, hands on hips, glaring at each other, then burst out laughing.

'Bee, I don't want to be in a hurry for us to part. I'm so used to you being there. I'd feel half a person without you. Would you mind it very much if we had to leave each other?'

'Sure would, you're my best mate. Anyway, we're talking daft. We'd better get a move on. The lads are probably miles ahead by now.' She whistled to Wolfie who reluctantly turned away from a clump of bulrushes. 'Get a move on hound! He must be getting old, letting common cows fret him.'

After a while, the reeds petered out, and the river, now out of sight below the steep bank, could be heard tumbling noisily over its rocky bed. The trees and bushes had started to take on an eerie menace, as if nameless things could be watching from the deep thickets. Once they thought they heard voices, but it was only the croaking of a pair of rooks perched on a low tree on the far bank.

Bird glanced up at the sun and frowned. 'It's well past midday. We should have caught up by now – we must be getting into Annunder Territory. Is that the sound of Brightforce in the distance? Do you think that's where they're going for a skinny dip? What a sight: Daffodil and Alaria dipping their podgy toes in the churning pool!'

Bee gave a scornful laugh. 'I can't see the sissies being brave enough to swim there – the water's too deep and cold. Could be that they thought of camping there, though: the sparkling foam from the waterfall is very romantic in the moonlight. If we get to join in, it'll stop Daffy's nonsense with Fin!

'I hope Lark's brought some of Grammer Nutmeg's mutton pasties,' she added. 'I'm getting hungry. Anyway, we're not scared of skinny dipping in Brightforce pool. Wait a mo, we didn't bring towels. I don't fancy having to get back into my clothes, dripping wet!'

Bird grinned. 'Would we need to get dressed?' She shifted her rucksack to a more comfortable position: it felt very light. When she'd packed, she hadn't thought about practical items, like towels; her priority had been to put in something pretty to wear – she'd a vague picture of them sitting under the stars, faces glowing in a flickering fire, toasting mallows, and drinking berry juice.

She noticed Wolfie had stopped where a small river ran beneath a bridge and was staring down a track branching off to the right. Wondering if the trail was an animal-run used by something large and dangerous, she urged him on.

'Come on Wolfie,' she said, prodding his rough fur flank, 'have you lost the scent?'

They didn't know the branching track would have led them to Plashydale.

'Poor Wolfie, we can't expect him to act the bloodhound,' Bee said, looking anxiously along the deserted path from where the roar of Brightforce came. 'I wonder if it's safe so far into wild Annunder lands? Hope we won't have to spend the night here, alone. I keep remembering that spooky what-ever-it-was climbing Mossy's wall.'

She shivered as she checked her crossbow was safe on her back, and the darts loose in the quiver. The twins were skilled archers, and even though their arrows were small, they could inflict a nasty injury.

Reaching Brightforce, they gazed up in awe at the tea-coloured peaty water thundering over the seventy-foot drop into a deep foaming pool.

'Look!' Bee shouted above the roar of crashing water.

Bird spotted flashes of white skin in the creamy foam. Scrambling excitedly over the rocks to the water's edge, they discovered a shoal of trout, frantically twisting and turning, trapped behind a wall of boulders. Disappointed, they sat watching them for a while, feeling the cold spray on their faces, the roaring water muffling all other sounds.

Wolfie, drinking at the water's edge, suddenly lifted his head. Bounding over the rocks back to the path, he stood listening, ears pricked. Fearful, the twins clambered up to join him.

'Do you think it's them?' Bee hissed. 'Quick, hide in these bushes, and jump out at them!'
'I hope it is them, and not something dangerous!' Bird muttered.

Slipping their crossbows from their backs and arming them with darts, they waited with hearts thumping. 'Watch out we don't shoot the lads,' Bird whispered.

After a few minutes, when nobody appeared, they assumed Wolfie had given them another false alarm. Thinking it best to get away from the noise of the waterfall, they took to the path again.

As they walked, the path, rising steeply, appeared to be leading to the high fells. The trees began to thin out, giving way to heather and juniper, with here and there patches of reed covered boggy ground.

They met nobody. Getting more and more tired and hungry, they began to regret they hadn't turned for home at the waterfall.

When finally, they reached the fell tops, the sun had dropped below the shadowy horizon. It was eerily quiet up here; no birds sang, the air sullen and still.

'It's strange – where could Fin and Lark have got to?' Bee muttered, looking nervously at Wolfie, who kept stopping to stare back down the path. The stink, which they had thought was from the cows, again drifted towards them on the heavy air.

'We're much farther west than I would've liked.' Bird's voice sounded loud in the silent gloom. 'We must have missed the lads somewhere back along the way. I've a feeling they went down that trail Wolfie wanted us to follow. Should we go back and have a look?'

'No way will we reach that turning before it's dark,' Bee said. 'Let's face it, Bird: we've made a mess of things. I hate this weird moor. Let's go back to the trees – we can hide in them until morning. We'd better hurry! The light around here isn't like Brightdale light, is it? It seems to be getting dark sooner than normal.' She pointed to a dark silhouette on the horizon. 'Isn't that where Withered Wood lies?'

The prospect of home and family began to have ever stronger appeal, even though they knew they would get a major telling off.

By the time they reached the trees, the foul smell had become nauseating.

'Yuck, whatever is that stink!' Bee muttered. 'Nothing we know stinks like that!'
Bird grabbed Bee's hand. 'What's up with Wolfie now?'

He'd dropped down on his haunches, hackles raised, and was staring down the path.
'I can hear thudding feet!' squeaked Bee. 'Quick, hide!'

They were too slow: as they dived towards a clump of juniper trees, out of the twilight galloped a huge long-legged bird.

Unknown to Bird and Bee, they too were being followed. On the far bank of the river lurking in some tall reeds, an orange-pelted simian creature, accompanied by a large, snake-necked bird, had been observing them.

'There's two tasty morsels, Peggy – one fer you, 'n one fer me,' thrummed Slicer's mechanical voice box as he got a tantalizing glimpse of two blonde heads above the reeds.

'Bet one's got that shiny jool. Be in Lord Gressil's favour if I got me dabs on that – nab it afore Mr Hot Smoke Raaum.'

Mounted astride his ganglefowl, close to where the Dandrum cows stood amongst the yellow water iris, the Frit was about to launch out into the river, when Peggy's smell spooked the beasts, sending them squelching noisily up the bank; the twins' ever-watchful hound alerted, Slicer's quarry hurried on.

Keeping to thick undergrowth above the river, Slicer and Peggy continued to where the far side bank rose high above the water. Finding a shallow spot, they waded across and hunkering down below the bank's cliff, waited for a Delphin ankle to come within easy reach.

Hearing approaching chatter, Slicer's camera-lens eyes snapped rapidly open and shut with excitement. Flexing his metal fingers in readiness to grab, he was thwarted once more by a warning growl from the hound, sending his small prey scurrying away along the path. Turning furiously on his ganglefowl, Slicer gave her a hefty swipe, sending up a cloud of fluffy feathers.

'Give over fluttering yer wings Peg, that scruffy hound can sniff yer B.O.'

Peggy's glittering eyes glared at her master. Darting out her beak, she yanked a tuft of orange nylon fur from his back.

'Behave yersel' stinky fowl!' Slicer snarled, jabbing viciously on Peggy's harness.

A short fracas ensued, ending with Peggy falling into the water, and Crud's vital electronics nearly flooding. Spluttering, they returned to shadowing their prey.

At Brightforce, Slicer nearly nabbed them but slipped on a wet rock, sending a shower of pebbles tumbling into the river, alerting the hound yet again. From behind some larger rocks, he watched in fury as the Delphins scrambled back onto the path. He decided he would try again away from the roar of the waterfall, confident that before the day was over, he and Peggy would be feeding on succulent fresh Delphin meat.

The opportunity came as evening fell: his victims had turned back down the path and were heading straight towards where he and Peggy waited hidden behind boulders.

'Here we go, Peg – no eating mind, afore I've checked which is one carrying the shiny jool!'

Saliva dripping from his rubbery lips, he mounted Peggy and kicked his metal heels into her feathery sides. With two great bounds, she landed on the path in front of their quarry.

Again, it was Wolfie who thwarted him: the huge hound launched himself at Peggy, clamping his powerful jaw around her long neck, choking her off, mid-squawk. Slicer lost his grip on the reins and fell off, hitting the ground with a tinny screech. Getting caught up in Peggy's gangling legs, she fell on top of him, with Wolfie on top of them both, his teeth still clenched about Peggy's neck.

'Run! Run!' Bee screamed, pushing Bird behind her at the same time groping for her crossbow.

Taking aim, she didn't spot the Frit escaping from the whirl of lashing ganglefowl legs and snarling hound. Slicer was swiftly upon her. Snatching a handful of her hair and baring his razor teeth, he made ready for his famous slicing death bite. He never made that bite: a small arrow slammed deep into his metal brow. With a shriek of rage, he let go of Bee's hair.

Twisting free, Bee saw Bird arming her crossbow again, preparing to let fly another dart.

But Bee and Bird didn't know that Frits are part machine, and the Delphin arrow embedded in Slicer's brow was no deterrent. Bird aimed again as the Frit lunged once more at Bee, razor teeth bared, ready to slice. Before he could bite, from out of the dusk leaped a tall figure wielding a great sword. A flash of steel blade: one swift scythe and Slicer's head came away from his neck. For a split second it hung mid-air, then thudded to the ground, to roll away down the path, Bird's arrow still stuck between the blank eyes, Slicer's body wobbling after it.

Finally escaping from Wolfie's jaws, Peggy staggered to her feet and leaving a cloud of feathers floating behind her, followed. Frit and fowl disappeared down the path, Peggy's choking squawks fading away into the twilight.

For a moment Bee stood gaping after the retreating figures, then, with a whoop of delight, grabbed at the drifting feathers.

'Noooo!' cried the sword bearer: but too late.

Bee screamed: 'Newt's knickers – they sting!'

Frantically shaking the feathers free of her fingers, she fell groaning to her knees. Fumbling for her pot of marigold ointment in the pouch at her waist, Bird rushed over and began slavering a thick layer over Bee's rapidly swelling fingers; but it didn't work. Rocking in pain, Bee stuffed her hands beneath her armpits.

Turning to their rescuer for help, Bird recoiled in shock: their rescuer was a Skwid.

She'd never been close to one before, only seeing bands of them in the distance as they passed through Brightdale, sometimes setting up camp for the night on the heights above Spinner Hall, causing a stir. Delphin children had long been warned not to go near them. 'They steal little ones and roast them for supper.'

Whether the Skwid was human or not, was hard to judge; the face was predominantly human, with small swivelling eyes and the skimpily clad body had human female form. But the skin was that of – perhaps – a lizard? Or a chameleon? At first glance dark green, but the reptilian scales often changed colour, brighter every now and then, with sometimes a rainbow of rippling colours.

Bird wondered what she could do if the Skwid turned nasty. Remembering the beheaded Frit, she wouldn't have time to shoot a dart before the creature slashed with her deadly sword. She plucked up her courage: 'Please can you help my sister?'

Hunkering down beside them, the Skwid pulled out Bee's hands from under her arm pits and studied them with her strange swivelling eyes.

'She needs her hands in cold running water,' she said. Her voice, curiously husky, seemed kind in tone and she spoke in the Common Language, which Bird found reassuring.

'There is a spring near here where we can bathe them.' She scooped Bee up into her arms. 'We must hurry – when that headless Frit gets back to base, his friends will come looking for us. Be quick, follow me as best you can!'

Gently cradling Bee, the Skwid strode off through the heather. Gathering up Bee's crossbow and arrows, and slinging their rucksacks over her shoulder, Bird stumbled after. Terrified she would lose sight of Bee, she clung to the rough fur of Wolfie's neck, keeping as close as she could. Every now and then the creature stopped to listen, twisting her head, sniffing the air. Once, scenting something unpleasant, Bird heard her mutter the word 'fowl!' Hearing Bee groaning in pain, she hoped they would soon reach the spring.

Darkness fell, making it hard to see their new companion as the hue of her skin blended with the night, showing only a faint moving shadow ahead. All Bird could do now was to hang onto Wolfie's neck as he trotted in the Skwid's tracks. Eventually the moon rose, flooding the landscape with silvery light. She saw they were going through scrubland of low growing bilberry and juniper, heading towards a forest spreading darkly below them.

At the tree line, Skwid waited for her and gently shifted Bee to her other arm.

'We are nearly there!' she called in her husky voice.

At the sound of running water, Bird's spirits rose. Plunging into the trees, they came to a dell where a small stream, sparkling in the moonlight, trickled through a curtain of ferns into a shallow pool. Instructing her to sit on a patch of moss, the Skwid set Bee in her lap, and taking her swollen hands, plunged them into the icy water, making Bee whimper.

'Keep her hands there until the pain eases,' the Skwid commanded.

As the cold water soothed the fiery stinging, Bird could feel Bee slowly relax. After a short while, sighing with relief, Bee pulled her hands out of the water. Tucking them inside her sleeves, she leaned against Bird's shoulder, and closed her eyes.

Bird twisted around to look up at the Skwid crouched on the bank above her. 'You have been very kind,' she said gratefully. 'Who you are?'

'My name is Shadow Dancer, but most people just call me Dancer. As you see, I am of the Skwid kind!' She stood up tall and proud, and thumped her chest. 'But I am also a Trekker Warrior!'

Recalling their reputation, Bird was surprised that a Skwid, let alone a female, could be a Trekker. Then, remembering her manners, she introduced herself and Bee.

'I'm Bird Spinner, and this is my twin sister, Bee.'

She timidly held out her hand to the Skwid, who took it in her strong scaly grasp.

'Greetings, Bird and Bee Spinner,' she said, sitting down beside them.

In the pale moonlight, Bird saw Wolfie crouching nearby, head drooping. To her dismay, a large white feather was sticking out of his mouth. 'Dancer, can you help our hound! He has one of those evil feathers caught in his teeth.'

Stroking Wolfie's head reassuringly, the Skwid took the hound firmly by the muzzle and gently prising open his jaw, pulled out the feather. Coaxing him to the stream, she tenderly bathed his mouth. When she had done, Wolfie licked her face in gratitude, making the Skwid chuckle: 'He'll soon recover – that was a pin feather, which do not sting; indeed, some prize ganglefowl quill feathers as the best writing pens!'

She now began to clean her sword. Plucking a handful of dry bracken, she carefully wiped away the acrid Frit oil from the long blade, paying special attention to the viciously sharp edge. Polishing the steel to a bright shine, she slid the sword back into the leather sheath strapped to her back. Then, stretching her arms over her head, she repeatedly drew the blade in and out, her action so lightning swift Bird could hardly follow.

'That's better – my precious sword is fettled,' Dancer said.

She turned her attention to Bee. 'How are you faring, little lass?' she asked, smoothing Bee's hair from her pain-racked face. Taking hold of Bee's hands, she examined her fingers and grunted in satisfaction. 'The swelling is going down! Tuck your hands away again to keep the chilly air off them.'

It was far into the night before the stinging in Bee's fingers finally faded. 'The pain's gone at last,' she sighed as she pulled out her hands from her sleeves. Leaning her head against Bird's shoulder, she gave a little sob. 'Sis, I'm so tired – how I wish I were at home tucked up in my own lovely bed!'

Bird twisted her head around to Dancer. 'Are we far from Brightdale? We must get back home as soon as we can, our family will be going frantic with worry!'

The Skwid remained silent for a moment; even though the light was poor, Bird could just make out the shadow of colours rippling over her face. Suddenly on her guard, she wondered if she could really trust the creature.

'It will not be safe for you to return by the way you came. That Frit which attacked you may have gone for help to Killhope Gate, which is the portal into the Land of Contagion – not far from here!' The Skwid pointed her long reptilian finger to the west. 'I fear his companions will be looking for us! On my own, I could not defend you from a troop of Frits. No, we must go by another way, which will take longer! We will move as soon it's light enough; the longer we linger here, the more we are in danger!'

Bird gave the Skwid a suspicious stare: she'd a feeling this wasn't the whole truth.

Dancer saw her look. 'You have to trust me: I do not intend to eat you, as I think your stories have warned!' Her face puckered into a frown. 'Explain to me: why did you little Delphins stray so far from the safety of your Dale?'

Bird felt herself blush. She was rapidly realising how silly she'd been, chasing after Fin. Avoiding Dancer's questioning gaze, she muttered: 'I've been very foolish, and dragged my sister into great danger.'

Bee scrambled off Bird's lap and glared at her. 'Don't talk daft, Bird! You didn't drag me into danger. If anything, it was me who got us into this pickle – "showing off as usual" as Lark would probably say!'

Bird shook her head crossly: 'It was because of me fussing over Fin, believing Daffy's nonsense about her and him going Skinny Dipping!'

She explained to Dancer: 'It's Delphin tradition to go Skinny Dipping as a ritual before marriage. I've always thought that one day, Fin and I would get married. Then I found out that a podgy lass called Daffodil was trying to muscle in. She said she and Fin were going for a Skinny Dip, and it made me furious. I went chasing after them without thinking things through. I didn't even pack properly, just silly things like make-up. Now, I just want to get Bee home, and look after her.' She sniffed hard, wiping tears from her eyes.

Dancer gave a low laugh. 'Love and romance! We females get into such a tangle over them – it was love that got me into being a Trekker!' She shook her head regretfully: 'I gave up my tribe to follow a handsome warrior, even though I knew he was high born and beyond my reach. I wish I could go, skinny dipping, do you call it?'

Bird gave the Skwid a watery smile. Suddenly her stomach rumbled, reminding her she was very hungry. She fished the bag of marshmallows out of her rucksack, offering some to Dancer and Bee. Remembering the bottle of berry juice, she got that out too.

Chewing the mallows, and passing round the juice, they listened to the little stream tumbling down towards the forest. The night was peaceful with no unusual sounds to alarm them. Now and then Wolfie lifted his head, his keen hearing picking up the rustling of small night creatures. Once Bee let out a squeak when a fox barked. They dared not sleep, Shadow Dancer always alert.

Chatting quietly, an easy friendship grew between the twins and the Skwid.

'It wasn't only that Frit creature giving us a scare,' Bee told her, 'last night we saw a proper monster in Market Place, crawling up Mossy's wall, like a fiery black duster with a bad cough!'

Recognizing Bird's description, Dancer looked sharply at her. 'You surely imagined that! What would one of those devils be doing in your little hidden land?'

'Grammer Nutmeg saw it too,' Bee said huffily, 'mothing after Lark and Fin: that's why we were watching Mossy's shop. She'd asked us to see if the lads had got there safely, and as we hid spying under a cart in Chippen's yard, we saw it – a devil did you call it? I reckon it was after Master Marlin's treasure, brought back from his wanderings – there are rumours too, that Master Marlin was not killed by a wolf, but something evil happened to him.'

After explaining to Dancer about the death of their Head, Bird said: 'I'm sure something worse than a wolf must have killed him: when I was helping Grammer Nutmeg prepare the body for the pyre, I saw the vilest wound in master's throat.'

Dancer shook her head in wonderment. 'There's a conundrum: I wonder what it was that your Master Marlin possessed, that one of Lord Gressil's devils risked coming into your Dale – where Zagzagel gives you protection?'

66

Leaping to her feet, she tested her sword again, swinging it about her head, before re-sheathing it. 'Come, we must hurry away from here! There is light in the east: it will be daylight soon.'

As the twins gathered up their rucksacks and crossbows, Dancer suddenly stopped to listen, her eyes rapidly swivelling as she stared down into the forested valley. Wolfie went to her side, his hackles raised.

'What is it?' Bird asked nervously. Then she too heard it, coming up through the trees: a sound like huge flat feet slapping wetly on rock, followed by a sighing swish.

'Curse them,' hissed Dancer, 'Maabella's babes have been allowed out to play!'

'What in all the world are they?' the twins chorused.

'Have you not heard of Maabella's babes? It is to be hoped you never meet them! Hurry, we must reach the river before they do!'

'Which river is that?' asked Bird. 'Couldn't we make for our own river, the Bright? It must be safe, now it's daylight!'

The horrid sound seemed to be getting louder.

Dancer's face and head flashed pink and red. 'I was not telling the whole truth when I said I would take you the long way back to your home. I have been commanded to take you to a safe place, not far from here, where you will meet up with the friends you have been following. Surely, you must have wondered what has happened to them? You are expected, and my boss will be anxious if we delay any longer.' She indicated the valley below them. 'We must follow the path along the river Durholm: it is our way to safety. But we must reach there quickly before the bugslugs!'

Expected by her boss? Bird wondered what the Skwid was talking about. 'How can your boss be expecting us?' she exclaimed, 'he wouldn't know about us.'

'And I bet Fin and Lark will be at home, raising the alarm because we're missing!' added Bee.

Dancer flashed them an extraordinarily colourful grin. 'No! Word came to our Trekker Squad that you needed help. Iskander, our boss, knows you were following the two other Delphins when you went astray. Have you not wondered why I am here? I was sent to find you!'

Bee looked at her suspiciously: 'How did this boss of yours know? We don't know anybody called Isk something!'

'He is a friend of Mr Mossy's, whom you do know. It was he who got word to us. We must head for a place called Stonetree. Luckily bugslugs move slowly. When we reach there, we can alert the others that those evil creatures are on the river!'

Bird looked anxiously at Bee's pale face. 'Is it far? Bee's still very poorly.'

'Your fine hound will carry her. Come – help me lift her onto his back.'

Bee smiled bravely. 'I'm feeling much better, but my fingers have started to sting again – my legs have gone all wobbly, too.'

Wolfie stood patiently whilst they slung their rucksacks across his back, before helping Bee scramble up.

Seeing Bee wince as she grabbed his rough coat, Dancer looked at her sadly: 'You will always have a great fear of the ganglefowl, Bee. And I think they will not forget you either,' she added darkly.

Bird looked up at the Skwid in dismay as she knelt to drink from the pool with cupped hands. But Dancer chose not to elaborate on her remark.

'I hope you can manage to walk nine miles, which is how far Stonetree is from here,' Dancer called, taking hold of the fur around Wolfie's neck, and leading him towards the trees.

Bird jumped determinedly to her feet and ran after them. Her stomach felt dreadfully empty; all she'd eaten since the funeral feast were six marshmallows. Hoping that Dancer was telling the truth, and that they would soon meet up with Fin and Lark, she wondered what they would say about her and Bee straying so far from home. Surely Dilly and Alaria weren't with them?

# 7
# CROW

From somewhere beyond his dark despair a distant voice called: 'Wake Fin! Wake!'
His palm burned with stinging pain.

He couldn't breathe. Cold, murky water was all around him, filling his lungs.

The voice called again, more urgently: 'Fin, you must wake now!'

He was being drawn up towards sunlight. Breaking the surface, taking gulps of air, he looked around. He was floating in a lake beneath a brilliant Highsun sky. Lily pads spread all around him, spangled here and there with scarlet and butter-gold blooms. On a far bank, willows swayed in a soft breeze, languidly dipping their green tips in the water. Beyond the willows rose a high yew hedge.

On a wooden jetty overhanging the lake stood a tall, hooded figure. 'Come Fin, come to me!' called the figure. As he beckoned a gemstone on his hand flashed blood red.

'Who are you?' Fin cried pushing his way through the thick lily stems.

'I am Fescue. I have come to wake you!' sang the beautiful voice. The figure threw back his hood and the blaze from his eyes dazzled Fin. Lake and lilies faded. The golden eyes filled all his vision. He smiled drowsily. 'Hello Fescue.'

'So, you've decided to wake up!' exclaimed familiar voice.

Fin sat up: Lark's pale green eyes were on him. It all came back: Phul's Hollow, the strange black stone, the descent into deep despair.

'Lark?' He looked about, bewildered, seeing trees and tumbled walls. 'Where are we? Where's Phul's Hollow?'

'We're in a place called Stonetree. Sandy carried you here.'

'Sandy? You found Sandy!'

A shadow fell across them and a tall man smiled down at him.

'Hello Fin Dandrum!' Sandy said, hunkering down next to him. 'I am glad you have woken. Zagzagel would never have forgiven me if anything dire had happened to you!'

Like Lark, Fin was surprised by the man's midnight-blue gaze: why hadn't Mossy told him about this kingly friend of his?

'How do you feel?' Sandy asked.

Fin grimaced. 'Pretty foul! But it's good to meet you, Sandy. I'm sorry I wasn't—' He turned to Lark. 'Did you say Stonetree? Never mind stone trees, I urgently need to get behind any tree!'

Hearing a chuckle, he saw a stocky dark-haired man crouched nearby, watching him.

'Meet Kenji,' Lark said, 'the best chef this side of the Humber!'

'Never mind the introductions, let the lad get behind a tree first.' Kenji laughed, pulling Fin to his feet and turning him towards the nearest tree trunk.

Back on his bed of fur pelts, Fin studied his sore palm. 'What's the matter with my hand?'

'You picked up a doomstone – it stuck to you!' Lark said. 'Fescue here saved you: pulled it off – so – so you wouldn't go mad!' He glowered in disgust at the sinister black stone lying by a wall, where Fescue had thrown it.

Fescue took Fin's hand, and as he massaged where the stone had stuck, it dawned on Fin that he was looking at a Gaiakin: he had never seen Gaiakin without their robes, faces always hidden inside deep hoods.

A fierce spasm of burning in his palm distracted him. He pulled his hand away and frowned. 'What happened at Phul's Hollow?'

Experiencing again the horror, wide-eyed, Lark explained. 'Mick's yelping woke me. I saw you slumped on the ground with a varmint Scav pawing you! I tried to catch him, but he was too quick – he got away. The creature had laid the doomstone as a trap, so he could steal from you!'

'Doomstones are known as eaters of joy – holding one can send you into dark despair,' Fescue added gravely.

Fin shuddered as he recalled picking up what he had thought was a piece of clinker.

'Come lad, eat some food – it'll make you feel better,' Kenji said, handing Fin a skewer of roasted meat. 'I've kept some pieces warm.'

Hungrily biting into the succulent morsels, Fin realised he hadn't eaten since last night's meal in Phul's Hollow. Whilst he ate, Lark sat next to him, applying more ointment to Mick's bites.

'They look nasty,' Fin remarked through a mouthful of squirrel meat.

'Aye, but Mick gave as good as he got – damn nearly killed the Scav's rat!'

Smiling at Lark's look of pride, Fin picked off the last pieces of meat and licking his fingers, settled himself on his fur blanket.

Across the clearing Sandy, Fescue and Kenji were sitting on a wall, deep in conversation. It didn't surprise Fin that Mossy should know such people. He recalled when he, Tissy and the twins were playing in the tree house, and Mossy had walked past with a tall man he now realised was Sandy.

Was Fescue also a friend of Mossy's, he wondered? He noticed the Gaiakin glancing in his direction and wondered if he might be the person to take charge of the cross; an unaccountable feeling of caution warned him to be careful.

He liked the look of Kenji, and like Lark, was intrigued by the man's skull-shaped belt buckle.

He and Lark watched amazed as Kenji stood up, and with one fluid movement reached back and pulled out his long sword from its sheath, scything the air before returning it.

'Right boss, I'm off – going to check on the bugslugs' slime you and young Lark found at Ireshope.' Slinging his crossbow over his shoulder, he strode off down the path towards the river, the glimpses of bright orange fur decorating the tops of his boots, reminiscent of some exotic bird fluttering through the bushes.

When he'd gone, Fin studied the surrounding clearing. Observing the ruined walls covered in ivy and moss, he wondered about the people who lived here, a thousand years ago. What had they been like? In Brightdale there was little trace left of those people. Like most Brightdale Delphins, he'd never ventured into the wild forests where many abandoned settlements could still be found, half-buried in undergrowth. He speculated what life must have been like in those distant times; Mossy had told him that the people made amazing mechanical contraptions, some of which even flew in the air. A wave of pity washed over him – their machines hadn't saved them from dying of plague.

Hugging his knees to his chin, he saw Sandy's eyes on him, making him acutely aware of his mix of Delphin and Rom features, and his odd coloured eyes. He would have been surprised to know that Sandy thought his Delphin and Rom mixture gave him a rare quality.

Strolling over, Sandy nodded towards the tumbled walls. 'Do not be sorry for those people, Fin. The folk who lived here long ago are now resting in joy, waiting for the coming of the new creation, and are to be envied!'

Kneeling beside him, he spoke in a low voice. 'Fin, I must ask you about what you carry – I would not trouble you, but Zagzagel has charged me to take care of you – and the Chi Rho. Is it safe?'

Fin drew out his leather purse and, careful to leave his mother's coin behind, took out the cross and laid it on the fur pelts. Looking again at the rich jewels glittering in the sunlight, he was filled with awe. That he, a simple Delphin, should be carrying such a precious object was hard to take in.

Sandy leant forward and lightly touching the clear crystal, frowned. 'This cross is thought to be dangerous, as well as of great power. Put it away! You must carry it for a while longer – at least until we reach Durholm.'

Fin sighed, rubbing his neck where the purse's cord had chafed. 'I'll be glad to pass it on: it's getting me down. I wish I'd never taken charge of it! Couldn't you look after it until we get to Durholm?'

'Indeed no! You should wait until we reach Durholm Garrison, where you can decide the fate of the cross – with the help of those wiser than me.'

Fin scooped the cross back into the purse and tucked it away again. Desperate to get to Durholm, he knew that first that he needed to get more strength back – his legs still felt like jelly. 'I hate this delay,' he muttered. 'That Scav needs – needs – sorting,' he finished lamely.

'I'd like to know more about the Scav – Crow is he called?' Lark asked. 'He sounds an evil tyke!'

'My father mentioned him in his letter to me, but didn't say what happened to him,' Fin said.

'Crow is a sly, secretive creature – I will tell you what I know. Let us sit closer to the cooking fire and I will recount his story.'

Lark, helping Fin walk unsteadily to a log, sat by him. Sandy sat opposite on a tree stump; the sunlight had turned his dusty red hair to gleaming copper, reminding Fin of a prince from one of Nutmeg's story books.

'Crow was born in one of the Scav settlements that sprawl along the coastal marshes of our three Northern rivers.'

Fin and Lark noticed he had the trace of an accent, unfamiliar but pleasant to listen to.

'I believe they come to Watersmeet with their stuff?'

The two Delphins nodded, thinking of the small grimy ruffians, stinking of rotting fish, with their bits and pieces of metal, glass and plastic for sale or barter on market day.

'Even though there are still Scavs able to find a living from scavenging in the estuaries, the accumulated detritus of plustic, metal and glass is now much depleted, and many have abandoned the mud and marsh of the coast, migrating south where they have become a nuisance. There are reports of ravening hordes swooping on towns and settlements, inflicting havoc, and destruction.

'Only the toughest Scavs survive to adulthood; they cake their bodies in a crust of salty mud, affording a kind of protection against the cold, their only clothing being a loin cloth, sometimes fashioned from plustic sheeting. Their bodies scarred, deformed by ill-mended broken bones, they often have fingers or toes missing; the detritus they dig for in the mud can be sharp. Most do not live long: poisons and fumes from the rubbish shortens their life.'

Lark frowned. 'Why wasn't Crow hurt by the doomstone?'

'Carrying the Chi Rho for all those years may have given him immunity,' Sandy explained.

'Did he come looking for me because he is drawn by the cross?' Fin asked. 'My father said in his letter that when he found Crow, the cross was embedded in his chest. Do you know how he came to have it in the first place?'

Sandy nodded. 'It is a strange story that I learned from the Holy Brethren who took him in and cared for him whilst his wound healed. The Brethren are kind folk and he told them more about himself than he would have told others.

'A Brother Aidan had care of him. Spending many hours tending the sad creature, he learned his story: how he was abandoned at birth, and taken in by a gang of orphans, who called themselves the Grubbies. These orphan gangs compete with the adults for a living, the older ones looking after the youngest, who are trained to be useful members.

'In appearance Crow is much like his fellows, undersized and scrawny. As a child, he lost an eye fighting a carrion crow for a scrap of meat, leaving him with an empty eye socket; he has a habit of searching the ground with his good eye, hopping like a crow, inquisitively pecking with his little pointed nose.

'When he grew to adulthood, he left the Grubbies, and so escaped the worst of the poisons that kill most Scavs. Years of roaming have made him skilled at living off the land. He is a lonely creature, friendless and bitter. He also steals. His best treasure is the chain-mail corselet he took from a dead Skwid child. In a pocket in the leather lining, he keeps his pet rat.'

'Aye, Mick knows all about that rat,' growled Lark, 'and my fingers still remember that chain mail jacket!'

Mick glanced up at his master proudly.

Sandy smiled. 'Down the years,' he continued, 'Crow has had many pet rats and he always gives them the same name: Sparkie.

'Now, Brother Aidan, with much patient questioning, learned of how Crow came to possess the cross. He was scavenging in the marshlands that surround the land of Contagion when he came upon it. (How it came to be there is another long tale.) Nosing around the stinking sewer that flows out from Gressil's fortress, something shining in the slime caught his eye. He told Aidan that when he put it close to his good eye, he saw that it was a richly jewelled cross. Lost in wonder as he gazed at his find, he was startled by a harsh cry: he had been spotted from one of the watch towers that crown Gressil's fortress.

Clasping his new-found treasure tight to his chest, he scurried away through the marshes, running for many miles to get as far from that evil place as he could. By the time he felt it safe to stop, he found the gold had latched onto his skin. Try as he would, causing himself great pain, the cross would not come away from his flesh. So, he left it there: it gave him no pain, and he found it pleasing to touch the crystal.

'Carrying his Burden, he travelled far and wide. One day, whilst wandering along the coast, he let his guard slip, and was attacked by a gang of Scavs, attracted by his chain mail jerkin. (He always kept the jerkin tightly closed over the cross.) The Scavs would have killed him, but for his rat, grown large and vicious, who fought them off with his wickedly long teeth and claws. Fin, that was when your father found Crow, and believing him dead, his rat nowhere to be seen, took the cross from him.

'A long time later, Brother Aiden came upon Crow crawling in the mud, and took him to their refuge: that is how Aidan learnt from Crow about what he called 'a thieving green imp', stealing his jool.'

Fin gave a wry grin. 'I never thought of my father as a green imp! Do you know how Crow found out that I'm the one who now carries the cross?'

Sandy sighed. 'I think he has been hanging about the borders of Brightdale for a while – the pull of the cross is very strong! We have tried to keep track of him, but he is very devious, and we must be watchful as even now he could be lurking in the undergrowth.'

He looked searchingly at Fin. 'Now you know why you must never wear the Chi Rho. Your father wore it and it caused him great suffering. Fortunately, Zagzagel saved him from the fate that has befallen Crow: never free of a desperate longing.'

'Now I've heard his story, I almost feel sorry for the piece of vermin,' Lark said. 'Even so, I bet he would happily give us away to the Evils. I wish I'd caught him when I'd the chance!'

'It cannot be helped, Lark; if you had fought with Crow you would not have escaped without serious injury!'

Lark peered nervously into the shadowy undergrowth beyond the ruined walls, wondering if the Scav could be watching them. Seeing the sun's rays filtering through the trees, he knew the farmers would be worrying about this dry spell during Saprise. But being dry and mild helps us living out in the open, what with Fin not being well, he told himself silently, glancing furtively at Fin, thinking he looked listless and depressed.

'Why is this place called Stonetree?' he remarked, studying the trees around them: a mixture of spruce, elm, and oak.

'Look closely at the tree trunks. Can you see one is different?' Sandy said, a gleam of amusement in his eyes.

Staring hard, Lark spotted a tree trunk of huge girth and darker than the rest, a broken branch lying beside it. Going over, he felt its rough bark. 'It's made of stone!' he exclaimed. 'It was a clever hand that sculpted this: it certainly fooled me, and I'm a woodsman born and bred.'

'It was not sculpted,' Sandy said. 'Once, millions of years ago, it was a living tree. When it became buried in mud, its centre rotted, and its trunk turned to stone.'

'Ah, a fossil tree!' Lark nodded knowingly. 'Well, I've come across fossil leaves and bugs inside rocks, but never a whole standing tree trunk.' He gave it a pat before coming to sit down again.

'Talking of fossils, that is what doomstones are – droppings from the monstrous body of the scorpion in which Gressil's dark spirit is imprisoned, a creature known as a Manticore.'

It was Fescue who spoke. He had returned unnoticed from a reconnoitre into the forest and was sitting quietly on a log close by. Fin and Lark stared at him, astounded.

Lark shuddered. 'Raddled rams – Gressil's dung?'

'Yes. Gressil's servants sometimes use them as snares: they cling to warm flesh,' Fescue explained.

'Makes me even more furious with that Crow,' muttered Lark, glaring into the trees.

Feeling sick, Fin wiped his itching palm down his trouser leg. 'Where are they found?'

'In the Doomstone Mines, over by Birdoswald – where they breed the ganglefowl.' Fescue waved in a northerly direction. 'The Sneaksouls send the Frits down to dig them out; being part machines, they are not affected by them. Even so, the Frits dread going down there, for it is where the Phraggmorgia lurk!'

A sudden sharp bark from Mick made them start. 'Oi, come back, yer cheeky tyke,' shouted Lark, giving a shrill whistle as, hackles raised, Mick shot off along the path.

Moments later he came bounding back ahead of Kenji and they jumped up in surprise as he called to them: 'Look who I've found!'

Bird was walking beside him, and behind her Wolfie with Bee riding on his back.

Seeing the tall figure walking by Wolfie's side, Lark's hand flew to his boning knife.

'It's one of them Skwid!' he hissed in Fin's ear, staring in horror at the creature, her reptilian skin rippling leafy green and twiggy grey, blending with the dappled forest light.

Sandy strode to meet them. 'Dancer! Thank the Creator!' he exclaimed, giving the Skwid a hug, sending vermilion and crocus gold rippling over her scales.

'We dreaded you may have tangled with the bugslugs!' Fescue called.

'No fear, Fescue!' Dancer said. 'We made haste! But the beasts are not far behind!'

Helping Bee down from Wolfie's back, she introduced Sandy and Fescue to the twins. 'This is Sandy, my Boss. And this is Fescue, of the Gaiakin people.'

The twins smiled shyly up at tall warriors.

Kenji turned to Fin and Lark and made the introductions. 'Lads, meet Dancer, the fourth member of our Squad. Dancer, this is Fin Dandrum and Lark Annunder: Delphins of Brightdale.'

'Ah, Fin and Lark,' Dancer said in her huskily warm voice. 'I feel I know you already – Bird and Bee have told me much about you!'

Fin took her proffered hand, finding the Skwid's rough skin warm. He wished Mossy had warned him how weird they looked when you got close.

Dancer's protruding eyes swivelled to Lark, gaping at her slack-jawed, and she gave him a broad grin, reducing him to utter confusion.

Embarrassed at his own rudeness, turning red and swiping off his floppy fish-hook hat, he bowed low. 'How-do?' he muttered.

He glowered at Bee and Bird. 'What in Phul's name are you two lasses doing here? What scatty prank have you been up to?'

'Don't fuss Lark – you sound like an old hen!' Bee said, collapsing on a tree stump seat.

Fescue looked at her with concern. 'Little lass, what has happened to you?' he asked, feeling her brow.

Blushing, Bee showed him her swollen fingers. 'I did a silly thing! I grabbed some stinging ganglefowl feathers.'

Bending, Fescue took hold of her hands. 'I have just the thing to soothe them,' he said, taking out a small pot from his pack. Removing the lid, a sweet smell of lavender filled the air.

Whilst Fescue applied cream to Bee's fingers, Bird told them how they were attacked by a Frit with its ganglefowl. 'Thank goodness Dancer came to our rescue!'

'Oh, Bird, what on earth possessed you to wander so close to Withered Wood?' Fin asked. Seeing her look away, finding it hard to meet his reproachful gaze, he felt sad: he didn't want awkwardness spoiling their friendship.

'As I've told you Fin – Bird's got some silly notion about you wanting to marry Daffodil,' Lark growled.

Fin sighed. 'Why won't anyone believe me: there's nothing going on between me and Daffodil Akest!'

Bee snorted. 'Are you sure? I'm certain I didn't misunderstand what Dilly said when we were cooking for the feast at Dandrum Den – about you and her going Skinny Dipping! Isn't that right Bird?'

Looking embarrassed, Bird nodded. 'That's why we followed you, to save you from the fat lump – she would've had you married to her before you knew what was happening!'

Kenji chortled. 'The porky Daffodil sounds formidable! Fin, it appears that you have been saved from a dreadful fate!'

They all laughed.

Growing impatient, Dancer turned to Sandy. 'Boss, as I said – Maabella's bugslugs are on the way! We heard them slapping along the river.'

'Maybe they were out playing and will soon go back down the tunnel at Killhope!' Kenji said, trying to sound hopeful.

Sandy shook his head. 'No, Kenji. They have been set loose for purposes other than play: I fear the Enemy's attention is drawn to us! We must set out for Durholm Garrison as soon as possible! We will go by the forest trail.' He waved towards the surrounding undergrowth. 'Maabella's babes are unable to travel on rough woodland terrain – they will keep to the river.'

'How far is it to Durholm?' Fin asked, not sure he had enough strength yet for a long trek.

'About fifteen miles, as the eagle flies,' Kenji said.

'Oh!' Fin said, dismayed.

Bird looked at him anxiously. 'What's happened to you, Fin? You look as poorly as Bee!'

'Yes, have you had a feathery encounter too?' Bee chipped in.

''course he hasn't,' Lark exclaimed, 'we know not to get caught by those evil feathers! No, Fin was attacked by a Scav.' He gave Bee and Bird a lurid account of what happened at Phul's Hollow. To Fin's relief, he didn't mention the cross.

Fin turned to Sandy. 'The twins' family will be frantic with worry! There's no need for them to come to Durholm – Lark must take them home!'

Lark glared at him. 'I promised!' he almost shouted. 'I promised Mr Mossy I wouldn't leave you, and I'm not, even if I have to lurk in the undergrowth keeping an eye on you.'

Sandy backed Lark. 'The journey to Brightdale would be too dangerous. There will be roaming gangs of Frits, seeking to avenge the attack on their companion. Lark would not be able to deal with a Frit or its ganglefowl on his own, and with the threat hanging over Durholm, I dare not spare any of my Squad to go with them.'

Feeling miserably guilty, Fin gave in. 'I respect your judgement, Sandy. I admit I was sorry to be sending Lark home so soon.' He smiled ruefully at him glowering, arms crossed. 'I hope Mossy will be able to reassure the twins' family that they are safe.'

Dancer gave an exaggerated sigh. 'Well, now that's decided, can we get away from here? Perhaps you people don't mind, but I don't fancy having my head sucked off by a bugslug.'

Lark stared at her in alarm. 'Just what are they – these sluggers?'

'Think of your ordinary garden slug, only the size of a sheep with shark's teeth,' Kenji said with a leer.

'Oh…' Lark wasn't sure if Kenji was joking.

'Anyway,' continued Dancer, irritably, 'whilst you're packing up camp, the twins and I must eat, or we'll faint; all we've had for supper last night and breakfast this morning are Bird's marshmallows – tasty but no staying power.'

'Yes, this little lass needs food and rest before taking to the trail,' Fescue said, bending down to look at Bee's fingers, his long golden hair brushing her face, making her go pink and giggly.

'Kenji, have you anything left over from that meal?' Dancer asked, eyeing the remains of his cooking fire.

Kenji's eyes gleamed. 'I've saved your favourite bits, Dancer. Raw livers sliced and marinated in peppery nettle juice, just as you like them. And for the young Delphin lasses, a roast squirrel each, cold but still juicy.' He eyed Wolfie doubtfully. 'I'm not sure about their fine hound: he'll have a right royal appetite. Would he eat a raw squirrel, skin and all? I have a couple I was going to stew tonight.'

Whilst Kenji, Fescue and Lark packed away the camp, Dancer and the twins, sitting on a log together, hungrily attacked the food. Mick watched Wolfie enviously as the deerhound tackled a squirrel carcass. The whole lot rapidly disappeared, including the pelt, and Mick turned away in disappointment.

Sandy beckoned Fin to sit with him on a moss-covered wall. 'Regarding the lasses, I believe that the Frit who murdered your father, wrongly assumed the twins were the ones carrying the cross, which drew his attention away from you.'

Recalling the wound in his father's throat, Fin shuddered. 'Thank goodness Dancer came to their rescue!'

As she ate, Bee glanced at Sandy and Fin talking. Soon inquisitiveness got the better of her and she came to sit beside them. 'Fin why are you and Lark here, so far from home?' she asked, picking the last meat off her squirrel.

Not wanting to speak openly of the cross, Fin frowned, wondering what to tell her. 'I'm delivering something for Mossy,' he said lamely.

Bird came and joined her sister. Taking Fin's hand, she timidly squeezed it. 'I was sorry about your dad, Fin. Getting away from Brightdale for a while is good for you.'

He smiled awkwardly. 'Thanks Bird. The thing is, my father left me something to take care of, something precious. I'm taking it to Durholm for safekeeping.'

Hearing the twins' questions, Lark looked up from adjusting the straps on his rucksack. 'You just hold in your nosiness, you lasses,' he growled.

He'd spotted Fescue watching Fin. At the mention of something precious a shadow passed over the Gaiakin's face, making Lark uneasy.

Everything packed away, Sandy asked: 'Is everybody ready? The hour is late, and daylight is fading, so we shall have to spend tonight under the stars. If all goes well, we will reach the Garrison by dawn tomorrow.'

Bird called to Wolfie. 'Come lad, stand still so Bee can climb up.' He pretended not to hear.

'Let the poor fellow alone,' Bee said, 'he didn't enjoy being a pack pony! Anyway, now I've had a good feed, I feel strong enough to walk. What about you, Fin? Would you like a ride?'

'Perhaps you would rather come up on my back?' Kenji suggested.

Fin scowled at him. 'I'm a Delphin,' he said, standing proud, 'not a weakling. It wasn't an afternoon stroll the Dandrum Delphins undertook when they travelled from our tropical lands to claim Brightdale as our new home. Besides, I also have Rom blood in my veins.'

Lark looked approvingly at Fin: his master had more backbone than he'd first thought.

Heading in a north-easterly direction, Sandy led the little group, single file, out of the ruins along a narrow path through the trees.

Silence descended on the clearing.

Crouched in deep shadow, still as the stone wall he was hiding behind, Crow the Scav watched Sandy's party leave the camp. When the voices faded away, he slipped out into the open, and pecked about with his little pointed nose, hopping around the dead fire, head cocked to one side, his one eye glinting. Finding a meaty bone, he sat back on his haunches and gnawed it clean.

After his meal, taking his injured rat from a pocket in his chain-mail jerkin, he laid it gently on the ground, where it lay twitching. Caressing it lovingly with long bony fingers, he squinted at the limp body.

'No fret little Sparkie,' he croaked, his voice gravelly from lack of use, 'that fullaflea mutt-dog, it pays for this – soon I get him tight by mangy fur.'

Trickling a few drops of water from his drinking flask between the rat's yellow incisors, he tenderly stowed the creature back in his jerkin.

Searching for more leftovers, he had to settle for a bit of squirrel hide that still had a trace of flesh. Chewing miserably, crouched by Kenji's cold cooking fire, he swayed to and fro, recalling how close he'd been to reclaiming his beloved cross.

'That long legged, gangly Delph with black grass-top – sticky stone almost fixed him,' he croaked, 'I skin-feel bag where beloved jool kept – fingers fizzed strong, oh they did! But pudgy Delph with yellow grass-top stop me. Me be 'venged on him – slit its gizzard, lightning quick!'

Pulling a short hunting knife from a sheath at his waist, he ran his dirty fingernail along the blade, relishing thoughts of revenge.

Much cheered, he sniffed the air. Listening hard, he heard in the far distance a strange sound, reminding him of rippling waves slapping against a seashore.

'Bugslug! Bugslug coming! We better be gone quick, Sparkie darlin' – get to Durholm afore them slimy raskols.' He grinned wickedly. 'Them at Durholm don't savvy what's coming! Maabella's baby gang on the move! Our chance come, oh yep, our chance come, little Sparkie.'

Agog with anticipation, hopping along sideways, his small pack bouncing on his back, skinny elbows sticking out like flapping wings, he headed along the path to the river. Instinctively, he kept to the undergrowth beside the main track, hopeful that when he came to Durholm, he would get close enough to steal back his 'jool', so wickedly taken from him.

# 8
# DURHOLM

Making their way through the forest, the setting sun slowly dipped below the horizon, and the whisperings and rustlings of night started to be heard. A drawn-out howl made them all start. Wolfie, hackles raised, plunged into the undergrowth. Mick tried to follow, but Lark caught him by the scruff of his neck.

'No, Mick – stay!'

'Wolfie! Wolfie!' the twins called, their high Delphin voices echoing through the gathering dusk.

'Quiet!' Sandy hissed, turning to frown at them.

'Let the hound be,' Kenji said, 'he's probably scented something – there's lynx and other big cats in these parts.'

Dancer stopped to sniff the air. An unpleasant odour had drifted from somewhere to their left.

Her fingers still prickling, Bee thought of her encounter with the ganglefowl feathers.

'Can I smell...?' she whispered, looking up at Dancer fearfully.

Dancer nodded. 'Yes, ganglefowl. The stench is distant, but powerful – there must be many!'

Wolfie burst out of the brushwood, teeth clacking as he downed the last of something long and stripy that looked suspiciously like a tabby cat's tail; Mick eyed him enviously.

Sandy and Fescue strode on, the others hurriedly following. Slowly, the sky turned dark velvet and the moon rose, bathing the forest silver.

At a great oak spreading above the stones of an ancient ivy-covered wall, Sandy halted. In the moonlight, they saw him smile reassuringly. 'We shall sleep here – you have done well, young Delphins!'

'Alas it will not be safe to light a cooking fire,' Kenji said, heaving off his rucksack, 'we'll have to make do with dry rations for our supper.'

They settled down to eat, backs against the tumbled wall. Kenji handed out his travelling supplies: raisins, dried sunflower seeds, and slabs of bilberry fruit-leathers. Bird had ten marshmallows left and offered them around, giving the last two to Wolfie and Mick. With a triumphant flourish, Lark added the half-full jar of Grammer Marigold's pickled onions to the meal.

Crunching on a pickled onion, Lark noticed Fescue casting glances towards Fin. Having eaten little, the Gaiakin had gone to sit apart on a thick oak tree root. He wondered what the awesome being was thinking. He recalled what Mr Mossy had told him about Gaiakins, that they were from a far distant place called the Universe of White Beams, or was it White Light? He'd said something about them being unmarred – whatever that meant. In any event, if Fescue was anything to go by, they were astounding.

He saw that Bee and Bird had finished eating and were sitting with Dancer on another part of the wall. In the pale light, he could just make out Dancer's head flashing warm gold and pink as she chatted with the twins. He would find it hard to get used to the weird creature; but looking at the long sword strapped to her back and remembering that she'd swiped off a Frit's head with it, he was glad she had befriended the twins.

Stuffing a handful of sunflower seeds into his mouth, he thought about Sandy's Trekker Squad; he'd like to know more about all of them: who they were, and where they came from.

He considered Kenji. Surely, he must be from a distant land? What with his beetle-black eyes and glossy black hair. Lark had never seen anyone like him before, not even on market days, when all and sundry came to Watersmeet from the Outside. But he was a skilled cook.

Good hunter too. He'd seen him with his crossbow – dead accurate. Shot a magpie this afternoon, the hardest bird to nab. Like the others, he carried a long sword on his back, and his sword practice was amazing to watch.

'As for Sandy, there's more to him than meets the eye,' Lark muttered in a low voice.

'What?' Fin peered at him.

'I was wondering about Mr Sandy,' Lark whispered, 'what do you reckon to him, Fin?'

Fin glanced towards the tall figure seated next to Kenji, deep in talk.

'I believe he's from a people known as the Lords of the Isles. There's a picture of one who looks rather like Sandy in one of Mossy's books. Their clan name was Cyning, which means king, but their kingdom is long gone.'

Fin raised his voice so that everyone could hear. 'What I'd like to know is – how do you become a Trekker?'

Kenji stopped chewing his mouthful of seeds to look at him quizzically. 'I believe we could have a recruit here, boss,' he said with a grin. 'It's the aim of many a youngster to become a Trekker. Specially to join Iskander's Squad. But their fighting skills must be best of the best – be as one with their bow and sword. They must have good survival skills in wild places, too. Fin, do you think you could learn?'

'I'd be willing to try,' Fin said fiercely.

Lark stared at him aghast. 'I hope you aren't thinking about becoming a Trekker. You're Head Dandrum now and going Trekking won't do!'

They all laughed.

'Why are they called Trekkers?' It was Bee who asked. The twins, ever inquisitive, moved closer with Dancer to sit beside them.

Sandy took up the explanation. 'Trekkers are the Warriors who protect the Geek Communities in what are called Motherhomes.

'Geeks are descendants of the people who built the Star Talkers which, when the world was full of humans, circled around the earth – before the Great Dying. The Geeks who lived during the time of the Dying were the first Keepers, protecting the Knowledge from the Enemy. Now there are hundreds of Motherhomes scattered all around the world. It would take all night if I were to tell you of the bravery of the Trekker Squads who give aid to any threatened Motherhome Communities.'

'Which Motherhome does your Squad belong to?' Fin asked.

'We are of the Yrvik Motherhome, to the south of here, where the ruins of a great cathedral lie hidden in the marshes. But because of the threat from Contagion, we have been seconded to Durholm Garrison, along with several other Squads.'

Kenji carried on explaining: 'Though Trekkers are brave, to my mind the Geeks are even braver: they spend their days underground guarding Knowledge, caring for the Motherboards in which the Knowledge is stored. My grandfather and my father were Geeks: they lost their lives when their Motherhome was invaded. One day I shall tell you their story!'

'Where did your grandfather and father come from?' Lark asked. 'Surely they were not of this land?'

Kenji smiled. 'I'm descended from the people of the Land of Cherry Blossom – far to the East. They worshipped strange gods who taught them new ways of fighting. Our clan came here many centuries ago when the global warming drowned our islands.'

'The Land of Cherry Blossom,' mused Bee, 'it sounds beautiful.'

Kenji eagerly described his ancient homeland, where in Saprise the countryside was blanketed in the pink blossom of a million cherry trees.

'The peopled loved the blossom; the short-lived flowers reminded them of the frailty of life – cherry blossom is our symbol for beauty, which is but fleeting. At holiday time, family and friends would gather beneath the blossoming trees to drink rice wine and retell legends of long ago.'

Bee sighed. 'How romantic!'

'Have you any family here, in our country?' asked Bird.

'Other than my grandmother who lives at Yrvik, I am the last of the Sanyo line.'

Dancer gave a gravelly laugh. 'You may be last of your line for the moment, but if your grandmother has anything to do with it, she'd have you married off tomorrow!'

Kenji groaned. 'She's ever hopeful that I'll find a suitable female among the round-eyes.'

'Thankfully, she hasn't yet,' smiled Sandy, 'you are too valuable a member of my Squad.'

'Has your grandmother thought of the possibility of a Skwid-eyed lady?' Dancer asked mischievously.

Seeing Kenji's horrified expression, the Delphins' peals of laughter echoed in the darkness.

'Ssh! You're making too much noise,' Sandy hissed. 'Now, no more talk, we must sleep if we are to rise at first light.'

Settling down beneath the oak tree, darkness gathered around them as the moon set. From somewhere near came a long sad cry, bringing a rumbling growl to Wolfie's throat. To Lark it sounded like the yowl of a lynx.

Tired out by their adventures of the last twenty-four hours, Fin, Lark, and the twins quickly fell asleep. Ears pricked, Mick and Wolfie crouched despondently nearby, Bird's marshmallows being all they had eaten for supper.

During the night, Bird woke from a dream of white downy feathers fluttering about her like snowflakes, prickling her skin. She turned over, trying not to disturb Bee. Coming unprepared for camping, the twins had had to make do with what could be spared by the rest of the company and were wrapped together in one of Lark's plustic sheets.

Her restless thoughts ran over the last twenty-four hours. She was full of wonder at the strange people she'd come to know; she never thought that she would make friends with a Skwid. She wondered if other Skwids were like Dancer, who beneath her strange exterior wasn't so very different from herself.

This morning, on the walk to Stonetree, Dancer had recounted how she'd become a Trekker. How she'd left her Skwid nest and had gone wild. How she'd been saved from drowning by Sandy when, fishing by a riverbank near Yrvik, she'd tripped on a root and hit her head on a stone, stunning herself.

'He took me back to his Yrvik Motherhome, where the Community cared for me, and it was there that I fell in love with him, but I shall never tell him! He is too high born for me, a Skwid female. I worked hard at learning Trekkers' skills, and after many trials I was taken into his Squad. Spending my days with him makes me content, but I know I shall never go, as you say, Skinny Dipping with him.'

Poor Dancer, thought Bird, at least I've got a chance with Fin.

Bee stirred in her sleep, and turning over, lost some of her covering. As Bird tenderly covered her sleeping sister, a wave of sadness washed over her. To others there was little difference between the twin sisters, but she knew inside they were as different as salt from sugar. Since they had come on this adventure, she felt Bee had somehow started to drift away from her, as if she were fading. It worried Bird: she hoped the cause was her feelings for Fin, then somehow it wouldn't be so bad. She was relieved that Daffodil Akest had turned out not to be a rival, but now that Fin had lost his father, he'd changed. She'd feeling that, even though he was making light of it, he was carrying something dangerous, and it concerned the evil Frit who had attacked her and Bee.

The next morning, as dawn crept through the trees, they breakfasted on the last of Kenji's rations. Sandy explained that they had saved several miles by taking the forest trail, but would now return to the river path, about half an hour's walk away.

Fescue who had slipped away to reconnoitre, returned to report that he had found no trace of bugslugs. Even so, fearing an encounter with sheep-sized slugs, Fin, Lark, and the twins kept close to their warrior companions as they walked.

Half an hour later, they reached the river, wider now and deeper, flowing below steep banks. The well-trodden path quickened progress. A few miles farther on, following a loop in the river, there came into sight on the far bank a massive building standing on a high cliff.

The Delphins stood amazed.

'Behold, Durholm Cathedral!' proclaimed Kenji, spreading his arms wide.

'It's like a fairy castle from one of Grammer Nutmeg's picture books!' breathed the twins in unison.

At first sight, the building looked to be in ruins, its two west facing towers open to the sky, their walls covered with ivy. Looking closer, they saw, beyond the ruined towers, slate roofs shining in the sunlight. Above the roofs a great tower rose tall and square. To the north, a high fortified wall ran from the cathedral, and circling around, rejoined it on the south side. Inside they glimpsed the thatched roofs of dwellings.

'When was this place built? It must be ancient!' Lark exclaimed.

'Building first began over two thousand years ago,' Sandy said, 'much has fallen, and much has since been added.'

'I was expecting Durholm Garrison to be a huddle of huts, not this massive place!' Fin gasped. As he gazed, his hand strayed involuntarily to where the Chi Rho lay in his purse inside his jerkin.

Fescue drew close and whispered in his ear. 'This is where the remains of Holy Cuthbert lie. His Shrine is guarded by the brothers and sisters of the Holy Community. If you were looking for somewhere safe to keep a treasure, it would be here.'

Watching Fescue suspiciously, Lark quickly came and stood by Fin. 'Have you got your sketch book to hand, Fin?' he asked pointedly, giving Fescue a hard stare. 'Mr Mossy will want a drawing –'

He was interrupted by the deep voice of a great bell ringing out from the tower.

'The call to Mass,' Fescue said bowing his head and tracing an invisible cross from forehead to chest, and from left to right shoulder.

As they waited for Fin to complete his sketch, the others watched the bustling activity across the river, where several boats moored alongside a wooden jetty were being unloaded and their cargoes hauled by ox cart up a zigzag path to the clifftop.

'Being the first line of defence against the threat from Contagion,' Sandy explained, 'the population of the Garrison has grown, with traders sailing up from the ports at the coast.'

'How do we do we get across?' Lark asked, looking up and down the deep river: he couldn't see any bridge or boat on their side.

Sandy gestured to where the river went out of sight around the cliffs. 'We continue round to the drawbridge – it is strictly guarded, but as you are in my charge, there should be no problem of entry.'

Satisfied his sketch had captured the grandeur of the cathedral, Fin put away his pad, and they set off once more, quickening their pace as the smell of cooking bacon drifted from a building across the river.

Allowing the others to walk ahead, Sandy held Fin back. 'We are coming to a place where the Christ is worshipped,' he said in a low voice. 'What you carry will be of great significance to the Holy Community here, and they would find great joy in adding the Chi Rho to the relics in Holy Cuthbert's Shrine.'

Fin brushed his hand against his chest. 'I'll be glad to be rid of the cross, but out of respect for my father's suffering, I won't hand it over without being sure I am doing the right thing.'

Sandy agreed: 'Yes, you should be careful. Whatever you decide, I shall support you.'

Drawing near to the crossing point, they saw the drawbridge was raised, and Wolfie and Mick, who had gone on ahead, were sniffing around the open door of a wooden sentry hut.

A fierce-looking, red-haired man in loudly clanking armour stepped out. 'Password!' he barked, pointing his sword threateningly at the dogs' twitching black noses. Then, spotting Sandy, he beamed. Cupping his hands to his mouth, he yelled across the water. 'Let down the drawbridge – Iskander and his Squad are back!'

'The password must not be ignored, Cedric,' Sandy called as he approached. 'I believe today it is Hope?'

'Hope it is, Lord Iskander! You and your Squad are free to cross.' He frowned fiercely at the Delphins. 'But mind you keep a close eye on your small green-skinned companions, and their curs.'

Across the river heavy chains rattled, and creaking ponderously, the drawbridge descended, landing with a thump near the sentry hut. Scurrying across after the others, Mick and Wolfie in tow, the Delphins had barely time to step off the bridge before it began to rise behind them. They waited nervously as the portcullis in the high wall lifted just enough for everyone to duck under the pointed bars before it descended behind them with a crash.

Going through a tunnel beneath the gatehouse, they entered a cobbled square surrounded by the dwellings whose thatched roofs they had glimpsed from the river. Along the enclosing battlements warriors could be seen staring out toward the forest, their crossbows armed and ready to fire. To the left on a hill, stood the cathedral, tall and proud.

It was market day, the square filled with stalls and thronged with many races: humans, Scavs, Roms and Skwids, jostling to buy foodstuffs and goods. On a stall next door to a couple of Scavs doing a brisk trade in metals, glass and plustic, Rom women were selling brightly coloured velvets, silks, and lace.

Searching their faces, Fin wondered if his mother could be one of them. What would she look like now, a woman in her late thirties? Would she still be beautiful? Or care-worn by life? To his dismay, his staring had attracted the attention of two raven-haired Rom girls who were fluttering their heavily blacked eyelashes at him. Bird glared at them challengingly and took Fin's hand in hers. From the battlements, a group of Trekkers had spotted the new arrivals. Clattering down a ladder, they strode over.

'Welcome back, Lord Iskander!' rasped one of the Trekkers, a tall broad-shouldered Skwid, the rough scales on his face flashing mauve and orange.

'Greetings, Drogon. Is all well here, at Durholm?'

'At present! But word has come that Maabella's Babes are on the loose.'

Looking worried, the warriors discussed this news, before dispersing to their duties.

'Come, Delphins,' Sandy commanded. 'We shall go to the cathedral.'

Hungry after their meagre supper and breakfast, their hearts sank at the prospect of being taken on a sightseeing tour.

Kenji smiled encouragingly. 'You don't want to offend Blessed Cuthbert by not paying your respects! But as soon as we have done that, I'll take you to the kitchen to meet the cook, a friend of mine. He'll provide us with a proper cooked breakfast!'

Trooping behind Sandy up a cobbled lane towards the cathedral, as they passed a row of cottages a group of small children stopped their play to stare, calling to their mothers to come and see the tiny green people. Their piping voices alerted a pack of dogs, who came sniffing around Wolfie. Setting Mick barking shrilly from the safety of Lark's jerkin, they were driven off by Kenji and Dancer.

Approaching the cathedral's great north door, they gazed up in awe at the edifice rising above from where grotesque stone gargoyles, devils, dragons, and other monsters, leered down, tongues out and teeth bared.

A group of Skwid, relaxing on a nearby patch of lawn, spotted the Delphins, their faces and heads flashing bright colours, eyes swivelling excitedly as they pointed at them.

Dancer, about to stride off purposefully to speak to them, Sandy called her back. 'Dancer, take the dogs to the kitchen: they will need feeding.'

Tucking Mick firmly under her arm, and grabbing Wolfie by the scruff, she headed for a path leading around the outside of the west towers.

Sandy explained: 'Dogs are not allowed inside the cathedral. At the kitchen, the cook will give them a hearty meal! Like most Skwids, Dancer is not a believer, and does not like going inside the cathedral.'

Watching her disappearing around the corner, Lark wondered again about the Skwid race and would have liked to ask more of their history, but seeing the others already heading into the cathedral, hurried after them as they ducked through a low portal set in the larger iron-studded oak door.

About to step over the threshold himself, he stopped, his eye caught by a large bronze knocker bolted to the ancient worm-riddled wood. Looking closer, he saw it was a stylised face of a fierce-eyed lion, an iron ring gripped in its snarling jaws. Unable to resist, he lifted the ring and let it go with a soft thud.

Fescue, who was waiting for him, pulled his hand away. 'Have a care Lark!' he whispered, 'the Sanctuary Knocker must only be used if you are in desperate need of help!'

Fearing the thud might have been heard, Lark dived inside, finding the others huddled by a wall of brightly coloured pictures, which they would later learn were made up of fragments metal, glass and plustic depicting various scenes from of the life of Holy Cuthbert.

Blinking in the incense-scented gloom, a vast interior stretched before them. Two rows of massive pillars divided the space into three, two shadowed aisles on either side of the wide central nave. From high in the vault, shafts of sunlight streamed down through two rows of arched windows, to shine on the brown and cream floor tiles, and lighting up the golds, blues, and reds of the heavily decorated pillars. Two-thirds of the way along, beneath the space of the square tower, a finely fretted, gold painted wooden screen blocked off the chancel and high altar, and high in the far wall beyond, sunlight streamed through a huge round, coloured glass window.

Sandy, Kenji, and Fescue had already joined the congregation gathered before wide shallow steps leading up to the gold screen. As they hurried to join them, Fin saw scattered amongst the crowd, figures in long brown robes, their heads covered by deep hoods, making him wonder if these were members of the Holy Community Sandy had mentioned. Peering over the heads of the kneeling worshippers, he spied the choir through the lattice of the gold screen. Dressed in red robes, small boys and girls on one side of the chancel, youths and men on the other, their singing was so achingly beautiful it brought a lump to his throat, and unlike anything he'd ever heard before, being familiar only with simple tunes sung to fiddle, flute, and harp.

Beyond the chancel, shallow steps led up to the sanctuary. Here the celebrant was performing the ancient rite of the Mass before the altar, his richly embroidered cloth-of-gold and scarlet garments gleaming in the banks of blazing candles, his servers, wearing long white robes, treading a stately dance around him.

As Fin watched, he became aware of eyes on him. Looking up, he saw hanging on a thick chain above him the carved figure of a man pinned by hands and feet to a great wooden cross. The painted blood looked so life-like he felt it might drip on him. The eyes, shadowed beneath a crown of thorns, seemed to be gazing directly at him. His nightmare of the crucified man and the hooded figure rushed back, bringing with it a yearning to take out the Chi Rho, to feel the jewels, to caress the great crystal. Shoving his hands deep in his trouser pockets, he looked away.

The singing stopped, and a harsh rasping voice from the altar made him start. The celebrant had started intoning a prayer in a strange language. The rasping tone made Fin's skin crawl and he sighed with relief when it stopped and once more the beautiful sound of the choir echoed around the cathedral. Finishing with a lingering high note from a lone boy chorister, the ceremony ended. The altar servers and choir processed out through a side door, but the celebrant lingered on the sanctuary, his fierce gaze peering through the screen. The penetrating stare rested on Fin, sending a shiver down his spine.

Sandy muttered in his ear: 'That is Brother Hardwick – he is the Community Superior. I know he will wish to speak to you when he has divested himself of his robes. In the meantime, we shall visit the shrine of Holy Cuthbert.

The congregation dispersed, and Sandy called to everyone. 'Come, follow me!'

Striding down the north aisle, they scurried after him. At the eastern wall, gazing up at the great round window, they wondered who the people were in the scenes depicted in the pieces of coloured glass, some with yellow circles around their heads. Here and there pieces of the original glass were missing, the gaps filled in with nuggets of worn glass, and in some places, bits of plustic.

'Come now and pay your respects to the Holy Saint,' Sandy called from where he stood by the heavy red curtain that screened off the back of the high altar. Here a slab of green marble had been set in the stone floor, with a tall brass candlestick at each corner, the flickering flames of their bees-wax candles filling the air with a honeyed perfume. An inscription, chiselled into the green marble, was so worn with age, it was barely discernible.

'Beneath this marble lies the remains of Cuthbert – reputed to be undecayed, as it was when the coffin was dug up on Holy Island all those years ago, when they found his body whole, his beard as if it had a year's growth!

'We shall now go to the west wall where you shall learn more; it is there that the story of the journey of Cuthbert's body is depicted in mosaic.'

He set off eagerly back down the aisle to where they had come in.

Before following the others, Fin lingered for a moment wondering if this grave would be a safe place to keep the Chi Rho. He studied the inscription on the marble slab. The faint markings reminded him of the writing in one of ancient scrolls on Mossy's bookshelves; Mossy had called the blocks of lines, circles and dots, runes, and he'd begun to teach Fin how to read them. Bending down he tried to decipher them, but even though he had made good progress reading Mossy's scroll, he found these too worn. Giving up, he hurried to catch up with the others.

At the wall, Sandy was about to launch into his story of the long journey of Cuthbert's bones, when he was interrupted by Kenji. 'Boss, our young friends are almost fainting from hunger! Breakfast calls!'

Sandy smiled resignedly, realising his audience had lost interest, their eyes following the brown robed figures heading towards a door in the south wall, from where wafted a tantalising smell of baking bread.

'Follow me, everyone, I'll take you to meet the cook.' Kenji called.

Walking with Sandy, Fin said: 'I'd better return here later to do some sketches. Mossy will want to know about the brilliant artist who created the mosaic.'

'You are keen on drawing?' Sandy asked.

Feeling guilty, Fin nodded: the only sketch he'd done so far, was of the outside of the cathedral.

As they neared the door, one of the brown robed figures strode towards them.

'Brother Hardwick,' Sandy muttered in Fin's ear.

'Iskander, thank the Lord, you are back, just when we need you!' The grating voice set Fin's teeth on edge.

'Greetings Brother,' Sandy called. 'This is Fin Dandrum with his friends Lark, Bird and Bee.'

The man's eyes raked them coldly. A chill ran through Fin – he'd seen the same sickly glitter in his uncle Roach's eyes. Unlike the coarse cloth of the robes worn by his community, his were made of a rich velvet and he wore a heavy gold cross decorated in red enamel with a large garnet set in the cross-piece.

Hardwick glared at the twins. 'You females,' he sneered, 'have an air of mischief. Are you prone to spying on matters that are none of your business?'

Not waiting for an answer, he clapped his hands, making them all jump. 'Go now to the refectory and find food!' Nodding dismissively to the Delphins, he addressed Sandy and Fescue: 'I wish a word with you both. Come to the Chapter House.'

Glad to escape, the Delphins ran after Kenji already heading out through the south door. They emerged into a courtyard surrounded by a covered walkway.

'This is the cloister garth,' Kenji explained. 'The kitchen is at the end.'

He nodded to a doorway from where came the alluring aroma of roasting meat and baking bread. Hurrying towards it, they passed the arched entrance to the refectory, where they saw people eating at long tables.

They found the kitchen busy with community members, snowy white aprons over their robes, preparing food: chopping vegetables, kneading bread, and rolling pastry. In front of a blazing fire, a Scav, dressed only in a loin cloth, was turning a massive joint of pork on a spit, the sizzling dripping juices filling the room with a succulent smelling haze. In a corner, a sweaty-faced baker with a long handled wooden shovel, was pulling plump golden-brown loaves out of a fiercely hot bread oven.

A potbellied man, all in white and wearing a tall starched hat, came over from a cooking range, where he was frying sausages in an iron skillet.

'Grantly, my friend!' exclaimed Kenji, greeting the cook with a gentle punch in his bulging stomach. 'I've brought some very hungry customers in need of a feed: they have travelled far, with only my travelling rations to sustain them.'

Wiping the sweat from his face with the hem of his apron, Grantly squinted at the Delphins with critical interest. 'How do, little strangers, from where do yer come?'

Fin bowed. 'Our land is called Brightdale. Do you know of it?'

Grantly shook his head. 'From your stature, it could not be a very plentiful land! You and your companions need feeding up!'

Fin drew himself up, his Delphin eyebrows dipping into a disdainful V. Clearly the man had never seen the Delphin race before. 'Our land of Brightdale has abundant food!'

'We may seem little to you, sir,' chipped in Lark, keenly eyeing the sausages frying in the skillet, 'but our appetites are huge, and we would very much like to try some of your tasty bangers!'

'Ah, a person after my own heart,' grinned Grantly. 'How about bacon and eggs to go with the sausages? And bread and butter on the side?'

The Delphins immediately forgave the cook his mocking.

They were startled by Mick giving a sharp yap of greeting from a corner where he and Wolfie were licking the last shreds of food from two large tin bowls.

'Mutton offal,' explained Grantly. 'The Skwid lady said they'd been on short rations like you. Said I was to feed 'em up. Took a big bowl of offal for herself, too.' He lifted the lid from a pot on his stove and gave it a stir.

'Aye, that'll do 'em grand!' Lark said, smelling the pungent aroma of boiling sheep's innards.

Leaving Grantly slapping bacon rashers into another skillet, they went into the refectory, where they spotted Dancer tucking into her bowl of mutton offal, with a side serving of parsley. She beckoned them to sit beside her.

The refectory started to fill as workers from the Garrison, Trekkers, and members of the Holy Community crowded in. Queueing for brews of tea at a serving hatch, many stared openly at the Delphins. Kenji and Dancer's annoyance soon grew, and there would have been altercations if Sandy and Fescue had not arrived accompanied by Brother Hardwick who, snarling sarcastically, rapidly emptied the place.

Soon dishes of food appeared at the hatch, and they eagerly collected their mugs of hot sweet tea and plates piled with bacon, eggs, sausages, and bread and butter.

Lark was starting on his third sausage when Brother Hardwick roughly squeezed between him and Fin, almost pushing him off the bench. Giving Hardwick an angry scowl, Lark picked up his food, and went to sit next to Kenji.

Hardwick leaned close to Fin's ear, his foul breath turning Fin's stomach. 'Iskander has told me of your errand,' he hissed hoarsely. 'When you have finished eating, come to my quarters, so I can help you to decide what should be done.'

Hastily putting down his mug of tea, Fin turned his face away.

Seeing Fin's discomfort, Sandy came and sat on his other side.

Frowning, he leant across to Hardwick and said in a low voice. 'Brother, I am full of foreboding! Since I was last at Durholm there have been happenings that have alarmed me greatly. It may be that the precious object Fin has in his possession is the cause!'

Fin looked at him in dismay. 'If my coming here has brought danger, I should never have come, and I'd better leave as soon as possible!'

'No! No!' Hardwick rasped. 'The cross must stay here! You, a mere youth, have no right to decide!'

Glaring fiercely at Hardwick, Sandy said: 'Brother, Fin has inherited this Burden, and it is his decision what should be done with it – not yours nor mine!'

Hardwick scowled. 'Even so, the Delphin has brought the cross here, putting us in danger, and because of that the Community has the right to know. We must call for a general meeting in the Chapter House as soon as possible – before disaster befalls us!'

He stood abruptly. Laying his hand on Fin's head as if in blessing, gave his hair a vicious tug. 'I will come for you later, young Dandrum, and before the meeting we shall find somewhere private, so I can look on the holy treasure!'

Staring down at his egg-smeared plate to avoid the sinister man's horrible eyes, Fin didn't reply.

Stalking out of the refectory, Hardwick stopped to call out: 'When you have eaten, go to the dormitory and find sleeping places.' He gestured towards a flight of steps at the far end.

Sandy strode after him, determined to make sure the Chapter House meeting would be organised by him and not Hardwick.

Calling the dogs from the kitchen, they climbed the stairs leading to the dormitory. At the top, they found themselves in a long room with lines of straw mattresses laid on the floor. Tall latticed windows set high beneath the wood-beamed ceiling let in soft restful light. Whilst Dancer took the twins and Wolfie to the female quarters, a curtained-off area at the far end, Kenji, Fin and Lark, with Mick under his arm, searched the mattresses in the main part. Most were spoken-for belongings left on them or occupied by sleeping forms beneath blankets. Finding three empty ones next to each other, they dumped their rucksacks on them.

'The night watchmen are getting their sleep, so we must be quiet,' Kenji murmured, nodding to the sleepers. 'Unpack what you need, and we'll go to the lavatorium in the cloister garth to smarten ourselves.'

'What about Sandy and Fescue, where do they sleep?' Lark asked.

'Sandy being an Alpha Leader, has his own apartment in the barracks and Fescue shares quarters there with his brother,' Kenji explained.

Meeting up once more with the twins and Dancer, they went downstairs to the lavatorium, then refreshed by ample hot water and soft towels, they sat on a bench in the garth to make plans for the day.

Sandy found them in heated discussion. Fin had let slip that he was to attend a meeting to which the others had not been invited.

Lark, arms crossed, his face red, glowered at Sandy. 'Fin needs me at this meeting, to give him support. He's my boss, and Head of our Dale!'

'Not just Lark, he needs all of us Delphins to back him up,' Bee said aggressively. 'Besides, I don't understand. Why has Fin got to attend a meeting? What's it all about?'

Lark turned on her. 'There you go again, Miss Nosey. Just because you've invited yourself on this expedition, doesn't mean you need to know all about Fin's business.'

Seeing Fin's agonized expression, Bird intervened. 'Before Fin even thinks of being questioned by strangers, he should rest on his bed.'

Shooting her a grateful smile, Fin shook his head. 'No, I'd like to go back into the cathedral. I thought of sketching the mosaic by the north door, to show Mossy.'

'Shall I come too?' Lark asked.

'No Lark – I want to be alone to do some thinking and prepare what I want to say at the meeting.'

'Oh, alright.' Lark was relieved; he didn't fancy going back inside the great gloomy place. It was a lovely Saprise day and he wanted to take the dogs for a run and to have another look at the strange Sanctuary Knocker Fescue said must only be used in an emergency.

'Where's the way out?' he asked Dancer, remembering she had come through the refectory with the dogs.

'I'll show you,' volunteered Kenji, 'I want a word with Grantly, to see if he can spare some cooking salt for my ration bag.'

Whistling to Mick and Wolfie, Lark and Kenji headed off for the refectory.

After a muttered conversation with Dancer, Sandy spoke to the twins. 'I am going to the Scriptorium to write a message which Dancer will send by carrier pigeon. If you would like to, you can go with her up to the pigeon loft in the great tower.'

Bee agreed at once, but Bird hesitated, wondering if she shouldn't go with Fin; it would be a chance to be alone to talk and make things up between them. The voice of her conscience told her: 'No! Your duty is to take care of Bee – she came on this adventure because of you.'

She called out to Fin making his way to the south door of the cathedral. 'We'll meet you back here, Fin! Don't get too tired,' she added in a motherly voice.

Fin turned and waved.

'Stop fussing!' Bee exclaimed, grabbing Bird by the hand. 'What harm can Fin come to in the cathedral?'

They ran to catch up with Sandy and Dancer, already marching along the far cloister toward the Scriptorium.

# 9
# PHRAGG

The heavy door groaned as Fin stepped inside the cathedral. No one was about; the smell of incense lingered in the air; a draught made him shiver. Thinking he'd heard a soft intake of breath, he peered into the brooding shadows: he could see no one there. He made his way to the mosaic, his footsteps echoing in the vast space.

At first, he stood back, marvelling at how the small pieces of copper and steel, intermixed with coloured plastic and glass, made up a series of scenes from Cuthbert's life story. Looking closer, he frowned at one picture. Cuthbert was wearing a cross: it resembled the ornate cross Hardwick wore. Pulling out his drawing pad and charcoal stick, he began sketching.

After a while, deciding he'd done enough, he thought he'd take another look at the high altar.

Standing in front of the gold painted screen below the figure on the huge wooden cross, he felt once more the shadowed eyes beneath the crown of thorns staring down at him. Avoiding looking up, he peered through the lattice screen where he saw suspended above the altar, a candle flickering inside a red glass holder. Its ruby-red light glinting off an ornate jewelled cabinet, made him wonder what could be inside that was so precious. A sudden yearning stole over him to hold the Chi Rho, to feel its golden weight in his hand, to touch the rough jewels, to stroke the smoothness of the crystal. His fingers strayed inside his shirt. Glancing furtively about, keeping the purse's leather thong about his neck, he pulled out the cross. Laying it on his open palm, a beam of sunlight from a window in the vault caught the jewels, creating flashing points of brilliant coloured light.

Hearing footsteps behind him, gripping the cross tightly to his chest he spun round.

A hooded figure was shuffling down the nave towards him. Leaning on a walking stick, head lolling crazily, a fiery cloud of black rags floated behind: the cloud had a face, angry red eyes, a grinning mouth showing yellow fangs. Deep inside the smouldering rags, a white-hot core pulsed like a beating heart. Suddenly the foul emanation sped towards him. Then, mid-way, it halted abruptly and whirled about as a powerful voice echoed around the ancient stone walls.

'WELL, PHRAGG? DO YOU DARE TAKE ON A GAIAKIN?'

Fescue stood there, tall and challenging. His golden sword drawn, he leapt at the spectre, lunging and slashing, lunging and slashing, flames and hot rags flying around him.

'Give me the Chi Rho, runt!' A harsh voice rasped close to Fin's ear. The hooded figure had come upon him. A bruising blow from the walking stick fell on his forearm. The cross slipped through Fin's numbed fingers. Skittering across the tiles, and landing by a pillar, he dived for it.

Thwack! Thwack! Again, and again, the stick hit his head and shoulders. Roaring filled his ears. Sliding into darkness, from far, far away he thought he heard Lark shouting....

'Hurry now!' Dancer called as the twins ran to where she and Sandy were waiting outside the Scriptorium. On their way, they passed a narrow iron-studded door with a small barred window. From inside came a stink of urine.

Holding her nose, Bee muttered: 'Smells like the lock-up in Watersmeet!'

Entering the Scriptorium, they found themselves in a lofty room lit by tall windows and lined from floor to ceiling with shelves of books and scrolls; the mingled smells of ink and glue reminding them of Mr Mossy's shop.

Three brown robed scribes sat at a long table cluttered with ink pots, writing quills and parchments. Looking up from their work, they stared curiously at the two Delphins. The twins noticed that one of the scribes was a Skwid, which surprised them as they thought their species couldn't read and write.

Sandy asked for writing materials. Splodges of inky blues rippling across his head, the Skwid handed him parchment, pen, and ink. Tearing off a small piece of parchment, Sandy wrote a swift note, and rolling it into a tight tube, gave it to Dancer.

'You know what to do,' he muttered urgently, 'it is vital that a pigeon flies immediately to Holy Island.'

Beckoning to the twins to follow, Dancer strode out into the cloister and immediately turning right took them to where a narrow stone stairway spiralled up through the thick outside wall of the great tower.

Aided by a rope banister, climbing swiftly, they reached a loft. Brightly lit by sunlight streaming in through two arched openings, one looking east and one looking west, the room was almost filled by great brass bell hanging from a beam in the roof down through a hole in the floor. Around the walls, pigeons in wire cages cooed and bobbed, greeting their visitors excitedly.

Picking a way over floorboards caked with feathers and droppings, the twins cautiously peeped down past the rim of the bell to glimpse the altar far below and the flickering light from the red candle holder.

Dancer opened one of the cages, setting up a crescendo of cooing. Catching hold of a pigeon and unscrewing a small metal tube attached to one of its pink scaly legs, she pushed Sandy's parchment roll inside before re-fastening the tube.

'This bird will fly back to its home on Holy Island, carrying Sandy's message with it,' she explained.

'Why does Sandy want to send a message?' Bee asked. 'Who is it to?'

'He senses that things are not right here. He wants to alert Mother Hilda, the Firstmother of the Holy Community.' Her Skwid skin turned dark green as she frowned sternly at Bee. 'It's vital that no one knows, so do not speak about this matter in public.'

'Bee, there you go again, being nosey!' Bird said in exasperation. 'You'll get us into trouble with Lark.' She turned to Dancer. 'Can I release the pigeon?'

Dancer nodded and laying it gently in Bird's outstretched hands, indicated the eastern opening. 'Holy Island is ninety miles or so to the north – how it knows the way is magic to me!'

Feeling Bee's envious gaze, Bird hesitated: it was her foolishness that had brought them to this place. She sighed: 'Go on sis, you launch the pigeon.'

Eagerly taking hold of the bird, Bee stroked the soft smooth feathers on its head for a moment, then leaning out through the eastern opening and lifting her arms, let it go. With whirring wings, it soared into the sky.

But even as the three of them watched it flying free, through the bell-hole from behind came a blood curdling shriek. Spinning about, the shriek was followed by several more, sending the terrified pigeons frantically battering their wings against the wire mesh of their cages.

Then, through the west opening came a crash of shattering glass. Black smoke filled the loft, and a stink of burning rubber. A dark shape shot past, momentarily blocking out the sunlight.

'Fin's down there!' Bird screamed.

'Come!' yelled Dancer, drawing her sword and speeding for the stairs.

The twins raced after her.

Following Kenji's directions, Lark shepherded the dogs across the refectory and out through a door leading down steps into a walled kitchen garden. Wandering between the beds of young cabbages, carrots and runner beans, the dogs gambolling around him, he headed for an archway and found himself in an orchard of apple and pear trees, their branches heavy with Saprise blossom. At the end of the trees, he came to a wide grassy area, beyond which lay the path Dancer had taken earlier with the dogs, leading around the west towers to the cathedral's north door. Taking the path, he stopped for a moment to look over a bramble hedge fencing off a high drop to the river and saw below on the far bank the way they had come earlier that morning.

At the north door, remembering the unfriendly pack of dogs they'd met earlier, he called Mick and Wolfie to heel, and looking again at the knocker hanging on the ancient nail-studded wood, couldn't resist gently lifting the iron ring gripped in the lion's jaw. As it fell, a loud shriek rent the air. He looked about, bewildered, hoping he hadn't set off an alarm. There came another shriek. Realizing it came from inside the cathedral he panicked: Fin was in there!

Flinging himself at the low portal door, sending it crashing inwards, tripping over the frightened dogs, he stumbled inside. Another hideous shriek rebounded off the walls. Blinking hard after the sunlight outside, he made out flashes of light at the end of the nave in front of the carved gold screen: Fescue was there, sword drawn, lunging at what looked like a fiery cloud of burning black rags. With every plunge of Fescue's blade came a long drawn out shriek of agony.

Mercilessly Fescue hacked and thrust, until finally with a last choking scream, from deep inside the burning rags spouted a stream of molten lava; smacking the floor, cracking like pistol shots, the tiles crazed in all directions. Fescue, his beautiful face contorted with exhaustion, his sword blade melted out of shape, stumbled back, and watched as the burning rags, flopping across the floor like a giant wounded bat, made for a nearby pillar. Leaving a trail of black smuts, it laboriously climbed to a window in the vault. Crashing through, sending glass shards tinkling down, it disappeared.

Desperately Lark searched for Fin and spotted him crouched on the floor, arms covering his head. A hooded figure, wielding a stick, was standing over him, raining down blows on his head.

'HOY, GERROFF MY MASTER!' he bellowed, racing after Wolfie, already bounding down the nave, Mick scrabbling behind.

The figure momentarily glanced at him, before continuing its attack.

'GERROFF!' he yelled as he drew closer.

The figure melted into the shadows, leaving Fin lying motionless, eyes closed, a pool of blood spreading around his head. Lark dropped to his knees, and taking hold of Fin's wrist, to his relief, felt a pulse.

Wolfie growled into the shadows, but Lark could see no sign of the hooded figure.

Fescue staggered over and collapsed beside them. 'Lark – the Knocker – use it – call for help!'

Lark looked at him uncertainly.

'Hurry! I can take care of Fin!'

Reluctantly, Lark got up, and stumbling back down the nave, half falling out through the low portal, he swung the knocker with all his strength. THUD! THUD! THUD! The sound echoed around the great building – as if in reply there came distant shouting.

Speeding back to where Fin lay, he saw Fescue had his hand pressed over a gash in Fin's forehead, blood seeping through his long fingers.

Finding the pad of moss he always kept in a pocket of his jerkin, Lark shoved Fescue's bloodied hand away: 'This will staunch the blood!' he said, pressing the pad to the wound. As he pressed, he noticed with a shock that Fescue had the Chi Rho in his other hand. He gave the Gaiakin a hard look. 'I see you have the cross!'

Fescue looked down in dazed surprise. 'Oh yes – I found it on the floor.'

Lark fished inside a pocket with his free hand and brought out his handkerchief. 'Here, wrap it in this and give it to me, Fescue. Fin would want me to take charge of the cross.'

Wrapping the cross, reluctantly Fescue dropped it into Lark's open palm. Awkwardly tucking it away in a pocket, to Lark it felt heavier than he thought it should, and he realised it was the first time he'd held the cross.

A moment later, there came a bang as the south door from the cloister crashed open. 'We heard the Sanctuary Knocker!' cried Sandy, running down the nave accompanied by Kenji; they were followed by several of the Community members.

Before Lark could call out, Dancer and the twins came rushing down the steps out from a small gate in the altar screen.

'A Phragg,' cried Dancer, 'a Phragg flew past the bell tower!'

Bird ran to where Fin lay on the floor. 'Lark, what's happened?' she wailed.

Kneeling to take hold of Fin's cold hand, seeing the bloodstained moss pad she shuddered.

'He's been attacked,' Lark answered curtly. 'Here, hold on to this pad whilst I get out a bandage.'

Hand trembling, Bird pressed the pad to the wound, whilst Lark found a bandage. Winding it about Fin's head, with a shaking voice he told everyone about the hooded figure with a walking stick.

'Who would do such a dreadful deed in our holy place,' groaned one of the Community members.

'Brother Hardwick must be told of this!' cried another.

Sandy looked gravely to where Fescue was slumped against a pillar, his face grey with exhaustion.

'Was there a Phragg here?' he called.

Fescue nodded dumbly.

'Fescue was so brave!' Lark said, giving the Gaiakin a swift look of reassurance. 'He stabbed deep into the monster over and over, ruining his lovely sword.'

Fescue weakly lifted the buckled sword lying by his side, but it fell from his grasp.

Kenji pointed at the pile of smoking black matter. 'Did the Phragg do that?'

Lark nodded. 'Yep, sicked up a load of red-hot muck, then crawled up that pillar and crashed out through a window.'

They all looked to the pillar, eyes following the trail of dark smuts up to the vault.

'We heard breaking glass when we were in the loft,' Bee said, her face sickly white. 'Then a dark shadow shot past!'

Dancer stared suspiciously at the little cluster of Community members: 'Did anyone see the hooded figure that attacked Fin?'

Shaking their heads and looking distressed, they peered about into the shadows.

'Kenji and Dancer, you must hunt for the attacker!' Sandy commanded. 'Indeed, all of you should help – I will take care of the young Delphin.'

The group quickly dispersed, some searching the side aisles, others going through the door in the screen onto the chancel.

Sandy gently lifted Fin into his arms. 'Lark, help Fescue," he commanded.

He turned to Bird and Bee. 'Lasses you must take charge of the dogs. Follow me. I am taking Fin to the Sanatorium!'

As Lark stumbled after Sandy supporting Fescue as best he could, the journey to Stonetree swam into his mind, when he'd followed Sandy carrying Fin, the doomstone stuck to his hand: it was happening all over again! Feeling the cross heavy in his pocket, it took all his will not to abandon Fescue, rush out and fling the dratted object into the river.

The sanatorium was a long room with whitewashed walls. A line of iron bedsteads with crisp white covers stood beneath the row of barred windows and a smell of vinegar and lavender pervaded the place. A pale faced man with a heavily bandaged hand lay in the only occupied bed, and they recognised the cook who'd been chopping onions in the kitchen. He was being tended to by a plump, grey-haired woman wearing a white apron over her brown robe; they learned later that she was called a goodwife.

Sandy laid Fin gently on a bed, and Lark helped Fescue collapse onto another.

'Dogs are not allowed!' the goodwife called to the twins as she bustled up. 'Take them to the kitchen: Grantly will take charge of them. And bring back mugs of sweet nettle tea for everyone.'

The twins hurried out with the dogs, and she turned to her new patients, going first to Fescue who had become alarmingly grey faced.

'Goodwife, I must guard the cross! I must guard the cross!' he sobbed, grabbing at her apron.

Gently hushing him, she took his wrist to feel his pulse, and frowning, she covered him with a blanket. 'Young Lord!' she called to Sandy, 'this Gaiakin has an affliction of soul. You must tend to him!'

Settling on a stool by his bed, Sandy took Fescue's hand. 'Do not fear, Fescue,' he said soothingly, 'the cross is safe!'

Sinking back on his pillow, Fescue closed his eyes.

The goodwife leaned over Fin. 'Ah, an injury!' she said, sounding more confident as she saw Lark's bandage around Fin's head. Lifting one of Fin's eyelids and studying his pupil, she reassured Lark, hovering anxiously by the bed. 'The lad is concussed, but not deeply.'

Eyeing Fin closely, she asked: 'Is he a friend of yours? Surely, he is not of your Delphin kind? He skin is swarthier, and from his long legs, he must be taller. If I am to physic him, I must know his race!'

'His mother was a Rom,' Lark explained.

'Ah, that is where he gets his dark hair!' She stroked Fin's pale cheek. 'My, he's a grand looking young man! Did he fall from a height?'

Lark shook his head. 'He was attacked!'

Unwinding the bandage, she gave a grunt of satisfaction. 'Was it you who applied the moss pad?'

Lark nodded.

'You did correctly. Moss, with its antiseptic properties, is the best treatment for cuts! We had better take off his blood-stained clothes to see if he has any other injuries.'

With screens around the bed, Lark helped her strip off Fin's clothes. Bringing a bowl of warm water, cloths, and towels from a side room, she gently washed him, searching for further injuries, but found only grazes and many bruises. After applying musky smelling ointment and fresh wound pad to the cut, she dressed Fin in a nightshirt and covered him with a soft linen sheet.

Taking away the screens, she said: 'We have done all we can for now. Young Delphin, I shall leave you to watch over him.'

Gathering up Fin's clothes, Lark remembered the cross, and unwrapping it from his handkerchief, dropped it into the leather purse. Tying the drawstring tight, he tucked it beneath Fin's pillow. Fetching a stool, he sat by the bed head, apprehensively watching Fin's stiff, pale face for any change for the worse.

Sandy came from consoling Fescue and murmured: 'Do you know if the cross is safe?'

'Yep, I've just put it back in the purse, and hidden it under Fin's pillow.'

'We must keep guard: Fin must not be left alone!'

Lark nodded, grim-faced.

A rattle of the door latch signalled the return of the twins with tea. 'Has he opened his eyes yet?' Bird asked anxiously.

Lark shook his head. 'The nurse said he's got concussion but he's moving his fingers, which is a good sign.'

Bird sighed, and finding another stool, sat beside Sandy, whilst Bee perched on the end of the bed.

'Are the dogs O.K?' Lark asked.

Bird nodded. 'Grantly was happy to take charge of them.'

Lark was relieved: he'd enough worry about. The door latch rattled again to announce Kenji and Dancer. Sandy drew them aside.

'Any sign of the hooded figure?' They shook their heads.

'I've a feeling you know who it was, boss!' Kenji said, giving Sandy a meaningful look.

Sandy frowned. 'Dancer, did you send my message by the pigeon?'

She nodded. 'Yes – fortunately it had flown before the demon appeared!'

Hearing Fescue calling weakly, Kenji and Dancer went to him.

'My sword! I left it in the cathedral,' sobbed the Gaiakin trying to get up.

'Don't fret Fescue!' Kenji pressed him back into his pillow. 'I took it to John Smithy. He promised to have the blade mended by sundown – his skill isn't to Gaiakin standard, but he'll do a reasonable job.'

Dancer put a mug of tea in Fescue's hand. 'This will cheer you, Fescue dear,' she said, trying to sound motherly. Fescue gave her a feeble smile.

Gathered around Fin's bed sipping the honey-sweet tea, they discussed the attack in the cathedral.

'That thing we saw flying past the loft did you call it a hag?' Bird asked tensely.

'No, lass,' Sandy replied, 'it is what they call a Phragg and very bad news indeed, even the Gaiakins are challenged by those black devils!' He glanced across at Fescue who, revived by the tea, was sitting up watching them.

'Who was that hooded figure bashing Fin?' Lark wondered.

Kenji frowned. 'Whoever it was, I believe it called down the Phragg.'

'We've seen a Phragg before!' It was Bee who spoke.

They all looked at her in surprise.

Bird nodded, wide eyed. 'Yes, we saw one crawling up Mossy's shop wall!'

Lark gave them a sceptical look. 'When was this?'

'After the funeral. We were hiding in Chippen's yard, watching Mossy's shop,' Bird explained.

'Whatever were you doing there, at that time of night!' Lark barked.

'You know what we were doing,' Bee muttered, 'checking if Fin had met up with Daffodil. Tissy was with us – she nearly fainted.'

Bird saw Lark's look of anguish. 'She was O.K., Lark. We looked after her. Took her safely to Spinner Hall.'

There came a crash from Fescue's bed: he'd dropped his mug and was trying feebly to get up. Sandy hurried over, and helping him back under his blanket, called urgently to Kenji: 'Find Mullein!'

As Kenji made for the door, Fescue, still struggling, cried: 'The cross! The cross! I must rescue the cross!'

'Do not agitate yourself, Fescue! It is safe in Fin's purse!' Sandy said softly, holding the Gaiakin in his arms. Looking pleadingly up into his face, Fescue whispered: 'It is not the jewels: you know that don't you, Iskander?' Sandy hugged him reassuringly.

'Who is Mullein?' Bee asked Dancer in a low voice.

'He's Fescue's brother, and like Sandy, he's an Alpha Leader.'

Moments later Kenji returned accompanied by a Gaiakin. He resembled Fescue, but his hair was the colour of moonlight, instead of warm gold, and his eyes were as silvery as sun on ice.

Striding to Fescue's bed, Mullein held him close. 'Fescue, dear one, the morning is bright with sun, come with me and soak its warmth!' Fescue tried to push him away. 'I cannot leave young Fin, he has been injured!' he groaned.

'He is safe in the care of the goodwife, and his friends – in your weak state, you are of no assistance to him!'

Gently, Mullein helped Fescue from his bed, and led him from the sanatorium.

Kenji explained to Lark and the twins that the Gaiakin brothers had gone to sit in the sunshine. 'When afflicted, their kind need sunlight for healing – it reminds them of their Universe of White Light.'

Sandy interrupted. 'Kenji, I fear we have been lax! A watch must be kept on the battlements, in case the Phragg should return! Go and gather a group of Trekkers.'

'I've a nasty feeling that not only Phraggs, but bugslugs could be on their way as well,' Kenji said, testing his sword in its sheath. Collecting his crossbow from by the door, he strode out.

'Should I go too, boss?' Dancer asked, testing her own sword action.

'No, you and I will continue to search for Fin's attacker.'

He spoke to Lark and the twins: 'I will leave you in the goodwife's care. Do not stray far from the sanatorium!' he added sternly.

When Sandy and Dancer had gone, Lark and the twins sat with Fin, hoping his eyes would open. After a while, Bee volunteered to go for more tea, and returned with three mugs and a plate of buttered toast. She reported that Mick and Wolfie were getting on famously.

'The scullery Scav has taken a shine to them. I left them by the kitchen fire, gnawing pork bones!'


The Saprise afternoon was turning to evening when, after another fruitless search for Fin's hooded attacker, Sandy and Dancer joined Kenji and a group of Trekker warriors on the battlements. Fescue, fully recovered, was there with Mullein, their eyes sparkling as if they'd drunk of the sun's elixir.

The group stared fixedly over the forest. The clouds around the setting sun had taken on purple and orange hues, like angry bruises. Now and again they could smell the unmistakeable stench of ganglefowl, faint but growing stronger, drifting towards them on the heavy air: the loathsome creatures were drawing near.

'Never have I felt such strong evil,' Kenji muttered.

'Do I hear Snoopers?' Mullein asked suddenly, his keen hearing picking up a distant angry thrumming.

One of the warriors groaned: 'Hopefully our defences will be strong enough to keep out Frit and 'fowl, but how are we to deal with flying Snoopers?'

'Your skill with bow and arrow will be needed, good Harold,' murmured Mullein.

'What has brought this evil on us, Lord Iskander?' asked another warrior, looking to Sandy for reassurance. Sandy said nothing, stony-faced as he stared at the ominous sunset.

A sudden deep sigh, like the gasp of a great creature, rose from the river. They watched in astonishment as the water level slowly dropped as if sucked up by a vast mouth, exposing the muddy banks.

'It is as I feared, Maabella's bugslugs are on their way,' hissed Sandy, 'how long we have before they reach us, we can only guess – a day or so, hopefully!'

'Surely they will not come to Durholm!' exclaimed a warrior.

'Bugslugs not only travel on water but can crawl up walls if the stone is smooth enough,' Kenji said, speculatively studying the stone wall below them. As he spoke, from the west they heard a distant, drawn out shriek.

'The Phragg has returned to its lair!' shuddered Fescue, covering his ears.

'Not for long, I'll bet.' Kenji muttered. 'It will be back, bringing an army from Killhope Gate!'

'Not only from Killhope,' Mullein added, pointing north-west to where the Doomstone Mines lay. 'I fear the Frits and their ganglefowl have been let loose from their breeding grounds at Birdoswald.'

Sandy took Fescue and Mullein aside. 'It is the Chi Rho that draws them,' he told them in a low voice, 'it is as I dreaded, Lord Gressil knows that the Chi Rho has come to Durholm.'

'I feel the creature Crow has had a hand in that,' sighed Fescue.

'I have sent for Mother Hilda,' Sandy said, 'It is clear Hardwick is demon-bound, so she must preside at the Chapter House meeting, when Fin is to decide the destiny of the cross. I am hoping he will take it from here. Where to, I cannot at present think. In the meantime, we must look to our defences! But first let us see how our young friends are faring.'

He called to Kenji and Dancer. 'Come, we will return to the sanatorium.'

Mullein nodded. 'Fescue, go with them and reassure yourself of the young Delphin's welfare, whilst I warn others in the Garrison of the danger. Join us as soon as you can, Iskander – your wise counsel will be needed!'

# 10
# DRONEBIRD

Late that evening, Fin opened his eyes. Groaning, he lifted his head, puzzled at Lark and the twins' anxious faces.

'What's the matter? Where are we?' he mumbled, wondering why every bone in his body ached.

'You're in what they call the sanatorium,' Lark said.

Fin groaned again. 'My head hurts something rotten,' he complained, lifting his hand to his head.

'Don't move the bandage,' Bird said, pulling his hand away, 'you've got a nasty cut underneath. I'll get something to cool your brow.' She went off to the dispensary.

'Would you like something to drink?' Bee asked.

Fin nodded gratefully.

'I'll go to the kitchen for a mug of nettle tea.'

Fin lay back on his pillow and closed his eyes. Memories swam into his mind: a hooded figure and a black cloud of fiery rags. Fescue slashing at it with his sword. He remembered dropping the cross as the hooded figure attacked him.

Frantically, he groped inside his nightshirt: 'The cross, Lark! Where's the cross!'

'It's O.K. It's here, safely hidden.' Lark pulled the purse from under Fin's pillow.

Snatching it from him, Fin felt its weight before tucking it back.

'I wonder who attacked me,' he said, closing his eyes again, 'all I remember was someone hitting me with a walking stick.'

Listening to Lark's description of the spectre, Fin recalled the horrid face grinning through the roof window in Mossy's attic: the black cloud in the cathedral also had glaring red eyes. Was it the same monster?

Bird returned with bowl and sponge. Pressing the cool lavender-scented water to his brow, the aching pain in his head eased, and he was able sit up without feeling sick and dizzy. Bee brought a mug of honey-sweetened nettle tea and, as he sipped, he tried to focus on the twins' dramatic account of a dark shadow flying past the pigeon loft.

'Sandy said it was something called a Phragg,' Bird said with a shudder.

He took another sip and, eyes closed, tried to marshal his thoughts. He had to deal with a pressing problem, even though he felt as if he'd tumbled down a hundred stone steps: it was time to tell his friends about the cross. Opening his eyes, he found the room spinning again, so he decided it would be better to wait until Sandy and the others were there too.

His opportunity came when Sandy, Kenji, Dancer and Fescue returned from the battlements.

'What's the news?' Lark asked.

'Nothing much to report,' Sandy said trying to sound reassuring, but betrayed by his worried face.

Seeing the goodwife leave the room, Fin called them all to his bedside.

'I've been thinking things over,' he said, glancing uncertainly to where the injured cook lay snoring peacefully. Beckoning them closer, he lowered his voice. 'It's my treasure the Phragg's after. I should have insisted at Stonetree, that the twins go back home. And now I've brought danger to them, and everyone, even to your Squad, Sandy.'

Dancer snorted. 'Danger! That's what us Trekkers do!'

Fin shook his head impatiently, making him feel queasy again.

'Give over fretting Fin, you're turning sickly again!' Kenji exclaimed.

'Fin, we're your friends,' Bird said, pressing her sponge to his brow. 'We couldn't possibly let you go into danger, without us coming too!'

The soothing scent of lavender calmed him, and he gave her a grateful smile.

'Anyway, what's this treasure that's so special, it's brought a monster from Contagion?' Bee demanded.

Lark turned to her, ready with an angry retort but Fin checked him, laying a hand on his arm. 'It's alright Lark, I've decided it's time they knew about the Chi Rho.'

He looked around at the mystified faces. 'Sandy and Lark know what I'm talking about.'

Bird frowned. 'Is this something to do with your dad?'

Fin pulled the purse from under his pillow. Carefully keeping his mother's coin hidden, he took out the cross and held it up. As it swung on its chain, light from the windows caught the jewels, creating a kaleidoscope of sparkling colour.

'That's a fine trinket you've got there, young Delphin,' grinned Kenji.

'Surely this is the famous Cross of the Legend?' breathed Dancer, leaning closer, her protruding eyes blinking rapidly.

'Wow, what a piece!' exclaimed Bee, squinting into the crystal lozenge. 'Did your dad leave it to you? Why ever don't you wear it?'

Fin pushed her away irritably. 'It's not a piece of jewellery. It's what is called a reliquary. It has special powers – sort of magic, and you don't wear magic crosses.'

'You're joking!' Bird giggled. He jerked it out of reach as she tried to touch it.

'Fin's dad left it to him, to take care of,' Lark explained, 'Mossy told us all about it on the night of the funeral, whilst you two were mucking about in Chippen's yard. Its ancient. Only certain people can even touch it, let alone wear it.'

He glanced across at Fescue, sat apart on another bed, shoulders hunched.

'Anyway,' Fin continued, 'Mossy said it must be taken out of Brightdale, to somewhere with more protection from evil, so I've brought it here. But after what's happened, I'm not sure. What do you think Sandy?'

'It seems to me, Boss' Kenji butted in, 'now that young Fin has brought the Chi Rho to Durholm, it's up to you to take charge of it.'

Sandy looked troubled. 'No, no, the Burden has been given to Fin, until he passes it on.'

'If this is the Chi Rho that was stolen from the Community on Holy Island,' Dancer said, 'it should be returned to them. If I know the legend right, it was stolen by a Skwid,' she added, a guilty sunset pink rippling across her scaly cheeks.

Sandy frowned in thought. 'I know that Zagzagel intended the cross should come here, into the care of this Community, but I fear something is badly wrong – news has come to me that Brother Hardwick has taken to his bed – with an injured knee,' he added meaningfully.

Lark glowered. 'I'm dead sure it was him attacking Fin.'

'I certainly don't trust the man – there's something of my Uncle Roach about him,' Fin muttered.

At that moment, the door latch rattled, and Brother Hardwick limped in. He was leaning heavily on a gnarled walking stick. Lark had a strong suspicion he'd been listening outside.

Slipping the cross under his pillow and closing his eyes, Fin dropped his head back, feigning sleep.

Hardwick's baleful gaze roamed over the group, stopping first on Fescue.

'So, Gaiakin, you have recovered. I hear that you confronted one of the Phraggmorgia. I hope you are free of any trace of evil?'

Scowling, Fescue didn't reply.

Hardwick turned his attention to Fin.

'I see the Dandrum has not yet recovered. Are all his possessions accounted for, and kept safe?' He glared at Lark.

'Yes, sir,' Lark replied, looking Hardwick's brown hooded robe up and down, before pointedly staring at the walking stick.

Hardwick shrugged impatiently. 'As soon as the Dandrum is well enough, we shall have the Chapter House meeting. Iskander, make sure that all the Alpha Leaders are ready with their reports: I hear there are rumours of Frits gathering!'

Not waiting for a reply, he hobbled from the sanatorium.

As Sandy and his Squad made ready to go, Sandy held Dancer back. 'Stay here Dancer, to keep an eye on the Delphins' safety.'

When Sandy, Kenji, and Fescue had gone, they gathered once more around Fin's bed.

'Have you thought what to do about the cross?' Bird asked. 'Now you know you can't trust Hardwick.'

'I think you should take it back to Brightdale and let Mr Mossy look after it, you've suffered enough because of it!' Lark said, folding his arms and looking challengingly at Fin.

Fin gave a weary sigh. 'Mossy wasn't at all keen to have it in his care! He kept going on about its power getting to him, making him do things that a person of his sort shouldn't do. Do you remember, Lark, when we took the cross out of its box, he wouldn't even look at it? I suppose I'd better see what happens at this meeting Hardwick keeps going on about.'

'Luckily for you,' Dancer said, 'it won't be Hardwick who will be in charge: it will be Mother Hilda. That was the reason we sent her a message by pigeon. She'll be here soon. She has much wisdom, Fin, and if I know her aright, you can trust her!'

Grateful for this crumb of comfort, Fin lay back on his pillow. He listened whilst Dancer and the twins relived their experience in the loft. He was amused that the twins had got over their fright, and that Bee was beginning to embroider the details, adding flourishes to annoy Lark.

In the morning, Fin felt well enough to get up, and they all met for breakfast in the refectory. When they had eaten, Fin returned to thank the goodwife, then went with Lark to the dormitory to reclaim his mattress.

To the Delphins, Durholm had taken on an ominous atmosphere, with a strong feeling of approaching evil. The weather having turned wet and windy, they stayed in the kitchen with Grantly and his cooks. Sandy, Kenji, and Fescue visited them occasionally, breaking off from helping to increase the defences. Dancer remained with the Delphins, polishing her sword, and chatting with Grantly.

They saw no sign of Brother Hardwick.

That night, up in the dormitory, Bee and Bird sat with Fin and Lark for a while. After their day of idleness, they didn't feel sleepy. Dancer had gone to check on the ramparts and apart from them, the dormitory was deserted.

Hearing hammering and shouting from outside, Bird nodded to the empty beds. 'I suppose everyone's on watch, or building up defences, and things.'

Bee shivered. 'What I wouldn't give to be back in Brightdale, this place is giving me the jitters.'

Lark bit back the retort that it was her fault she was there. Instead he said: 'I don't like the sound of those slugbuggers. And I hope they're on top of those evil fag creatures, too!'

Bird glanced at Fin sitting on his mattress hugging his knees; he looked tired. The goodwife had taken off his bandage, but he had an ugly bruised cut showing beneath his dark hair.

'It's time you got some sleep, Fin,' she said, 'come on Bee, we'd better go to bed, too.'

Calling Wolfie, who had made himself at home on a spare mattress with Mick snuggled by his side, the twins said goodnight and went to the female quarters.

During the night, Fin was jolted from a dreamless sleep by the sound of shouts from the ramparts. Through a window above his head, he heard the rattle of chains as the drawbridge was lowered, and the portcullis was raised, followed by hooves echoing in the tunnel beneath the gatehouse. He wondered who could be travelling in the dead of night, braving the threat of danger.

Next day the wind had dropped, the cloudless sky promising a fine day. Sandy came to the refectory where Kenji, Dancer and the Delphins were finishing breakfast, and Mick and Wolfie were cadging bacon rinds.

'You must make haste,' he told them, 'the meeting in the Chapter House will take place immediately: they wish to hear the Alpha Leaders' reports and discuss the ominous events that have occurred since your arrival. Come, follow me!'

Sandy led them across the cloister garth to the Chapter House. Its great doors stood open, revealing a large circular room with a lofty ceiling. Sunlight streamed in through tall windows. A long marble bench followed the curve of the walls, almost encircling two ornately carved wooden chairs on a dais. One was occupied by the elusive Brother Hardwick and the other by a lean-looking woman with close-cropped iron grey hair.

Warned by Sandy that dogs were not allowed, the Delphins sternly commanded Mick and Wolfie to 'stay!' and left them crouched mournfully by the doors. At the foot of the steps into the Chamber, following Sandy's example, they bowed respectfully to Hardwick and the woman, before seating themselves close to the steps where they could keep an eye on the dogs.

Fin studied the woman. Like other members of the Holy Community, she wore a coarse cloth robe. The hem was heavily mud spattered and he wondered if she was the rider he'd heard in the middle of the night. She looked young, despite her grey hair. Befitting the occasion, her face was set in a severe expression. Her intelligent grey eyes falling on Fin, the tightness of her mouth softened, and she smiled at him kindly.

'That is Mother Hilda,' Sandy whispered in Fin's ear, 'she is the Firstmother of the Holy Community, and has just arrived from Holy Island. Brother Hardwick was very put out, for she is his Superior, and he knows she will thwart whatever devious plan he has in mind.'

Feeling the cord of his purse pressing on his neck, Fin's fingers strayed inside his shirt. A hope grew in his mind: could he safely entrust the Chi Rho to this Firstmother?

More people arrived, bowing to Hilda and Hardwick before taking their places. A low hum of conversation filled the room. Skwids, faces flashing rainbow colours, stared curiously at the Delphins. Fescue and Mullein arrived with several other Gaiakins, and Fescue, remembering that Fin had not met his brother, introduced him.

After a few kind words to Fin, Mullein took Sandy aside to discuss the progress of the defences. Fin watched the two Alpha Leaders, heads close together, their expressions grave. He noticed for the first time that Sandy, even with his weary all too human face, bore a resemblance to the Gaiakin. He wondered again about this warrior they called Lord Iskander and regretted he hadn't asked Mossy more about him. Thinking of Mossy, a wave of longing washed over him, to see his dear face amongst these strangers.

He became aware of Hardwick leaning forward watching him, claw-like hands gripping his knobbly walking stick. A glint of gold in the folds of his rich velvet robe caught Fin's eye. He saw, half hidden, the gold cross with the red gem: it was damaged, with one of the arms bent.

Suddenly Hardwick struck the floor of the dais with his stick, making Fin start.

'Quiet everyone!' he grated. 'Before we begin our meeting, we will pray.'

All stood and made the Christian sign of the cross, touching their foreheads, chests, and shoulders. Out of politeness, the Delphins copied their action. Hardwick's prayer was muttered and brief and everyone sat down again. Hardwick glowered around at each person in turn, treating the Skwids to a particularly long, sour glare.

'Delegates, I have asked you here as a matter of urgency,' he began. 'As you may know, there is great danger coming upon us! There are reports of increased enemy activity in the forests to the west: an army of Frits mounted on ganglefowl are on the march from Birdoswald, believed to be commanded by Sneaksouls who are part of Lord Gressil's own household. Also, bugslugs' activity has been observed on the river – there are even reports of Gressil's Snoopers in the air!'

At this last news, a hubbub of gasps and exclamations broke out.

Hardwick raised his hand for silence. 'Do not be fearful, my children,' he cloyingly attempting to reassure his audience, 'something of wonder has come amongst us which will be a mighty weapon in defeating the enemy.'

For a moment Fin didn't take in what Hardwick had said, then fury gave him courage. He leapt to his feet. 'What are you talking about, Hardwick? The Chi Rho can't be used as a weapon!'

All eyes turned on Fin. Lark sprang up and planted himself firmly next to him, fists bunched ready for battle; he glowered challengingly at the amazed faces before him but didn't dare speak.

Sandy stood and put his hand on Fin's shoulder. 'Brother, did we not agree that it is the Delphin who must decide what he should do with that which he has brought?'

His voice was icy, his face like thunder.

Raking the gathering with his keen gaze, he continued: 'Brother Hardwick refers to the Cross that was stolen from Holy Island. When we have finished our business, I shall remind you of the story, but for now it must suffice for you to know that Fin Dandrum here, is the present guardian of the Chi Rho.'

Gasps echoed around the chamber as everyone stared at Fin in wonder.

Leading Fin and Lark back to their seat, Sandy called to Hardwick. 'Brother, time is passing, and we have much to do to improve our defences. Should we not hear the reports from the Squads?'

Petulantly shrugging his shoulders, Hardwick snarled for the Alpha leaders to stand up.

There were six Alphas, including Sandy and Mullein.

One of the Skwid Alphas raised his hand to speak first. Hardwick nodded curtly, and the Alpha came to stand before the dais. His clothes were blood-stained and muddy, he looked exhausted, his face dark grey. Forcing his body to attention, he called out his name:

'Alpha Haar. Reporting from the West: very bad. The enemy, spilling out from Contagion, came South. Much burning of settlements. Much slaughter. Motherhome Manchester under siege, but we fought off the foe. Now the evil has returned North. Reason not known.'

He hesitated for a moment, before, his voice breaking, he continued. 'Lost a Squad brother, Warrior Naginata. Died bravely.' Looking towards Kenji, his scales flashed dark red and black. 'Sorry lad!'

Kenji bowed his head: Naginata was of his race. 'How did he die?'

'Burnt to a cinder by a Phragg!'

Hearing this, Bee and Bird sobbed loudly, and hid their faces in their hands.

Brother Hardwick glared at them: his eyes had often strayed towards the Delphins. Leaning on his stick, he rose to his feet. 'We are indeed sorry to hear your sad news, Alpha Haar. You are not the only Alpha with bad news, I regret to say. We shall hear the rest of the reports in a moment.'

He stabbed his stick in the direction of the twins. 'First, may we know why these small females have become so agitated?'

The twins, leaning close to Dancer, all eyes turned on them. Pushing them aside, angrily Dancer stood.

'Trekker Shadow Dancer,' she growled in her husky voice, scales flashing bright pink and dark mauve. 'My companions were horrified by Alpha Haar's mention of a fiery Phragg that burned someone to a crisp.'

'And what do these little imps know about the Phraggmorgia?' Hardwick sneered. 'This meeting is too important to be interrupted by alien species, who should be outside with their dogs! Now, before we have any further childish interruptions, we will hear the next Alpha report. I call Alpha Mullein.'

Before Mullein could speak, a new voice rang out, clear and authoritative.

'Brother Hardwick, can we not learn the reason for the young Delphins' distress?' It was Mother Hilda who spoke. She remained seated, but leaning forward, smiled encouragingly at Bee and Bird.

Bird came forward, and in an unsteady voice explained: 'The Skwid's talk of Phraggs brought back the memory of the thing we saw, through the pigeon loft window, which glowed as if on fire!'

'We also saw one in our own homeland!' Bee called from the bench, her eyes wide with horror.

Murmurs rippled around the chamber.

Sandy called out in a commanding voice: 'Yes, my friends, you should well be afraid – a Phragg has been among us! This is the danger we face. Indeed, it could even be that another Phragg has infiltrated our community here, as a Sneaksoul!' His gaze settled for a moment on Brother Hardwick, who shifted uneasily in his seat.

His listeners stared at their fellows, bewildered and suspicious.

'Have courage my children!' cried Hilda. 'We must admire these small Delphins who have braved the sight of a Phragg – Brother, is it not time we were introduced to these remarkable Delphin folks?' She turned back to them. 'I am Mother Hilda. When we have completed our business here, however pressing the danger, I must hear a little of your history and of your country – perhaps over a glass of wine in my quarters?'

Her keen grey eyes searched out Fin, who bowed respectfully in acknowledgement of the invitation.

Sandy introduced the Delphins, pointing to each in turn, giving their names.

When he had done, Brother Hardwick, clearly exasperated, called on Mullein to report on the happenings and threats, this time from the south east. He had similar bad news to Alpha Haar, as did Sandy, who told them of the evidence of bugslug activity they had seen at Ireshope. When all Alphas had finished, and returned to their places, muttering broke out through the Chamber.

Mother Hilda stood and immediately silence fell. 'Friends, some of you must be wondering about the Chi Rho to which Iskander has referred.' She looked to Fin. 'May we have your consent to tell this gathering the nature of your Burden? I believe that you have been sent to us by Zagzagel, for help and advice?'

Fin nodded miserably: he felt trapped in a situation he'd never planned.

Lark, determination on his flushed face, stood protectively close, arms crossed. 'Have a care!' he said fiercely to Mother Hilda, 'my master has suffered much because of what he's carrying, and I don't want him being made ill again.'

'Do not fear, Lark,' Hilda said, 'your concern is admirable. Let me reassure you that no decision will be made without Fin's free consent.'

Brother Hardwick snorted in disgust. 'The Chi Rho does not belong to the Delphin. If any have the right to decide its fate, it is the Holy Community from which it was originally stolen!'

Now Fescue rose to his feet. 'Tell me Brother, was it the Holy Community or was it a Gaiakin, who saved the Chi Rho from destruction, when Jerusalem fell into ruin?' His tone was unusually sarcastic for a Gaiakin.

Brother Hardwick glared at him. 'Now we are in the realms of ancient history!'

The meeting erupted into argument. Fin and Lark sat down again. With a curt nod from Mother Hilda, Sandy clapped his hands, calling for order.

'Friends, if Lord Gressil could witness us now he would know his battle was won without lifting a claw! We must give careful and measured thought to how we can protect our people – but now is not the time to use the power of the Chi Rho. It would be a horror beyond imagining if we gave the demon the opportunity to steal it.

'We should remind ourselves why the Cross is coveted by Gressil. It is a tale I must tell, even though time is pressing, so I will be as brief as possible.'

The Great Chamber hushed. Parts of the story were already known to many; even so, all waited in respectful silence.

Shifting closer to Fin, Lark leaned forward eagerly, keen to hear Sandy's version of the history of the Chi Rho. Had it been only a few days since he sat in Mr Mossy's room above the shop? he asked himself silently. It seemed like a lifetime ago.

Sandy picked up a much-thumbed, tattered book from the marble bench. Propping wire-rimmed spectacles on his nose, he leafed through the book to the page he wanted.

'I will read an extract from the Polychronicon of the angel Zagzagel – of how Gressil and Queen Mab were imprisoned in their loathsome bodies – a tale which many of you have heard at your mother's knee!'

Some of the older warriors and Community Members nodded.

He began, his musical voice rising to the rafters, filling the room.

*'When THE CREATOR had completed the making the Universe of Stars, it was given to Zagzagel the task of nurturing life on the blue world of Gaia, filling her oceans with creatures and her lands with plants. Now, the devil Lucifer, seeing the wonderful living things that Zagzagel cared for, became mightily jealous and longing to spoil Gaia's beauty, sent his servants, the demons Gressil and Maabella to fight with Zagzagel and destroy his work.*

*But Zagzagel was more powerful, and after a battle that lasted a million years, he overcame those wicked demons, and as a punishment, he imprisoned their dark spirits inside the creatures of Gaia they had tried to destroy. Gressil, he forced into the monstrous body of an ancient sea creature. Maabella, he forced into the body of a great slug.*

*For aeons, Gressil and Maabella crawled Gaia's oceans' floors, trapped in these bodies, searching for a way to escape. With the passage of the ages, they were forgotten.*

*It was when the horror of the Great Dying came upon the human children of Gaia that Gressil and Maabella found hope. Crawling out of the sea, sometimes hiding in the jungles of the world, sometimes in muddy swamps, sometimes in deep caverns, they came in the end to the Land of Contagion, where Gressil built a fortress of stone. Here he made a nest for Maabella where she would find some relief from the pain of giving birth to her maggot children.*

*Over the hundreds of years that Gressil and Maabella have lived in the Land of Contagion, Maabella has grown weaker, and her black spirit is fading. Soon she will be no more. To delay her end, she feeds on the life spark of innocent spirits, and it is the demons, known as Phraggmorgia, who provide her with these souls.*

*But now her body too, is dying, for she has a suppurating wound in her side that is slowly poisoning her. She received this wound when a human ventured into Contagion and allowed himself to be captured, to enter the pit where the Queen Mab lay on her nest, so that he could kill her...'*

Abruptly snapping the book shut, Sandy sat, and polished his spectacles. His audience remained silent.

Eventually Mother Hilda spoke: 'Iskander, you have not explained how Queen Mab came by her wound!'

With a resigned sigh, Sandy stood once more, and began chanting the story, which he knew by heart.

'The year was 3333. The threat of evil hung over our northern lands where Gressil had his fortress in the Land of Contagion, his power ever-growing. A Gathering was called on Lindisfarne, better known as Holy Island.'

Sandy started counting on his fingers. 'Those present at the meeting were as follows:

'Aeronwen, the Firstmother of the Holy Community. (Brother Eadwig who had been their Firstfather and had carried the Chi Rho from Yrvik to Holy Island, weakened by his Burden, had passed the leadership to Mother Aeronwen.)

'From the Cyning clan came King Flaithri, and his son, Prince Cadeyrn, Lords of the Isles. (Come from their northern fastness, these two were descended from the first King Cyning, saved from death by the Gaiakins, when the Gaiakins first came to Gaia.)

'From the Gaiakin people, came King Guelder and Queen Fleur of Florain, with Fescue and Mullein.'

He paused to bow to Fescue and Mullein. Fin looked amazed at the two brothers: their faces unwrinkled, their eyes bright, but Sandy had said that the Gathering was in 3333, nearly two hundred years ago!

'Present too, was Zagzagel, known to the young Delphins as Mr Mossy.'

Fin noticed a soft gleam in Sandy's eyes when he mentioned Mossy.

'After long debate, it was eventually agreed that Gressil should be attacked where he was most vulnerable: by killing Maabella, his Queen. Her children, sometimes known bugslugs, or more properly Bombyx, were multiplying, their appetite for living flesh ever more voracious.'

Fin frowned. He'd read about such creatures in one of Mossy's books: the slug-like young ones growing into monsters with eyes on fleshy stalks, and bunches of tentacles, like long fingers, growing out of their fat slimy backs, each one ending in a jaw fringed with needle-sharp teeth.

Sandy continued his account.

'It was decided that one among them must volunteer to risk almost certain death, to venture into Contagion, to enter the pit where the Queen Mab lay on her nest.

'Prince Cadeyrn volunteered for this dread task – the legends of his bravery are written in the annals of the Cyning clan, stored in the libraries of the Motherhomes of the world. Suffice to say, that Cadeyrn, having seized a chance to get close to the heaving mass that was Mab's vile body, failed in his mission. The dagger hidden in his loin cloth was not long enough to inflict a mortal blow – when he stabbed Maabella her hideous screams alerted her servants, and Cadeyrn was discovered and killed.'

A groan rippled around the chamber. Sandy raised his hand for silence.

'So Cadeyrn failed, but Maabella's life force is seeping from the injury he inflicted. Gressil's servants are unable to heal the wound, and Gressil knows his beloved is slowly dying after years of agonizing pain. When word came to him of the miraculous healing powers of the Chi Rho, he sent out his scouts to search for this fabulous object, and it was by evil misfortune that they found it.'

He glanced at the group of Skwid. 'The Skwids know that tale, for it was a Skwid who stole the Chi Rho from the Community on Holy Island.

'But by mysterious chance, the holy relic was lost again before Gressil's servants could use it to heal the Queen – that is why Gressil still desperately seeks the Chi Rho.'

His voice faltering, Sandy drew his hand across his tired eyes. 'By strange accident, not long ago, the Chi Rho was found again, and by even stranger chance, it came into the care of the Delphin peoples. But I shall end my account here!'

He slumped back on the bench, drained.

'But Iskander, how did the young Delphin come to be the bearer of the Cross?' Hardwick rasped.

Feeling Brother Hardwick's greedy eyes on him, Fin's hand strayed to the cross in its leather purse. 'Time is passing Brother; cannot we leave that tale?' Sandy snapped.

'No, we cannot!' Hardwick snapped back, 'Many here wish to know how an insignificant Delphin has possession of this precious relic.'

From around the chamber there came cries of assent.

Sandy rose, wearily, for a third time. 'Fin, may I speak on your behalf?'

Fin nodded: he felt he could be sick at any moment.

Sandy gave a terse account of what he had learnt from Mossy, of how Marlin had found Crow with the cross embedded in his chest.

When he'd finished, Hardwick scowled. 'That Marlin Dandrum should have given the cross to us here at Durholm! I suppose Zagzagel mistakenly thought it would be safe in the little land of Brightdale. Now I hear that Marlin has been killed, and again the precious relic almost fell into enemy hands.'

He glared wildly around the chamber; his face contorted with rage. 'The Chi Rho must be in my care! I'm certain the runt called Crow, who lusts desperately for the Chi Rho, has alerted Gressil's minions of its whereabouts: that is why Gressil is gathering his forces!' He stabbed his stick in Fin's direction. 'The Delphin has brought great danger upon us!'

Mother Hilda rose to lay a hand on Hardwick's shoulder. 'Hush Brother, calm yourself. Before we decide what to do with the cross, should we not first complete our defences of Durholm?' She looked enquiringly at the circle of people.

'Yes, Mother – the people still have much to do to make their homes secure!' called Mullein.

'Cannot this Fin Dandrum leave and take the danger with him?' shouted one of the Skwid trekkers.

The room started to hum with angry mutterings.

Fin realised that he would have to speak. Taking a deep breath, he approached the dais. Lark made to follow, but Sandy held him back. All looked at Fin expectantly, the Chamber fell silent. He began to speak in a low unsteady voice, causing some of the older folk to lean forward to hear him.

'First, I beg your patience. I know only too well that the Chi Rho does not belong to me, but I have been chosen to carry it: Zagzagel can assure you on that point.

'Though I may be young and untried, the Chi Rho has fallen into my care, and it is my duty to decide what should be done. I came to Durholm for advice, and all I wanted of this gathering was guidance. If you cannot give that, I will leave, and take the danger with me—'

'No! No!' Hardwick screeched, 'this is not right. I insist that the Chi Rho be handed over to me to, to put with our other treasures! Yes, and, and, guarded by the spirit of Holy Cuthbert…' he finished lamely. Brandishing his stick, he stamped down the dais steps, coming so close Fin could see the glowing sickly green in his eyes. A thudding roar filled his head. He stumbled back, wondering if he might be going mad, before realising the sound was coming from outside the Chamber. Terrified the roof was falling on them, he ran to the bench, where Lark and the twins cowered together.

Looking around, they soon realized that, apart from them, nobody seemed troubled by the sound. Instead, a hum of amused chatter filled the Great Chamber, and many looked up to the roof, grinning.

'This is all we need, for complete chaos!' snarled Hardwick, limping back to his seat.

The insistent thudding turned to low rumbling, coughed, and died. Everyone looked expectantly toward the entrance. A short while later from the cloister the dogs could be heard snarling. A lanky, leather-clad man wearing a helmet and goggles appeared in the doorway. Unfortunately, he could go no further: Wolfie barred his way, hackles raised.

'I say, can someone deal with these dratted dogs!' the man called, attempting to shake off Mick, whose jaw was clamped to his boot.

Dancer ran up the steps and, amid general laughter, shooed the dogs back into the cloister, from where there came mutinous growling. The man loped nonchalantly down the steps and made several theatrical bows to his cheering audience.

'Wings, what brings you here?' Hardwick shrilled above the laughter.

Pulling off his helmet and goggles, the man's pale grey eyes scanned the bench, and stopping at the Delphins, gave them an exaggerated wink.

'Acting as a messenger for Zaggy,' he said, ambling over to sit by Sandy.

He shrugged off his grubby leather jacket. 'I've a message for a young Delphin by the name of Fin Dandrum,' he announced, wiping his grimy face with his oil-stained scarf, leaving a greasy smudge across the grey stubble on his chin.

Hardwick grumbled resentfully.

Ignoring Hardwick, Wings continued: 'Also, I should warn you chaps, you'd better finish your cosy chit-chat, and look to your defences. Any time now there'll be something pretty nasty knocking on your door.'

'You have seen the enemy?' Mother Hilda cried.

He looked across at her. 'Yep, Hilda! A Frit army, riding ganglefowl, heading this way along the river path from Killhope Gate. Had a dogfight with a flock of Gressil's Snoopers, too. Nearly went down in the river, which by the way, is chock full of bugslugs!'

At this, the meeting collapsed into uproar.

Hilda clapped her hands for order. 'Friends, what do you wish: look to our defences, or debate the question of the Chi Rho?'

'To the battlements!' called Mullein, making for the steps, his Squad close behind him.

'The fate of the cross is in the hands of the young Delphin,' shouted Haar, following Mullein with his own Squad.

Agreement came from all around the chamber. Sandy took Fescue, Kenji, and Dancer aside, for an urgent muttered discussion.

Huddled together, frightened and feeling forgotten, the Delphins were relieved when Mother Hilda came to them.

'Delphins, come to my room where we can decide what should be done with the sacred relic.'

She shepherded them up the steps. Sandy, Dancer and Wings joined them in the cloister.

'I know for certain now that Hardwick has been taken and is possessed by a Sneaksoul,' Sandy told them grimly. 'Fescue and Kenji are dealing with the matter – the lock-up will soon have an occupant!'

Just then they spotted Fescue and Kenji marching Hardwick, screeching curses, towards the lock-up Bird and Bee had seen earlier on their way to the scriptorium.

As everyone headed for Hilda's room, Wings called out: 'Wait a mo, Hilda! I haven't given Zaggy's message to young Fin.'

Fin stopped. 'What does he say?' he exclaimed.

Before Wings could answer, Hilda broke in. 'You can pass on the message whilst we drink wine in my room!'

Wings rubbed his hands gleefully. 'I could do with a drink after my dust-up with Snoopers!'

Lark grinned as they passed the lock-up: from inside came a stream of coarse swearing. Looking up at Wings walking beside him, he said: 'Hardwick won't like being in that stinking place, what with his fancy velvet robe!'

Mother Hilda's quarters were next to the sanatorium. They gathered around a brightly burning fire, whilst Hilda poured goblets of ruby-coloured elderberry wine.

Observing their strained faces as she handed the drinks around, she said: 'I think we should eat first and make plans after.'

'Good idea Hilda – could eat a whole hogget!' Wings exclaimed. 'Not had breakfast today, let alone lunch.'

Bird and Bee volunteered to go to the kitchen, bringing back trays laden with bowls of onion soup and hunks of bread. As they ate, the Delphins told Mother Hilda of their adventures.

Mopping up his soup with a piece of bread, Fin looked across at Wings. 'When were you in Brightdale?'

'Got there yesterday. Had a long confab with Zaggy and spent the night on his dratted uncomfortable sofa. Left at first light – Fin, he warns that you must get out of Durholm! He's heard news of the coming invasion.'

Fin sprang to his feet. 'Then I should go at once before all escape routes are closed!' Hesitating, he looked around at the circle of faces. 'But I don't know where to go! Should I try to get to the coast and find a ship?'

Wings shook his head. 'No, that wouldn't do! Zaggy reckoned Holy Island would be the safest place. That's why I've come – to get you and this cross-thingy away as quick as possible, and the fastest way is to fly!' He pointed to the ceiling with a flourish.

The Delphins stared at him, doubting the man's sanity; Lark had a vision of them leaping over the battlements, rucksacks on their backs, frantically flapping their arms.

Sandy chuckled. 'Wings means you should fly in his machine.'

'Yep, Wings' Airline Service,' grinned the pilot, jumping to his feet. 'Don't often carry passengers, I'm used mainly as a postal service. Come on chaps, it's time you met my Skyhook!'

He strode for the door, everyone trooping after him. Full of misgivings, Mick tucked firmly inside his jerkin, Lark brought up the rear: the talk of Fin flying away, and there being no mention of him coming along too, agitated him greatly.

Beyond the orchard, they came out on to the grassy area, where the Delphins halted, dumbfounded.

'Well, what do you think of the old girl?' Wings waved his arms proudly at the strangest contraption they had ever seen. 'I call her Skyhook!'

The machine was tubular in shape, a skin of tarred canvas stretched over the framework. It stood on three spindly legs with wheels, one at the front and one each side. Stubby wings stuck out either side of the body and rising vertically from the middle of the machine was a metal shaft, topped by a large horizontal propeller made of thin wood. A smaller vertical propeller projected forward from the nose.

'Is this what we heard overhead in the Chapter House?' Lark asked, suspiciously eyeing the propellers lazily turning in the breeze.

Wings nodded. 'Come and have a closer dekko!'

Tingling with excitement, Fin followed Wings, but Lark and the twins hung back.

Running his hand over the tarred canvas, Fin recalled another book in Mossy's library, this time with illustrations of flying machines. Suddenly it dawned on him: a grin spread across his face. He called to the others: 'It's a Dronebird! Weren't we daft, not realising a Dronebird was a flying machine?'

Stroking the beautifully carved smaller propeller at the front, he smiled at Wings. 'I never would've dreamt that I could get to fly in one!'

'Am I right in thinking Delphins have a superstition, seeing a Dronebird brings them good luck?' Sandy asked.

Lark nodded, gazing wide-eyed at the machine. Remembering the rare times, he'd seen a Dronebird thrumming along the horizon, he'd been certain it had been a great bird.

Watching Fin bending to inspect the underside of the body before getting on tiptoe to look inside the cockpit, he hoped his head injury hadn't addled his brains. Plucking up courage, he approached cautiously, but the twins stayed where they were, close to Sandy, Dancer and Mother Hilda.

Giving the small windscreen a quick polish with his scarf, Wings pointed out the machine's various features as Fin listened keenly.

'The rotor up there gives her lift,' he explained, flapping his arms, 'and the prop in the nose gives forward motion. The engine's in the front, and I sit here, in the cockpit.' He pointed to a seat made of woven bamboo. 'There's room for two passengers behind the central prop shaft.' He indicated two further bamboo seats, set one behind the other. 'I put cargo in the hold at the rear – light stuff only, papers and scrolls needing to go air mail.'

'What fuel powers the engine?' Fin asked, craning his neck into the cockpit to study the dials and knobs on the instrument panel.

'Specially distilled vegetable spirit – mainly from rapeseed oil. Power for the electric starter motor and the fuel pump come from these solar panels.' Wings patted one of a set of dull black plates screwed to the top surface of each wing. 'She's guided by a rudder at the back here.' He took Fin around and showed him a blade-like piece of wood sticking out at the rear. 'A shaft runs from the joystick in the cockpit, to the stern – she manoeuvres like a ship.'

Whilst Wings explained, Lark earnestly inspected the two passenger seats: determined that however dreadful an experience flying might be, he would occupy one of those seats. 'Fin's not going without me,' he informed Wings firmly.

Wings grinned. 'No worries, Lark. Zaggy gave me strict instructions that you were to come too. That was one of the reasons he didn't come to Durholm with me, there would be no room for you!'

Fin looked sharply at Wings. 'Has Mossy flown with you in this machine?'

'Yep, a few times – if he's in a hurry to get somewhere. But being a giant chap it's a bit heart-in-mouth getting off the ground. But more importantly—' Leaning close to Fin and Lark, he muttered: 'Mossy is needed in Brightdale, what with the kerfuffle at Spinner Hall.' Nodding meaningfully towards the twins, he added quietly: 'With the lasses not coming home!'

Standing back, he cheerily called out: 'Right, time we got going. Fetch your kit lads, and then we'll be off whilst there's still plenty of daylight. Pack only what's necessary! Even then, it'll be a fair fight to get the old girl into the air.'

Lark didn't like the sound of that at all: looking once more at the canvas and wood, he was amazed that it could lift off the ground, let alone fly in the air.

Whilst Lark and Fin ran to pack, the twins waited, listening forlornly to Sandy, Mother Hilda and Dancer discussing with Wings the route he should take.

'Make for the coast: you don't want another confrontation with Gressil's Snoopers,' warned Dancer.

'And then turn north for Holy Island,' added Sandy.

'We must also decide what is best for these lasses,' Mother Hilda said, putting an arm around each twin. 'Someone must take them home!'

Sandy frowned. 'I fear Hilda, that we cannot spare anybody to take them back to Brightdale! They must go with you to Holy Island.'

Seeing Hilda's uncertainty, Bird begged: 'Can we please, Mother Hilda?'

Hilda frowned. 'It could be a dangerous journey, what with Snoopers in the area – I would not like to have to answer to your parents if anything happened to you.'

'Would you like Dancer to go with you?' Sandy asked.

Dancer agreed eagerly. 'Please say yes, Mother! The lasses and I are firm friends now, and I would be sorry to say goodbye!'

Giving a sigh, Hilda reluctantly gave her assent. 'But we must be ready to leave as soon as we have seen the machine flying off!'

A moment later Fin and Lark returned. Doubtfully weighing their rucksacks, Wings stowed them in the cargo hold.

Fin turned to the twins, his mismatched eyes, one brown, one green, sparkling with tears. 'Take care, Bee and Bird – get back home safely!'

'You won't be getting rid of us that easily, Fin!' grinned Bee. 'Sandy said he can't spare anyone to take us home, so we're coming to Holy Island by land, with Mother Hilda and Dancer.'

Lark scowled. 'Then, you'd better behave yourselves, and make sure you aren't a bother! What your mum and dad will say when they hear of your gallivanting, I dread to think!'

'Yes, behave yourself, Bee,' Fin said, giving her a soft punch on the shoulder, before shyly turning to Bird and giving her a hug. 'See you on Holy Island, Bird!'

'Get there safely, Fin,' she said, trying not to cry. On an impulse, she took from around her neck a silver bird charm hanging on a chain and pressed it into Fin's hand. 'This has always brought me good luck!'

'I'll keep it safe with the cross,' he said huskily.

Wrapping the twins in a crushing hug, Lark said: 'Well, lasses, I still don't think you should have come on this trip.' He looked wistfully to where he thought Brightdale might be. 'I was hoping you'd be going home, so you could tell Tissy that, despite all the wonders I've seen, I mostly think of her.'

Turning away, he whistled to Mick, busy cocking his leg against a nearby apple tree. Guessing it would be very cold high in the sky he jammed on his floppy fish-hook hat and taking a big breath, climbed up into Skyhook, Mick under his arm.

'Farewell Fin,' Sandy said, ruffling Fin's dark hair, 'I have a feeling that you will find more than you ever hoped for on Holy Island.'

Fin noticed him give Mother Hilda a significant look, which she answered with a soft smile. 'God speed, young Delphins!' she called.

'Goodbye, Fin. Goodbye Lark!' Dancer said gruffly, helping Fin climb into his seat. 'Don't fear for the lasses. I shall take care of them.'

'Thanks Dancer.' Fin shot her a grateful smile.

Snapping his goggles down over his eyes, and pulling on large leather gauntlets, Wings leapt into the cockpit and, with a creak of bamboo, settled in his seat. Jabbing at the starter button, he grasped the joystick, and after a couple of throaty coughs the engine fired, settling into a steady rumble that made the aircraft tremble.

As he settled in his seat, Fin wondered what Sandy meant by his odd remark about him, Fin, finding more than he hoped for on Holy Island. Then the excitement of flying drove all else from his mind. The engine note rose to a roar, above him the propeller became a blur, and Skyhook ponderously lifted off the ground. Looking over the side, he saw the twins standing next to a frantically barking Wolfie, their faces full of apprehension.

Skyhook rose higher, the downdraught from her propeller snatching at the blossom-laden trees in the orchard, filled the air with clouds of pink petals. Lark grabbed wildly as the wind caught his hat, but he was too slow: snatched off his head, it soared into the air to land on the refectory roof, where its forest of fish flies could be seen glittering in the sun. During the days to come he often regretted its loss.

Those on the ground watched heart in mouth as Skyhook dropped behind the hedge, plunging towards the river, before reappearing a few seconds later. Just missing the treetops on the far riverbank, she circled round towards the east, and flying off over the forest, turned to a dot on the horizon.

On a rocky ledge beneath the cliff path, hidden deep in a tangle of brambles close to where Skyhook stood, Crow the Scav strained to hear the voices above him. His desperate longing for the Chi Rho had brought him there, ahead of the advancing Frit army.

Hearing plans being made for the long-legged Delph, with black grass-top, to take his, Crow's jool far, far away, he moaned in misery: 'Holy Isle – that land, such a longaway away!'

Suddenly there was a deafening roar. Terrified, he shrank deeper into the brambles as the flying monster dropped from the sky and hovered a moment in front of him before swooping upwards, almost snatching at the treetops, to disappear into the horizon. Alerted by the noise, Sparkie, the rat, poked its head out enquiringly from Crow's chain-mail jerkin. The creature, fully recovered from its mauling by Mick, looked sleek and contented.

Crow kissed the top of its head. 'Lik Sparkie, how we get jool now it gone away up sky, along a Holy Isle?'

The voices above faded as the watchers walked away. He buried himself deeper in the thorny tangle and began munching on a cache of hazel nuts he'd found earlier – probably forgotten by a squirrel last Leaf Turn.

From the cathedral, the shouting and hammering grew louder as the defenders prepared to repel invasion. Peering down through the brambles, Crow saw that the river had become strangely low. He shivered with anticipation: Queen Mab's bugslugs would soon be coming!

# 11
# FLYING

The steady drone of the engine vibrating through his spine turned Fin's terror into exhilaration: if he couldn't be Head Dandrum, he'd become a pilot and fly the world!

Craning over Wings' shoulder, he watched his gloved hands twiddling knobs and tapping flickering dials, tweaking the joystick a little left, a little right, keeping the flying machine on course. Twisting around, he saw Lark crouched deep in his seat, eyes tight shut, his face a sickly yellow. All he could see of Mick was a black snout poking out of Lark's jerkin. Braving a peep over the side, he saw they were entering a bank of cumulus cloud. Seconds later, a thick mist enveloped them, and Skyhook shuddered violently. Gripping the back of Wings' seat, he held his breath for a few moments until they emerged into clear sky, and smooth flight once more. Recalling Wings' mention of Gressil's Snoopers, he was alert for anything nasty, but apart from a few clouds, and a flock of starlings flying west, the sky was empty. Far below, the muddy brown river snaked through a forest of toy sized trees, shaded palely green in young Saprise leaf. He realised Wings was using the river as a guide, following its meandering course north-eastwards.

Remembering Bird's farewell gift, he pulled out the delicate chain and looked wistfully at the little silver bird in his palm – the pendant was the third precious thing he'd been given in these strange days. Dangling it, he watched the bird spinning and twisting in the wind, the two green gemstone eyes catching the light, reminding him of Bird's pretty eyes. A strand of her soft green-wheat coloured hair was caught in the chain, but before he could pull it off, the wind plucked it away.

Skyhook flew steadily on. The forest beneath thinned to scrub, and the river became a maze of rivulets running through reed beds. Occasionally, low flat-roofed buildings could be seen on scattered islands. These became more numerous, and soon the terrain was covered in a mass of roofs, intersected by winding channels of muddy grey water. Dotted amongst the islands, were mounds of what looked like middens or rubbish heaps. He realised these were piles of debris: they were passing over the home of the Scavenger peoples, and Crow's birthplace.

Beyond was a wide expanse of mudflats, from where every now and then a small grey face peered up, attracted by the engine noise. A glittering brightness ahead caught his eye and, leaning farther out, he saw a blue-grey expanse, flecked with white wavelets, stretching to the horizon: it was the sea. He'd never imagined that one day he would see the sea.

He turned excitedly to Lark. 'LOOK!' he shouted above the engine noise.

Lark opened one eye, and gingerly craning his neck out over the side, his jaw dropped. In his amazement, he forgot his misery, and a huge smile spread across his face.

Hearing Fin's shout, Wings turned to grin, but as he did so, his expression changed to horror: he'd seen something behind them. Fin and Lark spun their heads around. Silhouetted against the westering sun, four huge dark shapes were speeding towards them. As they drew nearer the shapes turned to giant hornet-like insects, their black and yellow striped bodies the size of sheep, their cruel faces dominated by black compound eyes, their whirring transparent wings stretching out over six feet.

'GRESSIL'S SNOOPERS!' Wings yelled, shoving his joystick hard to the right, sending Skyhook lurching left. Hitting his head hard on the prop shaft, Fin had to blink to clear his vision.

The giant insects were all around them, their ferocious buzzing audible even over Skyhook's engine. Thud! Thud! Thud! Thud! Skyhook shuddered as out of their fat backsides shot a volley of knitting needle-long stings. Her canvas skin peppered with holes, the snatching wind tore them to wide rents. One of the monsters, flying too close to Skyhook's main prop, instantly disintegrated sending a razor-sharp shard of striped carapace slicing through the fuel pipe; a thin stream of oil spurted past Fin's face. Skyhook's engine spluttered, hiccupped and died.

Their mischief done, the insects swung away, and disappeared into a passing cloud.

Wrestling the joystick, Wings kept Skyhook in a shallow diving glide: all was ominously quiet, the only sound the rush of wind through the now useless propellers. Her nose dipped sharply. Gritting his teeth, Fin clung to the back of Wing's seat.

Behind him, Lark groaned: 'Gnats nadgers! gnats nadgers! It's not the falling that's painful, it'll be hitting the ground!'

'Put your heads between your knees,' Wings called, 'we're in for a bit of a bump!'

Through a rent in the canvas, Fin saw the ground rushing to meet him: crazily he wondered if ever somebody found his body, what they would make of the Chi Rho.

'Stop your wriggling, Mick,' Lark screeched, 'we're not there yet!'

With a heavy thump, they hit the ground, bounced, hit the ground again and slid to a halt. Amazed he was alive, Fin rubbed his bashed nose and looked about: they'd come down in the soft mud of the estuary.

Wings turned and grimaced at his shocked passengers. 'All in one piece, chaps?' he enquired. He patted Skyhook's battered bodywork. 'Not the first time she's had to land without her engine, that's why I gave her wings. If all else fails, she can glide. Good place to land – in mud!'

Spotting a mob of small grey figures slithering over the ooze towards them, he groaned. 'Drat, we've been spotted!' Struggling out of the cockpit, his boots sunk in the mud. 'Get off, you thieving weasels!' he shouted batting at the Scavs as they descended on Skyhook, clawing off bits of loose metal and wood. Hauling his legs over the side, Fin almost lost his boots to grabbing hands and quickly retreated to his seat.

Meanwhile, Mick, wriggling out of Lark's jerkin, and leaping over the side, landed in mud up to his belly, and began furiously snapping at any bony ankle within reach. Drawing his boning knife, from his seat Lark joined in the attack, jabbing at a couple of Scavs picking at a black solar tile on the port wing. That was enough for them. Snatching a few bits of metal, the mob quickly retreated to higher ground where like, a flock of sparrows, they cheeped excitedly as they fought over the bits and pieces they'd filched.

Tut-tutting, Wings pressed his gloved finger over the gash in the fuel pipe, trying to stem a thin stream of honey-coloured liquid. Taking off his long scarf, he wound it around the pipe, and the flow slowed to a drip, then stopped.

'That'll do for now. I need every drop of fuel I've got. There's precious little around here of the special stuff I need. As for poor Sky's torn canvas, we're not far from Scavport.' He waved towards a distant settlement. 'It's a harbour town and I'm friendly with the ships' chandler there.'

Seeing Fin and Lark's weary, mud-spattered faces, he added encouragingly: 'We'll get something to eat at Rosie's Roost. She's famous for her fish stew.' He looked up at the sky. 'Anyway, it'll be dark soon, so we can't fly again until daylight.'

'What about Skyhook?' Fin asked, 'won't the Scavs come back when we've gone? I don't mind guarding her,' he added reluctantly. The mention of fish stew had made him realise how hungry he was.

'No, Fin,' said Lark, 'if anyone should be guarding, it should be me: I can deal with those muddy tykes with my boning knife.'

'No worries on that score, chaps,' Wings said, leaning into Skyhook's cockpit to rummage under his seat.

He brought out a bundle of orange fur, some flowery material, bamboo canes, and what looked like a swede-sized metal ball with staring eyes and a toothy grinning mouth. The Delphins looked on baffled as he began to erect something that looked like a drunken monkey in a nightie. Strapping this object to the prop-shaft, he jammed the metal ball on one of the canes.

'Meet Marjorie, my anti-theft device,' he said, inserting a key in the back of the ball, and turning it several times. The ball clanked into life, and began slowly rotating, the eyes and mouth snapping open and shut. 'That'll keep the little blighters off, never known it fail.'

'Wings, your engineering skills are amazing,' Fin said, awestruck.

'Why do yer call it Marjorie?' Lark asked.

'Named her after my mother-in-law,' grinned Wings.

'You've a family? Where do they live?' Fin asked.

The pilot's pale eyes misted. 'That was another life, Fin – when I had a family. Dead now – all dead...' Turning away, he swiped his leather sleeve across his eyes.

Turning back, he gave them a rueful smile. 'Going soft in my old age! Come on chaps, get your kit and we'll go in search of fish stew!'

Retrieving their rucksacks, Fin and Lark climbed out.

Squelching through the mud, Wings leading the way, they headed for the firmer ground where a track led to the town. Coming to a collection of ramshackle dwellings on the outskirts, several Scavs came out to stare and eye Mick speculatively: covered in mud, he looked like something unidentifiable from a sewer. When some started to follow, Lark made a show of drawing his boning knife and they fell back hastily.

They found the harbour crowded with mariners of every race. Freed from the confines of their moored ships, many were heading for the taverns, intent on a night of roistering.

Lying at the mouth of the Durholmwater, Scavport is a busy place. Vessels from faraway bring all kinds of cargo: spices, rich cloths, and other exotic goods. The main trade is with the Scavs, who barter metals, plustic and glass. As well as warehouses, shops and dwellings, there are several hostelries catering for the sailors and traders, providing a livelihood for townsfolk, but also attracting petty thieves, cardsharps, and other low life.

Embarrassed by their muddy appearance, Fin and Lark kept close to Wings as he headed purposefully for the chandlers. At one point, they paused to watch a bedraggled group of Scavs who, with much squeaky shouting, were hauling a dripping net from below one of the jetties. Landing with a heavy thump, it burst open spilling out sparkling lumps of metal and glass, washed clean by the seawater.

'Get a move on chaps,' Wings called impatiently, 'I want to get to Billy Rope's before he closes!'

Hurrying past shops and warehouses, they came to a yard where several ships were being repaired, their hulls propped up on wooden blocks. Inside a barn-like building they could see coils of different thickness of rope, rolls of canvas, jumbles of netting, anchors, lobster creels, drums of tar and marine varnish.

Sitting outside on an upturned barrel was a bald, ruddy-faced man, smoking a clay pipe. He smiled a greeting to Wings before looking enquiringly at Fin, Lark and Mick.

'Billy Rope, old chap, glad you're still open,' called Wings, 'I'm in urgent need of tar and canvas. Had to make a forced landing out in the estuary. Mud all over us; anywhere we can wash?'

The man rose stiffly and, pipe still gripped in his teeth, gestured to a standpipe across the yard.

'Aye, Wings. Help yourselves at yonder tap.'

They sluiced off the worst of the mud from their legs and feet, then Lark, to Mick's noisy outrage, rinsed him under running water until his coat was white again before roughly drying him with a piece of hessian sacking.

Whilst they washed, the chandler studied Fin and Lark.

'These are my friends,' said Wings, 'they are of the Delphin race – probably a novelty to you?'

Billy shook his head, sending sparks cascading from his pipe. 'No. I've met a Delphin before. Let me see, must be twenty years past. Hungry face. Cold eyes. Gave him a berth for the night in exchange for a bit of rat catching. Amazing skill with his bow: he killed two dozen, including a brown plague rat. Went off next day. Heard later he had made friends with the Holy Ones up at Jarrow.' He pointed with his pipe to the north.

Fin's throat tightened – had he meant his father?

'Anyhow Wings, my man,' Billy continued, 'if it's tar and canvas you'll be wanting, you know better than me what you'll need for your strange contraption – have a poke round.' He nodded towards the rolls of canvas and barrels of tar inside the barn.

Wings went in to search. Full of curiosity, Lark followed, but Fin lingered outside, working up courage to speak to the chandler.

'The Delphin rat catcher, did he give his name?' he asked, holding his breath in expectation.

The old man scratched his bald head and frowned. 'Nope, didn't talk much. One thing he did say was that he was looking for a certain Rom woman, and wondered if I had seen her, this being a port. What a Delphin would want with a Rom woman, I wouldn't know.'

Sudden tears smarted Fin's eyes. He turned away to wipe them with his sleeve. 'The Delphin was known to me. He was looking for his wife, she was a Rom.'

The chandler regarded Fin thoughtfully. 'You've a bit of Rom about you too, for a Delphin lad.'

Fin didn't reply.

Wings found all he needed: a roll of stiff grey canvas and a can of black tar. Leaving them with Billy Rope, who had offered them a corner where they could snatch a night's sleep on a pile of sacks, they went in search of food.

It was dusk by the time they came to Rosie's Roost; a low wooden building near the harbour-side. The windows heavily curtained, inviting light streamed out through the open door, along with raucous laughter and pungent smells of onions and fish.

Wings ducked through the low doorway, and with Mick tucked under Lark's arm, they followed, finding themselves in a long room lit by red glass lanterns hanging from the smoke-blackened ceiling. The place was packed, the air thick with the smell of sweaty bodies: humans, Skwids and Scavs, eating and drinking, some standing, some sitting at small round tables. Behind a bow-fronted wooden bar, a scruffy, grey-scaled Skwid was filling pewter tankards from a row of barrels. Small Scav boys scurried between the tables, almost tripping over their long white aprons, carrying over their heads wooden trays laden with the foaming tankards.

Near the bar was a cooking range on which a sooty cauldron simmered. A queue waited to be served bowls of stew and hunks of dark crusty bread by a bad-tempered looking cook with red hair and a patch over one eye. Progress was slow. Payment was in mixed currency: pieces of plustic, glass or metal, each of which the cook studied carefully.

Wings pushed through the crush to the last empty table, in a corner, out of the way of curious eyes. Stowing their rucksacks beneath the table, Fin and Lark sat down, and Mick perched on his master's knee.

'I'll get some stew,' Wings said, leaving them to weave his way to the cooking range.

They waited nervously, trying to look inconspicuous, thankful that the crowd was too intent on drinking and eating to bother with them. Across the room, the cook greeted Wings with a grin and a friendly cuff on the shoulder. Ladling three bowls of stew, and cutting three hunks of bread, he abandoned his queue of customers to help Wings carry the food.

'Best stew this side of Jarrow, so eat up lads,' growled the cook, slamming down the bowls before them. Firmly refusing payment from Wings, he returned to his grumbling customers.

'Me and Carlos go back a long way – known each other since we were lads,' Wings explained as he sat down, 'Once he owned a schooner, and travelled the world. Made and lost several fortunes.' He shook his head sadly, 'who'd have thought he'd end up cooking in this dive. His food is good though, mainly foreign recipes he picked up on his travels.'

Lark peered suspiciously into his bowl; amongst the onions and carrots, were an octopus tentacle and the whole head of an ugly looking fish, all in a rich tomato sauce. Bravely, he took a mouthful. Fin and Mick watched him questioningly as he chewed thoughtfully.

'Once you get past the fish bones and chewy bits, it's very tasty,' Lark announced, returning to his bowl with more enthusiasm.

As they ate, one of the little Scav waiters arrived with three foaming mugs. 'How do, Squat,' said Wings, 'is Rosie about?'

'Putting on 'er glad-rags for t'arantula,' squeaked the Scav.

When they'd finished, Lark tipped the leftovers into a bowl, and put it under the table for Mick, who hungrily dived in with loud crunching and slurping.

Fin sat back replete, picking fish skin out of his teeth. The noise in the room had begun to die down. Eager faces now turned towards a small stage with a beaded curtain at the side. The curtain rattled and a fierce-looking, hawk-nosed young man came out, carrying a guitar, and settled on a stool at the back of the stage.

'Rosie is going to dance the Tarantella,' Wings breathed in Fin's ear.

The young man tuned his guitar, bending his ear close to his instrument, eyes closed in concentration. Satisfied, with a flourish he brushed his fingers across the strings, filling the now silent room with a spine-tingling chord. The bead curtain parted to an uproar of whistling and clapping. In a swirl of scarlet silk and black lace, a lithe, dark haired woman pirouetted onto the stage, and the guitarist struck up an insistent haunting tune. Drumming her spangled high heels on the wooden boards, and clapping her hands rhythmically, the dancer began to gyrate, slowly at first and then faster and faster. Fin watched, spellbound as her lean body bent and swayed to the fiery tempo of the music. Caught by the intensity of his gaze, the dancer twirled nearer and nearer the edge of the stage, close enough for him to smell her strong sweet perfume: he knew from her dark chocolate eyes that she was a Rom woman. As the wild rhythm slowed, so she spun slower and slower. With a last lingering note from guitar, she dropped to one knee, her breast heaving, her eyes, full of fire, fixed on his face. There was a momentary silence, then the place erupted into an uproar of whistling and stamping of boots.

As the room settled back into its normal hubbub, the dancer came and sat down, so close to Fin he could see sweat glistening on her dusky skin.

'Who are your strange companions, Wings?' she asked, studying Fin's face. 'Have you befriended the little people now?' Her voice was rich and deep.

'No, Rosie,' laughed Wings, 'these lads are Delphins from Brightdale.'

'I heard tell of a Delphin who came here, several years back, looking for a Rom woman,' Rosie said. Taking Fin by the chin, she turned his face to the light, and considered his mismatched eyes. Her touch burned Fin's skin.

She gasped. 'You have the Blood! You are not wholly Delphin!'

'My mother was a Rom.'

'How strange. You said was – is she dead?'

He shook his head. 'I don't know – she left me when I was little.'

'So, she was not a good mother, and you should forget her.' The woman's voice had taken on a cruel edge.

Unnerved, Fin suddenly felt he must escape the stuffy room. Grabbing his rucksack from under the table, he jumped up and turned to Wings. 'Can we go now. I don't know about you; I need some sleep!'

Not waiting, he pushed his way to the door, and stumbling outside, took gulps of fresh air.

He understood now why his father had abandoned the search for his mother in this place; there was no one here who could be her. A desperate longing to see Bird, to hold her tight, brought a sob to his throat. He came to a decision: in the morning, he would ask Wings to take him back to Durholm, then he would take the twins home. On the way, he would find the courage to chuck the cross into the muddy waters of Scavport.

Wrapped in their plustic sheets they spent a chilly night in the chandler's shed on sacks smelling of tar. In the morning Billy Rope brought them a breakfast of rye bread spread with pork dripping, washed down with tea, thick and sweet as treacle.

As he sipped his tea, Fin thought about his decision last night. Soul searching, he knew he couldn't abandon his mission to find a safe place for the Chi Rho: he would have to go to Holy Island. But when that was done, come what may, he'd go back to Brightdale with Bird, and ask her to go Skinny Dipping.

After thanking Billy Rope for his hospitality, they made their way through the mud back to Skyhook.

Repairs took most of the day, with Fin and Lark tarring pieces of canvas to mend the rents in the bodywork, whilst Wings repaired the leaking fuel pipe, and checked the engine for other damage. The Scav gangs kept away; Wings reckoned the magical powers of Marjorie, his anti-theft dummy scared them.

Taking a break from their work, Fin and Lark came and looked at the exposed engine.

'Are there any more flying machines like Skyhook?' Fin asked, as he peered in.

Wings nodded. 'Yep, we've made several. VTOL's are what we call them, stands for vertical take-off and landing. The props are chain-driven by technology borrowed from bicycles. The four-stroke engine runs on ethanol – refined plant spirit.'

Digesting, but not quite understanding this information, they studied the screws, rods, wires, and chunks of metal, with lengths of rubber tubing snaking in and out.

'Did you make all these parts? It looks mighty complicated stuff,' Lark asked.

'An engine like this needs expert machining. I do it in the Foundry on our Island of Mann, where my home is.'

He waved vaguely towards the west. 'Mann lies in the Irish Sea, away beyond Contagion and the Great Ice Berg.'

'What's the Great Ice Berg? I've never heard of that!' Fin exclaimed.

'Like the Withered Wood, it's a barrier, keeping Gressil's evil in, and good folk out. Some say the Gaiakins put it there, but really it has more to do with the North Pole's ice cap melting, and drifting ice bergs.'

'The Irish Sea... now there's a sea I've never heard of!' Lark said, shaking his head in wonder. 'I thought Contagion went on forever an' ever into the West!'

Wings smiled. 'I see you'll have to learn a bit of geography, young Lark. Now, enough chit-chat lads. We don't want to spend another night on those dratted sacks.'

Fin and Lark returned reluctantly to their cutting and tarring.

By late afternoon, they were ready to take off. Muddy again and aching, they clambered into their places. Mick, who'd spent the time dozing on Lark's seat, refused to get inside his master's jerkin, but sat on his knee looking up expectantly at the propeller; Lark had a feeling his intelligent dog was getting the hang of how Skyhook worked.

'All settled, lads?' Wings asked, turning to check they were seated properly.

They held their breath as he pulled and jabbed at various levers and knobs. After a couple of stutters, the engine roared into life and the propellers spun into a blur. Rising from the mud with an ominous sucking sound, her engine working hard, Skyhook slowly gained height. Swinging her around towards the sea, Wings flew a few miles out, before turning north; to their left, white flecked waves washed a wide sandy shore, and beyond lay the buildings of Scavport. Fin shivered at the thought that if Skyhook's engine failed, they would plunge into the green grey expanse of cold, deep water below, but consoled himself with the thought that it would be better than hitting hard ground.

About a quarter of an hour later, they flew over another river mouth, where another settlement, even larger than Scavport, straggled along the banks. Pointing down, Wings yelled: 'JARROW!'

Fin remembered this was where his father had found Crow wounded on the shore. He wished they could have landed, in case his mother might be there. He sighed: in his heart, he knew that had she been, his father would have brought her home.

Leaving Jarrow behind, the Scavenger settlements gradually petered out, and the coastline turned to wide, golden beaches, backed by high dunes. Behind the dunes, a vast forest stretched away into the west.

Skyhook's engine droned on. Half an hour passed. The sun now hung low on the western horizon, and it had turned cold. Despite covering their knees with blankets, the Delphins' woollen clothes let in the wind, unlike Wings' leather jacket and trousers.

Realising he was getting hungry, Fin wished he'd eaten more of Carlos's fish stew last night: all they had eaten today, apart from Billy Rope's bread and tea, were a few raisins and sunflower seeds from Lark's emergency supplies. He twisted round to look at Lark; his blanket was up to his chin; his face a sickly yellow again. Mick perched on his knee, ears flattened by the wind as he peered over the side.

The engine note changed, and Wings pointed ahead to a small island lying not far from the main shore. 'Coquet Island! We'll spend the night there,' he shouted.

Hovering over the island they saw it was about quarter of a mile wide and half a mile long, fringed by low rocky cliffs. The only flat area was occupied by a large colony of terns and as they landed clouds of the birds rose into the air, some coming dangerously close to the whirling propeller. Wings switched off the engine and easing his goggles to the top of his head, massaged his tired eyes.

Climbing out, and stretching his long body, he indicating a ruined building not far away. 'Coquet Island lighthouse – I keep a stash of emergency supplies there: fuel and food rations. Even though it's a ruin, I can promise you a reasonably comfortable night.'

Clambering down to the ground, Fin and Lark stamped life back into their stiff legs. The air smelt fresher here, with a strong tang of seaweed.

Batting off a squawking bird that had landed on his leather helmet, Wings set off for the ruined lighthouse. 'Watch out for sharp beaks' he called. 'It's the terns' nesting season, and they don't take kindly to being disturbed!'

'You're right there,' Lark growled regretting the loss of his fish-hook hat as a beak stabbed at his head. He whistled sharply to Mick, leaping up and down, barking at the birds.

Bending low, holding their rucksacks above their heads for protection, Fin and Lark ran after Wings. As they approached the lighthouse, they heard a new sound above the shrill cries of the terns. Coming to a halt, they looked at each other, eyes wide.

'Lark, can you hear waves?' Fin asked.

'Yep! Proper sea! It'll mean a chance to bathe, and get all this muck off – come on, last one in washes the socks!'

With Mick bounding ahead, they set off around the tumbled lighthouse walls and at the top of a sloping beach stood gazing in wonder at the creamy crested waves washing up the sandy shore.

Lark sighed. 'Well Fin, when we first set out, I never would've thought that I would see such a sight. Do you think Tissy will believe me when I tell her?'

Fin didn't answer, his heart too full of a half-recalled memory of the sea: a deep warm ocean where a figure swam through waving seaweed. Then, realising that Lark was already down to his underwear, quickly tucking his leather purse into a trouser pocket, he dragged off his clothes.

Hopping and skipping over the sand, they ran down to the water's edge and gasping at the cold, plunged into the waves. After they'd scrubbed off the mud and tar, their skin tingling clean, they splashed about for a bit, whilst Mick pranced up and down in the shallows, yapping shrilly. Back on the beach, drying themselves hurriedly with their grubby shirts, they pulled on fresh underwear and shirts from their rucksacks, and carrying their muddy clothes went in search of Wings.

They found him in the shell of the ruined lighthouse where in a corner a thick mattress of heather, large enough for at least four people, lay beneath a crude canvas roof stretched over a frame of bleached driftwood poles. Draping their damp clothes to dry on one of the walls, they went to help Wings who was pulling off a tarpaulin from an irregular shaped mound. Beneath were boxes of food, dry firewood, and barrels of the special fuel he used to power Skyhook.

'We'll light a fire on the beach, so we can sit and watch the waves,' Wings said. 'Collect some logs and sticks, chaps, and I'll bring the food. I'm pretty sure there's something tasty left.'

Finding a spot in the shelter of a dune, they soon got a good fire going. With the flickering flames lighting the gathering dusk, they settled down to eat. Their swim had made them hungry, and Wings' food store, though plain, felt like a banquet: there was smoked fish, hard cheese, salty biscuits, and small apples, wrinkled but sweet, harvested from last year's Leafturn, all washed down with tin mugs of fiery fruit brandy, diluted with water from a spring that bubbled up in the heather by the lighthouse.

Mick, keen to stretch his legs, had gone off to inspect the island. He returned a while later, his white chest stained yellow with egg yolk, and a large gull's egg held delicately between his jaws which he carefully put down at Lark's feet. Fondly cuffing him behind the ear, Lark sliced off the top with his boning knife and balanced the egg in the sand to cook close to the fire.

'There's enough here for a tasty mouthful each.'

'Your mutt is a gem among mutts,' smiled Wings, wiping the yolk from Mick's chest with his oil-stained scarf, leaving a greasy black mark.

When they'd eaten, they leant back against the dune and under the star crowded night sky they watched the waves sparkling white against the blackness of the restless sea. Soon, with the fruit brandy coursing through his veins, Lark's eyes closed and, chin resting on his chest, he started softly snoring.

Troubled by doubts, Fin felt wide awake. Should he have given the cross to Mother Hilda whilst they were at Durholm, instead of bringing it on what might be a wild goose chase? He thought about the huge hornets Wings had called Snoopers, that had attacked Skyhook. Had flying out of Durholm drawn the evil away?

Wings poked the dying fire with a stick, sending sparks flying up into the night. The sudden bright flare lit up his thin face, criss-crossed with scars.

'Wings, what exactly are Snoopers?' Fin asked, searching the dark sky nervously.

Wings grimaced. 'Sort of flying scouts for Gressil. When they're about, you can be sure Gressil will know what's going on. Nasty critters – yesterday wasn't the first time I've nearly been got by their vicious stings.' He pulled up the sleeve of his flying jacket, and by the firelight, showed Fin two neat round white scars, one each side of his forearm. 'Got stung here a few years ago. Went clean through. Nearly the end of me!'

Fin shuddered. 'And those bugslug creatures, did you see a lot of them making for Durholm? What with them, and the army of Frits on ganglefowl, I hope Bird and Bee got away safely!' 'Don't you worry, Fin! Sandy and his Squad can deal with those devils. Besides, I'm sure that now the piece of ironmongery you carry has gone from Durholm, the evils will not waste any more time there – that's what Zaggy was hoping.'

Not much encouraged by what Wings said, his conscience still pricking, Fin scanned the darkness, hearing the waves sighing along the shore. Could bugslugs swim in the sea? He gave a start. 'There's something coming out of the water!' he hissed, gripping Wings' arm, 'Big animals – look!'

Wings tensed and, peering at the grey forms silhouetted against the white foam, chuckled softly. 'Keep still,' he said calmly, 'and you'll see something marvellous. Don't be afraid, they're just natural sea creatures. This is their island; they come this time of year to mate. I think they're curious about our fire.'

Fin leaned close to Wings and watched as six large animals emerged from the water. On woefully inadequate flippers, they slowly hauled themselves up the sandy incline.

Disturbed by Mick's low growling, Lark stirred and, opening his eyes, froze mid-yawn. 'What the….?'

Fin put a warning hand on his knee. 'I think they're seals,' he whispered, 'I've seen pictures of them in Mossy's book on Sea Life. I didn't think they'd be so big!'

'We'll leave them to get on with breeding,' Wings whispered as he carefully dampened down the fire with sand, keeping his movements slow so as not to jinx them. 'Come on chaps, I've one more sight to show you, before we settle down for the night.'

Stars lighting the way, he led them past the lighthouse, to the flat land where they'd landed Skyhook in the tern colony. The birds had settled down to roost, the night filled with their soft cheeps and squeaks; Skyhook stood above them, outlined against the starry sky, her freshly tarred patches standing out dark against her old canvas.

At a cliff edge, they stood, awestruck, gazing to the mainland where a rainbow dome of lights shimmered above the dark forest.

Wings spread his arms wide. 'The Garden of Florain – the home of the Gaiakins.' He looked down at Fin. 'The evils will have to get past that place of powerful goodness before they can get to us here.'

'Is that where Fescue and Mullein come from?' Lark asked.

Wings nodded. 'Yep, it's there that they craft their beautiful objects of silver and gold.'

Fin recalled Mossy's story of the two Gaiakins who had created the jewelled crosses, thousands of years ago, in a far-off jungle land; it seemed that with Fescue and Mullein the art lived on.

'Florain is also where Sandy's mother lives,' Wings added as a throwaway remark.

Lark chortled. 'I can't imagine Sandy having an ordinary mum!'

Wings grinned. 'Queen Ailis isn't ordinary! Anyway, no more chatting, it's time we got some shuteye: we must take off at first light. I don't know about you chaps, but I'll be glad to get to Holy Island.'

'Can't we fly to Florain first?' Lark asked, hoping to see the famous gardens so he could tell Tissy.

Wings sighed. 'O.K. then, tomorrow we'll fly over on a quick detour before we head north.'

Reluctantly turning away, they followed him back to the lighthouse, where their heather bed awaited.

Instantly falling asleep, Lark dreamed of graceful Gaiakin folk with shining hair, dressed in long flowing clothes, dancing sedately amongst flowerbeds dazzling with an array of scarlet roses, orange marigolds and deep blue delphiniums.

As Fin dozed off, his thoughts turned to Bird. He hoped Wings was right, and that the twins were with Mother Hilda, safely on their way to Holy Island. Or better still, on their way home to Brightdale, where their mother, Sable, would give them a good telling off, before their dad dealt with them. Snuggling deeper into his blanket, he felt his purse pressed against his chest. Careful not to disturb Lark and Wings, he sought out Bird's little chain. As the delicate links ran through his fingers sleep slowly carried him off into a dream.

He was in a cold murky sea, struggling to stay afloat, pale light all around him. Just as he thought he must drown, sinking, choking water filling his lungs, a hand caught him by his arm and pulled him to the surface. Coughing up salty water, he found above him a small rowing boat gently rocking. A woman was leaning over the side, long white hair tumbling from the deep hood of her brown robe. As she helped him clamber in, he saw her hands were rough and gnarled with heavy use. Sitting on the boat's wood-ribbed bottom, he stared at her. There was something familiar about her dark eyes.

'Who are you?' he gasped.

'Do you not know me, Fin?' She sounded sad.     Hope bubbled up inside him. 'Mother?' he whispered.

She held out her arms to him, but before he could scramble to her, his eyes snapped open. Pushing away his blanket smothering his face, he sat up. The sound of waves reminded him he was on Coquet Island. Bird's pendant chain was wrapped around his fingers. Tucking it back into his purse, he buried himself deeper into the heather mattress.

'Drank too much of Wings' booze,' he grinned to himself.

He was drifting off again when he sat up in alarm: the Dandrum sword! The night before, he'd left his rucksack unguarded in Billy Rope's shed: he knew he wouldn't sleep until he'd checked if the sword was still safe inside. Careful not to disturb Lark and Wings, he slipped from under his blanket. Mick looked up from where he lay in the crook of Lark's arm, and assuming Fin was going to cock his leg, snuggled back down.

Ducking out from under the shelter, Fin stood up. Above him, pale ragged clouds scudded across the star-studded sky. Shouldering his rucksack, he struck out for the headland where they had watched the lights of the garden of Florain. Following the silvery ribbon of the path, he passed Skyhook, her rotor blades lazily turning in the breeze; from all around came the low chatter of roosting terns. At the cliff, he gazed across the black water to the dome of light still pulsing above Florain. Below him, the waves gurgled and slapped against the rocks, their salty tang stirring his blood, as if they were tempting him to dive in and lose himself in their cold depths.

Settling on a patch of thyme, he delved into his rucksack. The sword was still there, within the folds of a spare shirt. On impulse, he drew it from its pearl-encrusted sheath and held it above his head. Watching the coloured lights from Florain shimmering up and down the highly polished steel blade, awe filled him. Should he have brought the sword with him? Or should he have left it in Mossy's care? He wasn't a warrior like Kenji or Sandy, nor ever likely to be. What use would he have for it? Nevertheless, he was now Dandrum Head, it was his by right to use it as he wished.

The trouble was, he didn't feel like he imagined a Head should feel; he was far from Brightdale, and the way was free for his Uncle Roach to take over. All because of the Chi Rho. With a surge of hate, he thought of what the cross had done to him and his father. He should get rid of it now. But how? Throw the malevolent thing into the sea? Let the ocean currents take it away – for Gressil to scurry after it? Wasn't he a sea monster? Let him go back into the sea, leaving the Delphin people in peace, and Brightdale safe.

Dragging his purse over his head, he pulled out the cross. Going to the cliff edge, and stretching out his arm, he let it dangle above the water: it was as if the waves were reaching up, wet fingers pleading. He couldn't do it, he couldn't let go. He staggered back, letting the cross fall from his grasp. Bouncing off into a patch of scrub, he averted his gaze from where it lay, glittering invitingly. Sitting down, he stared miserably towards Florain. Gradually heavy sleep overcame him, and he fell forward, his face buried in the thyme. The Dandrum sword lay unsheathed at his side.

Wings woke at first light and was instantly alert. He saw Lark and Mick sleeping soundly beneath their blanket, but there was an empty hollow in the heather where Fin had lain. Pulling on his trousers and flying jacket, he set out to search the island.

He found Fin, asleep on the headland. Spotting the richly decorated sword lying by his side, he frowned. Then a glint in the nearby scrub caught his eye.

'By all that's Holy!' he gasped, picking up the cross. Dangling the cross in front of his face, he gaze into the great crystal in the centre of the cross-piece.

His exclamation had woken Fin.

'No! Don't touch it. Give it to me.' Angrily springing to his fee, Fin snatched the cross from him, and savagely pushed it into his purse. At the sight of Wings' troubled expression, he slumped to his knees, his face in his hands. 'I'm sorry, Wings,' he groaned, 'I was trying to throw it into the sea, but just couldn't.'

'No worries young chap,' Wings said, his voice kind as he ruffled Fin's tangle of dark hair. 'Take the advice of an old airman – admittedly with no experience in the disposing of fancy crosses – you shouldn't leave it lying about for all and sundry to pinch.'

With a mirthless grin, Fin re-sheathed the sword, and returned it to his rucksack.

From behind the dunes came insistent yapping, and Mick shot into view, closely followed by Lark.

'There you are!' Lark called indignantly, 'Have I missed breakfast?' His eyes narrowed in suspicion when he saw Fin's drawn face, and Wings' wan smile.

'No, we haven't eaten yet,' Wings said, 'we'll grab a quick bite before refuelling Skyhook – we must get a move on if we're making a detour over Florain.'

They breakfasted on hunks of dry bread and smoked fish, washed down with spring water. When they'd eaten, Wings left Lark and Fin to tidy the camp, whilst he staggered off with a heavy can of fuel to fill Skyhook's tank. A short time later, rucksacks stowed, they climbed into their seats. Lark looked on proudly as Mick leapt nimbly up on to a wing, and then on to his lap.

Snapping on his goggles, Wings pressed the starter, and after a few coughing grunts, Skyhook roared into life, sending up clouds of indignant terns as she rose into the air.

Crossing the short stretch of sea to the mainland, Wings turned north, flying along a beach of golden sands, fringed by high dunes. A short while later they came to a river mouth, where on the southern bank stood the remains of a ruined castle. Below lay a harbour where a few fishing boats and sailing ships were moored along the stone jetty. A road ran from the harbour. Following the course of the river and bordered by fields of sunflowers, their yellow faces turned towards the sun, the road headed for the distant the roofs of another castle. As they drew near, Fin and Lark saw that this one was complete, the high white stucco walls and terracotta roof tiles gleaming in the rising sun. A moat covered with bright green duck weed surrounded the castle on three sides. Spanning the moat was an arched bridge leading to tall gates, shining so brilliantly they knew they must be made of gold.

Starting from one side of the moat, a high yew hedge curved out of sight into the distance, before circling around and reappearing to join the moat on the castle's other side. The hedge enclosed the garden of Florain.

Pushing the joystick forward, Wings dropped Skyhook lower, and they began a slow zigzag flight over the garden, which they discovered was a patchwork of different styles, each of immense size.

First came the formal garden with paths of smooth mown grass, winding between gaudy-hued herbaceous borders, leading to pergolas and gazebos, and where hammocks swayed invitingly in the breeze. Then came the woodland garden, where tomtits, chaffinches, blackbirds, and thrushes darted among the tall branches of beech, elm, oak and ash, so busy making nests, they appeared unconcerned by the roar of Skyhook's engine. Next the green gloom of a jungle garden rose toward them. Skyhook's wheels skimming the tops of trees of awesome height, they saw butterflies and dragonflies of enormous size lazily dancing in and out of orchids decking the draping lianas. A wooden walkway, swinging from ropes in the branches, wound a way just beneath the tree canopy. Leaving the jungle behind, they came to an alpine garden, its lush meadows spangled, red, blue, and yellow with alpine flowers, and where, to their disbelief, they spied patches of unmelted snow beneath rocky outcrops. Finally, they came to a desert garden, where tall cactuses growing out of the baking sand pointed their prickly fingers to a hot sky, and where hummingbirds hovered, sipping nectar from the trumpets of the cactus' gaudy flowers. Flying over a last lonely cactus, the yew hedge rose in front of them and beyond, in the outside world, the great forest stretched into the distance.

Swinging back towards the red roofs of the castle, Wings took them over a lake fringed with willows, its surface a carpet of lily pads, dotted with scarlet, yellow and white blooms. A wooden jetty jutted over the water where, stirred by the downdraught of Skyhook's propellers, a flotilla of small boats bobbed up and down. Fin recalled his dream at Stonetree: swimming in a lily covered lake, and Fescue standing on a jetty, waving to him, calling him to wake up.

At the castle they turned east, heading once more for the coast. As they passed over a walled vegetable garden, Lark narrowed his eyes to peer down at the neat rows of leafy greens, recognising cabbages, carrots, peas, runner beans, and beets. Then, as they flew over an orchard, spotting splashes of reds and golds among the frothy blossom, he blinked in amazement – surely those weren't fruits growing amongst the blossom-laden branches?

He had no more time to wonder as passing over the yew hedge, they saw in its shadow a long low brick building with a column of black smoke rising from a tall chimney.

Wings gesticulated down. 'The Gaiakin workshops,' he called, 'where they make their famous jewellery.'

Thinking of the exquisite gold and silverware the Gaiakins brought to Watersmeet market, Lark wished they could have landed to look inside.

Pulling back on the joystick, Wings took Skyhook higher and headed for the sea.

# 12
# INVASION

On the cliff path, the twins watched Skyhook vanish into the pale horizon.

Bee sighed. 'Well, that's that. Fin's gone again – after all our efforts to catch up with him!'

Unhappiness rolled over Bird: how she wished she could have gone in Lark's place! But she knew she could never abandon Bee – Lark would never have agreed anyway. She grabbed her sister's hand. 'Come on Bee, let's go and see what's in store for us.'

Whistling to Wolfie, they ran through the vegetable garden to where Sandy, Mother Hilda and Dancer waited by the refectory steps.

'Is it far to Holy Island?' Bird asked them.

'It's a day's ride to Scavport, and another day by sea to Holy Island – depending on tide and weather,' Hilda said.

Seeing their dismay, Sandy smiled. 'Have you never been in a boat?'

They shook their heads. 'We haven't even seen the sea, let alone sailed on it!' exclaimed Bee.

'It is to be hoped you have strong stomachs,' Hilda said, 'this time of year, the North Sea can be rough.'

Bird shuddered. 'When will Fin and Lark reach Holy Island?'

'If all goes well, and they don't have engine trouble, they should arrive by this evening,' Sandy said.

'Has Wings' machine ever crashed?' Bird asked in alarm.

'He has had a few mishaps, but as you have seen, he is alive, and reasonably whole.'

'I'd rather plod all the way on a donkey, than risk flying in that roaring contraption,' Bee muttered.

Hilda laughed. 'You'll find our ponies a little more willing than stubborn donkeys! But hurry now – enough chatter, go to the dormitory and collect your things.'

Sandy left them to search out the other Trekker Squads at the cathedral.

As Dancer and the twins headed for the dormitory, Hilda called to them: 'When you've packed, meet me at my lodgings.'

Their meagre packing soon done, the twins slung their crossbows over their shoulders and strapped their arrow quivers to their belts. Observing approvingly, Dancer tested her sword, swiftly drawing it in and out of its scabbard. Whistling to Wolfie, they hurried downstairs.

Crossing the garth to where Mother Hilda was waiting at her door, they spotted Fescue and Mullein looking in through the bars of the lock-up window.

From inside, Hardwick's voice screeched: 'Curse you, you traitorous Gaiakins!' His walking stick suddenly poked through the bars, catching Mullein a vicious jab in the ribs.

'Quickly now, follow me,' Hilda called, picking up her small canvas bag. Following her along a narrow passageway, they headed for the square. From ahead came sounds of shouting and hammering, and a scared looking man with a long plank on his shoulder shot past them, nearly knocking them down.

In the square, they found a frenzy of activity: mothers, some with babes in arms, crying children clinging to their skirts, were frantically filling boxes and bags, their menfolk piling them onto already heavily laden handcarts. More men were nailing planks over windows and doors. At the square's far end, desperate to escape, a crowd laden with sacks and bags were pushing their way into the tunnel leading to the drawbridge; for some unseen reason, their way was blocked by others struggling to get back in, their faces contorted with fear.

'We must find out what is going on!' Hilda called. 'Keep close!'

Fighting a way through the crowd to the tunnel entrance, Hilda and Dancer peered over the heads. They saw that the portcullis had been lowered.

'As I had dreaded,' Hilda cried, 'we are too late! The bugslugs are upon us!'

'Maabella's Babes?' wailed Bird and Bee in unison, their small terrified voices lost in the bedlam of screams and shouts.

Jumping up, they tried to see. Helped by Dancer to scramble onto a mounting block jutting from the tunnel wall, a horrific scene met them: swarming up the portcullis were the weirdest creatures – grey things, slimy like slugs but the size of fully-grown pigs. There were at least six of them. Through the bars they saw hundreds more crawling up the battlement walls, snot-like saliva oozing from their mouths, gluing them to the smooth surface as they attacked the stonework, their rasping teeth scraping out the mortar, sending great blocks crashing into the river.

'Look!' screamed Dancer, pointing across the drawbridge to the river path. 'The Frit army has arrived!'

Glimpsing bobbing ganglefowl heads, the twins remembered the imp-like creature mounted on a long-legged bird they had encountered back in Brightdale.

Crowding onto the drawbridge, the Frits leapt from their saddles to clamber up the ramparts, sharp metal fingers and feet digging into the bugslugs' slimy backs. From above, the defending warriors let loose volley after volley of arrows, fighting bravely, but the enemy was too numerous; the Frits quickly overwhelmed them, slicing and slashing with their razor teeth, sending bodies tumbling, some into the river, some smashing onto the cobbles in the square, blood spraying over people scrambling out of the way.

'Back to the cloisters,' Hilda shouted, 'we can escape through the refectory, onto the cliff path!'

Climbing down from the mounting block and clinging to Dancer they struggled after Hilda purposefully pushing her way through the melee. Suddenly from behind came a loud crash; they realised the portcullis, loosened by the bugslugs, had fallen.

At the passageway leading to the cloisters they turned to see charging out of the tunnel, a squad of Frits mounted on ganglefowl. The squad was led by a pale-skinned, cruel-faced man on a huge liver-coloured horse, its hooves mercilessly trampling on anyone unfortunate enough to be in its path.

Hilda groaned. 'The horseman must be a Sneaksoul, like Hardwick!'

Brandishing her sword, Dancer would have tried to get to him, but Mother Hilda dragged her back.

'Have a care, Dancer! You'll put the lasses in danger!'

They ran into the passage, away from the dreadful scene.

Back in the cloisters, they were too late: bugslugs were swarming on the kitchen and dormitory roofs, tearing out slates. The air filled with choking dust, heavy roof beams and ceilings came crashing down, crushing everything beneath: beds, tables, benches. There was no sign of Grantly, his cooking range mangled beneath a huge oak beam, the kitchen chimney, open to the sky, billowing black smoke.

Hilda stood for a moment nonplussed, before coming to a decision. 'We will go through the cathedral, and down the cliff path to the jetty – if all the boats have gone, we'll have to swim across!'

Hitching up the hem of her robe into her rope belt, she started climbing over fallen masonry towards the south door.

The others were about to follow when Bee let out a wail. 'Wolfie! Where's Wolfie?'

'Dancer, we can't leave him!' Bird cried, pulling on the Skwid's arm.

'There's no time to look for him!' Dancer yelled, dragging them sobbing after Mother Hilda.

Scrambling over the rubble, stonework crashing all around them, they finally reached the cathedral's south door, now hanging loosely from its hinges. Bruised and covered in dust, they stood aghast at the scene within.

A savage battle raged up and down the nave and side aisles. Frits on ganglefowl were locked in combat with defending warriors, Trekkers, and younger members of the Holy Community. The high vault echoed with the clash of weapons mingling with screams of agony, the tiled floor slippery with slicks of blood and littered with wires, screws, and other Frit parts. Clouds of stinging ganglefowl feathers, landing on bare flesh, were sending their victims rushing about, crazed with pain. Among the Frits they saw the Sneaksoul who had invaded the square on his liver-coloured charger.

Sandy and his Squad were in the thick of the turmoil. It was as if they were a single fighting machine; Kenji in the vanguard, his long blade scything through the forest of ganglefowl legs; Sandy following, his sword slashing left and right, inflicting appalling injuries on any that Kenji had missed. In their wake came Fescue who, his broken sword still with the smithy, had drawn his dagger, and was stabbing and slicing, his golden eyes ablaze with angry fire.

Grabbing Dancer by the arm, Hilda shouted in her ear: 'Go to the pigeon loft! Release them all – their mass arrival on Holy Island will raise the alarm – take the lasses with you – I must stay with my suffering Community!'

With that, she pulled a vicious looking knife from beneath her robe and, taking a deep breath, plunged into the tumult.

Dancer and the twins had no choice; they headed for the bell tower, speeding up the steps two at a time.

In the loft, the noise of battle from below made the great bell vibrate as if crying out in pain. Running from cage to cage, they released the pigeons, shooing them out until the last bird had flown. Climbing onto the cages to look down into the square, they saw just a few people remained, slumped on the blood-stained cobbles amongst the battered bodies of the dead. The only activity was a small group of Frits gathered round a familiar brown robed figure, waving his arms about, giving instructions.

'Hardwick!' Dancer hissed, 'the Frits must have freed him from the lock-up.'

Bee let out a quivering sob. 'Lark was right, we shouldn't have come on this jaunt – I can just hear mum and dad now, saying: "Bee my girl, we always knew you'd come to a bad end!"'

'I wish I knew what happened to Wolfie,' Bird choked, 'the old hound just came along to look after us, when he could've stayed at home by the fire.'

They both burst into tears.

But Dancer didn't notice, her attention was fixed on Hardwick and the Frits. Alerted by the clatter of the pigeons' wings, their faces were turned up to the tower; one of the Frits had a small arrow stuck in its forehead.

'We must get away from here,' she muttered, pulling the twins down from the top of their cage.

Even as they headed for the door, from the west opening of the tower came an angry thrumming. A vinegary stink filled the loft. Thud, a huge wasp-like insect landed on the ledge. They watched, frozen in terror, as it squeezed its fat black and yellow body inside. It was followed by another, then another. Rising into the roof space, papery wings whirring, the monsters hovered there, glaring down at them, scimitar-like teeth snapping.

In desperate fury, Dancer drew her sword and slashing wildly at the dangling legs, lopped several off. The angry buzzing changed to a high-pitched screaming whine.

Ping ... ping ... ping ... long skewer stings came shooting out of striped backsides. Ping ... ping ... ping ... stings peppered Dancer's face, arms, and legs. Her precious sword fell from her grasp and clattered to the floor. Plucking feebly at the stings, in her agony she staggered dangerously close to the edge of the hole beneath the great bell. Rushing to her, the twins snatched at her belt and using every ounce of their slight strength, feet scrabbling across the floorboards, slowly dragged her away. Dancer collapsed.

Crouching protectively in front of her, the twins unslung their crossbows from their shoulders, swiftly loaded, took aim, and fired. Time after time they shot, emptying their quivers, but their darts bounced harmlessly off the insects' hard carapaces.

With a last triumphant hum, the monsters turned about. Squeezing out one after another through the eastern opening, they disappeared into the blue.

Kneeling by Dancer, Bird and Bee dabbed vainly with their sleeves at the blue Skwid blood seeping from the sting wounds in her face, arms, and legs. Weakly, she pushed them away.

'Leave me – run!' she choked, her face so swollen she struggled to breathe.

'We can't leave you, Dancer,' whimpered Bird.

'No, no, you must get away from here! I am safe now – they have done their work. It is you lasses who are in danger.'

'We'll get help, Dancer, as quick as we can,' sobbed Bee, pulling off her jerkin, and tucking it beneath Dancer's head.

Snatching up their rucksacks, they headed for the stairs.

They were too late: their way was blocked. A dozen or so Frits crowded through the doorway. Sick with fear, Bird recognized her dart sticking out of a Frit's brow: it was the Frit she'd shot back in Brightdale; its head had been reattached by a couple of screws in its wiry, sinewy neck.

Razor teeth clacking, tinny voices humming, the group jabbed, kicked, and punched them down the stairs. Scraping the rough stone walls, losing their rucksacks on the way, they landed at the bottom battered and stunned. Their captors gave them no chance to run. Hauled brutally over the rubble to the lock-up, they were flung inside. Slamming the door and triumphantly shooting home the bolts, the Frits scuttled off, their metallic chatter fading away.

Head spinning, Bird sat up and gingerly probed her side. Feeling a sharp pain, she knew she'd cracked a rib. Eyes smarting from the stench of urine-soaked floor rushes, she peered around the small cell. The only light came in through a square barred opening set in the thick door. Distant cries and the clash of weapons could be heard from the battle in the cathedral. Immediately outside, everything seemed quiet; the bugslugs had finished their destruction.

In the gloom, she made out Bee, her face buried in the stinking rushes. Wincing from the pain in her side, she crawled over to her.

'Bee, are you O.K.?' Turning her over, and pushing back her soft pale green hair, she saw her face was contorted in pain.

'I think my arm's broken,' Bee groaned. Her arm lay at her side oddly twisted and swollen.

Searching her pockets, Bird found her jar of marigold ointment, but it had smashed to pieces, the ointment full of glass fragments. 'Have you still got your marigold, Bee?'

Bee shook her head. 'It was in my jerkin I put under Dancer's head.' She burst into tears. 'Poor Dancer! I hope she doesn't die!'

Bird tried to think. She'd nothing to bind the broken arm with; their rucksacks and crossbows were lost; all they had were the clothes they were wearing. The Frit with her arrow in its forehead had even seized their plaited leather headbands, tying them over his disgusting orange wig; it seemed a lifetime since she'd plaited those bands in Grammer Nutmeg's attic room.

Trying not to burst into useless tears, she searched through the rushes for something to use as a splint. Her hand came upon a knobbly stick; by the light from the door, she realised it was Brother Hardwick's; he must have left it behind when he was rescued by his Frit servants. It was longer than she would have liked, but it would have to do. Picking out some of the least smelly rush leaves, as gently as she could, she bound Bee's broken arm to the stick which protruded a good foot beyond Bee's hand but held the arm firm. Tying off the last ends of rush, she sat back, pleased with her work. Seeing Bee's eyes closed, she wasn't sure if she'd fainted or fallen asleep.

After a while Bee's dark lashes fluttered and her eyes opened. 'Well sis, we're in an even worse pickle now!' Grimacing with pain, she struggled to sit up.

'At least we managed to free the pigeons. Surely, they'll raise the alarm, and someone will come to our help?' Bird said, without much hope.

As she spoke, she heard scratching at the door, followed by a whimper. Joyfully, she scrambled to the small, barred window. Wolfie's face met hers, and his rough tongue shooting in through the bars gave her sore eyes a welcome lick.

'It's Wolfie!' Squeezing her hands through the bars, she ruffled his ears.

Bee staggered to her feet, and dragging Hardwick's stick behind her, came to greet Wolfie. 'Bird, do you think we could send him home with a message of some sort?'

'We could try!' Bird's face clouded. 'But we haven't anything to write on.'

'What about a piece of flat rush: it needn't be a long message, just "Help! love Bee and Bird."' Hampered by the stick, Bee tried to search for a suitable leaf, but overcome by pain she slumped down with a groan.

'I'll look,' Bird said, helping Bee lie down. Squinting in, his head on one side whimpering agitatedly, Wolfie watched her as she searched. 'Stay, boy, stay!' Bird called sternly.

She found a suitably smooth and clean piece of dry leaf, but her hopes were dashed: she had no pen or ink. An idea came to her. Hunting around again she found a strong thin stalk, and taking a deep breath, stabbed it hard into her palm, drawing blood and making Bee wince in sympathy.

'Well, I've got parchment, pen and ink now!' Bird said grimly. 'Who should we send the message to?'

'Wolfie would go to Mossy, wouldn't he?'

'Of course. We'll write the message in a code only Mossy can understand!'

Braving the soreness, Bird dipped the stick into her bleeding palm, and in wobbly lettering, wrote the following: "Dear M – D.G. invaded. Captured by Frits. Help, Bee and Bird." She dipped the stick once again into her wound, and added a P.S.: "F escaped with the C."

When she'd finished, she sat licking her sore palm, thinking – she'd yet another problem: Wolfie didn't have a collar to tie the message to. She searched for some long rush strands to tie around his neck. Wolfie peered in through the bars, panting heavily and yelping impatiently.

'Alright, Wolfie, I'm doing my best,' she called as she rummaged. Then, to Bee's surprise, she giggled. 'Well, luck must be on our side – look what I've found!' She held up a glittering gold chain strung with ivory beads, and a small gold cross hanging from it.

Bee grinned weakly. 'That belonged to Hardwick – I noticed it around his neck. Dancer told me they're called rosary prayer beads – he must've given up praying!'

With strips of rush, Bird deftly bound her message to the chain of beads, making the outer packet thick, to keep the message dry. With difficulty, she passed the rosary chain through the bars and over Wolfie's head and smiled fondly as he squinted down cross-eyed at the gold cross resting on his furry chest. 'Don't you try and scratch it off, Wolfie,' she said tapping him smartly on the nose. 'Now off you go. Seek Mossy! Seek Mossy!'

At first, he didn't seem to understand, and scratched at the door looking puzzled. After a few moments, his face disappeared from the window. With a lump in her throat, Bird waited in case he returned. When, after some time, there was no sign of him, she came and sat next to Bee, feeling very mournful.

'Poor old Wolfie, I hope he gets home safely, even if the message falls off.'

'He's our carrier-pigeon hound,' Bee said, attempting a joke through her pain.

'I wish he could fly like a pigeon,' sighed Bird.

The thought of flying, reminded her of Fin. She would give anything to see his strangely bewitching eyes once more: one a cold green, like his dad's, the other dark brown and full of fire. Wistfully, she wondered if he was thinking of her as he flew high in the clouds. She hoped he'd keep her pendant safe, a reminder of her, even if they never saw each other again. Thinking of her silver pendant brought back the memory of the day her Uncle Josh had made the small bird in the Spinner forge, melting down a silver goblet. He'd also made a bee pendant for Bee. She longed desperately to be back there, at the forge in Watersmeet.

She hadn't long to wallow in misery; from outside the door came a harsh voice. The bolts rattled, and the door flew back to reveal Brother Hardwick, his Frit gang crowded around him. What Bird thought of as her Frit, was studying her with a greedy gleam in his camera-lens eyes, his bloodied metal teeth grinning between slavering rubber lips. Her leather headband with its feathers draped about his head, looked like bedraggled earrings.

Brother Hardwick started back. 'What's this?' he shrieked, turning angrily to Bird's Frit, 'Stupid fool Slicer you've got the wrong Delphins. I told you to catch the half-breed and his servant – these females are no good to me!'

About to hobble away dismissively, he stopped, and turned back.

Eyeing Bird and Bee speculatively, he sneered. 'Yet perhaps I could have a use for them.'

Rubbing his hands, a sinister green gleam in his eyes as a plan evolved in his mind. His Sneaksoul voice took on an even crueller edge.

'Yeess, they could serve as hostages. We'll take them with us and lure the arrogant young Delphin into my clutches.'

'And when you've finished with 'em boss, these tasty morsels will cheer up the lads at Birdoswald,' drooled Slicer's humming voice box.

Leaping forward, he grabbed Bee's broken arm, making her cry out in pain.

Enraged, Bird lunged at him, twisting the arrow sticking out of his forehead. 'I hope that gives you the mother of all migraines!' she screamed.

Slicer yanked his head back, and the arrow came away in Bird's hand; snatching it from her, he broke it in half.

'Cease mucking about, Slicer!' snarled Hardwick, 'get your lads to tie up these irritating fleas – bind them well, we don't want them escaping and alerting their friends in the cathedral. Secrecy is vital, or you'll all regret it!'

'Count on me, Master Beliaal, sir. I'll see the lads do a good job – my old Master Raaum would've vouched for me, if that black-skinned angel hadn't driven him out of the ratty little Delphin called Roach!'

At his command, his fellow Frits, whipping out wire flex from their backpacks, trussed the twins' wrists and ankles tight.

'You two, go to the river and find a boat,' Hardwick said, shoving a couple of them out of the lock-up. 'Wait for us at the base of the cliff – the rest of you carry our captives. Go through the refectory – or what's left of it,' he added with a smirk.

'Come on lads,' called Slicer, keen to demonstrate his authority as he grabbed Bird by the feet.

'Not so fast, Master Slicer!' Hardwick said, catching hold of him by his nylon toupee. 'I've another job for you! I need you to pass on a message – stand still!'

With lightning speed, Hardwick spun the screws in Slicer's neck and yanked his head free. His fellow Frits laughed derisively as the now headless body, crashing against the door posts, pirouetted out of the lock-up to collapse in a heap of nuts and bolts.

Hardwick turned on the sniggering mob. 'Get a move on, runts! Take the Delphins to the cliff!'

The Frits hurriedly lifted the twins and scrambled off over the ruins. Out on the cliff path, they secured two long ropes to a fence post. Tying the other ends to the twins' waists, they heaved them over the bramble hedge, dropping them down the cliff to where the two Frits waited in a rowing boat.

Back in the lock-up, Hardwick delved inside Slicer's head. After a few more adjustments, Slicer's lips started to move, and his voice box sparked into droning life. Hardwick muttered instructions into the head, closed the lid and carefully replaced the orange toupee. Kicking up some floor rushes into a mound, he placed the head strategically on top, Bird's feather and leather headband draped over the blank eye lenses.

Satisfied, he hurried to join the Frits on the cliff top, and clambering down one of the ropes, landed clumsily in the boat, rocking it alarmingly. He glared up at the Frits peering down.

'If I hear you've been talking about what's happened here, you'll end up like your friend: headless,' he roared. The Frit faces instantly disappeared. Grumbling, Hardwick settled in the wobbling prow and the rowers set off.

On the far bank, more Frits waited with their ganglefowl, and the liver-coloured horse for Hardwick. The almost unconscious twins were heaved out of the boat, slung over the backs of two ganglefowl, and with Hardwick riding ahead, the party set off along the river path.

By dawn the next day the battle of Durholm was finally over. Rusty bugles blaring, the Frit force left as they had come, their ganglefowl jostling through the tunnel, over the fallen portcullis, and out over the drawbridge, to ride away along the river path, their raucous victory chants fading raggedly into the distance. Just beyond Stonetree, the army divided, most continuing along the path to Killhope Gate, where a deep tunnel wound for many miles, back to their H.Q. in the land of Contagion. A smaller group took a hidden path, north-west into the forest, to their garrison at Birdoswald. Exhausted by their destructive work, the bugslugs, surfing along the river, headed back to Maabella their loathsome slug mother.

In the cathedral, weary and dejected, Sandy and his Squad sat amidst the filth of battle: ganglefowl body parts muddled with the wreckage of dismembered Frits. Soft white feathers, swirling like snowflakes, still drifting in the air, landed on the congealed mess of blood and Frit oil. Clearing up had already begun. Sandy watched, pity mixed with admiration as humans, Gaiakins and Skwids, young and old, set to work with broom and shovel, determined their sacred building be cleansed and restored.

The sanatorium in ruins, a temporary hospital had been set up in the Chapter House. From there the goodwife and her stretcher bearers searched for the wounded, whilst grim-faced Trekker Warriors despatched any stricken Frit or ganglefowl still alive. Amongst the fallen they found the body of the pale-skinned, cruel-faced rider, possessed by a Sneaksoul, who had led the Frit attack. The foul emanation had reverted to Phragg form and fled his borrowed body, streaking away to its lair deep in the Doomstone Mines. The body was reverently laid out before the High Altar, along with the dead who had given their lives defending Durholm. No one had found Brother Hardwick's body.

Fescue, the fire of battle fading from his golden eyes, shook his head sadly as he surveyed the scene of destruction. 'It was an evil hour when the Chi Rho came to Durholm!'

Wiping his bloodstained face with his sleeve, Sandy nodded sorrowfully. 'Evil indeed. But at least we have the consolation that this destruction was not in vain – the cross is safe. It would have been even more disastrous if Lord Gressil's servants had seized it.'

'It is no consolation to the poor butchered bodies lying about us!' Kenji muttered savagely as he carefully cleaned corrosive Frits' juice from his sword. His embroidered padded clothes were torn in places, and his bare arms were livid red from ganglefowl feather stings.

Mother Hilda's commanding voice rose above the noise, giving instructions to the workers, and bringing encouragement to her flock. Spotting Sandy and his companions, she limped over.

'Are any of you in need of medical treatment?'

Looking with concern at Fescue who had a deep gash across his forehead, she took a bandage from the pocket in her robe and made to wind it around his head.

Fescue pushed her away. 'There are many with worse injuries than mine, Mother,' he snapped.

Sandy looked worriedly at the Gaiakin. 'Fescue, go and find Mullein. He will be glad to know that you are safe, just as I am sure you want to know how he has fared!'

Watching Fescue loping towards the north portal, shoulders bowed, Sandy remembered Zagzagel's warning that Fescue's relationship to the Chi Rho went deeper than many knew.

His thoughts were interrupted by Mother Hilda. 'Where are Dancer and the Delphin lasses? I sent them to the pigeon loft during the fighting. Could they still be hiding up there?'

Sandy groaned. 'May Zagzagel forgive me! I had forgotten them. Quickly, we must see if they are still there.'

Running to the bell tower, they found Dancer lying unconscious in a pool of blue blood at the foot of the steps, her twisted sword by her side. A trail of bloody footprints on the steps were witness to her brave efforts to follow the twins, who were nowhere to be seen.

'From her wounds, I fear she was attacked by Snoopers!' muttered Sandy grimly.

Gently lifting her into his arms he strode towards the Chapter House.

Here, they found the injured had been laid on straw bales, and the weary goodwife trying to bring comfort with the few resources she had salvaged from her ruined dispensary.

Showing where they could lay Dancer, she shook her head in consternation. 'Surely this is the young female Skwid who came with the little Delphin folk? Where are they now?'

Before they could reply, she was called away as more wounded were brought in, many of whom were children and old folk who had been caught up in the Frit and bugslug invasion in the square.

Mother Hilda took charge of Dancer, gently extracting the stings Dancer had not managed to pull out herself, staunching the bleeding with the goodwife's cloths, then dressing them with ointment from her own pack.

'She is lucky to have survived such an attack by Gressil's Snoopers,' she said to Sandy as he knelt beside Dancer, bathing her colourless face with cool water.

Deeply worried, Sandy said: 'I wonder if those were the Snoopers Wings saw when he flew here from Brightdale? I dread to think where they are now!'

Dancer groaned, slowly coming out of her deep swoon. 'The twins!' she mumbled, struggling to sit up.

'Be still, Dancer,' said Sandy, firmly holding her down by her shoulders, 'you have lost much blood.'

She plucked at his sleeve agitatedly. 'Have you found the Delphin lasses? A gang of Frit came to the loft and captured them!'

Sandy called to Kenji, who was helping carry an old woman with a broken leg. 'Go and search for the twins, they could have hidden somewhere and are too fearful to show themselves.'

But before Kenji could go, Fescue ran in. 'I have been with Mullein, surveying the damage to the cloisters. When we went to see if Hardwick was still in the prison cell, we found it empty and this laid on a mound of the stinking floor rushes!'

Swinging it upside-down by the stray wires hanging from its neck, he held up a severed Frit head.

Gasping in horror, they stared in dismay at the feather-decorated strips caught around the Frit's ear.

Dancer moaned: 'Ah me! Surely they are the twins' leather headbands.'

Suddenly the camera lens eyes started rapidly blinking. The rubber lips stretched into a grimace, exposing bloodied razor teeth. Feeling a sharp electrical tingling up his arm, Fescue dropped the head. Clattering across the stone floor it landed at Kenji's feet. Scooping it up by its orange topknot, he brushed his fingers over the soft grey feathers entwined in the headbands.

'What mischief was the imp up to?' he muttered, glowering in revulsion.

As if answering his question, from the Frit's mouth came a thin metallic voice: 'The K.... Ky.... Roohooo.... for Delfff lassesses.... bbring.... ttt…. Dooomstoone Mmmmiii….'

The message stuttered into silence. Kenji shook the head angrily, then threw the head down in disgust.

But they had no need to hear more: they understood only too well the meaning of the chilling message.

'This is the work of the Sneaksoul to which Hardwick is demon-bound,' Fescue snarled, giving the head a kick.

Seemingly dumbfounded, Sandy stared down at it.

Steely determination gleamed in Kenji's black eyes. He shot Sandy a challenging glare.
'Well Boss, with or without your permission, I'm off to rescue those lovely Delphin lasses: if they are taken to the Doomstone Mines, it will be their deaths!'

His words galvanized Sandy. 'Yes, you are right! We must follow Hardwick and his captives and catch up with them before all is lost.'

Fescue eagerly agreed. 'When Mullein and I were searching for Hardwick, we found a trail through the rubble to the cliff path, where two ropes hung down to the river. Hardwick must have climbed down to a boat and taken the lasses to the other side.'

'That gives me hope!' Sandy exclaimed. 'There is no time to waste! Fescue, you and I will climb down the rope to see if we can find evidence! Kenji go and search for a boat and meet us below the cliffs.'

But, as Kenji turned to go, Mother Hilda called out to him: 'Wait, Kenji!'

Kenji sat down impatiently on a nearby straw bale.

Hilda looked around at them pleadingly. 'We must give this matter more measured thought, I beg of you. Have we correctly understood that message left by the Frit head? How can we be sure that it is not some trick of Hardwick's to draw you away, so he can go in pursuit of Fin?'

'Hilda, what else can they do?' cried Dancer, 'We cannot let Bird and Bee fall into the hands of Gressil's cruel servants!'

Hilda frowned. 'I believe Fin must be told of what has happened. He is—'

Fescue interrupted her. 'Surely, Fin, a mere youth, should not decide whether he will or will not hand over the Chi Rho, in exchange for the little Delphins? Even if he complied with the demand delivered by the Frit's head, we cannot trust the Sneaksoul in Hardwick to return the Delphins unharmed!'

'I'm for going after Hardwick now. We can ambush his party more easily before he reaches the Mines.' Kenji snarled, glowering at Hilda.

A prickly silence fell.

Sandy bowed his head in thought, his face drawn with anxiety. He came to a decision. 'You are right Hilda. Fin must be told.' He gave a groan. 'The Delphin lasses should have been sent home as soon as danger threatened! But it is no good regretting what was not done. It is a hard choice we have! Do we allow Fin to hand the Chi Rho to Gressil's servants, or do we allow the lasses to be killed by the Evils?'

Hilda frowned. 'As I see it, Fin must be the one who decides: the burden of the Chi Rho has been laid on him. We must trust him. Therefore, I suggest that I return to Holy Island with all speed, with this dreadful object.' She gestured at the Frit head lying on the floor. 'Wings can then fly Fin back here. Regretfully we cannot send a pigeon with a message; in my stupidity, I commanded Dancer to release them all. I presume there are none left?'

Dancer nodded weakly.

Agonized, Sandy stared at the straw strewn floor. 'We already took a great risk with the Chi Rho, when we let Fin fly off. I hope he has arrived safely at Holy Island – I have in mind the Snoopers that attacked Dancer. But I agree we must wait for Fin to return. Then Wings must go on to Brightdale and bring Zagzagel – we are in desperate need of his wise counsel!'

Fescue hissed softly under his breath: 'These great matters should never have been left in the charge of humans, let alone a childish Delphin. The precious object should have been taken to Florain and kept safely there.'

Sandy glanced sharply at the Gaiakin but didn't speak.

They again fell silent, full of conflicting thoughts.

Finally, Hilda laid a comforting hand on Sandy's shoulder. 'Do not be so troubled Iskander,' she said, 'When I reach Holy Island, I will lay the matter before young Fin. He is now the Head of the Delphins of Brightdale, and he also has their welfare to consider. He is young, but he has mettle, and must be given a chance to prove himself. Besides, have you forgotten why we urged him to go to Holy Island: you know of whom I am thinking, do you not, Iskander?'

Sandy looked at her, his expression now full of hope. 'Yes, the Anchoress! She will be a great source of wisdom for Fin.'

'Whilst we are waiting for Fin to return, we shouldn't waste time!' Kenji exclaimed, jumping up eagerly. 'Can we not follow the trail that Mullein and Fescue have found, whilst it is still fresh? Make sure that Hardwick is indeed on his way to the Doomstone Mines at Birdoswald, and it's not some trick!'

'Yes!' Sandy said, relieved at the prospect of action. 'But first we must have something to eat. Let us go and see what Grantly can spare us.'

They found Grantly amidst the remains of his kitchen. A cooking fire glowed in the ruined fireplace, where a large cauldron bubbled and steamed; the odour having an unpleasant savour of ganglefowl.

His apron torn and dirty, his white cook's hat spattered with blood, Grantly looked a sorry sight, but there was a resourceful gleam in his eye as he stirred his cauldron with a table leg. They asked if he could spare some provisions, but he shook his head, saying that his store cupboards had been crushed beneath the rubble, and it would take at least a day to salvage any food. So, they returned to say a hurried farewell to Hilda before she left with her servant for Holy Island.

When she had gone, Sandy and his Squad made their own preparations, testing their newly cleaned swords; Fescue's sword blade, now freshly forged by the Durholm smith, gleamed as he pulled it from its sheath. Kenji checked his pack for emergency rations, finding reasonably full sacks of sunflower seeds and dried bilberries. Leaving the others, he went in search of a boat.

Watching them enviously, Dancer groped for her sword in the straw. Looking sorrowfully at the ruined blade, she wondered when a new one could be forged.

After feeble attempts to stand she miserably admitted to Sandy and Fescue they would have to go without her. 'I will come with you next time, when Fin returns,' she promised, laying back on the straw and shutting her eyes.

Sandy and Fescue picked their way over the ruins of the cloister garth, through the wrecked vegetable garden and orchard to the cliff path. Below where the ropes dangled down to the river, Kenji was waiting in a flat-bottomed pontoon – the only craft he could find. As they climbed down, looking out for clues, Fescue found a small shred of wool cloth, which he recognized as being from one of the twin's jerkins.

Kenji laboriously punted them across to the far side, where they found the bank churned up from the passage of Hardwick's gang. Kenji, being the most skilled tracker, crouched close to the muddy ground, studying the jumbled mass of Frit feet and ganglefowl claws, hoping to pick up any trace of Hardwick's human footprints, or even small Delphin's. Fescue found the boat Hardwick had used to cross the river, hastily hidden in some tall reeds nearby.

Sandy and Fescue watched impatiently as Kenji methodically puzzled out the tracks.

After what seemed an agonizing length of time, his face brightened. 'Hardwick mounted a horse. If we keep following these horseshoe tracks, we'll surely have confirmation of where the lasses were taken. Hardwick would not let them out of his sight.'

Fescue nodded in agreement. 'He must have carried them with him on his horse or put them on the back of a ganglefowl. Whatever was decided, he would have kept them close.'

Crouching down, he looked closely at the hoof prints. 'See, there is a jagged mark in one of shoe prints: this will make our tracking easier.'

Kenji eyes followed the trail. 'They have turned off the main path, along that narrow track.' He pointed into the undergrowth.

Sandy turned his anxious face up to the sky. 'May the rain keep away! Now we know in what direction Hardwick is going, we should return to Durholm and wait for young Fin. But I am very reluctant: we have a clear track to follow and any delay could be disastrous.'

He came to a decision. 'It is no good, I cannot turn away now! Come friends, we will follow the trail a while further.'

Kenji gave a muted whistle of relief.

Striking away from the riverbank, they plunged into the forest, eyes to the ground, following the path leading north-west. The going was desperately slow. Frequently losing the notched hoof print in the mass of ganglefowl claw and Frit prints in the dry leaf litter, they had to stop again and again to find it.

Their backs sore from crouching, they finally gave up. They searched frantically but the trail had gone cold. But now they knew for certain that Hardwick and his captives were heading for Birdoswald and the Doomstone Mines.

'I have knowledge of the Mines,' Sandy said grimly, 'I once ventured into the labyrinth of tunnels.' He heaved a sigh. 'Now we know where the young Delphins have been taken, we must turn back, the hour is late, and we are needed at Durholm. I pray that young Fin will quickly return!'

Fescue shook his head sadly. 'I fear it will not be for a while. Mother Hilda will not have reached Scavport yet, and when she finds a boat, it will take at least a day to sail to Holy Island – if the tides and weather are right.'

Weary and dejected, the companions turned back for Durholm.

After saying goodbye to Sandy and his Squad, Hilda did not linger. Carrying the Frit head, she hurried to what remained of her lodgings. Shaking the dust off a leather satchel, she buried the head deep inside. In the Square, few were about: most folk were still working in the cathedral or hiding in their homes. Her servant was waiting for her with two ponies by the ruined portcullis. They did not cross the river by the drawbridge but mounted and took the path along the outer skirt of the battlements. They were heading north-east, for Scavport; riding as hard as they dared, it would take them the rest of that day to reach there.

Hilda and her servant did not know they were being observed. Cowering deep in his hiding place, Crow had listened in awestruck terror as the bugslugs attacked: the crashing of falling masonry, and the din of battle seeming to go on forever. Now, spying Hilda and her servant astride their ponies, he realised they must be heading for Scavport, to find a passage on one of the supply boats that travelled regularly to and from Holy Island. He knew he would have to move fast. Gathering his bits and pieces and tucking Sparkie into an inside pocket of his chainmail jerkin, he climbed out of his den.

'Come little Sparkie, we must hurry!' he croaked, 'that Holy Missis. Follow her, oh yes we will – I ken her belong Holy Island and that home too, of my old mate – Boss Huw.'

Thinking of Huw brought a tear to his one eye. Wiping it from his scarred cheek, he remembered his childhood. Boss Huw had been the closest thing he'd had to a brother, protecting him from the cruel bullying of the other members of their Gang, fussing over his cuts and broken bones, and making sure he got his fair share of food. When Boss Huw had left Scavport for Holy Island to join the Holy Ones, Crow had left too.

'Boss Huw will give us shelter on t' island, you bet, Sparkie love. Then we get close to jool again.''

Dodging through the brambles, he monkeyed along the cliff face. Swinging beneath the drawbridge, he climbed on to the narrow path running beside the battlements. Keeping well hidden in the undergrowth, he followed the short-legged ponies as they trotted purposefully on their way to Scavport.

And so, as was foreseen by Zagzagel, Crow the Scav unknowingly continued to fulfil the destiny that had been laid out for him, from the time he had found the Chi Rho in the Land of Contagion.

# 13
# HOLY ISLAND

Wings flew along a coastline of golden sands backed by high dunes; the great forest beyond, a dark shadow stretching away to the west. Their flight smoothed by light winds, a gentle swell on the grey sea below them, Lark found the courage to gaze about in wonder. Perched on his knee, Mick leaned out, ears flattened, yapping at any bird flapping past.

They passed over a cluster of small islands, their cliffs white from the guano of countless generations of nesting guillemots and kittiwakes.

'The Farnes,' Wings called above the engine, 'where Blessed Cuthbert lived many years, as a hermit.'

Banking away to avoid the clouds of seabirds alarmed by Skyhook's engine, he pointed ahead: 'Holy Island Castle – we're almost there!'

Over his shoulder they saw a rock mount rising out the dunes, topped by an ivy clad ruin.

Fin wondered what he would find there, on Holy Island, help or hostility, or even worse, lustful greed? Would he be able to hand over the Chi Rho? To test himself, he felt inside his jerkin for the soft leather of his purse. No, it would be a struggle. Staring down through a small hole in Skyhook's canvas, he wished he could find the courage to drop the cross into the foam flecked sea, far below. He'd been shocked last night by how strong the pull was, when on Coquet Island he'd tried to throw the cross into the beckoning waves. If he'd done so, would he have become like Crow, a wanderer searching the world, hoping to find the cross, washed up on a far distant shore?

Skyhook's engine note changed: they had reached the mount. Flying around the ruined castle, her roar spooked a family of rooks nesting in the ivy, sending them fluttering into the air like black rags caught on the wind. On the beach below, a group of long-horned goats grazing on the seaweed splashed off into the sea. In a field bordered by stone walls, a flock of sheep scattered in all directions. The shepherd waved his crook at them, whether in anger or greeting, Fin couldn't tell.

Fin saw Holy Island wasn't large, more a peninsula of land, two miles or so across, connected to the mainland by a strip of marram-covered dunes. A line of wooden posts, almost obscured by encroaching sand, marked the remains of a stone causeway.

Wings headed for the south side of the island where a large building of weather-worn sandstone stood over a cluster of thatched cottages. Fin wondered if the building was Holy Island Priory, where the Blessed Cuthbert had lived and prayed, and from where the cross was stolen by the Skwid. Attached to it were some smaller buildings surrounding an inner courtyard, reminding him of Dandrum Den.

Beyond the Priory, a road led to a harbour, where, within the shelter of a sea wall, a dozen or so fishing boats were moored at a stone jetty. Tied up alongside them, a two masted vessel was being unloaded. Small figures, backs laden with baskets, ran up and down a gangplank. They stared up as Skyhook passed overhead.

Leaving the harbour behind, Wings circled over a small islet lying a few hundred yards offshore. As Skyhook wheeled about, Fin spied a small, thatched cottage tucked in the shelter of a high dune. A thin spiral of smoke rising from the chimney blew towards the distant Farne Islands.

On a dune above the cottage a woman stood looking up at them, the hood of her brown robe thrown back showing her pale face and her white hair. As she waved, Wings dipped Skyhook's wings in greeting, and swung away, back to Holy Island. Leaning as far out as he dared, Fin tried to catch another glimpse, but she had gone.

Passing once more over the harbour, the settlement and the Priory, they dropped down into a field of close-cropped grass, landing just as the shepherd and his dog had gathered the last of the scattered sheep into a pen.

Wings turned off the engine.

Stretching, Lark looked about him. 'Here at last!' he exclaimed, 'I wonder how many miles we are from Brightdale – I reckon it must be at least eighty.' He shook his head in amazement. 'I would've been right raddled, if you had told me a week back, that I would be going adventuring so far from home! And seeing such sights – cathedrals, castles, fairy-tale gardens, and the sea!'

He climbed down from Skyhook onto the rough turf.

Lost in thought Fin stayed in his seat, remembering his dream and the woman who had pulled him from the sea. Who was the lone woman on the islet?

Realising what Lark had just said, he felt a stab of guilt. He climbed out and helped him haul out their rucksacks.

'Are you missing home, Lark? Wings can take you back any time you like – there's no need for you to be here.'

Lark looked shocked. 'Now there you go again, Fin: I promised Mr Mossy I would keep an eye on you.' He turned and waved an arm at their surroundings, 'And I wouldn't have missed this jaunt, not even for a year of Grammer Nutmeg's pasties! Anyway, it's not so different to home, don't you think? The stone walls look just like ours in Brightdale.'

'Talking of pasties, I'm off to find lunch,' Wings called, finishing lashing down Skyhook with ropes and pegs. 'Do you want food, or are you going to spend all day chatting? I see Mick's gone to meet the locals,' he added, nodding to where the shepherd was leaning over a five-barred gate and Mick was sniffing noses with the sheepdog. Lark had to whistle twice before he trotted back.

As they set off to find food, a gang of boys ran across the field calling to them. A thick-set youth, bossily pushing his companions aside, strode up to Wings and pointed to Fin and Lark. 'Mister Pilot, are them youngsters? Last time you be 'ere, you'd not let us lads 'ave a go in yon machine – isn't fair they little 'uns 'aving a ride!'

Full of scorn, he looked Fin up and down. ''e looks as if t'first stiff sea breeze would whip 'im off t'sland!'

Wings grinned and ruffled the youth's dusty red hair. 'Aren't you Jed Arry's eldest? You might have grown a foot taller, but your manners have shrunk. I'll be having a word with your dad later. My friends aren't children, they're Delphin-kind, and in their manhood.'

Lark stepped forward, fire in his green eyes, black eyebrows furrowed to a sharp V. Twitching his boning knife from his belt, he pointed the blade at the youth. 'I might not be a door post like you, but I'm solid enough to give you a good sorting! Don't you talk of Fin in that fashion – he's Head Dandrum, king of Brightdale. Watch out he don't put a spell on you and turn you into a worm.'

Mick snapping at his heels, the youth scuttled back to shelter behind his cronies. Fin looked at Lark in awe as the gang sheepishly sloped off.

The shepherd, who'd ambled across from leaning on his gate, shouted after the boys. 'Go 'n warn Brother Rory of Mr Wings and his machine acoming.' Then beaming at Fin and Lark, said: 'Tak no ken to young'un, sirs. If you be friends of Mr Wings, you be welcome on our island.'

Doffing his woolly hat from his shaggy white head, he gave Fin a little bow. ''tis an 'onour to be acquainted, your 'ighness!'

'Sorry about the row when we flew over, Tom,' Wings said. 'Sheep none the worse for the kerfuffle, I trust?'

With a toothless grin the shepherd, shaking his head, waved his crook in farewell.

Wings set off towards the settlement.

'Hey, Wings wait a moment,' Fin called, as he and Lark snatched up their rucksacks.

Fin looked up at Wings, his expression tense. 'We need to decide what we should say. I'd rather it was not known yet, what I've brought to Holy Island: I'm hoping first to have a talk with Mother Hilda when she comes.'

Wings' grey eyes softened. 'Sorry Fin, I was so keen to get a bite to eat, I forgot. Maybe best if we don't shout it from the rooftops. But don't judge the chaps here too hurriedly. Brother Rory, Hilda's second-in-command, is a good fellow – not like that nasty bit of work, Hardwick. You mustn't forget the cross was very precious to these people; they'll be keen to get it back. They'll be suspicious, too – a couple of Delphins suddenly arriving on Holy Island – why? But I'll keep shtum if that's what you want. Anyway, come on chaps, I could eat a whole sheep.'

He strode across the field.

Lark hurried after him, but Fin lingered, still full of doubts.

Wings had brought home to him that not only Brother Hardwick knew about the Chi Rho. Other members of the Holy Community must know the story of how his father had found Crow with the cross embedded in his chest. Hadn't brother Aidan from the Holy Community looked after Crow at the place called Jarrow?

'I should have remembered that.' he told himself angrily.

Feeling a sudden stab of pain where the cross inside his purse pressed against his chest, resentment bubbled up inside him: these people couldn't expect him just to hand over the Chi Rho and walk away. An urge to get away from this place, to go back to Skyhook and leave immediately, almost overcame him. He was about to call out to Lark and Wings to stop, when from somewhere in his head, he heard a soft laugh: Mossy's dear brown face swam before his inner eye.

As quickly as his frenzy had come upon him, it was gone. Now he knew with a strange, calm certainty, that whatever lay ahead – hard choices, even horror and death – he would not be without help. What had Sandy said back at Durholm? 'I have a feeling that you will find more than you ever hoped for on Holy Island.' Squaring his shoulders, he ran after Wings and Lark.

At the Priory gates they were greeted by villagers calling eagerly to Wings, asking for news of the outside world. Three members of the Community were waiting for them: a man and woman who, with their freckles and red hair, resembled each other. An old Scav leaning on a walking stick stood with them.

The man stepped forward. 'Welcome, Wings!'

'Good to see you, Rory,' Wings said, gripping the man's proffered hand. 'Moyra, and Huw, too!' He nodded to the other two. 'Meet Fin Dandrum and Lark Annunder – they've come all the way from Brightdale, way down towards—' He waved vaguely towards the mainland, hidden from view by the Priory buildings.

Rory smiled at Fin and Lark, his keen blue eyes full of speculation. 'Welcome young Delphins.' The soft lilt of his voice reminded them of Sandy. 'It is a rare delight to meet Delphin-kind. My sister, Moyra, who has charge of the dormitory, will take care of your comfort whilst you are staying with us.'

Moyra laughed delightedly when they gave her a bow. 'You have brought us most polite guests, Wings,' she said, ruffling Lark's thick hair, making his cheeks turn red.

'And this is Huw.' Rory beckoned the old Scav forward. 'He has given up his Scaving days and is writing the history of our northern lands – he is eager to learn about your small country.'

The little Scav hobbled closer to peer at them. Both his hands had fingers missing, making them wonder how he could hold a pen. 'I be pleased to meet t'folk of Brightdale,' he squeaked. 'I'll be wanting an account from your honours, of that place so near to the evil land – never named here on Holy Island.'

Indignant at his home being thought a mere borderland to Contagion, Fin replied icily. 'We shall be happy to tell you of the beauty of our Dale, where there is peace and plenty, despite the neighbours.'

'Obviously doesn't know Mr Mossy lives in Brightdale – he'd put him right,' Lark muttered under his breath. Hearing tension in his master's voice, Mick growled at the Scav.

Wings hastily changed the subject. 'Rory, you'll be wondering about Mother Hilda?'

'Indeed! We have been waiting anxiously since Iskander's message came by carrier pigeon, summoning her urgently to Durholm Garrison. She arrived safely?'

'Got there, let me see,' Wings counted on his fingers, 'we flew out yesterday – no, the day before. She reached Durholm the night before the special meeting – three days ago.' He looked down at the Delphins, who nodded in confirmation. 'We don't know what happened after we left: Hilda insisted we got young Fin away, a.s.a.p. because of what he's carrying—'

Stopping abruptly, he shot Fin an apologetic look. 'Anyway,' he continued hurriedly, 'Hilda thought it best I brought Fin and Lark on ahead. She'll be coming by boat with Fin and Lark's friends. Dodgy situation there, Gressil's chaps were already on the warpath when we left.'

Rory looked dismayed. 'Your news fills me with dread, especially when, yesterday the whole loft-full of pigeons returned from Durholm, bedraggled – and none carrying a message!'

Alarmed, Fin stared at Rory. What had happened at Durholm? Were the twins in danger? Remembering Bird's anxious face looking up at him as Skyhook rose into the air, he felt as if a knife had been twisted in his heart. He grabbed Wings' arm. 'I knew we shouldn't have come here! We must go back!'

Lark groaned. 'Yes – if anything has befallen our lasses, without me to protect them, I'd never forgive myself!'

'Steady on chaps,' Wings said. 'Let's think this through. As I told you, I'm sure the Frit army will have given up any idea of attacking Durholm – won't be keen to risk combat with chaps like Sandy and his Squad. More likely the evils will try to follow us, now they know the— Damn! I'm sorry Fin, I keep forgetting.'

Rory frowned at him suspiciously. 'Wings, you are not telling me everything. Why are the enemy attacking the Garrison when they have never done so before?'

Seeing the pilot's agonised expression, he shrugged impatiently. 'We must discuss this further in the privacy of my room. I have asked a kitchen maid to bring us mugs of ale, Come, follow me!'

Turning abruptly, he went through the gates into the courtyard. Huw the Scav hobbled after him.

Moyra held out her hands to Fin and Lark. 'I will take your packs to the dormitory, where I shall prepare beds for you.' She gave Wings a knowing wink. 'Vera is airing a bed for you at the Fisherman's Friend.'

'Oh, righto, Moyra!'

Wings turned to Fin and Lark. 'I'll be along in a mo. You go and join Rory.'

Shouldering his rucksack, he strode off towards the harbourside inn.

Tempted to go with him, Fin watched his retreating figure, before changing his mind, and following the others.

Much like Dandrum Den, an array of buildings enclosed the courtyard. Facing the gates was a long refectory, with the kitchen, bakery, and dairy. To the right stood stables, byres, and kennels. To the left, was the ancient Priory church with its nail-studded oak door set beneath an archway, flanked by tall windows, their stained glass gleaming richly in the sunlight.

Crossing the courtyard, as they passed a stone column, Fin and Lark stopped to look. It was a statue, so worn the features were indiscernible: the head tilted back, the stunted nose pointing to the sky, and what had been a raised arm now a stump. As they studied it, they became uncomfortably aware of a group of watching girls milling around the open kitchen door giggling and nudging one another. The aroma of cooking meat from the kitchen proved too much for Mick, who set off eagerly.

As Lark chased after him, Fin was startled by a high-pitched voice. He turned, to find Huw the Scav waving his stick at the statue.

'Holy Aidan, it is,' squeaked the old Scav, 'he be worn away with sorrow!'

'Surely it was the wind and rain that wore the stone away,' Fin said, smiling in superior amusement at the earnest wrinkled face peering up at him.

'No! No! Aidan be forlorn, for years 'n years – ever since the wicked Skwid stole the precious Cross from him!'

Brother Huw pulled him to a small slab of smooth pink marble set in the cobbles at the statue's base: carved into the surface was a clear outline of the Chi Rho.

'Was this where they kept the cross?' Fin exclaimed, kneeling, and running his index finger over the familiar shape. Looking up he saw Huw's searching gaze on him.

'I think you knows of our Cross,' the Scav remarked thoughtfully.

Fin was saved from answering by Lark returning with Mick tucked firmly under his arm, and they headed to a cottage by the Priory, where Rory was beckoning to them.

Rory's room was simply furnished. A desk strewn with parchments and writing implements stood beneath a porthole-shaped window framing a view of the harbour and the sea beyond. Beside the desk stood a sheepskin-covered bed and across the room, sea-coals burned in a grate.

'Come, warm yourselves whilst we wait for the maid to bring ale.'

Rory motioned Fin and Lark to two stools set either side of the hearth. Bringing a bentwood chair from by the desk, he sat between them, and turning to Fin, studied his face.

'Fin Dandrum, for a Delphin, you have a look of Rom about you,' he observed.

Fin shrank back. 'My mother is of the Rom people,' he muttered uneasily, wondering where Rory's remark was leading.

'There was a Delphin who came to the Jarrow, looking for a Rom woman,' Rory said. 'His name was Marlin Dandrum. It was he who found the Cross that had been stolen from us – are you related to that Dandrum?'

As Fin and Lark exchanged agonized glances, the door latch rattled, and Wings ambled in.

Wings sized up the scene suspiciously. 'I say, Rory, don't go upsetting the lad. He's had enough aggro' from Hardwick.'

'What has Brother Hardwick done?' Rory asked sharply.

Perching on the end of Rory's bed, Wings explained their realisation that Hardwick was demon-bound. 'They had to put him in the lock-up!'

'This is worrying news indeed!' Rory looked apologetically at Fin. 'Forgive me. You must know that the theft of the Chi Rho is a great sorrow to our Community. When it was found again, we were angry that it was not returned here, to Holy Island, but taken away into obscurity by an alien race. I ask again, are you related to this Marlin Dandrum? Do you know of the holy Cross?'

Again, before Fin had to reply, they were interrupted, this time by a nervous knock on the door.

'Enter!' Rory called impatiently.

A plump girl with large blue eyes and blond curls came in bearing four mugs of ale on a tray. 'Cook says you're to hurry with your ale, Brother, or the stew will be burnt.'

'Thank you, Trixie, we shan't be long. Put the tray on my desk and serve our guests first.'

Handing round the mugs and bobbing a curtsy to each person in turn, as she went out, she fluttered her eyelashes at Fin and Lark. Shutting the door behind her, they heard giggling from her companions outside.

They drank in silence for a moment, then Fin put down his mug.

'O.K. Brother, I'll put an end to your speculation. Marlin Dandrum was my father. I inherited the Chi Rho when he was killed. I've come here on Mother Hilda's advice: she said that I would find help in deciding whether to leave the cross here or to take it elsewhere. Be assured: I certainly don't want to keep it! I've even tried to chuck it into the sea but found I couldn't.' He stared miserably into the fire. 'I'm beginning to hate it,' he muttered, putting his hand to his chest.

'Do you have it there?' Rory whispered in awe.

Lifting the cord from around his neck, Fin brought out the purse and impatiently shook out the contents. The cross, along with his mother's coin and Bird's pendant, scattered on the stone hearth where they glittered in the firelight.

Rory gasped, and falling to his knees, gazed down at the cross, his hands clasped in adoration.

Lark leapt up and put an arm around Fin's shoulder. 'Now look what you've done,' he hissed angrily at Rory, 'he hasn't got over being nearly killed by a phruggle in Durholm, you know!'

Wings, tut-tutting, gathered up the treasures from amongst the ashes, handing them back to Fin, who stuffed them into his purse.

'Rory, my friend, I'm beginning to wonder if we did the right thing – coming here.'

Brother Rory, recovering his composure now the cross was out of sight, stared out of the window, his jaw working with emotion.

'I hope Mother Hilda comes soon,' he muttered.

Looking longingly out to where the low outline of the islet they had flown over earlier, could just be seen, his face brightened. 'Of course, that is why Mother Hilda was insistent you come to Holy Island! She wanted you to visit our Anchorite on Cuthbert's Island.' He pointed to the islet. 'Fin, she too is of the Rom people! Come, drink up your ale: we shall go to the refectory, and whilst we eat you must tell me about the dreadful happenings at Durholm. After that, I will row you over to the island.'

The refectory was crowded with farmworkers sitting at long trestle tables. At the cooking range, a large, sweaty-faced female cook was ladling out bowls of rabbit stew from a steaming cauldron. Among the serving maids was Trixie, who had ogled Fin and Lark earlier.

Mouths watering from the wonderful meaty smell, Fin and Lark realised how hungry they were – their breakfast on Coquet Island seemed a long time ago. Finding places at one of the long tables, whilst they waited to be served, Wings gave Rory an account of what had happened at Durholm. 'We got away before the Frits and the bugslugs reached there. We hoped that if we took the cross away, the enemy would be drawn to follow us and pass Durholm by. Even so, I'm worried Gressil's Snoopers might have caused trouble. On our flight here, we were attacked by a squadron of the pests – had to do an emergency landing for repairs at Scavport, which is what delayed us.'

Rory shook his head. 'I shall indeed be glad to see Mother Hilda!'

As he spoke, the cook waddled over carrying a tray laden with bowls which she set before them. The last, a small tin bowl, she put on the floor for Mick, who dived in, slurping loudly. Gazing in awe at a huge fluffy dumpling floating in his bowl, Lark smiled his thanks before plunging his spoon into the rich brown gravy.

They ate in silence until, impatiently pushing away his bowl, Rory got up from the table.

'Come Fin! We will go down to the harbour, and I will row you across to Cuthbert's island.'

Leaving his stew half finished, Fin got up to follow him.

Hurriedly swallowing the last of his dumpling, Lark stood too, but Rory shook his head. 'No Lark, you must stay here with Wings.'

'Fin can't go off without me!' he cried in dismay.

'I'll be alright, Lark,' Fin said, 'this is something I must do on my own. As you saw, it's not far to the islet and I'll soon be back.'

Wings pulled Lark back onto his seat. 'Hurry and finish your stew, lad. We'll watch them from the harbour wall, and then I'll take you to the Fisherman's Friend for a drink. Vera's beer is uncommonly good!'

Walking beside Rory, Fin's mind seethed with speculation. Who was the woman who had waved up at them as they flew over the islet? Rory had called her the Anchorite, and said that she was a Rom. Could she be his mother? Surely not. He couldn't imagine the beautiful woman in his father's sketch being a Holy Woman like old Mother Gonebatty who looked after Aidan's Shrine in Watersmeet.

Rory rowed them out through the gap in the harbour wall, where Wings and Lark, with Mick under his arm, stood waving. He took barely ten minutes to reach Cuthbert's Island, beaching the little rowing boat in a small sandy bay.

As they climbed out, Fin saw her waiting on the dune where he had seen her earlier from the air, hood thrown back, white hair flowing over her shoulders. She beckoned to him. Hesitating, he turned to Rory for reassurance.

'Go!' Rory said, giving him a gentle shove. He pushed the boat back into the water, and leaping in, took up his oars. 'Someone will come for you when she gives the signal,' he called as he rowed away.

Fin looked up uneasily. Again, she beckoned. Reluctantly he started to climb the dune, pulling himself up by the strong stalks of marram grass, the soft dry sand running between his fingers. Almost at the top, he halted. Searching her face, he found no trace of the beautiful, dark-eyed young woman who haunted his imaginings: this woman looked old before her time, her face careworn.

She held out her arms. 'Do you not know me, Fin?'

Mutely, he shook his head, and turned to slither back down the dune. Rory, working against the tide, his back bent into his oars, had not gone far. If he hurried, he could just catch his attention before he was out of earshot.

Behind him, she started to sing:

'Gypsy boy, gypsy boy, my brown eyed, blue eyed son—' Her lilting voice, breaking with emotion, drifted into silence.

It was if sunlight had thawed a frozen wellspring: the tune and the words released deep hidden memories. Scrambling back up the last few yards, he ran to her and buried his face in her coarse brown robe that smelled of thyme and honey. For the first time since his father had died, he wept.

'There's so much to tell you, mother,' he sobbed, his voice muffled as she held him close. 'The worst is that father is dead – killed.' Looking up, he hungrily searched her thin face: the worry lines around her dark eyes, the tight line of her pale lips.

'I know! I know, my love. I have heard how—' she could not say more, she just held him, stroking his hair, waiting for the storm of grief to pass. And when it had, she wiped his tears away with her rough hands.

'Come to my home for hot sweet tea and then we shall talk for the rest of the day, and all night if we wish!'

Taking his hand, she led him along a narrow path through a spinney of sea-buckthorn bright with blossom and from where deep inside its thickets came the whistling cheeps of nesting eider ducks. At the end of the path, they emerged onto a piece of flat ground spread with a carpet of low growing thyme. Her thatched cottage nestled beneath the shelter of a high dune, a plume of smoke from the chimney rising into the clear sky. Looking out from a nearby shed, a cow chewed its cud, whilst chickens scratched around the door.

Her one-roomed cottage was windowless, lit by daylight coming in through the open door. A sea coal fire burned in the grate, its flames flickering across the scrubbed stone floor. Next to the hearth stood a rocking chair, with a high-backed pew bench facing it. A dresser with a few pots and mugs stood by the door. In the farthest corner, a hammock slung between two roof beams had a prayer kneeler beside it, with a plain wooden cross on the wall above.

'Come, warm yourself,' she said, gesturing to the bench.

Sitting on a long wool cushion that covered the seat, Fin ran his hand over the embroidery of dolphins leaping through foamy white waves. Deep inside him a memory stirred, and he wondered if the tapestry had come from Dandrum Den. He watched as she stirred a pot hanging over the fire, filling the room with the smell of fish stew. Pouring a mug of dark nettle tea from a teapot warming by the hearth, and adding a generous spoonful of honey, she handed it to him. Then seating herself on the rocking chair, as he drank, she eagerly studied him, but didn't speak.

When he'd finished, she got to her feet. 'Now I will show you around my island, and as we walk you shall tell me all about yourself: your growing years, your friends and what you wish for the future!' She took his hand.

Outside, they stood for a moment looking about. To the west, the mainland lay close by, its marshes tumultuous with the cries of wading birds rising and falling as they fed, the forest beyond, dark and forbidding. To the south, the Farne Islands rose out of the grey wave flecked sea, and to the north, on Holy Island, the roof of the Priory church could be glimpsed above the buckthorn, the castle mount beyond.

Walking through low dunes with her leaning on his shoulder, he told her about his life: Nutmeg caring for him like a mother, how he loved his cousin, Thetis as a sister, and his friendship with Bee and Bird. Then, he told her of his troubled life at Dandrum Den, how they resented him being Marlin's son, and that they didn't want him as Head. As he talked, bitterness bubbled up inside him.

He stopped and looked up at her reproachfully. 'Mother, it's hard being a half-breed. That's what I'm called by the Dandrums.'

Gripping him by his shoulders, she searched his troubled face. 'Fin, never be ashamed of who you are: you are from two proud races!'

He scowled. 'I wish you'd taken me with you when you left: I would have been better off growing up as a Rom child. What made it worse, was father leaving too. I was nine years old when, at last he came home – a stranger, with terrible moods.'

He was startled to see tears in her dark eyes. Wiping them away with her sleeve, she gazed wistfully across the water to the priory, its stonework golden in the sunlight.

When she finally spoke, her voice was husky with emotion: 'It was a hard, hard choice, Fin. You must remember I was very young – younger than you are now! After I gave birth to you, I was desperate for the comfort of my own mother. At Dandrum Den there was only Nutmeg who showed me kindness; she did her best, but she is a Delphin and did not understand the customs and ways of the Rom. I never dreamed your father would come searching for me!'

Her face crumpled with misery. 'I should have been there – at his passing, to ask his forgiveness!'

Shocked, Fin said: 'You mustn't feel guilty, mother! After his death, I saw his face, it was full of peace. I think I might have seen his spirit too, in a sort of waking dream, swimming in the warm sea. He looked very happy!'

Still holding him by the shoulders, she stared into his eyes. 'You saw his spirit? Fin, you are indeed a Rom – you have the Sight!' A smile softened the deep lines around her mouth. 'He looked happy, you said?'

Fin nodded.

She gave a wistful smile. 'When we married, your father and I, we loved each other so much.'

Fin realised she must have been about Bird's age.

Thinking of Bird reminded him guiltily of the twins, and the danger they might be in. He saw that they had walked around the island and were back at the cottage. To the west, behind the forest, the sun had nearly dropped below the horizon. What was he doing? He should get back; Lark would be worrying.

'It's almost sunset!' he exclaimed, 'I should be getting back before Mother Hilda and the twins arrive!'

She looked at him pleadingly. 'Stay a while longer, Fin. There is so much more I would like to know about you!' Her gaze searched the empty sea to the south. 'I can see no sign of a boat. Mother Hilda will not be arriving for some time!'

Leading him to a bench facing Holy Island, she beckoned him to sit beside her. 'From here we can look at the Priory church, where the spirit of my Saviour rests in the tabernacle,' she said.

Settling beside her, he studied her worn face, seeing no vestige of the fiery beauty his father had fallen in love with; once again he wondered what could have happened to her. Her talk of a tabernacle reminded him of the gold cabinet on the high altar in Durholm cathedral – Fescue had told him the cabinet was called a tabernacle.

He frowned, trying to put thoughts into words. 'Mother, in all my imaginings of you, I never dreamt that you would be what Rory called "The Anchorite". Are you happy here, alone on this small island?'

She pondered his question, gazing across at the Priory roof. 'What is happiness? If it is being at peace, even though I suffer pain, yes, I am very happy. I am never lonely, either. So many come to see me! And now, even my son has come!'

She stood. 'Come, eat supper with me. And then we shall sit in front of my fire and talk more. Zagzagel has told me of your skill with drawing. Have you brought any of your sketches?'

From his pocket, he produced the small sketch pad Mossy had made for him. 'There's not much to see,' he said ruefully, showing it to her. 'Lark keeps nagging me to do more!'

She smiled. 'Ah, young Lark, Nutmeg's grandson. You must tell me more of him, too!'

So, putting return to Holy Island from his mind, he followed her into the cottage.

Whilst eating the fish stew, Miryam looked through his sketch book, peering at the drawings by the light of the lamp hanging from a beam. Fin eagerly watched her admiring expression as she turned the pages, her bowl balanced on her knee, her rough fingers clumsy.

'My goodness, you have skill!' she exclaimed, studying the little sketches of landscapes, skyscapes and bits and pieces that had caught his eye. When she came to the sketch of Lark standing by the fossil tree at Stonetree, she bent close. 'He reminds me of old Nutmeg,' she said. Turning the page, she laughed at a quick drawing he'd done of the twins, heads together, sitting on a bed in the sanatorium in Durholm. 'They're alike as two chicks from the same egg!'

When they'd eaten and he'd put away his sketchpad, they talked more. He told her how he had come to live with Mossy, and more recently, his new friendship with Lark. He explained about the Spinners, and his friendship with the twins.

As they talked it was if he was under a spell: he forgot about returning to the main island and gradually drowsiness came over him. The recollections of that night became forever vague and unreal. Sometimes in later days, incidents would drift unbidden into his mind; he knew she had told him about her Smith family, and about what happened to her when she left Brightdale, about her wanderings searching for her own clan, how she had been befriended by the Holy Community at Jarrow, but try as he might, he could not remember in detail what she had said.

At last, he must have fallen asleep. When he woke, he was stretched out on the dolphin cushion on the bench, wrapped in a blanket, with daylight filtering in under the cottage door.

Crow reached Scavport late evening, an hour or so after 'Holy Lady' and her servant arrived. Hopping from cover to cover, exhausted from trying to keep up with the fast trotting ponies, he consoled himself with the thought that when Holy Lady reached Scavport, she would have to wait for the next high tide. If he missed her sailing, he could stow aboard another vessel; there were several daily sailings to and from Holy Island, carrying goods for the Community, with return shipments of the famous Holy Island mussels, and sea-washed grey wool from the island sheep.

He was ravenously hungry but, Scavport being one of his haunts, he knew where scraps of food could be filched. He tried his luck at Rosie's Roost, lurking by the midden near the back door, hoping to find leftovers. By lucky chance, a couple of Scav waiters were chatting by the kitchen door, getting some air.

'What were Holy Missus asking after, Squat?' Crow heard one of them ask. His ears pricked up.

'Had me seen Wings and his little chums. Said me had, spent night at Billy Rope's, I tole 'er.'

'Me heard her askin' Carlos cook about next boat t'Island,' his companion remarked.

Crow sucked in a wheezy breath of satisfaction. He grabbed a meaty looking chicken leg off the midden and, keeping to the shadows, hop-skipped to the harbour. His luck was in again when he spotted Holy Lady by the gangplank of a two-masted barque, talking to the captain. Darting behind a nearby stack of barrels, gnawing on his chicken leg, he listened carefully.

'Yes, Mother, the passenger cabin's free.' The captain's throaty voice carried clearly across to him. 'We'll be sailing at dawn, but you're welcome to come aboard now. Will it be the usual payment in kind?'

'Thank you, Captain Shell. A barrel of mussels in exchange for the passage? How will the weather be, do you think?'

'A front's blowing down from the north – if it gets too rough, we'll put in at Craster.'

'Oh, I hope not! I wanted to reach Holy Island as soon as possible.'

'Better to be safe than sorry, Mother!' Captain Shell exclaimed.

Pressing himself deeper into the shadows he peered out, watching Holy Lady's servant lead the ponies away. The Holy Lady carried her belongings, a bag and a satchel, up the gangplank and moments later a light appeared in a cabin porthole.

No one about, Crow scuttled to the gangplank and, clinging to the underside, clambered on board. Once on deck, he lifted the hatch to the cargo hold, and dropped down into the blackness. Landing on wet wooden planks, he listened for sounds of alarm: no one had spotted him. Still clutching his chicken leg, now stripped of all flesh, he sat dozing, waiting for dawn and the tide to turn.

Waking from a restless night's sleep, from the motion beneath him he knew the ship had set sail. Captain Shell's promised stiff northerly breeze was in full force, tossing the small vessel on the heaving waves.

Feeling sick, he peered blearily about. In the dim light from a chink in the ill-fitting hatch, he saw at one end of the hold bundles of new fishing nets, and at the other wooden casks which, by the slopping sounds, contained liquid of some kind. The rolling motion and the stench of old shellfish was playing havoc with his stomach, already protesting at the rotten chicken leg. Desperate for something to drink, he crawled amongst the casks, and finding one with a loose lid, prised it open. Scooping a handful of liquid into his mouth, he discovered it was lamp oil. Gagging and spitting, he crawled to the bales of new netting, which looked invitingly soft and dry. Climbing on top, he stretched out and tried to catch sleep again.

Remembering Sparkie, patting his chain-mail jerkin, he found it Sparkie-less, and assumed his rat had gone on a hunt for food, and perhaps friendship among the ship's resident rats. Hearing angry squeals from a dark corner, he guessed his rat had not found a welcome. He was not troubled for his pet; Sparkie could easily deal with any common rat. He thought resentfully of the evil mutt belonging to the Delph with the pale grass top, that had nearly killed Sparkie, and he longed for revenge.

'I bite his leggies off, I will. Oh, yep, I cut him low afore I kill him,' he muttered, burying himself deeper in the nets.

A while later Sparkie scrabbled back inside his jerkin. Crow grunted a greeting, and wrapping his bony arms around his thin chest, enclosed his pet in a hug. Peace seeped through his tired body. He gradually drifted into sleep, happy in the knowledge that as the boat struggled north through the rough sea, he was getting closer to his treasure, and comforted by the thought that the old Scav called Huw, his childhood protector, would give him a hiding place.

'Mind Sparkie, we mustn't tell Bro Huw why we come t'Isle! You be not forgetting, oh no ratty, my dear. He'll lust for special jool too, I'm knowing!'

# 14
# GRIM NEWS

After a breakfast of honey-sweetened porridge, Miryam took Fin to a tarn in the middle of the island. Here they watched the sun rise, the rays turning the smooth surface of the dark peaty water to blue and gold. High above them, a skylark sang.

'Mother why is there evil in the world, when the Christ is said to have overcome it,' Fin asked. 'Mossy says by his dying and rising everything is being made well, evil has been defeated, but how can that be, when there's still so much bad in the world?'

Miryam didn't speak but knelt and searched in the damp sedge. Finding a pebble, she threw it into the still water, sending shimmering circles rippling out to the reeds fringing the tarn. They stood in silence as the surface gradually settled, mirroring the sky once more.

She explained: 'The sky reflected in the surface of the water is Creation as God first made it. The stone that I threw in, is the evil which marred it – it only took a moment to distort the surface before the stone sank deep into the mud. The ripples continued for a while but now, as you see, it is smooth again, and once more the sky is reflected in it. Thus, it is with evil: the Christ has overcome it, but the ripples will continue until his New Creation is complete, when all will be mended...'

'Tell me, did Nutmeg give you my gift of the gold coin, with your secret name scratched on it?' she asked, suddenly.

Fishing inside his purse, Fin handed her the coin. The chain of Bird's silver bird had wound around it. She pulled it away, and holding up the pendant, the sun's rays caught the silver, creating small sparkling lights.

'This is a pretty thing: is it a keepsake from your girl?'

Fin shook his head, and grabbing the pendant, stuffed it back in the purse. 'I don't have a girlfriend. No sensible Delphin girl would want me, a half-breed. Bird Spinner gave me the pendant for good luck.'

Miryam sighed sadly but didn't say anything.

She studied the name she'd scratched into the coin, nineteen years before. Looking up, she searched his face, as if seeing him for the first time. 'Saroson, my own dear boy,' she whispered huskily, handing him back the coin.

Tears stung his eyes. 'Mossy told me your coin would protect me from the worst effects of the Chi Rho – it isn't doing a very good job.'

Annoyed with himself for mentioning the cross, he scowled and with a heavy heart, pulled it out.

Reverently, she laid it on her gnarled palm and bending close stared into the crystal lozenge. As Fin watched her, she seemed to fade, as if the cross were drawing her into another dimension. Sour jealousy twisted his stomach. Snatching the cross back, he immediately dropped it: the gold had turned fiercely hot. Holding his stinging hands in his armpits, he glowered down at the jewels glinting mockingly up at him.

'That thing might be holy to you! But to me it's hateful,' he hissed. 'I've tried throwing it away, but I couldn't – soon I won't be able to fight the temptation to wear it, and it'll bury itself in my chest, just like it did father.'

She stared at him, dismayed.

'When he was dead, I saw a Chi Rho shaped wound in his chest, as fresh and deep as it must have been when Mossy probed the cross out, years before!'

Her face contorted in anguish, making him ashamed at what he'd said. Pulling his sleeve down over his hand, he picked up the cross: it was quite cold. As he put it away, she tentatively put out her hand, as if to take it from him. For a fleeting moment, he wondered if he should give her the cross. Was that what was meant to happen?

A soft voice whispered in his head: 'Fin, there is neither bad nor good in the Chi Rho: it is the Blood on Wood that has the power!'

'Do you desire the Chi Rho?' he cried angrily.

She shrank away in astonishment. 'What need have I for it? Surely it should be put back from where it was stolen?' She turned her face towards Holy Island.

A shout startled them. Brother Rory strode into view. 'So, this is where you are!' he called irritably. 'I've been looking all over for you. I have come to take Fin back – Mother Hilda is home!'

Grim-faced, Rory didn't speak as he rowed. In the prow, Fin gazed back towards Cuthbert's Island: she was standing again on the dune above the little bay, outlined against grey clouds, her white hair blowing in the wind she waved farewell. He waved back, feeling lost and sad: he had so much more to ask her. Then realisation dawned on him: he'd found his mother! Not how he had imagined it would be. But he didn't mind. And now he knew what he must do with the Chi Rho: leave it with Mother Hilda. He, Lark, and the twins would go back home to Brightdale, to take up their everyday lives again. He heaved a sigh of relief and turned his face to the approaching harbour.

As they rowed in, he saw a newly arrived vessel moored against the jetty, sailors unloading barrels and bales of fishing nets. Rory made the little rowing boat's rope fast to a rusty iron ring at the foot of some stone steps. Lark and Mick were waiting for him at the top and Fin clambered up eagerly: he had so much to tell Lark!

Reaching the top, he grabbed Lark's shoulders. 'Lark, the most amazing thing – you'll never guess who lives on Cuthbert's island!'

'At the Fisherman's Friend they told me a wild woman lived there. It got me real agitated – I was afeared that if anything happened to you, Mr Mossy would turn me into something disgusting!'

Fin smiled. 'You needn't have worried. She's someone—' Noticing Lark's anxious expression, he stopped. 'Is there something wrong? Have the twins and Mother Hilda come?'

'Not the twins – just Mother Hilda. She landed at dawn, with a nasty looking greasy bundle, and she's in right distress.'

Fear clutched his heart. 'What's happened?'

'Hilda wouldn't say until you got back – they're waiting for you in Brother Rory's room.'

They set off after Rory, already striding purposefully up the lane to the Priory. On the way, Lark stopped and, panting for breath, turned to Fin. 'You were going to tell me something amazing about the woman on the Island?'

'I'll tell you later. Come on, we must find out what's happened – I can't understand why the twins aren't with Hilda!'

As they entered Rory's room, Mother Hilda jumped up, her face anguished. 'Ah, Fin! I have such dreadful news – the twins have been taken!'

Fin stared at her, uncomprehending. 'What do you mean, taken? Not – not demon-bound like Hardwick?'

'No! No! Not that. Hardwick has kidnapped them. He, or rather the devil who possesses him, left a ransom message using the voice in that Frit head there.' Her hand shaking, she gestured to Rory's desk where Wings stood peering at something lying there.

Joining Wings, Fin gazed in revulsion at the object: a Frit head, oil seeping from the severed neck had stained Rory's parchments. The lens eyes stared back at him, unblinking, the rubber lips grinned mirthlessly, exposing a row of bloodstained razor teeth. A plaited leather band adorned with grey dove's feathers was caught around a protruding tube-like ear. He'd last seen that headband tied in Bird's soft blond curls.

He tried to speak, but a burning pain from the purse pressing against his chest, took his breath away. From a long way off he heard Lark: 'Raddled rams, isn't that one of the twins' headbands....'

The floor heaved; the room spun. Wings' voice thundered in his ears. 'Watch it – young Fin's passing out!' Feeling the rough leather of the pilot's flying jacket grazing his cheek, everything went black.

He came to, slumped on a stool in front of the fire. Wings was holding a tin cup to his mouth. Taking a sip, the fiery liquid caught his throat, making him cough. Turning, he stared in abject misery at the Frit head lying on the desk.

Back in Rory's rowing boat, it had seemed so simple: he would leave the Chi Rho here in safe hands. They could all go home. He'd see Tissy and Lark married, then stand aside for cousin Kelp to be Head Dandrum. He would come back to live here on Holy Island – best of all, with Bird as his wife. That dream was dead.

Sick with horror, he listened as Hilda told them of the attack on Durholm; Bugslugs wrecking the kitchen and refectory, the Frit army invading the cathedral; finding Dancer badly injured, the realisation the twins were missing. Finally, Fescue discovering Hardwick had escaped from the lock up, leaving the Frit head with its garbled message, demanding the Chi Rho in exchange for the twins.

Rage and remorse burned inside him. He pushed Wings aside and staggered to his feet.

'IT'S ALL MY FAULT,' he shouted at the dismayed faces around him. 'I've been a stupid, stupid fool! I should have taken the twins back to Brightdale when we were at Stonetree. Wings, you must take us back to Durholme in Skyhook – immediately!'

Hilda gripped him by his shoulders. 'Fin – Fin! Do not despair! Even as I left Durholm, Iskander was making plans to go after Hardwick and his Frits – they are no match for him and his Squad.'

'Yes, Kenji's famous as a tracker throughout the North,' Wings added encouragingly, 'and Fescue's powerful Gaiakin eyes miss nothing. Dealing with a Sneaksoul and a pack of Frits is a way of life for those chaps – they'll soon get the lasses back!'

Lark moaned. 'But, if they're too late, what will the Sneaker inside Hardwick do to the twins, if he doesn't get the cross?'

Wings nodded. 'Lark's got a point there, Hilda.'

'I've no choice!' Fin said grimly, 'I must get back to Durholm, and go after Hardwick myself – let him know I'm willing to hand over the Chi Rho. And Wings you must go on to Brightdale, to get word to Mossy and the twins' parents—'

'No!' interrupted Brother Rory angrily, 'Mother Hilda, I beg of you, the Chi Rho must stay here! Surely Iskander can save Fin's friends without him deliberately handing the sacred relic over to evil hands!'

He turned on Fin furiously. 'Do you not realise, Delphin, that possession of the Cross would increase Lord Gressil's power to an unimaginable degree? Not only will you fail to save your friends, but you will also cause the deaths of countless innocent people!'

Fin looked at him scornfully. 'I don't intend to just meekly hand over the cross to Hardwick, but I can't let the twins die, while you piously ogle it. There's no choice – I have to use the Chi Rho to trick Hardwick, however dangerous that will be!'

Turning away, he stared out through the small window at the grey sea and Cuthbert's Island in the distance. His voice thick with emotion, he muttered: 'I'm – I'm hoping Mossy will help me.'

'Your good Mossy has no power over the might of Lord Gressil,' snarled Rory 'The Chi Rho belongs here, it is not yours—'

'Enough Rory!' cried Hilda, her face white with anger.

Suddenly, Lark let out a yell, giving them all a start. 'ENOUGH OF YOUR ARGUMENTALS! The cross was put in Fin's care, with Mr Mossy's approval, for a purpose that we don't know yet, and it certainly wasn't given to you, Brother Rory.'

His cheeks flushed, he turned to Wings. 'I reckon we should get back to Durholm and take our plans on from there. I've had a feeling for a while, that piece of jewellery has a nasty side – look at us arguing. As for the twins, I always knew the silly chumps would get into bad trouble.'

Fin gave him a bleak smile, then looked apologetically at Rory. 'Brother, perhaps one day, the journey of the Chi Rho will come to a safe end, here in Holy Island, but for now, a mere Delphin has been given charge over it; even though he probably will never know half of its mysterious power. I had decided, when I returned from the Anchorite on Cuthbert's Island, to leave the cross here in the care of the Community, but seemingly it was not meant to be.'

Brother Rory didn't reply but turned on his heel and stalked out of the room.

Hilda sadly watched him go. 'Iskander said he would wait for you two days at most,' she told them, 'I hope he has not already set out. Rough seas delayed me, and he and his Squad were desperate to follow Hardwick's trail while it was fresh.'

'Then we must get a move on!' Wings exclaimed, 'I'll drop you lads off at Durholm and then go on to Brightdale. I need to get there before nightfall: I hate flying in the dark. Thank goodness, I've already refuelled! Lads, fetch your rucksacks, and we'll meet at Skyhook.'

Returning from collection their rucksacks, they saw across the courtyard Brother Huw talking to Mother Hilda. The little Scav angrily waved his stick in their direction. He knew that Huw, like Rory, would hate the Chi Rho being taken away again.

Fifteen minutes later, they were all gathered around Skyhook, waiting for Wings to join them. He arrived carrying a large grey plustic sack. Shoving it into the cargo hold, he explained that Huw wanted him to take the sack to the brothers at Durholm. Stowing his own pack under his seat, undoing the ropes holding down Skyhook, he clambered aboard, and fiddled impatiently with his instrument panel, waiting for Fin, Lark and Mick to get seated. The moment they were settled, he fired up the engine. Skyhook rose into the air and with a look of grim determination Wings set off on a straight course, south: this time he intended flying over land.

Looking down, watching Hilda and Rory growing ever smaller, Fin saw Rory's face was contorted in bitterness. He wondered how it had come to this, that the Chi Rho still lay in his purse. Feeling the weight on his chest, he knew he probably wouldn't have found the courage to hand the cross over on Holy Island. He thought about the vile Frit head lying inert on Rory's desk: he was glad he'd had the presence of mind before leaving to salvage Bird's plaited headband. He put his hand inside a pocket in his jerkin, feeling the soft feathers.

As they flew over Cuthbert's Island, he scanned the dunes: there was no sign of his mother.

Unbeknown to Wings, he had another passenger on board. In the cargo hold behind Lark's seat, Crow, squashed in the almost airless plustic sack stowed there, let out an involuntary burp. Terrified that he'd been heard, he clapped his scrawny hand to his mouth to keep back the plume of bile rising in his throat. Panting for air, Sparkie poked his nose enquiringly out of a pocket in Crow's chainmail jerkin.

'We be quiet as mousies, ratty mine, or fulla-flea mutt kens us,' Crow snickered softly into his pet's tattered ear.

Despite the terror of being high in the air, and the rumbling roar of the engine shaking every bone in his thin body, Crow's heart glowed with joy: he was only a few feet from his beloved jool, with a good chance he'd soon get it back from the Delph with the black grass-top, and at the same time have his revenge on the mutt.

From leaving Durholm it had taken nearly two days for Hilda and Crow to reach Holy Island. Captain Shell's prediction had been right: a Saprise storm had sent their boat scuttling for shelter in the tiny fishing harbour of Craster, where Crow took the opportunity to sneak on shore to find food, raiding a fisherman's cottage larder for a smoked herring and a bottle of berry juice. Next day, leaving Craster before dawn, they docked at Holy Island as the sun rose, and as soon as the crew had gone to the Fisherman's Friend for breakfast, Crow had slipped out from his hiding place to search for Brother Huw. Using survival instincts honed over years of struggle in a hostile world, he soon nosed out Brother Huw's quarters: a snug attic room above the Priory kitchen.

Brother Huw, furious at being woken from a sleep mercifully free of arthritic pain, showed no pleasure at meeting Crow after so many years, angrily accusing him of wanting to steal the Priory silver. Cowering on the dusty floor as Huw shrilly berated him, terrified the racket would alert the entire Priory, in his panic Crow had told Huw of his hope to get his stolen jool back from the gangle Delph.

Peering short-sightedly into Crow's snot-glistened face, understanding dawned on Huw. 'Ah, you'm after t'Cross! I'm have you know, Cross not a piece of Scav tat for you to keep, but beloved by us here on t'Island – beloved, beyond telling!'

'Any road, Delph not here, gone to see t'Anchorite on Cuthbert's Isle. Spect he back soon – Mother Hilda has brung bad news, and I reckon he be gone again soon and take Cross too, if I knowed that Delph reet.'

'Dat not good, Boss Huw!' squeaked Crow, hopping up and down in agitation. 'Dat Delph mustn't take our jool away!'

A sly gleam flashed in his one pale eye. 'How bout I ketch jool back for you, eh, Bro?' he wheedled with a cringing leer, taking Huw's arthritic hand in his thin grasp. 'You know I good at stealin' – but you must aid Crow first.'

Brother Huw peered doubtfully at him. 'I don' know— What I do know is you wicked lad, Crow!' He shuffled up and down, muttering to himself. 'We love t' Holy Cross, us brothers and sisters, we all truly love t' Cross. We long to have it safe back.' He came to a halt in front of Crow. 'O.K. First I go and find out what goin' on.'

Leaving Crow hiding under his bed, taking his walking stick from by the door, the old Scav hobbled off down his narrow stairway. A while later he returned with the news that the Delphins intended to fly straight away, and the gangle Delph was to take the jool with him.

Crow flew into hysterics. It took all Huw's old kudos as a Scav gang's commander to calm him.

He then quickly hatched a plan: Crow would go in the flying machine. Hidden in the hold, he would try to steal the cross. Huw would persuade Wings to take a bag of documents to Durholm: a favour the pilot had done before, when Huw had wanted to exchange records with his fellow scribes. From his small Scriptorium, he brought a bulging plustic sack filled with old bits of parchment. He took out enough to let Crow climb inside, stuffed some parchment back around him, and loosely tied up the opening with string. This done, he went off to find Wings.

Inside the sack Crow waited in agonies, dreading that Huw might have betrayed him, but he soon returned, accompanied by Wings.

Lifting the sack, Wings immediately dropped it, complaining about the weight. In the end, tired of Huw's squeaky pleadings, he heaved it over his shoulder and stamped off, still grumbling.

So, that was how Crow came to be a stowaway on board Skyhook. Full of hope, he knew that if he kept his wits, his precious jool would soon be back around his neck. Despite his solemn promise to Huw, he had no intention of bringing the cross back to Holy Island.

He sniggered inwardly. 'Boss Huw wants me save the lovely jool for Holy Isle. Not likely me do that! Me loves it too much!'

Hearing a sharp canine yap from outside, he choked off a scornful snort.

With one stop to refuel from a stash Wings kept hidden in a clearing deep in the forest, they arrived at Durholm midday. Kenji was waiting for them on the landing area beyond the orchard, his clothes torn and dirty, his arms and face still livid from ganglefowl feather stings. As they climbed out of Skyhook, they looked in shock at the ruins of the refectory and kitchen. The thought of Bird and Bee being there during the attack made Fin feel sick.

Seeing his distress, Kenji squeezed his shoulder. 'No need to fret lad, we'll soon rescue your friends! Hurry now, collect your rucksacks. Sandy wants to follow Hardwick's trail as soon as possible. It'll be a hard slog, but nothing fit young Delphins can't manage! But first you'll need something to eat – to fettle you both for the journey: we'll go and see what Grantly can provide.'

Leaving Wings to attend to Skyhook, Fin and Lark set off after Kenji.

As they picked a way through the rubble, Lark realised Mick wasn't with them.

'Where's the dratted tyke?' he muttered. Returning to Skyhook, he found him crouched behind the rear seat, ears pricked, sniffing at the plustic sack still stowed in the luggage hold. 'Come on lad,' Lark growled, fishing him out by his scruff, 'even if you're not hungry, I am.'

Catching up with Fin and Kenji, he found them staring down into what had been a cellar beneath the kitchen, now open to the sky and filled with a crusted sickly yellow goo. Lark's stomach heaved: suddenly he wasn't all that hungry.

'The damage looks worse than it is,' Kenji said. 'They've cleared the muck from the cathedral and will start work on the kitchen today. Grantly's dug down to his larder, unearthing a whole cheese, squashed but edible, also a couple of sides of gammon, which makes a change from ganglefowl stew.'

The cook was in the garth, stirring a cauldron bubbling over a makeshift fire set in a circle of bricks. 'Iskander's with the wounded in the Great Chamber,' he said, ladling them out bowls of bacon and lentil soup. 'Help yourself to bread and cheese.' He waved his bent ladle at a trestle table on which lay a large slab of dusty looking cheese with a pile of grey bread beside it.

Between gritty mouthfuls, they gave Grantly and Kenji news of Mother Hilda and Holy Island. When they'd eaten, they headed for the Great Chamber. Mick trailed proudly behind, a meaty gammon bone in his jaws.

In the Chamber, they found Dancer lying on her bed of straw bales, her reptilian face still swollen from stings; Fescue was bathing her brow with lavender water.

She held out trembling hands. 'I'm so sorry lads—' she choked, unable to say any more.

'Now, Dancer,' Kenji said firmly, 'You put your life on the line singlehandedly tackling a flock of Snoopers: there was nothing more you could have done!'

'Aye,' Lark said gruffly, 'it wasn't your fault – as I've said before, the scatty chumps should never have come on this jaunt!'

Sandy came over from where he was comforting an old man with a bandaged head.

'Well lads, I wish things could have turned out differently. But the fact the Phragg in Hardwick is heading for Birdoswald, and not Contagion, gives me hope. I believe the Demon covets the cross for himself; his greed is even greater than his fear of Lord Gressil!'

'He can have it for all I care!' Fin said, glaring around challengingly. 'I just want to get Bird and Bee back safely.'

Fescue, dropping the bowl of lavender water with a clatter, leapt to his feet. 'No! No! You cannot hand the sacred relic to Hardwick!'

Wings' arrival stopped an angry retort from Fin. He gazed sadly at the rows of injured filling the Great Chamber. 'What a mess the whole place is in!' he exclaimed. 'You've got to admire Grantly, the man's a miracle worker!' He patted his stomach. 'His soup has fettled me nicely for my flight to Brightdale.'

He knelt for a moment at Dancer's side. 'I say, old girl, you'll have to buck up: by the time I get back with Zaggy, we'll need your famous Skwid tracking skills.'

He turned to Fin and Lark. 'I must be off, chaps. The sooner I go the sooner I can get back – don't want to be flying in the dark! Come and see me off!'

Skyhook, ready for take-off, Wings climbed into his seat and snapped on his goggles. 'I'll be back with Zaggy a.s.a.p. We'll stop off here, but knowing him, he'll want to fly on to catch up with you chaps – so look out for us!'

He frowned. 'Not sure about Dancer. Looks pretty done-in to me. Besides, I couldn't carry both her and Zaggy, too much weight – best if she stays here.' He jabbed the starter. Skyhook's engine burst into life.

'YOU'LL SEE THETIS FOR ME, TELL HER I'M ALWAYS THINKING OF HER?' Lark yelled above the noise. Wings gave him a thumbs-up.

Watching Skyhook rise into the sky and slowly turn to a dot on the horizon, Lark felt as if his heart would break. How he longed to see Tissy, to take her in his arms, feel her cheek against his, smell the lavender in her soft hair. Why ever had he come on this journey?

With a quivering sigh, he pulled himself together. What stories he would tell her, when – or if – he finally did come home. Swiping his sleeve across his teary eyes, he whistled thickly to Mick, and followed Fin back to the Chapter House.

Wings was halfway to Brightdale when he remembered Huw's plustic sack. Craning around, he saw it still in the luggage hold. He shrugged, there was nothing he could do about it now, he would have to hand it to the Brothers in the Scriptorium when he returned with Zaggy.

'They're probably too busy, anyway, clearing up the mess,' he told Skyhook, patting her instrument panel.

Sitting at the table in Mossy's bookshop in Brightdale, for a moment Tissy thought she heard Lark's familiar laugh outside the window. Looking up from grinding the lump of brown rock in the mortar, she saw Sparrow Chippen there with a chum, studying the books in the window. Sparrow's laugh was rather like Lark's.

Lark's face swam into her mind: how he looked at her in that special way, his sea-green eyes full of gentleness. Dropping the heavy stone pestle into its mortar, she touched her puckered lip, remembering how he liked to run his finger lovingly over the scar. What was he doing now? In all the excitement of his adventures, did he ever think of her?

She took out her handkerchief and blew hard. Flexing her aching wrist, she began again to grind the pigment. It was tiring work, but after a while she observed with satisfaction the fine rich ochre powder. She looked across the long table at Mossy, his face close to a page of creamy parchment as he added another word to the line of glistening black lettering. Dipping his quill into the inkwell, he smiled at her over his half-moon spectacles and she felt as if sunshine had suddenly come out from behind dark clouds.

The only sounds in the shop were her grinding, the scratching of Mossy's quill, and an occasional whiffle from Lass dozing beneath the table. It was early evening: from outside came the muffled noise of bustle as shopkeepers closed for the day. Taking that as a signal, she packed away her equipment, emptying the freshly ground pigment into a jar. Cleaning the pestle and mortar, she returned them to their shelf, lingering for a moment to straighten the jars and pots, putting off going home to Dandrum Den where her father lay inert, stretched out on the oak table in the Great Hall, his washed-out green eyes wide open but unseeing.

Nobody would tell Tissy what had happened after uncle Marlin's funeral. Mossy had come, white fire in his eyes, bringing turmoil to the Dandrum household. Ever since, Ramora, her old grandmother, had sat stony faced by her dad's side, refusing to move, whilst her mother and her sister had taken to their beds, leaving her brother Kelp to run the farm with Hollin Annunder the ghillie.

There was one bright incident: Grammer Nutmeg, who'd taken charge of the domestic life of the Den, had sent Daffodil Akest packing. Tissy couldn't help grinning as she recalled Daffodil stomping down the road to Watersmeet, dragging her clothes bundle behind her, wailing that Fin had cruelly abandoned her.

It was Nutmeg who decided that Tissy should spend her days with Mossy, away from all the misery and stress. Quick to learn, she could already name a dozen or so pigments, and knew what to mix with them: oil, egg, or vinegar, magically transforming the dry powders into glowing hues of blues, reds, greens, yellows, and browns. Mossy was so impressed he allowed her to add illuminated letters to the pages in some of the books and scrolls stacked on the shelves in the shop.

Given an advantage other Delphin lasses never had, she should have been happy, but always at the back of her mind was her fear for Lark, Fin, and the twins – gone into unknown lands beyond the safety of the Dale.

Her thoughts went back to the day after uncle Marlin's funeral, when she'd been woken from a deep sleep by Grammer Nutmeg, and found herself in Bird's bed, the twins gone.

When she told Nutmeg what they had seen creeping up Mossy's shop wall, the old Delphin had become so hysterical it had taken an age to stop her trembling.

'I knewed it, I knewed it,' Nutmeg screeched, 'like a cloud of burning rags, weren't it? Didn't I say there's a murdering devil roaming t'Dale! It's taken the lasses for certain!'

Scrambling into her clothes, Tissy found Bird's note tucked inside her left shoe. Reading what Bird had written, her mind became a turmoil as she imagined Lark leaping into the Brightwater where her sister, Alaria waited naked, her arms wide and a pretty piece of lace tied around her lank hair – instead of the grey strip of flannel she usually wore for swimming.

Reading the letter, Nutmeg snorted scornfully. 'Well, fancy snooping after Fin and Lark – as if they would go skinny dipping at this dreadful time, what with Master Marlin's ashes still warm up there on Kirion.'

'I hope you're right, Grammer! I couldn't bear it if Lark had taken a fancy to my sister!'

The old Delphin had laughed at the idea. 'Tissy, you know'd Lark's been moping after you, like a whippet that's lost its rabbit, for a year 'n more! Now finish getting dressed – we must go to Mr Mossy's and see what he has to say about all this.'

At the bookshop, Mossy was expecting them, his door opening as they knocked. 'Come in, come in, Mrs Annunder and young Thetis, too. Upstairs you go, and we'll put the kettle on.'

Seated on the sofa, sipping nettle tea, Tissy showed Bird's letter to Mossy, explaining about the weird thing she and the twins had seen crawling up his wall.

After reading the letter, Mossy put it down and began pacing the room. 'Things are not well here in the Dale!' he muttered broodingly. 'The dark emanation you saw last night is, as you Mistress Annunder feared, the reason for Marlin's murder. That demon is one of two who are roaming the Dale!'

They listened in horror as he explained about the Sneaksoul infesting Roach, which he had sent packing, and about its demon accomplice, whom he knew had been lurking around the bookshop on the night of Marlin's funeral.

'Those devils are searching for a precious jewel Marlin had in his possession, a treasure he brought with him from his wanderings. Now he is dead, Fin has inherited the jewel, which is the reason Fin has left Brightdale, to draw the evil away.'

In the heavy silence, Tissy and Nutmeg had tried to take in what Mossy had said. Tissy's heart went out to Fin: his dad murdered, and now an evil monster after him.

'Poor Fin – and Lark too – being so brave, going off into the unknown and danger!' It was hard not to cry at the thought of Lark not coming to say goodbye.

'Ah, Mr Mossy, whatever's happening to our peaceful homeland?' Nutmeg sobbed, tears running down her crumpled cheek. 'What with Master Marlin killed, Master Roach lying as if dead, and – and my Fin and Lark with evils after them!'

Patting her shoulder, Mossy tried to reassure her. 'Do not fear, Mistress Annunder. I have powerful friends who will protect Fin and Lark.'

Fishing a lacy handkerchief out of her sleeve, Nutmeg mopped her eyes. 'I'm sure your friends are mighty, but I shan't be at peace until I can clap eyes on my lads, knowing they've come to no harm. In the meantime, I'll put a bowl of bluebells by Phul's shrine up at the Den, for their safe return – but how come the twins have got themselves involved in all this?' she added, her small mouth working angrily. 'They need a good telling off by their dad!'

Mossy sighed. 'That is a very unfortunate complication! But it is no use fretting over green peas spilt on green grass, as you would say, Mrs Annunder.'

'I should have been braver!' agonised Tissy, 'if I hadn't taken sickly, I could have talked sense into them!'

'Now, don't you fret yourself, Tissy love,' Nutmeg said, 'you couldn't have stopped that naughty pair. I know my Lark: he'll send them home with salt on their tails!'

She shook her head in wonder. 'These are strange days, Mr Mossy, whatever is going to become of us?'

For a while they gloomily sipped their tea.

Glancing up at his mantelshelf, Mossy suddenly stood to take down a small box. 'Thetis, Lark asked me to give you this!' he exclaimed.

Handing her a small box, Tissy lifted the lid. Inside, a battered silver ring nestled on a pad of sheep's wool.

'Before leaving, Lark gave me that ring, asking me to tell you that he hoped you would wear it, so as not to forget him. He said it was his mother's: the only memento he has of her. He begs that you be patient and when he comes home, his greatest wish is for you to go Skinny Dipping with him,' Mossy added solemnly.

Tissy's cheeks burned as Nutmeg wrapped her plump arms around her. 'That's what I've always hoped for,' the old Delphin cried, 'you and Lark getting wed!'

Speechless with joy, Tissy studied the cracked green stone set in tarnished silver. Slipping the ring on her finger, it fitted perfectly.

Coming out of her reverie, Tissy twisted the ring on her finger. The dull green stone was more precious to her than any weighty jewel full of sparkling fire.

A sudden scratching at the front door made her look up in surprise. Under the table, Lass growled and stood, hackles raised. The scratching came again, this time more urgent. Putting down his pen, Mossy hurried out into the lobby, followed by Tissy and Lass.

When Mossy opened the door, they couldn't at first work out what was lying on the step: it looked like a muddy bundle of coarse fur. Sniffing it tentatively, Lass began licking it agitatedly. At one end, a thin bedraggled tail, sticking out from the heap, thumped weakly, and at the other end a bloodshot eye opened.

Tissy groaned. 'Oh Mossy, its Wolfie!'

Lifting the bundle into his arms, Mossy quickly peered into the shadows in Market Place before slamming and bolting the door. 'Go upstairs Thetis and get the kettle boiling,' he hissed.

Tissy ran up the stairs two at a time, Lass close on her heels. Mossy followed, calling out: 'When you have got a kettle boiling, put a pan of milk on to warm. Then fetch a bucket of water from the well.'

After struggling up the stairs with a heavy bucket, Tissy found Mossy had laid Wolfie on the sheepskin in front of the fire, with a thick towel beneath him. Lass was hunkered close by, her big brown eyes full of distress. Tissy poured hot water into a bowl, adding water from the bucket to cool it. Squeezing out a wetted rag, she gave it to Mossy who began washing away the mud and blood.

As he worked around the neck, he spotted something glinting in Wolfie's rough fur. Gently parting the matted mess, he drew a sharp breath. Leaning close, Tissy saw, almost embedded in the flesh, a fine gold chain strung with pearls. Gently, Mossy attempted to pull it away but stopped when Wolfie let out a whimper.

'Fetch my pliers,' he commanded. Leaping up, she searched through the tools on the table and came back with a jeweller's wire cutter. Snipping carefully at the gold links, Mossy teased the chain of beads away from the flesh.

Holding the pieces up to the light, he exclaimed. 'This is a rosary! It must have belonged to a member of the Community at Durholm.'

Taking the broken links from him, Tissy noticed a wad of some grassy stuff wound around one part of the chain. The wad gave off a strong smell of urine. Disgusted, she dropped it on the hearth, and turned back to help Mossy clean Wolfie.

A while later, Mossy sat back on his heels. 'That is most of the dirt off. I'll apply some balm to the wounds. When I've taken the wet towel from under him, you can feed him with the warm milk. Use a spoon and pour a bit at a time through the side of his mouth.'

Whilst Tissy spooned milk between Wolfie's teeth, Mossy picked up from the hearth the piece of chain wrapped with the wad of reed. At the table, he teased apart the stinking leaves with tweezers, eventually coming upon the inner, clean leaf on which Bird had written the message in her blood. Carefully spreading out the fragile leaf, and putting on his magnifying spectacles, he bent close.

'Thetis, here is something strange! Come, see with your young eyes what you can make of this.'

Taking up a magnifying glass, she examined the piece of rush. Wrinkling her nose against the smell, making out faint brown lines, she soon realised they were smudged letters.

'It's a message!' she gasped. Bending even closer, she attempted to decipher the smudges. 'Yes! I can read a word: dear, then some blotches, and then a capital letter D, followed by another word: in – in – invaded! Then I can just make out more letters: h, e, l and p – help!'

She turned pale as below help she made out the names Bee and Bird. 'The twins have written this!' She peered hard again. 'It gets clearer. I can read escaped, then smudges, then the capital letters F and C! Mossy, what ever could it mean?'

To her dismay, she saw tears glittering in his dark eyes. Turning to look at Wolfie, lying unmoving, scarcely breathing, dread clutched her heart.

Mossy paced the room. 'I must go there, I must go—' Seeing Tissy's anguish, he stopped and gave her an encouraging smile. 'But first things, first! The brave hound needs urgent attention. Come, Thetis, his wounds are terrible, if not mortal. We will take the poor creature to St. Aidan's shrine, to anoint him with the healing waters of the Holy Spring. Then we will take him to Spinner Hall, to lie by his own hearth in the care of his family.'

Carefully lifting Wolfie's limp body into his arms, he made for the stairs, Tissy and Lass close behind.

All was quiet as they hurried across Market Place. At the far end, they turned into a lane leading to a small stone shrine in honour of Holy Aidan. Laying Wolfie on the ground and taking the tin cup used for drinking the sacred water, Mossy gently poured water over the hound's head, at the same time softly whispering a prayer. A lump in her throat, Tissy knelt by Wolfie's side, tenderly stroking him. After a little while, Mossy again lifted Wolfie, and they headed for Spinner Hall.

As she trotted by Mossy's side, Tissy became aware of a thudding inside her head, and desperately hoped that she wasn't going to faint like she did when she had seen the monster with Bee and Bird. Slowly she realised that the noise was coming from the deep blue evening sky. Mossy stopped and looked up.

'Wings has come!' he exclaimed, 'thank our dear lord God! Hurry Thetis, we must take the hound to Spinner Hall, then quickly return to the shop.'

He strode on up the hill, Lass loping by his side, Tissy scurrying after them, Mossy's long strides making it hard for her to keep up.

Events became a blur for Tissy. At Spinner Hall, they gave Wolfie into the cook's startled care, and did not linger to see the family. Back at the shop, Mossy rushed upstairs and rummaged through the drawers of his bedside cabinet. Tissy looked on, worried and frightened.

'Thetis, come and see,' Mossy called, bringing out a box, richly decorated with silver and mother-of-pearl flowers. Unlocking it with a small silver key hanging on a chain about his neck, he brought out a shimmering blue cloth. 'The precious treasure I told you about, that Fin took away with him, used to be kept in this box, wrapped in this cloth,' he explained. 'The box and the cloth are very holy: I want you to take them for safe-keeping to Nutmeg Annunder up at Dandrum Den.'

He looked at her sadly. 'I have to go away for a while. I will leave you in charge of the shop. Take Lass home with you every evening.'

Heart racing, she stared up at him, not quite taking in what he was saying, but before she could ask any questions, there was a hammering on the shop door. They rushed down the stairs. Pulling back the bolts, Mossy flung the door open. A tall man stood there, dressed all in leather, with thick round goggles perched on top of his leather helmet.

'Zaggy, you're needed urgently!' the man gasped. 'I wanted to get here sooner but Skyhook had engine trouble!'

Tissy found his story hard to follow; he seemed highly distressed, saying the little lasses had been taken, gabbling about Fin and the 'cross thingy', and why had he called Mr Mossy 'Zaggy' – what did it all mean?

Mossy listened intently, and at the mention of having to risk flying in the dark, he nodded briskly before finally introducing the stranger to Tissy. 'This is my friend, Wings – Wings, this is Thetis Dandrum. Fin's cousin.'

The man shook her hand and frowning distractedly, his expression suddenly brightened. 'Of course – young Lark's special friend! Now let me see.' He rubbed the stubble on his grease-streaked chin. 'Yep, he asked me to pass on a message: 'tell her, I'm always thinking of her'.'

Tissy couldn't stop herself: she burst into tears.

Mossy wrapped her in his arms. 'There, there, little lass, all will be well, I promise you!' Taking out his handkerchief, he gently wiped her eyes. 'I am sorry, Tissy, but I have to go away now with Wings in his flying machine. There is no time to explain. I hope to return soon with Fin, and the others! But come, you can see us fly off!'

Grabbing his stick and firmly commanding Lass to stay, Mossy locked the door behind them, before handing the key to Tissy. Already loping ahead of them, the man called Wings led them to the stretch of river where, in Highsun, young Delphins went midnight skinny dipping. Staring in wonder through the gathering dusk, Tissy made out the bulk of a strange contraption that looked like a huge insect, standing on the small sandy beach.

Mossy hugged her again. 'When I have gone, go back to the shop, damp down the fire, and after locking up, take Lass with you to Dandrum Den. Do not forget the precious box! I shall be back as soon as I can!'

He turned away to climb into the machine. Making the frame creak, bending his knees to his chin, he eased himself into one of the wicker seats. Wings swung into the front seat and began fiddling with the controls. With a great roar, the contraption came to life, making her stumble back in fright. Grumbling and shaking, it rose into the air, soon disappearing into the darkening sky.

Clutching Mossy's key, as she listened to the flying machine's roar become ever fainter, a huge lump rose in her throat. When the sound finally died away, she set off for the shop. Sobbing as she ran, she tried to work out what had just happened: it had all been too sudden and strange to take in. Thinking of the crude cry for help scratched on the leaf, all she knew for certain was that Bee and Bird were in desperate danger.

Then she remembered the message from Lark, and her heart sang.

# 15
# TO BIRDOSWALD

Skyhook finally lost to sight, Fin and Lark rejoined Sandy and Fescue at the Chapter House. Saying goodbye to Dancer, once more they picked their way through the debris, out onto the cliff path. Climbing down the ropes left by Hardwick and his Frits, they joined Kenji, already on the pontoon he had used earlier. Once across the river, they set off in single file with Fescue leading, following the horseshoe trail they had found earlier. From the sun's position, it was already well into the afternoon.

Tucking Mick into his jerkin, Lark had firm words with him. 'Now you keep out of mischief,' he growled.

He kept close to Kenji, his eyes searching the undergrowth, fearful they'd attract the attention of any giant slug, orange haired imp or other unnatural creature that might be lurking there. He decided the terrain might seem like his Annunder forest; the same oak, ash and aspen, with the under-story of holly, willow, and brambles, but an alien stench lingered on the air, and he reckoned it was from those gangle birds they said had invaded Durholm.

All afternoon, they scrambled up steep hills and down into deep valleys, faces and hands scratched by brambles. Knowing for certain that Hardwick and his Frits were heading for Birdoswald, they soon abandoned tracking the horseshoe prints. Even so, they kept an eye out for signs of evil as they headed north-west. Most of what they came across was of little significance; Mick, free from Lark's jerkin, had a go chewing on a ganglefowl pin feather caught on a bramble, but spat it out; Fescue found a piece of torn rag, stained with Frit oil, which he tucked into a pocket, and Kenji found a sandal with a broken strap, which he recognised as Hardwick's, so threw it away in disgust.

The sun was dropping behind the trees when they came to an ivy clad ruin beside a shallow, fast flowing river. Sandy decided they should stop and rest; he told Fin and Lark the place was Blanchland, just as ancient and holy as Durholm, and the river, a tributary of the great River Tyne, was called the Derwentwater. They flopped down on the mossy ground, backs against a tumbled wall. Opening his supply bag, Kenji handed out portions of sunflower seeds and sour-sweet dried bilberries.

As he ate, Lark looked about the peaceful place; a purple haze of bluebells spread away into the green shade, dappled soft gold by the westering sun's rays. From the branches above came the comforting cooing of collared doves. Mick splashed belly deep in the river, taking gulps of cool water. Too tired to join him, Lark took a swig of lukewarm water from his drinking flask. Chewing moodily on seeds, he thought longingly of Grantly's ham and lentil soup they had eaten that morning.

He sneaked a look at Fin, slumped beside him, his Delphin brows drawn into a deep frowning V as he stroked the soft grey feathers that decorated the headband belonging to Bird. His seeds and bilberries lay untouched on a dock leaf beside him. Lark dreaded what Fin might be planning.

'I'll have to keep a close eye on him,' he told himself silently. 'Watch he doesn't do anything daft, like sneaking off after Hardwick – without me or Mossy.'

He wondered: if Tissy had been taken, would he be brave enough to face the evils to save her?

He didn't like the sound of the Doomstone Mines, either. Sandy had told them that to reach the Frit camp at Birdoswald they must go through those ancient coal mines that stretched under the Tyne river. To Sandy's annoyance, Kenji had turned unusually jittery, muttering something about the mines being the home of the Phragg monsters.

Lark glanced up at Kenji, perched on the wall, a distracted look on his face as he absent-mindedly polished his belt buckle with his sleeve. Lark admired that buckle, fashioned from a Frit's head, the lens eyes replaced by green stones. Kenji tightened the ganglefowl beak he used as a clip to tie back his glossy black hair and jumped down to sit beside him.

'Shall I tell you about this land?'

Lark nodded eagerly, glad to escape his troubled thoughts.

In his sing-song voice, Kenji began: 'This forest is my work-place! People, long since dead, built their homes here and farmed the land. Now deer, sheep and goats graze among the moss-covered ruins, and boar snuffle in the leaf litter beneath the thick tree canopy. Wolves and big cats have returned, and herds of aurochs roam freely, unhindered by wall or hedge, growing huge on the lush vegetation.' He threw back his shoulders and thumped his chest. 'I can read the animal runs like my own palm, track the spoor of deer, goat or boar, with the certainty of a good roast supper at the end of the day!'

Suddenly his voice went harsh. 'But on this trek, we are heading for the Doomstone Mines, and you don't go there, if you want to keep your sanity!' He glared at Sandy, stretched out, eyes closed on the grass nearby, and continued in a low voice. 'Now, I shall tell you Sandy's story, as told to me by my inestimable grandmother.'

His black brows puckered as he collected his thoughts. 'Iskander comes from a royal line: he is descended from King Flaithri of the Cyning Clan. You will recall that it was King Flaithri's son, Prince Caedyrn, who went into Contagion to try to kill the Slug Queen. Their ancestral home is in the north, way beyond the Wall.' He waved vaguely to where he thought that might be. 'But Sandy was born in the south. His parents were members of a Geek colony who lived in a Motherhome near the Holy Community of Yrving. His father was Flaithri the Tenth. His mother is Ailis of the Stuarts – she is also of the Gaiakin peoples.'

Lark looked across at Sandy in wonder; that confirmed what he'd always suspected: Sandy was part Gaiakin.

Kenji continued. 'When Sandy was a child, the enemy invaded their Motherhome, slaughtering most of the people, including his father. But Sandy and his mother escaped, taking refuge with the Gaiakins of Florain, where he grew to manhood. His mother still lives there.'

Kenji whispered in Lark's ear. 'Sandy has a girl in Florain; he wears her pendant on a chain about his neck. I've glimpsed it, a yellow enamel flower with a gold letter B, for Betony – that's her name. She's a stunner. You think Fescue is amazing to look at, but his looks are nothing compared to Betony!'

A little way off, Fescue sat on a wall, shoulders hunched, holding the Frit-oil stained piece of rag he'd found along the path. He flung it to the ground, leapt to his feet, and began pacing up and down, muttering to himself, every now and then shooting an odd look at Fin, making Lark wonder what was going on in his alien mind.

'Fescue has changed of late,' Kenji murmured as he studied the Gaiakin from under his hooded eyelids. 'His human side is showing; his shining eyes have clouded over. I wonder just what happened when he struggled with that Phragg in the cathedral?'

'Aye, there's something not right with him,' Lark agreed. 'I learned from Fin, Gaiakins could feel and see things beyond the scope of mere mortals. Is it true Gaiakins don't die?'

Kenji nodded. 'They are immortal unless they are killed.'

Lark looked in awe at Fescue as he paced the ground. 'Do you know his history, Kenji?'

'Only some of it – he has lived far longer than you or me!

'Fescue and his brother, Mullein, are half-human. From their mother, they inherited the Gaiakin longevity. Their father, who was human, is long dead. He too came from King Flaithri's line. Their sister, Tormentil, inherited their father's human traits, and is dead too; Fescue and Mullein still mourn her.'

A loud bellow from nearby interrupted Kenji, making everyone start to their feet.

'Raddled rams, whatever's that? Sounds enormous!' Lark yelped, peering fearfully through the trees.

Gathered close together, weapons in hand, they listened to loud crashing from the undergrowth. Moments later, a herd of huge oxen-like animals came into view: a bull and three females with calves.

'Keep very still! Aurochs!' Kenji commanded in a low voice.

The animals halted, swinging their great heads about, regarding them with their soft brown eyes, before lumbering on down to the river. Spooked by Mick's shrill barking, one of the females stopped and lowered her long-curved horns at him, but deciding the small dog was no threat, turned away with a derisive snort, to follow her companions to the water's edge.

Kenji chuckled. 'We must be more watchful of our surroundings!' he exclaimed. 'You have to be wary of aurochs when the females have young.'

Lark nodded sagely. 'It's the same with boar; the forest in Saprise is a dangerous place for those who don't have wood-craft.

'It is time to move on!' Sandy said. 'We shall now continue westwards for a while and make for a secret door that I know of, leading down into the Mines!'

Kenji frowned, but didn't say anything.

Puzzled and worried, Lark whistled to Mick. As he set off after Sandy, Fescue and Kenji, he realised Fin wasn't with them. He was sketching the aurochs drinking from the river.

'Get a move on, Fin!' he called softly.

'Sorry, Lark, I thought I'd better get in a quick sketch – Mossy would be keen to see a drawing of those animals!'

Lark tut-tutted impatiently as Fin, dropping his eraser, knelt to search for it. 'We mustn't get left behind!' he called.

'Here it is! I'm coming Lark!' Fin called, getting to his feet. 'I'll keep up I promise, I don't want to be last, and have to wash everyone's socks.'

Lark frowned. He certainly was going to have to keep an eye on Fin – he seemed to be going loco.

With the setting sun in their eyes, they trekked on. After a while, the terrain began to change. The deciduous trees and thickly tangled undergrowth were giving way to closely packed fir and pine trees, making their surroundings gloomy and the path slippery with dead pine needles.

Noticing the tired Delphins lagging, Kenji waited for them to catch up. 'Have courage, lads, the going will be easier now we are entering the borders of the Withered Wood.'

Lark looked about, frowning. 'Where's the thorn break? In Brightdale, you have to get through a thick barrier of thorns before you can get into the Wood.'

'Lark, you're forgetting our legend,' Fin said, 'the thorn barrier on our Delphin borders was put there by the Gaiakins for our protection – perhaps it's not just a legend after all, but true,' he added wistfully.

At the top of a steep slope, they looked down through the pine trees into a narrow valley, from where there came the soft sound of trickling water. Slithering down the sandy needle covered slope, a vinegary stench hung in the air, growing ever stronger.

Kenji stopped abruptly, causing Fin and Lark to bump into him. 'Can I smell hornet juice?' he murmured.

Fescue scanned the far hillside. 'There is a Snoopers' nest over there!' he hissed, pointing across. 'Iskander, surely you are not taking us that way?'

Sandy smiled grimly. 'Yes! We are going into the Mines through a Snoopers' nest – an unguarded back door used by the monster insects and not known to Frits – I do not intend knocking on their front door!'

Even as he spoke, from across the valley came a loud insistent thrum. Silhouetted black against the red glow of the setting sun, three of Gressil's Snoopers appeared from behind a stand of Douglas fir. They flew in V formation just above the treetops, following the line of the valley, their wings stretching out six feet on either side of their wasp-shaped bodies. As they flew, poison dripped from their backsides, the acid shrivelling leaves on the topmost branches of the trees. Then, as if in response to a command, the giant insects swooped away to the west, to where Contagion lay.

Reaching the valley bottom where a stream oozed sluggishly along the forest floor, Sandy came to a decision.

'Despite the smell, we shall have to rest here until first light.'

Finding a dry area away from the stream, they settled down to a supper of yet more seeds and berries. Then, wrapping their blankets about them, they lay down to snatch sleep. Mick, in protest at the lack of supper, after munching loudly on a mouthful of seeds, crept into Lark's blanket to whimper resentfully before falling silent.

Fin closed his eyes, pretending to be asleep. When he heard regular breathing from the mounds that were his sleeping companions, he lifted his head and peered about carefully, stifling a cough as the fumes caught his throat. No breeze stirred the branches criss-crossing the velvety sky.

Gazing across the stream at the dark hillside beyond, he considered what Sandy had said, that he knew of an entrance into the Mines up there. Bird and Bee were in that place, without protection. Kenji had referred darkly to Frit larders; the mental image of the twins strung up like pieces of carrion to be eaten as a delicacy by Frits, terrified him. He should get to them, sneak off now! Not wait for Mossy!

Pushing back his blanket, he hesitated: he had no plan! Only Sandy knew of the mine entrance. It had just been bravado when he'd told Brother Rory he wouldn't just swap the Chi Rho for the twins but find a way to save the cross too. If he got caught, Hardwick and his Frit thugs would take the cross from him anyway. And even if Hardwick agreed to let the twins go, would he let him go? He thought not. He must face it: his days were numbered. At best, he'd end up in the Frit larders, and find a quick death by having his throat cut. And at worst? Could he brave a lingering death in Contagion, like Prince Caedyrn? He covered his mouth to muffle an involuntary groan. Mick, giving a little yap in his sleep, made him start. Lark turned over, muttering a curse, but didn't wake.

Looking at Lark's dark form, affection washed over him. If he'd known the dangers they would face, he wouldn't have accepted Lark's companionship; his place was in Brightdale – being a ghillie and marrying Tissy. Should he wake him, and tell him he must go home, with or without the twins? There would be a huge row, and loyal, stubborn Lark would never agree. He wished he could turn back time, be in Brightdale with his simple day to day problems, like hating boar hunting.

Then came the memory of Cuthbert's Island: the feel of his mother's rough hand against his cheek, the smell of fish stew in the little cottage. No, he didn't want to turn back time – he'd found his mother!

A stab of pain where the Chi Rho lay inside his purse, reminded him why he was here, in this evil smelling place. Fighting dizziness, he lay back down. Closing his eyes, weariness overcame him, and he plunged into a dark dream of bony fingers clawing at his chest.

Bird suddenly woke. Sitting up, bewildered, she found herself on a thick bed of dusty straw. Above her glowed a glass ball of warm red light. In its radiance, she saw around her the glint of steel mesh, and realised she was imprisoned in a large cage. All about her in the straw lay huge eggs, the size of footballs, glowing pearly pink.

Puzzled, she tried to recall what had happened. Had it been a nightmare, or had she heard Bee screaming? The memories flooded back: their capture by Hardwick and his Frits, being roughly lowered down the cliff into the boat, rowed across the river and flung on the back of a ganglefowl. And the horror of the journey: her face pressed against the ganglefowl's stinking leathery side, the torture of thirst. Worst of all, hearing Bee's whimpers as the ungainly stride of the ganglefowl repeatedly jarred her broken arm. Eventually she must have slipped into unconsciousness.

She couldn't recall how she'd ended up in this horrid place. She scowled in disgust at the eggs, from which came a muffled chirruping. Shoving them aside, she probed about, in the half-hope that Bee might have buried herself in the straw. There was no sign of her. Pressing her face against the mesh, she saw a long dark tunnel lined with rows of cages, each cage with its own red light. They all contained clutches of giant eggs. Her spirits rose: they must have put Bee in another cage. Scrambling over the eggs, she peered to the right and then to the left, but nothing moved beneath the red lights.

'Bee! Bee!' she called, the sound of her voice dulled by the tunnel's dead air. The chirruping from inside the eggs stopped abruptly; she sensed things were listening as the silence pressed in on her.

Shuffling to the cage door, she rattled it, but it was chained and padlocked. She spotted a bottle of water outside the mesh, with a tube leading into the cage. Realising how thirsty she was, she sucked eagerly on the end. The water was wonderfully soothing, even though it tasted sour. A metal container was attached to the inside of the door. Gingerly putting her hand inside, she brought out grains that looked like dried insects. Trying a bit on her tongue, they tasted pleasantly salty-sweet. Shovelling a handful into her mouth as she munched, she searched about in the straw, hoping to find something, perhaps a piece of metal, with which to pick the lock.

A sudden loud crack from one of the eggs in her cage gave her a start. She watched in fascinated revulsion as the shell began to open and a yellow beak poked out. Around her more eggs cracked open. Soon all along the rows of cages, albumen-covered ganglefowl chicks tumbled out on to the straw, filling the tunnel with the sound of cheeping.

It wasn't long before the chicks were trying to stand, staggering up on their gangling legs, little bald heads swinging on snake-like necks, glittering black eyes examining their new world.

The hatchlings in her cage crowded around her, and fearful of their stinging feathers, she pushed them away with her booted foot. But two kept wobbling back to her, and before she could stop them, they hopped onto her lap, where they settled down to preen their new plumage. Accidentally brushing her hand against their feathers, she found they didn't sting, and she stroked the chicks, enjoying their comforting warmth. As she stroked, their heads flopped down over her knee, and they fell into a deep sleep. The rustling and cheeping stilled, as in cage after cage, the hatchlings went to sleep. Overcome by drowsiness, her head dropped forward onto her chest, and slumping over into the straw, she fell into an exhausted sleep.

'Here they are, Raaum. All fresh, souls intact.' The harsh voice dragged Bird back to consciousness.

A rubbery burning stung her nostrils. Hardwick rattled the door chain, setting off a commotion of cheeping from the hatchlings. Rage bubbled up inside her. Pushing the babies out of the way, she scrambled over to him.

'Where's my sister—' Her voice died in her throat: a smouldering black cloud hovered beside Hardwick, so close she could feel the heat from the white-hot heart pumping within the ragged depths.

Two fiery eyes studied her. 'Oh, yess, oh yess, friend Beliaal: female Delphin, soft and malleable! That'll do nicely,' crackled Raaum, the Phragg who had once infested Roach Dandrum.

Bird shrank back.

'But weren't there two female Delphins?' Raaum whined. 'Who's pinched the other? I deserve a choice – after what I suffered, being cruelly dragged out of the runt Roach by the black angel.'

Saying the word, angel, the fiend gagged, and a molten spume cascaded from its maw, spraying sparks across the tunnel floor.

Hardwick leapt aside. 'Yes Raaum, I heard you've had the Zagzagel treatment!' he choked in the acrid smoke. 'You're right. There are two Delphins, which one would suit you? This feisty one, or the more docile one?'

He searched along the rows of cages. 'Where's the other one?' he shouted to two Frits cringing in the shadows.

'It was nearly deaded, master,' thrummed one of them, its metal parts rattling in terror as it crept into the light.

'We took it to 't cookhouse fer roastin', whilst t'were fresh,' quaked the other, lurking behind its companion.

Hardwick turned apologetically to Raaum. 'Sorry, the other Delphin is not here: I'll send the Frits to the cookhouse to find it. By the by!' He pointed at Bird. 'I happen to know this particular Delphin is very friendly with the one who has you-know-what,' he tapped his hooked nose conspiratorially.

Crackling and hissing, Raaum regarded Bird with greater interest. 'I see what you're getting at, Beliaal my friend – if the other's too damaged, we could still have a use for this one – more reason for the half-breed runt to hand over the cross.'

Cowering amongst the hatchlings, Bird listened closely. What did the demon mean by the half-breed and the cross? Did it mean Fin and the Chi Rho? Was that why she and Bee were prisoners – to be used as hostages?

'We'll take this Delphin upstairs, whilst they find the other one.'

Hardwick swiped one of the Frits across its orange topknot.

'Make yourself useful, scab. Open the cage and catch this flea,' he snarled.

Metal claw trembling, the Frit unlocked the cage door and leaned in to grab Bird's leg. She was too quick, darting out of reach amongst the squirming chicks.

After several attempts, the Frit dragged her out. Some chicks escaped at the same time, disappearing into the darkness, leaving a cloud of floating baby feathers. Bird tried to scramble after them, but Hardwick, pressing his foot on her back, held her down. One of the Frits, whipping rubber-coated cable from its pack, swiftly lashed her wrists and ankles.

'If she's damaged, I'll twist your wiry sinews in knots.' Hardwick stabbed the Frit's lens eye with a forefinger. 'I'll take charge of her now. You two get upstairs and find the other Delphin – if it's dead you'll answer to this Phragg, here.'

Squealing in fright, the Frits scuttled off.

Hardwick gave Bird a vicious kick. 'You behave yourself flea, or you'll never see your sister again.'

Heaving her over his bony shoulder, he set off after the Phragg, already a fiery glow in the distance.

Bird could hardly breathe. Choking for air, she passed out.

She returned to consciousness in a vast cavern with daylight streaming in through a high arched entrance. Hardwick had dumped her at the top of stone steps that she assumed led up from the hatchery. Lying still, collecting her wits, she realised that whilst her hands were still tied, the wire binding her ankles had worked loose, so with careful movements she managed to free her feet.

The cavern was in uproar. In the centre, a mob of cheering, whooping Frits surrounded at a safe distance, two cock ganglefowl. The huge birds, armed with vicious spurs strapped to their thick legs, were slashing at each other. Scarlet wattles wobbling wildly, blood and pinfeathers flew as the two Frit handlers, grimly holding on to ropes attached to their headstalls, tried to control them. Outside the throng, Hardwick was hopping about shouting, attempting to make his hoarse voice heard above the yelling and honking. Its fiery rags swirling, the Phragg hovered nearby, more and more irate. A tongue of flame shot from it towards one of the fighting birds, instantly turning it into a ball of fire. Exploding into wild panic, the yelling Frit mob scattered, tripping over one another, desperate to escape from the gyrating inferno.

Bird seized her opportunity. Hands still tied, she staggered to her feet, and darting behind a row of large boulders along the cavern wall, dashed for the entrance. Outside, she dived into a thick privet bush, where she crouched, heart in mouth, listening to the pandemonium inside. Hardwick's voice still screeching above the metallic thrumming and squawking, she knew she must get away quickly. Peering out through the leaves, she wondered where they could they have put Bee. In front of the cavern was an area of beaten ground littered with rotting food crawling with maggots. Inside a circle of log benches, a cauldron hung over a dead fire. Full of dread, she remembered that a Frit had said Bee had been taken for cooking. Could she be too late? Surely, she would feel, deep inside her, if Bee's body were in that pot? She daren't go and look; she only had moments before the mob would rush out of the smoke-filled cave.

To her left, about twenty yards off, close to a rusty chain-link perimeter fence, was a short stretch of wattle screen. Beyond loomed a dark forest of pine trees: that was where freedom lay. Realising it was pouring with rain, she held up her face, licking the water thirstily. The wet, dripping down her arms, was making the rubber-coated cable binding her wrists slippery. Wriggling hard, her hands came free.

Dashing to hide behind the screen, she realised from the stink that the area was a urinal. Shaking the rusty wire fence, she found it was only loosely fixed to the ground, with places where she could slip underneath. She hesitated: if she got away now, she'd be free but would never see Bee again. Cooking smells wafted towards her from a ramshackle building nearby: it must be a cookhouse. Could Bee have been taken there? Breaking cover once more, crouching low, she ran for it, and dived behind a mound of rubbish sacks piled against the end wall.

Screaming and yelling from the cavern growing louder, she cautiously poked her head around the corner of the building to see black smoke belching out of the entrance, filling the air with a stink of burning feathers. Frits on fire were rushing out through the smoke, the flames hissing and spitting in the pouring rain. Others were sitting on the log benches moaning, a scattering of toasted bodies lying about them. One Frit looking like a torch on legs, reeling in her direction, collapsed into a puddle, to lie steaming peacefully. A moment later, Hardwick staggered out, batting at his smouldering sleeves, followed by the Phragg, still whirling frantically.

Diving back among the rubbish sacks, she hoped Hardwick hadn't spotted her. From an open window above came the sounds of clashing pans and raucous swearing. Climbing to the top of the sacks, she squinted in through a filthy net curtain. At a cooking stove a Scav was frantically scraping a burning frying pan. Around a long table, more Scavs were peeling and chopping mounds of mouldy potatoes, rotting onions and carrots. A gorilla-sized human was yelling instructions, belabouring them with a long-handled ladle. In the middle of the table was a suspiciously large package wrapped in dock leaves, loosely tied with string. Bird gasped: one end was open, showing the top of Bee's blonde head.

The kitchen door flew open, and a Frit stumbled in, well ablaze, splashing flaming oil over the Scav cooks. Flinging down their knives, as one they dashed for the door. Their boss followed, pursued by the burning Frit. The kitchen deserted, Bird scrambled over the window ledge and dropped down into a stone sink full of cold greasy water. Jumping out, dodging splodges of smouldering Frit oil, she ran to the table. Shoving aside piles of chopped veg, she clambered up and crawled to Bee's inert, leaf-wrapped form. Terrified of what she might find, she gently pulled away a dock leaf revealing Bee's chalk white face. Putting her cheek close to Bee's mouth, Bird felt warm breath.

Bee's blue-green eyes sparkled up at her. 'Is it morning already, sis?'

Bird gave a choking laugh. 'You're alive! You're alive!' she wailed, lifting Bee and holding her close.

'Course I am, silly. Just a bit battered.'

'Are you hurting, Bee?' Bird's voice trembled as she gently pulled away the dock leaves from Bee's body.

'Not much, apart from the pong coming from you, making me want to puke. Whatever have you been up to? Look at your hair, or what's left of it! I can see bald patches. You'll be in for a right telling off when Grammer Magette—' She groaned as the leaf binding fell from her broken arm.

'Sorry, sorry, love,' sobbed Bird, 'I'm trying to be gentle, but we've got to get away from here, quick. Do you think you can walk?'

Holding her broken arm to her side, Bee sat up gingerly. 'Every thing's a bit whirly, but if you help me, I reckon I can even run, if I have to.' She looked down at herself. 'But I'm not going anywhere like this, I'm as starkers as the day we were born!'

Bird grabbed a large grubby apron, and wrapped it around Bee's naked body, using the ties to bind her broken arm. 'Thank goodness, it's big enough – it must have belonged to that revolting cook.'

Bee picked disgustedly at the apron. 'I've got issues with that greasy bloke. It was him who trussed me up. As dad would say, I'll have his innards for braces!'

Bird gave her a hug. 'I've missed you so much, sis. But come on, we must get out of here. I've found a way to escape – under a rusty fence outside, and into the forest beyond. If we're lucky, we should be well away before they find we've gone.' Her voice quivered. 'I wish we had Dancer with us.'

Bee's face puckered. 'Do you think she's still alive? She was bleeding dreadfully.'

'I'm sure Sandy would have saved her,' Bird said encouragingly as she helped Bee down off the table.

To save Bee having to climb over the sink and out of the window, she decided to risk them being seen. Peeping round the door, she heard shouting from some buildings a distance away to the left, but the area outside was deserted.

Taking Bee's good arm, she hurried her round the side of the kitchen, to the rubbish dump. 'Sit here for a sec, whilst I look for a hole in the fence.'

Working her way along the bottom of the chain link, she came to a gap wide enough to get under. Running back to Bee, she pulled her to her feet.

'Quick! Run!'

She was pushing Bee under the wire, when a voice from behind chilled her to the bone.

'Got you!' hissed Hardwick. A heavy rope net fell over her.

'Run, Bee, run!' she screamed.

But Bee lay unmoving, her face grey with pain.

'Your sister a bit poorly then?' Hardwick guffawed.

Bird turned and spat, hitting him full in the eye. With an angry squeal, Hardwick slammed his fist into her face. Pinpricks of light danced before her eyes and everything went blank.

Fin woke with a start. A chill dawn light was creeping in through the trees: he saw the others were already up. Furious with himself for going to sleep and not slipping away, he chewed miserably on the sparse breakfast of sunflower seeds Kenji had provided.

'Would've chickened out anyway,' he muttered.

Scowling up at the gloom of Withered Wood, he remembered when he and Tissy were small, sitting in Grammer Nutmeg's room listening, with excited dread, to her warnings.

'Withered Wood is a dead place – never go there! It's full of evils, waiting to capture and torment you!'

He'd ended up here, anyway.

He searched the grey strip of sky, just visible between the topmost branches of the pine trees, hoping to hear the drone of an engine. Surely Mossy would guide Wings to the Doomstone Mines?

'Right lads, it is time we got going,' Sandy called, shouldering his rucksack.

Wearily they got to their feet, and leaping over the small stream, scrambled up the hillside, the pine needles slippery beneath their hands and boots.

The sun was well risen when they came upon the armoured face of a dead Snooper poking out from the rotting bole of a fallen tree, jaws set in a permanent snarl of fearsome incisors, its empty eye sockets glaring at them in warning.

Close by lay a pile of bleached bones, peppered with rusty Snooper stings, a tarnished scimitar was gripped in the skeletal hand. 'A Skwid Trekker, long dead,' Kenji muttered.

The vinegary Snooper fumes, drifting through the trees, became ever stronger, reminding them that they were heading towards what they dearly longed to fly from.

They almost stumbled upon the nest, half buried in the hillside, the tops of the surrounding fir trees scorched black by dripping venom of arriving insects. The nest was a honeycomb-like structure of dusty grey parchment, at least twenty feet across and twenty-feet-high. Most of the hexagonal holes were collapsed or blocked with debris, except for a hole in the centre which, gaping open like the beak of a baby bird, was large enough for the passage of giant insects.

Listening anxiously for the sound of buzzing, all appeared quiet. As they gingerly climbed, using the honeycomb of holes as footholds, the brittle papery structure threatening to collapse beneath their boots, the rising dust made them cough. At the central entrance hole, they crawled in one by one, and crouching together in the confined chamber, studied their surroundings. Through the grey light coming in through the translucent walls, they saw at the back of the chamber two tunnels burrowing into the hillside, each large enough for a Snooper.

'An entrance and an exit,' Sandy whispered, 'which is which, Fescue? Can you tell?'

Fescue shuffled over and, after examining each hole, indicated the left tunnel. 'This is the way the insects go in. If we do not wish to meet a hornet coming out, we must go this way.'

Taking a deep breath, he plunged in. Sandy followed, with Kenji on his heels.

Fin, about to crawl in after them, realised Lark was still crouched at the entrance. 'What's up, Lark?' he whispered sharply.

'Mick's still mucking about below!' Lark called anxiously.

Fin looked out to see Mick whimpering agitatedly at the base of the nest.

'Come with us, or go home with yer tail between yer legs,' Lark hissed savagely.

Swiftly cocking his leg against a nearby tree, Mick attacked the nest as if he were after a fleeing rat, tumbling through the entrance covered in dust. Terrified that the racket might have alerted a huge insect, Lark quickly stuffed him inside his jerkin. Taking in a great gulp of air, he dived into the tunnel.

As Fin followed, he desperately fought down the urge to turn-tail and escape. From within walls of the structure he heard sounds of scratching, and every now and then, a small face or waving tentacle would suddenly appear from a hole. To his relief, he realised they were natural: spiders, beetles, earwigs, and other small creatures.

From ahead came Sandy's low voice: 'Fescue, are you able yet to see with your inner sight? Can you locate the lasses?'

'Not so far, Iskander! In this foul place, it is difficult,' came Fescue's muffled reply.

Fin despaired. Were they too late? He pictured Bird cowering beneath a shower of Snooper stings. He recalled the time on Coquet Island when Wings had shown him the deep puncture mark on his arm. Could a Delphin survive such stings?

'I knew I should've drawn my sword before getting into this narrow space,' croaked Kenji. 'If I came upon the backside of one of the insects, I could have skewered it! It might have made tasty eating! My grandmother tells me the people in my lost homeland often hunted and ate giant hornets – I reckon Snoopers would give more meat!'

'But taste worser!' Lark muttered.

They crawled on miserably, until Fescue called softly: 'Take heart friends, here is a nook where we can rest for a few moments.'

One by one, they crawled into a cramped chamber. In the grey light, they saw that the floor was covered in dead insect cases, every movement sending up a cloud of wings and carapaces. Keeping as still as they could, listening to the scurrying of hundreds of creatures along hidden passages, they rested.

Suddenly Kenji let out a yelp. Frantically shaking his left leg, they watched in fascinated disgust as, from out of the orange Frit fur decorating his boot top, wriggled a long black body with hundreds of waving legs. Landing on the back of Lark's hand, before he could react, Mick leapt out of his jerkin, and snapped off the back end, leaving the front to wriggle rapidly out of sight through a crack in the wall. Crunching on the last morsel, Mick settled down to scratch.

Their expectant gaze returned to Fescue, sitting with his chin on his knees, his eyes closed in intense concentration, so still they wondered if he'd fallen asleep.

Eyes still tight shut, he began twisting his head from side to side. 'I can see— I can see close by, a – a faint light! Whether it is the soul of one of the Delphin lasses, I cannot yet tell.' He returned to silence for what seemed to his companions an age.

Abruptly, he gave a cry. 'I see a soul in torment!' He stared wildly about. 'Hurry, we must get into the Doomstone Mines – we must not delay.' Pushing past Kenji, he tumbled out into the tunnel.

Scrambling after him, they watched anxiously as he prodded the papery walls. Pausing to press his ear to the surface, he said: 'It is thin enough here to break through.'

Drawing his golden dagger, he hacked at the parchment-like surface, soon opening a jagged rent. A thin stream of dry black grit cascaded out, filling the air with fine dust. Kenji joined in, and soon they had a hole large enough to climb through. Peering into the darkness, they felt a warm draught of air blowing on their faces, recalling leather bellows at a forge.

'This is well done!' Sandy exclaimed. 'We can now get into the Mines without raising the alarm amongst the Frit folk. Fescue, your sight is keenest in the dark, you must again lead the way.'

Dreading what new horror might await them they started to crawl.

Fin, close on Lark's heels, wondered about the black grit that had fallen out of the hole. What was he was crawling in? Was he grubbing through Doomstone dust? He sniffed hard: the odour called to mind the sticky stone he'd picked up back at Phul's hollow. Were Bee and

Bird trapped, helpless, somewhere in this hellish place? Once again, he wished he'd plucked up the courage last night to sneak off: it must be easy to find the main entrance to the Mines – he would probably be guided by the stink of ganglefowl. Hardwick would be sure to be looking out for him, at what Sandy had referred to as the 'front door'.

But what would Mossy think, when he found out he'd handed over the Chi Rho to Hardwick? Surely the twins were more important than a piece of jewellery, however precious to some? He became conscious of the weight of his purse bumping against his chest. He had a strong suspicion that, when it came to it, he wouldn't be able to hand over the cross. A wave of resentment washed over him: Mossy should never have thrust this burden upon him. But then, how would Mossy ever find him here, deep underground, beneath tons of heavy rock?

Miserably he crawled on. He had been glad to escape the fumes of the Snoopers' nest, but in this lung-squeezing passageway, the suffocating dark seemed never ending. Fighting down panic, it was only Lark cursing close in front that stopped him from turning and escaping back into daylight and fresh air. Feeling out in the dark, his hand located the sole of Lark's joggling boot. Touching it every now and then, he forced himself to keep going.

After what seemed like an eternity, he became aware of a faint light ahead. Soon his elbows no longer bumped the walls, and his rucksack no longer scraped the roof. The tunnel was growing wider. It had also started to descend, steeply.

He heard Sandy calling anxiously to Fescue. 'I fear this way is leading us too far down. Should we not turn back?'

'There is light ahead, Iskander. Let us see what lies there!'

As Fescue called, a screech rent the air. A flash of bright light momentarily blinded them.

'What was that?' gasped Kenji.

From inside Lark's jerkin, Mick let out a muffled howl.

'Raddled rams, whatever have I got myself into!' whimpered Lark. Panicking, he tried to back down, but his way was blocked by Fin.

'Keep going Lark – no way am I turning back!' Fin croaked, his voice edged with terror.

'It is much lighter here!' Fescue's voice came from ahead.

Pushing onwards, they saw his tall figure silhouetted against a pulsating orange glow: the tunnel had come to an end. One by one they crawled out and stood, stretching their stiff backs and massaging their sore knees. Looking at one another in the light they saw that their faces were covered in black dust.

Lark shuddered as he wiped his hands on his trousers: 'I hope we haven't been crawling through Gressil's droppings!'

'No, this is good, honest coal dust,' said Sandy.

'I wonder where we are?' Fescue muttered, as they gazed about nervously.

They were standing on a narrow ledge high in a vast cavern, the roof lost in darkness. To their right and left rose rock walls, in front of them a deep abyss. The air was oppressive with malevolence. Edging closer to the rim they looked over: rising from the fiery depths were the tops of a forest of glistening black stalagmites, resembling huge pillars of animal droppings – turned to hard rock.

Sandy groaned. 'We have come to the Doomstone Pinnacles! These pillars are Gressil's ancient droppings.'

A gasp from Kenji made them start. 'What are those?' he cried, pointing across the chasm.

Clinging to the far wall, were row upon row of what at first looked like black bundles of rags, reminding them of giant bats; each bundle wheezed and squeaked restlessly, their insides pulsing red and white hot. One of the creatures flapped from its perch to hover momentarily on a thermal of hot air, before dropping onto one of the pillars. Opening its fiery maw, it sank its teeth into the glistening column. Tearing out a chunk, it munched greedily.

'Roosting Phraggs! We must get away from here!' Sandy hissed. 'Before they see us!'

Even as he spoke, Kenji and Lark, fell to their knees sobbing and moaning. Crawling towards the edge of the abyss, they would have hurled themselves over, had not Sandy and Fin rushed to pull them back.

Tears streaming down his blackened face, Lark fought to free himself from Fin's fierce grip. 'I want to die, I want to die. I'm sorry Tissy, you'll have to marry someone else, I'm never coming home,' he wailed.

He and Kenji had been overcome by the power of the doomstones.

Fin and Sandy heard Fescue calling, low and urgent, from further along the ledge from where he gesticulated to an archway.

'I have found a way out!'

Beyond him a flight of soot blackened stone steps spiralled upwards towards a faint red light. The Phraggs, alerted by Fescue's call, began to stir. Pushing and dragging Kenji and Lark, Sandy and Fin stumbled to the archway and up the steps following Fescue. As the loathsome cavern receded, Lark and Kenji's despair drained from them, and soon they were able climb unaided.

Losing count of the steps, overcome by weariness they sat down to rest.

Pouring water from his flask into his cupped hand, Lark gave Mick a drink. 'Well, whatever came over me!' he exclaimed. Turning to Fin squashed next to him on the step, he took hold of his hand and squeezed it. 'I was going to jump! I owe you one, Fin.'

'Why wasn't Fin overcome?' he asked, turning to look up at Sandy a couple of steps above them.

Sandy frowned in thought. 'The doomstone he picked up at Phul's Hollow may have given him immunity.'

Appalled, Lark shook his head in amazement. 'If those pillar things were Gressil's turds, he must have been huge when he deposited them! How did he ever get into the Mines?'

Quite restored to his usual self, Kenji grinned up at him from a few steps below. 'I reckon he'd got taken short, on his way to Contagion. Legend says he journeyed this way from the eastern North Sea. These ancient mines continue under Jarrow, and out beneath the seabed, for miles. Tunnels go under the land the other way too. One joins the Killhope tunnel, which is the main highway into the Land of Contagion – an easy route for any who have a yen to go crazy with fear.'

Fin shuddered. 'Do you think Crow would have come down here, to get his doomstone?'

'Who can say?' Sandy answered, 'it is a fearful place to venture into, but in his desperation for the cross, he could have done.'

'Do Phraggs need to eat? Did I imagine it, or did one of them take a bite out one of those – Doomstone Pinnacles, did you call them?' Fin asked.

From a step above Sandy, Fescue's deep soft voice echoed down to them: 'No, Phraggmorgia are dark spirits and do not need food or air. They eat the doomstone rock to fashion a more solid form for themselves, so to speak. Only when they take possession of a body and become Sneaksouls, do they relinquish this matter. When they abandon a body, they start all over again, plunging deep into the earth to consume the stones and to fuel their fiery form of the Phraggmorgia once more.'

'Where in the world did the Phraggies spring from?' Lark asked.

'They came with the Gaiakins, from the Universe of White Light, latching on to the tail of Universe Crosser, the ship in which the Gaiakin race travelled,' Fescue explained. 'There is a sculpture of it in the Great Courtyard at the Castle of Florain.

'Legend says that when Queen Maligne, first of the demons known as Phraggmorgia, entered the Universe of Stars, she landed on the dirty ice of a comet, and sailed across the Universe in search of a suitable ice nest where she could give birth to her children. But before she could find such a nest, two of them, the twins Hellion and Grimalkin, fell out of her body, and into a fiery volcano here on Gaia. That is why Phraggs love fire and molten rock. Some say that Maligne still lives, trapped in ice, and can never go near her many grandchildren, for fear of melting.'

'I've heard it said she lurks in the Great Iceberg, and you can hear her wailing for her lost children,' Kenji added, with a ghoulish leer.

Frowning disapprovingly down at him, Sandy said: 'Enough of that, Kenji. Come, we have rested enough – we must remember why we are here, in this evil place!' Rising to his feet, he looked up the steps winding towards soft red light. 'Hopefully, we shall soon come to the surface!'

So, Fescue led them once more, all eager to get away from the horrors behind them.

# 16
# STOLEN SOUL

Step by step the five trudged on up in silence, each lost in his own thoughts, until finally they stepped onto a landing. Before them were three tunnels: the left and right disappeared into darkness, from the wider and higher middle tunnel streamed red light.

Peering into the two side tunnels, Fescue breathed in the musty air: 'Those are the ways the Snoopers come and go – it is to be hoped those vile insects do not appear! Come, the way out will be through the centre tunnel!' He set off purposefully.

They found this tunnel easier going. As they marched, keeping close together, soon the sound of birds' cheeping could be heard, growing louder.

Lark held his nose. 'Pooh, can I smell chicken manure?' As he spoke, a cloud of fluffy white feathers drifted towards them.

'Raddled Rams are those stinging feathers?' he exclaimed, pulling his shirt collar up to his ears.

'No, these are from chick fowl, their feathers do not sting,' Kenji said, grabbing one floating past. 'Harmless – until the birds are fully grown and feed on stinging nettles.'

'This is good.' Sandy said. 'We are approaching the ganglefowl hatchery, which I know is close to the surface. It could be where Hardwick has imprisoned the lasses.'

Rounding a bend, they were confronted by lines of cages stretching along the tunnel, each with a red light above it.

Fin gazed in dismay 'There's hundreds of them – it'll take ages to check them!'

Mick scrambled out of Lark's jerkin, and running to the first cage, poked his snout through the mesh, setting off a chorus of squawking.

Dashing from cage to cage, they searched feverishly looking for a blonde head or Delphin face among the birds: there was no sign of Bee or Bird.

'Look, there is strong evidence that a Phragg has been here!' Fescue called from ahead. He indicated a puddle of glistening tar-like matter splattered on the rocky ground outside a cage.

Lark grimaced in disgust. 'Looks like something's sicked up oily burnt coal.'

Mick sniffed it, and leaping away howling, would have bolted back down the tunnel if Kenji hadn't caught him by a back leg.

'A Phragg has been here for certain!' Sandy exclaimed. 'A friend of Hardwick's, no doubt. Fescue, could they have put their captives in this cage?'

Fescue pressed his face against the mesh and closed his eyes. Ignoring the small beaks pecking at his chin, for a long moment he didn't speak. Then he uttered a shuddering sigh.

'Yes, a Delphin lass was here, which lass, I cannot tell – but I sense her brave spirit!'

Encouraged, they searched on, from cage to cage, finding only straw, broken eggshells, and hatchling ganglefowl.

All the cages checked, ahead was yet another flight of stone steps, wider than those from the mines they had just climbed. A soothing draught of cool air wafted down to them.

As they started upwards, Sandy scanned each step, and stopping at one, muttered: 'A Phragg has recently passed this way!' He indicated a nugget of still smoking black matter.

Higher up, Fescue gave a cry: 'Look, a tarred footprint! Could it be Hardwick's? This must surely be the way Hardwick and the Phragg took the Delphins!'

Hurrying on, as they stepped out into a lofty cavern with a high arched entrance letting daylight stream in. Fescue pointed to a twisted length of rubberised wire lying on the ground.

'That was used to bind one of the lasses. We are not far behind!'

The cavern was deserted. From outside, a clamour of honking reminded Fin and Lark of Brightdale at Leafturn, when flocks of geese came to feed on the stubble in the corn fields. A stench of burnt flesh lingered in the air, smouldering bodies lay strewn on the earth floor; mostly ganglefowl and Frits, with a few Scavs.

'What on earth happened here?' Fin asked, crouching down to a small burnt body, dreading it might be Delphin: it was a Scav.

Kenji held up a strip of charred leather harness. 'A Fowl Fight which got out of hand! Look, a piece of a headstall from a cock ganglefowl – the males have an evilly fiery temper.'

Sandy picked up a scrap of brown velvet cloth. 'I was hoping that the Frit army would be out on manoeuvres. But this fire indicates there are some about!'

Flexing his arm muscles, he unsheathed his sword from his back. 'Come – arm yourselves! We must be ready, even if we only encounter the cook and his Scav slaves.'

Kenji drew his sword and Fescue his golden dagger.

Scared, Lark hoisted Mick back into his jerkin. 'Get back inside,' he said in a shaky voice, 'this is no time for small dog's mischief.'

Drawing his boning knife, he saw with irritation Fin rummaging in his rucksack: surely, he wasn't going to start sketching! About to protest, he saw him unwrap the Dandrum sword from his spare shirt.

Sliding it from its pearl encrusted sheath, Fin held up the blade. The polished steel flashed in a shaft of sunlight. To his great satisfaction, Lark realised his master was at last showing his Dandrum quality.

'That's a pretty piece of weaponry,' Kenji remarked, 'but won't make much impression on a sinewy ganglefowl leg!'

Fin glowered at him as he tucked the naked blade into his belt: 'It's the only weapon I've got – until I become a Trekker like you, I'll have to make do.'

Sandy smiled indulgently. 'Right, are we all armed? Lead the way, Fescue!'

One by one they sidled out of the cavern, and from behind thick bushes scanned the compound.

Surrounded by a series of brick and wooden buildings, the compound was enclosed by a rusty wire fence. Beyond, Withered Wood loomed dark and menacing. Searching the empty sky, Fin listened for the drone of an engine: no such sound came.

'What is this place?' Lark whispered to Kenji beside him.

'This is Birdoswald. Long ago it was a military camp. You could say it still has military purposes, for the Frits use it as a Barracks: it is here they breed the ganglefowl.'

The compound appeared deserted, with no sign of either Hardwick or the twins. In an area of beaten earth where some log benches had been set about a now dead fire, several bodies lay smouldering.

Leaving the cover of the bushes, they dashed to the rear of a long hut where stained bedding had been draped over the windowsills, indicating the Frits' dormitory. Crouched beneath a window, from inside they heard a low moaning.

Suddenly a Frit's face appeared, and a stream of vomit cascaded down on Lark's head, directly below. Caught unawares, he let out a loud curse and the Frit gaped in amazement. Its tinny screech of 'BURGLARS! BURG…' was cut short by Kenji's sword slicing through its wiry neck. The head bounced to the ground, scattering oil and screws. Disgustedly Lark tried to clean himself up, picking bits of mouse fur and bones from his hair.

'Forget it, Lark,' Sandy commanded as he headed for a thicket of tall bright green plants.

As they ran, the honking that had reminded them of wild geese, became a cacophony. Nearing the plants, they realised to their alarm the thicket was a plantation of giant stinging nettles. Stems as thick as beanpoles, both stalks and leaves were covered in stiff, extra-long hairs.

Fescue and Sandy set off on hands and knees along a furrow between a row of plants. Before diving after them, Kenji called a warning to Fin and Lark.

'Cover any bare skin as best you can: these nettles are fed with a top dressing of ganglefowl manure!'

Collars and cuffs pulled over their hands and necks, as they crawled a stinging miasma radiated from the nettles, and by the time they emerged their skin felt as if it were on fire.

Wiping their burning faces with spit, an astonishing sight confronted them. Behind chain-link fencing, hundreds of huge, long-legged birds milled about. Spotting the intruders, they rushed to the wire. Stamping their enormous clawed feet and shaking their backsides at them, the air filled with downy feathers.

Struggling out of Lark's jerkin, Mick barked at them fiercely. The honking became deafening.

'Teg's knackers!' yelled Lark, swatting away feathers, his voice almost drowned by the racket. 'That's done it! We've gone and rung the front doorbell, alright!'

Dreading discovery, crouching low and running beside the rows of nettles, they headed for a large concrete building beyond the fowl pens. As they drew near, they realised from the smell of blood hanging heavy in the air that they were approaching a slaughterhouse.

Fescue halted, crying out in alarm: 'I can feel— Delphin— very near— also— also— Phragg!'

Sandy gestured to the building. 'Do you mean in there?'

Fescue grimaced in anguish. 'I fear so!'

Dashing to the ivy clad side wall, they peered in through a low window. Through the grimy glass, they made out rows of pale carcasses hanging from the rafters, the blood still dripping from gutted bellies onto the floor piled with viscera – glistening livers, coils of intestines, quivering pink lungs, still pumping hearts. The carcasses were mainly ganglefowl, but among them were several long-horned goats and a couple of deer. For one horrific moment, Fin thought a small corpse might be a Delphin, then realised the flesh didn't have the pale green Delphin skin but was Scav grey.

The scene and the smell of rotting flesh turning their stomachs, they became aware of an all too familiar, even stronger stench, acrid and foul, reminding them of the Phragg roost deep in the Doomstone Mines. Crowding together, in turn they squinted around the corner of the building to where a concrete ramp streaming with blood and viscera sloped down from wide open double doors. A smouldering black cloud hovered there: they had found the Phragg. In daylight, it seemed even more intensely evil, molten spittle dripping from its fiery maw. The blazing eyes were fixed gloatingly below on two small forms lying on the ramp.

Squirming past Fescue and Sandy to get a better view, at first Fin couldn't make out who they were, they were so covered in bloody filth. Then, seeing one move, he recognized Bird. Her clothes in tatters, her hair nearly all burnt away showing scorched skin beneath, she had started crawling towards the other small form wrapped in a dirty grey cloth, lying face down. Fin knew it was Bee.

Despair and rage banished terror. Drawing the Dandrum sword from his belt, he sprang into the open:

'NO PHRAGG! YOU SHALL NOT HAVE HER!'

Aiming his blade at the burning cloud, his boots squelching in the bloody mess, slowly he advanced up the ramp. The Phragg hovered, watching him interestedly. Forcing himself not to look at Bird, but at the demon's white-hot heart, he edged ever closer. The Phragg, grinning at him tauntingly, made a show of preparing to plunge on the small form below, pouting its crusted lips into a grotesque kiss.

A hoarse screech from inside the slaughterhouse distracted it; with a whirl of flames, it spun around. Fin made out two glowing green dots in the shadows by the doors: Hardwick's Sneaksoul eyes.

Stepping out onto the ramp, his rich robe torn and singed, Hardwick wasn't looking at the Phragg, but at him. Throwing back his hood, his thin lips grimacing greedily, he waved his claw-like hand at Bird and ran his long yellow thumb nail across his throat in a slicing motion, before stabbing his finger in the direction of Fin's chest.

Fin understood instantly what Hardwick's actions meant. He let go of the Dandrum sword, letting it sink into the muck on the concrete slope. Searching inside his jerkin, stiff fingers fumbled at the drawstring of his purse. As he put his hand in, it brushed the smooth crystal. A wave of exquisite longing brought a sob up from his chest: it was time to give up the Chi Rho. For a long moment, he fought to master his will, then slowly he drew out the cross. Gripping it fiercely, step by dragging step, he climbed the slope towards Hardwick. When almost within arm's reach, he opened out his palm. The Chi Rho had his blood on it: the hard, sharp jewels had nicked his skin.

'Nearer! Nearer!' Hardwick's voice wheezed.

Drawing closer, Fin could clearly see the malevolent sickly green glow in Hardwick's eyes.

'That's a good lad!' Holding out his trembling hand, Hardwick groaned in rapture. 'Give it to Beliaal, yess, to meee!'

But as he spoke his expression changed from gleeful greed to bewilderment and disbelief. Staring down at his chest, tottering forward, he grabbed hold of Fin's jerkin, choking on his own blood, then, arms flailing vainly, fell backwards. Behind him stood Fescue: his long dagger had skewered Hardwick straight through his heart.

Fin's senses reeled. Everything around faded.

*He was on the skull-shaped hill again, crouched on the bare earth beneath the man pinned to the wooden crossbeam. This time everything was more vivid: the jeering crowd pressing around him, reeking of sweat, the hooded stranger kneeling next to him, rocking to and fro, groaning from the burning pain of the blood that had splashed the back of his hand. As he threw back his hood Fin saw his beautiful face, bathed in the unearthly yellow light of that terrible day. He knew who he was...*

A sickening moan brought him back to his surroundings: Hardwick lay on the ramp, blood bubbling from a dark hole in his chest. Fescue stood over him, dripping dagger in hand. Twisting his head around, with his last breath Hardwick screeched at the Phragg hovering above Bird: 'DO IT RAAUM – STEAL HER SOUL…'

His voice died away, the evil green glow faded from his eyes, leaving just the face of a tired old man. From the hole in his chest a thin spiral of black smoke rose into the grey sky, drifted away, and vanished. The demon Beliaal was gone, his wicked spirit destroyed by a Gaiakin's golden blade.

Fin's despair turned to courage. Stumbling to where Bird lay struggling beneath the fiery rags of the Phragg, he held up the Chi Rho.

'HERE, TAKE IT! TAKE IT!'

A grip like steel clasped his wrist. 'The Cross is sacred: you cannot give it to the devil,' Fescue's voice spat in his ear.

'FESCUE, DON'T STOP ME!' Fin screamed, struggling to wrench free. But the bitter truth struck him: he was fighting a mighty Gaiakin. 'Please Fescue! Please let me save Bird!' he moaned.

Fescue's grip loosened slightly; desperate longing shadowed his extraordinary golden eyes. With shuddering sobs, he dragged Fin away from the Phragg.

At that moment Sandy's voice, powerful and commanding, thundered in an alien tongue. Eyes blazing with Gaiakin power, his sword scything above his head, he mounted the slope and raced towards the Phragg, sending it spinning wildly, shrieking in rage, sparks flying. He was within sword's reach of its white-hot heart when he slipped, his feet sliding on a coil of greasy intestine. Before he could regain his balance, the Phragg, lips pouting, plunged.

As it did so, a war cry rang out, as if every long dead Samurai had found voice again: Kenji, the warrior, with one great bound, hurled himself at the Phragg, thrusting his sword deep into its burning depths: in an instant, the blade melted. Molten metal pouring over his hand, Kenji fell to the ground writhing in agony.

Back on his feet, leaping over Kenji's prone form, Sandy was a fraction too late: sucking in a deep fiery breath, the Phragg fastened its cracked lips onto Bird's mouth. Her body slumped inert on the ramp. Raising its hideous visage, the Phragg leered: inside its maw, fluttering behind the imprisoning yellow fanged teeth, was the soft pearly glow of a small soul.

The maw snapped shut. The Phragg spiralled into the sky. Cackling with mirth, it streaked away, over the dark mass of Withered Wood towards Contagion, its trail of fire and smoke lost on the wind.

In the terrible silence that followed, gazing at the fading smoke, Fin wondered: would it have saved Bird if the Phragg had taken the Chi Rho? He suspected it wouldn't. Evils don't act honourably.

Without noticing, he hung the cross about his neck, and went to the burnt shell that was once Bird. Her face blackened by fire, he saw no vestige of Bird in the eyes, no life spark, but thankfully no sickly green glow. Taking his paring knife from his belt, he cut the cruel rubber-coated wire binding her wrists and ankles. On an impulse, he took out her silver bird pendant from his purse and slipped it over her head.

She struggled weakly as Sandy took her up to cradle her on his knee. Covering her with his cloak, she went still. Racked with misery, Fin clung to the hope that, because she moved and breathed, Bird must be somewhere in that seared husk. Leaving her with Sandy he went to Bee.

Fescue was holding her, his face pressed to her cheek, his tears washing the hurt from her scorched skin. Fin saw she was just alive, her eyes sparkling. Snuggling close to Fescue's chest, she took a long quivering breath before letting it go with a sigh. Fin waited, desperately hoping that her chest would rise again – it didn't. Fescue closed her eyes, drawing his gentle fingers over her lids.

Someone gripped Fin's shoulder; he looked up and found Lark, tears streaking his coal-blackened face. By his side, Mick pointed his muzzle to the sky and let out a high howl. Beneath Sandy's cloak, Bird shrieked in fear. Pushing the cloak away, her face appeared, her blank eyes searching wildly. She clawed at her burnt clothing, exposing raw skin. Fin tenderly covered her again.

Still holding her, Sandy got to his feet. 'Come Fin, come Lark, we must get away from here before the Frit army returns. I will carry Bird and Fescue will carry her sister.' He looked to where Kenji crouched, moaning softly, gripping his burnt hand. 'You must help Kenji.'

They were too late. From Withered Wood came the tinny blare of a cracked bugle and a hundred or so Frits on their ganglefowl galloped out of the trees. Streaming in through the compound's open gates and leaping from their mounts, metallic voices thrumming war cries, the Frits sped towards them. Hurriedly setting Bird down, Sandy drew his sword and strode to meet them. Fescue laid Bee's body beside Bird and followed with his dagger. Clutching the hilt of his melted sword in his good hand, Kenji tried to stagger to his feet, but the effort was too much, and he collapsed groaning.

Muttering a curse, Lark drew his boning knife, and fighting down terror, took his place by Sandy and Fescue. Mick followed close at his heels, his formidable ratter's teeth snapping excitedly.

Before facing the Frits and certain death, Fin knew he had one more task: to make sure the Chi Rho was safe. Lifting the cross from his chest, he felt a sharp pain as skin came away; swiftly stuffing the cross into his purse, he grabbed the Dandrum sword from where he'd dropped it in the muck on the ramp and wiping it on his trousers, ran to stand by Lark. The Frits, closing on them, the stink of rancid oil and grease turned his stomach. He planted his feet firmly apart, hoping to get in one killing blow before his throat was sliced open. He picked a Frit and as it charged him, its mouth snapping open, he carefully aimed at the uvula bobbing at the back of its gullet. Bracing himself for the impact, it dawned on him that he was going to meet the same death as his father – well, so be it.

The Frit was upon him. An agonising pain shot up his arm: it had ripped through his sleeve with its razor knuckle-duster, cutting deep furrows in his flesh. Spurred by rage he lunged, thrusting the Dandrum Sword down the Frit's throat. The metal jaws snapped shut, breaking the delicate silver blade almost at the hilt. The Frit fell backwards, drumming its metal heels in its death-throes. As the next Frit sprang at him a javelin flew past Fin's head, skewering the creature to the ground. Spinning around to see from where the javelin had come, relief flooded through him.

Out of the forest to the north thundered a squadron of Gaiakins, their huge horses seeming to fly, silver harness flashing. Leading the charge was Mullein, Fescue's brother. As he rode, he hurled his javelin into the midst of the Frits, skewering three in one go, as if they were meat for a barbecue. With blood curdling whoops, the Gaiakin fell upon Frit and fowl, swords slashing and scything until all were reduced to a twitching mass of flesh and metal.

The massacre swiftly ended, the Gaiakins dismounted. Fescue embraced his brother. Their comrades gathered round, cheerfully outdoing each other in boasting of the number of Frit and ganglefowl they had disposed of.

Calling them to attention, Sandy told them of the horror that had befallen them. As they listened, tears filled their shining eyes as they gazed sorrowfully to the abattoir's blood drenched ramp, where Fin and Lark crouched beside Bird and her sister's body, and where Kenji sat weeping, still nursing his burnt hand.

Anxious to leave the vile place with all speed, plans were quickly made. Some of the party searched the compound and buildings for any living Frits and their servants, others going into the great cavern to search there. They found it deserted, surmising that if any were still alive, they must have fled, either into the tunnels leading to the hatchery and the Mines, or into Withered Wood.

Sandy carried Bird to a woodshed by the gates and settled her outside on a pile of wood shavings. Fin, kneeling by her side, took hold of her hand. First helping Kenji to stagger to a log nearby, Lark returned to the ramp, and fetching everyone's discarded rucksacks, squatted next to Fin. Grief-stricken, he watched Fescue gently laying Bee's body by Bird's side and covering her with his cloak.

Leaving Fin and Lark in charge of the wounded, Sandy and Fescue carried Hardwick's body to where the Gaiakin warriors were piling up Frit and ganglefowl bodies in front of the cavern entrance, ready for burning.

Absent-mindedly stroking Mick leaning against his leg, Lark attempted to get his tumultuous thoughts into order: the horror of the fiery hellion, and then the pitched battle had numbed his senses. Everything had gone so horribly wrong. He tried not to look at the small mound of Bee's body beneath Fescue's cloak, but his eyes were drawn towards it. Bird, slumped in the wood shavings, was so scorched she looked like a cinder. Now and again she let out grunting sounds that made his skin crawl. Fin knelt, stony-faced, beside her, holding her hand, unheeding of the blood seeping through his sleeves. Lark couldn't pluck up the courage to talk to him – not with the strange, almost frightening mood Fin was in.

Nearby, Kenji rocked in pain as he clasped his blistered hand. 'My sword,' he groaned, 'my ancestral sword, handed down the generations, melted away!'

'Brave do on his part, stabbing the Phraggy,' Lark thought himself. He wished he could do something for him, but he knew his marigold ointment wouldn't be much use for such bad burns. What had happened just now? It was hard to take in: Fin had lost his head and marched off to hand over the cross to the enemy, as if it were just any old piece of ironmongery. And then Fescue had tried to stop him. Had he imagined it, or had he really seen Fin putting on the cross? Just what Mr Mossy had warned him not to do. Lark braved a peek at where Fin's shirt gaped open, and glimpsed blood.

'Serve him right if he's sent mad,' he muttered resentfully, disconcerted at how hurt he was by Fin ignoring him, when he was desperate to help – if Tissy (Phul forbid!) had been taken like that, he would have been grateful for any bit of comfort and support.

The smell of burning flesh and feathers, drifting from the Gaiakins' cremation pyre, broke his train of thought. Through a gap in the swirling smoke, he spotted Fescue and Mullein, heads close, silently communing. Was it Fescue who had called the Gaiakins to their rescue, with his weird Gaiakin powers?

It had been awesome to see the Gaiakin warriors scything down the enemy, not leaving a single Frit or ganglefowl standing. He looked to Gaiakin's horses tethered to a clump of willow saplings outside the compound gates. The powerful animals showed no sign of exhaustion, even though they'd galloped all the way from Florain, their stamping hooves shaking the ground as they pulled on their bridles impatiently, almost uprooting the saplings; the beasts would tower over the sturdy Brightdale ponies and he hoped he wasn't expected to round them up if they broke loose.

To his relief, he saw Sandy coming out of the smoke; he was accompanied by a female Gaiakin. Earlier, when she'd been introduced as Betony, Lark remembered that, when they were resting at Blanchland, Kenji had told him she was Sandy's girlfriend and that he wore her pendant shaped like a yellow betony flower. He agreed with Kenji, she was very beautiful, her warm brown eyes almost fox-like.

As they drew near, Mick set up barking, which frightened Bird, making her shriek in an odd creepy way. Betony went to her at once. Gently releasing Fin's tight grip on her hand, and taking her onto her lap, she cooed softly to her. Lark saw with dismay that Bird sniffed at her like an animal. From her pack, Betony brought out wadding, and wetting it with her water flask, tenderly washed the black from Bird's face.

'She'll get better, won't she, Miss Betony?' Lark asked. 'It'll break the Spinner's hearts if they lose her as well as Bee!'

Fin scowled at him, his face etched with misery. 'Can't you understand – Bird has gone, she's not there!' he snapped.

''COURSE she's there,' Lark shouted, both furious and frightened. Frantically he searched Bird's face for any sign of comprehension.

'SHE ISN'T, you great gollop!' yelled Fin, his voice cracking, 'the Phragg took her for his pleasure, and it's all my fault.' He stumbled away, his tortured face buried in his hands.

Lark looked pleadingly to Sandy, who shook his head despairingly. 'Fin may be right. I fear the Phragg has taken her soul – her poor little body is a dark, empty shell.'

'Then – then, we must stop the Phragger from getting there!' sobbed Lark, pointing a trembling finger in the direction of where he thought Contagion lay.

He glared at Fin, standing with his back to them, staring over the forest towards the brooding horizon. 'Fin might have given up on our Bird, but I haven't.' Snatching up Sandy's cloak, he tenderly draped it around Bird's shoulders. 'Lady, you must help her!' he pleaded to Betony.

'I will do my best, but I need time,' she said, exchanging doubtful looks with Sandy.

'Did you hear that, Bird lass, we'll make sure you're alright, just you be patient.' Lark patted her hand, making her cringe away from him.

Betony looked at Kenji rocking to and fro clutching his ruined sword. Leaving Sandy to hold Bird, she went over to him.

'Ancestral it was – melted, melted!' Kenji groaned.

'Well, Kenji, what do you expect – stabbing your blade into the fiery depths of a Phragg. A brave but foolhardy act.'

From her pack, she produced a small clay jar, and peeling off a thin seal of plustic film, released a pleasing scent of lavender and mint.

Curious, and glad of a distraction, Lark watched amazed. As she applied the creamy ointment to Kenji's raw burns, the pain faded from the warrior's face.

'What's in that ointment!' he exclaimed as Kenji, first shifting his Frit-head belt buckle to a more comfortable position, lay down in the wood shavings and closed his eyes in sleep.

'It is a mixture of herbs and oils.'

Betony dipped her finger into the jar and dabbed some on a blister where a spark had caught Lark's skin. He felt a pleasant tingling sensation creeping over his hand; gradually the soreness eased, leaving a warmth coursing through his body as if he'd drunk firewater.

'Are you interested in the Healing Arts?' Betony asked him as he blinked at her sleepily.

Lark shook his head to clear his vision.

'I've learnt simple healing skills by helping my Grammer in her still room, but I know she'd be amazed by this ointment; apart from willow-bark pills for the pain, the best she can concoct for bad burns is arnica mixed with baking powder.'

'When there is an opportunity, I will write down the recipe for her!' smiled Betony.

Lark thanked her politely but wondered what Grammer Nutmeg would make of it; there must be more to the ointment than just a mixture of herbs and oil – probably Gaiakin magic, with a pinch of Dragon's Blood.

Betony now went to Fin. Making him sit, she pulled up his tattered sleeve to expose the cuts.

'These wounds are deep, but I do not think they need stitching,' she said.

Fin seemed surprised, as if he'd only just noticed his injuries. Searching her pack again for a small glass bottle containing a purple liquid, Betony gently painted his cuts. Lark recognized what Grammer Nutmeg called purple gentian.

As she bandaged Fin's arm, Betony looked at him with concern. 'You must have come very close to a Frit's vicious razors,' she speculated.

'I'd no choice,' Fin said, pulling the Dandrum Sword from his belt to show her the hilt with its blade snapped off. 'My sword is for ceremonies, not fighting a Frit. Even so, I managed to ram the blade down it's throat.'

'Is this sword very old?' she asked, tracing her finger over the small bit that was left of the leaping dolphins etched in gold along the thin blade.

Fin nodded and tucked the hilt back into his belt. 'I shouldn't have brought it: the Dandrum Sword has been in our family for hundreds of years. But with the mess I've made of taking care of the twins: one dead, the other an empty husk, wrecking the Dandrum Sword hardly matters. A fine Dandrum Head I've been,' he added bitterly.

Betony watched him sadly as, shoulders stooped with misery, he slouched off to sit next to the rucksacks. Distracted by Mick sniffing at her hands, she bent down to scratch him behind his ear, and was rewarded by a lick on her nose.

'Well my friend, do I taste good?'

'Don't be fooled by Master Mick's soft tongue,' Lark said gruffly, 'he has teeth that are feared in the rat kingdom!'

Betony smiled.

Fescue, Mullein and their Gaiakin companions now returned, beautiful faces smudged with soot, their grim task done.

'We lit another fire inside the cavern to deter Gressil's hornet spies from flying out,' Mullein said.

'The smoke will have suffocated the baby fowl in the hatchery below!' Fescue added.

'I will be glad to leave this evil place as quickly as we can,' said a Gaiakin.

'We should burn it to the ground as we depart,' said another, looking over in disgust at the blood-soaked ramp leading to the slaughterhouse.

Fescue looked pleadingly at Sandy. 'Do we go to Florain, Iskander?'

Sandy stood in thought, and then nodded. 'Florain is where Zagzagel will head for when he finds us gone from here.'

Hearing this, Lark spirits lifted a little: they were going to Florain! And when Mr Mossy came, he'd cure Bird – get her soul back. Surely, he would? And on a personal level, he'd be able to wash off the sticky Frit vomit clinging to his hair.

'The way is long and the Delphins will soon tire on foot,' Mullein said, looking at Fin and Lark doubtfully.

'They will have to ride with you on your horses,' Sandy said. 'Also, Kenji!' he added, smiling down at him where he snored peacefully.

So, it was decided: Fescue and Mullein would walk, carrying Bee's body on a makeshift bier, whilst Sandy would ride with Bird on Mullein's horse.

Mullein and Fescue immediately set to, making the bier by tying Mullein's cloak to a couple of Gaiakin javelins. Then Fescue reverently laid Bee's body on it, covering her with his own cloak. Lifting the shafts to their shoulders, the Gaiakin brothers strode off, their heads bowed, the small body no burden to their backs, but heavy on their spirits.

Meanwhile, three Gaiakin warriors untied their horses, and led them, prancing friskily, to where the others waited. Lark stepped back nervously as he gazed up in awe at the animals towering above him.

He watched as Sandy, astride Mullein's steel-coloured stallion, took Bird from Betony. Seeing Bird struggling like a little tiger kitten as Betony handed her up, tears filled his eyes.

Turning away, he saw a young female Gaiakin had roused Kenji from his sleep and was picking wood shavings off his clothes. She wore peacock hued feathers twisted through her long shining hair, and Lark thought her very beautiful; he learned later that she was called Spring Spurge. Helping Kenji climb into the saddle of her horse, she leaped lightly up behind him.

Wondering which of the horses he would be riding on, and hoping he could go with Betony, he saw, with a stab of jealousy, that she had taken Fin up behind her. Seeing the utter misery on Fin's face as he held on to Betony, his arms tight around her waist, he immediately felt guilty, and resolved to make peace between them as soon as he had the opportunity.

Kenji, sitting behind Spring Spurge, gave a shout of laughter: he seemed to have got over the melting of his sword. He was quizzing Spurge about the food in Florain, doubting the Gaiakins' cooking skills, and speculating whether the Florain vegetarian diet would sustain his healthy appetite.

'Florain Gaiakin are the best cooks this end of the Universe of Stars,' laughed Spurge. 'Our skills with butterbeans are a wonder!'

Kenji grimaced.

A young Gaiakin called Herb offered to take Lark. Seeing his horse's kind eyes, Lark felt a bit more cheerful.

'This is a fine ratter, young Lark!' Herb called down, taking Mick from him, before helping him up into the saddle behind him.

Setting off at a brisk trot, Herb consulted him about a problem with his own ratter, a female called Flash, who had developed a fear of rodents.

As Lark offered his sage advice, all they'd been through overcame him, and weariness washed over him. His head nodded forward and fearful of falling off, he clung on tight to Herb's belt. To keep himself awake, he tried to concentrate on their route, speculating how far it was to Florain. He soon gave up; he could not relate the mysterious ferny way they now travelled to any terrain he remembered from when they had flown in Skyhook from Holy Island back to Durholm. Dozing fitfully, the journey became almost dreamlike, and ever afterwards when he tried to remember details, he couldn't even recall if they'd rested or stopped to eat.

He avoided looking at Bird, hidden inside Sandy's cloak, from where every now and then could be heard grunting sobs. He wondered yet again what had happened at the cursed place where Bee had died. Bird's blank dark eyes had shocked him to his depths; one moment he felt sorry for her, then, remembering what had happened to Master Roach, he feared her.

Desperately he wished Mr Mossy would hurry up. How often had he searched the clouds scudding across the sky, ever hopeful of hearing the drone of Skyhook's engine? It never came.

# 17
# FLORAIN

Emerging from the cool of a bluebell wood Florain lay before them, the red tiles of the castle turrets shining in the sun, its gleaming white walls towering above the duckweed covered water of the moat. Curving away into the distance was the great hedge they had flown over in Skyhook.

As Herb urged his horse across the bridge above the moat, Lark, perched behind him, blinked in amazement. A flotilla of swans, cutting a swathe in the weed, glided beneath them: their plumage was glossy black, not white, their beaks scarlet, not yellow. Would Tissy ever believe him when he told her? He'd have to see that Fin made sketches of them, including notes on their colour.

'It's about time he got out his sketch pad again,' he told himself.

The tall golden gates swung silently open and they passed through into a wide sunlit courtyard. The sky above was of such deep blue Lark felt certain they'd come to a foreign land. In the centre stood a large metal structure standing low on three legs; to Lark's mind the structure resembled a huge dinner plate, with small round windows around the rim. Then he remembered Fescue's story of the Gaiakins' flight across the Universe in a mysterious flying ship called The Universe Crosser – hadn't Fescue said there was a sculpture of it in the Great Courtyard of Florain? He decided it looked a most unsuitable vehicle to go travelling in.

Their horses' hooves ringing on brightly patterned tiles, they rode across the courtyard to a flight of shallow steps leading up to a pair of tall mahogany doors. Lark saw that these were inlaid with silver and mother-of-pearl, depicting wondrously fantastical flowers, reminding him of the box that had contained the Chi Rho.

At the steps, Betony dismounted and helped Fin down from the saddle, before going to take Bird from Sandy. Covering her with Sandy's cloak, she hurried away through a nearby low door. Fin attempted to follow, but Sandy drew him back.

'No, Fin! Betony is taking Bird somewhere quiet and peaceful, where she will wash her and tend to her burns. I promise you can see her later.'

Seeing Fin's anguish, Lark longed to comfort him, but such was Fin's mood, he knew he would be rebuffed.

'Even so, I'd better made sure he doesn't do something daft again,' he muttered to himself, climbing down from Herb's horse and releasing Mick from his jerkin. Massaging his stiff backside, he looked about, seeing fruit trees growing against the courtyard walls, their blossom filling the air with perfume. He recognised most: pear, apple, plum, peach, cherry, and even the more exotic lemons and oranges; the Gaiakin folk occasionally brought baskets of oranges, lemons, and grapefruit to Watersmeet market which were much prized by Brightdale's cooks for jams and other preserves.

But several species of trees were unknown to him. Hung with yellow and green fruits, resembling multi-fingered hands, their leaves were like large green handkerchiefs growing on thin branches straight out from hairy trunks, whilst others had huge fan-like leaves, their branches hung with ridged pink fruits.

What puzzled him most was, even though the trees were frothy with blossom – as they should be at Saprise – they were also laden with fruits, as if it were the season of Highsun too. He sighed: Fin must get going with his charcoal stick, it would help to distract him.

About to ask him if he'd got his sketchpad to hand, the mahogany doors were flung open, and a party of Gaiakins came down the steps, their melodious voices calling out a welcome as they crowded around, eagerly asking questions.

Before meeting Fescue, Mullein and their warrior companions, the only Gaiakins Lark had seen were the ones who came to Watersmeet market, so covered up it was impossible to see them properly. But these Gaiakins, with joy in their shining eyes, laughter in their soft voices, wore the most amazing silken garments, their shimmering hues ever changing as their wearer moved: silver, then golden green, then kingfisher blue, like morning dew caught in sunlight. Then, with a jolt, he recalled the dragonfly-blue cloth in which the Chi Rho had been wrapped, when they had opened the box in Mossy's room – so this was where the cloth came from!

Amongst the crowd, he noticed a woman holding Sandy's hands and talking to him earnestly. Although dressed in Gaiakin garments, she didn't resemble them, her long auburn hair in places pewter-grey, her pale face still beautiful though lined with age. Lark remembered what Wings had told him: that Sandy's mother lived in Florain.

Conscious the smell of Frit sick in his hair was attracting disapproving stares, he wondered if there was somewhere he could wash. Looking around, he saw Fin had joined Fescue and Mullein in a far corner, where they had laid Bee's body beneath the spreading boughs of a blossom-laden apple tree. Making sure Mick kept close on his heels, he made his way over.

A young female Gaiakin kneeling by the bier was weeping softly as she brushed away the apple blossom falling on the cloak covering Bee's body. Her garments were of the same shimmering fabric as those of the older Gaiakins, but close fitting, outlining her slender body and long legs. Her long shining hair was held back from her pretty face by a band of soft pink feathers; a pair of lovebirds sat on her shoulder, nibbling her ear, and cooing softly.

Fin sidled up and whispered in his ear: 'Mullein tells me her name is Weeping Willow.'

Lark grinned, then remembering that they'd fallen out, said in a wintry voice: 'It's good that Bee is getting a proper mourning!'

'I wish Mossy would hurry up and come,' Fin sighed, looking up at the empty blue between the red tiled roofs. 'Surely Wings must have got to Brightdale by now?'

The sight of Fin's ravaged face was suddenly too much for Lark. Lurching towards him, he grabbed him in a desperate hug. 'Fin, please let me help you!'

Scowling, Fin pushed him away. 'There's nothing you can do – I wish you'd go home!' he muttered, turning his back on him.

'But Mr Mossy said I must be your helper!' Lark whimpered, plucking at his sleeve.

'I'm not a kid, I can look after myself,' Fin hissed, pulling his arm away.

Their angry voices alarmed Willow. Leaping to her feet, sending her lovebirds fluttering into the air, she rushed over to them, almost smothering them as she took them in her arms.

'You poor, poor darlings. You mustn't argue – you're in Florain!'

Her tearful cooing, setting Mick off howling, brought Sandy over from the crowd at the steps.

'What is going on here?' he demanded sternly. 'Mullein and Fescue – take the wee lass's body to the embalming house! And you, Willow, go to help with the laying out.'

Blushing, Willow released Fin and Lark from her embrace, to follow Fescue and Mullein, carrying Bee's bier as they processed to the door through which Betony had taken Bird.

At the doorway, Willow turned and gave Fin and Lark a theatrical wink, breaking the tension hanging heavily in the air. Lark let out an involuntary snort of laughter, and blushing scarlet, he noticed a pair of young male Gaiakins who had come to stand beside Sandy, were studying him. Like Willow, their garments were close fitting, showing their long muscular limbs. To Lark's amazement, clouds of flying insects were darting in and out of the numerous strands of their plaited silver hair, the sight reminding him of the hooks adorning his sadly missed fishing hat.

Turning to the young Gaiakins, Sandy addressed them briskly: 'Foxglove and Snapdragon, you too can do something useful – take our Delphin guests to the wash house!' He turned back to Fin and Lark. 'When you have washed, you are invited to my mother's cottage, where she is preparing a meal and beds for you.'

Fin shook his head firmly. 'It's very kind of your mother, but I must be with Bird.'

'Do not be concerned for Bird! She is safe with Betony. When she has washed and newly clothed her, she will bring her to eat with us – so you can see for yourself how she fares. Now go with Foxglove and Snapdragon to the washhouse and I will come for you there.'

As he turned away, Fin ran after him. 'Wait a moment, Sandy!'

Fin drew him into a secluded space between the gnarled trunks of two old pear trees. 'I need a favour – I don't want to leave my treasures unguarded whilst washing – can you take care of them?'

He held out his purse to Sandy who frowned at it discouragingly.

Seeing his expression, Fin said: 'The purse also contains a piece of Rom gold, which is supposed to lessen the power of the Chi Rho.'

Sandy raised his eyebrows in surprise. 'It is a rare thing – to own a piece of Rom gold! It explains why you have not succumbed to the notorious power of the Chi Rho!' Reluctantly taking the purse and tucking it in a pocket inside his jerkin, he sighed. 'Your father was not so lucky – Zagzagel told me that Marlin wore the cross, causing a deep wound.'

Fin nodded miserably. 'Yes, after he died –murdered – I saw the scar on his chest. When we were at Birdoswald I put on the cross too, to keep it safe when the Frits arrived. It was only for a short while, even so it wounded me.'

He touched his chest lightly and, feeling ashamed, looked away to avoid Sandy's searching gaze.

'I have not done a very good job of taking care of you, have I, Fin? Zagzagel will not be pleased with me!'

Fin couldn't help a lopsided grin. 'I'll do my best to defend you from Mossy's wrath!'

He saw Lark looking about for him. 'I'd better go, I see Lark's fretting. Will you please tell your mother we look forward to meeting her?'

Re-joining Lark and the two young Gaiakins, he suddenly felt more cheerful, as if a black cloud in his head had blown away; he knew it would only be temporary – when Sandy gave him back his purse, the cloud would return.

The Gaiakin called Foxglove, introduced himself: 'My full name is Digitalis Purpurea, but I insist on being called Fox,' he added solemnly, and bowing low, the creatures living in his numerous braids rose in a whirling cloud about his head which, to Fin and Lark's astonishment, were black and yellow furry bumble bees.

'And I liked to be called Snap, or if you must, Snapdragon, never Antirrhinum Majus!' said his companion, tossing his head proudly, sending up a cloud of dragonflies, their iridescent wings catching the sunlight.

Gazing at the swirling insects, Lark couldn't help sniggering, and then, in a release from the tension of the last days, the sniggering turned to chortling, then hearty laughter. Catching Lark's mood, a happy grin spread across Fin's face and, jumping up, he tried to catch a dragonfly, but they were too quick for him, diving back into Snap's mass of plaits.

At first, the two Gaiakins glowered at the Delphins, but indignation turned to mirth when they spotted Mick, excited by his master's merry mood, rolling on his back, frantically pawing the air with his short legs.

'What a crazy dog!' Fox laughed, tickling Mick's pink stomach. Then, becoming aware of Sandy frowning at them from across the courtyard, exclaimed: 'Oh, oh, Lord Iskander's on the war path! Come Delphins, and specially you Lark, it's time to get that disgusting mess off you!' Playfully catching Lark by his thatch of pale green hair, he rapidly let go in disgust. 'I don't like your hair oil, young Lark!'

Outraged, Lark growled: 'It's not hair oil! I don't use hair oil – that stuff's Frit sick.'

'Really?' Fox and Snap chorused, eyeing Lark in awe.

'We'll want to know how you came to be so close to an evil Frit – and survived!' exclaimed Snap.

'And how you came by your wounds!' added Fox, looking admiringly at Fin's bandaged arms. Then spotting the hilt of the Dandrum Sword tucked in Fin's belt, he raised his brows. 'We'll want the history of that amazing weapon too, don't you agree, Snap?'

Their strange guides led them across the courtyard, through an archway into a long chamber dimly lit by small windows set in the low roof. Rows of wooden lockers lined the walls.

'Right, give me your packs.' Snap said, grabbing their rucksacks and stuffing them into lockers.

'And I'll help you with your boots,' Fox said, firmly pushing them down onto a bench, and untying their laces.

Wondering what they were in for, Fin and Lark eyed a doorway at the far end of the room from where came the sound of running water.

Starting to unbutton his jerkin, Lark glanced uneasily to the entrance from the courtyard. 'What if that Willow comes in?'

Fox grinned. 'She'll shut her eyes!'

'Don't rag him!' laughed Snap. 'This bath house is males only. Is it not the same in your country?'

'We don't have bath houses. We mostly wash under the pump in the yard. The only time we take all our clothes off in public is when we go Skinny Dipping on Highsun Eve, when us young males and females dive naked into the Bright – that's when marriages are arranged,' Lark added solemnly.

'Rather drastic, to my mind,' Fox said, 'you won't have to marry anyone in our pool. Come on, we'll strip off too.'

As they flung off their beautiful shimmering clothes, the attendant clouds of insects dived into their hair.

Encouraged, Fin and Lark quickly emptied their pockets, giving it all to Snap, including the Dandrum sword, to put in with their rucksacks in the lockers. Then, with great relief, they pulled off their filthy clothes. Unwinding the bandages Betony had bound around his arms, Fin was surprised to find his cuts had already healed to faint scars, but looking down at his chest, he saw he still had a livid red mark from the Chi Rho.

'What about my dog?' asked Lark indicating Mick, cowering in a corner, 'he doesn't take kindly to hot soapy water.'

'I'll sort him,' Fox said, grabbing Mick and sprinting off with him under his arm to the door from where steam and bubbles seeped out.

Fin and Lark hesitated, wondering about the fate of their piles of dirty clothes.

'Don't worry,' Snap called impatiently, 'they'll be washed and ready for you later! In the meantime, when you've bathed, we'll fit you out with Gaiakin clothes.'

Plunging in after the Gaiakins, Fin and Lark found themselves in a bubble-filled steamy chamber. Dimly lit by small glass windows set in the roof, from the misty steam ahead came indignant howling from Mick. Following Snap's example, they moved slowly forwards through the jets of water shooting out of the walls, feeling the hot soapy foam washing away the filth of the horrors they had lived through. Nearing the far door, clear water jets rinsed them off before Snap handed them soft white towels to dry themselves.

Refreshed and invigorated, they self-consciously stepped into a great chamber bright with sunlight streaming in through a cupola high above. Before them stretched a long pool where several Gaiakins could be seen swimming amongst lily pads that almost covered its surface. On a tiled walkway surrounding the pool more Gaiakin, wrapped in soft white towelling, lounged on deeply upholstered couches set against the marbled walls.

Kenji's dark head bobbed up out of the lily pads. 'Come on in lads, the water's warm,' he called, 'but be ready for the nipping fish!'

They saw he had a look of utter ecstasy on his face. Turning on his back, he scudded off, paddling his arms and legs vigorously, drawing glares from his fellow swimmers.

Dropping gingerly into the water, at first the pleasant warmth soothed their aching muscles. Then Lark let out a yell and at the same moment Mick shot out of the water.

'Oi, whatever's that!' Fin yelped, batting at something beneath the surface.

Grinning hugely, Fox and Snap swam over. 'It's just the fish cleaning off any lurking bugs from Birdoswald! Keep still and enjoy them!'

Clinging to the edge of the pool, they felt little pinpricks, starting with their toes, rapidly spreading all over them as the fish did their job. When they'd finished, Lark gave a contented sigh.

'Eee, that was grand! Come on in Mick, it's your turn now,' he called encouragingly to Mick, whimpering agitatedly from the edge of the pool.

'Leave him be,' Fox called, 'he's had a scrubbing in the soap tunnel. Look, his white parts are simply dazzling!'

'When he's dry, he shall have a reward for his bravery,' Snap said. 'Is he partial to rabbit? If he is, he can have a whole one to himself.'

'Hey, I thought Gaiakins are vegetarians,' Kenji called indignantly, 'why am I not allowed rabbit?'

A Gaiakin called down from a bench above them: 'Rabbit meat is only for the dogs – as a reward for ratting in the grain barns!'

'I'm a good ratter too,' grumbled Kenji, plunging back beneath the surface.

Tingling all over, Fin and Lark enjoyed a good wallow until, conscious that Sandy could be waiting for them, they reluctantly climbed out.

Kenji bobbed up to call out, 'You're privileged to be staying with Sandy's mother. Queen Ailis' cooking is plentiful and homely.'

With a farewell wave, he disappeared below the surface again.

In another chamber, Fox handed out fresh dry towels, whilst Snap busied himself searching shelves for child sized Gaiakin clothing.

Towelling himself down, Fin looked about. Unlike the basic slate and wood of the locker chamber, the dark marble walls and floor of this chamber were richly decorated with silver and mother-of-pearl flowers. 'Reminds you of the box that Mossy kept the Chi Rho in, doesn't it?' Said Lark. Pointing out the decoration, Fin asked Fox who had made them.

'Oh, Fescue and Mullein – the brothers are Florain's metal smiths. If we get a chance, we'll take you to their workshop. Some of their artefacts are fabulous, but their craft has been sadly neglected since they became Warriors.'

Among the clothing Snap found two long sleeved tops in soft maroon velvet, with matching trousers, which he measured against Fin and Lark, making them feel self-conscious about their small stature.

'What about underwear?' Lark asked, 'I always wear linen next to my skin – my Grammer would be shocked if I didn't. We've got clean smalls in our rucksacks. Can we go and get them?'

Fox, now dressed, grinned. 'Your Grammer sounds a mite fussy! I'll fetch your kit.'

When he returned, Fox eyed Fin as he dried his hair. 'We would be interested to learn how you came by that strangely shaped chest wound,' he said, looking pointedly at the livid scar left by the cross.

Scowling, Fin didn't reply, but searched his rucksack for clean underwear. He had laid the broken Dandrum Sword on a bench. Snap reverently picked it up and whistled in admiration. 'This must be as ancient as King Guelder!'

Finishing vigorously drying Mick, Fox took the sword from Snap. In wonder, he traced his finger over the silver tracery near the hilt. 'Tomorrow, after we have taken you on a tour of the Gardens, we shall go to the forge, to get the blade mended.'

Lark looked up eagerly from tying the cord tighter around the top of his velvet trousers. 'A tour of the gardens! That's just what I've been longing to do!'

Fin frowned at him. 'Thanks for the offer Fox, but we won't have time,' he said curtly, 'our friend Bird needs us.' Taking back the sword, he buried it deep inside his rucksack.

'Fin, surely we can have time for a tour of the gardens?' Lark exclaimed.

About to argue, they were interrupted by the arrival of Sandy.

'Good! You are ready!' he said, eyeing their Gaiakin garments with mild amusement. 'My mother has a meal prepared for us. Bring your rucksacks: she has made up beds for you.'

Queen Ailis' cottage stood down a leafy lane outside the castle walls. Black and white timbered, its small diamond paned windows peeped out from beneath a fringe of deep thatch. A silver knocker in the design of a thistle hung on the green door. Sandy led them through the white picket gate along a crazy-paved path. Growing in the flowerbeds on either side, was a higgledy-piggledy array of vegetables and flowers: lavender, hollyhocks, lupins, roses, larkspurs, calendulas bloomed amongst raspberry canes, cabbages, scarlet runner beans, peas, and sunflowers. In a secluded corner by the hedge, an apple tree with a bench around its gnarled trunk, reminded Fin of the old apple tree and bench in Mossy's back garden.

Queen Ailis greeted them at the door, and Sandy introduced them. 'Mother, this is Fin Dandrum, a prince of Brightdale,' he said with a twinkling smile. 'And this is Lark Annunder, with his dog, Mick.' Hearing his name Mick wagged his tail furiously.

Bobbing a girlish curtsey to Fin and Lark, Queen Ailis bent to chuck Mick under his bearded muzzle. 'It is an honour to meet Delphin folk! Sandy has told be of your terrible trials and of your bravery,' she added gravely, her voice having a soft lilt like Sandy's. 'Come inside! The meal is prepared.'

Leaving her son to scoop up Mick, taking Fin and Lark by their hands, she led them into the cottage. Squeezing past an umbrella stand containing not only umbrellas and walking sticks, but also spears, bows and swords, along with fishing rods, nets, and arrow quivers, she showed them into a sunlit room, where a steaming copper kettle whistled a greeting from the fireplace.

A high-backed bench padded with cushions faced the fire, taking Fin and Lark back to Grammer Nutmeg's attic room; only here the view from the window was framed by tall hollyhocks and sunflowers, instead of the roofs of Dandrum Den. Fin began to hope that this was a place of peace where Bird might find healing.

'Now, I know you have been swimming and will be hungry, so we shall eat as soon as our guests arrive,' Queen Ailis said, indicating a round table in the bay window set with an assortment of food laid out on a flowery cloth. Around the table stood six chairs, three of which were heightened by cushions for the benefit of Delphin guests.

Lark looked appreciatively at the pies and sausage rolls, and neatly cut sandwiches, accompanied by different coloured jellies, iced buns and slabs of fruit cake: a spread every bit as good as Grammer Nutmeg's best efforts for a birthday tea.

Before Sandy could stop him, Mick struggled out of his arms, and leapt at the plate of sausage rolls. With a mortified cry, Lark rushed to haul him away by his scruff.

'I'm sorry, your majesty! Mick's usually better behaved, but he's desperate for a decent meal, as he's been living only on sunflower seeds!'

Queen Ailis laughed. 'I have a special package in the larder for your Mick, delivered by young Snap; from the smell, I think it is a freshly killed rabbit!'

She turned to her son: "Skander, whilst I take Mick to be fed, you must show our guests their room!' Tucking Mick under her arm, she went out to the kitchen.

Fin and Lark gazed after her in wonder, astonished that Lord Iskander could be spoken to in such a manner. Hiding smirks, they followed Sandy to a winding flight of stairs in a corner of the room that took them to a small landing where doors led into two bedrooms. Through the door on the left, they entered a low-ceilinged room, simply furnished with a dresser against one wall, and two beds beneath a small round window overlooking the front garden.

Gazing wistfully at the dresser, Sandy said: 'Have a play if you like!' He indicated a set of carved wooden warriors on a chess board next to an array of childish weapons, with a shelf of books on the wall above, their leather bindings worn from much use. Leaving them to settle in, he clattered back down the stairs.

Dumping his rucksack on one of the beds, Fin studied the spines of the books; the titles were varied: Kings and Queens of Scotland and Modern Warfare beside Wildflowers and How to Identify Them, and Poetry, Ancient and Modern. Lark picked up a small, beautifully modelled sword, and tried to decipher the strange inscription engraved beneath a pommel cleverly forged into a silver thistle flower. Then, hearing the door knocker below, they knew Betony had arrived with Bird. Glancing in a mirror on the wall, they smoothed their hair, and hurried downstairs.

Betony and Bird were already seated, with Bird perched on a pile of cushions. Washing off the grime of Birdoswald had exposed her sore skin, which shone raw and pink through a film of ointment. Thoughtfully, Betony had dressed Bird in a soft sea-green velvet dress to enhance the pretty colour of what was left of her hair, but this couldn't distract attention from the burnt patches on her scalp. There was no light in Bird's blank eyes, but Fin knew Betony could never heal that: Bird wasn't there, her body just an empty shell.

He couldn't stop himself cringing when Betony gave Bird a sandwich which, like an animal, she sniffed before blindly tearing it apart with her hands. Clucking like a mother hen, Lark climbed up next to her, and gently guided pieces of sandwich to her mouth, which she gulped down without chewing. Torn between disgust and pity, Fin knew he should have sat next to Bird, but was guiltily glad Lark had got there first.

Taking his seat next to Lark, he helped himself to a sausage roll and listened politely to Queen Ailis talking to Sandy and Betony of everyday matters. He tried to look as if he was enjoying himself, but unhappiness made the food dry in his mouth.

Queen Ailis brought up a problem with her chickens. 'I am being plagued with bumble-foot,' she sighed.

Knowing a lot about chickens, Lark asked with authority. 'Have you checked their perches lately? Splintered perches can be a cause of bumble-foot.'

'Lark Annunder, you have been specially sent to me!' Queen Ailis exclaimed with delight, 'come, I shall take you to my chickens.'

By this time everybody had eaten enough, even Sandy and Lark. Taking him out to her chicken run, on the way through the kitchen they stopped to collect Mick, crouched under the kitchen table, gnawing on a last rabbit bone.

In the living room, after tenderly wiping the crumbs from Bird's mouth, Betony lifted her into her arms. 'The little lass needs rest.'

'Where will you take her?' Fin asked, jumping down from his seat.

'Back to the Healing House – I think she feels safe there.'

'May I come with you? Until Mossy arrives, I should like to be there, looking after her.'

Betony shot Sandy a querying look.

He laid his hand on Fin's shoulder. 'Have you forgotten I have something of yours, Fin?' He put his hand to where he'd hidden Fin's purse inside his jerkin.

Fin turned pale: he'd forgotten about the Chi Rho!

Sandy smiled kindly. 'Come, we shall go with Betony and Bird, so you can see for yourself the room where she sleeps, and then we will return here and sit for a while on the old bench beneath the apple tree; I shall return your treasures to you there.'

The Healing House, a long thatched single-story building set in a quiet glade, surrounded by a garden filled with healing herbs: rosemary, sage, thyme, lavender, parsley, wormwood and many more, was not far from Queen Ailis' cottage, in a lane running down to the River Coquet. Bird's room looked out on the river, where swallows skimmed the water for flies.

Whilst Betony helped Bird into a nightdress, Fin went to the window and watched the swallows dip and dive. Craning his neck to see farther along the river, he spied the ruined castle they'd seen from the air when Wings had flown them over Florain. Then he'd been full of hope that he would hand the cross over to the Holy Community of Holy Island, before returning home to Brightdale – he hadn't known about Bird and Bee being already captured by Hardwick.

He turned back miserably to watch Bird settling down to sleep, curling up in her blankets as if she were a wild creature. Unable to bear the sight any longer, he hurried from the room to join Sandy waiting outside.

Back at Queen Ailis' cottage garden, they sat beneath the apple tree. Taking the purse from his pocket, Sandy held it out to Fin. 'Well Fin, have you decided what you are going to do with the Chi Rho?'

Fin pulled a face as he took the purse. Fishing out the cross, twisting the chain around his fingers, he balanced it in his open palm, and gazed down at the gold and jewels. Watching him, Sandy wondered how it was that such a person, so young and untried, had not been overcome by the mysterious and powerful burden of the Chi Rho – was it his Delphin or his Rom blood, he wondered? Or was it the power of the Anchorite's Rom gold?

Fin breathed a long sigh. 'It was good to be free for a while. It has made me realise what a horrible influence it's having on my mind. Despite the protection of my mother's gold coin, there have been times when I weakened, desperately wanted to put it on, to wear it close to my skin!'

He felt inside his shirt where it still felt sore. 'Sandy, I don't suppose there's a chance you'd consider—?' The words choked in his throat. Taking a deep breath, he managed to gasp: 'Take care of the cross – just until Mossy gets here?'

Reaching out as if to take the cross, Sandy hastily pulled his hand back. He looked anxiously into Fin's eyes. 'Has it become too much for you, Fin? It is vital that you do not succumb to the power of the Chi Rho, as so many have. Even in the short time I have been in possession of it, it has been a sore trial to me – the folk of Brightdale are fortunate indeed that you are their Head!'

Fin scowled. 'I'm just a half-breed – they don't want me as Head! Besides, I'll have forfeited any Headship rights over the Delphins of Brightdale, when I return with two of their daughters, one dead and the other in a living death – that is, if I dare return!'

He glowered down at the cross in his palm: it was already taking hold again. Brusquely, he stuffed it away. As he did so, his fingers brushed against his mother's coin, and he came to a decision.

'I shall go back to Holy Island, Sandy. When Wings comes with Mossy, I'll ask him to take me there in Skyhook. I'll try and persuade Lark to go home—'

He stopped abruptly, alerted by Queen Ailis and Lark's voices as they rounded a corner of the cottage. Mick was trotting ahead of them, carrying in his jaws a meaty looking chicken gizzard.

'Young Master Annunder is a fount of wisdom!' called Queen Ailis, 'not only did he find the cause of the bumble-foot, but he has also given me wise advice on the anaemic state of my raspberries: liquid comfrey.'

'Now that your problems are solved, mother, it is high time we had supper,' Sandy said with a grin. 'If your guests are not hungry, I am. Will there be roast chicken for us?' he asked, speculatively eyeing Mick's chicken gizzard. 'The few sandwiches and jelly we had earlier were not enough for me!'

After a supper of roast chicken, stuffing, and Queen Ailis gizzard gravy, (a special treat for Sandy), they sat around the fire sipping honey-sweetened mint tea. To entertain her guests, Ailis recounted the story of how she and Sandy came to live in Florain.

She began in a chanting, sing-song voice:

'Now, the Geek Community where we lived was called Yrvik, and was the original Motherhome, hidden amongst the reeds and marshes on the banks of the river Ousewater – where it meanders, wide and deep through the forests of the plain of Yorvale. Encircled by a deep trench filled with sharp wooden spikes, even so, Yrvik's defences were not enough: it was attacked, overrun, and most of the people murdered. The precious Scrolls of Knowledge were destroyed…' her voice trailed away as she gazed sadly into the fire.

Sandy quickly explained: 'Motherhomes are places where Knowledge in all its various forms is kept, guarded by the Geeks who protect it from corruption and decay. There is now another Motherhome at Yrvik, one of many found all around the world. Yrvik was where my Squad, Fescue, Kenji and Dancer, were based, until we were called north, to guard Durholm.'

Coming out of her reverie, Ailis took up her story. 'The enemy that attacked us came from the south, an ill-equipped hungry mob, led by the vile creatures known as Sneaksouls. Sandy's father, my dear husband Flaithri, was one of those killed. Sandy was six years old at the time. Those who survived were scattered, many to die in the forests of Yorvale, but after a fraught journey, often hunted, always hungry, Sandy and I reached the safety of the Holy Community of Yrving. It was from Yrving we made our way north, to our people here in Florain.'

Sandy looked meaningfully at Fin and Lark. 'You know already that it was the brothers and sisters from Yrving who journeyed to Holy Island to establish their new Community – bringing the Chi Rho with them.'

Fin wondered how it was that Sandy and his mother were related to the Gaiakins of Florain. He decided he would ask Mossy about these two awesome beings who were not wholly human.

'It is time we all went to bed!' Ailis said, taking the tray of mugs to the kitchen.

Sandy stretched his tall frame. 'I must be going. I am meeting with Kenji and Fescue to discuss our plans.' Wishing them a good night's sleep, he strolled out into a starlit night.

In their bedroom, Lark, overcome with sleepiness, dropped his Gaiakin clothes in an untidy heap on the floor, crawled under his blankets, and fell instantly into deep slumber. Mick snuggled up beside him.

Fin found it harder to catch sleep, tormented by images of Bird's scorched scalp swimming before his closed eyes. Listening in the dark to Mick's stomach rumbling, he remembered he'd promised Lark that tomorrow he'd sketch some scenes in Florain, to show Tissy when they got home.

Throwing back his covers, he felt his way to his rucksack and found the block of parchment and small bundle of charcoal sticks, bound with string, and placed them on the top. Back under the blankets he tried to calm his mind by planning what he would draw: the castle, the bridge over the moat, and perhaps Queen Ailis' cottage.

When they woke next day, they found their Delphin clothes neatly folded at the end of their beds, jerkins and trousers brushed, shirts and underwear washed. After dressing, they went downstairs to a breakfast of boiled eggs, laid by Queen Ailis' hens. They were dipping buttered toast fingers into the last of the bright orange yolks when Snap and Fox arrived, their clouds of dragonflies and bees buzzing excitedly above their heads.

'Hurry up, lads!' Snap said, 'We've been instructed to take you to meet King Guelder and Queen Fleur before our tour of the Gardens. You must be smart, so Lark make sure you wipe the egg yolk from your chin!'

'Where's Mick?' Fox asked, looking under the table.

'Doing the necessary in the back garden,' Lark said, rubbing his handkerchief over his chin.

Fox went out to find Mick, returning a few moments later with him under his arm; he'd tied a red ribbon with a big bow, around Mick's neck: Mick looked furious.

When they were ready, Fox and Snap took them back to the castle courtyard, past the spaceship statue, up the steps, through the tall mahogany doors and into a spacious hallway. To the left and right, flights of stairs covered with gold and silver carpet rose to other floors. Following Fox and Snap across the polished black marble floor, they headed for a tall archway from where there came the sound of splashing water and the low hum of many voices.

At the archway, Fin and Lark stopped at the top of steps to gaze in wonder. Before them lay a wide sunlit courtyard. On three sides row upon row of balconied windows looked down out of high walls, their delicate golden balustrades festooned with swags of gauzy silk that floated on the soft air like coloured clouds. In the middle stood a circular pool, its centrepiece a fountain of three white marble dolphins. Standing on their tails, fins touching, jets of water arced from their beaks, splashing back down onto a surface of bobbing and spinning silver balls. On the low wall around the pool, trailing plants cascaded out of tall silver urns, their leafy tendrils heavy with waxy purple blooms, filling the air with heady perfume, which Lark learned later were a species of jungle orchid, brought from their abandoned African jungle garden.

Around the courtyard were marble topped tables where groups of Gaiakins lounged on deeply upholstered sofas, eating richly decorated cakes set on silver dishes and drinking sparkling purple juice from crystal goblets.

Eyed curiously by the diners, they followed Snap and Fox between the tables, and made their way to a raised dais where two Gaiakins sat side by side in throne-like chairs, apparently waiting for them. Mounting the steps, Snap and Fox bowed low. Copying their example, Fin and Lark also bowed.

'Glorious King Guelder and Beauteous Queen Fleur, we bring before you the princeling, Fin Dandrum of Brightdale with his servant, Master Skylark Annunder,' Snap announced grandly.

'And this is Master Annunder's ratter, who is named Mick,' Fox added, holding up Mick, his red bow obscuring his furry face.

Leaning forward to greet their guests, the imposing couple could have been any age, their long lustrous hair gleamed like snow, but their faces were smooth and their eyes clear and alert.

'It is an honour to meet you, young Fin Dandrum and your redoubtable servant!' King Guelder said.

Seeing the kindness in the Gaiakin's midnight blue eyes, Fin realised to whom Queen Ailis and Sandy were related: it was to the King of Florain.

Rising from her chair, Queen Fleur held out her hands. 'Welcome, Fin and Lark!'

Fin thought her beauty had more of the look of Mullein, the silver light in her sapphire eyes mesmerising as she searched his face.

'I think young Fin, that you desire to know more of our Gaiakin history,' she observed.

With a shock, he realised she had read his thoughts.

'Your spirit of curiosity does you credit. An enquiring mind shows your worth as a prince.' She turned to her king. 'My love, shall I tell the Delphin folk the history of our people?'

'Indeed, you must!' exclaimed King Guelder.

'Come and sit!' Queen Fleur said, leading Fin and Lark to two low stools facing the thrones. 'And whilst I tell my tale we shall partake of refreshments!'

She looked pointedly at Fox and Snap who, their clouds of insects firmly under control, scurried to a table at the side of the dais where a crystal pitcher sat on a tray with four silver goblets, and a silver dish of small cakes, excitingly decorated in a thick layer of gold and pink icing. First serving the King and Queen, then Fin and Lark, Fox and Snap sat on the dais steps nearby awaiting further command.

Biting into their cakes, popping explosions filled their mouths, as if the cakes contained miniature fireworks, making Fin and Lark grin at each other.

Taking another cake from the plate, Lark spotted Fox surreptitiously dropping one on the carpet for Mick. Lunging forward to stop Mick eating it, he was too slow: with a gulp, the cake was gone. The next instant it reappeared, to be deposited in a neat pile on the richly decorated gold carpet – along with other bits and pieces Mick had consumed while foraging in Queen Ailis' garden.

Politely ignoring this unfortunate incident, Queen Fleur embarked on her history of the Gaiakins of Florain.

'Now, when the Gaiakins came into the Universe of Stars,' she began, 'so long ago that there is no record, they made their home in the tropical lands of Gaia, finding joy in her lush rainforests filled with fruits and flowers. In those days, Rowan and Stachys were King and Queen. They had only one child, a daughter named Eyebright, who when she grew to adulthood married a human Prince, called Cadeyrn.'

'Was he the one who wounded Gressil's slug Queen?' Fin asked eagerly, unable to contain his interest.

Queen Fleur shook her head. 'No, the Prince Cadeyrn who went into Contagion was his descendant. The Prince Cadeyrn who married Eyebright was from the clans who lived in northern Britannica – four thousand years before the Great Dying.

'How Cadeyrn met Eyebright of the Gaiakins and married her, is another long tale which perhaps one day, Lord Iskander will tell you. Suffice it to say, the brothers Fescue and Mullein are also of that line. As are Queen Ailis and Iskander, but they have mainly human traits,' she added, giving Fin a meaningful look.

'How did the Gaiakins come to live here, in Florain?' Lark asked, spreading his arms wide, his face a picture of wonder.

'It was during the time of the Great Dying. Our jungle home became diseased, the trees and the plants blighted, growing ugly and twisted. Many of the Gaiakins returned to our own Universe of White Light, including our King Rowan and Queen Stachys.

'But some of us decided to search on Gaia for a new home. We found this place, where once there had been an ancient garden, and we called it Florain, after our lost tropical garden. As is the way of Gaiakins, we have a deep love for the flowers, trees and grasses of Gaia: there are none in the Universe of White Light.'

She fell silent, a wistful look on her beautiful face.

Lark sighed. 'Well that's very satisfactory, your Highness. Thank you for putting us in the picture, so to speak. But someone from your people must come and explain to my Thetis just how amazing Florain is, she just won't believe me!'

Fin said nothing but sat hunched in thought. Some of his curiosity was satisfied but there were still questions he would have liked to have asked but didn't dare. One was: how could a person of Fescue's quality be tempted by the Chi Rho?

King Guelder murmured to the Queen and they rose to leave. As they descended the dais steps, all the Gaiakins in the courtyard stood and bowed. Fin and Lark jumped up and they too bowed deeply. Their attendants forming up behind them, the royal couple processed out of the courtyard.

Snap sighed with relief. 'Now that's done, we can at last take you on a tour of the gardens.'

Lark gave a little jig. 'I've been looking forward to this ever since I learned we were coming here— hoy, wait a mo!' he called to Snap and Fox, already half-way down the dais steps. He turned to Fin. 'Did you remember to bring your sketch pad and charcoal sticks?'

In triumph, Fin brought them out from his trouser pocket, and they set off.

Fin did his best, his charcoal drawings skilfully portraying the forms and light of the gardens, but charcoal sticks could not capture the scents and colours. Lark was grateful for his efforts, but remembering their flight over the gardens in Skyhook, now they were on the ground he found them even more magical, and he passed the next hours in a dreamlike haze.

'Like rooms,' he muttered under his breath, rehearsing what he would tell Tissy, 'divided not only by walls of stone and brick, but hedges too: yew, copper-beech, box and privet.'

He tried to memorise all he saw, but he knew a lot would just fade away, never to be recalled. He would try hardest to remember the highlights: the cottage garden, red brick paths snaking between beds full of flowers and vegetables, buzzing with bees, and loud with blackbird song, reminding him of a Highsun morning. Also, the woodland garden which reminded him of the woods in Plashydale with the drifts of bluebells, snowdrops, celandine, ragged robin, red campion, and wood anemones, all blooming in one season. And the alpine garden, the grassy meadows brightly jewelled with flowers of red, blue, yellow, and white, and stony cliffs cut by sparkling streams, where, amazingly, patches of snow lay in the deep shade.

He would certainly never forget the tropical garden; going along the alarmingly bouncing wooden walkways high above the densely growing ferns and huge gunneras, where he was sure dangerous creatures lurked beneath their giant leaves. But he didn't like that garden, it was too humid and full of biting insects. He wasn't too keen on the hot desert garden either, especially when Snap warned him not to step off the sandy path on to the rocky ground, where snakes hid, ready to sink fangs into a careless ankle.

In the end, he decided his favourite garden was what Snap and Fox called the formal garden; a picture-book come to life, where kings and queens could take a stately walk among the dancing butterflies along smooth grass paths between dazzling flower beds, coming every now and then upon cool ponds where fountains of wondrous statuary splashed down on lazily swimming golden fish of enormous size. In places, almost hidden in the thick hedges, shell grottoes could be found where if you peeped through the windows, you could see statues of nymphs and unicorns.

Leaving the last garden, a rose garden filled with heady scents, they passed through a gate in a wall of weathered red brick and found themselves by a wide lake fringed with yellow iris and kingcups, its surface covered in scarlet, lemon, and cream waterlilies. On the far bank, tall willows swayed in the gentle breeze, their leaf tips brushing the water. Beyond them rose the great yew hedge, marking the far boundary of Florain, and behind the treetops of the forest could be seen stretching away into the haze of the outside world.

A wooden jetty jutted out into the lake, with a flotilla of rowing boats moored alongside, their brightly coloured pennants fluttering on the balmy air. Snap and Fox led them to the jetty's end, where a tartan rug and picnic basket awaited them.

'From Queen Ailis,' Fox said, pulling off with a flourish the picnic basket's red and white checked cloth, to reveal neatly cut sandwiches, slabs of fruit cake and two green bottles containing an interesting looking sparkling liquid.

'Shall we sneak a sandwich?' Snap asked Fox. Then spotting, tucked among the cakes, a couple of greasy pig's trotters wrapped in clear plustic, intended for Mick, he grimaced. 'Perhaps not – chores beckon: it's our turn to muck out the stables.'

Turning to go, Fox said: 'Enjoy your lunch. We shall come later to take you to the forge, so Fin's sword can be mended.'

Fin smiled his grateful thanks.

The two young Gaiakins loped back along the jetty, their clouds of dragon flies and bees streaming behind. At the gate into the rose garden they turned and waved.

Lark called out: 'Would you like us to save one of the pig's trotters? Mick would be honoured!'

'No thanks!' Snap called back, pulling a sour face.

Settling down on the rug, boots dangling over the water, they started on the cucumber and radish sandwiches, before moving on to other delicious titbits between swigs from their bottles, which they discovered was elderflower fizz, and every bit as good as Grammer Nutmeg's. Mick crouched a distance off crunching a pig's trotter, his paw over the other, guarding it from theft. To his relief, his red bow had come off somewhere in the gardens.

The last sandwich and cake eaten, Lark asked if he could look at Fin's sketches. Whilst he leafed through the pages, Fin sat, dozing a little, watching the lily pads bobbing on the lake: he'd been here before, in his dream when Fescue had called to him, the blood red beam from his ruby ring flashing across the water. The hooded figure in his other dream, also wore a red ruby on his finger. Now he knew for certain who that figure was kneeling beneath the man on the cross: it was Fescue.

A grunt from Lark brought him out of his reverie: he was holding the sketch pad at arm's length, admiring a picture. Fin studied Lark's face, seeing with a shock how he'd aged: fresh lines etched around his mouth and eyes, traces of the recent terrors he'd been through. With a pang of remorse, he wished he'd been kinder to him.

'I'm sorry Lark, I've been bloody rotten to you these past few days,' he blurted out.

Lark looked up from the sketchbook, and Fin, seeing the relief flood into Lark's face, felt even worse.

'Apologies accepted Fin. Just make sure you don't try to cut me out again – never forget I'm here to help you!' He took Fin's hand and squeezed it, then grinned. 'But calling me a gollop, what kind of word is that?'

'I made it up – not brilliant.'

'Yep, daft, and I'll need a forfeit.'

Fin looked at him in alarm.

'Nothing too bad. Just when we get back to the castle, you can do a sketch for Tissy – of me standing by that monstrous dolphin fountain in the courtyard where the Gaiakins were having breakfast.'

He heaved a sigh and opened his arms wide. 'She's not going to believe all this – pansies, snowdrops, poppies, daffs, peonies, hellebores – all flowering together! And those other plants, looking as if they were made of coloured wax, and so bright you need sunglasses – and the tulip trees – gob-smacking— I'm beginning to think it's all a bit over the top, this Gaiakin Garden. Makes me appreciate the seasons in Brightdale; snowdrops in late Dormant, primroses in early Saprise, buttercups in Highsun, ripe apples in Leafturn...'

Glancing at Fin's drawn pale face, he lapsed into silence. For them both, but Fin most of all, the horror of what had happened at Birdoswald was still very raw.

'Fin, what about Bird?' he asked gently. 'What are we to do? You know I'll do anything to help!'

Fin frowned. Should he tell Lark the ever-changing plans that had been churning in his mind since they'd brought Bird here? The latest was that if Mossy didn't come soon, Lark should take Bird (or what they must think of as Bird) back home, whilst he returned to Holy Island, where he would give them the Chi Rho. He hadn't even acknowledged to himself what he would do if Mossy couldn't cure Bird – he might even go to Contagion to find her soul, whatever that looked like.

He picked his words carefully. 'If it's decided that Bird should be taken back to Brightdale, one of us should go with her. I – I think it should be you.'

'And what do you intend to do, Fin?' Lark asked suspiciously. 'Hope you haven't got some daft idea in your head. Any road, we shouldn't decide anything until Mr Mossy gets here – surely he and Wings must come soon!'

They both turned their gaze towards the pale horizon beyond the yew hedge, from where they reckoned Skyhook would appear: the sky was empty.

'How about a dip, eh Fin?' Lark asked, attempting to cheer them up. He looked meaningfully down at the invitingly cool water.

'Last one in—' he began, unbuttoning his jerkin and starting to undress.

'—WASHES THE SOCKS!' Fin shouted, jumping to his feet.

Whipping the purse from around his neck, and stuffing it into a pocket, he quickly stripped down to his underwear, and leaving his clothes in a pile, dived neatly between two lily pads, leaving Lark gaping at the circle of ripples he'd made.

# 18
# DANCER ARRIVES

As he swam in the cool green water, pushing through the forest of lily stems, Fin thought back to his dream on the fell, when he'd seen his dead father's spirit swimming amongst the seaweed fronds. How he wished he could have told his father that he'd found Miryam. But perhaps Marlin knew? Could the dead watch over the world of the living? Feeling the silky soft mud of the lake's bed between his toes, he remembered his purse, lying unguarded on the jetty. He knew he shouldn't have left it there, but he didn't care. He had a feeling that in this place, his treasures would be safe.

A shadow fell across the surface above him. He spun round on his back, sending up a stream of bubbles from his nose. A familiar lizard-like face peered down through the water. Pushing his feet into the mud, he shot to the surface.

'Dancer! At long last!' he exclaimed, spitting out muddy water. Taking hold of her proffered hand, he scrambled up on to the jetty. 'Where's Mossy?' he asked, looking eagerly behind her.

Dancer didn't speak, anguish contorting her Skwid features. He saw Sandy at the far end of the jetty, helping Lark get dressed. Lark seemed to be weeping, his shoulders heaving. Fescue was there too, slumped on the boards, holding a bundle of blue cloth to his chest.

It couldn't be! It mustn't be! He sprinted down the jetty, Dancer running after him, carrying his belongings. Kneeling in front of Fescue, he reached out and touched the dark stain spread over the familiar inky-blue cloth: he felt dry blood. Bewildered, he searched Fescue's stricken face but saw no hope there. Hearing a loud sob, he dragged his eyes away. Kenji was crouching on the bank, transfixed by something lying on the grass: it was a boot – it looked like Wings' left boot. And it contained part of a leg, torn off just below the knee, the flesh all ragged, the bone sticking out. Sickened, he looked to Sandy, hoping for reassurance, but Sandy had his head bowed.

'Come Fin, you must get dressed,' he heard Dancer say, as if from far away. Looking up, he saw she was holding out his trousers and shirt. 'We shall tell you what has happened when we return to Queen Ailis' Cottage.'

In a daze, Fin dressed. Taking the purse from his pocket, he hung it around his neck. The Chi Rho added no extra burden to his stricken heart. Before turning away, he looked once more at the empty sky beyond the yew hedge: Skyhook would not be coming now.

Trailing through the gardens, listening to Lark's sobs, he wondered if he were in one of his dreams, that he would wake up soon. Fescue had given him the blue robe to carry, and to test if he was awake, he pressed the stain to his face, feeling the dried blood rough on his skin: the honey-sweet smell beneath the iron tang smote his heart, sending his mind spinning back to the sunlit fells above Watersmeet. A storm of rage hit him. What was Mossy doing, dying? Angels don't die! As he stumbled along this thought became a chant: Angels don't die. Angels don't die. Angels don't die.

'Come Fin, drink,' Queen Ailis said. Fin took the mug from her. Between sips, he looked about, not remembering how he'd got there. Her living room was full of shadows. Through the window, he saw it was almost dark outside. He was sitting on the sofa with Sandy, his face stony, but grief in his eyes. Lark crouched on the floor, staring down at the carpet, hugging Mick close. Dancer, Kenji, and Fescue sat at the table by the window, Wings' booted foot placed incongruously amongst the cups and plates.

Queen Ailis handed around mugs of steaming chamomile tea, urging them all to drink. 'I have added poppy juice: it will comfort us!'

Sandy looked across at Dancer. 'Now, you must tell us tell what happened.'

Purples and dark greens rippling across her face, a sob in her husky voice, she began haltingly.

'It was— it was a few days back when we feared something might be very wrong. A – a group of Scavs turned up at Durholm with unusual salvage for sale: lengths of twisted tubing, lumps of buckled metal, pieces of tarred canvas.

'One of Haar's keen-eyed Squad brought a piece to me and I knew at once something dreadful had happened. I went with him to the Scav stall, where a piece of black tile from one of Skyhook's wings confirmed my fears. The Scavs were reluctant at first to talk, but unsheathing my sword made them suddenly keen to help. The Scavs told us they had found the wreckage scattered in the forest. Haar organised a search party, taking one of the Scavs as guide. By— by this time I had regained sufficient strength to go with—'

Dancer's voice broke as she summoned up courage to continue.

'There— there was little wreckage left, mostly larger pieces, too heavy for the Scavs to carry: part of the frame, bent and buckled, and the pilot's seat, distorted and slammed into the smashed engine. Skyhook must have hit the ground with considerable force. Haar thought it was an attack by Gressil's Snoopers, but— but as everything was so damaged or destroyed by fire, it was hard to be sure. There was no telling how long ago the crash had happened.'

'Were there no— no bodies?' Kenji asked huskily.

Dancer shook her head. 'No, apart from that,' she gestured with a shudder toward the leg, and the bloodstained robe. Strangely, they were found quite a way from the wreckage. Haar reckoned a hungry big cat of some kind might have— have—' her voice broke once more.

After a pause, she continued in a firmer voice. 'After returning to Durholm, I was torn as to what to do: Haar wanted to take his Squad to Birdoswald. Then a carrier pigeon arrived from Florain with a message from Sandy, saying you were all here, so here I came.'

She fell silent.

No one spoke – grief a living presence in the room.

Eventually, Ailis got up and lit lamps. Lark had fallen asleep on the hearth, so Sandy carried him upstairs to bed. Dancer reverently wrapped the booted leg in a piece of plustic.

Not bearing to watch, Fin went out into the hallway where Mick crouched mournfully by the front door. Letting him out, he followed him down the star-lit path and sitting on the bench beneath the old apple tree, watched the flashes of white fur, as Mick dived in and out of the deep shadows, investigating rustling noises.

Taking out the Chi Rho, he laid it on his open palm. The jewels gave off a soft glow as if they had their own internal light. He knew now what he must do: go to Contagion and search for Bird's soul. He would take the cross with him, as a bargaining treasure. What he would do after he found Bird – if he survived – he didn't know. He didn't know what a soul without a body looked like, let alone how to put it back inside the person's body. Mossy was supposed to do all that, but he was dead. Perhaps his mother would know? Yes, he would go first to Cuthbert's Island: she might know what a soul looked like.

The cottage door opened, flooding the flower beds with light. He heard Queen Ailis calling a soft goodbye to Kenji and Fescue as they went out through the picket gate. Quickly tucking the cross away, he waited as Sandy and Dancer came to sit either side of him.

Fin glanced down at the bundle at Dancer's feet. 'Is – is that Wing's foot?'

Dancer nodded. 'Tomorrow I will bury it in a quiet spot down by the lily lake.'

Fin shivered. 'Poor Wings! He told me and Lark that he had no family – that they were all dead.'

Sandy sighed. 'Yes, they were killed: his wife and two daughters—

'This is the story he told me: he was born in the huge city of London. When he grew up, he was taken as an apprentice by the machine makers, known as the Engineers. In the basement of the workshops, he discovered a store of books, hidden for centuries in sealed metal boxes. These books were full of diagrams of flying machines, and from them he began constructing prototype models. But his fellow engineers scorned his efforts, so he decided to escape into the countryside, where he could work free from interference.

'After some time wandering, he met a farmer willing to let him live in a cottage on his farm, with a workshop attached where he could construct his amazing machines. Soon, he became close friends with the farmer and his family, eventually marrying the farmer's daughter. They had two little girls and it was a happy time for him.

'Over the years his engineering skills grew famous and the farm became a thriving centre of cutting-edge flying technology.

'It was during the early hours of a winter morning that disaster struck. A horde of Plague Scavs, rampaging through the area, attacked the farm, stealing what they could and destroying the rest.

Wings was flying home from a night test of a new aircraft, when he saw the glow of fire on the horizon, and realised it was from the farm. He found devastation. The Scavs gone: the farmer and his wife, Wings' wife and daughters all brutally killed, his engineering works burned to the ground. All he had left was his flying machine.

'Fleeing from heartbreak, navigating by the stars, he undertook his longest journey, on the way begging, or stealing the special fuel he needed. After several months, he reached the Island of Mann in the north-west sea, and the good people there gave him a refuge and encouraged his inventions.'

Fin sighed sadly.

'Yes, Wings told Lark and me about the foundry on the Island of Mann where they make machines – I suppose someone will have to go there to give them the news.'

The three of them sat for a while, thinking of Wings.

Then Fin spoke. 'I have decided that I should go back to Holy Island, to see my – the Anchorite. Perhaps she can give me guidance – now Mossy's dead.'

He turned to Sandy. 'But I'll need help getting there.'

Sandy didn't offer any argument. 'I will take you: I have a small sailing dingy moored in the harbour down by the old castle. As a lad, I often sailed along the coast. It is about time I had some practice – it has been too long.' He looked up at the sky, sniffing the air. 'The weather looks fair here in Florain, but what it will be like in the outside world, who knows? We will sail with the dawn tide.'

He looked questioningly at Fin. 'What about Lark? Will he come with you?'

Fin sat for a moment, his thoughts still in terrible turmoil. 'When I set out on this journey, Mossy appointed Lark as my companion. He has given me more loyalty than I deserve. I owe it to Mossy, and to Lark, to ask him to come on this last journey – then I'll send him home without me.'

Fighting back tears, he continued. 'Someone must take Bird home, someone she can trust.' He turned to Dancer, who was watching him closely, searching his face with her enigmatic eyes.

She gently laid her hand on his, her scales glimmering silver in the starlight. 'I've been to see Bird: she seemed to know me when I held her. Perhaps she remembers that we're friends. I'll willingly take her home – you can trust me to take great care of her.'

Fin breathed out a long quivering sigh. 'It would be for the best,' he said. 'Thank you, Dancer.'

'And what about you, Fin?' Sandy asked softly. 'After you see the Anchorite? Have you a plan?'

'What I will do, will depend on what she advises. I— I might have to go to Contagion—' A desperate weariness washed over him.

Rising to his feet, he walked back into the cottage.

Not wanting Fin to find him asleep, Lark sat on his bed, trying to keep his eyes open. As he waited, he again mulled over what had happened at Birdoswald, when Fescue had stopped Fin from handing over the cross.

'At least Fin won't have to decide what to do with the dratted thing,' he muttered to himself. 'The Gaiakin covets it, and he'll most certainly get it in the end!'

The door latch rattled, and Fin came in. 'Well, Fin? Have you decided? Are we to leave Florain?' he asked challengingly.

Fin nodded. 'Yes, Lark. Do you think you can come with me on one more journey?'

Lark breathed a sigh of relief. 'Of course, I can! Where're we going?'

'Back to Holy Island. Sandy will take us in his boat, tomorrow with the dawn tide. Do you remember, I promised to tell you about my time on Cuthbert's Island? But then Hilda bringing the Frit head, changed everything.'

'Yep, I haven't liked to ask, but I'd heard that a woman lived there, all by herself. A kind of Holy Woman. But when they said she was a Rom, I worked out that she might be your mum – was I right?'

Fin nodded and smiled wistfully. 'When I think about my time on Cuthbert's Island, I sometimes wonder if it was a dream. She's an amazing person, Lark! I really would like you to meet her.

'I thought my mother might help me decide – perhaps leave the Chi Rho with them on Holy Island. After that, I'm not sure what to do – I might stay there. One thing I am certain of though, is that your job will be done, and you should go home.'

Lark looked at him in dismay. 'But Fin, you're Head! You must come home too – the Dale needs you!'

Fin looked at Lark's troubled face. 'You have to understand, Lark. I might not be able to find the strength of will to be parted from the Chi Rho. I thought if I stayed close to where it was, after a while, I'll get used to not having it. It won't be forever, I'm sure. Anyway, I'll return one day, to see how you are getting on in Brightdale, what with you marrying Tissy!'

Lark stared at him suspiciously. Then he asked the question that had been hanging in the air like a black cloud. 'And what about Bird? You're not letting me in on your plans there, are you? You should, you know – Mr Mossy would have wanted me to stay with you until things were put right, and I've every intention of doing so, so you're stuck with me, Fin Dandrum, even if Tissy doesn't wait for me, and – and marries someone else.' His face crumpled with unhappiness.

Fin put his arm around Lark's shoulders. 'You're as stubborn as your Mick,' he said, looking at Mick dozing peacefully on Lark's pillow. 'Once you get your teeth latched onto something, it takes a lot to make you let go!' He rubbed his tired, itching eyes. 'But I'm too tired to argue with you. If I don't get to bed, I'll drop asleep on the floor!'

Knowing Sandy wanted to sail on the dawn tide, they woke before first light. Fin told Lark the plan for Dancer to take Bird home to Brightdale and that, on Sandy's orders, Kenji would accompany them with Bee's body. At the same moment, they both realised it would be an opportunity to send messages: for Lark to write to Tissy, and Fin to send his sketches to Nutmeg for safe keeping.

Begging a sheet of parchment from Fin's sketch pad, and a piece of charcoal, Lark lay on his stomach on his bed, and with much grunting, did his best to explain to Tissy that he would be away longer than he had intended.

'Does promise have a 'c' or an 's'?' he asked, wetting his finger, and trying to rub out a word.

'An 's', I think. Have you got any message for Grammer Nutmeg?'

Lark frowned. 'You can say it all. You'll tell her about Mr Mossy? Whatever they'll think in Brightdale when they see Dancer, I dread to think! You'd better warn Grammer: explain that Dancer is very trustworthy!'

Sitting on his bed close to the window, his sketch pad on his lap, Fin stared blindly out at Queen Ailis' nodding hollyhocks. Thinking about Dancer and Kenji's terrible mission, and the Spinner family, he couldn't imagine the depth of their grief.   As they finished, Sandy's head appeared round the door. 'Are you ready lads? Mother has breakfast prepared.'

Fin stuffed the letters and sketches in a sock that had lost its partner, tying the top with a piece of string.

Whilst they packed, Sandy fiddled with the chess pieces on the dresser. Picking up the small sword with the silver thistle knob, he looked at it thoughtfully. On an impulse, he held it out to Fin.

'As your sword is broken, would you like to borrow this one? It would suit your height. I was twelve when Mullein forged it for me in the Florain foundry.'

Deeply touched, Fin looked up at Sandy uncertainly. 'Are you sure? I really would like that – it would remind me of you and Queen Ailis when I'm far from here.'

Taking the sword, he studied the strange lettering beneath the silver thistle. 'What language is that? What does that say?'

'It is an ancient Celtic language, it says: beware my downy flower, a thorn lies beneath. An appropriate legend for you, Fin,' Sandy said with a wintry smile. 'Now, no more chattering! We must get a move on or we'll miss the tide.'

They were sorry to say goodbye to Queen Ailis and her cottage; it had been a refuge of peace. After giving each of them a long hug, and tickling Mick behind his ears, Ailis stood at her door watching them go. At the gate, Fin turned and waved. He promised himself: one day, in better times, he would return.

They went first to the Healing House to see Bird, finding her asleep and Dancer sitting by her bed, her head bowed in weariness. Fin wondered if she had been up all night. Bending to kiss Bird's forehead, she opened her eyes: they were blank, there was nothing there. As she gave a small squeak, he smelt scorched clinker on her breath.

Taking Bird's limp hand, Lark bent close to her burnt ear. 'Get better soon, Bird,' he whispered gently. He looked pleadingly at Dancer. 'Take care of her, Dancer!'

'We'll be waiting for you in Brightdale – come soon,' she said.

Fin fished the sock package from his rucksack and handed it to her. 'Please can you give this package to Grammer Nutmeg when you get to Brightdale. It contains letters and some of my sketches for her to keep safe. Sorry, they're in a sock – that's all I had to wrap them in.'

'There's a letter from me too, for my girl, Tissy,' Lark said. 'Can you make sure she gets it? Can you tell her I'm O.K? She'll be worrying.'

Jumping to her feet, her face rippling orange and purple, Dancer took him in a crushing hug. 'I'll tell her of your bravery too, Lark Annunder!'

Fin and Lark turned away, their hearts too full to say more and, without looking back, joined Sandy outside.

They walked along the river road beside the sunflower fields, to the harbour beneath the ruined castle, where Sandy's single-masted sailing dinghy was moored to the stone jetty alongside several fishing boats: the lettering on the prow read Puffin.

Sandy climbed down a metal ladder into the dinghy, his weight rocking the small craft alarmingly and Kenji handed down their rucksacks, which Sandy stowed beneath a canvas covering in the prow. 'Come on down lads,' he called, his face full of boyish anticipation.

'Surely, we're not going to sea in that!' Lark exclaimed, clutching Mick to his chest, his face already turning green at the thought.

'Yep! Don't worry, the weather's good, and I'll soon hone my sailing skills.'

Climbing down the ladder, Fin cautiously settled on the bench behind the mast. Lark still dithering on the jetty, Sandy called to him impatiently. 'Get a move on, Lark!' He held up his arms: 'Pass me Mick.'

Muttering a curse under his breath, Lark handed down Mick, then taking a deep breath, slid shakily down the ladder, collapsing beside Fin, making the boat rock wildly.

'Safe journey, Delphins,' Kenji called, throwing the mooring rope to Sandy. 'I hope we shall meet again soon, in happier times!'

Sandy unfurled the sail, and pushing away from the jetty, busied himself with ropes and the tiller, gaining confidence as they drifted to the middle of the river. Then the current caught them and took them towards the open sea.

As he looked back to give Kenji a last wave, Fin's eye was caught by a gleam of gold: Fescue was standing on a castle wall, his golden hair shining in the sun. Fin raised his hand, but Fescue turned away and disappeared through an archway. Had he imagined it, the tortured expression on Fescue's face? He glanced at Lark, and was glad that he hadn't seen Fescue, being too occupied anxiously watching Sandy fumbling with ropes.

Rounding a last marram-topped spit of land, they came to open water, where they were hit by a stiff breeze.

'Hold on lads – mind your heads!' Sandy called as the limp sail billowed, sending the little craft yawing sideways. The wooden boom swinging just above their heads, almost scalped them. Heaving on the tiller, exhilaration sparkled in Sandy's midnight eyes. A youthful grin spread across his face, peeling away his years.

'YER COULD HAVE WARNED US A BIT SOONER!' yelled Lark, as he clutched Mick, gripping the gunwale with his other hand.

As the sail dragged over the surface of the water, he was convinced the boat would be sucked under, sending them all to a salty wet death.

Tweaking the tiller to left, to right, Sandy gradually got the little craft upright, and tacking like an expert to use the wind to advantage, they were soon skimming along, leaving a white wake behind them.

They made good time: an hour later they were passing between the Farne Islands and the shore, following the route Wings had taken in Skyhook.

Watching the clouds of birds restlessly swirling above the cliffs, Lark sighed. 'Didn't think we'd be coming back here again so soon.'

Fin nodded dumbly, a lump filling his throat as he remembered Wings' watery grey eyes behind his goggles. He turned his face to the north, hoping to catch sight of the castle on Holy Island, and was surprised to see a billowing white mist rolling towards them.

'Blessed Neptune, what are you up to?' groaned Sandy, 'that's just what we don't need – a sea fret!'

A moment later, they were enveloped in a dense fog; the wind dropped, and the sail fell limp. Furling the idly flapping canvas to the mast, Sandy pulled out a pair of oars from beneath the Delphins' feet.

'This'll take longer than I expected, lads. Luckily, it's not far. Move out of the way so I can sit where you are. Lark, go into the prow, and Fin, take the rudder.'

Settling the oars into the rowlocks, Sandy began rowing.

'Should we take turns?' Fin asked.

'I'll see how I get on.'

Sitting in the stern, tiller in hand, Fin discovered that if he moved the rudder to the right, the prow turned to the left, and vice-versa. He soon got the hang of keeping the boat on course, helped by Sandy, with his instinctive sense of direction, giving occasional instructions as he rowed, turning every now and then to peer intently into the white mist. After half-an-hour, handing the oars to Lark, Sandy took the rudder back from Fin.

Whilst Lark rowed, Sandy told them of his plan. 'I think it best if we do not go to the main island, but to Cuthbert's Island, where I will leave you with your mother.'

'I was hoping that would be the plan!' puffed Lark as he rowed. 'No offence, Sandy, but I wouldn't have put up suffering in this wooden bucket, if I hadn't been looking forward to meeting Fin's Ma.'

Fin was greatly relieved: Sandy understood his desperate need to talk to his mother about Bird. Peering through the rolling mist, hearing a distant muffled mewing, he recalled the sound of eider ducks when he and his mother had walked through the buck-thorn spinney to her cottage: they would soon be there.

On Cuthbert's Island, Crow the Scav could hear the eider ducks clearly. Lying in a makeshift den, deep in the marram grass covering the dunes, the mist enveloped him in a clammy blanket, obscuring the sandy bay below, from where came the muffled slap and slurp of the sluggish waves.

Pulling Sparkie out of a pocket in his chain-mail jerkin, he kissed the top of its ratty head. 'Sparkie, little love, can you tell me, how come we live here with holy lady? She called antikrite? Not sure? Anyroad, I call her Aunty Krite.' He gave a quivering sigh. 'She says me belong her now.

'What a day that was when we comed here! First, her push me in hot wet-wet, making me big mad. But me forgive her when she gived me cosy box in woodshed for nest – make me safe from nasties, it does. Lux-lux too, with fat bed, stuffy with fluffy feathers from duck bums, and hook to hang jangle-vesty at dark time. Keep Sparkie cosy too, eh? Tucker good too – got fat belly now!'

He patted his little paunch and burped loudly. Relaxing back on the soft powdery sand, the memory of what had befallen him, before he arrived in his haven, loomed to the surface. Sitting up and clasping his bony arms around his thin knees, he rocked to and fro, reliving the horror.

It started at Durholm. The pilot-man had returned too soon and nearly caught him climbing out of Huw's plustic sack; he'd just managed to dive beneath the rear passenger seat without being spotted. Pilot-man had made the machine roar, and there had been nothing Crow could do, but stay where he was whilst the sky came racing down to catch the flying thing once more and drag him and the pilot-man up into the blue. After ages of roaring, the flyer let go of the sky again, and settled down on the safe ground. Not knowing where he was, Crow stayed quivering with fear under the back seat, with dark time swooping around him.

Not too long later, the pilot-man returned, bringing a friend. What a friend! Crow's stomach churned at the memory.

'Girt black giant, Sparkie. You see him too, don't argue!'

The rat, sleepy after a feast of eider chicks, blinked and yawned.

Crow shook his pet vigorously. 'Yep, black giant gets in, and sky picks us up again. Him kenned my hiding place! Eyes burning hot, he reads me, deep down, deep in me secret places! He hooks me out and straps me in seat.'

Crow shuddered. 'Then terrible happenings come, quick, quick! Gressil Waspies hit us! O, ratty darling' what could Crow do! We fall, fall, down, down, thump, crash, hit hard ground. Me sure I was all broken! You too!'

He crushed Sparkie to his thin chest, sobbing at the memory. After the crash, his recollections were just snatches of horror: the gobbets of blood, not his – the pilot man's – dripping on his face. Being dragged long times in dark, and even when he managed to run away, another giant, this time a bushy tree giant, caught him.

'Rough, nasty twiggy fingers, pinching me skin, Sparkie. Bark hands cover me gob, lost breathings – near dead, I was! What do Aunty Krite calls them bushy giants – Bossies? No, no ratty! Boskies!

'The walking goes on for ever, up and down, branches cracking, grass swishing, two times of dark and two times of light. Me no see, just hearing rumbling, creaking voices like trees falling in wind. Then I sleep and wake and finds me with Bro Huw, but far, far, from jool. He brings me here where I so comforty! Aunty Krite heal me, washing away horrid memories along with blood, and giving me love.

'Her loving making me heart thump, thump. But now, I feel in me bones things change!'

A tear trickled from his one good eye. A ray of sunlight, piercing the sea fret, searched out crannies in the crumpled skin around the other, empty, eye socket and peace filled him once more.

'I go make sure me stuff still safe in woodshed,' he muttered, scrambling to his feet and hopping back to t'anchorite's dwelling.


Suddenly Cuthbert's Island loomed out of the thick mist, and Sandy beached the dinghy on the pebble shore. Scrambling up the dunes to where Miryam was waiting, Fin buried his face in her rough robe, his body shaken by a storm of grief.

As Sandy and Lark climbed into view, Miryam looked at them in questioning dismay.

'We believe Mossy is dead!' Sandy said brusquely, hiding his emotion.

'What! Dead? Surely not!'

'We fear so – we have heard nothing from him or Wings, since Wings set out several days ago, to bring Mossy from Brightdale – then Scavs brought evidence to Durholm that Skyhook had crashed.'

Pushing away from Miryam's embrace, Fin pulled the blue robe from his rucksack. 'Look, it's all bloody!'

Miryam lightly touched the dark stain. 'I have been dreading this. A few days ago, Brother Huw came to me with an injured Scav for healing – he said the pathetic mite had been found in the forest, babbling about a black giant, and a roaring monster that had fallen from the sky. Thinking his injuries had dazed his mind, I did not question him further. But I did wonder–'

'They found part of Wings' leg, too! Chopped off at the knee!' Lark put in, 'but we left that in Florain.'

She shuddered. 'I never liked that flying machine! So noisy and dirty! Come to my cottage and tell me more!'

But Sandy shook his head. 'No, I'll not stay, Miryam. I will sail on to Holy Island to bring the news to Mother Hilda.'

He turned to Fin. 'Fin, for a while our ways part, but I leave you in comforting hands!'

Wiping tears from his cheeks with his sleeve, Fin took Sandy's proffered hand, and gripped it hard. 'Thank you for bringing me here. Now I'm with my mother, it will be easier to– to — decide!' His voice broke into a sob.

Sandy took him in a hug. 'May Zagzagel be near you!' he whispered.

He turned to Lark and ruffled his thatch of pale green hair. 'I will not forget Lark, that when we first met, you were expecting me to have the appearance of a Scav!'

Lark grinned up at him. 'Glad to have met you, Sandy! When – when things are back to normal, you must come and hunt deer in our Annunder forest.'

Down at the beach, Fin and Lark helped Sandy shove Puffin back into the water. As he took up his oars, Fin called to him: 'Will you tell them on Holy Island that I am here?'

'Do you wish me to?' Sandy called back.

'No! Not – not until I've decided what I should do.'

Sandy nodded in understanding.

As the little craft disappeared into the mist, Lark called out. 'Hey – Sandy, don't forget to take the news about Wings to Vera at the Fisherman's Friend!'

Sandy's muffled voice came drifting back through the mist, but they couldn't hear what he said.

Sad that he had gone, Fin and Lark turned away and climbed back to where Miryam waited with Mick.

Miryam studied Lark's face. 'It is good to meet you, Lark Annunder. You have a resemblance to your Grammer Nutmeg – I have not forgotten how kind she was to me.'

Her sweet smile resembled Fin's. When Lark had first seen Miryam he'd felt disappointed; he was expecting her to be brightly dressed and wearing gold bangles, like the dancing woman at Rosie's Roost, not this careworn woman with her coarse brown robe, stained and threadbare.

She led them through the sea-buckthorn to her cottage. Inside, a black pot hung over the fire hissed and bubbled, filling the room with the sweet smell of cooking oats, making them realise how hungry they were. Dropping their rucksacks in a corner, and seating themselves on the pew, they warmed their chilled hands at the fire. Mick settled on the rag rug in front of the hearth, disturbing a ginger cat, which shot out through the door.

Looking around, Fin tried to recall his last visit, but the time he'd spent here had a dreamlike quality; the only vivid memory was the tapestry cushion embroidered with dolphins, on the pew where they sat.

'First, you must eat,' Miryam said, concerned at their strained faces, as she ladled out bowls of porridge.

After a cautious first taste, Lark dived in enthusiastically.

Noticing Mick's mournful expression, Miryam set down a smaller bowl of porridge, on the floor by the door. Diving in, he sent the bowl spinning across the stone flags and Lark had to jump up to rescue it before it broke against the wall.

Taking Mick by his scruff, Lark pushed him out through the door. 'Go'en find your catty friend, you badly behaved tyke,' he muttered.

When Lark had returned to his place, Miryam sat expectantly in her chair by the fire. 'You must tell me all that has happened!'

Putting his spoon down, Fin began falteringly. 'You heard about Bee and Bird – how they were taken hostage by Hardwick?'

Miryam nodded. 'Mother Hilda came to tell me the dreadful news.'

'When we returned to Durholm, Wings immediately flew on to Brightdale, intending to fetch Mossy. Meanwhile, knowing that Hardwick had taken the twins to Birdoswald, we set out with Sandy and his Squad, tracking their trail through the forest.'

Lark butted in: 'Dancer didn't come with us, because she was too badly stung by the Snoopers.'

Fin continued. 'When – when we reached Birdoswald, we were too late, we – we couldn't save the twins: the Phragg killed Bee, and – and stole Bird's soul —'

He fought with himself before he could continue. 'The – the Phragg dropped on Bird like a fiery vulture – took her little pearly soul inside its evil mouth—' his voice turned to sobs as he stared blindly into the fire, his face twisted in misery.

Lark put a comforting hand on Fin's shoulder and took up the tale. 'The – the Frits then attacked us – we'd have been killed too, if the Gaiakins hadn't come to save us. We went with them to Florain – which is where we've been since.

'Betony is taking care of Bird,' he added. 'When she's a bit better, Dancer is going to take her home to Brightdale, with Kenji to guard them.'

'And there was no sign of Zagzagel?' Miryam whispered.

Fin shook his head. 'I used to believe he had the power to do anything, but now I know he was just an ordinary old man – who got killed.'

'But Fin, you did all you could to save Bird!' Lark exclaimed. He turned to Miryam. 'He was very brave – even if foolish. He tried to bargain with Hardwick by giving him the cross but was thwarted by Fescue's treachery. The Gaiakin folk aren't all good, you know!'

Fin glowered at Lark. 'You don't understand the power of the Chi Rho. It can take over even the strongest will!'

Miryam leant forward and caught hold of his hand. 'Fin, what you did, you did out of love. But tell me about the blue robe and Wings' boot. Where were they found?'

Fin explained about Dancer and some Skwid trekkers finding evidence that Skyhook had crashed.

'The Scavs who found the debris guided them to the crash site, not far from the Durholmwater. Yesterday, Dancer arrived at Florain with the news, bringing the robe and the booted leg with her.'

'From the evidence, Dancer reckoned it was Gressil's Snoopers that made Skyhook crash,' Lark said.

For a while Miryam sat frowning, then asked: 'What do you intend to do now, Fin?'

He sighed heavily. "Last night I decided to come and see you – perhaps live with you for a while, whilst Lark returned to Brightdale—'

'But then we remembered Bird,' Lark interrupted grimly.

'Yes, we remembered Bird.'

'There is no choice, is there, Fin?' Miryam said, her question more a statement.

'Nope. To get Bird's soul back, I'll have to use the Chi Rho – go to Contagion and bargain with Gressil. I've a feeling that's what he's been planning all along. He must be hopping a victory dance on his eight clacking legs at the news of Mossy's death! The trouble is, I don't know how to get to Contagion. All I know is that it lies beyond the Withered Wood, which is virtually impossible to get through. There must be another, longer way, but if I am too late—Bird's soul will be—' He shuddered. 'I've – I've heard Maabella eats souls!'

'I bet there are secret ways which, with my tracking skills, I could find.' Lark said in a low, frightened voice.

Fin looked at him unhappily. 'Are you sure you should come with me, Lark? Tissy needs you. They all need you in Brightdale.'

Lark groaned, and in frustration thudded his head against the back of the pew. 'You just don't get it do you, Fin? I'm sticking to you, come what may. I promised Mossy, and I couldn't face him, when he and I next meet — most likely in the next world!' Sniffing hard, he stared fixedly at his boots.

Fin was about to argue when he was interrupted by shrieking from outside. Miryam rushed to the door.

'Your dog, Lark! He must have gone to the woodshed. Come, quickly! You too, Fin!'

Thinking Mick must be fighting with Miryam's cat, they rushed after her.

The woodshed was behind the cottage, from where there came a pandemonium of squealing and snarling. Rounding a corner, they stood gaping: it wasn't the cat Mick was fighting, but a very large rat; blood and fur flying in all directions. A little bird-like person was hopping about the whirlwind of rat and dog.

'Et 'im Sparkie, bite its leggies off!'

Unlike at Phul's Hollow, this time Lark was ready: he lunged.

'Got you!' he yelled, catching hold of a stick-thin leg. Flinging the figure to the ground, and sitting on the skeletal chest, he whipped out his boning knife, ready to slice the scrawny neck, and would have done, if Miryam hadn't caught his wrist.

'No Lark! Don't hurt him!'

Lark blinked up at her in amazement. 'What?'

Then, seeing Fin was in danger of losing fingers in the snapping ball of dog and rat, he let go of his victim and rushed to his aid. After an agonising few moments of curses and scratched hands, Lark managed to pull the rat away from Mick. Catching it by its long rope-like tail, he whirled it about his head, intending to dash it against the side of the woodshed.

'NO! No kill Sparkie!' screamed Crow, struggling to escape Miryam's imprisoning arms.

'Stop, oh, please stop, Lark!' Miryam sobbed, at the same time laughing hysterically as she fought to hold Crow. 'You mustn't kill his rat! You have to be friends with the Scav!'

Lark gaped at Miryam. Letting go of Sparkie's tail, the rat flew to the woodshed, and disappeared inside. Mick tried to dash after it, but Lark caught him by his back leg. ''nother time, young Mick,' he growled.

'Mother, did I hear you right?' Fin glared at Crow, struggling in Miryam's arms, desperate to get to the shed from where there came loud squeaks. 'Did you say we must be friends with that evil Scav?'

'Use your head Fin,' Miryam panted, trying to control Crow, 'the Scav has been to Contagion, he knows the way there – he will be your guide.'

'NO WAY!' shouted Lark, 'he'd cut our throats long before we got there.'

'Mother, this vile creature tried to kill me with a doomstone.' Fin looked at Crow as if he were a bit of dog dirt. 'Anyway, how come he's living here, with you?'

Crow had stopped struggling, and was hiding his face in Miryam's robe, from where there came sounds of muffled weeping.

'There, there, no cry, little one, no cry,' Miryam cooed, stroking the top of his head, smoothing his feathery hair over a scarred bald patch. She looked sadly at Fin.

'As I told you and Iskander, he was brought to me injured, so I have given him a home. It was his desperate longing for the cross that drove him to try to steal it from you. Can you not give him a chance to redeem himself? You should know only too well how the Chi Rho can warp the mind.'

Crow pushed Miryam away, and bringing himself to his full diminutive height, faced up to Fin, his scarred face contorted in a mixture of anger and fear.

'Aunty Krite, this gurt Delph stole me jool. I hates him, an' I no take him Contagion.'

Crouching down, Miryam gently shook him by his bony shoulders. 'How come you treat me bad, young Crow? What I do to deserve dat? I told you: you don't need treasure. It bad, evil! Make you sick. You an' Fin must be friends. Aunty Krite loves Fin – he's my child. You'd never hurt my child, surely? He needs Crow so, so much, to show him way to Gressil's land. Please help Aunty Krite, little Scav one!'

Mesmerised by Miryam's dark unblinking eyes, Crow crumpled to the ground. Helping him up, Miryam led him to the woodshed. 'Come, little Scav,' she coaxed, 'come see if Sparkie O.K. He needs his Crow now, pretty-damn-quick. Him needs mending. I bring bandages and salve for you to tend him.'

She winked at Fin and Lark as she gently pushed Crow into the shed. 'Go young Scav child, you go an' tend rat, and I'll bring tasties for you to share with him.'

Astounded by Miryam's treatment of the Scav, they returned to the cottage in silence, sinking bemused on to the pew, whilst Miryam collected salve and bandages and returned to the woodshed. Lark got out his jar of marigold ointment and taking Mick on his knee, gently applied some to the rat bites, which, despite the ferocity of the fight, were superficial. Still fizzing with excitement, Mick soon got impatient with his master's ministrations. Wriggling free, he settled on the rag rug next to the ginger cat, who had reconciled herself to putting up with an intruder rather than spending the night out in the cold. Sniffing him, she had a go at licking the unction off his fur, spitting it out in disgust.

Lark offered the jar to Fin, and as he smoothed the ointment on his scratches, Fin looked at him earnestly.

'Lark, have you really thought it through – coming with me? There'll be little chance of you ever getting back home to Tissy.'

Lark's face puckered in anguish. 'Don't say that Fin! There must be some hope – we'll get the job of rescuing Bird done, and then do our best to get back home. I love my Tissy too much, not to succeed! Grammer Nutmeg says that good comes to those who do right. Anyhow, I've put it all in old Phul's care: he won't let us down.'

Whipping out a grey-looking handkerchief, he snorted loudly into it. 'But we'll have to keep a close eye on that evil little Scav if he's coming with us!'

'I don't deserve having you as a friend, Lark,' Fin murmured, taking his hand and squeezing it. 'Mossy knew your worth!'

Lark laughed thickly through his tears. 'Now master Fin, that's a bit over the top.' He pulled his hand away. 'Listen to us, going on like a pair of old grammers! Here, give me back my pot of ointment before it's all gone: the scratches I got from that foul rodent are fair itching – I wouldn't be surprised if they turn poisoned.'

At that moment Miryam returned, having finally settled Crow and his rat.

'What a to-do that was!' she exclaimed, collapsing in her chair with a relieved sigh. 'I think Crow has understood he must behave himself.' A shadow of guilt passed over her face. 'I've threatened him with all kinds of weird magic – not that I know any.'

Seeing the impish sparkle in Miryam's dark eyes made Fin realise why his father had fallen in love with her.

'Do we have to bring Crow along with us? Is there no other way?' he asked.

'It is as Zagzagel would have wanted it. I know he had plans for Crow,' she said mysteriously.

To avoid further explanation, she busied herself with a large cauldron, which she stood on the trivet over the fire, beside the pot of porridge. After giving it a stir, she tasted the contents, adding a spoonful of salt from a box on the mantle shelf.

Fin resigned himself to having Crow as a guide. He knew it would be impossible for them to find the way without Crow's knowledge of the terrain; there would be dense forests and fast rivers. And, in Contagion itself, they had to find the way to Gressil's lair without being spotted.

'Mistress Miryam, what did the Scav call you?' Lark asked; he'd been thinking about the fracas with Crow and the rat, recalling the Scav's squeaky voice calling Miryam something.

She smiled, and wiping her hands on her robe, sat down. 'Crow has taken to calling me Aunty Krite. Brother Huw must have put the idea into his head. Brother Huw refers to me as 't'ancorite', meaning the anchorite.'

'So, Crow knows Brother Huw,' mused Fin. 'Did you know Crow had come to Holy Island?'

She nodded. 'According to Huw, he turned up in his room on the day Mother Hilda returned. Brother Huw reckoned he must have first stowed away on her ship, and then stowed in Skyhook when you flew back to Durholm.'

She stared into the fire, lost in troubled thoughts, and didn't elaborate on who had brought Crow, injured, and frightened, the second time to Holy Island. They would have been amazed to know the extent of her friendships, not only with Mossy, but also the hidden people of the forests.

A bubbling hiss from the cauldron startled them. The room had filled with shadows; through the half open door, they saw dusk was falling, and a wind had risen, dispersing the sea fret. Miryam lifted the lid of the cauldron, releasing a rich aroma of fish, garlic, and wine.

With a taper from the fire, she lit the lamp hanging from a beam in the low ceiling, bathing the room with warm yellow light.

'Supper is ready,' she said, filling bowls with mussels in a rich sauce. She put a cod's head in Mick's bowl and placed it in front of him. Needing no encouragement, he dived in, crunching noisily. 'Your dog is amazing, Lark!' she laughed as she watched Mick – he'd gripped the bowl between his two front paws to prevent it from skidding off.

Their food finished, with satisfied sighs they relaxed against the soft tapestry of the pew.

'That was the best fish stew I've ever eaten,' Lark said, stretching his short legs towards the fire, 'not that I'm an expert, having only ever eaten the fiery stuff, full of fish-bones and crab shells Carlos the cook serves at Rosie's Roost.'

'Simple recipes are the best,' smiled Miryam, 'chilli peppers and tomatoes are not easily come by on Holy Island; we make do with what we can gather or grow locally. It helps that the Island's mussels are the best you can find anywhere along the coast.'

'I think I could get to like sea-fish,' Lark said, 'mind you, river trout and salmon take a lot of beating. Do you remember the river crayfish in Brightdale? Grammer Nutmeg's recipe – ah!' he sighed.

Miryam smiled wistfully.

As Lark and Miryam quietly chatted, Fin watched them: these two were the only ones left to him that he loved, now that Bird and Mossy were gone.

They were interrupted by a scratching at the door. Miryam got up and found Crow standing there, bowl in hand, looking forlorn. 'I'm so sorry Crow, I forgot to bring your tasties! Come in, come in!'

Crow shuffled to the threshold but would not enter. Sniffing mournfully, he glowered at Lark and Fin, eyeing him over the back of the pew. Then scowled at Mick, busily cleaning the last traces of fish gravy from his bowl; Lark suspected he would have given Mick a kick if they weren't watching.

'It's mussels tonight!' Miryam, her voice cheerfully forced as she spooned stew into Crow's bowl. 'I'll put in a cod's head as well, it has extra meaty cheeks which I know Sparkie particularly likes.'

Crow muttered some grudging thanks under his breath, and snatching the steaming bowl, hopped out into the windy darkness.

'Does he like living in the woodshed?' Fin asked.

'He seems happy. He sleeps in an old wardrobe, wrapped in a blanket on a thick eiderdown mattress.'

Lark rubbed his sleepy eyes, then sat up straight, looking at Fin and Miryam. 'Before going to sleep, I'm hoping we can work out a strategy for Crow and his rat. For a start, how do we tackle the, ahem, ill feeling, between Mick and the vermin?'

'I've thought about that,' Miryam said, rummaging in her locker. She produced a brown leather satchel with straps.

'It's a bible bag, used for carrying books on journeys. Look, it's strong with ventilation holes along the top.' She undid the straps to show them the inside. 'Crow must be made to keep his rat in here – usually it lives in a pocket of his steel-ringed jerkin and comes and goes as it likes.'

Lark looked amused. 'Yes, that'll do nicely. When the rat needs to stretch its legs, I'll keep Mick out of the way in my jerkin.'

'I hope Crow doesn't try anything, once he thinks he's safely out of reach of your magic,' Fin said.

'We'll just have to keep a close eye on him,' Lark said, 'there's two of us: we can take turns sleeping, for a start.'

'An unknown is what he might do if the draw of the Chi Rho becomes too much for him,' Fin said, 'especially when it dawns on him that he's never going to get it back. But we'll sort that problem if, or when, it crops up. For my part, after I've got Bird safely home, he can have his jool for all I care.'

He gave a great yawn. 'Anyway, let's get some sleep.'

Wrapped in their blankets, Fin and Lark settled at each end of the pew, their heads on eiderdown stuffed pillows. Waiting for sleep, Fin listened to his mother's quiet movements as she busied herself tidying up. The thought of once again having to say goodbye, made him sad. How he wished he could have stayed with her, here on this island, or even nearby on Holy Island, perhaps one day becoming a Brother, like Rory and Huw. Maybe one day...

# 19
# BLOOD IN THE WOOD

Fin was woken by Miryam gently shaking him. It was just before dawn, the dying embers in the grate still glowed. 'I would like you to myself for a short while,' she whispered, 'come with me to the tarn and watch the sunrise.'

Leaving Lark and Mick snoring gently beneath their blanket, he pulled on his boots and tiptoed after his mother. Arm in arm they strolled to the tarn as pale light slowly flooded the horizon. At the water's edge Fin sat on a tuft of sedge grass, and stretched out his legs, his heels sinking in the boggy peat. Settling down beside him, Miryam searched in the mud, and finding a smooth pebble, threw it into the tea-coloured water, sending ripples circling out to the tarn's banks. Fin remembered the last time she'd done that; when she had explained about why there was still evil in the world.

On an impulse, he pulled out the cross and laid it on his palm. Bending close, he stared into the clear crystal where the thin line scarred the blue enamel background.

Sensing his mother's gaze on him, he glanced up to see fire in her dark eyes. 'Fin, there is neither bad nor good in the Chi Rho, it is the blood in the wood that has the power.'

Nearly dropping the cross, he shied away from her. 'What did you say? What do you mean, by 'the blood in the wood'? What blood? What wood?'

'Look closely into the crystal, at the blue enamel – what do you think that small dark blemish is?'

Setting the crystal at an angle, he studied the enamel sideways on. As he did so, from nowhere his dream rushed up: the hooded figure beneath the cross, digging with the tip of his gold dagger at the blood-soaked wood. Understanding hit him like a physical blow.

'It's a splinter! A splinter of wood!' he exclaimed. 'I thought, being ancient, the enamel had cracked, or it might be a bit of hair or something, trapped there; but no, it's a splinter of wood from the cross on which the poor man died!'

Jumping up, holding the cross tight to his chest, he paced the damp sedge, his thoughts in turmoil. His mind went back to Mossy's room, when Mossy had told the story of the making of the Chi Rho by the Gaiakin brothers.

'The hooded figure was Fescue – when my dream came back to me at Birdoswald, I saw him! It was he who chipped the wood from the cross, and it was he who put the splinter into the Chi Rho.'

He turned the cross over and read the inscription etched on the back: 'Having slept a short sleep on the tree, the King of all, The Word, who is both God and man, gave the wood virtue.'

Stunned, he stared at Miryam as he struggled to take in the significance of the words.

'But why is this blood so powerful? Loads of people die, some in horrid ways like the poor tortured man in my dream, but nobody bothers keeping some of their blood.'

Miryam searched for another pebble and standing, threw it into the tarn. 'You remember how I explained to you why I threw the stone into the water? The smooth surface represents Creation, and the stone represents the evil with which Lucifer marred the Creator's work.

'In your dream, you saw the Christ. His dying on the cross, being buried, and rising to life again, mended everything. It's like when a seed is buried in the ground and is transformed into a new plant – very different from the dry inert seed. But it must die and be buried before it can rise from the ground as a plant. It was thus for the Christ, being buried and rising from the dead. The drop of blood soaked into the splinter that Fescue took from the cross is the last remnant of the blood that Christ shed: it has not been buried, so in some strange way a mixture of evil and healing lingers there.'

Fin desperately wanted to understand what his mother was saying, but somehow the significance of the Christ dying and rising to life again was beyond him. Glancing at the last of the ripples made when his mother threw the stone, he shook his head in bewilderment.

Miryam continued. 'This cross is what they call a reliquary, a container for holy relics. This type of reliquary is called *enkolpion*, which means "*worn on the breast*". Your Chi Rho was intended to be worn against the breast.

Fin recalled Mossy's words: '*When the Gaiakin made this cross, he was overcome by a burning desire to hang the chain about his neck, and lay the cross close to his flesh, over his great Gaiakin heart.*'

Miryam's explanation almost overwhelmed him: it had been hard enough coping with the Chi Rho before, but he knew now it was of far more significance than he could ever have imagined. He tried to recall what else Mossy said that night. *'This cross has, shall we say, a reputation. Some believe it has healing powers, even supernatural powers.'* He, Fin Dandrum, intended to take it to Gressil to trade in exchange for Bird's soul!

'What *on earth* should I do, mother?' he whispered, looking at her, agonized.

She put her arm around him. 'Search your heart, Fin – what does it tell you?'

He tried to think, but his mind remained obstinately blank. The sound of a skylark, its sweet song rising and falling on the clear air, made him look up: 'I love you Fin! I love you Fin!' It was Bird's voice.

Grinning stupidly, he laughed out loud. He shoved the Chi Rho back in the purse, hiding it firmly away, determined not to take it out again until he stood before Gressil.

'I'll stick to my plan – to rescue Bird's soul, and the sooner I get going, the better!'

As he finished speaking, a gleam of golden sunlight flashed across the grey sea, momentarily blinding him. With it came a deep peace: he had made his decision.

Miryam took his hand. 'Let's go for breakfast – Lark will be wondering where we are!'

As they strolled past the woodshed, they heard snuffling squeaks from inside: Crow and Sparkie were awake.

Back at the cottage, Miryam poked the fire back to life and hung the pot of porridge over it. Fin sat on the pew, disturbing Lark who woke with a huge yawn.

'Well, I never would've thought I could have slept so soundly on a church pew!' he remarked, scratching his chest inside his shirt. He looked about him. 'Where's Mick? I'd better go and see what he's up to.'

Miryam went out with him, to milk the cow and feed the hens.

A while later, their porridge eaten, Mick still licking the last remnants from his bowl, Miryam brought out a tattered parchment from a drawer in her dresser. 'This is a copy of the map the Holy Ones drew, when they journeyed from Yrving to Holy Island. It shows the landmarks along their route. Legend has it that Prince Cadeyrn carried a copy when he went to Contagion to kill Queen Mab. You must bring the map with you on your journey, to check if Crow is taking you in the right direction. Come, we'll study it outside in better light.'

Spreading the map on the thyme covered ground, they knelt and pored over the faded markings, scattered with sketches of the flora and fauna the travellers had encountered: birds of prey, wild cats, aurochs, wolf, and boar, with warning notes written beside them.

Startled by a loud sniff, they turned to see Crow behind them.

'Ah, Crow love, good morning,' Miryam cooed, 'are you waiting for your porridge? We are studying the route you should take – come and see the map.' She traced her finger along the line of a river: 'Will you take the path along the Tillwater?'

Pushing his skinny frame between Fin and Lark, Crow peered at the faded brown ink lines and the little drawings of trees, rocks, and creatures. He sniffed again.

'Don't ken this stuff,' he muttered, 'but yep, I takes us along Tillwater, like you said – but shall keep away from Chill'am! Mustn't get caught by ghosty cows there!' He stabbed at a picture of a long-horned cow.

Spotting a mischievous twinkle in the colourless iris of Crow's one eye, Lark glared at him suspiciously.

Miryam folded up the map with an impatient sigh. 'Go back to your shed, Crow. I'll bring your breakfast!'

Crow slouched off. When he'd disappeared inside, Lark wrinkled his nose. 'He's so whiffy, there'll be no danger of him creeping up on us without us first smelling him!'

The day was well on when at last they were ready, the delay mostly caused by the struggle to get Crow to put his rat in the bible bag. After more dire threats of magic from Miryam, including turning his rat into a jellyfish, Crow finally gave in, weeping as he pushed the squealing Sparkie into the bag, and allowed Fin to close the straps.

'It's for Sparkie's own safety,' Fin told him yet again, his tone so severe that Crow quailed.

Lark snorted in disgust.

Miryam rowed them to the mainland in a little boat she kept in the dunes. As they crossed the water, Fin looked anxiously towards Holy Island, hoping they weren't being watched.

Reaching the shore, Miryam nosed the dinghy into a muddy inlet, deep in the undergrowth fringing the shore. Fin peered into the dense forest beyond and shivered. How was he going find the courage to venture into this wild, lonely place, with only Lark's boning knife and Sandy's childhood sword for defence?

Making the little boat fast on a low branch, they all climbed out on to the muddy bank. Enveloping Fin in her arms, Miryam whispered huskily close to his ear: 'My son, whatever happens, be true to yourself and remember you are in the care of the dear Lord.'

She turned to Lark. 'Farewell Lark Annunder. May the light of Phul be with you.' Laying her hand on his head in blessing, a warm glow spread through Lark, filling him with courage.

About to push her boat back into the water, a howl went up from Crow. 'Aunty Krite!' he wailed, snot starting to drip from his crooked nose, 'you not said 'bye Crow. You no love him anymore!'

She abandoned the boat and ran to him. 'My little chick, a course I love you.' Taking his hand, she pressed it to her breast. 'Feel the beating in here? You be in my heart always, young Scav!'

Giving him a quick hug, she climbed into the boat, and Lark, holding onto a branch and leaning over the water, shoved her off. Fin and Lark stood watching until the little craft disappeared around a sand bar. Crow sat sobbing in the sandy mud, clutching the bible bag to his chest. Mick gave a long, high howl from where he stood on higher ground.

Like shrews, they scurried after Crow pecking his way through dense undergrowth, following a path visible only to him. Signs of late Saprise were all around, the trees and shrubs full of fat bud about to burst open into leaf, the air loud with bird song.

They encountered little to alarm them; once a squadron of Gressil's Snoopers flew overhead, sending them diving into a thicket of holly, and later they spied a group of Skwid camped on a distant hill, forcing Crow to take them on a wide detour, before re-joining his chosen path.

Lark wished Sandy and Kenji were with them, with their reassuring knowledge and hunting skills, even Fescue, with his keen eyes; not Crow, muttering and grumbling, sometimes losing his way, forcing them to double back, and go in another direction. When he was lost, he murmured under his breath as he searched about; they caught the words: he stole me jool, and then when he found the way again, they would hear: Aunty Krite loves her Crow. Lark suspected the Scav was turning devious, now he was out of his Aunty Krite's influence; he caught him once, eyeing Fin's chest where he knew the Chi Rho was hidden.

'It's his stink I can't stand,' Lark muttered to Fin, his face wrinkling in disgust as he watched Crow hopping along, pecking the ground with his crooked nose, his stick-like body looking as if it had no muscles, just sinew and skin laid on bones. 'He smells as if he's rolled in a rotting carp carcass, like Mick sometimes does.'

Fin felt pity for the pathetic creature. Was it intended that Crow should be their new guide? Planned by someone? By whom? Gressil or Mossy? Gressil, more like, as he was bringing the Chi Rho to Contagion. Once, when Crow had opened his precious chain-mail jerkin to scratch, Fin had seen the clear white scar of the cross on his skeletal chest.

It started to rain heavily. Fin and Lark quickly got out their sheets of plustic, glad they'd always packed them on top. Crow didn't seem to have anything to protect him, but he didn't appear bothered; plunging into some denser undergrowth, they heard the snap of thick fleshy stems, and he reappeared with a large gunnera leaf draped over his head and shoulders.

Starting off again, Lark shook his head. 'Do you reckon he's taking us in the right direction?' he whispered, turning to Fin following behind. Fin shrugged. 'Until the clouds disperse, we can't see where the sun is, so we'll have to trust him.'

At a shallow, fast flowing river, they topped up their water bottles, and sitting in the lee of an overhanging rock, had a snack of seeds and berries. When he'd finished eating, Fin opened out the map on a patch of dry ground beneath a laurel bush. 'Have we reached the River Till?' he called to Crow, sat beneath his gunnera leaf at the water's edge, soothing his bare gnarled toes.

Crow eyed the map antagonistically. 'Reckon you don't trust me?' he asked curtly. Fin heaved a sigh and put the map back in his rucksack.

It was late afternoon when they came upon the swollen, worm-eaten body of a goat, half-hidden beneath a rocky outcrop.

'Tigger! Tigger!' shrieked Crow pointing a trembling finger at the gouged-out throat.

Wrapping his bedraggled gunnera leaf tightly around himself, he sat down and firmly refused to proceed. Try as they might, they couldn't get him to move. In desperation, Lark volunteered to go on a recce to see if the tiger was anywhere close. Taking Mick with him, he returned a short time later to report that he could find no evidence of fresh pug marks.

'I reckon the kill's several weeks old,' he said, drawing on his experience in the Annunder forests, where tigers were occasionally spotted. Only slightly reassured, Crow grudgingly relented and they carried on their way.

They spent the first night near the river, sheltering inside a small cave where they sat shivering in their damp clothes, starting at every sound from outside, and dreading yellow eyes staring in at them. The only bright spot was their tasty supper of salt herrings and barley bread spread with dripping which Miryam had packed for them that morning. When they'd eaten, they slept fitfully until they were woken at dawn by sunlight streaming in through the cave entrance.

Stretching his stiff back, Lark saw Crow was missing. 'Where's the little tyke gone now?' he growled. 'Must be near, I can smell his stink.' He glowered at the vibrating bible bag from where came loud indignant squeaks. 'Look, he's left his rat behind – can't have gone far. That's right Mick keep an eye on that bag: make sure the rodent doesn't get out. I still think we should have dealt with the vermin by slitting its throat.'

'Lark, stop chuntering on! You sound like an old wemmer!' Fin snapped as he stowed away his plustic sheet. 'Between your grumbling and Crow's muttering, I'm going crazy.'

Crow returned a moment later. 'Sun's face up!' he croaked, his crumpled features almost cheerful. He rubbed his stomach. 'Belly full o' squirrel nuts.'

'You could have brought some for us,' Fin said indignantly.

Lark scowled. 'You must be joking Fin – I wouldn't want to eat anything that bit of scum has pawed!'

Surprisingly, Crow didn't take offence at this remark, but grinned impishly. Slinging the bible bag over his shoulder, he crawled out of the cave.

'What yer lingering for?' he called, 'get move on Delphs!'

Sniffing the ground, he set off along his invisible trail. Grabbing their rucksacks, they hurried after him. A breeze had risen, blowing away the last of the rain clouds, and with the sun warm on their backs, they soon cheered up.

Later in the morning, Lark tucked Mick firmly inside his jerkin, so that Sparkie could be released from his bag. The rat spent most of its free time clinging to the chain mail on Crow's thin shoulder, occasionally leaping off and running ahead, reminding the Delphins of a tracker dog. Watching its antics, they reluctantly admired the magnificence of its glossy coat and the richness of its diamond collar sparkling in the sunlight.

'You've got a fine beast there, Crow,' Fin called, attempting some sort of bonding with the Scav. Crow turned and gave Fin a leer.

In a spurt of jealousy, Lark growled: 'Don't overdo it, Fin.'

They followed the river, stopping for short rests to eat handfuls of seeds and dried berries, until at sunset they came to a ruined building. Crow hissed in satisfaction.

'Come Chill'am, long last! We resty here. We find cosy place outside ruin – ghosties inside.' He pointed with a shudder to the tumbled-down ivy clad walls.

Lark snorted. 'Much rather find shelter inside the walls than outside, where something alive and nasty could get us! What do you reckon, Fin? I'm going in to have a look.'

Fin followed him through an opening into what must have been a hall, now open to the sky, the crumbling walls supported by the gnarled trunks of ancient oak trees. The floor was smooth and dry, with areas of brown and cream tiles still showing. Spreading their blankets in a corner by an old fireplace, they ate the last of the dried herring with some of the bread and dripping, to which Lark added a few young dandelions shoots he'd picked along the way.

'Crow, come and have some food,' Fin called softly.

There was no answer: apart from the wind sighing in the trees, all was quiet. It was turning chilly; night had begun to fall, the shadows growing around them.

'Tempted to light a fire,' Lark remarked, 'I'll go to find dry wood and at the same time see what the Scav's up to.'

'Mick stay!' he commanded as Mick got up to follow him.

Suddenly a bellow rent the night air. As it did, Crow shot in squealing with fright. A thundering of mighty feet outside the walls made the ground shake. Quaking in terror, they saw the treetops lashing about as if in a gale. Cowering in the old fireplace, not daring to move, the rumbling and roaring continued for hours, finally fading away as dawn came, and with it a blackbird's morning song.

Lark and Mick were the first to recover their wits. Peeping over a wall, Lark gaped. 'Well I'll be—' was all he could find to say.

Fin found he couldn't move his legs: Crow's thin arms were clamped around them. Unhooking them, he hobbled stiffly over and peered out: nothing seemed to have happened, not a twig, not a blade of grass had been disturbed.

Clutching his bible bag with Sparkie inside, Crow still looked terrified.

'Chillam ghostie cows – get away quick, quick, afore they come back!' he screeched.

Fin eyed him suspiciously. 'You knew about this strange thing, didn't you Crow? Had you some idea of scaring us?'

Crow shook his head vigorously.

The River Till now swung west, running shallower and swifter. Remembering the map, Fin worked out that Crow was heading towards its source in the high hills.

An hour or so later they came to the source, in an area of marshy ground reminding them of the borders of Annunder Territory, where lay Phul's hollow – and their first encounter with Crow. Stopping to rest, Fin spread out the map on the dry heather. He saw the hills around them were called the Cheviots. An arrow with an exclamation mark pointed to the west; beyond that, the parchment was blank.

Leaning over his shoulder, Lark pointed to the blank area: 'I suppose we have to go that way, don't we? It's where Contagion lies.'

Fin nodded. 'We'll have to rely on Crow for the route, even though I don't want to. We'll use our own common sense too: for a start, we know that Contagion lies beyond Withered Wood, which I reckon must be somewhere south of here.'

He called to Crow. 'Do we go through Withered Wood?'

Crow spat in disgust and shook his head vigorously. 'Nope, we don't want go that nasty place! We find big lake first, then go down Gressil land from there.' He waved his skinny arms first into the west and then in a vague southerly direction. 'It long, long way but safer. Mind you, we got to watch for strong-arm, grassy boskies!' His face contorted with the memory of some horror. "'don' wan' meet 'em again. Oh, no, no!' He covered his face with his hands and shuddered.

'What do you reckon he's on about? Whatever are boskies?' Lark muttered.

Puzzled, Fin racked his memory. What had he read in Mossy's books? He couldn't for the moment recall anything about boskies. 'He's probably trying to scare us. Anyway, we'd better get a move on, we've still got a long way to go.'

Following a beaten path through the heather they continued for another sixteen or so miles, before coming to a viewpoint looking west. Below them, for mile upon mile, stretched a great forest, pale green and gold in the light of the mid-day Saprise sun. Crow called the viewpoint Carter's Rest.

An icy breeze blew in their faces, smelling of what? Rotting flesh?

'A pinch of Doomstone?' Lark muttered to Fin.

'More like ganglefowl,' he answered.

'Aye, with a soupçon of Frit oil,' chuckled Lark.

'No laughs,' Crow hissed, 'dat niff comes from t'iceberg – nasty, nasty.'

Suddenly, lit by a ray of sunlight spearing the banks of black clouds, they saw on the horizon the gleaming outline of a grey-white mountain.

Fin gasped. 'Do you remember Wings mentioning the Great Iceberg? Do you think that's it? If it is, it couldn't be so far to Contagion!'

Hitching his rucksack higher on his shoulders, and staring challengingly towards the ice mountain, he said: 'Right, let's get going – the sooner we get there, the sooner we'll find Bird!'

They plunged down the steep, heather covered hillside into the tree-filled valley.

Loud with birdsong, Lark's spirits lifted. 'This forest reminds me of Annunder Territory more than anywhere we've been so far.'

Whistling a soft tune under his breath, he strode after Crow who turned to glare at him. 'Shut noise!' he squeaked, looking about nervously, 'there be creatures in these parts, dangerous beasties, not like Delph lands.'

It was evening when Crow found the lake. Emerging out of the trees on to a grassy bank, they gazed in wonder at a vast expanse of water, so big, the far side was only a dark haze of trees silhouetted against the red sunset. To left and right a reed lined shore disappeared into the distance.

'It's like a sea!' exclaimed Lark looking down at the waves lapping the sandy beach below them. Hopping down, Mick stood in the shallows having a long drink. Taking off their boots and socks, they too paddled their weary feet and dug their toes into the soothing damp sand.

For a while they watched the birds dipping and bobbing on the choppy water, whilst others dived in and out of the reeds along the bank, the air full of their cries. Farther along the shore they saw a huge auroch drinking, whilst out in the middle of the lake, a white winged eagle, hovering in the air, suddenly dived and rose again with a silver fish wriggling in its talons.

A short distance to the north, a lone ruined tower stood on a rocky outcrop. Seeing the remains of a wall jutting out from it into the water, it dawned on Fin that the wall and tower were part of an ancient reservoir, and that the lake was man-made.

'Is this Kielder?' he asked Crow.

He and Lark turned and found Crow wasn't sitting beside them. A fierce hissing drew their attention to nearby reeds, from where they saw him gesticulating to them agitatedly. Gathering up their footwear and rucksacks, they hurried over to him.

'Daft Delphs!' Crow exclaimed, pulling them into the reeds, 'you'm be seen by all and sunder – not good!'

He pointed to where, half-obscured by the long evening shadows, a wolf crouched at the water's edge, not far from where Mick had just located a coot's nest; luckily, being down wind, it hadn't picked up his scent. Hearing Lark's low warning whistle and seeing the wolf, Mick backed away and came quietly through the reeds to his master's side.

'Thanks for warning us, Crow,' Fin said.

'Shall we set up camp here for the night?' Lark asked. 'It seems dry enough in these reeds. Is the water sweet, Crow? Can we fill our water bottles?'

Peering uneasily out of the reeds, Crow nodded.

Pulling his socks and boots back on, Fin sniffed the air, smelling traces of the Iceberg.

'Is that the south-west?' He indicated the shoreline winding away to his left. 'Do you reckon, tomorrow we should keep to the rushes as much as we can, and skirt the lake?'

Crow grunted distractedly, still staring nervously into the surrounding reeds.

Fin and Lark took out their blankets and began sorting what food they could spare for supper.

'Right Crow, I'll stow Mick in my jerkin,' Lark said, 'and you can let your vermin rat have a run.' He paused and looked around puzzled. 'Where's he gone to now! Did you see, Fin?'

Fin looked up from unwrapping the packet of barley bread and called softly into the reeds. 'Crow, Crow.' There was no answer, just the wind rattling the dry reed stems.

Leaping to his feet, he let out a yell. From out of nowhere, a dried bracken and willow thicket had appeared. The thicket had a face, two little round eyes studying him inquisitively.

Hearing a smothered cry from behind, he spun round. He saw Lark caught in a pair of bracken-covered arms, a big brown hand covering his mouth. At that moment, a warm leathery hand covered his own mouth. Two strong arms lifted him and slung him head down over a broad twig-covered shoulder. Squirming around, he saw another bushy thicket, also with arms and legs, grab Mick and stuff him, snapping and snarling, into a woven reed bag, before gathering up their rucksacks and blankets. The three humanoid bushes set off briskly, their long, leaf and twig covered legs swishing through the dry reeds.

At first Fin struggled to free himself, but though gentle, the sinewy arms holding him were too strong and he soon gave up. Hanging over his captor's shoulder, his face pressed against the leaf-covered back, he picked up a fragrance of herbs and flowers, and realised there was warm skin beneath, and that the strange person was wearing a camouflage of nettle stalks, woven with dried meadow plants.

As they strode along, the bush men called softly to each other, their voices sounding like a breeze rustling through corn. Listening hard, Fin found he could pick out a few words, but most was unintelligible. Wondering where they were being taken, he consoled himself with the thought that whoever these strange beings were, at least they were taking them in the right direction for Contagion. He saw no sign of Crow. He understood now what Crow had meant when he'd referred to not wanting to meet grassy arm boskies.

He tried to remember if he'd read anything about them in Mossy's books. (Fin had yet to read the short entry in *ZAGZAGEL'S BOOK OF HOMINOIDEA: The Boskies are from the Subfamily PONGINAE, the same root as the Pongo from which orang-utans originate.*)

Evening turned to night, but the hominids sure-footedly kept up their long loping strides. The moon had risen by the time they came to the bush men's camp by the lake's edge. Lowering Fin and Lark gently to the ground, they shepherded them to a shelter made by weaving together the whippy stems of growing willows. Pushing them inside, they left them sitting on a bed of dried bracken.

Peering nervously out, Fin and Lark watched the shadowy figures of their captors moving about quietly, talking in low voices. The bush man who'd put Mick into the reed bag, brought it over, and loosening the drawstring, made a theatrical slicing movement across his throat as a warning that Mick must be kept under control. Lark nodded vigorously, and as Mick's furious panting face emerged, he quickly grabbed him by his scruff. Another bush man brought their rucksacks and signing to them that they should eat their own food, the group gathered in a circle at the entrance, watching curiously as Fin and Lark took out and began eating what was left of Miryam's barley bread.

In the moonlight, Fin and Lark could now see them clearly, finding their captors' faces ugly, with small pig-like eyes, bulbous noses, and wide thin-lipped mouths, their hair and beards festooned untidily with twigs and leaves.

'Not much to look at, eh Fin. Remind me of apes,' Lark whispered as he bit a chunk from his bread.

Fin nodded distractedly. Blowing off fluff from a piece of berry leather he'd found at the bottom of a food bag, he started to chew; he'd remembered a picture in one of Mossy's books: a tall ape with long arms that touched the ground, his body covered in orange hair.

'I wish I could talk to them properly. I'd like to get across to them that it's important we get to Contagion – they might know the way.'

Lark shrugged. 'Look, they've gone now, and they're sorting out their own food. Whilst they're busy, should we have a shot at escaping? I've still got my boning knife in my belt.'

'And I've got Sandy's sword in my rucksack, but with their keen eyesight, they'd soon catch us in the dark. Best to wait until daylight and see what they intend to do with us.'

Lark nodded. 'They couldn't be all that dangerous. Not unfriendly, really. Mick seems to find them O.K. Look, he's gone to check on what they're eating – roots of some kind.' He took a swig from his water bottle and frowned. 'I reckon I might have come across these types before.'

Fin looked at him in surprise.

'Thought I glimpsed one on the borders of Annunder Territory, when I was a lad. Got a notion Grammer Nutmeg knows about 'em too. I remember her warning me not to go near the hedge people from Withered Wood – I thought she was trying to frighten me, because it's well known that nothing can live in Withered Wood, it being totally dead.'

Looking thoughtful, Fin started packing away the last of their food. 'Wherever they come from, if they know a way through Withered Wood into Contagion, they could prove useful, so we should try and get friendly.'

Lark turned and peered through the latticework of their willow prison at the dark surface of the lake glittering in the moonlight. 'I wonder where Crow is. Glad he's gone – he and his rat were bad news.' He gave a cavernous yawn. 'I'm too tired to fret any more. Can I have first turn at some shut-eye?' He took out his blanket from his rucksack. 'Wake me in an hour,' he grunted as he grabbed Mick, returned from some dog's errand, and snuggled down.

Fin didn't wake him in an hour; weary beyond fear, wrapping his blanket about him, he too fell into deep untroubled sleep.

At first light, they were woken by their captors, who signalled that they should refill their drinking flasks from the lake. Sitting by the water's edge, Fin and Lark finished the last few scraps of Miryam's salt herrings, whilst the bush men packed up around them, dismantling the woven willow shelter and scattering the dried bracken. Soon there was no evidence that there had ever been a camp.

The Boskie who appeared to be their leader crouched beside them. He cleared his throat and, after a short hum to test his voice box, spoke.

'Me, Aspen.' He thumped his chest, before pointing to his two companions. 'Ilex, Oak.' Waving his long arms towards the south, he pointed at the Delphins. 'You, us,' he indicated his companions, 'go Boskie home.'

Fin shook his head vigorously, and pointing to himself and Lark, said: 'Contagion. We must get to Contagion.'

Aspen nodded, showing he understood. 'Boskie home,' he frowned, searching for a word, his expression brightening when he found it: 'Boskie home, first. Contagion after!'

Fin smiled his understanding, but Lark frowned. 'Should we go with them? Do you think they're to be trusted?'

'With nobody else to guide us, I suppose we must – we're not a million miles from Birdoswald, and I don't fancy ending up there again!'

'O.K. But I'll keep a close eye on 'em.' Glaring at Aspen, Lark twitched his boning knife from his belt. 'If you get up to any nonsense, you'll have me to reckon with!'

Chuckling, Aspen delved into the depths of his greenery and produced his own knife. Recognising the knife as Rom work and not forged by the Evils, Lark felt more at ease.

Watching the Boskies having an earnest whispered discussion, every now and then gesticulating to the Delphins, Fin said: 'I think they're doubtful we'll keep up! Looks like we're in for a major slog.'

Aspen pointed to his companions' backs. 'We fast! You ride.'

Before Fin and Lark could argue, Ilex and Oak unceremoniously swung them up onto their shoulders. Seeing Mick cocking his leg against a willow and in danger of being left behind, Lark whistled to him sharply. Aspen scooped him up and tucked him under a leaf-covered arm. That accomplished, the three Boskies set off through the forest, following a path away from the lake.

Swaying along on the foliage-covered shoulder, Lark groaned. 'Whatever would they think back in Brightdale, riding on a bush!' Even so, despite the indignity, he knew he would never have kept up.

At mid-day, they rested in a clearing where the Boskies had hidden a stash of last year's hazelnuts. Raiding their rucksacks, the Delphins could add sunflower seeds to this supply, greatly pleasing the Boskies, who munched them with relish.

As they ate, Fin studied the surrounding forest. The trees to the south, mainly deciduous, were beginning to thin out, with stands of closely growing pine trees looming among them. Remembering what Kenji had said about there being no thorn break in these parts, he realised they had come again to the borders of Withered Wood.

When they had eaten, the Delphins hoisted on their shoulders, the Boskies once more set off southwards.

They were soon amongst pine and fir trees, their trunks so close that their branches had become entangled. A deep layer of pine needles made the path slippery, and even the sure-footed Boskies stumbled occasionally. Deep silence descended, no bird song could be heard, no rustle of a woodland creature; everything had become lifeless, dried up, the atmosphere heavy and stuffy. They felt as if they'd plunged into an airless tunnel.

They'd been going an hour, when Fin and Lark recognised the all too familiar reek of Snooper. Above them, the pine branches had blackened and curled in death, confirming their suspicions: they were near a Snooper's nest making them anxious that Birdoswald might be near. The Boskies loping stride turned to a sprint, their footfall hardly sounding on the path. From ahead came a sinister metallic rattling. Mick, tightly gripped in the crook of Aspen's arm, set up a low growling. A turn in the path revealed a skeleton hanging from a branch by a rusty chain. It looked to be the bones of a Scav. A crudely written wooden sign nailed above it read: KEP OWT.

The memory came back to Fin of the little Scavs hanging in the abattoir. A picture of Bird's burnt body rose into his mind and he couldn't stop a sob.

From behind, Lark called in a low voice: 'You O.K. Fin? Bet you're glad we're here with these guys and not with Crow – dread to think what trouble he'd have got us into!'

Twisting around, Fin gave him a wintery smile.

As the afternoon passed, the fir and pines started to thin, letting in more light. Patches of low growing plants appeared on the forest floor, becoming more numerous as they progressed. A beam of sunlight, falling on a pathetic cluster of wood sorrel, gave them hope of a world outside, of fresh air and sunshine.

A little later, they heard sounds ahead of birdsong and running water.

Reaching the top of a cliff, the Boskies halted. Helping Fin and Lark down from their shoulders, they looked down on a wide green valley. Its floor a patchwork of fields, the surrounding steep hillsides covered in trees and shrubs rising to the fringes of Withered Wood. Immediately below them a path zigzagged down through rows of earth terraces to a settlement of grass huts clustered around an enormous oak tree. A sparkling stream tumbled down through the terraces to a broad reed-fringed lake. On the far side a small river from the lake meandered through fields, eventually disappearing between a gap in the hills.

Following the Boskies down the zigzag path, Lark was intrigued by what had been planted in the terraces. At the very top fruit trees; apples, cherries, plums, and rowans, all resplendent in their Saprise blossom. On the next terrace varieties of soft fruits; blackberries, gooseberries, currants, bilberries, and crow berries. On the lower terraces, swathes of herbs; dandelions with golden button flowers already in bloom; jack-by-the-hedge, smelling of garlic; alexanders, their buds not yet ripe for pickling; bistort, just beginning to flush purple; bitter cress, invitingly succulent, ready to slap between two pieces of bread and butter. All along the terrace edges, spider's webs of goose grass clung to the retaining walls, and banks of alpine strawberries grew beside the stream, jewelled white with small flowers, promising a sweet harvest when Highsun was at its zenith.

Coming to the valley floor, they followed a path between the lake and fields, where Lark saw some fields were still brown soil, awaiting newly sown seeds coming through, others were flushed fresh green with the shoots of what might be oats or barley, and yet others beginning to haze steel-blue with young flax. To his great satisfaction, he spotted a large patch of young-leafed comfrey, with a heap drying nearby, which he knew was being composted to make manure.

Giving a long happy sigh, he turned to Fin behind: 'This is what I call proper vegetarian farming! If I weren't so fond of Grammer Nutmeg's mutton pasties, I could happily settle here with Tissy.'

Nearing the village, Fin and Lark were surprised that there were no stone buildings; the dwellings were larger, more permanent looking versions of the shelter their Boskie companions had woven by the great lake, the leafy walls made not only of growing willow stems, but of birch too.

Their arrival had attracted attention: Boskie families emerged from their huts, voices sounding like a soft breeze as they gathered around the Delphins. Aspen introduced Fin and Lark in the Boskie tongue, and they all bowed politely. Unlike Aspen, Ilex and Oak, these Boskies were without a leafy covering of camouflage, and Fin and Lark could see their faces clearly. They still thought them rather ugly, but their kind and welcoming expressions were reassuring.

Some were obviously old, their faces lined, skin a leathery mottled brown and their copper beech coloured hair beginning to fade, whilst others looked in their prime, tall, and muscular, with conker brown hair, skin with a sheen like the backs of bay leaves. The children, called saplings, as Fin and Lark learned later, had lively inquisitive faces, their hair like fresh green grass, their skin light-coloured, smooth, and soft. All the Boskies, male and female, young and old, wore the same plain linen garments: sleeveless vest tops and short trousers woven from flax. The only individuality was in the way they decorated these garments: the females featuring flower blossoms and the males preferring ferns and grass, whilst the little ones sported a variety of feathers and empty snail shells.

Fin and Lark's diminutive height was a cause of keen curiosity with younger Boskies who crowded close, indicating their amazement by exaggerated gestures, and they were relieved when Aspen, Oak and Ilex came to their rescue, beckoning them to follow.

'Come, must meet with Midori and Llinos,' Aspen said solemnly, pointing to a large round hut standing close to the great trunk of the old oak tree they'd seen from the top of the terraces; this hut was more substantial, the walls built of rough wooden planks instead of woven growing shoots, the roof covered with bark tiles.

Scooping up Mick to rescue him from being prodded and poked by a group of very small Boskies, Lark grinned back at them as they pranced and danced behind him giggling and laughing.

'They might not talk like us, but they laugh like us!' he called to Fin.

Oak and Ilex did not enter the hut but waited outside, taking charge of Mick, whilst Aspen ushered in Fin and Lark.

As their eyes adjusted to the windowless gloom, they saw the interior was bare of furniture, apart from a low table set against the far side of the curved plank wall on which lay various metal objects. A thick carpet of hay covered the floor, smelling fragrantly of herbs.

Two Boskies sat near the table and, in the light from the doorway, Fin and Lark saw that the couple, one a male with a bushy beard, the other a female, were much older than the Boskies they had met so far, their skin like deep mahogany bark, and their hair the tints of dead autumn leaves. Leading Fin and Lark forward, Aspen bowed deeply and introduced them in their own language.

Peering up at them from his couch of hay, they saw a twinkle in the male Boskie's eyes.

'Welcome to our small country, Fin Dandrum and Lark Annunder,' he said, speaking in the Common Language, his voice deep and clear. 'My name is Midori, and this is my wife, Llinos.' He gestured to his partner.

'You know our names!' Fin gasped.

Midori bowed in acknowledgement. 'We learned about you from our dear friend, Zagzagel.'

'You have seen him! When?'

'He came by not so long ago.' Midori frowned, trying to remember. 'We do not note time here, as you do in the outside world. It could have been last sunrise, or twenty sunrises ago. He warned us that, one day, you might be passing our way and that we should give you shelter.'

'Then you don't know!' quavered Lark, tears starting to his eyes.

Midori looked at him is dismay. 'What is this? You weep!'

Fin sighed miserably. 'Zagzagel's dead – he was flying in Skyhook with Wings when they crashed.'

Pulling the bloodstained blue robe from his rucksack he showed it to Midori. 'Look, we have this as evidence.'

Llinos plucked Midori's sleeve. 'Dear one, show smalls our finding.' She was not as fluent in the Common Language as her husband.

Midori got up on creaking legs and led them to the low table. Set out on it were various carpentry items, including an axe, a fine-toothed saw, several chisels, and a hammer, all shining clean, obviously much cherished. Amidst the tools was a pair of pilot's goggles.

'Do you recognise this?' Midori asked, reverently picking them up.

Seeing the familiar elastic strap, caked in dried blood, Fin drew a sharp breath. 'Where were they found?'

Midori pointed east. 'Near to Durholm.'

Fin nodded sorrowfully. 'We learned they crashed not far from Durholm: they found the blue robe and – and a leg in a boot.'

Grief caught him unawares, and he sank down on the hay. 'Mossy wasn't supposed to die – it's all gone so horribly wrong!'

Dismayed, Aspen loped over from where he stood at the entrance, and helping Fin to his feet, took him by the hand and sat him down by Llinos, who put her arm around him.

'Poor small, poor small,' she crooned, stroking his dark hair with her large leathery hand.

Lark slumped beside them. 'Fin has had such troubles, Mrs Llinos. First his dad got killed – murdered. Then his girl's sister was killed, and worst of all, his girl's soul has been stolen by the Evils!'

He turned to Midori. 'You see, that's why we've got to get to Contagion, to rescue Bird's soul from Gressil's slug queen.'

Fin looked at Midori pleadingly. 'If one of your people could guide us on our way, we would be forever grateful – we must get to Contagion before it's too late.'

Midori nodded as if expecting to hear this. 'On the sunrise, Aspen, Ilex and Oak shall take you to the borders of that putrid land – I would not want them to go further, nor would they wish to.'

Fin gave a grateful smile. But when Midori translated to Aspen what was being said, a spasm of horror crossed his face, and he shook his head vigorously. 'Bad, bad land! You die there!'

Fin shrugged. 'I've no choice.'

Leaning down, Aspen squeezed his shoulder in understanding sympathy.

'But soon it will be moonrise,' Midori said with a broad smile, suddenly clapping his large hands together, making Fin and Lark jump, 'for a short while you must forget your sad task and feast with us!'

His hand clap appeared to be a signal to Oak and Ilex, who carried in two finely woven linen cloaks, dyed deep brown, which they tenderly laid over the shoulders of the elderly Boskies.

Mick rushed in with them, yapping hysterically as he frantically licked Lark's face.

Chuckling with delight, Llinos scooped him into her arms, and cradled him like a baby. 'Beautiful creature,' she crooned, 'is cat?'

Outraged, Lark shook his head indignantly. About to explain that Mick was a terrier, he was interrupted by loud chattering. A squad of younger Boskies trooped in carrying a large piece of canvas, which they spread out like a tablecloth on the hay. After them, a more senior group brought baskets filled with sprays of violets and primroses, which they strew over the canvas. That done, a procession of adult females came in and set out wooden platters piled high with all kinds of vegetarian food: seeds, nuts, roots, dried mushrooms, dried bilberries, rowan, and hawthorn leaves; the centrepiece being a tower of chunks of waxy honeycombs, dripping with honey, which made Lark's eyes gleam.

The aroma of fresh baking heralded yet more females carrying flat baskets piled with barley loaves and soft oat cakes. The last to enter were the males, with trays of wooden mugs, followed by their fellows rolling several wooden barrels which, the Delphins were soon to learn, contained a heady berry wine.

Everyone settled down on the hay in a wide semi-circle, facing Midori and Llinos.

'Come sit,' Llinos said to Fin and Lark, patting the hay between herself and Midori. 'Feasting will give you small people courage for your perils.'

All bowed their heads whilst Midori led prayers to their wood gods. Then the feasting began. Generously filled mugs of wine handed round, everyone unceremoniously dived in, eating and drinking with relish. Realising they were very hungry, Fin and Lark also set to.

Though the food was simple, it had been lovingly prepared, and dressed in different sauces. Lark particularly liked the dandelion leaves, tossed in hazelnut oil, bilberry vinegar and thin shreds of dark brown truffle. Munching on a cake of nuts and seeds, he detected sweet fruit cordials mixed with spices. He decided his favourite food was the flat breads, and copying his fellow diners, soon got the hang of using them as a kind of container, wrapping them around a variety of morsels, before taking big bites.

As he slipped Mick a chunk of honeycomb, Fin nudged him in his ribs. 'The berry wine's good,' he whispered, plunging his face back into his mug.

Lark nodded. 'Grammer Nutmeg could learn a thing or two here about brewing.'

Several mugful's later, they were as merry as their fellow diners, showing their appreciation by grins and arm waving.

As the wine barrels emptied, the Boskies started to hum, and by the time the meal ended they were all singing, their lilting voices trilling tunefully. The more expert started up a chorus of bird song, to Lark's ears so realistic he thought the dawn chorus had begun inside the hut.

Midori plucked Fin and Lark by the sleeves. 'I tell you the hishtory of our Boshkie family,' he announced, pushing his ceremonial cloak off his shoulders, and settling more comfortably in the hay.

'It ish believed tha' in ancient timesh, Delphshs and Boshkies came from the same jungle lands, both tribes trav'ling north.'

The Delphins had to lean close to hear his slurred speech.

'Many died in the crowded southern lands. Our clan escape into the Wesht – kind people of the Holy Community cared for us there. Shlowly, shlowly we travel north, creeping through the thick foreshts...'

Fin and Lark, stupid smiles on their faces, watched as he wobbled his long fingers in a walking motion over the hay.

Slowly Midori's head fell forward, and he began snoring loudly. Wrapping the cloak tenderly around the old Boskie, Lark keeled over next to him.

Blinking dazedly, Fin shook Midori by the shoulder, hoping to hear the end of his story.

'With...Withered Wood, when did Boshkies...' Finding his tongue wouldn't work, he shrugged, and leaning against Lark's back, grinned foolishly around at everyone. For some reason, Mick seemed to be chasing a cat around the hut, encouraged by shrieks of laughter from the smallest Boskies. He knew he ought to do something, but sleep hit him like a sledgehammer.

# 20
# CONTAGION

Fin was woken by Mick licking his face. His head spinning, he sat up cautiously, finding he was still in the round hut, but there was no sign of Midori and Llinos, or evidence that there'd been a feast. He was covered by his blanket but couldn't remember getting it out of his rucksack. Next to him, Lark lay beneath his blanket, snoring gently. Fin listened for sounds of activity outside, but nobody seemed to be about. Lying down again, he felt his purse weighing heavily on his chest. He remembered a jumbled dream: of Mick, wearing the Chi Rho, chasing a baby tiger around the hut.

Lark stirred and sitting up, looked blearily about him. 'Where's everybody?' he groaned, holding his head.

'I think we're the first to wake – do you remember much of last night?'

Lark shook his head, then as the hut swirled about him alarmingly, wished he hadn't.

Fin frowned in thought. 'I was surprised old Midori said he knew Mossy. Mossy never mentioned anything about Boskies to me.'

Lark yawned and massaged his stiff neck. 'Who could have told Aspen and his mates where to find us? It certainly couldn't have been Mr Mossy – he's dead. Could it have been one of the Gaiakins? Or might your mum have told them? I sensed she knew a lot more than she let on. Anyway, my head's too thick to do much cogitating. Let's sit outside and wait for folk to stir; fresh air might help. While we're waiting, why not do a bit of sketching? I'll need a record of this place for Tissy.'

Outside the hut they found log seats, and Fin began sketching.

'I wonder who lives where?' Lark speculated, scratching Mick behind the ears as he sat on his knee. He studied the surrounding leafy huts. 'They don't seem to have family groups like us. Have you noticed there aren't any dogs? No farm animals, either, no sheep, no cows, no chickens, just cats. Thinking of cows, I could do with a strong cup of milky tea.'

Fin sniffed the air. 'It's very beautiful here, but there's a smell – a whiff on the air. Could it be from Contagion? It must be quite near.'

Lark shuddered.

Fin had just sketched the lake with the terraced hillside rising behind, when Llinos appeared with two mugs and a dish of honeycomb on a tray.

She smiled kindly at them. 'Drink!' she commanded, handing them the mugs.

Taking a sip of the dark liquid, the Delphins grimaced.

Llinos laughed. 'Liquorice good after too much wine.'

Grimly sipping the strange concoction, they soon felt better. By the time they'd got to the dregs and eaten the honeycomb, the rest of the Boskie community were stirring. In a few minutes, the place became a bustle of activity.

Midori arrived and took them back inside the round hut where he carefully chose two chisels from the oiled and gleaming display on the low table. 'One for you, Fin Dandrum, and one for you, Lark Annunder,' he said, solemnly handing each of them a chisel. 'These belong to our ancient clan and have been handed down through the generations. They will be a memento of the time you spent with us.'

'This is a prize indeed,' exclaimed Fin politely, 'when I return to my home, I will hang the chisel in a place of honour on the chimney breast of Dandrum Hall.'

Lark found one of his socks, and carefully tucked his chisel inside. 'Mine shall be used for one purpose only: to carve a wooden piece so beautiful it shall stand for more than a thousand years, upon the hearth of the clan that Tissy and I will start.' His face turned red as he buried the sock deep inside his rucksack.

On an impulse, Fin tore his sketch of the lake and garden hillside from his pad and held it out to Midori. 'I don't see any pictures in your hut. Would you do me the honour of putting this on your wall?'

Speechless with emotion, Midori peered at the drawing, tracing his gnarled finger over the charcoal lines. Reverently he laid it on the table with the other precious objects.

They went out to find the whole Boskie community waiting. Some of the children were crying as they stroked Mick. They'd made him a plaited nettle-string collar, decorated with primrose flowers.

Llinos stepped forward and taking the Delphins in her long arms and giving them a fierce hug, pressed two bulky leaf-wrapped packets of food into their hands. 'Sweet-berry leather and honeycomb,' was all she could mutter as tears streamed down her face.

Other Boskies crowded around; the females stroking their heads, and the males patting them on the back. By this time, Aspen, Ilex and Oak had appeared, once more wearing their leafy camouflage and ready to guide Fin and Lark on their way.

They headed south through the fields to the end of the valley. There, they climbed through woodland of hawthorn, birch, maple, juniper and elder, until they reached the dark fringes of Withered Wood.

Taking a last look back into the peaceful hidden valley, Fin and Lark saw smoke rising from a line of charcoal bread ovens. On the far hillside the stream sparkled in the sunrise as it tumbled down past the terraces.

Yet again, Lark felt he might have happily settled there, even learnt their language, but he knew he would soon miss a good roast, swamped in rich meaty gravy. Reluctantly he turned away and plunged after the others into the oppressive gloom of Withered Wood.

Aspen led them south-westwards, up steep hills and down into deep ravines. The carpet of pine needles muffled their footsteps, the branches of the closely packed trees cutting out most of the light. Dejected, the Boskies walked slowly enough for the Delphins to keep up.

As the day wore on, Fin and Lark noticed some of the trees looked sickly, the red-brown bark crumbling from their trunks, the topmost branches either drooping, or fallen to the ground, opening the canopy to give glimpses of a bruised-looking sky.

'I reckon we are in Withered Wood proper – like it is beyond the thorn break at home,' Lark muttered as he plodded behind Fin, Mick tucked in his jerkin.

Finally, Aspen stopped and turned to Fin and Lark. 'Contagion not far,' he murmured in halting Common Language, his expression full of dread. 'We go Shap View, have look-see down into that evil land!'

An hour later, at the top of a high cliff, before them lay a parched land of valleys and craggy mountains, cowering beneath a jaundiced sky. No living thing moved: no birds flew, no trees to be stirred by the sluggish wind. On the western horizon the long line of the Great Berg could be seen, its icy tops glistening in the outside world of sun and fresh air.

Lark gave a despairing groan: 'Fin, what's happened here? Where are all the trees? Where's the grass? Is there nowhere green?'

Fin's mind went back to Mossy telling him about the Land of Contagion.

'A thousand years ago, Contagion was full of life – blue lakes, green hills, wooded valleys – but humans built a factory there to extract radiation from uranium, to make electricity to run their machines. When the Great Human Dying came, there was no one left to guard the dangerous toxin, and the radiation leaked out into the air and onto the land, poisoning all living things around: animals, birds, trees, grasslands. The fells turned to arid rock, and the rivers and lakes to putrid, sickly slime—'

'Humans caused this,' he snarled, 'and I'm glad they all died!'

Lark's face contorted in horror: 'And this is where you and I have to go – to rescue Bird!'

Fin nodded dumbly.

They inched to the edge of the cliff and looked down. A worn track wound down through a cleft in the rocky face towards a lake. The lake's surface an oily black scum, was fed by sinister dark streams trickling down the rocky sides of the surrounding high hills.

Aspen pointed towards the southern horizon where bile-coloured clouds glowered above distant crags. 'Gressil home there!' he muttered.

Fin, picturing Bird's trembling soul caged inside a maw of yellow fangs, hissed: 'And that's where I must go!'

Just as he said this, from somewhere among the barren hills came a hideous shriek. 'What in Phul's name was that!' he gasped, leaping back, sending a shower of pebbles skittering down the cliffside.

'Sounded like someone learning to play the fiddle – badly,' Lark tittered apprehensively.

They turned to Aspen, who was struggling for the right words: 'Queen Mab's young ones!' he croaked, waving his arms about. Seeing their bewildered expression, he cried impatiently: 'Bombyx! Bombyx!'

Ilex and Oak tried to help by snapping their fingers like mouths, as if they were playing a weird game of charades.

Aspen's face crumpled in distress. 'Bombyx! Many – many! Don't go. Take you home, Brightdale, yes?'

Fin shook his head. 'We've no choice! It's where my friend is held captive.'

Completely dejected, his camouflage drooping, Aspen turned away.

Oak grabbed Lark's arm. By elaborate hand mime, he illustrated water, very hot, or perhaps poisonous. Lark nodded, half understanding. 'He's warning us there's some sort of liquid down there that we should be careful of.'

Fin racked his brains to remember what else Mossy had told him about Contagion. 'It could be lye – or did Mossy call it vitriol? Anyway, we'll have to be careful. I'm glad we filled our water bottles in the Boskies' stream – there'll be nothing drinkable from that lake.'

Now Ilex warned them of another danger, flapping his hands above his head, then flinging his arms wide.

'Black stuff from ground. Boom! Boom!' The Boskie held his nose as if he could smell something bad.

'I think he means Dark Fire, like you get in mines,' Lark said.

'Anyway, whatever the dangers, we can't dither here any longer,' Fin said, making his rucksack more comfortable on his shoulders. 'Give Mick a whistle, and we'll get going.'

Shaking each Boskie firmly by the hand, he picked his way, skidding and stumbling down the path in the cleft. Lark followed with Mick safely inside his jerkin. At the bottom they dusted themselves down and calling a last farewell up to the still watching Boskies, turned to face the black lake.

'Well this is it: we're in Contagion,' Lark muttered, releasing Mick from his jerkin.

'Yes, and we know which direction we have to go!' Fin said, indicating the sky glowering above the south-west fells. He winced as from far away there came another ear-piercing shriek.

Uneasily, Lark studied the track winding between boulders in the direction of the black lake. 'Looks well-trodden – must be used often – by creatures, or perhaps something on two legs. We'll have to keep a keen lookout.'

With one last longing look up to where the Boskies had been, they set off determinedly.

At the black lake side, Fin frowned up at steep fell on their left and the lake on the right, the way ahead half-hidden by the remains of landslides. 'I don't like being boxed in like this.'

'We'll just have to keep a careful listen-out – there's nooks and crannies where we can hide.'

Lark pointed to boulders and fallen rocks scattered along the side of the track. Clumps of viciously spiked thorn bushes grew among them, and he noticed several dried-up little bodies caught in the branches. He reckoned it was how the plants made their meagre living: sucking juices from any insects or small creature which had the misfortune to stray into Contagion. In one clump, he saw the desiccated body of a sparrow, still clothed in feathers.

He turned to the lake, and staring down into the dark liquid, grimaced. 'I don't reckon much to this stuff – what do 'yer think it is?'

The fumes coming off it made his throat sore.

Fin leaned down and tentatively touched the surface. 'It's got a greasy feel,' he said, rubbing the stuff between his fingertips. Sniffing it, he wrinkled his nose. 'Reminds me of something, but I can't think what.'

'To me it smells of Contagion.' Lark muttered. He whistled to Mick lingering behind. 'Get a move on lad, stick close!'

They set off again, ever ready to jump off the path and hide. Several times they came across pathetic piles of bones, which could have been sheep or goats.

After about half-an-hour, from behind them came the regular thump of heavy footfalls, accompanied by the hum of tinny voices. They'd only just ducked behind a boulder when two Frits riding ganglefowl, galloped by and disappeared into the distance.

'I thought the Frits only used the tunnel at Killhope to get to Gressil's place,' Fin whispered.

Lark shivered. 'Obviously not! Even more need to be careful.'

Listening hard, they crept out from their hiding place.

A while later a Scav came towards them. They thought at first it might be Crow and waited by the track. But when they saw he was feeling his way with a long stick, they realised the Scav was blind, his thin face filled with terror. Standing very still, they allowed him to shuffle past. After that, other frightened creatures appeared, stumbling and tripping. A little flock of bedraggled ducks and a badger with only three legs; they all had empty eye sockets.

When they were out of hearing, Lark said: 'Poor things – do you suppose they could have escaped from some horrid place where Gressil does his torturing?'

Fin said thoughtfully: 'Whatever place they've escaped from, it means there's a chance of us escaping too – after we've found Bird.'

Keeping up a steady pace, they had just started to relax when a tiger limped silently into view on soft pads. Diving into a narrow crevice between some rocks, they watched it stopping to sniff the air. As it gave a feeble growl, they saw the mangy animal had lost all its teeth.

'I know tigers are merciless killers,' Lark whispered, sliding his boning knife back in his belt, and breathing a sigh of relief as it limped on down the path, 'but I can't help feeling sorry for it – I hope it gets back safely into the real world!'

Shaken by the encounter, they waited awhile before plucking up courage to come out of their hiding place.

'I wonder if we could find another way,' Fin said peering uneasily up and down the track.

Lark studied the steep hillside again; covered in jagged rocks and loose scree, any attempt to climb it could bring down an avalanche, and the danger of a broken leg, or worse. 'Don't think we've much choice, for now. We'll have to keep going until this valley ends – just have to be on our guard.'

Picking up Mick by his Boskie-made nettle-string collar, and tucking him inside his jerkin, they tramped on.

They hadn't gone far when they came across a greyish, dried up insect's case lying in the middle of the track: it reminded them of a woodlouse, but this one was football sized and turned to powder when Lark kicked it.

'I wonder if it's a dead one of those things that make that foul noise,' Fin speculated as another nerve-scraping screech reverberated on the air, this time sounding much closer.

Lark shook his head. 'No, whatever's making that racket must be bigger!'

As they progressed, the ground between the track and the fellside started to change. Patches of marsh grass, crusted in green slime, were appearing, and more and more of the strange insect cases lay scattered about.

Hearing a faint sound of water ahead, hoping to fill their drinking bottles, they hurried forward to a small stream trickling from a crevice in the rocks. Struggling out of Lark's jerkin, Mick began lapping thirstily. He'd only taken two gulps, when he cringed back whining, frantically batting at his mouth with his front paws.

'Must be poisonous,' Lark groaned, dashing water from his water bottle over Mick's foaming mouth.

Bending close, Fin sniffed the trickle of water. 'Yuck, smells of rotten eggs – must be contaminated with sulphur.'

'What a twit yer are, Mick, making me waste my precious water on you!' Lark said, shaking his bottle. 'Half full – I'll have to be careful from now on.' Damping his handkerchief, he wet Mick's mouth with a little more water before tucking him away again. 'Poor lad, I reckon he must be really thirsty to have done such a desperate thing.'

Fin sighed. 'I hope we find some drinkable water soon. Surely it rains sometimes in this loathsome place!'

They trudged on for another hour, coming across ever more dried insect cases. As the light faded, to their surprise they saw the green slime on the patches of the tough marsh grass had started to give off a soft blue-green light.

'Weird – I hope that stuff's not dangerous,' Fin said, looking thoughtful, 'I remember Mossy saying something about a glowing radiation that makes people very sick.'

'What are those!' Lark exclaimed. 'Could they be the creatures that leave those dry cases we've been seeing?'

With a soft rustling sound, hundreds of giant woodlouse-like creatures began appearing from cracks in the rocks and boulders. Scuttling over Fin and Lark's boots, they began grazing the slime covering the marsh grass as if they were rabbits in a meadow. As they grazed, their shells pulsed a soft green light. Crouching for a closer look, Fin recalled a picture he'd seen in one of Mossy's books, of a creature which, if he remembered right, was called an armadillo.

'Eating that stuff doesn't seem to make them sick, so I expect its O.K.' Lark remarked.

Fin grinned. 'Perhaps I should try some – my Rom skin might turn more Delphin green.'

Lark chuckled. 'I wouldn't chance it. Anyway, your tanned skin is much admired by the Brightdale lasses.' His face puckered. 'By Phul, I wish we were back there!'

Fin took his arm. 'Come on, the sooner we find Bird and rescue her, the sooner we'll get home.'

Night came, a dark shadow spilling down the fellsides and across the black lake. What they had both been secretly dreading was upon them: they would have to spend the night in this forsaken place. They looked to their left, where the clefts and crannies in the rocks and boulders had filled with deep shadows and wondered if they dare crawl inside one.

Fin plucked up the courage and stuck his head into one of the larger openings. 'This one seems to be unoccupied,' he called in a low voice to Lark waiting on the track with Mick.

Easing off their rucksacks, they crawled in through the narrow gap, finding the space deeper, wider and drier than they'd expected. First taking out their blankets and bags of food, they stuffed the rucksacks into the entrance to block it against unwanted visitors. Then spreading their blankets on the sandy floor, they took stock of their dwindling food supplies: two small half-full sacks of sunflower seeds and dried berries, two chunks of Miryam's barley bread, turned bone hard, two pieces of soft sticky honeycomb and a couple of strips of fruit leather that old Llinos had given them. To ease their thirst, and to save their precious water, they sucked on bits of the fruit leather before eating a handful each of the seeds and berries. Lark smeared some honeycomb around Mick's sore mouth to soothe it.

As they ate, they listened apprehensively for any sound that might spell new danger.

'I wonder how long it will take to get there,' Lark said looking out at the gap above their rucksacks.

The night sky had taken on a bilious hue, making him wonder if it was the light from Gressil's Compound. 'Have you any thoughts as to how we're going to find Bird?'

Fin frowned, trying to recall what else Mossy had told him about the Land of Contagion: it hadn't been much. He'd got the impression that Mossy didn't like talking about Contagion; he'd spoken of Gressil's stone fortress, looming over what he called 'the Compound', where Maabella lay on her Nest. He vividly remembered Mossy calling her Nest 'a pit of ordure'.

He'd learnt more when Mossy was out: he sneaked the key to a locked cupboard and looked in a book Mossy kept hidden there. Tattered and stained, the book was written by many hands, most of it in a foreign language. On the last page, he'd found a short description of Gressil's Compound written in the Common Language. He recalled vividly the description of a place called the Treatment Shed, where they made the stolen souls ready to be 'fed' to Maabella. There was something about the souls being sucked from their bodies, into pods and stored on racks. He wondered if Bird's soul could be inside one of those.

Ashamed that he'd sneaked a look at the book without Mossy knowing, he didn't want to speak about what he knew. Instead he answered Lark's question with another question. 'Do you recall the story Sandy told in the Chapter House at Durholm, how Prince Cadeyrn went into Contagion?'

He made out Lark nodding in the murky yellow light.

'I remember him telling us about the Bug Queen lying on her nest, laying Slugbuggers,' Lark said. He suddenly slapped his forehead. 'Of course! He called them bombyx or something – that's what Aspen and his chums were warning us about. We should have remembered!'

'Yes, I'd forgotten too. I saw a picture of a Bombyx in a book called Exotic Evils on one of Mossy's shelves. It had a big fat slug's body with a pair of eyes on stalks, and a bunch of wavy arms growing out of its back with jaws on their ends instead of hands, filled with pointy teeth.'

Lark thought for a moment. 'I reckon that's what Ilex and Oak were trying to tell us with their hands.'

They sat in speculative silence, both hoping such creatures were just the stuff of an artist's wild imaginings.

After a while, peering at Fin's dark outline, Lark summoned up the courage to ask him something that had been troubling him throughout this journey into Contagion. 'Fin, what do you reckon Bird will look like? Will she be kind of faded and misty? I've never seen someone with only a soul for a body, so to speak.'

To his dismay, Fin burst into tears. Reaching for Fin's hand in the dark, he held it tight without speaking. Gradually, the storm of grief passed.

Wiping his sleeve across his eyes, Fin gave a quivering sigh. 'I don't know what a stolen soul looks like, Lark. All I know is that Bird is there, in Gressil's Compound, and we'll know when we see her.'

A blood chilling screech brought them to their feet in terror. 'I reckon that was one of those Bombyx sluggers,' Lark hissed through chattering teeth. 'They seem very close – can they move fast do you think?'

'With their legless slug bodies, I don't reckon so,' Fin said.

Lark was doubtful. 'I think we should take turns sleeping – you first. Come on, wrap yourself up in your blanket.'

Too miserable to argue, Fin lay down and Lark tenderly tucked his blanket round him.

Sinking into exhausted sleep, a dream came to Fin, so poignant that it hurt: he was dancing with Bird. He wasn't sure where, and the music wasn't pipe, fiddle, and drum, but singing voices, so beautiful it caught his breath. Holding Bird softly against his chest, he pressed his face into her honey-scented silky hair. 'I love you Bird, so much,' he whispered.

She turned up her face to him, her green eyes sparkling with tears. ''course you do, my knight in shining armour! Just get a move on and rescue me from the ogre!'

Bending to kiss Bird's mouth, he drew back in revulsion: in her place, he held in his arms a voluptuously beautiful woman, with liquid brown eyes and thick scarlet lips. Fluttering her long black lashes, she leered at him invitingly. Pressing herself against him, something sharp jabbed into his chest. Looking down, he saw she wore the Chi Rho against her breast. Enraged, he snatched at the chain. The woman's scarlet lips parted to let out a scream so piercing he felt he was being cut in two.

He woke to another of the sickening screeches that had plagued them since they entered the Land of Contagion, and the pale light of dawn. Sitting up, he found Lark watching him worriedly.

'Lark, you're worse than old Nutmeg,' he snapped, 'have you had any sleep? The bags under your eyes are so huge, you could keep all your spare socks in them!'

'I was asleep, but you were yelling such a racket you could've woken all the Bombies in Contagion! Anyway, no more argumentals, we need breakfast before we start again.'

Breakfast was a mouthful of dried berries, washed down with a few sips from their water bottles. Mick ignored the offered seeds, but sat dejectedly in a corner, his head drooping. He thirstily lapped a little water from Lark's cupped hand.

Blankets packed, they returned to the path.

An hour later, the lake petered out into a sump of oily black sludge. Ahead the track became steep steps cut in the fellside rock before disappearing over a high ridge. On the south west the skyline the glow from Contagion looked closer.

Halfway up they stopped to rest, sitting on the steps looking back over the black lake. They could just make out in the far distance the misty outline of Shap View.

Lark spat out the mouthful of sunflower seeds he was chewing. Twisting around and looking to the ridge, he sniffed.

'Can you smell it, too?' Fin asked.

Lark nodded. 'Yep, like rotting meat. I've a feeling it's coming from the other side of that ridge.'

Gazing up anxiously, they became aware of an ominous slurping sound.

'I wonder what that is,' Fin muttered.

Lark leered. 'Sounds as if something huge is letting off wind as it wallows in its bath.'

A series of teeth-jarring screeches, followed by a terrified scream of pain, made him jump to his feet. 'I'm for going back!' he gasped, snatching at Mick, already on his way down, tail between his legs.

A moment later, a small flock of goats appeared at the top of the ridge. Panicked at the sight of Fin and Lark they took to the fellside, leaping down the scree, sending stones and boulders crashing onto the steps below: their way back was blocked. They had no choice but to continue towards the stench and the noise.

Summoning their courage, they climbed to the crest of the ridge, and cautiously looked over: below them lay a deep ravine, its jagged sides dropping fifty feet or so. At the bottom, squashed together on the muddy floor, was a heaving squirming mass of what looked like giant slugs. The screeching, and the stink of rotting flesh, sent their senses reeling.

'Are those bugslugs?' Lark gasped, staring in wide eyed horror. 'I can't believe nature had anything to do with these sluggers.'

'These are the Bombyx – older bugslugs.' Fin mumbled, covering his mouth with his sleeve, trying not to vomit. 'No, they certainly aren't natural: they are born of Maabella, who is a Demon. These are not the same as those that attacked Durholm. These are the grown-up version.'

He tried to take in the hideous bodies: pairs of bloodshot eyes on the ends of fleshy stalks, popping in and out like snail's eyes, bunches of sinuous tendrils growing up from their fat slimy backs, waving about like long fingers, each ending in a jaw fringed with needle-sharp teeth. Some of the waving tendrils stood tall and stiff, others intertwined with each other, seeming to caress themselves. From a dark tunnel, yet more were lumbering out, their rumbling farting filling the air with a putrid stink, the disgusting sound echoing off the ravine walls. Fighting for space, the monsters had nowhere to go but crawl over others, the only exit being blocked by a massive fall of rock. Some of the slugs, squashed by their fellows, lay inert on the muddy floor.

The steps, cut into the side of the ravine, continued down towards the heaving mass, almost to within reach of the snapping jaws, before climbing again to another ridge on the far side. Fin and Lark looked about, desperately hoping for another way. On one side, a steep, shale-covered slope fell several hundred feet towards another huge black lake. On the other side, beneath the narrow ridge, the cliff dropped sheer into the ravine: they must follow the steps.

'Well, this is it, we have to go down!' Fin said. Scrambling to his feet, he brought out Sandy's small sword from his rucksack. Tucking it into his belt, he turned to Lark. 'Are you up for it? I'd understand if you want to try and find a way back.'

Lark glared indignantly. 'What yer on about Fin! I'm in this to the end, whatever that'll be!' He noticed Fin's different coloured eyes, one brown and one green, had both turned muddy grey. Hitching his rucksack higher on his shoulders, Mick inside his jerkin, he started down the steps. Fin followed.

Finding what hand holds they could in the rock face, now and then they had to stop and spit to get rid of the sickly stench clinging to their tongues. About halfway down, they paused to rest. Looking over the edge to check their progress, a sea of snapping teeth and bulbous eyes stretched up to meet them.

Pressing back against the cliff, Lark felt wet running down his neck. Twisting round, he found a small stream trickling out of a ragged clump of ferns into a puddle at his feet. 'Well, I'll be!' he gasped. 'Who would've thought it: real water! Blessed Phul be praised!'

Mick's twitching black nose poked out of his jerkin. Struggling free, he jumped down and started frantically lapping.

'Any hope of topping up our drinking flasks?' Fin asked.

First allowing Mick to quench his thirst, Lark peered into the crack in the rock. 'It's only a trickle, but I reckon we can.'

Filling their flasks, they reluctantly continued their descent. The narrow steps, caked in slime, had become so slippery that, terrified of falling, they bumped down on their backsides. Soon they were so close to the monsters, they felt their rancid breath on their faces.

Refreshed by his drink and still wearing his nettle collar, the flowers all gone, Mick hopped jauntily down ahead of them. Overconfident, he nearly met his end. Straying too near the edge, snapping jaws reared up at him. Leaping back with a terrified yelp, Lark came to his rescue. Whipping out his boning knife, and leaning over the edge, he slashed at a gaping jaw, the shrieking creature spitting out several sharp fangs – doing, what he thought he would tell Tissy later, a nifty bit of dentistry.

Reaching the lowest step before they climbed again, they found it covered in blood. Close to the step a carcass of a goat was being torn to shreds by a couple of the Bombyx, and they realised the scream they'd heard earlier must have been from the poor creature.

The monsters distracted by their feeding frenzy, they slithered through the blood slick, and scrambled upwards. A dozen steps later, they were out of danger. Fin now made a mistake: he decided he ought to memorise a Bombyx for a later sketch. Peering gingerly over the edge, snapping jaws rose to meet him, one so close he felt spit on his face. Whipping Sandy's sword from his belt, he stabbed deep into the bulging tongue. Rearing back, the tendril crashed down into the writhing mass below.

That's a blow from the Prince of Brightdale, yer sluggers!' Lark yelled. Full of fire, swinging dangerously out, he sliced off a whole jaw with his boning knife.

Chaos broke out, the screeching increased to a crescendo; they knew now how the Bombyx produced their ear-splitting noise: by scraping their needle-like teeth up and down their tendrils, as if they were playing a violin. More and more Bombyx started scraping, sometimes emitting high pitched shrieks, sometimes low throbbing vibrations, the mass of tendrils swaying so violently, it looked as if a hurricane had hit the ravine, the wall of noise so powerful, Fin and Lark felt they were being battered against the cliff. Heads spinning, they crawled the last few steps to the top.

Staggering to their feet, they surveyed their surroundings. The track continued south-westwards across a dry boulder-strewn plateau towards the foothills of a mountain range. Beyond, the white bulk of the Great Berg could be seen, closer now, gleaming on the skyline of grey clouds. The noise from the Bombyx ravine behind, slightly muffled, they were able to hear a distant low groaning as the ice shifted on its bed. Their thoughts went back to when they were mending Skyhook's canvas, recalling what Wings had told them about the Berg:

'Some say it's a wall of ice, keeping Gressil's evil in and good folk out, and that the Gaiakins put it there, but I have my doubts. It has more to do with the melting of the north pole, and drifting icebergs. The Irish Sea lies beyond, and that's where my home is, on the Island of Mann – when this jaunt's over I'll take you there.'

Wings wouldn't be taking them to his home now.

They forced their tired legs to march on, the screeching from the Bombyx valley growing ever fainter.

Two hours later they reached the foothills of the mountains. The path climbed once more, taking a winding route between two cliffs. Too tired to go on, dumping their rucksacks, they slumped against a cliff face and closed their eyes.

A little while later Fin was startled out of an exhausted stupor by Lark's voice. He was standing a little way away, studying a dark patch on the ground.

'There's a pond here!' Lark called, kneeling to sniff. 'Yuk, tar – not something we can drink.'

Wandering disconsolately back and collapsing next to Fin, he took a sip from his flask. Mick instantly sat in front of him, pleadingly. 'O.K. lad, open yer mouth.' He let a few drops fall on Mick's tongue, then shaking his flask, sighed. 'If we want to conserve our water, we'd better make do with the berry leather.'

Fin nodded. He took a sip from his own flask, and firmly replaced the stopper.

Raiding their food bags, they bit off pieces of fruit leather and chewed gloomily, their dry throats making it hard to swallow. Gazing miserably across the arid plateau, they could see no green anywhere, not even the green slime they'd encountered by the long black lake.

Nothing stirred. Lark picked up a small pebble, and taking aim, threw it into the middle of the tar pool. Landing with a plop, he threw another, and then gasped.

'Did you see that – a flame!'

Fin raised his weary head and watched as Lark threw a third pebble. As it hit the surface, a small blue flame flickered and died.

'Better not do that, Lark. We don't know what that stuff is – it might give off poisonous gas, or even explode.'

Suddenly Mick sat up, ears pricked, staring towards the mountains beyond the foothills.

Slowly, from over a ridge flew three of Gressil's Snoopers.

Terrified, they pressed themselves against the cliff, and watched as the great insects headed in the direction of the Bombyx ravine: they didn't appear to have spied the small cowering figures.

Halfway across, the insects hesitated, and hovering a moment, tasted the air with their curled spring-like tongues. Paddling their dangling legs, they swung around to face Fin and Lark. Speeding across the plateau, seconds later they were upon them, papery wings whirring, their cruel armoured faces so close Fin and Lark could see themselves mirrored in every lens of their multi-faceted eyes. Baring their fangs, the insects dived, just stopping short of smashing their brittle bodies against the cliff. Buzzing angrily, they rose again and wiggling their fat yellow and black backsides, ping, ping, ping, a volley of long needle stings, each tip glittering with a globule of venom, rained down, hitting the ground all around Fin and Lark. Pressing themselves against the cliff, half blinded by the poison spray, they desperately searched behind for somewhere to hide.

Hearing muffled barking coming from somewhere above, Lark looked up and saw Mick peering out from a ledge. Wondering how he'd got up there, he spotted a narrow crevice.

'Mick's found an escape!' he yelled, grabbing Fin by the arm and shoving him into the crevice. Stings hitting the ground all around him, he scrambled after, but his rucksack snagged on a jagged rock. Frenziedly working it free, he felt a fiery stab in his foot. Looking down, he saw blood oozing from where a sting stuck out of his boot. Sobbing with pain, he was hauled to safety by Fin.

They found themselves in a narrow tunnel. From outside came an ominous thud, thud, as two Snoopers landed. A face full of fangs filled the gap in the crevice, luckily too narrow for the rest of the insect's body. Crawling deeper inside, a patch of grey light appeared ahead: they realised the tunnel climbed upwards. From above came Mick's shrill barking. Squeezing through the narrow gully, hindered by the bulk of their rucksacks, a few lung-bursting moments later they climbed out into a small cave. Barking hysterically, Mick licked their faces.

'Alright, alright, lad, don't let 'em know where we are!' Lark groaned through gritted teeth, pushing Mick away. He looked in disgust at his blood-stained boot with the sting, the length of one of Grammer Nutmeg's knitting needles, sticking out from the toe. 'There's no choice, you'll have to pull it out,' he said, giving Fin a weak grin.

Firmly grasping the sting, Fin pulled hard and Lark gave a moan as with a sickening squeak of wet leather, it slid out. Throwing the sting aside, Fin loosened the bootlace and gently eased off the boot. 'Now your sock,' he muttered, slipping it off and examining the foot. He whistled in relief. 'It didn't go deep – just made a hole in the side of your big toe.'

'I'll get that buzzer wasp!' Lark growled, grabbing his rucksack, and hunting for his marigold ointment.

Leaving Lark to anoint his sore toe, Fin searched the cave, which was more of a hollow gouged out in the cliff. It wasn't possible to stand up, and the only way out was either back down from where they'd come, or through a low opening onto a narrow ledge; thankfully too small for the huge insects to squeeze in.

Crawling out on to the ledge and sticking his head out as far as he dared, he saw twenty feet or so below, the Snoopers buzzing angrily around the crack leading to the tunnel. He knew it wouldn't take them long to discover the cave above. Having seen their shooting skills, he knew they could easily fire a few stings inside. Not far off, gleaming darkly, lay the black pool where Lark had thrown the stones. Turning on his back and stretching his neck, he looked up, hoping for some way of climbing upwards: the cliff wall rose sheer above him. He crept back inside.

'Lark, can you crawl? We'd better get as far back in the cave as we can.'

''course I can crawl – my toe just feels stingy from the poison.'

Gritting his teeth, Lark carefully put his sock and boot back on, and holding his sore foot in the air, wriggled on his bottom to join Fin and Mick where they'd taken shelter behind a few small boulders. As he went, he noticed stones littering the cave floor. Picking one up, with the vague idea of using it as some sort of weapon, an idea dawned on him. 'Fin, the black tar pool! Could we throw some of these stones into it, and create a diversion?'

Fin grinned. 'Brilliant! Come on!' Grabbing a couple of the larger, flintier stones, Fin crawled once more onto the ledge.

Shoving Mick to the very back of the cave and telling him to stay, Lark gathered two more stones and shuffled to join Fin.

'We'll chuck together,' Fin said. 'One, two three…' They threw, watching the stones arc into the air, only to land with heavy thuds a few paces short of the pool: the sound alerted the Snoopers, who sped over to investigate.

'I'll chuck another,' Lark muttered excitedly, carefully choosing a smaller lighter stone. Going out on the ledge and wobbling on his uninjured foot, he weighed it in his hand. Narrowing his eyes, he threw, spinning it as if he were playing ducks and drakes on a pond. As it left his hand, one of the Snoopers spotted him. Buzzing furiously, it shot towards him. He didn't have a chance to see where the stone landed. Diving back inside, he fell heavily on his face, crying out as a sharp pain shot up his leg. The cave was plunged into darkness as the insect's body filled the entrance. Realising it couldn't get in, the Snooper hovered just outside, making ready to shoot its sting. As it aimed, there came from behind it a strange gurgling sound, then a throaty roar, followed by a huge rumbling burp. The giant insect wobbled, then fell away, its sting tinkling harmlessly on the rocks below.

Scrambling to the entrance and cowering low, Fin and Lark looked out. They gasped: a black column of molten matter had risen from the pool. For a moment, a white-hot flame flickered up and down it. Then, with a loud boom, it exploded into an enormous fire ball. There was nothing left of the pool but a deep black crater.

Spitting out oily dust, wiping soot from their faces, Fin and Lark gaped as bits of Snooper carapace and tattered wings fluttered past them to the ground, already littered with broken insect bodies. Only one Snooper remained intact, twitching in its death throes before becoming still. A hush descended, even the distant screeching from the Bombyx valley stopped.

Horror-struck, Lark groaned. 'That's torn it, I might as well have banged on Gressil's front door!' He turned and saw Fin grinning stupidly.

'Wings would've have loved that,' he choked, his voice on the edge of hysteria. The terror had all got too much, and to their shame, they both burst into tears.

'Dat good job!' croaked a voice from above. Hiccupping into startled silence, Fin and Lark peered up. Crow's soot-blackened face leered at them. With a thump and a squeak, the bible bag landed beside them. Swinging nimbly down, Crow followed it.

# 21
# GRESSIL'S BACK YARD

'So, yer stinky wemmer – decided to join us, have you?' Lark's voice was still shaky as he pulled Mick back from nosing the bible bag.

'Me good lad!' Crow whined indignantly. 'I's promised Aunty Krite me take daft Delphs Gressil place!'

Spotting Crow's sly glance at the Fin's jerkin, where the Chi Rho lay hidden in his purse, Lark's fingers itched to take the Scav by the throat and strangle him.

Crow pointed his claw-like finger scornfully at the track below, winding towards the mountains. 'What yer doing, going dat path? I take Delphs secrit way. Come!' Giving Mick's snout a sneaky kick, he grabbed the bible bag. Dropping out of sight below the ledge, his face reappeared. 'Get move on!' he croaked impatiently before disappearing again.

Looking over the ledge, Fin called down. 'Crow, wait for us by the crevice – we're coming down by the tunnel!'

As he left the cave, Lark snatched up the Snooper's sting Fin had pulled from his boot and tucked it into his rucksack. 'A trophy to show Tissy,' he muttered to himself as he squeezed into the tunnel after Fin and Mick.

Crow was waiting for them amongst the scattered remains of Snoopers. 'Get move on Delphs!' he croaked, sniffing the air, and glancing fearfully towards the mountains. 'I smell more Gresslie's flighters, quick, quick, fast come our way!' Bible bag bouncing on his back, nose pecking the ground, he hopped away from the main track, towards the cliff faces of the foothills.

Limping past the deep crater that had been the dark pool, Lark looked down in awe, amazed how much force there must have been, and that he'd caused it.

They'd just reached the first rock outcrop when they heard the dreaded buzzing and smelt the vinegary stink. Cowering beneath an overhang, they couldn't see the insects, but they knew they were hovering over the scene of their companions' death. After what seemed an age, the buzz took on a higher note and gradually faded away in the direction of the Bombyx ravine.

Crow scrambled out. 'Hurry, hurry, Delphs, they be back soon, for sure!'

Keeping well out of sight of danger from the air, he took them through the narrow gully of a dried-up stream running between the high cliffs. Tired and thirsty, Fin and Lark found it hard to keep up, sometimes almost losing sight of him. Mick ignored the bible bag from where there came an occasional squeak, but trotted, head down, close on Lark's heels.

They kept up Crow's pace for half an hour but, Lark dragging his injured foot, began to lag. Finally, he gave up and collapsed heavily on a low rock to take a sip from his water flask. Tongue hanging out, Mick looked up at him pleadingly; shaking his flask, Lark found it was empty.

'Hey Crow, wait for us!' Fin called, helping Lark to his feet.

Crow came hopping back. 'No stop now Delphs! Soon, nice place I knows. Lots of wet for thirsty ones, and cosy nest to sleep safe! Come on, don't want be here long – tiggers!'

He glanced nervously to the top of the cliffs, before setting off once more along the winding gully. With Lark leaning on Fin's shoulder, they stumbled on.

Just as they thought they could struggle no further, from ahead came the wonderful sound of running water. Crow gesticulated excitedly. 'We come place – lots wet!'

Eagerly they limped after him. The gulley opened into a wide ravine where they stood in wonder. From every nook and cranny in the rock, ferns grew, green fronds tumbling to a floor covered in mosses and wild herbs. At the far end, a spring trickled out through the fern curtain, splashing into a shallow pool scooped out of the rocky floor and overflowing onto the mossy ground. They felt as if they had arrived in another world, a place where the poisons of Contagion had passed over.

'Well I'll be—' Lark gasped, his sore eyes drinking in the scene.

Swinging his bible bag off his back, Crow undid the straps and Sparkie's twitching nose appeared. With a leap and a bound, the rat darted to the pool. Mick followed close on his tail. Enmity temporarily put aside, rat and dog crouched together at the pool's edge, quenching their desperate thirst. Crow, Fin and Lark quickly joined them, falling on their knees, and scooping up the cool clear water with their hands. They made an odd scene: a rat, a dog, a Scav and two Delphins around a drinking hole – as if in some long-lost Arcadia.

When they'd drunk their fill, and refilled their flasks, they sat for a while on the cool moss, soaking in the blessed greenness of their surroundings.

'Do you reckon this place got forgotten by Gressil?' Lark speculated.

Crow sniggered. 'Delph talking daft!'

Fin considered for a moment. 'No, nothing to do with Gressil – he came to Contagion when the damage had already been done by the humans. This ravine is probably a last vestige of how it was before the contamination: a small toe-hold of nature, clinging on and sheltered somehow from the radiating poisons.'

Lark rummaged in his rucksack. 'I don't know about you, but I'm hungry.'

He took out a bag of dried berries and one of Llinos' leaf packets. Had it only been this morning when they'd had their breakfast in that cave by the long black lake, he wondered? It seemed years ago.

Fin brought out another leaf packet and the bag of sunflower seeds. Crow watched them enviously as they laid out the food – he had no food in his small pack.

'Right, we'll divide all the food into three lots,' Fin said, noticing Crow's hungry look, 'each person responsible for their own store – we don't know when we'll find more food.'

Lark grinned at Crow. 'You've been in these parts before, can you recommend a café or pub?'

Crow glowered at him. 'Grass-top talk daft again. No Rosie's round here, only deaded rotting ganglefowls to eat!'

The food shared out, they munched hungrily: a disreputable-looking trio, filthy faced, their clothes stained and torn. As he ate, Lark sneaked a look at Crow feeding Sparkie some sunflower seeds. Both Scav and rat looked haggard, and he guessed they couldn't have had an easy time lately.

As the light faded, they found an area of dry grass, safely hidden from the ravine entrance. Wrapping his blanket around him, Fin fell into an exhausted sleep. Crow fussed over Sparkie for a while, persuading him to get back in the bible bag. Then wrapping himself in the bit of sack that was his blanket, he curled up and he too was instantly asleep.

Lark bathed his injured toe in spring water where it flowed out on to the ground, taking care not to dirty the pool. Sitting on his blanket next to Mick, he examined his injury as he massaged his toe with marigold ointment; in the poor light, he couldn't see if it were healing. He hoped it was. Limping worried him: he needed to be fit if he were to help Fin, now they were getting nearer to the action that would decide their fate.

Looking up at the night sky, he noticed that the familiar sullen glow to the south appeared stronger and he reckoned they couldn't have many more miles to go. Sniffing the air, he picked up a faint chilly saltiness. Hearing a distant rumbling, he wondered if it was the Great Berg stirring on the seabed.

Next day, Fin woke with a start, a dream still fresh. He'd dreamt of Bird again. She was trapped inside a transparent bubble, pushing at the flexible sides, calling to him pitifully.

He saw the others were already up and about. Lark was washing his foot. Mick was searching for fleas in his nether regions. Nearby, Crow was carefully packing away his food, whilst Sparkie groomed his rope-like tail.

'Woken at last!' Crow croaked sarcastically.

Fin grunted and stuffed his blanket inside his rucksack. 'I'll eat as we walk,' he muttered, taking out a piece of fruit leather. He called to Lark. 'Hurry up Lark, let's get this over with!'

Back in the gully, Crow stopped every so often to search the cliff face. After a couple of miles, he halted at a cleft in the rock, and chirruped in satisfaction. Slipping in through the narrow gap, he called: 'This it! We climb now.'

Squeezing in, Fin and Lark found themselves in a deep gorge, with just a crack of grey sky showing above their heads. A tar-like substance covered the ground, recalling the black pool Lark had blown up.

'Wherever have you brought us, Crow?' Fin asked in disgust. 'I hope this isn't a trap you've set for us!'

'No, stupid Delph,' Crow squeaked indignantly. 'Look, steps!' He pointed to where a rusty-looking ladder climbed the rock face.

'Isn't there an easier way?' Lark grumbled, wincing as he stamped his injured foot to test it.

'No other way – unless you want Gressil sees you!' They saw in Crow's eye a glint of mischief. His bible bag slung over his back, he hopped across the oily floor and monkeyed up the ladder and disappeared over the top.

Spotting Fin eyeing his injured foot, Lark cursed inwardly. 'I'll go next,' he said firmly, determined to avoid any suggestion he should go home. 'Come Mick, inside my jerkin.'

Boots sticking in the tar, they lurched to the ladder. Giving it a vigorous shake, Lark found it wasn't as rickety as it looked. Testing the first rung, he started to climb, heaving his way up painfully, Mick peering down out of his jerkin. Eventually, with much grunting, he reached the top. 'Your turn, Fin!' he called. 'The view's amazing: you can see the Great Berg clearly!'

Fin climbed quickly and in moments scrambled off the last rung to join him.

They were on top of a high cliff looking over desolate marshland spreading westwards ten miles or so. To the south lay yet another black lake. In the distance, the bulk of the Great Berg cut off any sight of the sea. Above its jagged icy peaks, the passing ghost of the sun rode high and golden in the outside world.

'Is that Gressil's fortress?' Fin pointed to a dark mass outlined against the Berg's icy grey face.

Crow shuddered. 'Yep, I know secrit way there – alonga Gressil's sewage drain, stinky but safe!' He shot them a leering smirk.

Lark swiped him across the top of his head. 'You'd better not try any sneaky trick, young Crow,' he growled.

'No tricks, no tricks,' Crow squeaked. 'It safe way. Bin there afore, have I, when I finds my jool!'

'Well, be warned, yer little bum boil, I'll tell on you to your Aunty Krite if you get up to anything devious.'

Giving Lark a poisonous scowl, Crow dropped over the cliff edge, and slithered down the scree covered slope.

'If getting into Gressil's Fortress means going through the sewers, then that's what we'll do,' Fin muttered as he and Lark followed.

Crow leading the way along the bank of a sluggish river winding through the marshy sedge, by late morning, they were over half-way between the cliff and the Berg. The growling and groaning was much louder now, sounding as if the ice mountain was having an argument with itself. Finding a reasonably dry tussock of the spiky grass, they settled down to eat.

'Time to put mutt away!' Crow suddenly exclaimed, pointing to where Mick was nosing around a patch of smooth flat sand. 'That sucky sand. Bad news for mutts and peoples!'

Giving a sharp whistle, Lark patted his chest. 'Mick – jerkin!'

Mick safely stowed away, Crow opened his bible bag and his rat jumped out. 'Sparkie lead way now, nose good for sniffing out sucky sand!' He lovingly stroked his pet between its pink ears as it eyed Lark's jerkin. Twitching its whiskers, the rat tested the air and picking up the stink drifting across the marsh, hopped off purposefully from tussock to tussock.

They kept in single file, careful to keep to the rat's path as it scampered around the patches of sand. The ground became more and more waterlogged, and soon turned to a quagmire of salty mud, making it hard to lift their feet.

Squelching and slipping, Lark's injured toe began to throb badly; he dreaded the wound had opened, but he daren't stop to take his boot off to look in case Fin made a fuss – even now Fin could decide that he should go home: Brightdale wasn't all that far beyond the high hills to the south east.

Finally coming within the shadow of the looming Berg, they stared up in awe at the glistening wall of dirty grey ice, the smell of decay so pungent they could taste it. From beyond the ice mass came the faint cries of sea birds, filling them with a longing to be there. To the south, they saw the ominous bulk of Gressil's fortress, closer and clearer now, its outer wall caught in the Berg's icy grip. Its inner wall bounded by the black lake.

Shadowy things were entombed behind the clouded, sweating ice surface: rocks, boulders, the remains of trees – trunks, branches, roots, even a small stand of pines. Creatures of all kinds were trapped there too: a huge whale, an octopus, small and large birds, some with their wings spread as if in flight, rats, dogs, sheep, even a whole horse, lying on its back, its legs frozen in a prance. There were also pieces of metal and machinery. A silvery tube-like object with round windows running the length of its sleek body, reminded Fin and Lark vaguely of Skyhook, but much bigger. Marbling the glassy ice, twisting, and turning through and around the debris, was a network of what looked like black veins. The ones at the surface were dripping out a steady stream of black oily liquid. From the smell, they realised it was the same flammable stuff as in the black pool Lark had blown up.

Crow led them to a low brick wall running between the edge of the marsh and the base of the Berg. Standing on the top and looking down, the river of sewage oozing below them seemed almost alive. From the wall of the Berg on the other side came a constant drip, dripping of melting ice, and they noticed some debris had started to emerge, as if it were trying to escape. Suddenly, in a whoosh of meltwater, the remains of a large fish tumbled out and splashed down into the filth of the sewer: Fin recognized a basking shark, its gaping mouth packed with dirty ice.

Crow pointed to a large opening in the base of the ice wall from where there came an occasional belching rumble. 'That called Sewer Sump – where poo goes out to sea.' He eyed Fin's front. 'We go alonga sewer now, eh? Or perhaps go home? Keep jool safe from Gressil?'

Clutching the front of his jerkin, Fin shook his head. 'No, we go alonga sewer!'

Glowering resentfully, Crow whistled shrilly to his rat, grubbing about in the marsh nearby.

'Doan want my Sparkie getting dirtied by stinking filthies!' he muttered, tucking the rat back in the bible bag.

Mumbling curses about thieving gangle-leg Delphs, he set off sullenly along the top of the wall toward the dark bulk of the Fortress. The brick surface made the going easier than the muddy marsh, and they made good progress. Above the Fortress the bilious clouds loomed ever closer as twilight closed around them, and a chilly vapour creeping off the marsh, swirled wispy tendrils about their ankles. Flickering pin pricks of light began to appear, flashing bright then dimming. Every now and then a little glowing face would pop up out of the shadowy grass by the brick wall, to quickly disappear again.

Far away across the marsh, a sudden bright flash caught Fin's eye. Stopping, and scanning where the marsh met the black lake, he spotted two points of golden light bobbing and dipping in and out of tall reeds. Suddenly they disappeared. He stood staring hard, and when they didn't reappear, wondered if his eyes were playing tricks. Looking around for the others, he saw they had stopped a little way ahead. In the dim light, he made out Crow's agitated outline: he'd dumped his bible bag and was gesticulating down into the dark sewer. Lark and Mick stood watching him.

'What's up, Crow?' Fin asked, catching up. Crow pointed an accusing finger at him. 'Some place here, long ago, I find jool you stole from me.'

Crow's hate-filled face made Fin feel sick. He staggered as a fiery pain shot through his chest.

Lark turned on Crow. 'You're a lying bum boil,' he spat, 'it's about time you got it into yer thick head that the jool wasn't yours in the first place!'

Scowling, Crow aimed a gob of spit at Lark's boot, before grabbing the bible bag and setting off once more along the wall.

Moments later, stopping again, he stared fearfully out into the marsh. 'Ghostie lives there – last time I come, it skin touched me! Could be wanting to get me proper this time!' They made out a line of white stones, standing tall and straight, rising out of the marsh like grinning teeth.

From a little farther along they heard Mick give a sharp bark: he was peering down into the sewer, his tail wagging excitedly. They saw he'd found a short flight of steps cut into the side of the brickwork. It led down to a narrow ledge running just above the flow of sewage.

'Dat good! Dog find place!' squeaked Crow as he hurried down the steps. 'Quick, quick, Delphs – down we go. We keep hidden now – Gresslie's folks mustn't see us!'

About to follow, Fin and Lark hesitated as a familiar sound of honking came drifting across the black lake. In the fading light they saw a troop of Frits on ganglefowl galloping along a stone causeway towards the fortress.

'Get down Delphs!' shrieked Crow from below.

'O.K., O.K!' Lark growled as he and Fin, coughing from the foul reek, descended the steps.

Quickly tying their handkerchiefs over noses and mouths, dreading they might slip off into the stream of excrement, they gingerly made their way along the ledge, following Crow and Mick trotting ahead, seemingly unfazed by the stench.

Drawing nearer to the Fortress, the sewage's gurgling and bubbling flow became more and more agitated. The ledge started to slope downwards, becoming wider, with the wall to their left rising higher until the top came well above their heads blocking out any view of the marsh and lake. From ahead came an ominous thundering roar and rounding a bend, they came to a halt. Before them rose a cliff, sheer and smooth. At its base, the dark mouth of a wide tunnel spewed out a steady stream of dark brown sewage.

Above the cliff face stood Gressil's Fortress, its seaward side held by the Berg's icy grip, the inland sides standing proud and free, their crown of encircling watchtowers pointing to the lowering sky like the fingers of a hand. Small windows pocked the towers, out of which lights flickered like blinking eyes, staring north, south, and east.

Leaving Lark and Crow gazing up awestruck, Fin gingerly made his way down the slope towards the tunnel mouth. First peering in dismay into the roaring darkness, he looked up to search the smooth cliff face: he couldn't see any way up and into the Fortress.

Turning, he gestured in revulsion at the filth rushing out of the tunnel. 'Crow, do you intend us to go in there?' he called above the roar.

Scuttling to him, Crow dragged him back up the slope. 'No, no! We seed Gresslie's house, now we go home, eh?' He leered up at him hopefully.

'But I must get inside Gressil's Compound,' Fin cried angrily, 'my friend's there and I've got to save her!'

Crow scowled and said in a high wheedling voice: 'I never been into Gresslie's – don't know way! P'raps you find it and give Special Sparkler to Crow, to take care of, eh?'

Without warning, he pounced, snatching at Fin's jerkin, his clawing fingers groping inside. Lark leapt on him and grabbing him by the neck, dragged him to the ground.

'Showing your true nature now, aren't you, you bit of Scav manure!' he hissed, tightening his fingers around Crow's scrawny neck. Choking for air, Crow tried to bite him.

'You're strangling him, Lark,' Fin gasped, pulling at Lark's fingers.

'It's what he deserves! I'm going to tell on him to his Aunty Krite!' Pushing Crow away, Lark spat at him in disgust.

Crumpling into a ball, Crow sobbed hysterically. 'I tired, so tired! Can't go any longa,' he wailed. Licking snot from his upper lip, he crawled off to where a small nook had been cut into the brick wall. Inside, he crouched with his back to them, muttering into his bible bag.

'Better leave him be for a while,' Fin said. 'Anyway, we need to rest, too.'

Lark sighed and nodded. 'I suppose so – it'll be getting too dark soon to do any exploring.'

Wrapping their blankets around their shoulders, they perched on the ledge, half in the nook where Crow was hiding, the steady roar of rushing sewage drumming in their ears. They didn't feel like eating: the smell was too bad.

Lark found his ointment, and gingerly pulling off his boot and sock, massaged his sore toe. Leaning against his master, Mick busied himself with his tongue in his soft parts. He was filthy; earlier, he'd gone off into the marsh in search of something to quench his thirst, returning with his mouth and fur caked in mire.

Pushing off his blanket, Fin got up and using a crack in the wall as a foothold, pulled himself up to look over. Below him the dark lake lay oily and smooth, with the marsh to the left. To the right a high rubble wall butted up against the bulk of the Fortress. On the causeway they had seen earlier, a squad of Skwid on horseback were driving a group of small captive figures towards tall iron gates. At the gates, they milled about waiting for them to open, then, after they trooped inside, the gates shut with a distant clang. Fin knew there was no way into the Compound there without being seen.

He jumped back down and went once more a little way along the ledge towards the sewer opening. Studying the cliff face above him, he estimated its height with his eye. Returning to sit with Lark, he leant over and called in his ear: 'Roughly measuring the height of the cliff, I reckon that the sewer tunnel may not go in too far beneath the Fortress. When daylight comes, we should go in and have a look.'

Lark didn't answer. He'd fallen into exhausted sleep, sitting upright with his sock and boot lying by his bare foot; Mick lay on his back beside him, his muddy mouth open as he slept. Fin gently covered them both with Lark's blanket. Then, putting his head into the nook, hearing whiffling snores, he called softly: 'Crow, Crow.' There was no answer.

Wrapping his own blanket back about his shoulders, he gazed miserably up at the Fortress, thinking of Bird, somewhere inside. Letting his hand stray to his jerkin, he searched for his purse. Loosening the drawstrings, he brought out the Chi Rho, and laid it on his open palm. He spoke to it as if it were alive. 'Well, my friend, what am I to do?' he asked softly.

His thoughts drifted back to when he was with his mother by the tarn. There she'd given him the revelation that what he thought was a flaw in the enamel beneath the great crystal, was in fact a splinter of blood-soaked wood. Shivering, he put the Chi Rho away, and leaning his head back against the brick wall, closed his eyes.

*Once more he was kneeling on the skull shaped hill. Not far away stood a town, its whitewashed buildings silhouetted against dark clouds.*
*The man hanging on the cross craned his neck forward. His breath rasping, he called to the figures standing nearby. A young man, supporting an old woman, came forward, and the man gasped something, his voice almost lost in the jeering crowd around them. Hearing what he'd said, the old woman's face crumpled in grief.*
*Finding strength from somewhere deep within him, the crucified man flung back his head and gave a great cry.*
*'IT IS DONE!'*
*His head fell forward. Fin knew he had died. The ground beneath him juddered. A finger of lightning streaked down, flickered for a moment above the hanging body, brushing the bowed head as if in blessing, then vanished heavenward, into the vault of sky. As if someone had switched off the sun, the world plunged into night.*

Lark woke with a start, gagging from the stink. Bleary eyed, he peered about. Fin was asleep, slumped on the ledge, boots dangling just above the brown sewage.

Mick stretched and yawned, and after pottering off to cock his leg, scrambled out of sight over the sewer wall. Knowing he'd gone in search of drinking water, Lark didn't bother calling him back.

The nook where Crow had taken refuge was empty, apart from a neat pile of rat droppings. Had he gone back to his Aunty Krite, Lark wondered? Probably not, the pull of the cross was too strong; it had even overwhelmed Fescue of the mighty Gaiakin race.

He gave Fin a gentle shake and called softly in his ear: 'The Scav's done a runner again!'

Fin's eyes snapped open and sitting up he frowned in at the empty nook. 'Oh well, as he promised he's brought us to Gressil's Fortress, it's up to us to find the way in.' He looked uneasily at the watchtowers' windows staring down at them.

Lark studied Fin's tired face; in the murky light that served for day in Contagion, this time his strange bi-colour eyes appeared more striking: one iris icy green, so like Master Marlin's that it made Lark shiver, the other melting brown, recalling the anchorite on Cuthbert's Island. A bleak thought struck him: how surprised Grammer Nutmeg would have been, to learn that Master Marlin's wild Rom girl had turned out to be a Holy Woman. But Nutmeg would never know. He and Fin almost certainly would never come home, instead ending up in Gressil's larder.

He shook himself, impatient at his own pessimism: never give up hope. There was a job to do. Help Fin save Bird, and the sooner it was done the better. He eyed the stinking torrent spewing out from the dark tunnel at the base of the cliff; he'd a dreadful suspicion that they would have to go in there.

Hoping that last night in the gathering dark Fin might have missed another way, he climbed the wall and looked across the lake to where the oily liquid lapped against the rubble of the Compound's perimeter wall: the stones rose straight out of the water, no way could they swim in that black muck, and then climb up. In the marsh directly below, he saw Mick lapping at a small pool in a patch of sedge. Whistling to him, and helping him back over the parapet, they both jumped back down.

'Could you see a way?' Fin asked.

Lark shook his head and nodded towards the sewer outlet. 'We've no choice but to go that way. But before we do, we need to eat something, or we'll be fainting.' Hunkering down, he got out a fruit leather from his rucksack and tearing off a bit, handed it to Fin.

Chewing doggedly, Fin got out his sketch pad, and started sketching some of the objects trapped in the frozen wall of the Berg. Trying to capture the contorted body of a dolphin caught in the hazy depths, he scribbled through it: it looked more like a fat cow than a dolphin.

'This stench makes my tongue taste like a badger's privy,' Lark growled, spitting out the last of his mouthful of fruit leather.

'It's time we were going,' Fin muttered, throwing his half-chewed piece away. 'I reckon we'd better cover our faces again.'

Handkerchiefs tied over noses and mouths, rucksacks shouldered, they made their way along the ledge to the tunnel.

Up close, the great gobs of excrement spewing out almost made them lose their courage; only the thought of Bird, imprisoned somewhere in the fastness above, drove them on. Pressing themselves to the wall, with Mick leading the way they inched along the ledge, terrified of slipping into the rushing torrent below them.

Their hopes rose when, in the darkness ahead, they made out a faint grey light. Nearer to, they found it was daylight filtering in through a grid high in the sewer roof.

Here the ledge ended, opening out onto a concrete platform; beyond, the torrent of sewage roared out of darkness. A ladder attached to the tunnel wall led up to the grid. Lark gave it a shake, making it wobble alarmingly.

'I'll go first!' he called in Fin's ear.

'NO! I'll go first,' Fin shouted. 'You need to go carefully with your injured foot.' Before Lark could argue, he started to climb.

Holding the ladder steady, Lark watched him anxiously: each time he put his weight on the next rung it bowed scarily. Halfway up, shifting his rucksack to a more comfortable position, Fin almost slipped, just managing to steady himself. Reaching the grid, he shoved at the rusty mesh with his shoulder. With a metallic squeal, it gave way, sending rust fragments cascading down onto Lark's upturned face.

Dashing them from his eyes, Lark saw Fin's legs disappearing out of sight. In panic, stuffing Mick inside his jerkin, he heaved himself on to the first rung, and ignoring the shooting pains from his injured toe, started climbing. Near the top, a rusty rung collapsed beneath him. Mick let out a howl.

'Shurrup, yer tyke, you'll kill us both!' Lark screeched, clinging on, and blindly searching about with his boot before finding another rung. Resting for a moment, he glanced up to see Fin's face close above him.

'Keep going! You're almost there,' Fin called down.

With one last mighty effort Lark heaved himself up and out, collapsing with his rucksack beneath him.

'Raddled wemmers,' he groaned, struggling to sit up. 'I thought I wasn't going to make it! Visions of me being swept away out to sea along with the liquid turds!' He looked about. 'Anyway, where've we come to?'

They were in a wide courtyard within the encircling battlements and were relieved to see that the watchtowers were windowless on this side, rising high to block out most of the sickly yellow sky. From somewhere outside came an eerie wailing.

All around them were mounds of dark brown matter. Lark groaned. 'Not more manure!'

Buzzing with clouds of black flies, the brown swirls reminded him of the chocolate piping decoration on Grammer Nutmeg's fancy cupcakes. Poking out of swirls were bits of half-digested ganglefowl – hunks of grey skin, beaks, and bones.

Glowering in disgust at the brown columns, Fin noticed some had dried and were turning hard. A sudden violent itch from where the doomstone had stuck to his palm reminded him what the stuff was. 'I know what these are – they're doomstone pillars, like those we saw in the mines at Birdoswald, only fresher.'

Lark gingerly prodded the base of a nearby pile with the tip of his boot. 'Yep, I reckon you're right. I think we've found Gressil's outside privy! And if we have, we'd better not linger – he may come to visit at any moment!'

He frowned up at the walls, rising fifty feet or so above them. 'I dread to think what that howling noise is outside – reminds me of those Bombyx creatures!'

Recalling what he'd learnt from Mossy's book about Contagion, Fin wondered if the wailing might be Queen Mab on her nest, but not wanting to give Lark the jitters, he didn't say anything.

Searching the walls for a way out of the yard, they saw that on the top of the seaward facing battlement the Great Berg had formed a thick layer of ice. Spreading down into the yard, the ice started at the northern watchtower and continued round south-east, ending not far short of the square bulk of a massive stone keep. The rest of the walls were all solid stone without any door or open window – apart from the opening to yet another, larger tunnel at the base of the keep.

'Do you reckon that's the way into the Compound?' Lark nodded towards the ominous looking opening. 'If so, I don't like the look of it!'

Fin shuddered. 'No, nor do I! But I suppose we'd better go and have a look.'

They weaved their way around the manure mounds and peering in uneasily were met by a foul reek. From the darkness deep inside came a rumbling, as if something very large was having trouble with its digestion.

'Fin, I really, truly, don't fancy going in there,' Lark whispered. 'I think I'd rather go back down into the sewer and find another way.'

Fin gazed miserably at the blank walls. 'I can't understand why Crow brought us this way. And it's all taking far too long! I dread that we might be too late for Bird.'

Lark scowled. 'I reckon the devious bum boil led us to a dead end on purpose!'

In desperation Fin looked again at where the Great Berg gripped the top of the battlements. Dirty stalactites had grown down into the yard. There were pieces of debris sticking out of the ice; animal bones and tree branches, forming likely hand or foot holds, making the slippery surface climbable.

'I reckon we could get to the top of the wall there,' he said, nodding at the icy roots, 'and then make our way along to the keep, where there might be a side door or window to get in through, and hopefully a way down.'

Lark's spirits plunged at the thought of more difficult climbing; his injured foot was still throbbing from the effort of tackling the sewer ladder. He looked back into the tunnel, wondering if the rumbling was just a draught. Shouldn't they at least go in a little way and have a look? Then, recalling Grammer Nutmeg's graphic stories about Gressil, he gave a hopeless sigh.

'I suppose I'd rather fall and break my neck, than get stung and eaten by a scorpion with snapping—' His voice froze in his throat.

From within the tunnel came an eerie scraping and tapping. Two huge pincers appeared out of the darkness, tap, tapping the walls and floor. Ducking behind a nearby coil of half-digested droppings, trembling in terror, they peered out through a bunch of damp ganglefowl feathers. From the tunnel emerged a huge crablike face, followed by an enormous swollen body, the armoured back scraping the tunnel roof, the pale flabby belly rubbed along the floor.

'It's his nibs himself – Gressil!' Lark squeaked.

Mick, perched on a rusty Frit head close to Lark's cheek, let out a yelp.

'Fin, look at the size of his knackers!'

'Shush, shush!' Fin whispered, gripping Lark's arm.

The head swung around. Two stalks ending in clusters of berry-black eyes, swivelled about and homed in on their hiding place. Dripping strings of spit, the jaws dropped open and a long blue tongue, snaking out between multiple rows of yellow fangs, tasted the air.

Lumbering on creaking multi-jointed legs towards their hiding place, the body now in full view, they could see the segmented tail arching over the back, spiked here and there with bunches of short stiff black hairs. A swollen sting on the tip of the tail dripped venom. Searching about, the claws brushed the top of Lark's head, their draught parting his Delphin thatch into crooked line.

Suddenly from deep inside the bloated belly came a rumbling. The huge body shuddered. The tail uncurled and stretching up to the jaundiced sky, from between the back legs spewed a torrent of dung. Hitting the ground with squelching thuds, a choking stench filled the enclosed space of the courtyard. Bowels emptied, the scorpion tail sprang back, arching again, sending a ball of dripping poison on the tip swinging to and fro, ludicrously reminding Fin and Lark of a bauble, like those hung in the Great Hall of Dandrum Den at festive times.

The bauble had hardly stilled when there came a new sound, a sound they dreaded: the drone of Snoopers. Pressing themselves into the manure, they cowered as a squadron of Snoopers appeared over the towers, flying from the north. Monotonous buzzing vibrating around the walls, multiple glittering eyes searched the courtyard, spying their Lord, they hovered, dipping their heads in homage. Brushing his hard-shelled head with their dangling legs, they rose again, and dropped out of sight behind the Fortress keep.

Joints creaking, the great creature lumbered back into the tunnel.

Frozen in terror, they waited until all was silent, then creeping to the tunnel entrance, peered in.

'I reckon he's gone to chat with his Snoopers,' Lark muttered.

He suddenly giggled. 'Dang it Fin, where was your sketch pad, you've missed an opportunity! Tissy won't believe me when I tell her what we saw: Gressil in the flesh looks far worse than any tale Grammer Nutmeg has told us!'

Fin smiled bleakly. 'I could almost feel sorry for him, I shouldn't think it's pleasant stuck inside that great creaking shell. Anyway, knowing now what lurks inside the tunnel has decided it – we'll have to climb the ice.'

Shouldering his rucksack, he began picking his way through the manure towards the far wall.

'Hang on,' Lark called, 'where's Mick!'

He spotted him inside the tunnel entrance sniffing a large meaty bone crawling with maggots. Dashing over, he grabbed him by the scruff.

'Stay with us!' he growled, 'I don't want to come back, to pick over Gressil's dung, searching for yer furry pelt, fer – fer burying alongside your ma, Dinah.'

'Get a move on, Lark!' Fin called impatiently hearing Lark give a loud sob.

Halfway across the courtyard, crouching behind an extra-large manure pile, they paused to listen for sounds of danger.

Suddenly Lark let out a low groan.

'What is it?' Fin looked about in alarm.

'Look, in this turd!' Using the tip of his boning knife, Lark exposed soft blonde hair. Digging down, he found a head, but as he lifted it out, it disintegrated in his hands. 'Bird! Bird!' he wailed.

'Lark – it can't be Bird,' Fin exclaimed, 'her mortal body isn't here – it's safe in Florain!'

Tears streaming, shoulders shaking, Lark crumpled to the ground. 'I forgot! I forgot! I wish I knew what Bird would look like in this dreadful place.'

It dawned on Fin that the fresh doomstones were starting to have a bad effect on Lark: he must get him away as soon as possible. 'Come on, the quicker we're out of this stinking yard the better!' Dragging Lark still sobbing, he set off through the mounds of manure.

Safely reaching the ice-covered wall, he shivered; the air felt colder here, the columns of ice growing down the wall full of the creaking sounds of melting ice. Mentally planning a route to the top, Fin saw to his relief the bits of stuff poking out, mostly animal bones, would make reasonable hand or foot holds. At the top, an auroch's horns stuck conveniently out like handlebars and he wondered vaguely how the huge beast had ended up trapped in the ice. Rummaging in his rucksack, he found the coil of rope Lark had given him back in Brightdale, which he wound around his waist.

'Right, I'm going first,' he said in a business-like voice. 'You guard the rucksacks, and when I get to the top, I'll let down the rope, so I can haul them up.'

Lark didn't argue, but sank to his haunches, head bowed.

Blowing warmth onto his cold fingers, Fin tested his weight on a jutting thigh bone: he wasn't going to enjoy the next few minutes. Gritting his teeth, he began to climb. Halfway up he stopped for a few moments to rest, wedging his boots in the ribcage of what might have been a cow, or perhaps a horse. Face pressed into a mat of wet fur, he suddenly felt it move. The fright almost made him lose his grip; for a shocked moment, he thought the animal might be alive. He cursed under his breath as Mick came scrambling past him over the fur, his sharp ratting claws digging in like crampons. Waiting until he saw Mick's face appear over the edge at the top, pink tongue hanging out, he continued his climb.

Reaching the auroch's horns, he found it firmly fixed into the ice. Risking his full weight on it, he hauled himself up and landing in the ice gulley running along the wall lay panting, Mick's rasping tongue licking his face. The Berg looming above him, he felt the ice beneath him crack and shift and realised that it could break up at any moment. Searching for somewhere to tie his rope, he decided on one of the auroch's horns. Leaning precariously over the edge, he used what he hoped was a secure hitch knot.

'Right, I'm sending the rope down!' He called down to Lark where he sat slouched with his back against the rucksacks.

Lark didn't respond. Fin dropped the end, aiming it to land on Lark's head. Lark started, shook himself, and looking up gave a thumbs-up sign, before tying the rope to the straps of the rucksacks.

Planting his feet as firmly as he could in the slippery gulley and praying that the rucksacks wouldn't catch on any of the debris sticking out, Fin successfully hauled them up. 'Right, you next,' he called softly, throwing down the rope end.

Climbing laboriously, Lark eventually reached the top. 'Thanks Fin!' he gasped, dropping beside him. The influence of the doomstone pillars was quickly waning.

'Right,' Fin said, 'let's see what goes on over by the keep tower.'

Rucksacks on their backs, sliding along the ice gulley and coming to dry stone, they stood up. Outside to their right below the ramparts, the weird wailing sounded much louder. Climbing onto a ledge, they peered over.

Before them lay Gressil's Compound.

Roughly a square mile in area, it was enclosed on three sides, one side by the Fortress and the perimeter wall they'd seen from the sewer, which ran eastwards, taking in the causeway gatehouse, before circling southwards, then westwards, to join the mass of the Great Berg, which made up the seaward side. Not far beyond the gatehouse was the opening to another vast tunnel.

Fin knew this tunnel must be the way into the network of tunnels that Sandy and Mossy had referred to, dug by Gressil's slaves when he first came to Contagion. Running deep underground, these tunnels served as highways for Frit ganglefowl riders, bringing captives and supplies to Contagion: one branch led to Killhope, whilst another ran deep into the Doomstone mines.

The loud wailing drew their attention to the far side of the Compound. Looming above a picket fence of bleached bones, was the grey mass of what looked like an enormous slug. At once they knew they were gazing on Gressil's Queen Maabella. Sometimes partly obscured by a swirling green miasma, she lay twitching and throbbing on a swampy bed of rotting matter, which they remembered was known as her Nest.

They reckoned she was about twenty feet high, and fifty feet long, and even from this distance they could see in her side the deep gash inflicted by Prince Cadeyrn; a cloud of flies buzzed around it, feeding on the suppurating matter seeping from the wound which she was unable to drive off, her ten short pairs of legs waving uselessly.

They saw no sign of eyes in the quivering mass; at one end, a thick lipped mouth sucked in food (some of it still alive, little arms and legs waving desperately as they disappeared inside), whilst from the other end, every now and then squirted the maggoty body of a baby bugslug. Waiting to catch them was a team of slime-caked Frits: each time a bugslug was born, one of the waiting Frits, deftly catching the wriggling blob, would wade off through the mire to a nursery enclosure nearby, adding it to the seething mass of baby bugslugs already there.

On the edge of utter despair, Fin wondered how he would ever find Bird's soul in this nightmare place without seasons, where neither Saprise nor Highsun could ever penetrate, a place diseased beyond healing, full of the dreadful cries of tortured things?

Lark groaned. 'Surely our little Bird couldn't be down there!'

Mick looked anxiously up into his master's stricken face and whimpered.

Fin gave a start: from somewhere below he heard a small cry.

'Where are you, my knight in shining armour? Hurry and rescue me from the ogre!' called Bird's faint voice.

Frantically searching the nightmare scene, he saw directly below them the corrugated tin roofs of a group of shacks. Looking like rafts on a swamp of filth, miserable creatures of all kinds crawled along the network of muddy paths between the huts: humanoid, animal and avian, so filthy it was impossible to identify their species.

'Bird's in there!' he cried, pointing fiercely to the roof of the largest shed where Frits could be seen coming and going, driving mud-caked creatures before them; it seemed to be the centre of activity. Once again, he recalled the description he'd read in Mossy's secret book, of the Treatment Shed, where bodies were prepared for being 'fed' to Maabella – their souls sucked out and put in pods, to be stored on racks.

'We've got to get down to that shed!'

'Right!' Lark pointed to the solid stone walls of the square keep towering to their left. 'There could be steps down to the compound in there – come on, let's have a closer look for a door or window.'

Keeping low, they scurried over to study the stone face: it was blank.

'Let's look over the parapet once more,' Lark muttered. 'This time, take a chance on not being seen, and lean right out, so we can see what goes on directly below us.'

Climbing back up on the ledge, and craning their necks as far as they dared, they saw, twenty feet or so below them, the top of Gressil's head. He was on a wide ledge, his body half out of what seemed to be the entrance to a cavern, his eyes swivelling, claws tapping the wall around him. Hearts racing, they sprang back.

'Warty wemmers we've found the front door!' Lark gasped.

On the edge of hysteria after the relief of hearing Bird's voice, Fin giggled. 'Warty wemmers? That's a new one, Lark!'

'It's what my Granfer Fox used to say when I'd botched skinning a rabbit: "You've made a right warty wemmer's bum of that, Lark lad!"'

He gave a sob. 'What I wouldn't give to have him with us!' Wiping his nose on his sleeve, he said. 'Anyroad, where do we go now? Any ideas?'

Once more risking discovery, leaning far out again they scanned the horror of the Compound. A squad of Frits was driving a new clutch of victims towards Queen Mab moaning on her nest. Gressil sat viewing the scene, his probing claws swinging uncomfortably close to the top of the battlement. Below him, slightly to Gressil's right, they spotted something they'd missed the first time. A little further along below the battlement, protruding from the wall was a brown mushroom-shaped construction, with a wide, flat top. It reminded Fin of a variety of mushroom growing in the woods at home which Mossy called Dryad's Saddle, but of huge size. A network of sinuous knobbly tendrils grew from it, burrowing into the crumbling stone wall and spreading to the ground like monstrous roots.

'You know what that is, don't you?' Fin whispered.

Lark nodded, wide-eyed. 'It's another Snooper's Nest.'

'I've a feeling it's their Mother Nest.'

Studying it, Fin saw on the top of the spongy surface, ventilation holes rhythmically opening and closing like mouths. 'We could try climbing into one of those holes and down into the Nest, then find a way to the ground.'

Lark dreaded what could be lurking inside. 'We haven't any choice, do we Fin?'

Fin shook his head. 'We've got to try. We've been inside a Snooper's nest before, and know what to expect, and anything's better than trying to sneak past Gressil's great stinking hulk! But if you don't want to, I'll understand.'

Lark scowled at him but didn't say anything. Checking his boning knife, he shoved Mick inside his jerkin. Together they swung their legs over the rampart. Gressil's bulk was very close, his claws restlessly tapping the rock around him. The spongy top of the Nest looked a long way down. Taking a deep breath, they jumped, landing with a bounce. The Nest shook violently. Gressil's endlessly searching clusters of berry-black eyes swung round to home in on them. Driven by terror, they scrambled to the nearest open hole, just squeezing in before it snapped shut.

## 22
## MELT!

Sliding helter-skelter down a twisting tube, a warm honey-sweet smell wafted up to them, reminding them of the inside of a beehive. Landing on a springy floor, they were confronted by a looming yellow and black striped rump: a Snooper – bigger and fatter than any they'd encountered before. Waving its long antennae, the huge insect swung round to face them, and they saw it was blind, its bulging multi-faceted eyes misted over. They froze, not daring even to breathe, as its antennae probed inches from the tops of their heads. Just missing them, it turned about and lumbered away, and they breathed again.

In the half-light filtering in through the translucent roof they saw they were in a chamber of parchment-like walls lined with rows of hexagonal cells made of a pale waxy substance. Each cell contained a wriggling creamy-fleshed grub – the size of fat piglets, but without legs. They had landed in the Snooper Nursery. Two more Snoopers, both blind, emitting a constant low motherly hum, were patrolling up and down the rows, stuffing food into the grubs' gaping mouths: naked baby mice, fluffy yellow chicks, little frogs – many still alive.

Cautiously creeping around the blind insects, Mick leading, they made for an opening at the far end of the chamber. But as they stepped through, the shriek of an alarm shattered the whispering peace. Confused by the clamour, four tunnel entrances confronted them. From out of three sped angry shrilly buzzing Snoopers: these insects could see – evil eyes glittering. Taking the initiative, Mick raced off down the wider fourth tunnel, at present empty of Snoopers. Pursued by the furious insects, Fin and Lark bounced on the spongy tunnel floor after him. Then from ahead more Snoopers appeared out of side tunnels. Fangs snapping, the Snoopers closed in. Quickly drawing his boning knife, Lark faced them. As he stabbed and slashed, Mick began frantically digging with his long ratting claws at the tough papery wall. The huge insects, diverted by the small fierce figure attacking them, gave Mick and Fin time to tear a gap big enough for them to get through. Mick dived in first, followed by Fin, but just as Lark turned to jump a snapping jaw caught his rucksack. Lightning quick, he swung about and his blade sliced through its waving proboscis. Screaming in agony, the Snooper staggered back, and Lark fell through. Thrumming with fury, another Snooper shoved its bulk in the gap and with a war-like howl, Lark stabbed at its eyes.

'Come on Lark!' Fin's voice echoed from the gloom.

Staggering away from the furiously struggling insect, in the dimness Lark made out Fin and Mick's shadowy forms silhouetted against a flickering light.

'Where are we?' he called feeling his way along rocky walls.

'I think we're in a tunnel somewhere beneath the Fortress. Come on, let's see where it goes!'

As they edged towards the light, the all too familiar stench of burning rubber filled them with dread: they were faced with an awful dilemma, meet a Phragg or turn back to meet the Snoopers. Arming themselves, Fin with Sandy's sword and Lark with his boning knife, Mick close on his heels, fearfully they pressed on. Stumbling over the uneven floor, the way began to descend steeply, and they desperately hoped they were heading for the outside world – whatever that might bring.

The burning smell of grew stronger. Hearing a crackling and hissing, Fin's mind rushed back to the abattoir at Birdoswald, and Bird's body lying beneath the hovering Phragg. Without noticing, his hand strayed to his purse hanging heavy around his neck. Pulling on the drawstring, his fingers froze as a high scream echoed through the tunnel.

'Nooo, don't nasty cut me – me don't know where Delph is—!'

'Raddled rams, that was Crow!' Lark gasped.

His scream came again.

Fin groaned. 'He's been captured!' He gripped Sandy's sword tighter. 'Come on, we've got to help him!'

They plunged on. Coming out into a long, low cavern, mounds of rotting meat piled on the floor and carcasses hanging from the roughhewn roof, told them they'd come to one of Gressil's underground larders.

At the far end, close to an exit tunnel, hovered a fiery cloud of burning rags. Beneath it cowered Crow's small figure. A group of gloating Frits danced around him, waving razor knuckle dusters, their excited whining echoing off the rock walls.

'Master Raaum, please can we kill it now, can we? Whilst it's still full of juicy meat?' Drooled one of the Frit torturers. Leaping forward, it slashed at Crow's thin chest, and again his agonized scream resounded in the stinking cavern.

Rage welled up in Fin. Jumping up on to a pile of meat, he drew out his purse. Fumbling for the cross, he waved it by its chain, high above his head.

'IS THIS WHAT YOU'RE AFTER, PHRAGG?'

His clear young voice cut through the Frits' taunts: momentarily silent, Phragg and Frits stared in amazement. Jumping down, weaving through the piles of meat, Fin ran towards them, tantalizingly brandishing the cross. Sapphires, rubies, and gold glittering in the fiery glow, he dodged past, heading for the exit tunnel.

Open mouthed, Lark watched bewildered as the Phragg, spitting sparks, gave a shriek of rage. Abandoning Crow, it sped after him, Frits close behind.

Lark knew he must act – fast. In the moments it him took to snatch up Mick, Crow had mysteriously disappeared. Terrified of losing Fin, he didn't linger to search for him but ran for the tunnel.

Inside, as he ran, he sensed the floor rising. Straining his ears, the Frits' thrumming grew ever fainter. Ahead, the Phragg's fiery glow flickered and suddenly died. He was plunged into total, silent blackness: he was alone, and he'd lost Fin. Slumping to the ground, he burst into tears.

Feeling Mick's wet tongue on his cheek, he hugged him close. 'Oh, Mick, whatever's Fin gone and done,' he sobbed.

A hand covered his mouth and strong arms lifted him up. With a muffled shriek, he squirmed around: golden eyes blazed down at him, reminding him of sunlight flashing on rippling water. For a fleeting moment, he thought he'd woken from a nightmare, that he was back by the river, with Sandy on his way to Stonetree. Then he realised.

'Oh, Fescue!' he whimpered.

Fin ran on, waving the cross aloft. Now and then he stopped to clang Sandy's sword against the tunnel wall and call tauntingly: 'Catch me if you can! Catch me if you can!'

From behind, the fiery glow of the Phragg grew brighter, the Frits' mechanical thrum louder. Like Lark, as he ran, he felt the ground rising.

A faint voice called to him: 'Fin! Fin! Please hurry – I don't want to die here!'

Desperately he sped on. As daylight appeared ahead, he realised his pursuers had gone, and the tunnel came to an end. He was confronted by a mountain of bones: ribs and skulls, hips, jaws, all bloody, some with skin and fur still attached. Panting from the chase, he cautiously sidled around them. He was in a vast cavern. At the far end daylight streamed in through a high archway. On a ledge in the archway crouched Gressil, his bulk outlined against the dirty white mass of the Great Berg. The Phragg was pinned down by one of Gressil's back legs, its fire quenched, now just a pitiful pile of dusty black rags. Nearby the gang of Frits stood like statues, terrified grins fixed in death.

Gressil was tearing greedily at an auroch carcass, one cluster of berry-black eyes concentrating on his food, the other cluster swivelling on its stalk, keeping watch on the Compound below, from where there came the mournful cries of Maabella on her Nest. A Snooper hovered above Gressil's head, tapping the hard shell with its legs, trying to attract his attention. Lazily lifting a claw, Gressil batted it away and carried on ripping at the auroch. Persistent, the Snooper buzzed back, and continued tapping. Gressil's blue tongue shot out and sucked it into his wide mouth. Crunching it up, he spat out shards of insect casing.

Sickened, Fin looked away.

'Help me Fin, help me, I can't breathe...' Closer now, the voice called to him again. Twisting his head about, he tried to work out from where it came, but Gressil's loud slurping and Maabella's wailing muddled him. He had to get out of here!

Searching for a way, he saw at the back of the cavern a wide dark tunnel from where there came a strong stink. He realised it was the way into Gressil's back yard; no way did he want to go back into that foul yard. Then he remembered the roots he and Lark had seen growing from the Snooper's Nest down to the ground. He noticed some of the tendrils had spread onto the ledge where Gressil was crouched. Surely, he should be able swing to the ground from there?

But first, he must get past Gressil, and the only way he could do that – and not be killed and eaten – was to use the Chi Rho, to distract Gressil and draw him away from the ledge.

He was still holding the cross. Should he wave it, like he did to lure the Phragg and its Frits? Or should he get nearer before showing it to Gressil?

Tucking Sandy's sword in his belt, he wound a length of the cross's heavy gold chain around his shaking hand. Mossy's warning thundered in his brain: 'Never wear the Cross!' He didn't intend wearing it, just using it as a lure; saving Bird was more important than any piece of jewellery, however precious.

Stomach churning, for a moment he shut his eyes as he summoned up all his courage. Legs stiff with fear, he stepped forward.

Halfway across the bone-strewn floor, he stooped to pick up a heavy thigh bone. He aimed and hurled it. It landed with a thud by one of Gressil's legs. Gressil's jaws stopped working mid-munch. Heaving his great body up on to its eight creaking legs, Gressil swung around, and pincers snapping, lumbered in from his ledge. His eye stalks swivelled searching the cavern.

Keeping tight hold of the chain, Fin raised his arm and slowly waved the cross to and fro. Catching the light, the jewels sent sparkling rainbow colours dancing across the ground. Enraptured, Gressil drew closer. To give himself courage, Fin fixed his eyes on the cross. As it swung, twisting on the chain, he saw a small white flame flickering in the crystal around the tiny sliver of wood at its heart. With a mighty effort of will, he concentrated once more on the approaching hulk, close enough now to smell the rancid breath. With his free hand, he pulled Sandy's pitifully inadequate sword from his belt and pointing the blade at the grotesque face, advanced, inch by slow inch. A gleam in the darkness to his right distracted him for a second. Turning back to face the monster, sliding the gold chain off his hand, tensing his arm, aiming for the dripping maw, he prepared to throw.

A great cry rang out: 'NO! THE BEAST SHALL NOT HAVE THE CROSS!'

From the shadows leapt Fescue, eyes flashing molten fire. Slamming Fin to the ground, his knee on Fin's chest, with one hand he groped for the cross, with the other he pressed the tip of his golden dagger to Fin's throat. Slashing Sandy's sword wildly, the blade bit deep into Fescue's hand.

But Fescue was not deterred. Fingers slick with his blue Gaiakin blood, he overcame Fin's weakening grip. But even as he took hold of the cross, Gressil's powerful claw clamped around Fescue's arm, dragging him off Fin; the cross slipped from his wounded fingers and skittered off beneath Gressil's fat belly. Fin seized his chance. Quickly rolling amongst the forest of kicking legs, he snatched up the cross and hugging it to his chest, curled into a ball, bracing himself for the searing pain of Gressil's sting. Instead, someone grabbed his leg and dragged him clear.

'GET OUT OF THE WAY!' Lark yelled, hacking with his boning knife at one of the monstrous back legs.

As if he were a wisp of dandelion fluff, Gressil sent Lark spinning across the cavern floor. Snarling furiously, Mick leaped up at Gressil's left eye cluster. Sinking his canines deep into the soft flesh, as he darted away, he nearly lost his tail to Gressil's snapping jaw.

Drawing his sword, newly forged in Florain, Fescue pounced, his blade slicing neatly through the joint between Gressil's left claw and tentacle. The claw clattered to the ground, still clacking. Dancing out of reach of the right claw, he gathered his powers and dived in again, this time amongst the legs. Dagger in one hand, sword in the other, he slashed and chopped: two legs buckled and crashed to the ground. Gressil wobbled wildly, then toppled heavily on to his side. Attacking a third time, Fescue drove his sword deep into Gressil's exposed throat.

Boning knife in hand, Lark darted between Gressil's remaining flailing legs, to cut deep into the soft flesh of the underbelly. At the same time, Mick worried at the fleshy stump from one of the missing legs, as if he were gnawing a bone.

Fin, desperate to join in, tried to stuff the cross back in his purse, but the drawstring had knotted. Slinging the chain over his head, and tucking the cross inside his shirt, he leapt at Gressil, and with one mighty thrust, drove Sandy's sword deep into the remaining uninjured cluster of eyes. As they burst, liquid sprayed over his hand and arm. This last onslaught was too much for Gressil: his remaining legs collapsed, and with a final quiver, he slumped and lay still.

Fin gaped, stupefied, at the inert body. Shoving Sandy's sword back in his belt, he realised Lark was yelling at him.

'WHAT YER DOING, DITHERING ABOUT – GET THE CROSS AWAY FROM HERE!'

Staring at him, he took in what Lark meant. 'But – but what about you – I can't leave you—'

'YES, YER CAN!' Lark bellowed, giving him a shove. 'GO! NOW! Get the cross away from here.' His hand shaking, Lark pointed his knife towards the ledge, and gave Fin another hard shove. 'Go'en find Bird! Fescue and I will sort out the monster.'

Fin glanced towards Fescue watching them, the fire of battle fading from his golden eyes. Turning away towards the ledge, he forced his trembling legs to walk, half-expecting to feel the Gaiakin's strong hand pulling him back. From outside, the wailing had become frantic screams as if Queen Mab knew what had happened to her mate. Becoming aware of pain biting into his chest, he halted. Putting his hand inside his shirt, he felt hard gold. The cross had latched onto his skin. Dropping his hands to his sides so Lark wouldn't suspect anything, he marched unsteadily on.

Almost at the ledge, from behind him came the sudden clacking of a claw, followed by a strangled cry. He spun around. Gressil was not yet done. He was still just alive, his remaining claw had clamped around Lark's neck. Blindly Gressil lifted Lark towards his gaping maw. His eyes popping, his face turning blue, Lark's feet had disappeared inside when Fescue sprang. His golden dagger flashing, he hacked the claw from the joint; Lark hit the ground with a thud, the claw still tight around his neck.

Fin raced across the cavern. Grabbing hold of the pincers and heaving with a strength he didn't know he had, with a crack like a gunshot, the pincers broke apart.

Struggling to sit up, Lark gestured wildly to Fescue. 'Never mind me. Help Fescue!' he choked.

Turning, Fin saw Fescue had climbed onto Gressil's back, and was frenziedly stabbing at the hard shell, first with his sword, then his dagger. As he raised his arm for another stab, Gressil's tail twitched and shot straight up. Fin yelled a warning, but he was too late. The tail curled down towards Fescue's back. The poisoned sting stabbed twice, in and out, in and out, right through his body. For a long moment, Fescue stared down at the hole in his chest, his beautiful face bewildered.

Then, as the venom coursed through his veins, his sword and dagger slipped from his paralysed fingers and hit the ground with two metallic clangs. He tumbled after them. Squealing in ghastly triumph, Gressil's blue tongue snaked out, found Fescue's neck, and curled around it.

But in his glee, Gressil had forgotten the age-old lore: to pierce a Gaiakin's heart is death – by fire – fire from the Universe of White Light. A column of white flame – a heat of an intensity unimaginable in the Universe of Stars – blazed from Fescue's chest. Searing Gressil's tongue and hideous face with an explosive roar, the huge crustacean body became engulfed in fire. From inside the inferno there came a drawn-out shriek – never had there sounded a cry so terrible.

Desperate for relief from the agonizing pain, Gressil found new strength. Heaving up onto his leg stumps, blindly crashing against the cavern walls, molten fat dripping from the cracks in his shell, he crawled towards the light. Reaching the ledge, he wavered for a moment before toppling out of sight. Only a stench of cooking flesh remained.

As Fin and Lark watched in awe, from beneath the ledge rising skyward a huge ball of fire shot towards the Great Berg. Crackling and sizzling, like fork lightning, the ice fractured sending an earth tremor vibrating across the cavern floor followed by a thick cloud of steam stinking of rancid sea water.

Galvanized into action, they groped through the fog to where Fescue lay in a pool of blue blood. Kneeling either side of him, they searched his face for signs of life. Slowly, his golden eyes opened. Moaning, he raised his head, and whispered urgently. 'Save— save the poor creatures down— down there—!' His wounded hand fluttered towards the outside.

He grabbed Fin's wrist, 'Fin Dandrum, I bequeath my Chi Rho to you! Use it to destroy the vile Slug that is Queen Mab. The power of the blood in the wood will—' his voice faltered as he choked on blood, his eyes anxiously searching Fin's face.

Lifting Fescue's limp hand, Fin lightly touched the red mark on its back, and smiling at him through tears, said: 'Fescue, I was there – when the blood dripped on your hand.'

'Ah me,' Fescue sobbed, 'that was my greatest sorrow!' Breathing a great sigh, he laid his head back. 'But at last, the desire has gone!"

With breaking hearts, Fin and Lark watched the wondrous light of his eyes flicker then mist over. His body began to fade. Soon, all there was to see on the rocky ground, was a faint shimmer of blue-gold. Lying close by, his beloved sword and dagger slowly turned to rust, then fused with the rock. Fescue the Gaiakin had no more need of them, he had gone home to his Universe of White Light.

They sat for a while, full of sorrow, two small ghosts in the billowing fog, mourning the first Gaiakin they had known. From outside, came thunderous crashing as the melting Berg shed ice and debris.

Lark stirred, pushing Mick's licking tongue away from his bruised neck. He passed his hand above the shimmering stain. 'He's disappeared,' he said, remarking on the obvious, his battered voice box hoarse. 'Did I hear Fescue aright? Did he tell us to use the cross to kill Queen Mab? Have you any idea how we're supposed to do that? It would mean getting up close, for a start!'

Fin put his hand inside his shirt, feeling the gold firmly stuck to his skin. As he gingerly attempted to prise it away, he heard a small cry: 'Fin, I can't breathe!'

He jumped to his feet. 'Our priority is to find Bird. Then we'll see about dealing with Queen Mab.'

Relieved there was no talk of sending him home to Brightdale, Lark didn't argue.

'Right,' he croaked, 'I'll get our rucksacks – I dumped them by that huge pile of bones, when Fescue and I came into the cavern.' He disappeared into the fog.

Fin took a bit of rag from his pocket to clean Sandy's sword. As he did so, he glanced at the blue and gold stain where Fescue had died. Spotting Fescue's ruby ring, he picked it up; the beautifully cut red stone had dulled, its sparkle dead. Pulling out his purse, he found the drawstring had mysteriously untangled. Frowning, he put the ring inside: perhaps one day, he would be able to give the ring to Mullein.

By the time Lark returned, the fog of steam had almost dispersed, just a few wisps swirling in the roof. Lark had forgotten where he'd hidden the rucksacks, eventually finding them beneath a pile of mouldy fur.

Gazing sadly once more at where Fescue had died, they saw the stain had disappeared, leaving no sign that the Gaiakin had ever lived. Alert for Phraggs and Frits, they made their way towards the ledge.

Stepping around chunks of lobster-pink cooked scorpion flesh, Lark grimaced when he saw Mick take a bite. 'He'll be wanting a dab of tartare sauce next,' he growled.

Coming to the metal remains of the Frits, Crow's torturers, they saw they had fused into spiky stalagmites. A sooty streak was all that was left of the Phragg.

Out on the ledge, they saw where Gressil lay on the Great Iceberg. He'd managed to crawl halfway up. The extreme heat of his white-hot hulk was melting the Berg, sending cataracts of water cascading down the shrinking sides. Deep inside, the black flammable liquid trapped in the veins marbling the ice had caught fire. Blazing veins ran in all directions, one hitting a grove of ice-bound pine trees, setting their cones alight, sending small exploding bombs shooting skyward. Another vein, reaching an oily pool of whale blubber – all that was left of a Minke whale – ignited yet more black veins. Fire soon spread along the length of the Berg. More and more melt water rushed down the icy slopes.

As the inferno relentlessly ate into the berg, in the Compound, a rapidly rising tide of muddy filth swirled around the huts and sheds. Scavs, Frits, ducks, chickens, sheep, goats, dogs, cats, tumbled out of windows and doors. Some had managed to swim to the perimeter wall, but the gates leading out to the causeway had jammed shut. A group of Frits, using a roof beam as a makeshift battering ram, could be seen trying to break them open.

Across the Compound, Maabella thrashed on her nest, frenziedly waving her tiny useless legs, her just-born grubs disappearing beneath a rising sludge. Nearby, where the more grown-up bugslugs were corralled, the muddy water had risen over their bone fence, allowing them swim out. Enjoying their freedom, the wriggling mass were happily riding the swirling water, heading for the entrance to the tunnel network at the far end of the Compound, where a contingent of Frit, on bedraggled ganglefowl, were futilely attempting to stop them escaping.

A stinging pain reminded Fin he was still wearing the cross. He tried again to pull it away from his chest, but the agony sent his head reeling. Closing his shirt tight, he looked in despair at the chaos below. How was he ever to find Bird in all the confusion? Would her soul perish in this nightmare, never reunited with her body? Gazing at the bulk of the Berg, he saw the fire inside had spread to the ice gripping the Fortress. Panic seized him – he would have to hurry if he were to rescue Bird from drowning.

'Don't give up on me Fin …' her distant voice sobbed.

He groaned out loud. 'I won't my love! Just tell me where you are!'

'In the big shed! Look for the blind eagle…'

Frantically he searched for an eagle in the chaos around the sheds: all he saw was a small sparrow hawk, flapping helplessly in circles, its legs shackled by a chain to a dangling pole.

'Are you sure you mean an eagle?' he cried, bewildered.

'Did you say something?' Lark called.

'I heard Bird's voice! She was calling to me from inside there.' Fin gesticulated wildly down at the roof of a large shed.

Lark's heart sank. Had Fin finally gone loopy? Covering his ears against Maabella's screams, he stared at the seething mess below him. All his instincts told him to get away from this loathsome place as quick as he could. But no, he'd made a promise to old Mossy, to take care of Fin – his dream of marrying Tissy had evaporated with the steam from the Berg drifting off over the fells.

Whirring wings made him look up. A squadron of Snoopers had emerged from their Nest, carrying baby pupae between their legs. For a moment, he had a fanciful longing to grab a leg and cadge a lift. With an enormous effort, he looked down to the shed Fin had pointed to. A group of terrified Frits were driving a flock of geese out through the door; the birds' feathers were clipped, and they were unable to fly. Seeing one sucked beneath the watery mud, filled with wretchedness, he looked away.

'Are you sure Bird's down there?' he called.

'Yes! Yes – in that big shed! It must be the Treatment Shed!' Fin gesticulated down at the roof, a wild look in his eyes.

Seeing Fin's hand creeping inside his jerkin, Lark knew he must act quickly: put an end to the voices in Fin's head – in fact, put an end to everything, up here on the ledge, and in the Compound.

'RIGHT!' he shouted. 'First thing to do is get down there!'

Dropping on his stomach and leaning perilously far out, he planned a route from the Snoopers' Nest down the network of roots, twisting fifty feet or so to the ground. Directly below he spotted a group of Frits clinging to the roots as the lumps of ice and debris swept past. Some of them had missing parts: no arms or legs, one hadn't even got a head, just eyes and lips on the end of metal stalks.

Seeing how fast the water was rising, he wondered, once they were down, how could they get to the big shed – the Treatment Shed, Fin had called it. He saw not far out from the cliff, floating debris was piling up around rocks and boulders.

'Do you see those islands of rubbish? If we could reach them, we could get from there to the shed – we'll be in for a swim, so if you're last in, don't worry about washing the socks!'

He gave Fin an encouraging grin. To his relief, he saw him smile in response.

'Right, I'll go first,' he said, tucking Mick inside his jerkin.

Swinging his legs over the ledge and grabbing hold of a root, ignoring the stabbing pain in his sore toe, he found a foothold, and started to descend. Looking up, he was reassured to see Fin following.

Halfway down, a familiar sulphurous reek sent them cowering into the roots. Peering up, they saw two Phraggs hurtle out from one of the watchtowers. Outlined against the grey clouds, they fluttered for a moment, showers of sparks cascading off them. Then, black rags streaming behind them, streaked off south. Fin and Lark doggedly continued their descent.

Reaching the water, a powerful current snatched at them; losing their grip on the roots they were dragged amongst a jumble of part-made Frits, ice, and debris towards the gaping darkness of an opening. Swept in by the force and tumbling down a flight of steps, on the way they crashed into terrified Frits vainly trying to fight their way up. At the bottom, clinging desperately with his fingertips to the rough wall, Lark saw they were being dragged along a rough wall to where a flight of steps, cut into the rock wall and fenced off by chain banister, led up to a platform. At the steps, he judged his moment and lunged, catching hold of the lowest chain on the banister, and hanging on grimly, as Fin swept past, he managed to grab him by his collar. Hauling themselves on to the first step and climbing, at the top they collapsed soaked and dripping onto the platform, where Mick, scrambling out of Lark's jerkin, choked up a stream of muddy water.

Heaving off their sodden rucksacks, they took stock of their surroundings; high above them strings of lights in thin glass tubes shone down on a vast cavern. Below them, on a raised area, stood rows of strange machines. Spread out on work benches behind them were parts of Frits: coils of wire, tubing, and rolls of orange fur pelts. Some Frits were partly assembled, heads and limbs attached to metal-framed bodies, waiting for razor blades to be screwed onto fingertips, rubbery lips to be put in place, and jaws to be armed top and bottom with steel razors. On other benches stood jars containing fleshy legs, arms, hands, and feet floating in a clear liquid, where almost completed Frits awaited skin, muscles and sinews to be grafted on. It dawned on them they were in an underground workshop; that this was where the half-mechanical, half-biological ape-robots were manufactured.

The melt water rapidly filling the cavern, some of the benches had started to float, some tipping over, Frit parts sliding off, the relentless flood sweeping everything towards the back of the cavern from where came an ominous gurgling roar. They realised that there must be a drain there that took the muck from the factory floor down to join the sewer beneath the Great Iceberg where Crow had led them.

To their alarm the water level had now reached their platform and was lapping over their boots. Wading to the rock walls at the back they searched for another way out but found the walls solidly blank. Then they noticed a cage in a dark corner and trapped inside was a gorilla. The cage was so small, the great barrel-chested animal could barely move. Grunting in terror, long muscular arms thrust through the iron bars, he was trying to break out, but the door was chained and padlocked. Frantically hunting for a key, they couldn't find one. In desperation, Lark drew his boning knife, and urged on by the gorilla's distraught grunting, attempted to pick the padlock. For agonizingly long moments, he had no luck. But at last with a click, the padlock opened, and the chain rattled down into the water. Squeezing out of the cage, the gorilla staggered stiffly to his feet.

'Hurry! The water's rising fast!' urged Fin, dragging on Lark's arm.

Coaxing the limping gorilla along as best they could, they waded back to the steps.

As Lark stooped to pick up their rucksacks, Fin cried: 'Leave them! They'll drag us down!'

Reluctantly abandoning them, Lark thought sadly of all his precious stuff, his fishing tackle, his nets, the bits and pieces he'd picked up on his travels to show Tissy. As he turned away, the gorilla, gently gripping his arm, lifted the rucksacks out of the water and swung the straps over his powerful shoulders. Going to the edge of the platform and slipping smoothly into the water, making encouraging guttural sounds, he held out his arms to them. Too amazed to be frightened, taking hold of his big soft hands, they climbed onto his broad back and grasped the coarse silver fur. Mick followed; first leaping onto the thick muscular neck, he took refuge in Lark's jerkin.

Cautiously, the gorilla launched himself into the deep fast flowing water. His powerful legs battling against the flow, half swimming, half wading, he fought his way to the steps. Climbing to the cavern entrance, standing waist deep, he gripped the rocky walls to stop himself from being swept away. From his back Fin and Lark stared aghast. In the Compound many of the smaller huts had disappeared, submerged below the surface. Terrified creatures, drowned bodies, chunks of ice, hut roofs, walls and doors, everything was being inescapably sucked towards the far tunnel into which the escaping bugslugs had long gone. In the Berg itself large gaps had appeared, letting in a pale light; glimpses could be seen of the grey sea beyond, from where there came a fresh salty tang. Fire raged inside the still frozen parts of the Berg, flaring up in violent explosions as fresh pockets of inflammable liquid were reached, sending huge ice shards crashing into the water. Of Gressil's great hulk just a few glowing lumps remained.

(Fin and Lark could not know that his evil spirit had quietly slipped into the sea, his black shadow weaving through the kelp. Many days and sea-miles later, on the ocean floor the dark shadow will slink into a deep ravine, where a bobbitworm – of the species Eunice aphroditois – was waiting, ready for the Lord Gressil's rehousing. Here he will lurk, soothing the scars of his wounded pride, waiting to rescue his beloved mate, Maabella.)

To his relief, Fin saw the Treatment Shed was still standing, the water level not yet up to the windows. Queen Mab's mountain of wobbling flesh thrashed about, the water threatening to engulf her nest. Urgently thumping on the gorilla's back, he gesticulated towards the shed. At first the gorilla looked back at him, puzzlement in his small brown eyes. Understanding dawning, he nodded and launched into the water, promptly sinking up to his neck. Fin and Lark disappeared beneath the surface, coming up seconds later, with Mick half out of Lark's jerkin. Coughing and spluttering, the three of them scrambled higher up on to the gorilla's shoulders.

Swimming through the water, his toes feeling in the mud for footholds, the gorilla headed for a floating island of pieces of broken shed caught around a large flat-topped rock. Catching hold of a protruding plank he leaned forward, allowing Mick, Fin and Lark to scramble off his shoulders onto the rock, then climbed out to join them. Crouching together, covered in filth, the four of them could have been mistaken for creatures that had crawled out of an ancient primordial soup.

Surveying the situation, they saw the Berg had finally lost its grip on the Fortress. In the far wall, the entrance to the tunnel had now disappeared, but the Frits were still trying to batter the gates open. With a sudden squeal of fracturing metal, they finally crashed outwards. The causeway, the black lake, and the section of Berg above the sewer were now visible. In this part of the Berg the fire in the ice was still fiercely burning. One of the veins of black oil, well alight, was racing towards a cache of metal drums, marked 'jet fuel'. As the flames engulfed the drums, they exploded, shards of hot metal and great lumps of ice hurtled into the air to crash down into the sewer, filling it with debris. Finally, the Berg gave way, sending vast boulders of ice thundering down into the black lake. As they watched in horrified awe, in slow motion a huge wave rose, sucking up the lake, the filth from the sewer and mud from the marsh. A tsunami of oily black water surged towards the Fortress. Gaining momentum as it raced onwards, overwhelming the causeway, dislodging boulders from the rubble wall, and funnelling through the gates, it rushed into the Compound. Debris, creatures, and ice wildly swirling before it, the wave smashed against the wall beneath Gressil's ledge. The Snoopers Nest was torn from the rock face and disappeared, taking baby Snoopers and their blind nurses with it.

The torrent rushed on into the underground Frit factory. For a few seconds, the electric lights in the factory's roof flashed like lightning, then the entrance turned ominously dark. From deep inside the cavern came a menacing rumbling. Moments later a gigantic tide of brown muck blasted out of the mouth: the wave had met with the blocked sewage drain which had backed up, having no way to the sea. The brown tide raced towards them, breaking up their island of debris and washing over their rock, pitching them floundering into the filthy water. Paddling for their lives, they swirled towards the Treatment Shed, for the moment still firm on its foundations. Bumping up against the corrugated iron wall, the gorilla's long reach grabbed the roof gutter, and one by one he hauled them onto the roof, then swung up himself. Slithering on slippery mud, they scrambled up to the roof ridge.

The death of the Berg was not yet done with them. As they clung to the ridge, a wave, only a little smaller than the first tsunami, burst through the gateway from the black lake, and surged towards them. As it broke around them, the shed shifted violently sideways. Caught unawares, the gorilla lost his hold. Tumbling down the sloping roof, their rucksacks still slung on his shoulders, he disappeared beneath the murky water to reappear moments later, but without the rucksacks. A huge lump rose in Lark's – all his precious things had finally gone.

But he had no time for regrets. As the gorilla climbed back onto the roof, the shed finally parted from its footings and, like a great raft, began drifting ponderously towards where Maabella screamed and squirmed on her rapidly disappearing nest.

As they drew closer, it dawned on Lark that if the Chi Rho were to destroy her, they must kill her before she could swim away out to sea: otherwise, this nightmare would never end.

Leaning over, he yelled in Fin's ear: 'THIS IS IT! Get the cross out – destroy Queen Mab – like Fescue told us!'

Fin stared wildly at the mountain of slug flesh. He could clearly see the gaping wound in Maabella's side, blood and pus seeping out. Her high-pitched shrieking made his head spin. How was he supposed to finish her off? Stab the wound with the Chi Rho? Sliding his hand into his shirt, he felt the cross gripping his skin. Giving it a tentative tug, the fierce, biting pain made him feel sick. The bitter truth hit him: he hadn't the courage. Fumbling blindly for his purse, he drew out his mother's gold coin. Holding it against his cheek, peace washed over him: he was the son of Saro, he need fear nothing. Tucking the coin away, he drew the cord in his purse tight. Taking hold of the cross and breathing in, he tugged. The pain was unbearable: he couldn't do it.

'Fin, where are you? I don't want to die here!'

The faint panicky voice, on the very edge of hearing, seemed to be coming from beneath his feet. His hand froze inside his shirt. He stared down at the tarred roof.

'Lark, didn't you hear? It's Bird! She's calling from below!' He stabbed his finger downwards.

Lark looked at the roof blankly. Mab's screams were deafening.

Gritting his teeth, Fin pulled hard. The gold came away, ripping his skin. Agonising pain coiled around his heart, hot blood seeped through his fingers, he almost lost consciousness.

Out of a grey mist floated Mossy's voice: 'Fin Dandrum, you know what you have to do!'

'WHERE ARE YOU, you great black, dead, angel!' he yelled. 'Why aren't you here when I need you.'

'It's O.K Fin, it's O.K.,' said a voice.

Opening his eyes, he found Lark had his arm around him. He looked down at his hand. Why was he holding the cross? Why was it all bloody? Oh yes, of course, he'd torn it from his chest. Mossy was right – he knew what he must do: give the Chi Rho to Lark. Lark was the chosen one who would do the task.

He grasped Lark's clenched hand: 'Lark Annunder, I give you the Chi Rho. It will be your task to destroy Queen Mab.' He frowned, trying to remember what else he must say. 'I've – I've got to save Bird – can't leave her to die in this filth.'

One by one, he prised Lark's stiff fingers open and laid the cross in his palm. It slipped through unresponsive fingers. Sliding down the roof, the chain caught on a loose nail.

Tears coursing down his face, Lark rocked to and fro. 'I can't do it, I really can't, Fin.'

Fin shook him by the shoulders. 'There's no can't anymore – you're going to do it. Fescue said it's the only hope of saving the creatures suffering in this evil place. You must use the Chi Rho, to finish what Cadeyrn started.' Snatching up the cross, he hung the chain around Lark's neck.

Dumbfounded, Lark stared down at the cross lying on his jerkin. But when he looked up, Fin saw fierce determination on his open, honest face.

Clambering to his feet, wobbling precariously on the ridge, Lark faced the writhing mass of slug. 'Go on, Fin! Find Bird and save her! I'll destroy Queen Mab!'

Scooping up Mick, he threw him to Fin. 'Here, take him! Go with Fin, Mick lad,' he sobbed, 'show your worth as Dinah's pup: sniff out our Bird for Fin.'

Sliding down the roof, he stood teetering on the gutter. 'WATCH OUT, you pile of slug's shit,' he yelled, 'today's the day you die!'

Slipping down into the water, he turned and looked up at Fin sitting as if turned to stone. 'GET GOING, YER GREAT GOLLOP!' he shouted. Pushing out, he began doggy paddling towards Maabella.

The gorilla, who had been grunting agitatedly to himself, suddenly came to a decision: after thunderously pounding his chest, he slid down the roof and plunged into the water. Catching up with Lark, he lifted him up onto his broad shoulders and waded on.

Agonized, Fin watched as Lark drew his boning knife, and thumping the gorilla's head with his free hand, pointed his blade at Queen Mab's great bulk. Turning to wave to Fin, he called out something.

'Tell Tissy I...' The rest was drowned out by Mab's screams.

7'Lark, I'm sorry, I'm sorry....' Fin choked. Hugging Mick close, he could feel the little dog's heart thumping. Tucking him firmly into his bloodstained jerkin, he slid down the roof. Crawling along the gutter to an open window, he swung down, and balancing on the window ledge, looked inside.

## 23
# DROWNING OF THE COMPOUND

Something was very wrong. Bird's world was full of smoke and flame. She was lying on her back, the sky obscured by a fiery ragged cloud. In her pain, she thought she heard a familiar voice:

'NO PHRAGG! YOU SHAN'T HAVE HER!'

Fin? She squinted through the choking smoke. He was running towards her, waving something shining. Was it a sword? Yes, the silver Dandrum sword! When they were preparing Master Marlin's body, Grammer Nutmeg had found it missing. Why had Fin taken it?

Another voice rang out, a man's strong voice, in a strange language she didn't understand. The burning cloud above her rose higher. The smoke cleared, revealing Sandy's tall figure. Kenji appeared next. What were these warriors doing here, in her dream? It was so ridiculous! She shouldn't have had that second tot of fire-whisky at the funeral feast. She'd wake up soon, at Spinner Hall, tucked up in bed with Bee, because Tissy was sleeping in her bed.

Bee! Now she remembered – being captive in a cage deep underground, baby ganglefowl all around her – finding Bee wrapped in a leaf parcel in that horrid filthy kitchen – Hardwick throwing a net over them, hurting Bee with her broken arm.

She tried to call out to Sandy and Kenji: not to bother about her, to go to Bee, but the words wouldn't come. A cackle. A squeal. Hot rags enveloped her. A hideous mouth with cracked black lips and foul yellow teeth plunged towards her. A searing heat scorched her throat, sucking at her soul. Down and down she spun into nothingness.

The heat and pain had gone. She was in a world of green water full of shimmering sunbeams. A figure darted out of a thicket of sea kelp and waved to her. Granfer Joshua? Wasn't he supposed to be long dead – not young and laughing, with a fin tail instead of feet and legs? Why was he here, swimming with her in the sea? Granfer Josh waved again, beaming delightedly. She realised he wasn't looking at her, but past her, at someone behind. She turned: Bee was there! She too had a fin tail instead of legs.

Laughing, Bee swam up, and gave her a hug. Then, with a flick of her tail, she shot off.

'Bye, sis. Love you!' she called, blowing her a kiss, silvery bubbles rising from her mouth. Diving into the seaweed forest after Granfer Josh, fish tails gleaming, they disappeared.

Was this dying, Bird wondered? If it was, it didn't seem too bad. Pushing through the water with her arms and legs, she tried to follow them, but the sea world faded.

She was flying in a cloudless, brilliant sky. She could see Fin on an island far below, sitting on the edge of a dark tarn. Rising and falling on the wind, she called down to him, her voice trilling like a lark:

'I love you Fin! I love you Fin!' she sang.

Looking up, he grinned.

Fin and sky disappeared. Now she was floating in a thick clear liquid. Looking down at herself, she found she had a different body, a lovely, pearly-skinned, naked body. Putting out her hands to feel around, she came upon a translucent surface that sprang back like elastic. Frantically swimming about, she felt over the surface searching for an opening: there was none – she was trapped inside some sort of bubble.

'Fin, Fin, where are you? Come and rescue me!' she screamed.

Pressing her face against the elastic surface, she made out a large gloomy room, pale light filtering in through wide windows. Closer to, she saw the bubble she was in was hanging from a beam in the dark roof. Either side of her were more bubbles with moving figures inside, their bodies pearly pink, like hers.

Hearing muffled howling sounds, she looked down. Below her large cages stood on tables. Inside the one directly beneath her, she saw what she took to be a tabby cat, striped grey and yellow, but bigger than any cat she'd ever seen – almost the size of a tiger. It was pressing against the cage bars and yowling in terror. To her horror, when it turned its face upwards, she saw that its eye sockets were empty.

At the far end of the room, an enormous eagle was flapping its wings, its cruel yellow talons gripping a perch the size of a tree trunk, pecking futilely with its hooked beak at the chain attached to its leg.

Lifting its great head, it let out a mournful cry: 'SKEEW! SKEEW!' It too was blind, its eye sockets empty.

What kind of hell she had come to? Panic seized her, making her head spin.

'Fin! Fin! Please hurry – I don't want to die here!' she whimpered, beating her fists uselessly against the stretchy wall. There was no answer: he couldn't hear, her voice was too tiny.

Suddenly a giant lens-eye filled her view, quickly replaced by a grinning razor mouth, then a Frit's metal fingers enveloped her bubble. The liquid around her sloshed wildly, squeezing her lungs.

'Fin, I can't breathe…' she sobbed.

Glimpsing between the Frit's fingers, she saw she was being carried towards the eagle. One of the eagle's eye sockets loomed very close. With a sickening, sucking sound, suddenly she was in darkness, the bubble walls squashing in on her.

'Where am I? I don't know where I am—' she screamed, blindly flailing about in the swirling liquid.

'SKEEW! SKEEW! Hush! Hush! Do not let them hear you!' The shrieking voice close to her ear, nearly deafened her.

One side of the bubble cleared, and she could see out, clearly now as if the outer surface had been wiped clean. The liquid around her settled.

On the edge of a scream again, she called out: 'Who are you? Get me out of here!'

'Skeew! Skeew!' came a low cry.

She realised it was the eagle calling, softly now, reassuring her. 'You are safe now, in my eye socket. They will not send your little soul to be eaten by the Slug.'

'What slug? I don't want to be eaten by anything! Who are you?'

'I am Quilla. We must be friends. You are my eyes now! You will help me to see, so we can fly away from this evil place. Skeew! Skeew!' he called again softly.

'I don't want to be your eyes! I want to get out of here! Please let me out! Please! Please! I want to go home. My sister's dead and I want to tell mum and dad she's with Granfer Josh…'

'Skeew. Skeew.' The eagle cooed. 'Child, you must not leave your pod. It is keeping your soul safe – you must stay there until you are reunited with your body, otherwise your body will die.'

Bird looked down at her body, running a hand over her silky pink skin. 'But I can't get into my proper body!' she wailed. 'It got all burnt by the disgusting Phragg that brought me here!'

She felt a judder as the eagle's wings flapped impatiently.

'Then I do not know how you can come alive again if your body is dead. All I know is, from the time I have been imprisoned in this loathsome place, when a soul is stolen, they are put into a pod, like you. Some are put into the eye sockets of blinded creatures, and some are given to the Slug to eat – she is particularly fond of cat – but the more fortunate ones like you, are put into the eyes of birds, the birds to be trained as spies for the devil who lives in the Fortress. At least they live—'

She felt the eagle shudder and her pod went dark as the eagle closed his eyelids.

Floating in the blackness, thinking about what the eagle had said, she sensed Fin was nearby.

'Don't give up on me Fin!' she sobbed quietly.

'I know, my love, I know! Just tell me where you are!' Joy washed over her – he could hear her!

'In a big shed! Look for the blind eagle. Hurry!'

Fin's reply was drowned by squawks of terror from the eagle. 'SKEEW! SKEEW!'

Quilla's eyelids opened as his body lurched sideways.

'What's happening? Eagle! Quilla!'

'Shed moving! Water! Water rushing in! We shall be drowned.'

His body heaved up and down. The liquid around her swirled. To the sound of muffled screams, she saw cages crashing out of sight as tables fell over. With another violent lurch, her liquid world sloshed around again, making her dizzy. The eagle's legs were above her. His talons still gripping the perch, with frantic wing beats, he righted himself. Gradually her view settled, wobbling as the eagle shook out his wet feathers.

Below her she saw cages floating in the rising water; some with creatures still trapped inside, whilst others, their cage bars broken open, their occupants had managed to escape, and several bobbing heads were swimming towards an open door.

Suddenly, an open window close by filled with movement: over the sill came long legs, followed by a giant body, then giant shoulders and arms. After that, a huge, lovely, familiar face.

Pressing against the bubble wall, she shouted as loud as she could. 'FIN! I'M HERE! IN THE EAGLE'S EYE!'

Fin swung in through the window. Gripping the window ledge, he sat for a moment taking in the chaotic scene. As the shed rocked, tables and cages crashed about, some with terrified animals and birds still trapped inside. Creatures that had escaped were swimming for the doorway, their howls adding to Maabella's shrieking outside. Beneath his feet, a weakly scrabbling cat, eye sockets empty, reminded him of the blind tiger he and Lark had encountered on the path by the long black lake. In the dark roof space, a network of sinuous tubes ran the length of the shed with fleshy lip-like fixings dangling from them. Between the tubes hung strings of balloon-shaped objects. They were glowing softly. Was that what Bird meant when she said she was being squashed, he wondered? Could her soul be trapped in one of those? When he'd sneaked a look in Mossy's hidden book about Contagion, in the description of the Treatment Shed there'd been something about souls being sucked out of bodies and stored in pods ready to feed to Maabella who drew strength from the stolen living spirits. If Bird's soul was inside one of those pods, she must be minute!

At that moment he heard Bird call out. 'Fin! I'm here! In the…' The rest was lost in the uproar. He must act, now!

Dropping onto a table floating past, he wobbled wildly. As he grabbed the wall to steady himself, Mick slipped from inside his jerkin and doggy-paddled to the safety of a nearby floating bench.

Crouching on his half-submerged table, Fin looked about in despair: where was Bird in all this mess? Not knowing what a soul looked like, he had no idea what to look for.

Sliding off the table, he waded to a bench beneath the strange containers and climbed up to peer into one. Swimming about in a clear fluid was a tiny, pearly creature. Reaching up, he shook the ball: a tiny rodent face pressed up against the skin. Examining several more pods, he saw some contained human shapes. His heart leapt when he saw one that might be a Delphin, but the tiny person pressing his face against the membrane looked more like his Uncle Roach. Full of hope, he edged along the floating bench, peering into more pods.

Bird called again, her voice now so tantalizing close. 'Fin, I'm not there! I'm over here – in the eagle's eye!'

She'd said something about an eagle before. He searched about helplessly. In the shadows at the far end, the bedraggled bodies of birds hung in the murky water by chains from perches. He recognized a goshawk, a tawny owl, and what in life could have been a vulture.

Mick was standing on a broken cage, his front paws on the drowned vulture. Ears pointed forward, tail wagging furiously, he was barking excitedly at an eagle with sodden feathers, crouching miserably on a perch above him.

Fin splashed over. 'Good lad Mick,' he exclaimed, patting his head.

Like the other creatures, one of the eagle's eye sockets was empty, but in the other something gleamed: it looked like one of the pods hanging from the roof. Heart racing, he spotted behind the semi-transparent film, a tiny shimmering figure dancing about. A face pressed against the elastic skin: it was Bird's face.

'I can see you, Fin! I can see you!' came her muffled cry.

Horror-struck, he saw her body was the size of a tadpole. How was he going get her out of there? She looked so fragile!

'Oh, Bird, what I should I do?' he whimpered. Braving the eagle's stabbing beak and slashing talons, he reached up to its eye socket.

Held by the chain around its leg, the great bird lunged away. 'SKEEW! SKEEW!' it shrieked.

'No! no! You mustn't take the pod from his eye – you'll kill me!' Bird screamed.

'Bird, I can't leave you in there! The eagle's going to be drowned, along with everything else in this place.'

'He says— he says—'

Shielding himself from the eagle's wings beating on his face, Fin leaned closer, trying to hear her small voice. 'You must free him, so he can fly.'

Casting about for something he could use to break the chain, he wished he had Lark's axe. The water was nearly up to his chest and rising steadily: if he didn't hurry the eagle would drown, taking Bird with it. In a fury of desperation, he wrenched savagely at the perch. The rotten wood fell to bits in his hands. Free of the perch the eagle flapped to the roof, thumping its head on a beam. Catching hold of the chain dangling from its leg, Fin guided it to land on his shoulder, wincing as the talons dug through his jerkin. Keeping tight hold of the chain, Mick tucked under his arm, he waded waist deep through the mayhem of crashing cages, tables, and desperate animals. Reaching the door, he fell through into deep water. Losing hold of Mick, the little dog's brown and white head disappeared beneath the filth, then bobbed up nearby. As Fin lunged for him, Mick disappeared again. The eagle's chain in one hand, frenziedly feeling about beneath the water with the other, all he brought up were slimy lumps of unrecognisable body parts. Ducking beneath the surface, the water was too murky to see anything. Coming up choking out water, he continued his frantic scrabbling, but his fingers rapidly grew numb and useless.

He gave up: he had to accept that Mick was drowned. 'Lark, I'm sorry...' he gurgled, spitting out vile tasting mud. Grief stricken and exhausted, misery crushed him. Knees buckling, he began to sink into the water. The eagle tugged violently at the chain, pulling him up.

Bird's voice called to him. 'Quilla says let go of the chain, so he can fly to somewhere safe!'

'I can't, Bird. I'll lose you if I do!' he wailed. 'Tell him you want to stay close to me!'

'Fin, he'll drown if he can't fly! I'll drown with him, and so will you! You must let him go, so I can guide him – I'll make sure we keep you in sight!'

Hope draining away, he nodded resignedly. Hampered by the eagle's wings flapping in his face, laboriously doggy paddling, he made his way to a nearby pillar of rock where bits of broken shed and tangled bodies had snagged around it to form a small island. Clambering on to a shed door, he let go of the chain. Unhooking its claws from his jerkin, the eagle rose ponderously into the air. Its wings stiff from lack of use, it hovered for a moment, gaining strength. Inside its left eye socket Fin could see the pale gleam of Bird's pod. Fighting a longing to grab back the chain, he half raised his arm, but let it drop.

Flapping clumsily, rising higher, the eagle landed on the crumbling ramparts of Gressil's fortress, then flew to the top of a wrecked tower. Head held proud, it stretched its wings wide. Incongruously Fin recalled a picture of an Eagle Standard he'd seen in one of Mossy's books about Roman history.

With a joyful cry, 'SKEEW! SKEEW!' the eagle soared gracefully into the sky. Moments later, all Fin could see was a black dot against the grey clouds.

Taking in a long, deep breath, he cried out as loud as his lungs would let him: 'I LOVE YOU BIRD!'

There was no reply.

Despair overwhelmed him. He'd failed in everything: he hadn't passed the Chi Rho into safe hands, he hadn't brought Bird and Bee home, he hadn't killed Queen Mab, and he hadn't even saved Mick from drowning.

Crouched shivering on his shed door, he gazed miserably across the muddy water to where Queen Mab's grey mass squirmed and writhed. As he watched, her great slug body twisted back on itself, exposing her underbelly. Silhouetted against the pale flesh, he saw the gorilla dancing agitatedly. There was no sign of Lark.

Stumbling and slipping, every wading step perilous, the gorilla made his way through the water towards the slug. Sick with fear, Lark clung tight to his silver-furred back. Bodies floated by. Death was all around them. The foul stench grew stronger. Thrashing and screaming on her nest, Maabella's bulk grew closer, a loathsome shape, a horror beyond nightmare. The cross lay heavy on his jerkin; he knew he shouldn't be wearing it but feared to lose it in the water if he held it in his hand. Over and over, Mossy's words of warning dinned in his mind like a mantra: 'Never wear the Cross... Never wear the Cross...'

The gorilla rested for a moment, balancing on a flat boulder hidden beneath the water. Time was running out. The Berg was now so low the sea was lapping over the disintegrating ice. They would have to get a move on. He must kill her before she could swim away out to sea. Lark prodded the gorilla with his heel, and he waded on, reaching the base of the muddy slope leading to the Nest.

Maabella's swollen body was close enough now to see the pustules and clumps of short black spiky hairs scattered over her slimy grey skin. Her shrieking abated for a moment as she plunged her thick lips into the foul soup that was part of her food. Shuddering violently, from her other end poured a stream of white maggoty babies. Gagging on the released fumes, Lark looked up at the wound, bubbling out pus and blood, fifteen feet or so above his head.

The time had come. He, Lark Annunder a humble Delphin of Brightdale, must finish the job Prince Cadeyrn had begun. Where would he find the courage? Tissy's lavender-coloured eyes, full of trust, filled his inner sight. Terror fell away: this was for his Tissy.

A strange calm possessed him. Assessing his task, he wondered how he should slay the unnatural monster. Fescue had said something about using the cross. Lifting the chain over his neck, he placed the cross on his palm, and stared in wonder at the glittering jewels. Surely it was too beautiful, too wonderful, to use it as – as what? – a dagger? No! He just couldn't do that! No, the most certain way to kill Queen Mab was to stab her with his own trusty boning knife: plunge the long, keen blade deep into the foul wound.

Fumbling for his dagger with his free hand, his fingers froze: from behind the mountain of slug flesh rose a Phragg. Red eyes blazing, yellow-toothed maw gaping, the monster rushed towards him. Gibbering, the gorilla cowered away. A fire came into Lark's sea-washed eyes: he'd had his fill of those stinking clouds of evil. Slamming his boning knife back in its scabbard, balancing on the gorilla's broad shoulders, he stood tall and defiant.

'OH NO, YOU SCUM! You won't get the better of me!' he yelled. Holding the chain, he swung the cross at the white-hot heart: the Phragg, turning instantly to vapour, was carried away on the breeze. Half astonished, half triumphant at what he'd done, Lark dangled the cross before his eyes: the gold was unmarked, the jewels still glittered, the crystal as clear as it had always been. He hung the cross back round his neck, this time inside his jerkin against his shirt, careful not to let it touch his skin.

Climbing down from the gorilla's shoulders, he dropped into the waist deep sludge. Clinging to the ape's thick leg, as if dealing with Mick he gave its thigh a thump: 'Stay!' he commanded.

Gathering the tattered remnants of his courage, and taking a deep breath, he set off to climb the Nest.

Reaching the wall of flesh, his figure tiny against the mountainous slug, he planned his route up to the wound. As he pulled himself up by a bunch of the short black hairs, a stinging pain struck his chest: the cross had slipped inside his shirt.

A voice boomed hollowly in his swirling head: 'LARK ANNUNDER – DO NOT WEAR THE CROSS!'

'I know! Mr Mossy, I know!' he whimpered, dropping back down onto the mud, 'don't go on so! Yer expecting too much from a mere Delphin lad from the Dale.'

Tears blinding him, he pulled the cross and chain from around his neck. What could he do? For a start, he couldn't climb and hold onto it. On impulse, he clamped it between his teeth. Once more taking hold of a bunch of stiff spiky hairs, he started to climb, hand over hand, grabbing the hairs above him, feet on the bunches below. The gorilla watched, mouthing grunts of anxiety. When he reached the wound, fighting down nausea from the stink, gripping hairs with one hand, he drew his boning knife. Sucking in air between his teeth clenched around the cross, he raised his arm and, not giving himself time to think, plunged the blade deep into the bubbling wound, his forearm squelching into the rotting flesh. A spume of blood and pus squirted out, hitting his face. The huge body gave a great shudder. Twisting his knife deep within the wound, with his free hand he swiped the filth from his eyes.

Maabella's great bulk contorted, writhing in on itself. Her slimy underbelly rose before him. Feeling about with her fat pink tongue, blindly she searched him out. Her mouth puckered, and lunging down, her lips latched onto his face. Smothering blackness enveloped him. Her tongue filled his mouth, curling around the cross, sucking it from between his teeth. His boning knife slipped out of the wound. Still clutching the handle, he lost his foothold and tumbled down into the Nest. The foul body crushing him, squashing his face into suffocating filth, as life slipped away, Lark grinned to himself: what a way to die! Tissy would never believe…

A strong hand gripped his leg and heaved. Blessed air, wonderful, stinking, life-giving air filled his lungs. He opened his eyes and gazed into the gorilla's distressed face. Slinging Lark over his shoulder, the powerful animal half fell, half jumped into the water, and started to swim away.

From his floating shed door, Fin stared across the water in disbelief as Maabella contorted herself. He spotted, through the miasma surrounding her nest, the gorilla outlined against the pale body, leaping up and down, long arms waving wildly. Something odd was going on. Maabella's wails and screams had changed to faltering moans, sounding ever weaker.

The moaning stopped. An eerie silence fell, as if the world were holding its breath: no screeching, no screaming, even the roars of melt water, the Berg's death throes, seemed stilled. The ghostly vapour around the Nest thinned, leaving a few drifting green wisps. Now he could see clearly. The great slug stretched out on the rapidly sinking Nest, seemed to be shrinking, shrivelling in on itself, the slimy flesh turning dry and wrinkled like leathery parchment. A shape was emerging, bulging out of the taut stretching skin: Fin thought of the pupa of a butterfly.

The papery skin crackled and split: a head appeared. As the split lengthened, a moist, velvet fur-covered slender body slithered out – a woman's perfect body, marred only by a gash in her side seeping blood – the Chi Rho had failed to heal Queen Mab's wound.

Writhing sensuously on the remains of the nest, the velvety arms rose and fell, the long legs flexed. Slowly the figure stood. From her back, sagged crumpled damp wings. Opening to dry in the breeze and watery sunshine, they smoothed out, to reveal swirls and roundels of peacock-blue, icy turquoise, pansy-brown, mustard, silver and scarlet. When the wings had opened to their full width, their multicoloured hues shimmering ever more brilliantly, she made a few tentative beats. Suddenly she hesitated. Looking down, she lightly touched the wound in her left side just below her heart and bowing her head, for a moment her shoulders drooped. Then, the wonderful freedom of release from her vile slug body giving her new courage, she rose a little way into the air and pirouetted about, testing her lovely body in slow voluptuous movements. A flash of gold caught Fin's eye. He cried out in anguish: on her breast lay the Chi Rho. She heard him. Spinning around, she gazed across provocatively.

'Lovely boy am I not beautiful?' she trilled mockingly. 'Shall I give you a kiss?'

Confident now of the strength of her wings, she fluttered across the water. Twisting and turning coquettishly, she floated just above him. Reaching down, she took his chin in her hands, and pouting her luscious ruby lips, planted a fierce kiss on his mouth. Ecstasy coursed through Fin: he forgot Bird, he forgot Lark, he forgot everything, all he wanted was for this wonderful being to keep kissing him for ever. Unbidden, his hand slid inside his shirt to where his mother's gold coin lay inside his purse. Feeling the coin through the soft leather, he came to his senses. With angry disgust, he swiped the grotesque lips from his mouth.

Laughing scornfully, she leant forward once more to latch her lips on to his. Heavy gold brushed his face. He snatched at the cross and tugged hard: the thick chain did not break.

'Wicked boy! How dare you!' she shrieked, slapping him viciously across his mouth.

Rising, she kicked out at him, hitting his face with her dainty foot. Wobbling wildly, he caught hold of the edge of a wing, tearing a rent.

Screaming with rage, she rose higher and glared down at him. 'Evil boy, you shall be punished for that!' she spat.

Turning about she faced the sea. Enormous butterfly wings at first beating laboriously, holding a hand over her wound, she gathered speed. The butterfly form grew smaller, soon turning to a distant dot, faded into the grey horizon. Fin fell to his knees, his body racked by sobs.

A hand gripped his shoulder. 'Well, that's it, Fin: we've made a right warty wemmer's bum of the whole enterprise.'

Lark, caked in grey slime, was crouched beside him on the shed door. The gorilla sat nearby, his expression striving for understanding as he searched their faces.

Lark gazed around at the devastation: Gressil's Fortress reduced to a ruin, towers toppled, walls crumbled; what could be seen of the Snooper's Nest looked like a dirty wet bath sponge. There was no trace of the treatment shed or Mab's nest.

He frowned. 'Fin, where's Mick?'

'I'm s – so sorry, Lark—'

Tears glittered in Lark's pale eyes. Wiping them away, his slime-coated sleeve left a snotty smear across his cheeks. He heaved a shuddering sigh.

'Not even a bit of fur to bury next to Dinah?'

Fin shook his head.

'Fin Dandrum, you can't be trusted with anything!'

'Nor can you, Lark Annunder! You let that disgusting butterfly pinch my cross!'

Deeply distressed, the gorilla whimpered and moving closer began stroking the tops of their heads.

'Sorry Lark,' Fin muttered.

'It's O.K. Just have get have to get used to not having Mick around.' Lark couldn't find words to ask Fin about Bird.

They were startled by a superior-sounding sniff. Below them, a small, mud-covered creature sat on a floating roof beam. They gasped and grinned. The gorilla squinted at the object, mystified.

'So, you've decided to turn up, have you, yer little bum boil?' Lark growled.

The bum boil held up a wriggling body by the tail: a hoarse yap of indignation came from it.

'Grass-top don't deserve Crow save mutt – he gives Mab my jool!'

'Mick!' yelped Lark, reaching down to grab him. 'Where've yer been little lad, where've yer been!' He giggled idiotically as Mick's tongue slavered over his face.

Climbing up on to the door, Crow slumped next to them in a dejected heap.

'I not find Sparkie – Aunty Krite bible bag gone, deep down, deep down, in wet,' he sobbed.

Apart from his filthy loincloth he was naked, a layer of mud covering several nasty looking cuts on his bony chest.

'Never mind, little mucky tyke,' Lark said, patting Crow's thin shoulder. 'I'll find you another Sparkie – maybe a huge Sparkie, all glossy furred and feisty. Or better still, you can have one of my kit ferrets!'

Crow's one eye glowered at him. 'Ferrets disgusting! Any road, who our new giant chum? Looks dangerous!'

He inched away as the gorilla, peering at him in profound curiosity, dabbed with a thick finger at the tears on Crow's cheek.

'He's O.K. He saved us from drowning,' Fin said. 'Where've you been lurking Crow – whilst we've been fighting monsters, eh? I notice you kept well out of the way!'

Crow squeaked with indignation. 'Didn't I tell you grass-top not bring jool here! I warned, but no, you brung it here! How will Crow get it back now! Flutterby take it far, far away....'

He pointed a trembling finger at the horizon and gave a howl so loud it seemed impossible that such small lungs could produce such a sound.

As if in sympathy, the last remnant of the Berg gave a rumbling groan as it broke from the land and floated away. The Compound was now an inlet of the sea.

Hugging Mick tight in his arms, Lark looked worriedly at the rising water. 'Any ideas what we should do now?' he asked. 'It seems to me we're goners – going to drown and our bodies float out to sea – which is right and proper for a Delphin. And there I was, only a few days ago, hoping Tissy and me would…'

His voice trailed off as he gazed miserably at the body of a Frit floating past. Noticing something glittering jammed on its head, he leaned down to grab it, bringing up a sodden piece of cloth covered in bedraggled feathers and wire hooks: it was his fishing hat. Putting it on, it sat limply, dripping water into his eyes.

Fin searched the empty sky, hoping to see the eagle. A beam from the setting sun, flashing across the grey surface of the sea, lit his face for a second. A freshening wind whipped up white crested waves, racing through the gap between the hills where the Berg once stood. He wondered if one of these could be the wave that would drown them.

Rocking their flimsy refuge, he suddenly stood up, shading his eyes, and stared into the horizon.

'Is that a sail?' he whispered, hardly daring to breathe as he gripped Lark's shoulder.

A white dot had appeared where the clouds met the sea. The dot became a billowing sail, running before the wind. A sleek yacht took shape, almost flying on the creamy foam. They watched, transfixed, as it drew closer. Moments later the boat was gliding past the ice floes, into the inlet that had, so little time before been the nightmare of Gressil's Compound.

As recognition dawned, Fin couldn't hold back a sob of pure joy. Overcome with relief, Lark giggled manically.

Outlined against the setting sun, a tall figure stood in the prow, his ebony features recognisable even in shadow, his inky blue garments floating in the breeze.

In the stern, tiller in hand, sat another familiar figure, plaited red-gold hair streaming behind him. Swinging the tiller about, Iskander brought the boat alongside their makeshift island.

A third figure, helmet flapping, leaned across to grab a length of door frame.

'Climb aboard, lads!' called Wings, balancing on one leg.

Grasping his outheld hand, Fin scrambled over the gunwale onto the deck and rushed to Mossy's open arms. Crushed to his chest, the honey-sweet smell of his inky blue robe sent his mind spinning back to the sunlit fells above Watersmeet.

Lark, tears of joy streaming down his filthy cheeks, scooped up Mick, threw him over to Wings, and clumsily jumping, landed face down on the rocking deck. Staggering to his feet, he saw Crow in the water scrabbling frantically at the boat's smooth planks. Grabbing his plustic loin cloth, he heaved him up on to the deck. Making encouraging grunting noises and gestures, he coaxed the gorilla to climb on board just as their makeshift raft sunk beneath the waves.

Swinging the tiller about, Sandy set course for the open sea.

# 24
# ORCA

Sailing down the coast for an hour, they dropped anchor for the night in what, to Fin and Lark's surprise, Sandy said was a Boskie fishing harbour.

As the yacht sailed, they had stripped off their sodden, filthy clothes and cleaned themselves up as best they could with buckets of seawater. Mossy had found them some seafarer's clothes in a locker – overlarge, faintly fishy-smelling, but clean and dry.

The yacht swinging gently at its mooring in the sheltered estuary, they settled below decks on bunks in the narrow cabin: Crow and the gorilla with Mossy and Wings on one bunk. Sandy, Fin and Lark, with Mick heavily asleep on his lap, on the other. Lights could be seen through the porthole, winking from the Boskie village. Sipping tots of Boskie distilled sloe gin, too tired to eat or talk, Fin and Lark gazed at Mossy as if they couldn't quite believe he was real and not a ghost.

The warmth of the fiery spirit starting to course through his veins, Fin at last found the courage to begin the story of their adventures, starting with their journey to the great lake.

He was in the middle of telling how they were captured by the Boskies, when Crow fell asleep. Slumped against the snoring gorilla, mouth open, gin dripping down his fisherman's sweater, he'd been too distraught to tell them what had happened to the bible bag, his chain mail jerkin and small pack.

Emotionally drained, Lark too succumbed to the warmth of the gin. Listening to Fin telling them about the feast at the Boskie village, the sound of his voice faded and for Lark, everything went blank.

Next day, as the sun rose above the hills behind the harbour, weighing anchor, Sandy set a course for open sea. They were bound for the Island of Mann, where decisions would have to be made and plans laid.

The boat's movement woke Fin from a dreamless sleep. Flinging off his blanket and rolling up his over-long trousers and his thick sweater's sleeves, he clambered up the ladder to the deck. The yacht, speeding merrily through the waves, the sail billowing and snapping above his head, the fresh wind in his face brought him fully awake. Either side of the boat, chunks of ice and debris from the Great Berg swept past, and beyond the stern he saw the outline of coastal cliffs.

Wings was steering, occasionally resting a hand on his bandaged stump. The gorilla, perched on a barrel next to him chewing a carrot, watched fascinated as Wings twitched the tiller, to left to right.

Lark and Mick stuck their heads out through the cabin hatchway, ducking as the boom swung above them. Briefly retreating into the cabin, Lark emerged, also in seafarer's trousers and sweater, legs and sleeves ingeniously shortened with bulky knots.

'Skeew! Skeew!' To his joy, Fin saw the eagle, swooping and diving beneath the white clouds, wide wings flashing gold and rust in the rising sun.

'Skeew! Skeew!' There was a jubilant note in the call.

Waving his arms high and wide, the eagle flew lower.

'BIRD! Can you see me!' he shouted.

'You're the size of a shrimp!' came Bird's faint voice.

'Tell the eagle to come down so we can get the chain off his leg.'

For a moment, the eagle hesitated, before swooping down to perch on the cabin roof.

With a hacksaw Lark had found in the boat's toolbox, Fin set about cutting away the chain. All too aware of the eagle's vicious beak inches from his head, after a few minutes careful sawing, the chain – the last remnant of the horror of Contagion – fell away and was tossed overboard by Lark.

'Quilla says he's hungry – going hunting – back later—' Bird's voice faded as the great bird rose into the air and streaked towards the distant shore, its dark form soon blending into the grey cliffs.

'Lark, Fin, come and get your breakfast!' called Sandy, waving a greasy-looking paper packet from where he and Mossy sat in the prow on a bundle of fishing nets.

Collapsing beside them on the nets, they eagerly took the thickly sliced bread filled with smoked herring. These sandwiches, they learned, had been provided by the Boskies at Haverigg. Mick, having already demolished several whilst they removed Quilla's chain, settled on Lark's lap.

Lark suddenly gave a cry of delight. Two mud-caked objects leant against the mast: their rucksacks.

Hearing Lark's shout, Crow poked his head out of the cabin, and watched resentfully as Fin and Lark delved inside, finding everything filthy and waterlogged.

'Look at this vest!' Lark exclaimed, holding up a limp brown piece of cloth. 'Never get that white again!'

Sandy explained that he'd spotted the rucksacks floating on a large chunk of ice as they headed out of the harbour.

'When we reach Mann, we'll see what we can salvage,' Fin said, delving down, feeling the hard outline of the pearl scabbard and the broken Dandrum sword still wrapped in his sodden shirt. With a pang, he remembered the blade had never been mended as Fox and Snap had planned. Yesterday, he'd found Sandy's sword, miraculously still tucked inside his belt. Resolved never to use a sword again, he had firmly returned it to Sandy, despite his protests.

Leaving their rucksacks to drain, Fin and Lark returned to the last of the sandwiches. Finally, Fin turned to Mossy.

'Mossy, what happened, when – when you and Wings crashed?'

For a moment Mossy stared bleakly out across the grey ice strewn sea. Fin saw he had a faded look which he'd not noticed before.

Mossy began his story. 'It was dark when we flew from Watersmeet. With my extra weight, Skyhook struggled to take off. Skimming the treetops, we had been going a short while when, from behind us, came the sinister buzz of Snoopers: a squadron of least twenty. Wings did his best to avoid the shower of stings, tipping Skyhook on her side, so her underbelly took the majority, peppering her like a pincushion—— but her prop caught on a high branch, dragging–
—' He choked on his words.

Fin looked at him in dismay. Was an angel supposed to be so vulnerable? Surely not.

Stretching his arm across the Delphins' heads, Sandy squeezed Mossy's shoulder. 'Tell them another time, Zagzagel?'

Mossy shook his head firmly.

'No, let us get this over with! When we crashed, I was not seriously hurt, just momentarily stunned. Crow was still in his seat where I had tied him – from his twitching I knew he was alive. I couldn't see Wings – his seat was empty – I found him not far away. He was not moving – a dark blood stain spread around his left leg.'

Fin and Lark looked across at Wings in the stern; they saw how thin he'd become, the lines around his eyes etched even more deeply than before.

Mossy continued. 'If Wings were not to die, I knew I must get help quickly. Carrying him over my shoulder, with Crow stumbling behind me clinging to my clothes, I struggled on in the dark, hoping to reach Durholm. But in my stunned state I found it hard to think coherently, becoming more and more alarmed for Wings, who was losing so much blood. In the end exhaustion overcame me and I passed out. When I came to, Crow had gone – I could not leave Wings and go in search of him.

A little sniffling sob made them start: Crow had sidled close to listen.

'Just like you, yer bum boil, abandoning Mr Mossy!' Lark growled at him.

Crow squealed indignantly. 'Nasty Boskie took me – ketched me tight! Rough twiggy fingers biting me skin – lost breathings – near deaded, I was!' He crept back down into the cabin, from where they heard him howling: 'Where's jool – want jool – flutterby needs catching!'

Mossy shivered as if a fever had gripped him. 'Crow is referring to being found by the Boskies. From him they learned what had happened. It was he who guided them to Wings and me, and after a long struggle, we staunched Wings' bleeding.

'Desperately worried not only for Wings but for Bird and Bee, I asked if they could help me reach Durholm, and was horrified when they told me we were miles away! During the night, in my dazed condition, I had been going in the opposite direction – south!

'Wings being so seriously injured, they would not take him on the long journey to Durholm. They told me that they were the Fisher Boskies, and their village was about a day's walk away – on the coast, south of Contagion.'

Fin interrupted: 'So, these Boskies weren't the ones from Withered Wood – not related to Aspen, Oak and Ilex?'

'Not directly related. Fisher Boskies live on the coast, south of Withered Wood, in a place called Haverigg – where we moored last night. It is many years since I last heard of them. Indeed, I did not know there were some living so near Contagion!'

Lark frowned in puzzlement. 'But how come old Midori and Llinos had Wings' goggles? They showed them to us – all bloody they were!'

Mossy nodded. 'Yes, the Fisher Boskies told me that their Withered Wood cousins had found Skyhook's wreckage.

'It was whilst we waited for Wings to recover enough for the journey to the Boskie village, I managed to persuade one of them to take Crow to Holy Island – he kept wailing for Brother Huw, wanting his 'brother' to take care of him. I hoped the Boskie could explain to Mother Hilda what had happened.'

Lark turned to Sandy. 'But how come you're here, Mr Sandy? Though I'm mighty glad you are, what with your sailing skills!'

Sandy grinned and ruffled Lark's hair, still patched with crusty mud.

'Well, it's a muddled story! After leaving you and Fin on Cuthbert's Island, as you know, I went to Holy Island where Mother Hilda told me of the arrival of the Boskie with Crow. Not understanding Boskie language, Hilda gleaned only a vague notion what had happened. From the Boskie's sign language, she understood that Crow had fallen from a great height. She learned a little more later from Crow, who told her a wild, hysterical story about a black giant, covered in blood, dragging him through the forest.

'But how come Crow was back living with my mother?' Fin asked.

'That was Brother Huw's idea. Crow was so traumatized by his experiences, old Huw couldn't cope! He thought Miryam would be much better able to heal him.

'By the time I arrived on Holy Island, the Boskie who brought Crow had returned to the mainland forest, which was unfortunate. Knowing a smattering of the Boskie tongue I could have learned what had happened, and even found out where Wings and Mossy were. I decided, straight away, to go in search of that Boskie. But it was three days before I found him.'

It was Lark's turn to interrupt: 'Three days from when you left Holy Island? I reckon Fin and I were probably looking down into Contagion from Shap!'

Sandy nodded. 'You can imagine my relief when, catching up with the Boskie, he took me to Haverigg, where I found Mossy and Wings safe in the care of the Fisher Boskies. With much pleading, I managed to persuade one of them to take a note to Brightdale. I hoped Kenji and Dancer had reached there, having set out with Bird and little Bee's body the day we sailed from Florain. Whether the Boskie ever got there, we do not know.

'We hadn't been long in Haverigg when we realised something dramatic was happening to the north, where Contagion lay. Huge chunks of ice and debris of every kind were drifting into the estuary beyond the harbour. Mossy and I decided to investigate. We persuaded the Boskie fishermen to lend us this boat. Wings insisted on coming with us – he had made a remarkable recovery, thanks to Mossy's healing skills and the Boskies' nursing care, as well as his own strength of will. We set sail immediately, dreading what we might find.'

Fin looked up at the billowing sail. 'What kind of boat is this, Sandy? She's very fast in the water!'

'She's what's known as a cutter. Fore-and-aft rigged – makes for swift passage but tricky to handle – took a bit of getting used to, compared to my Puffin! Being Boskie-owned, they named her Twig!'

Lark sighed. 'I don't mind what type of boat she is. I'll never forget what a sight that was, seeing her, sailing towards us!'

Later that day, Crow, keeping a vigil at the boat's side, ever hopeful that he would spot his bible bag, suddenly let out a shriek. He saw it just ahead, lying on a dirty ice floe. Leaning out to grab it as it floated nearer, he nearly fell overboard. The gorilla bounded to his aid, holding on to the gunwale with one long arm and reaching out with his other, snatched it up as it floated past.

Inside, Crow found Sparkie's bedraggled body; he was still wearing the jewelled collar. Sandy organized a special ceremony of burial at sea. Wrapping the little corpse in a cloth, Crow insisted the collar should stay on. They watched reverently as, saying some appropriate words, Sandy dropped the bundle over the side.

Crow, tears streaming down his thin cheeks, sobbed: 'Ahmen. Alulla!'

The Island of Mann came in sight late afternoon, rising out of the grey sea, crowned by bare mountains, and fringed by rocky cliffs.

Quickly handing the helm to Sandy, Wings, grabbing anything he could for support, dragged himself to the gunwale, and gazed in dismay. The coves and inlets of his island home were piled high with filthy ice.

Calling to Sandy, he pointed to the south: 'We must make for Peel – on the west side!'

Swinging his tiller over, tacking sharply, Sandy set a new course for the southernmost tip of the island.

The sun was setting when they entered Peel harbour. Crowded with vessels, moored among the skiffs and corbels of the local fishing community were ocean-going ships, brigantines and tall-masted clippers. Rising above the roofs of the town, an imposing castle looked down on the harbour. Beyond the town could be glimpsed the corrugated iron roofs of the Engineers' workshops, their tall chimneys belching out black smoke.

They tied up among the fishing boats, and Wings eagerly grabbing his make-shift crutch, clambered ashore. Everyone hurried after him as he headed for the town. Halfway up the cobbled slipway, they were met by tall young man who halted and staring hard at Wings through pebble-lensed spectacles exclaimed: 'Wings? Is it really you?'

'Boff!' cried Wings, hobbling up and wrapping his arm around the young man's thin shoulders.

Three more people followed the young man, a middle aged man and woman, and a girl. All three greeted Wings with cries of delight.

'Whatever's happened to you!' exclaimed the man, eyeing Wings' empty trouser leg.

'Crashed! But I'm O.K. chaps. Never mind that: you must meet my friends.'

Introducing everyone he included Crow and the gorilla, who was doing his best to lurk unassumingly behind Sandy. Shaking their hands, his friends nervously eyed the gorilla, but Wings reassured them he was harmless by jovially ruffling the thick silver fur on the gorilla's back.

The young man now introduced himself and his companions. 'I'm known as The Boffin on account of my engine designing skills, but most people just call me Boff. And these are my parents, Vi and Ed Spanner, and my sister, Tabitha, better known as Tubs.' Like Boff, they all peered through thick spectacles.

Whilst introductions were taking place a crowd had gathered on the top of the harbour wall; word had got around that Wings had returned accompanied by a strange motley group: two warriors, three small people in grotesquely oversized clothing and a great ape. Uncomfortably aware of their curious audience, the Spanners invited the new arrivals to stay with them.

Going through the narrow streets, they took them to Peel Castle where they shared apartments with other families, all highly skilled Engineers. Taking them up a spiral staircase in one of the round turrets to where two bedrooms were kept for guests. It was decided that Mossy, Sandy and Wings would sleep in one bedroom and Fin, Lark, Crow and the gorilla in the other, so after dumping their rucksacks, supper being imminent, they went down to the Great Hall to meet the four other Engineering families, all very much like the Spanners.

Introductions over and everyone seated at a long table, supper was served: a rich meaty stew of Manx mutton with mountains of mashed potatoes and washed down with a heady brew of strong ale. A bowl of stew was placed under the table for Mick and being the first meat meal he'd eaten in days, he dived in eagerly.

Supper over, all gathered on benches around a fire blazing in the vast fireplace and Ed Spanner invited the visitors to recount their terrible experiences and what had happened in Contagion.

Mossy began. Carefully avoiding Fin and Lark's part in Gressil's downfall, he told a dramatic tale of the burning of the giant scorpion, the melting of the Great Berg, and the drowning of Gressil's Compound. Shaking their heads in wonder, everyone then turned to Wings, who described Skyhook crashing and the loss of his leg with such good humour there was a scattering of laughter among the tut-tutting and shocked dismay. Some of the more thoughtful, wanting more details, began sharply questioning Mossy and Wings, especially about the destruction the scorpion.

As the talk flowed, Fin, Lark and Crow found it harder and harder to keep awake. Taking pity, Vi Spanner took them to their bedroom, where she had made up the enormous four-poster bed with fresh linen and blankets. She had also set up a thick nest of straw in a corner for the gorilla who, clutching the remnants of a bunch of carrots, bedded down, huffing delightedly as he pulled the straw over his head. Mick sidled in beside him, full of left-over stew, and settled down to a good scratch.

In a bathroom next door, a giant tub was filled with hot water from the castle's ingenious plumbing system. Stripping off their fishermen's clothes, Fin and Lark gratefully plunged in, glad to wash off the last of the filth of Contagion. Then, tumbling between the crisp sheets, they fell instantly asleep. Crow, after a quick nervous dip in the soapy water, mournfully clutching his empty bible bag, crept in beside them. Restless at first, eventually he too fell asleep.

They awoke next day to find their rucksacks had been emptied. All the contents, including the broken Dandrum sword and pearl scabbard, the Boskie chisels, the Snooper's sting, even Lark's fishing-hook hat, had been carefully laid out to dry on rush mats. Their clothes were laid at the end of the bed, washed, dried and neatly folded, socks all fluffy, vests sparkling white, all courtesy of the Castle's hardworking electric laundry. (Laundry Tech is advanced on Mann – in the castle basement, two hard-working machines whoosh, rumble and gurgle night and day, the electricity produced from the power of a windfarm lying on the north side of the island.)

Happy to be back in their own clothes, they joined the others for breakfast in the Solarium, a sunny room with wide windows looking out over the battlements towards the sea. After Manx kippers and toast, they all went separate ways.

Ed took Mossy and Sandy to the Town Hall, to give the Mayor and other dignitaries a more detailed report of the melting of the Great Berg and the destruction of Gressil. The gorilla and Mick were taken by Tubs down to the docks on a foraging expedition as she'd heard a cargo of tropical fruits had arrived the day before from Florain.

Vi took Crow into her motherly care, applying ointment to the cuts he'd suffered at the hands of the Frit torturers in Gressil's larder. She found him a pair of small leather shorts, a woolly jumper and a striped navy and white T-shirt, as well as cotton underpants to replace the bit of plustic he'd worn as a loin cloth.

Fin and Lark went with Wings and Boff to their Engineering works.

Following them through the narrow streets, every now and then Fin glanced up at the sky, hoping to see Quilla: there was no sign of the great eagle. Before breakfast, he and Mossy had gone onto the castle ramparts, where they stood for a while searching the empty sky, before reluctantly joining the others.

At the Engineering works, tall gates led them into a wide yard stacked with piles of ironmongery around the high perimeter fence.

Lifting a tarpaulin, Boff exposed a jumble of wood, metal sheets, rubber tubes, chains, and wires.

Wings sighed wistfully. 'I intended this lot for a new machine – Skyhook Two! Now I'm back, I'll start working on her as soon as I can, making her bigger with a more powerful engine.'

Boff rubbed his hands eagerly. 'Yep, I've got ideas for several new features – longer wings, Perspex windows, better seating – perhaps a large prop in the nose.'

Wings rubbed his chin doubtfully. 'Won't be a VTOL, though – will need a runway.'

The two engineers discussed the design heatedly for a few moments before remembering that Fin and Lark were on a tour of the works.

For the next hour, Fin and Lark trailed behind Wings and The Boffin, through cavernous sheds filled with thumping, rattling machinery, trying to understand their enthusiastic explanations. Finally, they watched in awe as muscular workers, faces protected by masks and wearing thick leather aprons, wielding long hooked poles, dragged ingots of glowing molten metal from the mouth of a huge roaring furnace, sending them sliding on rollers to other workers who, sparks flying from the hammer blows, beat them into thin sheets. Shouting above the din, Wings told them proudly that the monster was the only blast furnace north of the Humber.

As they headed out, they passed a stack of rusting metal boxes piled in a dark corner. Boff shuddered. 'Old Tech. Not been used in hundreds of years – not since the Engineer who invented them was captured and taken across the Grey Sea, to Gressil's fortress where he was forced to design the Frits.'

'Even so, that type of robot tech is still being developed in other places,' Wings added keenly, 'mostly in the big towns in the south. One day, when my leg's fixed, we'll go there, and you can see for yourself!'

Fin and Lark gave him an encouraging grin.

Glad to be back in the fresh air, they saw Sandy striding towards them. To their amazement, Kenji was with him. Rushing up to him delightedly, Fin and Lark fired questions.

'Did you get to Brightdale safely? Is Bird O.K.? What did they think of Dancer?'

'One question at a time, lads,' Kenji laughed. 'Yes, we took Bird safely to Brightdale – Dancer is still there, looking after her. Once they got over her being a Skwid, she's proving a comfort to Mr and Mrs Spinner, what with little Bee—'A shadow passed across his face. 'Dancer has a special way with poor Bird's body, understands the odd outbursts. She's also become close friends with Tissy, which is good, don't you think?'

Fin nodded miserably, in his mind comparing Bird crouched on the cushions at Queen Ailis' tea table, to the flea-sized pearly body floating in the bubble.

'Did Dancer give Tissy my letter?' Lark asked anxiously.

'Aye, and Tissy's given me a letter for you! It's in my pack. I'll give it to you back at the castle.'

'Kenji, when did you get here?' Wings asked.

'This morning – the Boskie carrying Sandy's message reached Brightdale the day after Dancer and I arrived. What strange creatures Boskies are! He certainly caused a stir in Brightdale. Luckily, Mrs Annunder, who knows about them, was able to tell the Boskie that Sandy said in his letter that he must take me back to his village on the coast. We reached there early this morning, and immediately sailed here in his fishing boat.'

Kenji glanced down at Wings' empty trouser leg. 'Glad to see you're walking Wings! Not daunted, eh?' he gave the pilot a friendly punch on the shoulder.

Wings grinned. 'I'm planning an artificial leg – already got some ideas.'

'More talk later,' Sandy interrupted impatiently. 'Hurry now, we are to have a meeting – decisions must be taken, and plans laid! We are gathering in the Solarium where we had breakfast.'

As they walked back to the castle, Kenji told them more about when he and Dancer set out for Brightdale. They had left Florain the day after Fin, Lark and Sandy had sailed in Puffin for Cuthbert's Island. Dancer looked after Bird, and a pony carried Bee's coffin. Betony had wrapped Bee's body in shimmering sea-blue silk decorated with silver and mother-of-pearl bees designed by Mullein.

Walking beside Sandy, Fin thought of what Kenji had told them: Bird crouched, like a trapped wild animal, by the kitchen fire in Spinner Hall, and Bee's ashes scattered across the meadows down by the Bright. How on earth could it all be put right? He looked up at Sandy.

'I wish I knew where Mab has gone. I must get the cross back– it's, it's the only way— to put Bird back together again—'

Sandy laid a reassuring hand on his shoulder. 'Zagzagel and I have talked long about this matter. We believe Queen Mab will fly south, to warmer climes—'

'Then I must go after her! But how? I can't fly— Wings hasn't even made a start on his new machine!'

'I have thought about that,' Sandy said. 'We shall need an ocean-going vessel. Mann is an ideal place to find one! When our meeting is over, we will go down to the harbour and consult with the sailors.'

Fin's spirits lifted: what a comfort it was to have Sandy with him!

'Skeew! Skeew!'

To his joy, he heard the familiar call. Looking up he spotted the eagle swooping low out of the clouds. Bird's voice came faintly down to him: 'I can see you Fin!'

He waved madly. 'Tell Quilla to come down – there's to be a meeting in the castle!'

Hanging on the air for a moment, the great bird flew down and landed on one of the castle turrets.

Sitting around the table in the Solarium, for a while no one spoke, their thoughts troubled. Through the wide windows, Quilla could be seen perched on the nearby battlement, his golden feathers gleaming in the sunlight. Lark's face was buried in his letter from Tissy, already dog-eared from being endlessly read and re-read. Crow was crouched in a corner, scratching his chest underneath his new T-shirt and sweater.

His one eye tight shut, rocking rhythmically, he was hissing under his breath: 'Want jool – it hurt bad – bad – bad – need jool!'

The gorilla and Mick weren't there. Tubs had taken them to a sandy cove on the other side of the harbour, to 'throw sticks' for Mick, and find a special iron-rich seaweed to make a tonic for the gorilla. 'To build up his muscles and get his skin healthy,' she had explained.

Watching Mossy, head bowed, wooden rosary beads running through his long brown fingers, Fin broke the silence. 'Mossy, I don't understand how the Chi Rho can save Bird. Is it the Splinter that will save her? The blood-soaked chip from the cross on which they crucified the Man-God? I saw Fescue prising a piece off!'

Noticing the others giving him a sharp look of surprise, he muttered. 'It was a strange dream I had: a man nailed to a cross and Fescue chipping at the blood-soaked wood with his golden dagger.'

Mossy's fingers stopped working his beads. Tucking the rosary away, he got up and began pacing the room, talking more to himself than his mystified companions. 'Fin is right! It is the Holy Splinter beneath the great crystal that heals, not the gold nor the jewels – yes, the splinter soaked in sacred blood must rise again. First buried with little Bird, and then up, up, to New Life!'

Seeing their mystified faces, Mossy attempted to explain. 'That is what Christian Baptism is… going down into water and rising to New Life… Bird's body and her soul must go down into healing water with the Splinter … to rise whole, body and soul joined once more.

'There is a place – The Pool of Siloam – far, far from here, in the City of Jerusalem – where Bird's soul and her body and the Chi Rho must be plunged together. It is there you must go with the eagle and Bird's soul. It will not be easy – the task will depend on getting the cross back, and whether Bird's soul can reach Jerusalem before it fades – and of course, her body must be brought there too! Which is where Dancer and Thetis will come in – they will have to take her body there. Wings – you must make haste to build the new Skyhook and fly them from Brightdale!'

'No problem there, Zag! Boff and I have already begun drawing up plans. With the Engineers' help and a lot of hard work, we'll soon get Skyhook Two built.

'But just as important, we'll need a map to show the way!' Eyes sparkling with excitement, he hobbled to a chest against the wall and flinging the lid open, took out a tightly folded wad of parchment.

Spreading it out on the table, he said: 'This map was drawn after the Great Dying and very old. The Gaiakins brought it with them when they abandoned their Garden in Africa and came to Florain – getting on for a thousand years ago. It's been on the Isle of Mann for years! How we came by it I've never learned. As you see, the chaps who acquired the map have marked the changes after the humans all but died out.'

All gathering around, they studied the ancient parchment. Cracked along the folds, stained with damp, and marked with inky fingerprints, it showed all the world. The continents and countries were marked with the old names: Russia, Asia and China in the East, Africa, the Middle East, and Europe in the centre, and across the ocean, North and South America, with

Australasia to the South. Some unknown map maker had added drawings to show physical features: deserts, mountains, rivers and lakes, coastlines with cliffs and beaches, huge tracts of forest, grown up over the thousand years since the Great Dying. Inland regions, sparsely inhabited, were dotted with miniature sketches of castles surrounded by towns and villages, with farmlands beyond. Jungles were indicated by delicately drawn wild animals: lions, elephants, and monkeys swinging among trees. On the seas, sharks swam, dolphins leaped, and octopus waved their tentacles.

Jabbing at a drawing on the African continent, Mossy explained. 'The Gaiakins first made their jungle garden there, at the source of the River Gambia where it rises on the Fouta Djallon plateau. It is there that Queen Mab will go with the cross, for it is rumoured that some of the Phraggmorgia lurk there: a place of death and misery, as evil as Contagion!'

Leaning closer, they saw a scene of tiny trees, with the blue line of the River Gambia winding away to the coast.

Mossy now swung his finger across Africa and far to the east of the Fouta Djallon plateau, and touched on a city of whitewashed buildings surrounded by high walls. In the centre stood a building with a great golden dome.

'Jerusalem, where the healing Pool of Siloam lies – that is the place you must reach, once you have the Chi Rho!'

Starting from Brightdale, Wings traced with his index finger a route towards the city.

'It's a long way: I reckon close on two thousand miles!' He collapsed back onto a chair, his face contorted in pain. Massaging the stump beneath his leather trouser and frowning in concentration, he followed the route with his eye. 'But it's doable. My first stop will be Felixstowe. I'm friendly with the chaps there who refine the special fuel for flying machines. Then we'll hop over the sea to Rotterdam. After that, I expect there'll be other places on the way to find fuel. I'll make enquiries down at the harbour – there's sure to be a well-travelled mariner or trader who'll know.'

He grinned at his audience and rubbed his hands gleefully. 'What an adventure! Never would have thought I'd be flying again – what with losing a bit of me!'

He lifted his stump and waved his empty trouser at them.

While Wings was talking, Fin studied another part of the map, his finger tracing a route south from Mann, where the Irish Sea joined the huge blue expanse of the Atlantic, then along the shores of lands marked Spain and Portugal, and on down the African coast, to the thin blue line of the River Gambia, his finger halting at its source in the Fouta Djallon plateau.

'It is so far!' he groaned.

'Aye, and the butterfly has a long head start!' Sandy said. 'Goodrick, the town mayor, tells me of reports from sailors lately arrived, of seeing what they thought to be an exotic bird, flying south. I have already been down to speak with them. When we have finished here, we must go in search of a suitable vessel – the sooner we sail the better!'

Then frowning, he said: 'But we have a serious problem – how to we pay for such a vessel?'

Looking helplessly at one another, no one spoke.

Suddenly Fin jumped to his feet, startling them. 'The Dandrum Sword!' he exclaimed, 'or at least the scabbard – it's encrusted with pearls! Surely some of those would pay for a seagoing boat?'

His face fell. 'But it's one of the Dandrum Clan's greatest treasures – how could I ever face them back in Brightdale?'

Mossy rose and clasping Fin by the shoulders gazed into his face.

'Do not reproach yourself Fin. What you are doing is for a greater good – to save the beloved child of one of the Dale's oldest families. You will be forgiven for that!'

Fin squared his shoulders. 'Even if I'm not forgiven, I don't care – Bird's more important to me than getting into trouble with the family!'

Smiling indulgently, Mossy sank back onto his chair.

'Hang on!' Lark exclaimed. 'Before we go haring off, we must decide who'll go with us. Me, of course— an' – an' no arguments!'

He glared challengingly at Fin. 'T'was me who got up close to that unnatural excuse for a slug – can still taste its foul spit on my tongue,' he growled, rubbing his mouth with his sleeve.

Crow crept out from his corner. 'I need to come: an' – an' no argues either,' he squeaked in a small frightened voice.

Lark shot him an indignant look. 'We don't want you, bum boil. Go back to your Aunty Krite – with your bible bag and find a new Sparkie.'

Crow hopped in front of Lark, fists in a tight ball, ready for a fight. 'You're a bum carbuncle, worser than boil!' he shrieked. 'An' I don't need a Sparkie, got mouse family in bible bag now, all glossy and fat – an, an if yer mutt come near, I cut its leggies off!'

Lark gaped at him astonished, as the others burst out laughing.

'Lark, you've been told off good and proper!' grinned Kenji.

'Crow, if you want to come, I'll understand,' Fin said kindly. 'You've been a Cross Bearer and have every right.'

Crow muttered: 'Me miss jool bad – really bad!' He returned to his corner, and turning his face to the wall, sobbed quietly.

'If Crow's coming, so should Grilla!' Lark said – a name for the gorilla had suddenly come to him. 'He saved our lives more than once. He belongs in warmer climes – maybe he might find his family.'

Fearing that, after the destruction in Contagion, stray evils might invade Brightdale, Mossy said firmly that he would not come. 'I must return to Brightdale and alert Thetis and Dancer to Wings arriving with the new Skyhook.'

It was agreed that Kenji would accompany Mossy back to Brightdale, then with all speed return to Haverigg harbour, where he would meet up with everyone on their way south.

'So, lad!' Kenji exclaimed, slapping Lark on the shoulder. 'If you've got a message for your girl, get writing! Mossy and I will be off tomorrow morning!'

Alone in their bedroom, from the depths of his rucksack Fin took out the scabbard of the broken Dandrum sword. Firmly reminding himself again that Bird was more important than the ancient family heirloom, he chose four near perfect tear-drop shaped pearls and using his charcoal stick sharpening knife, carefully prised them off. Wrapping them in a handkerchief, he tucked them into a pocket in his jerkin.

Later that day in the Solarium, sitting by a window, Lark started his letter to Tissy. Outside the eagle was perched on the battlements, Fin sitting on the wall close by. Lark's heart went out to him: he looked so miserable.

As always, Lark found letter writing a struggle. It was even worse this time as he didn't want to mention anything that would alarm Tissy. After several attempts and a pile of scrunched-up parchment at his feet, finally satisfied, he tucked the thick wad inside a leather wallet Boff had given him.

Not long later, Kenji came into the Solarium, accompanied by Ed Spanner, who handed Lark a square of thick card with a picture pasted onto it.

'Is that me?' Lark exclaimed, staring at the picture. 'Do I look like that?'

'Yep,' said Kenji, looking over Lark's shoulder. 'Your girl will love it – put it with your letter.'

Lark frowned at the blurred sepia-tinted image. Earlier, overhearing Lark asking Fin to do a sketch of him to enclose with his letter to Tissy, Ed had snorted scornfully, and had insisted on what he called 'taking a photo'.

He took Lark down to his Lab in the castle cellars, a small windowless room smelling of chemicals, with a workbench covered in a jumble of glass jars, metal dishes and assorted scientific objects. Telling Lark to straighten his jerkin and smooth his hair, Ed had him sit on a stool. Then, going behind a wooden box standing on three legs, flinging a heavy blanket over his head, making a few adjustments to a glass-covered hole in the front of the box, he called: 'Say cheese!' A second later a loud bang and a blinding flash of light sent Lark diving under the workbench in fright.

Lark looked again at his startled face: he knew Fin would have done a better job with his charcoal. Sighing, he stuffed the picture in with his letter.

Out on the battlements, stretching his wings impatiently, the eagle gave a cry: 'Skeew! Skeew!'

From the pod in his eye socket, Bird called to Fin. 'Fin, Quilla's hungry! He wants to find food!'

Fin peered at her tiny, floating figure. Putting out his finger, he tried to touch the minute hand pressed against the bubble's skin. Quilla backed away, opening his hooked beak threateningly.

'Don't touch!' Bird's voice became fainter as she struggled to regain her balance. She said something sharply to Quilla and he crouched, shoulders hunched.

Bird's voice, clearer now, called from the bubble. 'I'm going to guide Quilla along the sea cliffs, where the gulls are nesting – he has a fancy for gulls' eggs.'

Quilla rose into the air. 'We'll be back before…' Bird's voice faded on the air.

'Skeew! Skeew!' The eagle soared higher and higher, before wheeling about to head towards the sea. With a heavy heart Fin watched as the great bird shrank to a small dot, then disappeared.

A hand rested on his shoulder. He looked up to find Mossy standing there.

'Have hope Fin! One day, when all is done, you will take Bird home.'

Early next day, they went down to the harbour to watch Mossy and Kenji sail away in the Boskie's fishing boat that had brought Kenji to them. With aching hearts, they wondered when they would next see them. As they waved, Kenji's anxious voice floated across the water, as for the third time he called: 'Don't forget to wait for me at Haverigg!'

The days passed in a blur of activity as they made ready to sail. They had found Orca moored up in a corner of the harbour, alongside some battered old fishing boats. Sandy's eyes gleamed when he saw the beautiful ocean-going cutter. Newly built, her woodwork smelt of fresh paint and tar, her sails and rigging unworn. The owner, a villainous looking seadog, had acquired her as payment for a gambling debt.

When he named his price for her, Fin pulled his packet of pearls from a pocket. Laying open the handkerchief on his palm, the sailor's shifty eyes glinted greedily when he saw the four spectacular pearls.

'Aye, I reckon all o' them 'll do. Where did yer steal 'em from, lad?' he asked suspiciously, holding one, the size of a quail's egg, up to the light.

Sandy, shouldering Fin aside, grabbed the sailor by the throat and pressed him against the wall.

'Hold your insolence, man – you'll take the four pearls and ask no questions, or you'll have me to answer to!' Seeing the cold fury sparking in Sandy's midnight blue eyes, the sailor sullenly agreed to the deal.

With the help of Ed Spanner and his friends among the town's chandlers, Fin and Lark set about buying the supplies needed for a long sea journey. To pay for everything, his conscience hardened, Fin stripped off a dozen of the smaller pearls from the scabbard.

Meanwhile, Sandy spent a lot of time down at the harbour, buying drinks for the sailors. Quickly becoming very popular, the more experienced mariners were happy to offer him good advice. A trader in tin, who travelled the Irish Sea along the Welsh and Cornish coasts, proved a valuable ally. As they pored over sea charts in the corner of a cosy bar, he advised Sandy to make first for the island of Ynys Mon, then sail down to the Bristol Channel, where they should head out into the Atlantic and make for the Tin Isles, before entering the notorious Bay of Biscay. In the end, he offered to sail with them as far as the Tin Isles.

In the town's bars there were more reports from sailors off newly arrived vessels of sightings along the Welsh coast of a strange exotic 'bird' flying with stately wing beats. Fin was desperate to set off. He fretted so much, Lark had to make sure he didn't forget to pack important items, including his sketching materials.

Finally, all was done. At dawn one late Saprise morning, Orca slipped her moorings, heading for the mainland harbour of Haverigg, where they hoped Kenji waited for them, bringing letters and news of Brightdale.

## End of Part One

## PART TWO – THE POOL OF SILOAM

## FROM THE SEA CAME A BOBBIT WORM ...

Dawn on the River Gambia. The jungle is waking. Pale sunlight caresses the tops of the lamba and obeche trees. Golden shafts filter through the twisting liana ropes to the balconies of bromeliads where frogs swim in watery lodges, tending their newly hatched tadpoles. A roosting horn-bill blinks in the morning light and a troop of colobus monkeys quietly stretch and yawn on their leafy nests. On the forest floor, palms and ferns strain towards the elusive sunrays. In the green carpet of macaranga, buzzing bluebottles, drawn by the stink of rotting meat, swarm around a newly opened corpse flower. A pangolin is woken with a start by the rustling of an aardvark returning to its burrow from a night's foraging. At the river's edge, a leopard probes among the mangrove roots, trawling for fish with a clawed paw. Overhead a fish eagle hovers.

Suddenly a cacophony of screeching shatters the peace. The colobus, whooping and gibbering, scatter in all directions. A flock of Go-away-birds take to the air, shrieking in alarm. A mousebird dives for safety into a hole in a tree trunk. High in the canopy a troop of Batfrits have arrived, crashing through the branches, their leathery wings flapping, razor-sharp claws snatching at the liana ropes. The Batfrits pause to await their leader, twitching as they hang upside-down, electric waves pulsing through their robot muscles. From behind and below them an even greater tumult bursts on the jungle morning. On the forest floor, the bulk of King M'Bopo heaves into view, belly wobbling, his moth-eaten fur festooned with jangling jewellery.

Grabbing a liana, swinging by his short back legs, he flaps his great chicken-skin wings to cool his mangy body. Glaring up through the cracked lenses that are his eyes, his rusty voice box barks out an order to his nervously watching troop. He has heard rumours: a butterfly is heading for the river. No ordinary butterfly, but a magical, giant butterfly with wondrous iridescent wings and, strangest of all, a human body – a woman's body, clothed in soft velvet down. Wonder of wonders – if the rumours are right – on her breast she wears a fabulous jewel! He was told it is a jewel more glorious than all the thousands stored in a great heap, deep in his caverns. M'Bopo desires that jewel!

He lurches off along a jungle path, heading for the river mouth. Breaking stems and scattering leaves, clumsily his squad trail after him, jabbering voice boxes echoing tinnily through the trees, sounding like a pack of bush dogs.

The river is teeming with water birds dabbling on the wide muddy banks and among the mangroves: pelicans, egrets, storks, ibis. In the distance the sun shines on the Atlantic Ocean.

M'Bopo raises a wing, and hisses for quiet. Immediately his troop hush, their rustles, squeaks, and thumps as they jostle one another softening to the sound of a gentle breeze. They creep into the mangroves, swinging from root stilt to root stilt. Above them, the nesting pelicans chatter quietly. Snap! One of the Batfrits has broken a branch. Great beaks clacking in alarm, the pelicans take to the air. The troop glare at the culprit. It's Iddy, of course. It's always Iddy!

Clinging to the mangrove roots like dusty brown sacks, the troop wait for the birds to settle once more. M'Bopo moves quietly to where Iddy hangs and hisses something through his rubbery lips into Iddy's trumpet ear. Iddy shudders, but terror of his boss is more than the terror of the command.

Reluctantly he slides down into the swamp, pushing slowly through the brackish water so as not to make waves. He waits, only his fleshy snout and lens eyes above the surface, hoping nothing nasty is eyeing him for a meal. A ripple disturbs the surface, then a splash. Could it be a croc – or a hippo? Neither are fussy eaters – their powerful jaws crunch up Batfrits' mechanical parts just as easily as Batfrits' fleshy parts.

From the sea, a new sound, growing louder: a steady whump, whump, as a butterfly of enormous size slowly rides into view, great wings flashing iridescent peacock-blue, icy turquoise, pansy-brown, mustard, scarlet and silver. A flash of gold catches King M'Bopo's eye: on her velvet breast lies a heavily jewelled cross, rainbow gems sparkling in the sunlight. M'Bopo chatters softly in excitement. Dainty toes skimming the water, she glides to settle wearily on a swaying bush. Massaging her tired shoulders beneath drooping wings, as she twists and turns her beautiful velvet fur-covered body he glimpses a deep gash in her side.

Cautiously, Iddy swims closer. Now he's beneath the butterfly. He reaches up, his hooked claw just centimetres from a dainty velvet covered foot. He doesn't see the two wicked eyes watching him beneath the water. A fang-lined mouth grins evilly. Iddy is just about to snatch... when a thin tongue darts... and gulps. Iddy the Batfrit is no more.

The bobbitworm's long segmented body sways out of the water and reaches up to the butterfly woman. She bends down, her lovely wings wrapping around the worm's writhing coils. Caressing the hideous the face, she presses her thick ruby red lips on the vile mouth. Queen Maabella has kissed her Lord Gressil.

Lumbering into the air, chicken-leather wings creaking, M'Bopo squeals a harsh command. His gang swing into action: they swarm out of the mangrove and fall on the swaying, tightly embraced couple, dragging them apart. Gressil's snapping bobbitworm jaws swallow two Batfrits. M'Bopo swoops, and lunges at the gold chain around Maabella's neck. Screaming with rage, she kicks out with her powerful legs sending him crashing into the water. Gaining height, she tries to take refuge amongst the terrified wheeling pelicans, but the Batfrits, wings flapping wildly, rush after her. Their powerful beaks jabbing, the pelicans force the Batfrits back down into the mangroves. His sodden wings too heavy for flight, M'Bopo can only watch as Gressil's plaited coils stretch like elastic out of the water and snaps at a Batfrit. With a gulp is gone.

The great butterfly sets off upriver on torn wings. The bobbitworm, head above the water, red eyes glittering, swims below her. Smiling down at her lord, Mab drops lower, the jewelled cross dangling just above his ugly head. Lazily paddling her wings, she begins to fly backwards.

But M'Bopo's troop have regrouped, and she is flying into their trap. Gliding behind her in twos, a few feet apart, in their claws hangs a fine mist net, almost invisible. Mab, unaware, flies straight into it. Swiftly the Batfrits twirl about her, wrapping her in the strong mesh. Fighting to break free, Mab's weight pulls them down towards the mangroves. Frantically M'Bopo yells commands. More of his gang rise to grab the net until their combined strength outmatches the butterfly's weight.

Leathery wings flapping the mob set off with their captive. Making steady progress, following the river. M'Bopo their boss, gibbering and cursing, crashes through the undergrowth in pursuit. They are heading for their cave lair beneath the Futa Jalon highlands. Behind them, Gressil's long sinuous body snakes through the water, desperate to keep up.

# 1
# VOYAGING THE SEA

Orca sped through the waves, her sails billowing. Standing in the prow, Fin gazed down into the blue-green sea, watching the dark shapes of dolphins skimming just below the surface. Narrowing his eyes, he saw one dolphin was different: almost human in form, arm-like fins and feet-shaped tail effortlessly cutting through the water. Spinning onto its back, it looked directly at him, and waved, then with a flick of the tail was gone. For the third time, Fin thought he'd seen his father.

'Skeew! Skeew!'

The cry made him look up. Brushing his dark hair away from his eyes, he made out a blotch against the white clouds. The blotch spiralled down to become a golden eagle.

Grinning, he waved his arms. 'Bird – can you see the dolphins?'

'Yes, I can see!' came a faint voice: 'Quilla, lower please! There's hundreds of them – playing! Having fun——'

A shriek of terror drowned her words.

Fin turned to see Crow's small, callused feet disappearing over the port side, followed by a line rapidly uncoiling from where he'd been peacefully fishing amidships.

'SANDY! Crow's overboard again!' Fin shouted, racing across the deck and snatching up the wooden batten at the end of Crow's line.

Sandy pushed the helm hard to starboard, and the sleek cutter immediately lost the wind. Yawing sideways, her mainsail flapping wildly, her boom swinging violently, she almost came to a standstill.

Kenji amidships scouring his cooking pot, bounded over and grabbing the line further along its length, he and Fin began hauling. Hooting agitatedly, Grilla swung down from the rigging and joined them. Lark's suntanned face popped up through the below-decks hatchway followed by Mick's brown and white head. Scrambling on deck, they rushed to the side, and Lark leaned over the gunwale, searching the waves, Mick beside him jumping up and down trying to see. A tiger shark broke surface, the line disappearing into its wide tooth-filled maw. Egged on by Mick's yapping Fin, Kenji and Grilla heaved. The twisting and thrashing fish landed with a wet thump on the deck. Springing back Kenji seized a boat hook lying nearby and smashed down hard on the snout. Bucking violently, the shark's jaws gaped, and Crow's slime-coated body slithered out. The shark, turning on Kenji, Lark leapt and plunged his boning knife into its head just behind an eye. The great creature shuddered and lay still.

Crow lay squirming, struggling for breath, his face covered in slime. Briskly, Kenji grabbed his ankles, dunked him over the side and hauled him back on deck. Trembling with shock and squealing indignantly, Crow sat up in a pool of seawater. 'I hate the sea!' he wailed. 'Want Aunty Krite! Want jool!'

'There, there, little chap,' Kenji cooed, patting Crow's dripping head of sparse hair.

Fin eyed the massive fish in awe. 'Cheer up Crow – what a whopper you've caught this time!'

The gaping jaw lined with rows of vicious teeth fascinated Lark. 'Wow Crow! That was a fine bit of fishing!' Hunkering down, he sliced into the thick hide with his boning knife. 'Good eating, do you reckon, Kenji? Shark meat would make a change!'

'Tuna tastier!' Crow said, giving a superior sniff.

'Skeew! Skeew!'

Fin smiled up at the eagle perched on top of the mainmast. 'Fin – Quilla's hungry. He wants a chunk of meat!' Only he could hear Bird, his ear tuned over the weeks to her faint voice.

Swooping down, Quilla landed clumsily on the shark. Talons digging deep into the leathery skin, he blindly stabbed and ripped with his powerful beak, ravenously swallowing chunks of flesh.

Leaning as close as he dared, Fin peered into to the eagle's eye-socket holding the bubble where he could see Bird's tiny figure.

'Hi Bird love!' he whispered. 'You O.K in there?'

Bird's voice came, soft and halting: 'I'm— I'm fine— Well not really, Fin. Sometimes I think I'm still in my body. I can feel straw pricking my sore skin, and my mouth sometimes feels so dry, it makes me desperate for a drink, but— but—'

Hearing a small sob, Fin's face twisted in misery.

Watching him, brought a lump to Lark's throat. 'Don't give up Fin!' he said gruffly, squeezing Fin's shoulder. 'We'll soon be catching up with that sluggy butterfly woman—'

Dumbly shaking his head, Fin stumbled to the hatchway and disappeared below.

Sandy called from the stern. 'Standby, everyone! We must get underway again and make land before nightfall!'

Pushing the tiller hard to port, he brought Orca once more into the wind. Back on course, she gave a kick as a sudden gust of caught her sails. Lark's stomach heaved as yet again the taste of slug rose in his throat. Spitting overboard, he swiped his sleeve across his mouth. Would he ever get rid of the vivid memory: plunging his knife into the pus-filled wound, the slug's fat tongue slithering into his mouth? How he wished for things to be put right – Bird saved, her body and soul joined once more. Then they could all go home to Brightdale and get on with their lives: him marrying Thetis, Fin coming into his Headship, Sandy, Kenji and Dancer, a Squad once more, patrolling their northern homelands, keeping the people safe. But of course, Fescue wouldn't be with them; he was dead, his mighty spirit gone back to the Gaiakin's Universe of White Light.

Lark saw Kenji had begun butchering the shark, sending Quilla back up into the rigging.

After a little while Fin returned on deck, and once more stationed himself in the prow, staring down into the sea, watching the dolphins, this time with his precious sketch pad and charcoal sticks in hand. At the start of the voyage, he had determined that, to give himself some little respite from his wretchedness, he would try to keep a record of their journey – Mossy would want that.

Four days out from Corunna they were passing the Gibraltar Straits heading for Tangier in north Africa.

Picking up Kenji at Haverigg and sailing south along the Welsh and Cornish coasts, passing a shoreline fringed by deep forests, rocky cliffs and deserted golden beaches, with sometimes a ruin, a relic of past habitation, they had seen no towns or cities; the only communities they encountered were small fishing villages. A week later they reached the busy port of St. Mary's on the Tin Islands. Lying in the Atlantic Ocean, these islands, once known as the Scillies, were a major stopping place for seafarers.

The tin and copper trader who had advised them on planning the trip and had helped Sandy master sailing such a powerful vessel as Orca, had travelled with them from the Isle of Mann. He left them when they put into St Mary's for supplies before the long passage through the Bay of Biscay. On the charts, he had pointed out the countries they would pass, still marked with their ancient names: France, Spain, Portugal. He explained that the people of those times, grown soft with easy living, had swiftly succumbed to the Great Dying. Their cities and towns fell into ruin, and forest reclaimed the land, leaving only fishing settlements on the wooded shores.

It took them three days to sail the Bay of Biscay. Tacking into the face-on westerlies blowing from the Azores, the rough seas severely tested their sailing skills, and they were thankful to reach the small bustling port of Corunna in northern Spain. The dark-haired swarthy people of Spanish origins reminded them of the Roms who came to Watersmeet Market to trade.

Even though at first, it was hard to make themselves understood, they found them friendly folk. But then Fin began asking around, showing his sketch of the butterfly woman, hoping for news of Maabella: had they seen a strange exotic bird in the sky? Some shook their heads in puzzlement, others looked at him as if he were crazy, and friendliness quickly turned to hostility. Glad to have obtained free water and provisions before the atmosphere turned sour, they hurriedly sailed from Corunna, south along the wild coast of Portugal. Stopping for supplies at a couple of larger fishing villages, anxious not to cause trouble, the others very firmly told Fin not to show anyone his sketch of Maabella.

'And here we are – shearing time not far off – more than a thousand miles from home,' Lark told himself as he sat untangling Crow's fishing line. He shook his head in wonder. How was it that he'd ended up on this boat in the middle of a great ocean?

When he'd set out this Saprise on his jaunt with Fin, he fully expected to be home long before hay making time; then he would ask Tissy to marry him. That wasn't going to happen. But what sights he'd seen! Great cathedrals, wondrous gardens, deep dark mines where fiery monsters lurked.

As for the horrors of Contagion – best not to dwell on that.

Think instead about the amazing people he'd met! There was Fin's ma for a start: once a wild Rom girl, now a Holy Woman on Cuthbert's Island. But the most amazing of them was Sandy. He glanced at Sandy seated at the tiller, his keen midnight-blue eyes searching the horizon. Trekker warrior turned sailor, his awesome sword was now kept in a locker below decks, along with his crossbow and quiver of arrows.

Kenji stored his sword under his bunk, the Samurai blade newly forged by the Gaiakins in Florain. Lark watched him cutting steaks from the shark, his hands badly scarred from the burns suffered when he valiantly plunged his sword into the evil inferno that was the Phraggy monster. Like everyone else, he'd adopted sailors canvas shorts. But he still wore his Frit's skull belt buckle and tied his glossy black hair back with the ganglefowl beak.    Then there was scrawny little Crow. Fancy him coming along on this trip, when the devious Scav had tried to kill Fin! But to be fair, he'd redeemed himself by saving Mick from drowning in the filthy meltwater of Contagion. Healthy and clean now, and smart in the clothes Mrs Spanner had found for him back on Mann, all carefully looked after, and regularly washed.

The Scav was crouched nearby, pinched face peering into his bible bag. He'd adopted a mouse family, a mother and one young – there had been six, but Kenji found them in the flour bag and had set Mick on them. The mother mouse still sported the now tatty, tinsel collar Tubs Spanner had made before Orca sailed from Mann.

Lark looked up as a heavy hand patted his head. Grilla had climbed down from the rigging. He too looked healthy, fully recovered from his ordeal, caged in Gressil's Frit Factory, his silvery fur shining after a course of seaweed tonic brewed by Tubs. Holding a battered black and white plustic football, the gorilla's small brown eyes peered eagerly into Lark's face.

'No! Grilla!' Lark said firmly. 'Can't play footie just now – got to sort out this line, people'll be tripping over it.'

Grilla looked hopefully to where Mick was stretched out asleep in the sun.

Lark chuckled. 'Yep, chuck ball to Mick – make him jump!' Lark had noticed Mick was starting to get tubby from too many fish and very little exercise.

Watching the gorilla skilfully bouncing the football along the deck, Lark was amazed that such a wild animal could be so intelligent. He'd grown very fond of the gentle giant, and he'd miss him if – or more likely, when – he found his family in the mysterious African jungles, where their pursuit of the butterfly was leading them.

Lark shivered in dread. From what he knew of jungles – creatures with poisonous teeth and insects with deadly stings – he didn't fancy going there at all. Shaking off the thought, he threw Crow's fishing line and hook into the tackle box and clutching the gunwale for support made his way along the swaying deck to join Fin in the prow. Staring across the choppy waves he made out a distant shadow of what could be land.

He nodded towards the horizon. 'Fin, could that be Africa? Didn't Sandy say we'll be coming there soon, to a place called Tangier?'

Narrowing his eyes, Fin looked to where Lark pointed.

'Yep, North Africa – where the Berber people live.'

'Do you know what kind of people they are?'

'Sandy told me they're an ancient race of people with black skin.'

'What! Black like Mr Mossy? They should be alright then!' sighed Lark.

Talk of Mossy brought an ache in Fin's throat – his time with him, on the Isle of Mann had been too short. There was so much more to ask. Kenji, on his return from Brightdale, had reassured Fin that Dancer was there with Tissy devotedly caring for Bird's burnt body. The thought of Bird, robbed of her soul, spending her days curled up in a box of straw like an animal was like a knife twisted in his heart. Unbidden, his hand strayed to the scar on his chest left by the Chi Rho. Even though the wound was healed, he still had a desperate craving to hold the cross, to feel the weight, the sharp jewels pressing against his palm, to run his finger over the clear smooth crystal. The thought of it glittering against Queen Maabella's velvet breast enraged him.

Turning his gaze to the sea below the prow, he wondered again about the figure he'd seen swimming with the dolphins. Was it his father? He thought back to when he was on the fell above Watersmeet searching for Blue Gentian flowers for Mossy, before he knew Marlin had been killed by the Frit, when he'd seen his father in a dream swimming in a tropical sea.

A shout from Sandy brought him back to the present.

'TANGIER IN SIGHT – READY ABOUT CREW! LOWER FORES'L!'

Grilla, grabbing Mick and Crow, swung over to the safety of the hatchway, from where they looked out as Fin, Kenji and Lark, now a well drilled team, sprang into action, their routine honed to perfection over two weeks of sailing.

Pushing his helm hard over, Sandy brought up Orca head-on into the wind. Her sails flapping wildly, Sandy quickly reefed in the mainsail, bringing her once more under control. Kenji dived to port, while Lark lurched over to starboard. Ropes singing through the blocks, they lowered the foresail. In the prow, Fin leaned out to swiftly gather in the billowing spinnaker, before methodically lashing it to the bowsprit. Foresail and spinnaker down, Sandy trimmed the mainsail, ensuring it was filled with wind and keeping an expert eye on the short lengths of ribbon fluttering along its edge.

Tasks done, the deck cleared of stray tackle, whilst Sandy skilfully steered Orca into the bay, they leant on the gunwale gazing to the shore where a city rose above a harbour thronged with boats being unloaded and loaded. To the south, where a sandy beach curved around to the open sea, more boats were pulled up on the strand, some, propped up on blocks, being built or repaired, whilst on other boats fishermen worked on their nets. They were amazed how large and busy the city of Tangier was, its creamy-white and ochre walls topped by red and gold domed roofs gleaming in the evening sun.

Seeing no place along the stone jetties and wooden piers for them to tie up, Sandy decided to moor amongst the boats riding at anchor in the bay. 'Attention crew!' he called. 'Get ready to strike sail!'

Again, they jumped to it. Lark and Fin hauled down the great mainsail, then lashed the canvas to the mast, whilst Kenji dropped anchor, the heavy chain rattling as it uncoiled.

As well as teaching them the skills working with sails and ropes essential to keep Orca moving, Sandy had also assigned each of them other tasks. He was concerned that, if they were not kept busy, Fin and Lark particularly might brood on the horrors of the recent past.

He was teaching Fin the rudiments of navigation. An enthusiastic pupil, Fin quickly learned to read charts, plotting the correct course using the ship's compass. Sandy had shown him how to use the Cross-staff, an ancient hand-held device for navigating by the sun and stars, with the help of a fine brass clock in the cabin and a musty book of navigation tables, which Fin was sure he had last seen in Mr Mossy's Bookshop back in Brightdale. He was also getting to grips with the Sextant, a handsome instrument of brass and mahogany, to find their latitude. Lark, being skilled with his hands, was appointed ship's bosun, repairing any damaged woodwork, sails and ropes, tasks vital to the success of the voyage. Kenji was cook and quartermaster, taking care of supplies; whilst Crow, as well as catching fish for their meals, looked after the fishing tackle, making sure lines were kept untangled and ready for use. Grilla's allotted task was keeping things clean. He dusted and swept their sleeping quarters with a will, but he wasn't very good at swabbing the deck. Several times Lark demonstrated what he should do, lowering a bucket over the side to draw up water for swilling over the boards, but Grilla just looked bemused and poured the water over himself.

With night coming on they settled down for the evening. Around them other boats' riding lights began to appear, and voices drifted across the calm water. They made plans for the following day as they ate their supper. Kenji had made sushi with the meat from the shark, his grandmother's recipe, handed down through the generations. Quilla had the shark's liver whilst Grilla ate the last few now tired looking carrots and a small bunch of over-ripe bananas.

'We'll need to get more supplies tomorrow,' Kenji said, eyeing the black skinned banana Grilla was fastidiously peeling – like all apes, he preferred his bananas still green. 'Tear me a piece of parchment from your sketchpad, Fin and I'll start a list.'

Sandy frowned. 'Yes Kenji, but I'm thinking it would not be a good idea to leave Orca unguarded: you, the gorilla and Crow must stay on board.'

Kenji sighed. 'O.K. Boss – but be warned: the list will be long! Not only do we need fresh fruit and vegetables, but we also need more rice, as well as charcoal and lamp oil.' He nodded in the direction of the city. 'I've a feeling too, that in this place we'll have to pay for it. The traders won't give us free stuff, like the kind people in the fishing ports we've called at so far!'

'I suppose I'll need to chip off more pearls!' Fin said resignedly. 'But I'm reluctant to use them to purchase low value things like food and fuel!'

They sat in thoughtful silence for a moment, then Lark jumped up, exclaiming: 'Nuts and bolts!'

The others watched him in bewilderment as he went astern to his toolbox, kept beneath the helmsman's seat. He returned triumphantly waving a clutch of small canvas bags.

'There are loads of screws here too! Should have thought about it before! Everyone needs nuts, bolts, screws and such – these bags are full of 'em. Me being bosun, Ed Spanner insisted I should have a good supply: 'You won't find the Isle of Mann forged metal parts anywhere else in all the world', he'd said.'

Sandy's eyes gleamed with amusement. 'You are right, young Lark. We'll bring some of them, but I think we'd better have a few small pearls hidden away, too – just in case!'

Their plans for the next day decided, a relay of night watches was agreed, Sandy taking the first watch, the rest of them went below, glad to sleep on the still waters of the harbour.

Early next day they were startled awake by loud shouts and banging on the hull. Grabbing their swords, Sandy and Kenji were first on deck, followed by Fin, Lark, and Grilla. They rushed to the gunwale where Crow, having fallen asleep on watch, was now engaged in an unintelligible shouting match. Alongside was a flat-bottomed boat filled with sacks of rice, bunches of green bananas, oranges, pineapples, string bags of vegetables, carrots, onions, cabbages, bright red tomatoes. Amongst this plenty stood two traders from the town calling their wares, holding up samples of their goods. After days of meagre rations, the sight was too much for Grilla. Swinging a long arm over the side, he grabbed the biggest bunch of bananas. The sellers screeched their outrage. 'Impshi! Impshi! Give cash! Give cash!' they chorused. Traders and Grilla firmly gripping the bananas, a tug-of-war ensued.

For a moment all were nonplussed; then Lark dived below deck, bringing back a small handful of screws, nuts, and bolts.

'Hoy! Hoy!' he shouted, showing the boatmen his shiny collection. 'Look! Look! How many for 'nanas?'

The traders let go, and triumphantly hugging his prize Grilla retired to the cabin roof to pluck one, and swallow it whole, unpeeled.

Lark handed down a brass bolt, a nut, and a washer. Heads close, muttering together the men reached up and rummaged through the other pieces of metal in Lark's open palms. Satisfied with a couple of stainless-steel wingnuts and some screws, they pointed to the other provisions.

'You want?' one of them asked.

Kenji, who had been looking on with huge amusement, quickly replied: 'Yep, want!' He pointed to a sack of rice and various bags of vegetables.

With Lark's metal parts an acceptable currency, he was soon stocked up with fresh produce and the sellers headed off for nearby boats.

Carrying the goods below deck, Kenji said to Fin and Lark: 'This'll save you a lot of shopping, lads! I'll write my list for the rest of the stuff – for a start, we'll need lamp oil.'

Half an hour later, Sandy, Fin, and Lark lowered Mini-Orca, their Jolly boat, a rowing dinghy stored amidships, leaving Kenji, Crow and Grilla on board. Lark, deciding against taking Mick, firmly told him to 'stay!' – Grilla immediately taking charge of him.

They had given Crow a small cutlass. As he swished it fiercely, knock knees showing below his leather shorts, stripy shirt, and a spotted handkerchief tied around his scrawny neck, Lark grinned: 'You look a proper little seadog, Crow!'

Fin and Lark settled on the benches in the Jolly boat, whilst Sandy took the oars to join a small flotilla of similar boats rowing away from the craft moored around them, all heading for the harbour. Inside his battered canvas shorts, Sandy had hidden a serviceable steel dagger in a leather sheath: its razor-sharp blade had been carefully forged for him by Ed Spanner. Lark, as always armed with his boning knife, had two small bags of nuts, screws and bolts tied at his waist. Fin's only weapon was his knife for sharpening charcoal-sticks in a sheath at his belt. His canvas jacket held his sketching materials, and in a secret pocket in his shorts lay a few of the smaller Dandrum Pearls.

As they rowed away, Quilla took to the air from his roost in Orca's prow. Bird guided him towards the beach, where fishermen were sorting their latest catches. Above them clouds of raiding gulls and pelicans swooped and dived.

Nosing in among rowing boats lining a wooden pier, they tied Mini-Orca to a mooring ring, then hopped across other boats climbed a ladder to the walkway leading to the dockside. Making their way through the bustle on the dockside, they passed a variety of moored ships:

cutters like Orca, two-masted caravels, sleek multi-masted clippers and schooners, along with flat-bottomed dories ferrying cargo to and from ships at anchor out in the bay. Workers, backs loaded with baskets, sacks, bolts of brightly coloured cloth and multi-patterned carpets, ran up and down the gangplanks. Cranes hauled up cargo from ships' holds, boxes, crates, even live animals cradled in nets – terrified, wildly kicking horses, cows, donkeys, and – most amazing to Fin and Lark's eyes – long necked, dun-coloured camels with wobbling humps, great flat feet flailing the empty air.

As Fin and Lark stopped to watch a group of richly robed merchants supervising the unloading of their cargo, two of the large sacks of roasted coffee beans fell and split open, spewing their contents on the cobbles. The aroma of coffee along with the merchants' yells and curses attracted a band of ragged street Scavs who fell on the beans like a flock of raiding starlings. Whip in hand, a dock overseer lashed out, sending them scurrying off gleefully triumphant through an archway into the city, handfuls of coffee beans bulging beneath their grubby T-shirts.

'Get a move on lads!' Sandy called.

They passed through the same archway, into a narrow alley lined with shops and cafes and crowded with people carrying sacks and boxes on their backs, others driving donkeys and camels, laden with goods. The pressing throng carried them along, up wide steps into to a great square surrounded by imposing buildings. Around the square, arches disgorged even more people from the city's maze of alleys.

It was market day, but many times bigger than Watersmeet's market that Fin and Lark had grown up with. Wandering from stall to stall, taking in the exotic smells, listening to the hum of voices all around them as people argued and bargained, the variety of stuff for sale amazed them. Meat sellers sat behind tables, idly swatting at clouds of buzzing flies dancing above trays of butchery. Fishmongers with boxes of ice topped with every kind of fish and shellfish, some they had never seen before. Vegetable and flower sellers, tables piled high with colourful produce. Spice merchants sitting among mounds of brightly coloured herbs and spices. Grain sellers, silos overflowing with flour, rice and grains. Stalls selling bolts of cloth and silks, leather goods, carpets, rugs, others offering metal goods, jewellery, wooden furniture.

At a seller of lamp oil, Lark pointed enquiringly at one of the glass bottles of honey coloured oil, holding a selection of screws, washers and nuts in his outstretched hand. Frowning and muttering, the stall holder carefully picked through them, whilst Lark and Sandy watched anxiously.

Whilst Lark bargained, Fin wandered to the next stall, drawn by the array of ornamental trinkets hanging on silver chains, butterflies, dragonflies and birds, created from sheets of coloured glass and silver and gold foil, fluttering and spinning, flickering in the sunlight. A wrinkled old woman, all in black, sat at the stall. Giving Fin a toothless grin, she held up a small silver and silk butterfly, reminding Fin of his sketch of Queen Mab. Fishing it from his pocket, he showed it to the old woman. Bending close she squinted at the voluptuous woman with butterfly wings stretched out behind her slender body. At first she seemed puzzled, then curiosity turned to horror and outrage. Screeching in anger, she snatched the sketch from him, and tottering from her stall, thrust it in the faces of passers-by.

In moments a crowd grew, its mood turning ugly. A chant went up: 'Commandant! Call the Commandant!'

Lark and Sandy, their oil buying done, realised something was going horribly wrong.

Lark groaned. 'Raddled wemmers, Sandy! Fin's showing his sketch of Mab, the great twit!'

A scarlet robed dignitary, a long peacock feather in his turban, was approaching preceded by his deputy, a weaselly-looking man in dusty black, a mere chicken feather in his turban, clearing the way, imperiously swatting with a baton at anyone who did not cower aside.

The old woman thrust the sketch at the Commandant. His expression of irritated scorn rapidly changed to fury. Long black beard wagging indignantly, brandishing the parchment, he shrieked: 'Blasphemy! Blasphemy!'

He stabbed an accusing finger at Fin. 'This devil imp has brought evil into our sacred city!'

'TO THE SCAFFOLD WITH HIM! CALL THE EXECUTIONER!' roared the crowd.

The deputy, roughly grabbing Fin and tying his arms behind his back, shoved him stumbling through the crowd. Following the Commandant, his peacock feather swaying, they headed for a high platform in the centre of the square. The mob faces contorted in anger and fear continued bellowing: 'DEATH TO THE EVIL ONE! DEATH! CUT OFF HIS HEAD!'

'Release him! Release him! It is all a mistake!' Sandy yelled, as he and Lark fought to get closer. As the crowd pressed in on them, Lark's bag was torn from his grasp, and the bottle of lamp oil smashed on the ground.

Sandy drew his dagger. Reaching the deputy, he pressed his blade at the man's throat. 'I said release him!' he snarled.

Staring up into the fierce midnight blue eyes, the official cringed away. His hold on Fin's arms slackened.

From the back of the crowd, came a shout. 'The big man and the little fellow with him are devils too!' It was the lamp oil seller, at the head of a squad of Civil Guards. Pushing through the mob to the Commandant, he opened his fist to show the gleaming stainless-steel wing nuts and screws with which Lark had paid him. 'Look! Look! Never have I seen such shining iron – they are devil forged!'

The crowd closed in on Sandy and Lark. Hopelessly outnumbered, resistance was futile. From somewhere, a wooden club smashed Sandy's dagger from his hand, sending it clattering to the cobbles.

'Seize the devils!' shrieked the Commandant.

Civil Guards grabbed Sandy and Lark, binding their arms to their sides. The Commandant mounted the platform, and the three captives were pushed up the ladder behind. Fin was forced to his knees whilst Sandy and Lark could only watch helplessly. To loud cheers, a tall, broad shouldered man, waving a heavy, two-handed sword, crossed the square and climbed onto the platform. His teeth flashed white as he leered at Fin cowering before him.

'Blindfold the imp!' he rasped running a long fingernail down the blade of his sword.

Roughly the Commandant's deputy tied a grubby rag around Fin's face. The swell of noise slowly faded, and an expectant silence filled the square.

Blindly turning his head about, for Fin everything became strangely unreal: in all the weeks since the Chi Rho came into his life, several times coming close to death, he'd never thought it would end like this: his head chopped off in a far distant land.

He could hear Lark sobbing nearby. The floorboards creaked as the executioner moved about: he seemed to be performing a ritual dance. He cringed as he felt the draught of an experimental swish of the sword above his head. Another creak from the floorboards. He turned his head to the sound and braced himself: was this it? A picture floated into his mind of his father swimming through seaweed fronds, kicking with fish tail legs.

'SKEEW! SKEEW!' He heard the thump, thump of powerful wings.

'FIN, DUCK YOUR HEAD!' Bird's voice yelled in his ear.

He lunged sideways, the blindfold slipping from his eyes. Hot blood splashed his face – not his – the executioner's.

Quilla's talons slashed at the executioner's face. Shrieking in agony, the man fell to his knees, blood pouring from a gouged-out eye.

'QUILLA, ENOUGH!' Bird screamed.

'SKEEW! SKEEW!' Quilla pulled away. With slow beats of his mighty wings, he rose into the air, hovered for a moment, then flew for the city walls. Thwack! Thwack! From a tower, a volley of arrows sped after him, one arrow passing harmlessly through his tail feathers. He soared higher and, as the crowd shook their fists at him, he disappeared into the heat of the blinding blue sky.

With a roar, the mob turned back to the scaffold. The executioner lay in a widening pool of blood, the Commandant kneeling over him. Their captors distracted, Sandy and Lark, struggling wildly with their bindings, managed to free themselves. As the first of the blood-crazed crowd made to swarm up the ladder, Sandy snatched up the executioner's sword ready to face him. Pulling out his boning knife and standing by Fin, Lark thought with a sick grin, at least they would die together!

Sword held high Sandy's clear, firm voice rang out above the roar of the crowd. 'Citizens of Tangiers! We bring no evil. We mean no blasphemy. Stand aside and let us depart in peace. Or…who will be the first to die?'

His startling Gaiakin eyes roaming the mob, silence fell. The Commandant and his Guards edged away. Then from the far side of the square, sounded a blare of trumpets. All heads turned. Four horsemen entered the square. Blowing fanfares on long silver instruments, their white Arab steeds prancing proudly, they scattered the crowd before them. Sitting tall in their gaudily fringed saddles, faces coldly expressionless beneath golden turbans, they rode before a great pink and white palanquin, resembling a huge wedding cake, lavishly ornamented with gold and silver baubles. Beneath the delicate dome of its roof, a shadowy figure reclined behind draped gauze curtains. Eight heavily muscled men bore the carrying poles upon their shoulders, two at each corner, richly embroidered boleros stretched over bronzed chests, with baggy pink silk trousers caught at the ankle. At each side of the palanquin marched three similarly attired guards with fearsome cutlasses sheathed at their waists, and in their right hands lances with which they marked their strides by ringing strikes on the stones. Two more brought up the rear.

Awed murmurs rippled through the crowd like a gentle wind: 'Queen Rami! Queen Rami has come.' Stepping back respectfully, eyes lowered, the procession made its stately progress to the foot of the scaffold. An expectant silence filled the square.

One of the riders beckoned to Commandant to come down. As he descended the ladder the chiffon curtains parted for a graceful, white-gloved hand to emerge.

'Come! Show me this blasphemous drawing.' In the hush, from within the palanquin a husky voice could easily be heard.

Taking the sketch from the Commandant's trembling hand, the gloved hand withdrew. Then from inside there came an exclamation of surprise. The curtains parted and there appeared a silver face mask, painted with large blue eyes and red lips. The mask gazed up at the prisoners on the scaffold.

'You three! Lay down your weapons and come to me!'

Sandy let the executioner's sword slide to the ground and Lark sheathed his boning knife. As they descended the ladder, Fin desperately searched the sky: there was no sign of Quilla. Calmly, the masked figure studied the sketch, then each of them in turn.

'Who drew this thing?' the husky voice asked.

Fin stepped forward. 'I did! It is mine alone.' He gestured to Sandy and Lark. 'These two are nothing to do with me!'

The old woman from the trinket stall, who had pushed herself to the front of the crowd, cried out: 'The imp is lying! These two are his friends – they were buying oil with him.'

'Aye!' called the oil lamp seller. 'They tried to bribe me with devil-forged iron!'

The masked figure gestured for silence, then turned slowly to study the captives once more. 'Bring them to the palace – I wish to question them more! Commandant, you and your men return to your quarters. Attend to the executioner!'

The mask withdrew, the gauze curtains closed. Bowing, the Commandant and his deputies fell back, and wordlessly the foot guards surrounded Fin, Lark, and Sandy. With a clash of lances on the paving, the party formed up behind the palanquin and with stately measure headed for the largest of the arches leading out of the square.

# 2
# QUEEN RAMI

With their silver trumpets resounding through the narrow streets, the four riders led the procession towards the dazzling white walls and shining roofs of Queen Rami's palace. As they approached, tall gates swung open to admit them to a wide courtyard. Within the mosaic-covered walls were kitchens, stables, forges, and laundry rooms, all bustling with activity. The gates closed behind them, shutting out the noise of the city. The retinue halted, the palanquin was borne away through high golden doors, and the prisoners were marched across the courtyard to an iron-studded door where a gaoler waited with jangling keys. By the light of a blazing torch that flickered over glisteningly damp walls, he led them down steep steps and along a narrow passage to unlock a barred door. The three companions were roughly pushed in, the door clanged shut behind them, and they were left in the gloom to survey their prison. High in the wall a small window let in a feeble light, enough to show on one of the slimy walls, the white bones of a skeleton hanging by rusty chains.

'Well, we're in a right mess now!' growled Lark. 'What a daft thing to do, Fin – showing your sketch! Didn't you learn your lesson when they made that fuss at Corunna?'

Sandy gave a mirthless grin. 'You had a close shave there, Fin!'

'Aye,' grumbled Lark. 'Close shave alright – nearly lost his head! Mind you, Fin doesn't need a close shave!' He explained to Sandy: 'Us Delphins don't start shaving until we're close on twenty-five!'

'Never mind me having a close shave!' Fin exclaimed. 'I'm far more worried for Bird and Quilla. They were nearly shot down!'

Lark nodded. 'Brave do on their part! Hope they got back to Orca to warn the others. If Bird could make herself heard, that is.'

Restlessly pacing up and down, Sandy stopped beneath the small window, measuring the distance to it with his eye.

'Fin, you are the slenderest – if you stood on my shoulders, could you reach the window? The bars look rusty – might be able break them.'

Fin looked doubtfully up at the narrow opening. 'It looks very small – besides, I don't want to leave you two here, whilst I escape!'

'If you got free,' Lark said, 'per'aps you could get to speak to that Queen person – explain the situation—' he stopped suddenly, listening intently.

From the back wall came a scraping noise, made loud by the silent gloom. To their surprise, a hidden door slowly swung open. The cell filled with light from a flaming torch as a cowled figure appeared. The figure beckoned to them urgently.

'Come! Hurry! Hurry!' hissed a female voice.

Following the torchbearer up winding stone steps, as they climbed the light from above grew brighter. Reaching a landing, they stepped into sunlight streaming in through a tall window. Their guide snuffed out her torch, and pulling back a heavy curtain, gestured to them to go through, before noiselessly disappearing down a passageway.

They found themselves in a spacious airy room, where gauzy silk curtains at high archways stirred languidly in a soft sea breeze. The mosaic tiled floor depicted scenes of cedar trees and snow-capped mountains; the walls, also tiled, were decorated with elaborate geometric designs in rich golds, reds, and blues. In one wall, a gilded spout gently cascaded water into a lily-covered pool.

In the centre of the room, still masked and gowned Queen Rami reclined on one of four deeply upholstered sofas arranged in a square. She was alone except for a young dark-haired maid kneeling at a low marble-topped table preparing mint tea in a silver urn set on a small spirit stove. Next to the urn lay a tray of glistening honey cakes. The maid beckoned them to sit opposite the Queen. All too conscious of their scruffy appearance, they sat silently together, whilst Queen Rami studied Fin's sketch from behind her silver mask. When the maid had handed around delicate cups, napkins and plates for the cakes, she was dismissed with the wave of a gloved hand.

The Queen's blue enamel eyes turned on Fin. 'This drawing is a remarkable likeness – you are skilled, Fin Dandrum!'

Startled, all three of them exclaimed their astonishment.

'You know my name!' Fin gasped.

'Yes indeed! I have been expecting you – you, Iskander and Lark, with your other companions. A message came to me that you are in pursuit of a butterfly – an unusually large butterfly, with the body of a woman, who is wearing a fabulous jewel.'

'You had a message? How could you have a message about us? We have come from far away – we've been sailing for days! No one knew where we were going – apart from Mos – apart from our friends.' Almost speaking Mossy's name, Fin rapidly corrected himself.

Leaning forward, Sandy stared suspiciously at the blank blue eyes. 'Queen Rami, who are you? Or should I say, what are you? There are those who would do anything to possess the jewel the butterfly wears, and they are mostly evil!'

'Aye, Gressil for a start!' Lark said bitterly. 'Fin and I got the measure of him and his missus – sorted him out good and proper! Least we would have sorted Mab if she hadn't done the dirty on us, and took the cross—'

Sandy gripped him fiercely by the arm. Turning red, Lark shut his mouth.

Fin addressed the Queen again. 'You said you have been expecting us. I ask again, who told you?'

'You call him Mossy – I know him as Zagzagel. His message warned me to look out for you!'

Lark glared at the silver mask. 'Fin, she's lying! Bet she knows about us because she's a friend of Mab. She couldn't possibly know Mossy! He's miles 'nd miles from here! Even if he flew in a Skyhook-type machine, he couldn't have got here any quicker than us!'

Behind the mask, the husky voice laughed softly. 'Lark Annunder, you are very wise! I understand why Zagzagel allotted you as Fin's friend!'

The mask turned to Sandy. 'Iskander, your young Delphin friends are singularly ignorant about Zagzagel. Do they not know he is an angel?'

Before Sandy could speak, Lark burst out. 'Oh, we know about Mr Mossy being one of those angels who stood by the empty tomb when the Christ rose up from being dead! We worked that one out, didn't we Fin?'

Fin was gazing steadily at the Queen. 'Tell me, Queen Rami, how can I be sure you are not possessed by one of the vile Phraggs, sometimes known as Sneaksouls? They cannot hide the sickly green glow in their eyes – take off your mask so we can see!'

Without warning he lunged across the low table, sending teacups and honey cakes flying, and dragged off the mask.

They gaped at the face revealed: for a fleeting second Lark thought he was looking at Dancer, so like her did the Queen look.

Alerted by Fin's raised voice and the crash of china, from opposite doorways two pairs of foot guards dashed into the room with drawn cutlasses. Her reptilian head rippling pink and orange, the Queen dismissed them with an impatient wave.

Swinging her legs down from the sofa and sitting tall, she stared defiantly at them: 'Yes, as you see, I am of the hated Skwid kind! Come closer, Fin, look into my eyes. Can you see green grinning faces?' Deeply ashamed, Fin shook his head. 'Majesty, I shouldn't have done that. Please forgive me!'

Sandy put his arm around Fin's hunched shoulders. 'Queen Rami, you must understand. Young Fin has suffered much at the hands of Sneaksouls. It was the demon Raaum who murdered his father and stole his sweetheart's soul. That is the reason we are chasing Maabella – to retrieve the Chi Rho and use its healing power to save Bird.'

Nodding sympathetically, the Queen leaned forward to take Fin's hand in her gloved one. 'Do not fear me, Fin. It is my desire to help you.'

She stood up. 'Time is passing! We must make plans! Eat and drink whilst I take off these tiresome garments.' She put the cakes back on the plate and poured out more mint tea.

With a hand clap she summoned her serving maid. 'Take off my robe!' she commanded, peeling off her gloves.

Sipping tea and nibbling cake, as the maid unbuttoned the back of her long silk robe and lifted it over her head. they were surprised to see she wore beneath a warrior's garb: her lithe muscled body covered in a close-fitting leather jerkin and trousers with knee length soft leather boots on her feet. At her waist hung a long dagger set in a jewelled scabbard.

Lark asked: 'Why do you have to disguise yourself, Your Majesty. What's wrong with being a Skwid? There's a Skwid in Sandy's Squad – Shadow Dancer. She's ace with a sword! Cut off a Frit's head!'

Her hoarse chuckle reminded them strongly of Dancer. 'I wear this disguise when I am in public – the Berber people have a hatred of the Skwid kind, ever since the Gold Wars, when the Skwid destroyed the Berber city of Timbuktu, and stole the secret of how to glean gold dust from the sand – but that is a long story!'

She smiled proudly. 'Like you Iskander, I too am a warrior leader – a sailor warrior. My true name is Kassabel! My crew and I patrol the African coast, controlling the brutal pirates that infest these waters.

'But enough talk! We go now, down to my private jetty where my crew are making my vessel, Aurora, ready to take you out to your Orca – your friends will be anxious for you. We shall moor alongside for the night in the bay, and in the morning we will sail for the Gambia – in pursuit of the devil butterfly woman!'

Her maid drawing aside a billowing silk curtain, they passed out on to a balcony looking across the bay. Below, a steep cliff dropped down to the sea. To the left, through tall cypress trees could be glimpsed the harbour, and beyond, the sweep of beach, with the fishing boats drawn up onto the sand. They descended winding steps cut into the sandstone to a jetty where Kassabel's boat, the Aurora, was moored. Running his now expert eye over her, Sandy recognised a caravel, shallow drafted for sailing close to shore. He reckoned she was about 75 feet long, longer than Orca by several feet, with a raised deck in the stern, and three masts: the two main masts lateen-rigged, her third, the mizzen, square-rigged for speed.

Her crew, all in uniforms of navy and white, were making ready to sail, loosening ropes to raise the sails; oarsmen were at their places on benches along the bulwarks, oars thrust through rowlocks, ready to row.

Four Skwids, like Kassabel dressed in leather, crossbows on their shoulders and broadswords at their sides, stood at attention by the gangway. One of them saluted Kassabel smartly.

'Is all prepared, Zahhak?' she asked him.

'Yes, Boss, enough water and supplies for a long trip – cook's down the hold, stowing the wine.'

'Good! First, we shall take my companions to their ship in the bay. We will anchor alongside them for the night. At dawn, we will set sail in convoy, heading south for the Gambia – hopefully meeting no trouble on the way!'

'If we do meet pirates, Boss, our quivers are full, and our swords sharpened!' exclaimed one of the other Skwids.

'Aye, my Sophie's fettled and keen!' hissed another, swiftly unsheathing his sword and swishing it through the air alarmingly close to the top of Fin's head.

'Watch what you're doing, Sobek!' Kassabel exclaimed. 'Fin has already almost lost his head once today!'

'Sorry Boss!' the Skwid muttered, his scales rippling orange and red.

With a curt nod, Kassabel ran lightly up the gangway. They hurried after her, Fin and Lark glad to escape the four Skwids' superior gaze. Each crew member saluted briefly as Kassabel led them to the stern and up steps onto the upper deck, where the captain, a hook nosed, brown skinned man with fierce dark eyes, and thick grey hair, stood at the ship's wheel.

'Well, Missy Kass? Are we off at last?' he asked in a soft voice, at once respectful and affectionate. 'The crew is becoming lazy – spending too much time in the taverns!'

'Yes Jamal, we're off again!' chuckled Kassabel. 'Chasing a butterfly this time – let pirates live another day! We are sailing in convoy with my new friends' cutter. They're making for the Gambia.

'Iskander, Fin, Lark – meet Jamal Salim, my Captain. What he doesn't know about seamanship, isn't worth a penny rush light!'

Jamal Salim eyed Sandy thoughtfully, then considered Fin and Lark. 'These imps, your crew, sir?' he asked. 'Used for climbing the rigging?'

Sandy's eyes twinkled. 'No – they would be hopeless! Fin is my navigator and Lark my bosun! Another member of my crew climbs the rigging – a hairy silver-back we call Grilla!'

'You are mocking me!' exclaimed the captain. 'I will be interested to see this tub of yours!'

'Enough talk Jamal,' Kassabel interrupted. 'Let's get under way – you'll see their cutter soon enough.'

Leaning over the balustrade, Jamal called to his crew, his voice now deep and commanding. 'Cast off, my children – prepare to sail!'

'AYE, AYE CAP'N!' the sailors chorused, setting about untying the moorings.

The oarsmen pushed away from the jetty, and settling into a rhythm, rowed swiftly out into the bay. Passing the flotilla of Jolly boats, they recovered Mini-Orca. The captain expertly spinning his wheel, brought Aurora close enough to the line of bobbing boats for a sailor to swing down and untie the little dinghy, then make her fast to Aurora's stern.

As they drew alongside Orca, the rowers shipped their oars, whilst two crew dropped straw fenders down Aurora's side, and another two leaned over with ropes to secure the two vessels together.

There was no sign of Kenji, Crow or Grilla.

'Ahoy Orca! Permission to board!' called Jamal Salim.

Silence.

He called again.

At his command, an Aurora crewman jumped on to Orca's deck. At that moment, the lid of the fishing tackle box flew off with a crash. Crow leaped out, waving his small cutlass, closely followed by Mick who clamped his powerful jaws on the unfortunate sailor's canvas shoe.

Lark whistled shrilly. 'IT'S US! MICK, DROP FOOT!'

Yelping with joy, hardly touching Aurora's side, Mick flew across into Lark's outstretched arms.

'Sorry mate!' Lark called to the sailor hopping about clutching his bleeding foot.

With his one good eye, Crow peered up suspiciously at the faces looking down from Aurora's top deck.

'Well, Crow, do we have permission to come aboard?' Sandy called, amidst general laughter.

Crow smirked and tucked his cutlass into his belt.

Kenji's head and shoulders appeared through the hatchway his crossbow primed with an arrow. Climbing out, he glared furiously up at the laughing audience. Grilla's bulk emerged next, teeth set in a snarling grin. The laughter turned to uneasy murmuring.

Sandy and Lark jumped over onto Orca. As Fin made to follow, he tripped and almost slipped between the two hulls. A sailor quickly put out a hand to save him.

'SKEEW! SKEEW!' From nowhere Quilla swooped and dug his vicious talons deep into the sailor's arm. Beneath the howls of pain from the sailor, Fin heard Bird's faint voice: 'Don't touch him, you vile man!'

'BIRD! STOP QUILLA! STOP HIM – THESE PEOPLE ARE OUR FRIENDS!' Fin yelled.

From Aurora's upper deck, came Zahhak's harsh voice. 'SQUAD! READY TO AIM!'

With an ominous hiss of arrows swiftly drawn from quivers, the Skwids took aim at Quilla, perched now on Fin's shoulder, wings drooping.

Kassabel quickly took command. 'Zahhak stand down your squad! The eagle misunderstood the sailor's action and was defending his master.' Leaping down onto Orca, she inspected the sailor's wounds. 'One of you – come, take him to the sick bay!' she called to the watchers on Aurora, adding. 'And you with the dog bitten foot, go with them!

Jamal and Zahhak, who had watched events with increasing amazement, jumped across from Aurora to join Kassabel and Sandy introduced Kenji and Crow.

'You have a Western Gorilla as part of your crew?' Kassabel exclaimed stepping back nervously as Grilla politely offered her his large soft paw.

'Aye, Mrs Kassabel,' Lark said, patting Grilla on his silvery back. 'He's perfectly safe – saved Fin and me from drowning!'

Jamal eyed the gorilla dubiously. 'I do not allow pets on board the Aurora – not even small dogs.' He scowled down at Mick standing close by Lark. 'They bring bad luck.'

His bible bag clutched to his thin chest Crow hopped forward. Glaring up with his one eye at Jamal, he squeaked: 'My mouse not pet! Mrs Mouse be innocent widow with baby – look see!'

Holding up the open bible bag he thrust it at Jamal who had little choice but to peer into its depths.

Lark grinned. 'He might be a shrivelled little Scav, Mr Jamal, but our Crow doesn't let anyone mess with his rodents!'

Stepping back from the bible bag, Jamal glared at his smirking crew watching from the Aurora. 'Well, pets or pests, if I find the Scav's mice in our grain store, they'll be thrown overboard.'

Zahhak's reptilian eyes focused on Quilla. 'The eagle's eyes are missing!' he exclaimed. 'Surely the bird is useless for hunting?'

Quilla turned his head towards him, giving the Skwid the uncomfortable feeling that behind the film misting the left eye, someone was glowering at him. With slow wing beats, Quilla left Fin's shoulder and flew to the top of the main mast.

Kenji chuckled and shook his head in mock horror. 'Dear me, Skwid! You've offended our Quilla – you'd best keep out of his way, or you might lose an eye!'

Zahhak scowled.

Kassabel studied Kenji interestedly. 'We do not often meet your race in these parts!' she told him. 'Having said that, there is a tribe in The Gambia. Sanyo is their name. Keepers of the Motherhome there.'

Kenji's dark eyes gleamed beneath his narrowed lids. 'Did you say Sanyo? That's my name! We must be related! Let me see…' He started counting with his fingers. 'Yes, they must be my great, great – great grandfather's second cousins' descendants, who went to Africa. But I would have to check with my esteemed grandmother. It doesn't surprise me that some of my people are keepers of a Motherhome! Guarding Knowledge, caring for the Motherboards, runs in the family. My grandfather and my father—'

Sandy interrupted him with a groan. 'Kassabel, you have opened a dam! It'll be cooking next!'

She laughed. 'Well Kenji, then you must meet our cook! Mokele's goat tagine is famous! Indeed, you are all invited aboard Aurora tonight for supper.'

Sandy bowed. 'We shall be honoured!'

'I look forward to hearing of your adventures,' Kassabel smiled.

With a farewell wave she jumped across to Aurora after Jamal and Zahhak.

Once alone Sandy, Fin and Lark recounted their adventure to Kenji and Crow, explaining how Kassabel had rescued them.

Lark apologized to Kenji for not bringing lamp oil.

Kenji frowned. 'Not your fault. But we'll have make do with rush lights until we call in at another port, unless…'

He looked across to Aurora from where a meaty aroma drifted from a porthole. 'I wonder if the cook will give us some oil. In return, I could offer to help with the cooking, and might even learn a new recipe! I'll go and call on him.'

He spotted Mick, whining behind the gunwale as he sniffed the drifting cooking smells, and whistled to him. 'Come on lad! Let's see if there's a bone for you!'

Later, in the brief African twilight, Sandy, Fin and Lark, hair tidied and wearing clean shirts, made their way onto Aurora, to be greeted by Kassabel.

Grilla and Crow stayed on Orca, dining on the fresh fruit and vegetables bought that morning from the boat traders. Mick was also with them, in disgrace after fighting with the cook's cat on Aurora. Before joining the others in the mess cabin, Fin lingered, searching the sky and was reassured to spot Quilla on the hunt for food: a dark silhouette against the last rays of the sun.

Below deck, he found a place at the long table between Lark and Captain Jamal, the rumble of voices loud as straw-covered bottles were passed around, mugs filled and refilled. At the far end, Sandy, Kassabel and Zahhak were deep in talk together, Sandy's copper-gold hair gleaming in the lamplight. He had taken on what Fin always thought of as his kingly air, making him wonder whether Kassabel and Zahhak realised he was part Gaiakin. Did they know about Gaiakins, he wondered? He hadn't seen any so far.

His thoughts were interrupted when, to a chorus of appreciative shouts, the cook's young cabin lad staggered in bearing a basket piled high with flatbreads. Behind him the cook proudly carried a large terracotta pot with a tall conical lid. A grinning, sweaty-faced Kenji followed with a similar pot. Placing a pot at each end of the table, at the same moment the cook and Kenji lifted the lids with a flourish, filling the crowded room with a mouth-watering aroma. Conversation halted as everyone ladled steaming stew into their bowls, then tearing chunks of flatbread to dip into the thick dark red gravy.

Kenji squeezed between Fin and Lark. 'Well lads, what do you think of the tagine?' he asked piling stew high into his bowl and grabbing a flatbread.

Coughing, Lark raised his mug for a gulp of rough red wine. 'Volcanic!' he managed to gasp.

Kenji laughed. 'Mokele's keen on chilli peppers – two dozen went into each pot – to cover up the taste of old goat, he told me!'

From the other side of Fin, Jamal gave a scornful snort as he helped himself to more stew and flatbread. 'Chilli is full of goodness. Gives strong muscles!' The Aurora's formidable Captain proudly flexed his bulging biceps.

The stew too fiery for him, after a few more mouthfuls Fin pushed his bowl away. Nibbling a flatbread, he saw that Kassabel and Sandy, also finished, had cleared aside mugs and bowls to open out a map. Zahhak had gone to sit with his Squad. Watching Kassabel, head bent low, her eyes swivelling as she studied the map, yet again he wondered about her. What was the real reason she disguised herself when she went into the city? The heady wine giving him courage, Fin turned to Jamal wolfing down his abandoned stew with appreciative grunts.

'Captain, forgive my asking – what is the story of Kassabel – how is it she came to be the Queen of Tangier, when— when the Skwids are so hated by the Berber people?'

In theatrical astonishment, Jamal twisted around to stare at him. 'Young Delphin!' he exclaimed. 'Surely you know the ancient Legend of Maghreb? Berber children are told the tale from the cradle!'

Fin frowned, trying to recall if he'd read the story in one of Mossy's books. 'No, it's not a tale us Delphins tell our children.'

Overhearing them, Lark, once more sitting next to Fin, Kenji having gone back to the galley, looked pleadingly at the Berber Captain.

'Tell us please, sir. Delphins are mighty keen on hearing stories!'

The Berber looked wistful. 'Telling the tale always brings memories of when I held my little son, Youssef in my arms...' Lost in thought, he fell silent.

Then, topping up the wine in his mug, he cleared his throat. In a soft singsong note, he began the story.

*'Now Hanno the Great, King of Carthage, gave his daughter Maghreb in marriage to Tingis, ruler of Tangier. Their marriage was happy but after several years, they still had no children. In desperation, Maghreb undertook the long journey to the Oracle at Delphi, to consult the goddess, Pythia.*

*Seeing her sorrow, the goddess had pity on her, foretelling that she would be given a child, but as she had sinned by marrying a heathen Berber, she would be punished: she would be given the child only when her husband Tingis lay on his death bed.*

*Fearful and saddened, Maghreb returned to Tingis, and they lived for many more happy years together, Maghreb becoming much loved by the people of Tangier.*

*Then Tingis became mortally ill with fever. To cool his brow, Maghreb went down to shore beneath their palace, to fill her flask with the sacred water of the bay of Tangier. Whilst she was bent filling her flask, she heard a small cry from the sea. Looking up, she saw a wicker basket floating towards her on the waves. Wading out a little way, she caught up the basket and carried it to the shore. Taking off the plain linen cover, she found a tiny lizard-like Skwid child there, wrapped in a blue silken cloth. Maghreb's heart was filled with pity for the tiny whimpering mite. Taking the creature home, she gave it to her maids to look after.*

*A few days later her husband Tingis died. Maghreb fell into inconsolable grief and mourned for many years.*

*One day, as she stood on the shore of the bay beneath her palace, she remembered the tiny Skwid child. Recalling what the Oracle at Delphi had said, she called for the maid into whose care she had given the Skwid and asked what had happened to the creature.*

*'O, great Queen – she has grown!' exclaimed her maid. 'She has lived in the palace for many moons and is much loved by the people. Going out disguised in robe and mask so that no one will know she is of Skwid kind, she works among the poor of Tangier, bringing them food and tending them in their sickness.'*

*Maghreb asked to see the Skwid and looking at her dressed in her raiment as a Berber princess, she recognized the creature as the daughter promised her by the goddess.*

*Maghreb took her to live in her own apartments and came to love her dearly. The name she gave her was Kassabel, and when Maghreb lay on her death bed, she decreed thereafter all future Queens of Tangier shall be called by that holy name.'*

Jamal stopped speaking and wiped his eyes. Lark sighed. 'That was a beautiful tale!'

Recovering his composure, Jamal shrugged: 'It is purely legend – make of the puzzle what you will! I tell you this though, if I were cornered in a fierce battle, I would rather have my Queen Rami at my side than anyone else! There is no one who has such fighting skills as she!'

'I bet they're no better than Sandy's,' Lark exclaimed hotly, gesturing down the table to Sandy. 'Iskander's Squad is famed throughout the North! Iskander is Sandy's real name – Lord Iskander. He's got royal blood in him as well as being part Gaiakin!'

Jamal gave a scornful laugh. 'How is it then that this mighty Lord has ended up captain of a small cutter with a rag-tag crew of Delphins, Scavs and monkeys?'

The wine coursing through him, Lark was about to come indignantly to Sandy's defence, when Fin's elbow dug him savagely in the ribs. 'Don't make trouble Lark!' he hissed fiercely.

Just then the benches were scraped back: supper was over.

Back up on deck, darkness had long since fallen. Across the bay, the city lights twinkled over on water.

The next day, Orca and Aurora left Tangier in convoy, heading south for The Gambia.

# 3
# EVIL COMES TO BRIGHTDALE

Hunkered down inside a gorse thicket, Tissy looked up through the branches criss-crossing the darkening evening sky; Dancer crouched beside her. They were watching the crags above, keeping an eye on a Snoopers' nest.

When Dancer had first told Tissy about the fearsome insects it had terrified Tissy; she'd nearly fainted – like when she'd seen the horrible fiery cloud outside Mossy's shop. She firmly told herself she mustn't be frightened: Dancer was a warrior – and now so was she. To calm her nerves, she took a sip from her water flask. The stopper squeaked as she pushed it back in and she felt Dancer's body by her side tremble. In the gathering dusk, Tissy made out green shades of fear rippling across her reptilian face. The Skwid's eyes swivelled down at her.

'Hush!' she hissed in a throaty whisper. 'The insects have the hearing of a lynx!'

Tissy searched for her hand, giving it a comforting squeeze. She knew Dancer was even more scared than she was. Dancer had encountered these monsters before, their needle-like stings peppering her body, almost killing her.

Their hiding place had a rancid stench, stronger even than the vinegary fumes drifting down from the Hornet Snoopers nest in the crags above. Dancer had shuddered at her first smell of the stink, muttering about it coming from a creature she called a ganglefowl, but she didn't elaborate. Unknown to them, a ganglefowl had once lurked in their gorse thicket. The huge ostrich-like bird had hidden in the thicket with its master, the Frit who ambushed and murdered her uncle Marlin, slicing deep across his throat.

In the sandy soil at Dancer's feet stood a small clay pot containing a lump of glowing charcoal. Beside it lay a torch, the end bound with tar-soaked cloth. After dark, they planned to creep up to the Snoopers Nest and set fire to it, killing the giant insects inside.

Dancer suddenly tensed. 'Look!'

Two insect feelers waved over the lip of the ledge above them: Tissy sensed they were listening. An armoured face with searching multifaceted eyes and fanged mouth, loomed into view. Its long proboscis tasted the air. Papery wings rattling, the insect thrummed excitedly. The black and yellow striped body, the size of a sheep, rose ponderously into the air. Long spindly legs dangling, it hovered above the gorse bush where they were hiding. Had it sniffed them out? Ping! A long sting, its tip glittering with a globule of venom, shot from its backside, hitting the ground in front of the bush.

Quickly Dancer set her torch to the glowing charcoal ember: a flame blazed up.

'Take it!' she hissed, shoving the torch into Tissy's hand. Springing from the tangled gorse, with a whistling swish Dancer drew her great sword from its sheath on her back. Almost flying, she slashed at the insect and three of the six dangling legs fluttered to the ground.

No time to feel faint: this was the moment to prove herself. With the loudest yell she could muster, Tissy leapt after Dancer. Brandishing the burning torch, she aimed for the striped body and threw: her aim was true. With a whoosh, the insect exploded into a ball of flame. But even as it fell to the ground, from the ledge flew another angry insect, then another. Tissy and Dancer froze in terror.

From above the ledge came a war-like whoop: a figure stood on top of a crag. It was Sam Spinner, his face lit by the blazing torch he carried. Jamming the torch into a crevice, he set the tar-soaked arrow on his crossbow to the torch flame then let fly. Thwack: it plunged deep into a Snooper's brittle carapace, turning it instantly into a fireball. From his crossbow flew another fiery arrow. Thwack. Thud. The second insect was engulfed in fire. For a moment, the screaming bodies danced in the air, then slowly tumbling, landed next to their charred companion.

For a moment, there was silence. Then from above came an explosive roar as flames shot into the evening sky. Through the fog of smoke Dancer and Tissy saw Sam Spinner's triumphant jig. He'd thrown his torch into the Snoopers' Nest: the waxy paper construction was now an inferno.

As they stood, awed by what they had done, from the valley below came shouts and the baying of hounds. A moment later, Tissy's brother Kelp ran towards them, followed by Hollin Annunder the ghillie, then Sparrow Chippen. Carrying torches, and armed with spears, their pack of hunting dogs around them, they slithered to a halt, gaping at the Snoopers' smouldering husks. They saw Sam on the ledge above, still doing a war dance in front of the flaming nest.

'SAM, ARE ALL DEAD?' Kelp yelled.

'BURNT TO A CRISP, NEST AND ALL!' came Sam's triumphant reply.

Kelp plunged his spear into a crumbling heap of glowing ashes, sending up a cloud of sparks. 'You've done a decent job, Skwid!' he said, looking admiringly at Dancer.

Dancer gave a hoarse chuckle. 'It wasn't me that set fire to that unnatural creature – you have to thank your little sister!'

Kelp turned to Tissy in surprise, noticing her for the first time.

'You here Tis? Well, I'll be——' He stared in amazement at her soot smudged face, then his gaze took in her clothes: her leather jerkin, trousers and sturdy boots.

Tissy glared at her brother: 'Oh, stop gawping Kelp! If you must know, Dancer and I are a team!'

'Yep!' Dancer grinned, rainbow colours rippling over her skin just visible in the light of their torches. 'You'll have to get used to your timid little sister being a fighter!'

'Enough talk!' Hollin Annunder growled. 'We must damp down these fires before the heather catches!'

He turned to Sparrow Chippen, still staring open-mouthed at Tissy. 'Get up the cliff, lad – Sam needs help there beating out the flames!'

A while later, satisfied that all fires were out, as the Saprise night gathered, the little war party set off for Dandrum Den, where Grammer Nutmeg was anxiously waiting for them, ready with a supper of rabbit stew and dumplings.

Walking beside Dancer, trying to match her long stride, Tissy wondered what Lark would think if he saw her now: a war-tested fighter teamed up with a Skwid. She grinned in the dark – how surprised Kelp had been!

Was it only twelve days ago, that she'd watched Mossy disappearing into the night aboard the flying machine, with the tall man called Wings?

Moments before he left, Mossy had solemnly entrusted to her care a box such as she had never seen before, the outside richly decorated with intricately inlaid silver wire and mother-of-pearl flowers, the interior lined with scarlet velvet. Set in the centre of the lid was a strangely shaped cross, in the form of an X intersected by the letter P. Inside, neatly folded, was a piece of shimmering blue silken material.

True to her promise, she'd carefully hidden the box behind a loose wall panel in her room at Dandrum Den. She'd told no one.

Several days later Dancer and Kenji arrived at Spinner Hall with their dreadful burdens: Bee's body in a coffin, and Bird only just alive, her body scarred with burns still raw red, most of her hair gone, scorched bald patches all over her head. Worst of all were her eyes: blank, as if the light of life had gone out. The silver bird pendant around her neck was a heart-breaking reminder of the Bird they all loved so dearly. Horror followed upon horror:

they also brought news that Wings' flying machine had crashed somewhere, and that Mossy and Wings were almost certainly dead.

Never had the Dale encountered such extraordinary persons as the two warriors who had arrived: one a Skwid, as fearsome looking as her sword and crossbow yet so gentle with Bird; and her companion with his glossy back hair tied back with a giant bird's beak, also armed with a formidable sword. The Dale seethed with gossip, more lurid with each retelling. All however were agreed on one thing: you would not mess with these two.

Spinner Hall was in turmoil, the twins' family inconsolable. Tissy and Grammer Nutmeg did their best to help, but without Mossy's wise and comforting presence it was hard to know what to do. Bee's funeral had been a particularly hard trial for Nutmeg and Tissy, who had the agonising task of preparing her small body for the funeral pyre.

Taking Lass, Mossy's old dog, Tissy left home to stay at Spinner Hall. She helped look after Bird, who crouched in a box by the kitchen fire with loyal Wolfie guarding her. Still weak from the wounds suffered on his heroic journey carrying the twins' desperate message from Durholm, he would growl fiercely at anyone who came too near Bird.

Over the days Bird gradually grew thinner, her skin becoming shrivelled.

'Her poor little body's like a plum turning into a dried prune!' moaned Nutmeg as she gently applied marigold ointment to the worst of Bird's burns.

They found Dancer a comforting help. She had a way with Bird, dealing with her wild outbursts of animal-like screeching that made Tissy's skin crawl. In their anguish, Bird's mum and dad, Absolem and Sable, found it hard at first to accept the Skwid but seeing how Bird trusted her, and the Skwid's tender care, they had come to like and rely on the strange nurse.

To soothe, if only briefly, her heartbreak Nutmeg busied herself raiding her clothes chest for her fancy underwear to make lace trimmed silk vests and knickers for Bird to wear under the beautiful green velvet dress a Gaiakin called Betony had provided.

Two days after the funeral Kenji left, called away by the oddest-looking man. Looking like a walking hedge, all covered in grass and twigs, small brown eyes peering out of a thicket of leaves, he arrived one evening in the courtyard at Dandrum Den. With few words of Common Language, waving his long arms, he just repeated over and over: 'Sandy say – Kenji come! Sandy say – Kenji come!' Greatly alarmed, Kelp and the cowhand tried to see him off, threatening him with spears. Luckily, Grammer Nutmeg heard their curses and threats, and was able to reassure them the strange man was not dangerous. She'd come across the likes of him before, on her wanderings near Withered Wood. Mr Mossy had said they were the Boskie folk who dwell in the Wood.

After Kenji had gone with the Boskie, in answering the question: 'Who was this Sandy?' Dancer explained that he was their boss – leader of their Squad, and if Sandy so commanded, it was vitally important that Kenji go with the Boskie.

As the news of Mossy's likely death spread, the question arose: what would become of his Bookshop? Some Dalers, especially the Akests, still bitter about the way the Dandrums had treated their daughter Daffodil, thought it was a good thing if he didn't come back.

'All those useless scrolls and books should be cleared out,' Mr Akest had said. 'A good building like that mustn't go to waste.' He was Watersmeet's barber and fancied extending his business. 'Doesn't Thetis Dandrum have the key?'

Several Dalers tried to bully Tissy into handing it over, but with a new-found confidence that startled them, they were sent packing. Furious, Grammer Nutmeg backed her up: 'Tissy Dandrum has enough troubles, what with her dad lying as if dead in the Hall at Dandrum Den, and her ma and sister taken to their beds, moaning and groaning like a pair of useless wemmers!'

That Absolem Spinner was standing behind them with his pitchfork also discouraged further argument.

Determined not to give up hope, Tissy went every now and then to dust the bookshop. Lass came too, crouching mournfully in front of the empty fire grate in Mossy's upstairs room.

A great comfort to Tissy and Nutmeg were the letters Kenji had brought from Fin and Lark. With his letter for Grammer Nutmeg, Fin had enclosed his sketches which she and Tissy pored over: ruined castles and exotic looking people, as well as quick sketches of the twins in strange landscapes. Tissy's favourite sketch was of Lark beneath a huge leaf. Fin had added the title: Lark in the jungle garden of Florain, beneath a gunnera.

Lark's writing was wobbly, making his long letter difficult to read. On the outside, he'd written: 'Thetis Dandrum: for her eyes only', with a picture of two eyes above the word 'eyes'.

It was an amazing tale he told; how the twins had been captured by an evil man who had taken them to a place called Birdoswald, a Frit army's camp, and how he and Fin had chased after them with their new warrior friends, Sandy, Kenji and someone called Fescue. But they were too late: they couldn't save the twins from being attacked by what Lark called a 'Phraggy monster': Bee so badly burned that she died, and the monster flying off with Bird's little pearly soul, trapped behind its evil yellow fangs, leaving her body an empty shell.

After that horror, he told an exciting tale about the Gaiakins, who had saved them from death at the hands of the Frits and had taken them to their garden home of Florain. His letter ended with the news, already known from Kenji and Dancer, that Mossy was believed to be dead, and that he and Fin were sailing from Florain to a place called Holy Island, in the warrior Sandy's boat.

Tissy kept Lark's letter inside her jerkin, close to her heart. Before Kenji left, she'd hurriedly written a letter back, in the desperate hope that Lark and Fin could be with Sandy.

She and Dancer soon became firm friends. Taking breaks from looking after Bird, they explored the Dale, with Lass ever at their side. On these rambles, Tissy listened spellbound to Dancer's descriptions of how Sandy's warrior squad fought the evils and protected the people. It was then that Dancer suggested Tissy should start learning fighting skills.

'Your small country may be safe at present, but there's great danger beyond your borders, and you should be prepared.'

'For a start, you can't wear those clothes – they would get in the way!' Dancer had added laughingly, helping Tissy unhook the frill of her skirt from a bramble bush.

Sitting in the kitchen at Spinner Hall making plans, Bird's grandmother Magette suggested that Tissy should have Bee's clothes: her jerkins, breeches and boots, just the right garb for a would-be warrior.

'Bee would be right chuffed, young Thetis – knowing you're turning into a little tom-boy like her!' she quavered, dabbing her eyes with her apron.

Suitably clad, and with Dancer's careful training, Tissy soon acquired the confidence to see off such as those who would bully her for Mossy's keys.

As the excitement of the warriors' arrival and the grief at the twins' terrible fate faded, the Delphin Dalers' thoughts turned back to their everyday lives. Highsun was around the corner when haymaking would start.

But all was not right in the Dale. Rumours were growing of blind creatures, with empty sockets where eyes should be, wandering on the borders. One or two people even reported seeing monkey-like imps, with orange hair, but nobody believed them – other than Grammer Nutmeg, who knew them to be Frits.

Then, one morning, Fox Annunder appeared in the kitchen at Spinner Hall just as the Spinner family and their farmhands were finishing breakfast. Dancer and Tissy were there too, attending to Bird's needs as she crouched in her box by the fireplace.

His face red and swollen, hands heavily bandaged, Fox told them a dramatic tale of an encounter with a flock of enormous flightless birds with stinging feathers. 'Huger than geese or turkeys – snaking, twisting necks and long legs with powerful claws!'

Hearing yet more rumours of blind, sick creatures appearing on the border between Annunder Territory and Durholm Dale, he had gone with his brother Fir to investigate. On the heights above Ireshope, they came upon the birds feeding on the heather – a flock of a dozen or so, bedraggled and frightened. They shot two with their crossbows, before the rest fled back down to the river path that led to Killhope Gate. Fired with excitement, Fir chased after them with his pack of hunting dogs, leaving Fox to butcher the two dead birds. As he started plucking the soft rump feathers of the first bird, a terrible fiery pain spread over his face and hands.

Listening to his story, Dancer became ever more agitated, dark colours of alarm rippling over her scales.

'A flock, did you say? Those birds are the vile ganglefowl the Frits ride! The vermin must be dealt with as soon as possible.'

She turned to Absolem. 'Are you able to muster a force of fighters, skilled with crossbow and spear?'

'Aye Skwid, we can gather a force!' Absolem said scornfully. 'We deal with boar and wolf – a few birds are naught to us!'

As he spoke, the kitchen door crashed open. Sam Spinner staggered in, supporting Rook Chippen, the Wheelwright. Rook was grey with fright, gibbering about a fiery black rag streaking across the sky. 'It spotted me – swooped down it did, molten spit dripping from its yellow fangs!'

A chill ran through Tissy: she remembered the monster outside Mossy's shop.

'In me cart I were, delivering logs to Smithy – knocked me off me perch it did. If Sam here hadn't come charging out with a bucket, and thrown water at it, I'd – I'd be burnt to a crisp!' Trembling violently, he collapsed into a kitchen chair.

Dancer looked around grimly: 'The monster is a Phragg – a servant of Lord Gressil! With the death of Zagzagel, evil has come to you – sooner than I expected. We must make plans to defend the Dale!'

'The Skwid gives sound advice!' Absolem Spinner growled, scraping back his chair. 'Come Sam, come workers – to the Great Hall to collect weapons from the wall!'

'And when we're armed, we'll go into Watersmeet to gather a force!' Sam cried, heading eagerly for the door.

'And they must be told up at Dandrum Den,' added Absolem.

'Yes – Kelp Dandrum and Hollin Annunder will be handy in a fight!' exclaimed Fox, the pain of the stinging feathers quite forgotten.

So, eager to show their fighting abilities to the warrior Skwid, every able-bodied Delphin rushed to arm themselves.

Then Tom Gotobed, the Dandrum shepherd, caused even greater alarm when he ran down from the fell to report to Sam Spinner that he'd seen huge flying insects up at Donkey Crags.

'Like giant fat wasps the size of sheep buzzing around – looked to me like they were making a nest!'

When Sam told Dancer, for a moment she trembled, her scales flickering blue-black. Then mastering herself, she hissed fiercely: 'Gressil's Snoopers! Those monsters were nearly my death! We must search them out, burn their nest – destroy their young!'

She turned to Tissy. 'Tissy, show me the place! Sam, come too, with a torch and your crossbow!'

That was this morning. As she walked beside Dancer back to Dandrum Den, triumphant pride filled Tissy: they had killed the giant insects and torched their nest. She'd proved to Dancer, and to herself, that she was a warrior.

Lovingly twisting the battered ring on her finger, she recalled the moment Mossy had given it to her, with a message from Lark: that it had been his mother's, his only memento of her, and he wanted Tissy to have it as a reminder of him. It was then that Mossy had told her about Fin inheriting a precious jewel from his father: a treasure he'd brought when he returned from his wanderings. That treasure had brought a demon to the Dale.

'It is the reason Fin has left Brightdale, to draw the evil away,' Mossy had explained.

Coming out of her reverie, she saw they were nearly at the Den. How she wished Fin and Lark were there, waiting for her! Were they in danger? Where were they? For reassurance, she put her hand inside her jerkin, and touched Lark's letter.

It was twelve days after Kenji had left with the Boskie, when everything dramatically changed. Early one morning in the Spinner's kitchen, Dancer and Tissy were coaxing Bird to eat her breakfast porridge, watched anxiously by Madgette, when there came a rapping on the oak door and Mossy walked in. Kenji was there, behind him.

For a moment Dancer, Tissy and Madgette stared in disbelief.

With a yelp of joy, Lass danced to her beloved master, her tail frantically wagging. Wolfie, making weak gruff barks, staggered after her.

Dropping her spoon in the porridge, Tissy rushed to Mossy.

'You're alive! You're alive!' she sobbed, grasping Mossy's outstretched hands. Eyes swimming, she hungrily studied his beautiful dark face wondering if she was dreaming.

'As you see, Thetis: all whole, nothing missing!' laughed Mossy, giving her a hug.

Swiftly going to Bird, screeching as she struggled in Dancer's arms, he laid a calming hand on her head. 'Is there any change, Dancer?'

Dancer shook her head. 'No — she eats too little! See how thin she is and so small. We fear there'll soon be nothing left of her!'

Bending, Mossy looked deep into Bird's blank eyes. 'There is a spark there,' he muttered. 'Small but alight in the dark place left empty by the theft of her soul. The Phragg did not take all of her valiant spirit – a shred is left behind!'

He straightened up. 'There is no time to waste – Mistress Madgette, take care of the small lass!

'Thetis, Dancer and Kenji, with me to the Bookshop – plans must be made! Mistress Nutmeg is already there, lighting the fire.'

With Bird settled on Madgette's knee and Wolfie lying by the hearth, they set off for Mossy's bookshop, Lass prancing before them.

In Mossy's room over the shop, Nutmeg had got a fire blazing, a kettle boiling, and was busy preparing tea. Dancer and Kenji sat on the ancient sofa, and Tissy settled on the sheepskin rug gazing lovingly at Mossy in his rocking chair by the fire. Lass lay beside her, the flickering flames warming her pink stomach.

Dancer leant across and took Mossy's hand. 'Mossy – what happened to you and Wings? When I found the wreckage in the forest, I was so frightened that you were killed!'

Mossy sighed. 'Skyhook crashing was indeed unfortunate!'

He told them about the attack by the Snoopers and Wings losing part of his leg. 'He nearly died! Thankfully, the Boskie folk came to our rescue!'

'Aye, Wings told me what happened,' Kenji said, 'he's recovering famously – hopping about on his crutch like a young lamb and planning to make a hinged metal foot!

As they drank Nutmeg's tea Mossy told them of the dramatic events in Contagion: the melting of the Great Iceberg, and the flooding of Gressil's lair. Fin finding Bird's pearly soul inside an eagle's eye, and Queen Mab turning into a huge butterfly, stealing the holy jewelled cross that was needed to heal Bird and flying away with it. Lastly, he told of how he, Sandy and Wings had rescued Fin and Lark from drowning in the flood and sailing to the Island of Mann, where they were planning to find a ship and sail after Queen Mab.

For a while, finding it hard to take in the horrific happenings, everyone sat in grim silence.

Tissy had a feeling there was more to the story than Mossy had let on: perhaps to spare her feelings, he'd left out what part Lark had played in it all. Nestling safe in an inside pocket of Tissy's jerkin was another letter Kenji had brought from Lark, and she longed to be alone to read it.

Setting down her mug, Dancer got up to pace the room, her scales rippling black and green.

'Those evil Snoopers have caused so much trouble! Some even came here, to this peaceful Dale!' She smiled at Tissy. 'But we've dealt with them!'

She told Mossy and Kenji how she and Tissy had joined forces with some of the Dalers to destroy the Snoopers and their nest. She also told them about Fir Annunder's encounter with the ganglefowl, and how Sam Spinner drove off the Phragg that had attacked Rook Chippen.

Nutmeg began gathering the tea mugs. 'Now you're back Mr Mossy, we won't be troubled by those Evils anymore. Mind you, I can't help feeling sorry for the poor bedraggled, blinded creatures that have appeared in the Dale – cow byre and kennels up at Dandrum Den are full of 'em: cats, sheep, goats, even a tatty old toothless tiger. Yesterday, some half-starved little Scavs, their eyes put out, came scratching at the gate! Whoever did such dreadful things deserve to be strung up for crows to peck! You'll need to get up there and see what you can do, Mr Mossy! Hollin Annunder is doing 'is best, but some creatures have died, poor beasts!'

Suddenly overcome, collapsing onto a chair, she threw her apron over her face and let out a long wail. 'Oh, Mr Mossy, what you've told us is all so dreadful! Will poor little Bird ever get her soul back? Will she end up like Roach, a shrunken pile of bones, his blank eyes staring at nothing?'

Mossy went to her, putting his arms around her heaving shoulders. 'Hush – hush, Mrs Annunder! Do not despair!'

'Mossy! Should not Tissy, Kenji and I take Bird to join the others?' Dancer exclaimed. 'Surely, when they catch up with Queen Mab and retrieve the precious cross, Bird's soul and her body must be together?'

'Yes, Dancer. Bird's body must be there with her soul. But it would do no good if you were to join them chasing after the butterfly. No, you must make for where they are all heading – including Queen Mab with the cross – the holy pool of Siloam – far, far from here. The sacred waters and the cross together will make Bird whole once more. That is why Mab has stolen the Chi Rho: she hopes the cross and the water will heal the deadly wound in her side and save her from dying. You must take Bird's body there and meet up with Fin, who will come with Quilla, the blind eagle, in whose eye socket Bird's soul is safely kept. I have already explained these matters to them on the Island of Mann.'

'Tell us where this holy pool is!' Dancer exclaimed. 'Tissy and I are willing to travel over land and sea with Bird's body!'

Jumping up to stand at Dancer's side, Tissy looked fiercely around at everyone. 'As Dancer says, I'm certainly not going to be left behind – I know how to take care of Bird – she trusts me!'

Mossy smiled. 'Have no fear, Thetis! Wings will take you and Dancer there in his new flying machine.'

Kenji nodded. 'When we left the Isle of Mann, Wings and his engineering friends had already started building his machine.' He grinned teasingly at Tissy. 'It sounds a devilish contraption – sooner you than me!'

'Dancer and I are warriors – we're not scared of any machine!' Tissy retorted defiantly.

Then recalling the night Mossy roared off into the sky, with the strange leather-clad man, wearing thick round goggles, she gulped nervously.

'Do not frighten the lass!' Mossy exclaimed, frowning at Kenji. 'From the plans, Skyhook II will be a sturdy machine – a metal frame, a reliable engine, padded seats and even, what the engineer Boffin, called Perspex windows, to keep out the cold! They are working day and night to complete her, and soon he will be coming for you and Dancer.'

Once more Nutmeg became agitated. 'Oh dear, oh dear! It's all so dreadful! Tissy going off too! I don't know how I will bear it!'

'Dear Grammer, don't fret yourself!' Tissy gave her old nurse a hug. 'We'll be back in no time, just you see. Bird all better! And Lark and Fin home too! Isn't that right, Mossy?'

'Indeed yes! Mrs Annunder, when they have gone, I shall need your help with the poor injured creatures. Time will fly!'

He looked round at everyone. 'Whilst we are waiting for Wings, there is still much to do in the Dale. We must find and clear a place for Wings to land his machine, as well as deal with any evil invader from Contagion. There are sure to be more Frits and ganglefowl on the way, and maybe more Snoopers.'

Hearing Mossy talking of Snoopers, Kenji looked worriedly at Dancer. 'Are you able to tackle those monsters – after your experience at Durholm? I intended to return to Haverigg in the morning, to wait for Sandy and the others to arrive in their ship, but it looks as if my sword and crossbow are needed here!'

Dancer scowled in irritation. 'As we have already told you, Kenji, Snoopers are no match for Tissy and me, with our band of brave Delphins. Don't forget there are several dead, up at Donkey Crags where they had started to build a nest – all burnt to a crisp!'

So Dancer and Tissy returned to Spinner Hall, having said goodbye to Kenji who, after spending the night on Mossy's sofa, left at first light to make his way to Haverigg where he was to meet up with the others on Orca,

That night, sitting up in the beds that had been Bird and Bee's, Tissy and Dancer discussed the amazing arrival of Mossy, whole and unhurt.

'Dancer,' Tissy asked, 'do you think Mossy could be an angel? Lark says he is – one of those who stood by the tomb when the Christ rose. Do Skwids believe in angels too?'

Seeing Dancer frowning in thought, she hoped she hadn't offended the Skwid. Perhaps their alien species didn't believe in the Christ's angels, like humans did. After all, Delphins weren't sure if they should either. They had Phul to worship, as well as myriad spirits: wood spirits, river spirits, sea spirits.

'Yes, Skwids believe in angels. Our special angel is called Kassabel. She's a star maker! More powerful even than Phul or Mossy, whose only concern is with the making of Gaia.'

Tissy wriggled excitedly. 'Tell me about her! Where does she live? In a star? Mossy says our sun is a star. Does she live there?'

Dancer chuckled. 'Who knows?' She gave a cavernous yawn. 'I'm too sleepy to think about that now! Come on Tiss, it's about time we got some sleep.'

Blowing out their candles, they settled down for the night.

Her mind in turmoil, Tissy found it hard to catch sleep. She thought about Lark's letter which she'd found a chance to read earlier. He'd enclosed a picture of himself, looking startled with his hair on end. After starting to write of being kissed by a giant slug, and a gorilla saving him from being smothered, he'd cut the story short, emphasising that he was alright, and she was not to worry – whatever Mossy told her.

'All you've got to do, is make sure you're safe, and I miss you dreadfully. And you're to trust Wings – he's a brilliant pilot and I'm sure he'll get you, with poor little Bird, to that healing pool.'

She thought about Wings, the strange man who'd come to the shop to take Mossy away. She couldn't quite believe she would be flying in his new machine, leaving her home, venturing far, far away, into the dangerous unknown! How she wished Lark could be with her – he would have given her the courage she desperately needed.

She stifled a whimper of fear. Pray – that's what she should do. Ask Phul to help her. No, better still, she'd ask the angel, Kassabel. Didn't Dancer say she was more powerful even than Phul or Mossy?

She conjured up what she thought Kassabel might look like. A picture swam into her mind of Dancer, with great white feathered wings sprouting from her back.

'Kassabel, keep us all safe …'

# 4
# THE GAMBIA

'Did you speak?'

Kassabel looked up at Lark, her needle poised over a hole in the fishing net she was mending.

Lark stared at her in surprise 'Me? Didn't say a thing.'

Kassabel frowned. 'I heard a voice – someone calling me.'

Lark nudged Crow, dozing on the bundle of nets he was supposed to be sorting. 'Stop talking in your sleep, Crow. You're distracting Queen Kass, when she's doing us a favour, mending our nets.'

'Weren't asleep!' Crow squeaked indignantly. 'Resting fingers – nets full of sharp fishy scales.' He nodded at Fin wandering along the water's edge, Quilla on his shoulder. 'Queen Kass must've heard tiny voice coming from eagle's eye.'

Kassabel smiled sadly. 'Yes, perhaps that's what I heard – the tiny voice in the eagle's eye.' From the look on her face, she didn't really believe it.

Kassabel had been showing Lark and Crow how to fish with the weighted circular nets the locals used: standing in the shallows watching for tell-tale ripples that indicated a shoal. Not having much luck, they realised the nets were too full of rents, and to mend them they settled on the soft yellow sand, their backs against an upturned dinghy.

Behind them loomed the African jungle, the chorus of chinking, clicking and trilling of the birds and insects were most of them of species unfamiliar to Lark. Farther along the beach could be seen the shanty outskirts of the small port of Banjul where the River Gambia opened into the Atlantic Ocean. Out in the deep water of the river mouth, beyond the lines of wooden jetties, Aurora and Orca rode at anchor. From Aurora came the sounds of hammering as the crew carried out running repairs after their voyage.

It was mid-day, the sun at its highest. A little way off, Mick and Grilla were enthusiastically digging for land crabs, spraying sand in all directions. Behind them, where the beach fringed the jungle, Sandy, Kenji and Captain Jamal sat on a veranda beneath the banana leaf roof of a ramshackle bar, drinking palm wine with local fishermen. Jamal, knowing the Mandinka language, was gleaning information on the conditions upriver.

Their journey had gone smoothly. With the hurricane season looming Captain Jamal had been keen to make all speed to reach the Gambia, so Sandy had asked Kassabel to join them on Orca to use her sailing skill to keep up with Aurora. The two vessels, skimming the waves like flying fish, she stood in Orca's prow leaning out like a figurehead as if encouraging Orca to keep up with Aurora.

They spent the first night in the bay of Ras but did not go ashore. The following nights they moored wherever shelter could be found. As they sailed, pushed along by wind and current, the shore gradually changed from desert to jungle. On the fifth day, they reached the mouth of the River Gambia, fifteen hundred miles south of Tangier, dropping anchor off Banjul with its settlement of grassed roofed round huts. To Fin and Lark, its rickety wooden jetties were reminiscent of Scavport back home.

Watching Kassabel's needle flying through the net Lark was reminded of Tissy embroidering the Dandrum cloak. Trying not to stare, he studied the Skwid's face. To him, Kassabel didn't look like an ordinary Skwid, not like Dancer, or the other Skwids he'd got to know at Durholm, their chameleon-like eyes flicking about inquisitively, scaly skin rippling bright colours with changing emotions. No, Queen Kass, as they had come to call her, had what he thought of as an 'atmosphere' about her, a glimmer to her skin. Once he'd caught a light in her small round eyes. Like – like shining stars, he explained to himself. Realising she'd stopped sewing and was smiling at him, he felt his cheeks turn red beneath his suntan.

'Pearl for your thoughts, young Lark?' she quizzed.

'Just thinking about my girl back home, in Brightdale. Watching you, with your needle and thread, reminded me of my Tissy – she's a mighty skilled embroiderer!' A lump rose in his throat. 'I hope she's alright – in her letter she said she's teamed up with Dancer to fight the evils that have come into the Dale – after the drowning of Gressil's Compound. She said they'd set fire to a Snoopers nest! I just can't see my Tissy doing—'

He stopped to whistle shrilly at Mick, who was chasing a large crab scuttling at startling speed up the beach towards the tangled bushes and coconut palms edging the sand. Mick chose not to hear, so Lark dashed after him, Grilla close behind him. Plunging into the undergrowth, they stopped to listen. From close by came Mick's excited yelping. Hooting agitatedly, Grilla crashed through the undergrowth in the direction of the yelps.

'Grilla! Grilla! Mick! Mick!' Lark shouted. Heart thumping, he listened to the unfamiliar buzzing and chirrups of myriad insects, only now remembering Jamal's stern warning not to venture into the jungle, where poisonous snakes lurked. At home, in Annunder Territory, he might hear the growl of a tiger or lynx, but he knew how to deal with them. Silent, coiling creatures spitting venom were another matter! Fearful, he searched the thick vegetation: any slight movement might be a snake, a giant rat, or a huge dragon lizard. Fighting panic, slashing with his boning knife through the tendrils festooning the branches he struggled towards the sound of Mick's barking and Grilla's hallooing, quickly becoming disorientated. In moments, he'd no idea in which direction the beach was.

Thud! A black sinuous body dropped from a branch in front of him, a fanged face reared up: sss! A stream of venom hit his left cheek, just missing his eye. Terrified, he turned and lunged blindly through the tangle of bushes, twice falling headlong. Chancing on what seemed to be a path, he glanced back: the snake was slithering fast behind him. Suddenly, from his right, Grilla crashed onto the path, Mick under his arm. Grabbing Lark with his free hand, the great ape swung him up onto his broad silver back. Clinging to Grilla's fur Lark sneaked a look back: there was no sign of the snake. A moment later, they burst out onto the beach where they saw Fin, Kassabel, Jamal, Kenji and Sandy running towards them, waving and shouting.

Trembling with shock, Sandy helped him down from Grilla's back. 'A huge black serpent spat poison at me!' Lark wailed.

Sandy grinned. 'You were warned that the jungle is full of mambas – black and green, both deadly!'

A raucous squeak from the bible bag announced Crow's tardy arrival.

'I seed snake too, a long, long, huge fat snake, pretty patterns on its serpent scales. Saw it when I went looking for Sparkie Two, here.'

Crow's mother mouse with her child had abandoned him for life with Aurora's mice. But he'd found a creature even better: the furriest rat he'd ever seen. He'd spotted it whilst wandering along the jungle's fringe. Skilled with rodents, he'd coaxed it into his bible bag with the lure of a ripe mango dripping with juice.

'You've got another Sparkie?' Fin exclaimed. 'Come on Crow, show us!'

Crow undid the bag's straps, and triumphantly lifted out the rat.

'Me saved Sparkie Two from being swallowed whole – he so furry, snake slow getting it in mouth. Bet snake would have had Mick, easy as anything!'

Stroking its dense soft fur admiringly, Fin asked Jamal: 'What sort of rat is it?'

'West African Shaggy Rat,' Jamal growled, 'the Scav better not bring it on my Aurora! Eat us out of corn in a day! Come – enough talk – time we returned to our ships; night will soon be falling.'

Striding to the water's edge, he waved his arms, and through his teeth let out a piercing whistle. On board Aurora, a sailor whistled back. A few moments later Aurora's jollyboat set off across the water.

They had supper on Aurora. As usual, Crow and Grilla stayed behind on Orca to dine on fruit and veg. Mick was with them gnawing on a goat bone given to him by cook Mokele who had come to admire his ratting skills.

When everyone had eaten, Zahhak, his squad and the ship's crew went up on deck to take the cool evening air and drink palm wine, whilst Fin, Lark, Kenji, Kassabel and Jamal gathered around Sandy who had spread a salt-stained, tattered map out on the table.

'I bought this map from one of the fishermen we were talking to on the beach. How a poor fisherman had got hold of it, I dread to think. It must once have been very precious to someone – it's beautifully drawn!' Sandy smiled apologetically at Lark, 'but I showed him a handful of our nuts, washers and screws, and he agreed to part with it for some copper screws.'

With a gasp of amazement, Jamal whipped out wire framed spectacles, to peer closely at the map. 'This is worth more than a few pieces of copper! It is from the ancient library of Tombouctou – look, there is the library mark!' He pointed at a small drawing in a corner, showing an eye inside a triangle. 'It is almost priceless – you must take the utmost care of it.'

Heads together they studied the beautifully drawn illustration of the Gambia river. Meandering eastwards, the terrain bordering the river depicted representations of savanna to the south and mangrove swamps and jungle to the north.

Sandy pointed out a drawing of jagged rocks and rough water several miles upriver. 'Those are the Barraconda rapids – a village headman drinking with the fishermen told me that is as far as the river is navigable. Sadly, there we shall have to abandon Orca and take to the jungle if we are to continue in our pursuit of Mab.'

Kassabel pointed her scaly finger further along the river to a drawing depicting a rocky plateau. 'The Fouta heights where the River Gambia rises. That was where the Gaiakins made their enchanted garden – abandoned when the Great Dying struck. It is now a place of horrific evil! That is where the butterfly demon intends to go, I am certain!'

They all shuddered – it seemed as if evil emanated from the drawing.

Frowning in concentration, Fin traced his finger along the serpentine river towards the Barraconda rapids. He looked up at Kassabel. 'You mentioned a Motherhome on the river – it doesn't appear to be marked.'

Kenji leaned in eagerly. 'Yes, where's the Motherhome? I was looking forward to meeting my relatives!'

'The map is too old. It is not marked – the Motherhome lies hidden in mangroves, somewhere on the north bank. There is a creek, somewhere here…' Kassabel indicated a spot just below the Rapids. 'I have been there. The way in to the Motherhome is underwater, through an old beaver lodge. It was a while ago – I hope it is still there and I can find the way in!'

An exclamation of dismay from behind startled them. Zahhak was standing in the cabin doorway, his scales rippling orange in alarm. 'Do I understand aright, my Queen? You cannot go with our friends! You are too precious to us! They must find their own way.'

Sandy agreed. 'Zahhak is right, Kassabel. This is our fight, not yours. It is a dangerous mission, but we shall not get lost with this map as our guide.'

Kassabel turned to Fin. 'And you, young Fin Dandrum, what would you wish me do? Zagzagel says you have a wise head on your shoulders. Tell me, do you still want me as a guide?'

Worriedly Fin ran his fingers through his hair. He recalled their first meeting, when Kassabel had told him she knew about their mission, that Mossy had sent her a message. She'd said: 'Do not fear me Fin, I am here to help you.' Having Kassabel by his side would be almost like having Mossy with him.

Watching Fin's unhappy indecision, Lark noticed his face had become thinner. The horrors he'd been through had taken a toll on him – his dad murdered, Bee dead, Bird's burnt body far away in Brightdale, her soul trapped inside an eagle's eye, and the hideous constant reminder of it all: the wound on his chest left by the Chi Rho.'

'Queen Kass, having you as a friend is a great comfort to me, and I know to my companions too.' Fin swept his arms open to include Lark, Sandy and Kenji.

'But as Zahhak said, your people need you. How about a compromise?' He looked nervously at Zahhak scowling by the cabin door. 'Could you come as far as Barraconda? Show us how to find the Motherhome? From then on I hope the people there will help us.'

About to agree, Kassabel was interrupted by a cry from outside.

'HELP! HELP! EAGLE'S GOT BIBLE BAG!'

They rushed on deck. Across on Orca, Crow was jumping up and down, thin arms waving desperately. Quilla was perched on a high spar, bible bag dangling from his talons. Cheered on by Aurora's crew, Grilla had started climbing the mast, whilst below Mick bounced about, barking excitedly.

'Stop 'im, stop 'im!' wailed Crow, 'he musn' eat Sparkie Two.'

Thinking quickly, Lark grabbed a large fish, a John Dory, that Mokele was gutting on deck and waved it above his head. 'Hoy!' called Mokele indignantly, 'that Dory was for the crew's breakfast!'

Quilla let go of the bible bag, sending it tumbling into Crow's arms knocking him flat, and swooping over to Aurora, Fin could hear from inside his eye Bird's small voice calling: 'Left a bit, right a bit! Stop! Stop!'

Snatching the Dory from Lark's outstretched hands, Quilla sped to the shore and landing on the beach began tearing voraciously at the carcass.

Captain Jamal shook his head in resigned reproach. 'I warned them, pets on board ship cause trouble! But they wouldn't listen.'

Next day, with the sun rising red out of the jungle, as they prepared to sail Sandy was given by Jamal detailed instructions on sailing on a river; forgetting Kassabel was perhaps the best sailor of them all, he was worried about the safety of his precious Queen.

'You must not mess up a tack – keep your sheet ropes loosely cleated – otherwise, disaster! Keep to the deeper water in the centre of the river, where the flow is fast.'

Sandy nodded humbly. 'Yes, yes, I will remember.'

Only partly reassured that Sandy would be a competent sailor, Jamal reluctantly returned to Aurora.

Raising anchor and unfurling the mainsail, Orca set sail. Standing in the stern watching Aurora grow smaller and smaller, glancing up, Fin was reassured to see Quilla had returned from his foray for carrion and was perched on top of Orca's mainmast.

Zahhak and squad member Sobek, ordered by Kassabel to accompany them, busied themselves setting up a deck tent.

Kassabel took the tiller, soon showing how Jamal need not have worried, calling out instructions to Sandy, Fin and Lark, who were kept busy adjusting the sails, frequently tacking from left to right, taking turns in the prow watching for rocks hidden beneath the surface; the extra passengers as well as supplies of water and dried goods made Orca low in the water.

For miles they sailed past a green wall of dense mangrove. As they passed, noisily quarrelling pelicans flapped into the hyacinth-blue sky to wheel around before settling once more among the branches. At intervals along the high muddy bank, a stork, heron or crane stood motionless half hidden in the undergrowth. Crocodiles, watching the arrival of Orca, slipped quietly into the water, eyes and snout just above the surface. Once they saw a swimming leopard, its bedraggled head searching the bank for prey. Another time, they were startled by hippos rising in front of them like grey leather hills, churning the water as they splashed off to an islet near the far bank.

Each night they dropped anchor in the middle of the river. Zahhak and Sobek cooked a meal, spicier than Fin and Lark would have liked, but they were too tired and hungry to complain. Through the night, to a ceaseless background of the booming of bull frogs, they kept watch in twos. Kassabel, Zahhak and Sobek slept on deck in the tent, the others in the cabin.

With each day the river became narrower and the current against them stronger, making it harder to maintain progress, Sandy and Kassabel, taking turns at the tiller, repeatedly calling to the deck crew to be ready to tack. The vegetation changed from mangrove to jungle, the trees growing ever taller, the undergrowth ever denser. To pass the time between their duties of keeping tackle in order and sweeping, Crow had been teaching Grilla how to fish. This was regularly interrupted by troops of monkeys swinging by, sighting Orca and setting up a hullabaloo, at which Grilla would rush down to hide in the cabin. Mick sat with them always hopeful of a juicy fish coming his way.

On the fourth day, they came to a village set back among the trees: the first human habitation they had seen. Men in dugouts fished mid-stream, women washed clothing at the water's edge. Excited by the novelty of strangers, children ran squealing and waving along the bank. They didn't stop: Kassabel was keen to reach the Barraconda Rapids and find the hidden Motherhome.

As evening fell, from ahead came the unbroken roar of rushing water growing ever louder. Rounding a bend, they came to the Barraconda Rapids. Orca could go no further. Zahhak and Sobek lowered the sail. Guided by Fin in the prow Sandy steered to calmer waters nearer the bank, and they dropped anchor. They ate supper on deck, fascinated by the foaming curtain of water cascading over high rocks down into the swirling boulder strewn river.

As night turned to dawn, Fin and Zahhak, who's turn it was to be on watch, became aware of a shrill yelping sound above the roar of the Rapids. Growing steadily louder, Fin was reminded of the shrieking swallows darting among the eves at Dandrum Den on a Highsun morning. Giving a low gasp, Zahhak pointed to the jungle. In the shadowy trees Fin saw flashes of light: he was sure they were eyes, twenty or so of them, flickering as they danced through the branches. A familiar oily stink drifted towards him: the smell of Frit. Shrieking and squealing, leathery wings clattering, bat-like shapes rose out of the jungle, their bodies silhouetted against the morning sky as they whirled and dived in ragged formation.

Kassabel crept silently out of the deck tent. 'Be still!' she hissed in Fin's ear, gripping his shoulder as a warning: 'Batfrits!'

Alerted by the shrieking, heads appeared in the hatchway, first Lark and Crow, then Mick and Grilla. They climbed on deck as Sobek came from the tent.

'All hush! They have not spotted us!' Zahhak whispered sharply.

Sandy and Kenji appeared; their crossbows armed.

It was as if the creatures were playing a game of aerial acrobatics: 'Eeekkk! Eeekkk!' they squealed; their cry so high pitched that only poor Mick with his dog's ears could hear the full force of the sound. Cringing, he shot whimpering back down into the cabin.

'Skeew! Skeew!'

From nowhere, Quilla flew into the group and snatching at a Batfrit with his talons, soared away and landed on the top of a tall tree. His great beak tearing at the mangy body, the Batfrit disintegrated, metal, leather and fur fluttering down through the branches. Fin gazed in horror: what were Bird and Quilla thinking of! Other Batfrits dived on Quilla, stabbing at him with their long metal fingerbones.

Sandy and Kenji aimed and fired.

Zip! Whoosh! Zip! Whoosh! Thud!

Eeekkk! Thud! Eeekkk! Two Batfrits spiralled down out of the sky.

Again, two arrows flew, this time Zahhak and Sobek's viciously barbed Skwid darts. Two more Batfrits fell.

Rearming in unison, all four warriors let fly another volley. Their aim was true. Four more Batfrits fluttered down.

'Skeew! Skeew!' Quilla fell on another Batfrit, his talons sinking into the metal and fur, tearing the leathery wings to shreds. The surviving Batfrits streaked away, their panicked screeching echoing over the jungle.

'Halloo! Halloo!' A high clear voice sung out above the roar of water. A long dugout canoe sculled by two rowers shot out from an inlet hidden by the clouds of spray just below the Rapids. As it drew near, they saw one was a pretty young woman, with glossy black hair tied in a ponytail, the other a grizzled male, a pigtail coiling down his back; both were drenched, hair dripping, their leather jerkins dark with water.

Kenji, thrilled to see that the pair were of his own race, rushed to the prow with a shout of greeting as the dugout pulled alongside. The woman, grabbing one of Orca's rope fenders, stared back at him, her eyes full of wonder.

The man cried to Kassabel in joy: 'Queen Kassabel! Tis wondrous indeed to find you here!'

'Hail, esteemed Yasuo. I am glad to see you still full of youthful vigour!'

Kassabel held out her hand to him to help him aboard. She looked at his companion, who swiftly swung up on deck. 'And who is this girl?'

'Do you not remember me, dearest Kass? It's your Suki!'

'Suki! My, you are a young woman now! Is it that long since I saw you?'

'Aye, it is too long since your last visit!' said Yasuo. 'Thank the Holy Ones, all is as when you left us – nothing has changed in our Motherhome! But tell me, who are your friends? They are indeed skilled with crossbows – we watched in admiration as they shot down the foul Batfrits. It is a shame some escaped, for they are sure to report back to M'Bopo!'

'Also, it is to be hoped the great eagle is not a servant of the Evils – never have we seen such a bird in these parts!' Suki observed.

'No!' exclaimed Fin vehemently. 'The eagle is with us. He's our – er, companion.'

Suki and Yasuo becoming aware of Kassabel's odd little band, looked bemused at the two Delphins, the Scav and a gorilla with a terrier perched on its shoulder.

Kassabel introduced them, starting with Sandy and ending with Kenji, who, wrenching his star-struck gaze from Suki, tapped his chest proudly.

'I am of the Sanyo tribe!'

'That is our name too!' exclaimed Suki, gazing admiringly at his handsome face and muscly arms cradling his crossbow.

Yasuo looked hard at Kenji. 'We received a message warning us to look out for two Delphins and their companions, but there was no mention of a Sanyo – we thought we were the last of our tribe! Where do you come from young Kenji?'

'From the North.' Kenji waved vaguely over the jungle. 'There's only my grandmother and myself left in our family. We were from the Leeds Motherhome – destroyed long ago. The survivors of our tribe escaped to Yrvik Motherhome before that in turn was destroyed. But I am a Warrior in Iskander's Squad – seconded to Durholm Garrison.'

Yasuo turned his attention to Sandy. 'Iskander? That name is familiar.'

Kassabel chuckled. 'Yasuo, to you Sandy may look like one of my ruffian sailors, but this is indeed the mighty Lord Iskander.'

Yasuo bowed. 'I am honoured to meet you sir! Why have you and your companions come here?'

'We are in pursuit of a very large and strange butterfly – a demon woman disguised as a butterfly. Have you seen such a creature? She has stolen a precious holy relic which we must recover!'

Fin brought out his sketch of Queen Mab. 'This is her – Maabella! We believe she's come to The Gambia – to the ancient Garden of Florain. We're desperate to get the jewel back to – to save our friend!'

Yasuo frowned. 'There is more to all this than the message told us! You must come with us to our Motherhome where we can learn the full story! We also have news – of a disconcerting nature! Rumours of sightings of something swimming in the river –thought to be a dragon worm, also known as a Bobbit! You must speak with Kisho, our wise leader.'

'Yes, we shall come.' Kassabel said. 'But not all of us!' She turned to her warriors. 'Zahhak and Sobek, you must guard the ship.'

Eyeing the newcomers suspiciously, her two guards growled their reluctant consent.

Taking in Suki's and Yasuo's soaked clothes, Lark asked warily: 'How do we get to your Motherhome? Will we have to go underwater? Queen Kass told us your refuge is only reached through an old beaver lodge?'

Suki smiled. 'That's right: for extra security, the entrance to our Motherhome is underwater.'

'Well, that's fine for Fin and me, being Delphin kind, we're at home underwater, but it won't do for Crow, Grilla and Mick! They'd better stay with Zahhak and Sobek.'

So, it was agreed: Sandy, Kenji, Fin, Lark and Kassabel would go to the Motherhome, and the others would stay on Orca to await their return.

Commanding Zahhak and Sobek to keep a sharp look out for Batfrits, Kassabel followed Fin and Lark down into the dugout. Stowing their crossbows back below deck, Sandy and Kenji climbed down after them, their added weight making the dugout low in the water. From Orca's prow Crow, Grilla and Mick, and Bird in Quilla's eye up on the mainmast, watched forlornly as Suki and Yasuo paddled the canoe to the foaming white water at the base of the Rapids, and disappeared into the clouds of spray.

Brushing through overhanging foliage, they entered a narrow gully with high rocky sides. Suki and Yasuo paddling hard against the rush of water, moments later they shot out into the calmer water of a small lake. Contained by a dam of tree trunks and branches at the far end, rose a tall mound of sticks and logs.

'A real beaver lodge!' Exclaimed Lark excitedly.

Paddling with easy strokes, Suki and Yasuo made for the mound and tying up to a log and diving over the side, disappeared beneath the surface of the water. Taking deep breaths, the others followed. Kicking hard, they swam after Suki and Yasuo's shadowy figures as they headed through the murky water down to the dark entrance hole at the base of the mound. Entering single file, they emerged a moment later into an air-filled chamber about five feet wide and four feet high lined with soft bark and lit by a soft green light filtering through the roof of moss and sticks.

Relieved to be breathing air again, they scrambled up onto the floating grass floor, and crawled after Suki and Yasuo along a dark narrow tunnel. Dimly lit by small glass-covered lights set in the earth walls, the floor sticky with damp mud, miserable in their sodden clothes, it seemed an age before they reached a heavy metal door. Suki pressed a sequence of numbered keys in a panel in the wall and flashing briefly, the door swung smoothly open. Stepping into a square chamber, as the door closed automatically behind them, from behind metal grilles in the roof fans suddenly roared into life, and a blast of hot dry air almost knocked them over. In a few moments, their shirts and shorts were completely dry, crackling with baked-on mud. Then following Suki and Yasuo's example, they took brushes from hooks on the wall and cleaned themselves off as best they could.

As the fans slowed to a halt another metal door swung open before them, and they stepped out into a lofty cavern where they gazed about in astonishment. The far wall consisted of tall wide plate-glass windows, taller and wider than any window they had ever seen. Beyond the windows cascaded a silvery curtain of water, its roar muffled by the thick glass. In front of the windows sofas and chairs were arranged to form an observation area. They realised they were looking out from behind the Rapids. In the centre of the cavern stood a long table and benches. To the left curtained alcoves in the rock indicated bedrooms, and off to their right, a well-equipped kitchen, the chimney of its cooking range rising through the rock above. They would learn that spray from the Rapids camouflaged the smoke.

Above them, a wooden platform, half the width of the cavern, formed an upper floor reached by a ladder, and from where came sounds of throbbing engines, interrupted every now and then by crackling and buzzing – this was the tech area. They became aware of a continuous background hum, which Yasuo explained was from a turbine in the Rapids, generating electricity – using the principle of the Archimedean screw.

A small grey-haired woman, busy at the kitchen range, wiped her hands on her apron and trotted over to greet them. 'Welcome friends!' she exclaimed, a beaming smile creasing her old face.

Kassabel, bending low, gave the old woman a hug. 'Dear Shika, how glad I am to see you – so hale and hearty, too!'

The old woman peered up at Kassabel. 'Kass, is it really you? What a joyful day this is! And who are your companions?'

Kassabel turned to the others and pointed each of them in turn: 'Lord Iskander, Fin Dandrum, Lark Annunder, and—'

Suki interrupted her. 'Grandmother dear – this is Kenji! He too is a Sanyo!'

Peering up at Kenji, Shika's face crumpled into tears. 'A Sanyo? Is this true?'

Kenji nodded eagerly. 'Yes, I am a Sanyo – of the Northern Island tribe. Sadly, there is only myself and my grandmother left.'

Shika sighed. 'I remember the story! After the drowning of our islands, your tribe dispersed to the northern regions, whilst my Southern Island tribe took the road to Africa, where most of us perished in the Great Dying. Even so, there are rumours that some survive in the lands far to the west, over the great ocean…' she waved her hand in a vague westerly direction.

'Shika, you can catch up with Sanyo history later,' Yasuo said impatiently, gesturing to where a wizened looking old man was waving to them from an armchair near the window. 'Can you not see, Kisho is waiting to meet our guests!'

Yasuo led them over.

'Welcome! Welcome!' wheezed the old man.

He looked up at Sandy. 'It is an honour to meet you, Lord Iskander. I have heard of you from Felixstowe Motherhome. We received a message from them, to watch for people of the Delphin Race – a certain Fin Dandrum and his companion, Lark Annunder. We have learned they are on a quest – to retrieve a precious jewel from the Evil Ones!'

'How did they know?' Fin exclaimed. 'Did they hear from Mossy – I mean Zagzagel?'

'Dear me, no! We of The Gambia Motherhome, are far too humble for Zagzagel to speak with us! No, we have received messages through the radio from the Felixstowe Motherhome. Even now, Mamoru is sending messages back, with confirmation of your arrival!' He gestured to the tech area above them.

'Come, I'll show you,' Suki said enthusiastically.

'I shall stay here,' called Kassabel. 'I have much to talk about with Shika and Kisho.'

Keen to hear her news, Yasuo stayed behind too.

Climbing the ladder onto the tech platform, Kenji exclaimed in delight: 'You have a radio!' He turned excitedly to Sandy: 'Do you remember the radios at Yrvik? In Leeds they had their own walkie-talkies! I wonder what happened to them…' He looked wistfully at all the equipment.

Seeing Fin and Lark's bewilderment, Sandy explained that radios were for sending and receiving messages. 'The electrical waves pass through the air, invisible, carrying messages to and from radio receivers.'

A young man with black spiky hair and round spectacles, sat at a bench intently studying rows of dials on a large metal box: the Motherhome's radio. From the radio, a wire led to one of two round disks clamped over his ears.

'Headphones,' whispered Suki.

Holding a round flat object close to his mouth, he was speaking into it in a low voice.

Over by the huge windows sat a young woman closely resembling Suki, her eye pressed to the base of a tube ascending through the rock roof.

Suki introduced Rinie and Mamoru. Turning to give a 'thumbs' up', Mamoru, smiled before returning to his microphone. Briefly taking her eye from the pipe, Rinie waved.

Mamoru's radio burst into life. Over a background hissing and crackling, a tinny voice barked out: 'Felixstowe calling Barraconda… Felixstowe calling Barraconda…. Have they arrived, over?'

The young man flicked a switch and spoke into a disk attached by a wire to the radio. 'Barraconda here… we confirm arrival, over…'

'Felixstowe calling… any problems? Over…'

'None so far… Over and out…'

Keen to show Fin and Lark how things worked, Mamoru let them take turns in wearing the headphones, so they could listen to the hums and hisses of radio waves.

Remembering Mossy's promise, to teach him what he had called electro-magnetism tech, Fin felt sad there had never been time: he hadn't even looked at the tech books in the shop – there'd been so much other stuff to study.

For Lark, the whole thing smacked strongly of magic. 'Do you mean to tell me, that voice,' he gestured to the box, 'was a real person's voice and it came from where?'

'Felixstowe,' Rinie said. Amused by Lark's amazement, she'd come from her pipe by the window, to join in the explanations.

'But that's – that's in back at Europe!' Fin exclaimed. 'How do the radio waves, did you call them, come into the box?'

'There's a radio mast outside that picks up the waves,' Rinie replied. 'Come I'll show you – we can look through the periscope.'

She took them to the pipe she had been looking through. 'With this device we can keep an eye on what's going on outside. It was through it that we saw you arrive and watched your battle with the Batfrits. You put your eye to the hole and move the periscope around with these.' She indicated handles on either side of a square glass-covered hole. 'Come Fin, sit here and look! You'll be able to see the radio mast, by the side of the Rapids.'

Putting his eye to the glass, through the misty spray Fin made out trees and the sky. Swinging the periscope around, he spotted a tall thin metal pole, taller than the trees, with a wire dish at the top.

'Yes, I can see the mast!' Swivelling the pipe again, he gasped: 'And I can see Orca on the water – she's so small! Come on Lark, have a look!'

Staring hard into the pipe, Lark whistled through his teeth. 'I can see Grilla – he's playing footie with Mick! They're —'

He was interrupted by old Shika's voice calling from below.

'Come children – food is ready!'

They scrambled down the ladder to gather at the long table, where Shika served up steamed river fish wrapped in banana leaves, with slices of fried breadfruit dipped in wild honey. Wondering if the fish would taste muddy like the river fish at home, Fin and Lark were impressed by Shika's cooking, finding it delicious.

Whilst they ate, they took turns in explaining what brought them to The Gambia. The Sanyos listened in wonder, then horror, as Sandy told the story of the destruction of Gressil's stronghold, and how Queen Maabella transformed into a giant butterfly, to escape with a fabulous jewel, and had headed for The Gambia.

Fin took up the explanation. 'The jewel Mab stole is known as the Chi Rho – a holy and precious relic. It was in my possession, and I have to get it back – not because of its beauty or richness, but because it will save my friend Bird, whose soul was stolen by a Phragg who took her to Contagion, and – and she ended up—' his voice choking, he fell silent.

Lark intervened. 'Mr Mossy said, if we don't get the cross back soon, her poor little burnt body will die – it's getting mighty urgent! So, if you could point us in the right direction, we'll carry on chasing after that vile butterfly woman!'

'Aye, we can point you in the right direction!' old Kisho growled from his end of the table. 'But I warn you, you are heading into great danger! We have indeed seen Mab, the butterfly: captured by M'Bopo the Batfrit! A few days ago, we spotted him and his troop with the butterfly, making for his lair in the caves beneath old Florain!'

Rinie shuddered. 'Yes, I saw the Batfrit gang through my periscope, skimming the water, carrying a heavy bundle wrapped in a net!'

'Suki and I had a close encounter also, out on patrol.' Yasuo added. 'We heard the evil M'Bopo cursing as he clattered through the undergrowth, sending up clouds of squawking pelicans – hippos crashing back into the river – monkeys screeching through the trees!'

Glaring around fiercely, Kisho exclaimed: 'We know how to deal with Batfrits! It was what was following them, that sent a chill through my old bones. A huge worm, a Bobbitworm, sometimes called a Terminator, swimming in the river! I feel certain it was the Demon Gressil in a new embodiment!'

Sandy drew a sharp breath. 'Zagzagel was right! He warned me that Gressil was not yet finished, even though his scorpion body was destroyed by Fescue!'

He turned to Fin and Lark. 'Natural Bobbitworms are creatures of the oceans. There is a description of them in a book on Mossy's shelves. Like you, Fin, I am interested in sea creatures, and I can remember the description:

'Eunice aphroditois, colloquially known as Bobbitworm, can grow to ten feet long. There is a narcotizing or killing toxin in its bite, which inflicts a long, slow death. It digs into the sea floor, exposing a few inches of its face, to wait for passing prey, snapping with its powerfully muscled mouth parts. Armed with sharp teeth, it attacks with great speed and force.'

'That, boss, is more information than I want!' Kenji exclaimed. 'Even so, I'll be ready for it! Whether Gressil's inside, or not!'

Suki grinned from across the table. 'I've yet to deal with a Bobbit! As I shall be coming with you, we can tackle it together!'

Old Shika gave a cry. 'Little Suki, you must not go!' She turned to her son. 'Yasuo, you shall go!'

'No, mother. I must stay to guard the Motherhome!'

Kassabel, sitting next to Shika, put a comforting hand on the old woman. 'Do not fear for Suki! I have learned from grandfather Kisho that she has grown into a formidable fighter!'

'Besides,' Lark added, 'she'll have Sandy and Kenji with her. Their skills with sword and cross-bow are formidable!'

Shika eyed Sandy and Kenji doubtfully. In their mud-crusted sailor's clothes they looked less than impressive.

Mamoru got up and headed for the platform. 'I must return to my radio,' he muttered, 'expecting a message from Trans Motherhome.'

Half-way up the ladder, he called down: 'Suki, you'll need Electroshockers for everyone if you're dealing with Batfrits! We must make sure they are fully charged.'

Suki jumped up and ran after him.

As they waited for her to return, Kisho told them what to expect when they reached M'Bopo's cave lair.

'Phraggs are known to be lurking in caves deep beneath the ancient garden of Florain, on the Fouta plateau above. Recently, more have arrived which I realise now is due to the destruction of Gressil's Fortress. We know also that the garden is not completely abandoned either: some Gaiakins still live there, but they have turned to evil, some have been taken by Phraggs and are Sneaksouls – a dreadful thought: a fallen Gaiakin infested by a Sneaksoul!'

Fin and Lark stared at the old man in dismay.

'Surely, you are wrong!' Fin gasped. 'Zagzagel says that Gaiakins are unmarred.' Kisho didn't say anything, just shook his head sadly.

Breaking the ominous silence, Sandy asked Yasuo where they stored 'The Knowledge'.

Yasuo got up. 'Come all of you, I will show you.'

Leading them to the back of the cavern he drew back a heavy leather curtain blocking off a deep alcove where clay tablets were stored on rows of shelves. Taking down one of the tablets, he showed them the writing, drawings and symbols etched into it.

'These are the more recent records, from the past thousand years. The cylindrical ones at the back are more ancient. Some are tens of thousands of years old, long before printing was invented. Knowledge from the time of the Great Dying, known then as 'data', we cannot store, it would corrupt in our high humidity.'

Suki clattered down the ladder, carrying a waterproof knapsack. 'The Electroshockers are charged,' she called, bringing out a bundle of sinister-looking short metal sticks, each with a handle and wrist strap. 'These are very effective against Batfrits. They fire a wave of electricity to deliver a nasty shock, disabling Batfrits' sensory and motor nerves, shutting down their tech systems. I'll keep them safe for now. We'll only use them when, or more hopefully, if, we need to.'

She looked around at everyone. 'Are you ready to go? If so, I'll just get my pack, and we'll be off!'

Whilst they waited Kenji praised old Shika's cooking. 'I hope one day to cook some of my grandmother's favourite recipes for you,' he laughed.

Dabbing her eyes with the edge of her apron, the old lady smiled tearfully.

Suki returned with her waterproof knapsack now bulging with the Electroshockers. After heartfelt farewells to their new Sanyo friends, they made for the door to the hot air chamber, then into the damp tunnel and out onto floating grass floor. From the water Suki drew up an airtight plastic container attached to a long rope. She sealed her pack inside it, and gripping its handle dived below the surface with it. As they all followed, the container shot to the surface.

# 5
# JOURNEY TO M'BOPO'S LAIR

Swimming up from the Motherhome, Fin was the last to break surface. Scrambling onto the canoe and settling on the bench, Quilla flew from a tree above and landed heavily on his shoulder, almost knocking him back into the water.

Leaning close, Fin whispered softly to Bird: 'Hi! You O.K.?'

'You've been ages!' she called irritably. 'I was getting so scared!'

'Sorry, love. We're returning to Orca now – join us there.'

The great bird launched into the air. Suki watched, puzzled and suspicious, as she retrieved her rucksack from the airtight plastic container but didn't speak. The current now in their favour, she and Kenji paddled them swiftly across the lake and out into the river. Emerging from the clouds of spray and heralded by Mick's excited yapping and hoots from Grilla, they climbed on board Orca.

When calm was restored, they sat on deck, drying their clothes in the hot African sun.

Whilst they waited, Suki told them of her plan: to follow the river on foot, along the south bank, where the going was easier.

'It's mainly light jungle, with a clear path. Eventually we must cross to the north bank, and into dense jungle. There we must find the way into M'Bopo's Cave.'

She eyed them critically. 'You'll need more suitable clothing: shorts won't be any use when we reach thick jungle – you'll be stung and scratched to death!'

'No worries!' Lark exclaimed eagerly. 'The chandlers on the Isle of Mann kitted us out with all the stuff we'd need for the tropics: floppy hats, strong leather boots, long-sleeve shirts, lightweight canvas trousers, and other gear. The whole lot cost Fin quite a few pearls.'

Taking Suki below deck, she was shown the brand-new jungle kit. The chandlers had even found smaller sizes for Crow; trying on his boots, he staggered about, sobbing resentfully: 'I hate boots! Want jool! All I need is jool!'

Eyeing his horny-skinned soles, Suki relented and let him go unshod.

'What about weapons?' she asked, after approving the clothing.

Sandy and Kenji, the only ones to be properly equipped for fighting, produced their crossbows before bringing out their magnificent swords, hidden away whilst at sea. Drawing Kenji's sword from its scabbard, Suki whistled in admiration as she ran her finger along the razor-sharp blade, newly forged in Florain. Kenji explained the original blade had melted in his desperate efforts to save Bird from the Phragg. He decided sadly, he would have to leave his ganglefowl beak and Frit buckle behind on Orca.

In their much loved, battered old rucksacks, Fin and Lark packed underwear and spare socks, wrapped in their trusty waterproof plustic sheets. Conscious of the need to travel light they had the agonizing task of choosing which few precious possessions to put in.

Fin took only the Dandrum sword and its scabbard, now stripped of many pearls; Lark, his fishing hook-covered hat, shrunk in the melting of the Great Berg, but now, to him, a lucky talisman, the Snooper sting a memento of his injury in Contagion, and Midori's chisel – Fin had already given his chisel to Boff on the Isle of Mann as a farewell gift.

Items they would frequently use they tucked in the many pockets of their new canvas shirts: Fin his sketch pad, charcoal sticks and eraser, his mother's gold coin and Fescue's ruby ring were safe in the purse hanging around his neck inside his shirt; Lark his jar of marigold ointment, flint, tinder and candle stub, before purposefully sliding his boning knife into its sheath on his belt. His bags of screws, nuts and bolts he left to be given to Captain Jamal for use on Aurora.

Crow discarded his clothes from the Isle of Mann in favour of his new jungle outfit, keeping only his striped T-shirt, spotted handkerchief and small cutlass which he stuffed in his small kit bag. His new rat coaxed into the bible bag he announced he was ready.

Sandy and Kenji as seasoned Trekker Warriors knew the art of travelling light. In the top of his rucksack, Sandy tucked a medical bag of soft red Tangier leather, provided by Kassabel and containing anti-mosquito cream, antiseptic, and water purifying filters. The map bought from the Banjul fisherman he put in an outside pocket for easy reference. At Suki's insistence, Kenji abandoned his bags of seeds, dried fruit and other rations.

'There'll be enough good hunting to keep us going!' she exclaimed impatiently as she watched him packing. 'Your knife and crossbow are all you'll need to keep alive!'

'What about salt? Can't leave my precious salt bag!'

Suki sighed. 'Go on – bring your salt!'

Zahhak provided Sandy, Kenji, Lark and Fin with a machete each. Despite Crow's indignation, he was firmly told he was too small to wield a machete, and would only injure himself, so must be content with his cutlass.

Grilla rather aggressively tucked the battered football under his long arm: no one fancied attempting to part him from it. Last but certainly not least, Mick, brought his keen ratting and guarding senses.

Preparations completed, they said a sad goodbye to Kassabel who solemnly blessed them, laying her scaled hand on each head.

'I wish I could come with you…' she said, gazing wistfully towards the distant misty heights rising above the jungle to the north-east.

Clambering down into the dugout, and crowding together, Suki paddled the short distance to the far bank, where she made the little craft fast to a branch to be collected by Yasuo later.

Scrambling up onto the bank, they watched Kassabel, Zahhak and Sobek preparing to sail. Raising Orca's anchor, Sobek punted with a long pole into midstream, where the current was strongest. Zahhak took the tiller.

'Take care of her!' Sandy called as Orca disappeared round a bend in the river. There was a catch in his voice. Kassabel, standing in the stern, raised her hand in acknowledgment.

To Fin she seemed bathed in an aura of shimmering light, and again he wondered about the Skwid – who she really was. He glanced up to see Quilla wheeling high in the sky. Reassured, he followed the others already making their way along the bank.

At the rapids, they lingered for a moment, gazing at the foam rushing over the rocks where they knew the glass windows looked out through the curtain of water.

Fin tried to spot the periscope, wondering if Rinie was watching them. Catching up with Suki and walking beside her, he asked: 'Are you, Rinie and Mamoru the only young ones left in your Motherhome?'

Suki sighed. 'Sadly, that is so. Rinie and Mamoru lost their parents when they were small, taken by Gambia Fever. My own mother, was also taken.' She shuddered: 'It's a vile disease – no cure!'

'And your father?' Kenji asked, from a few paces behind.

'He was killed by a hippo.'

Stopping abruptly, she gave them a stern lecture. 'Be warned – you must do as I say! Hippos may look lumbering clowns but are very dangerous – more than any other river creature – more dangerous than crocs!'

Lark gulped and, instinctively twitching his boning knife, knew it would be totally inadequate as a weapon against such creatures.

Crow, cowering behind Grilla, muttered: 'Me shall hate Africa jungle!'

For two days they followed the river along the south bank, keeping to a well-beaten path made by animals Suki said. The vegetation was lush, thickets of tall palms and baobab trees with an understory of ground plants. Suki, ever on the lookout for hippos in the shallows, allowed Grilla to lead the way, Mick trotting at his heels. It was the start of the rainy season and each afternoon rain thundered down, drenching them in moments – drip, dripping down their necks into their collars. Each night they camped beneath the trees, hanging Fin and Lark's plastic sheets between the branches as shelter.

On the third day, the terrain changed, the land gradually rising, the vegetation becoming sparser. The river too began to change, now shallower, more rock strewn, sometimes dropping below steep cliffs.

At dawn on the fourth day, Suki led them on a detour. She explained that it being the start of the monsoon, on the grasslands to the south there would be a wondrous sight.

'In the olden days, it was called "big game country". Come and see!'

Leaving the path, they scythed a way through the tall grass with their machetes. An hour later, coming to the brink of a high escarpment, they stood gazing in wonder at the scene spread out below them: a seemingly endless vista of lush grasslands bordering a vast lake stretched away to the horizon. Great herds grazed there: zebra, antelope, buffalo. Beneath the acacia trees, giraffes reached up with their long necks to leaf-laden branches. At the lake's edge, herds of elephants, rhinoceros, warthogs, troops of chattering baboons, slaked their thirst and wallowed in the mud.

The scene reminded Fin of a picture in one of Mossy's books. The title below the picture read 'Paradise – A new Eden.'

Not far from the lake, in the hot blue sky a flock of vultures wheeled above a pride of lions feeding on a freshly killed bushbuck. Circling packs of hyenas and wild dogs, snarling and shrieking in a feeding frenzy, dashed in every now and then to grab pieces of bloodied bone.

Above the vultures soared another bird, a majestic golden eagle. Fin tensed in alarm: Quilla and Bird were on the hunt. Folding his wings behind him, Quilla dived, plunging down through the vultures, to fall on the carcass. Lions, hyenas, wild dogs scattered. Seconds later, he rose into the air, wings working hard with the weight of half a leg hanging from his talons. Flying slowly up onto the escarpment, he settled on the ground close to Fin and began tearing at the flesh.

From his eye, Fin heard Bird's faint voice: 'Fin, wasn't that great!'

Fin shuddered. 'That was so dangerous – don't ever do that again!'

Glaring at Fin with a suspicious frown, Suki abruptly turned away, saying: 'Come, we must return to the river, I am hoping to get to the Banto's village before nightfall!'

Despite Suki's urging, it was dark when they reached the Banto village. The trail led towards the glow of a fire lighting up the night sky, an enticing smell of roasting meat came drifting through the trees. Reaching the village edge, they watched warily from the darkness. In the centre of a clearing surrounded by round grass-roofed huts, a group of people were roasting a bushbuck carcass on a spit, their diminutive figures silhouetted against the glow of their charcoal fire. The sound of their chattering, a mixture of low whistles, hoots and clicks drifted across the clearing.

Gesturing to the others to wait, Suki stepped into the circle of firelight.

'Yo! Yo! Bantos!' she called softly.

The chattering stopped. Then, with whoops of delight, the villagers came crowding around her, their welcoming cries echoing among the trees. Clad only in loin cloths and feathers, the tallest only came to Suki's waist, and she had to bend low to give one of the little people a hug.

From his hiding place Fin stared in amazement: listening to Suki trying to communicate with them, attempting their strange language, he couldn't believe what he saw and heard.

'They're Delphins! Look Lark – Delphins!'

Lark gasped: in the firelight illuminating their faces, he could see the dark line of V shape brows below thatches of dusty green hair.

Moving out of the shadows, at first Fin and Lark weren't noticed. Then as they stepped forward into the clearing, a Banto child spotted them, giving a cry of fright. The rest of the Bantos turned to stare, fear and uncertainty written on their faces. Those carrying spears pointed them threateningly.

Desperately Fin tried to recall the jingle in Delphin language that Grammer Nutmeg had taught him when he was little, a ridiculous tale of a cat and an owl getting married. Haltingly at first, he uttered a series of clicks and whistles. At first bemused, the Bantos started to chortle, then broke into delighted laughter. Not to be outdone, Lark followed with a walking song his Granfer Fox had taught him. A natural gift for imitating the cries of birds and mammals helped make his clicks and whistles more expert. The song familiar to the Bantos, whooping and clapping their hands they soon joined in.

Taking advantage of the distraction, Sandy and Kenji stepped into the clearing, followed by Grilla, his football firmly under one arm, Mick close at his heel. Clutching his bible bag to his chest as a form of shield, Crow cowered behind them.

The Bantos' laughter died away. With shrieks of fright, the females herded the children behind them. The menfolk stepped forward boldly and rattled the coral beads on their spears threateningly.

Suki quickly acting as peacemaker, speaking carefully and slowly in Common Language, repeated the word: 'Friends! Friends!'

The Head Banto, distinguished by a crown of mother of pearl dolphins leaping through a sea of shells, strode up to Sandy and Kenji, and haughtily studied the tall warriors.

Sinking to one knee, Sandy touched his forehead respectfully: Kenji followed his example. The Bantos gazed in awe at the swords on their backs and the crossbows on their shoulders. An elderly female Banto, spotting Crow behind Grilla, went to him, and softly cooing, started smoothing the thin covering of hair on his scarred head.

Lark led Grilla forward by his large soft hand and patting him on his shoulder uttered a few low whistles which he hoped conveyed that the great ape was no danger. Reassured, some of the braver Banto boys stroked Grilla's silver-furred back. Grilla carefully dropped his football and kicked it across the clearing. Delighted, the boys ran to kick it back: a full-blown football match would have started, if the adult Bantos hadn't called the boys to order.

Invited by signs to join in the Bantos' feast, they sat on grass mats in a circle around the fire.

Seated between Sandy and Suki, the Head Banto introduced himself. Contorting his lips painfully, he attempted Common Language. 'Me, Bonito, Head of Banto Clan.' He gestured to his fellow Bantos around them. Then, pointing to two males either side of Fin and Lark, again with heroic effort, said: 'Sons: Guppy. Blenny.'

Sandy shook hands with Bonito, before bowing politely to the circle of Bantos. Then, repeating their names slowly, he pointed to each of his own party, including Mick on Lark's knee.

Introductions over, it was time to feast. Expertly wielding machetes, two Banto men carved the roast, placing succulent slices onto wooden platters laid out on a rough-hewn table. Two females ladled out potato-like manioc stew swimming in dark red gravy from bubbling pots by the fire. Everyone with a laden platter, calabashes of palm wine passed around, the meal began. From her hut the elderly Banto auntie who had adopted Crow produced a large bunch of bananas for him and Grilla.

A calabash coming to him, Lark took a hearty swig then coughing and spluttering passed it to Fin. 'Watch out, its fiery,' he croaked hoarsely.

'So's the veg stew,' Fin replied, taking a small sip before handing the calabash to Kenji who was thoughtfully chewing on a piece of bushbuck, trying to work out what spices the cook had rubbed into the flesh before roasting.

'Cloves, ginger, dash of nutmeg,' he muttered. 'Wherever would they have got those spices from?'

Sitting beside him, Suki gurgled with laughter. 'They gather them from their forest gardens.'

'Wow,' exclaimed Lark. 'I'd like to have a look at those!' Struggling with clicks and whistles, he turned to Guppy to ask about them. But the Banto just shrugged and shook his head, mystified. Lark gave up and returned to enjoying the food.

After the meal, two warrior Bantos brought drums from their huts, and starting an insistent rhythm, were soon joined by chanting and singing. Heads spinning from the palm wine, Fin and Lark repeated their childhood songs, the villagers enthusiastically joining in. The feast finally over, the Bantos ushered their guests to a grass-roofed shelter where they could sleep for the night – Banto huts being too small.

When he woke next day, Fin searched the treetops for sight of Quilla, spotting him perched high in a baobab tree beyond the clearing. Not wanting to alarm the Bantos, he didn't attempt to call to the eagle.

Everyone else was already up. Lark and Suki were sitting on the grass mats, talking to Bonito, the Head. Mick was crouched by the dead cooking fire with a motley gang of village curs, picking over bones. Crow had a crowd of smaller children around him. Bible bag open, he was allowing them to stroke his magnificently furry rat. At the far end of the clearing, Sandy and Kenji were demonstrating their crossbow skills to an admiring audience of young Bantos. He learned later that Grilla had gone with some of the Banto women and girls to their forest garden to gather mangoes.

At a gesture from Bonito, Fin went to sit with him beside Lark and Suki. Observing the old Banto in the daylight, he saw his skin was a darker green than Brightdale Delphins, and more markedly shark textured. Keen to compare physical features, he showed Bonito the frill of gills behind his ears, and grinning in delight, Bonito drew aside his greying thatch to show his own gills.

Drawing on her limited range of Delphin creaks and whistles, Suki butted in, impatient to explain to Bonito their mission and that they needed guides to M'Bopo's cavern. Eventually – after Lark did a masterful impression of a Batfrit – understanding, mixed with alarm, dawned on the clan head's face. Giving a piercing whistle he summoned his sons, Guppy and Blenny away from watching the crossbow shooting. Shouldering their crossbows, Sandy and Kenji followed. Speaking rapid Delphin, Bonito explained Suki's request. At first, the two brothers looked shocked, and protested vigorously, but after a lot of pleading whistles and clicks from Lark, shrugging their shoulders, they nodded assent. Guppy pointed to the sun, and counting by the fingers of a raised hand, indicated they must leave in ten minutes.

Collecting their packs from the night shelter, they haltingly thanked Bonito for his village's hospitality. As Lark hoisted Mick out of a ruck of village dogs squabbling over ownership of an extra meaty thigh bone, Grilla appeared with two handfuls of mangoes, which he proudly handed over to Lark and Crow to store in their packs.

Blenny and Guppy, armed with spears and machetes, led them out of the village, the whole clan trailing behind. Passing through cultivated fields, Lark and Kenji asked Suki to identify some of the plants, and she pointed out yams, cassava, sorghum, and groundnuts.

At the edge of the forest, the villagers, not wanting to go further, called a farewell in Suki's language: 'Sayonara! Sayonara!'

As the Bantos' voices faded, they entered deep forest along a well-worn path. In the distance could be heard the river's roar. All around was thick jungle: trees of huge girth reaching to the hot African sky, heavy with fruit and blossom, their branches hung with lianas. In the dank leaf-litter of the forest floor grew clumps of ferns, gunnera and macaranga. The unfamiliar whirring, buzzing, humming, booming, chinking and clicking of countless creatures filled the humid air.

Recalling his encounter in the bush at Banjul, Lark dreaded that a snake might drop on him out the branches at any moment.

'Are there dangerous creatures in this jungle?' he called to Suki.

She halted, calling everyone to gather around. Blenny and Guppy rested on their spears.

As if recalling a childhood rhyme, she ticked off on her fingers the creatures of the forest: 'Of the big cats, leopards are the most common, and of the primates, red-colobus monkeys and chimpanzees. Of snakes, there are mambas, but also cobras and puff adders. The non-venomous reptiles are python, lizards and of course chameleon, which always remind me of dear Kassabel. Then there are porcupines and mongooses – I could go on for ever!'

'And insects?' Sandy asked, slapping a gnat that had landed on his neck. 'I've heard there are mosquitos whose bite causes serious illness.'

'Yes, the Anopheles mosquito, which passes on malaria.'

Fin, recalling the pictures of insects he'd seen in one of Mossy's books, remarked: 'I've read that bullet ants inflict the most painful stings!'

Suki shuddered. 'Yes, bullet ants are the worst. Their sting is like a lightning bolt. Fortunately, I have never experienced it!'

Lark anxiously searched the jungle around him. Seeing a line of fat red-bodied ants crawling up a tree trunk, he hurried after the others.

Conscious that any injury would be disastrous, their progress slowed as the path grew ever steeper, now slippery with mud and criss-crossed with thick roots. The roar of the river grew louder, and half an hour later, they arrived at a cliff top. Below them the river rushed fast and wild through a deep gorge. The enormous trunk of a fallen kapok tree bridged the gorge, its ancient roots clinging to the cliff on the near side, its branches embedded in rocks on the far side. Along the top of the trunk ran a walkway cut into the dead wood, with a rope handhold strung above.

To their surprise, Blenny and Guppy didn't cross, but gesturing that Sandy, Kenji, Crow, Grilla and Mick should wait, led Fin, Lark, and Suki down steep steps cut into the cliff to a ledge jutting out a few feet above the river. A shallow hollow had been dug out of the rock face. On the side walls were crude charcoal drawings of stick men armed with shields and spears chasing lions, antelopes, and giraffes.

It was the back wall that made them gasp: a full-sized painting of a Delphin man, the lines of his gently smiling face so perfect, it could almost be a portrait taken from life. His ankle length robe painted gleaming white, with delicately outlined silvery wings behind, around his head glowed a bright yellow halo. Laid in front of the figure were bowls of scarlet hibiscus, purple and white orchids.

'It's Phul!' breathed Fin.

Reverently Blenny and Guppy knelt before the figure and Fin and Lark sank down beside them.

Fin leaned close to Blenny and whispered in his ear: 'Phul?'

Blenny nodded with a smile.

Lark shook his head in wonder. 'Looks like someone has drawn him from real life! Just as good as your efforts, Fin! Do you think old Phul ever came here when he lived on earth?'

Fin didn't reply, he was thinking about Mossy and Kassabel, and the significance of who they were: Phul was one of their kind too.

Standing behind Fin, Suki whispered in his ear: 'The Bantos believe Phul is still on earth, and often comes to this cave.'

Overhearing, Lark looked at her in disbelief. 'That can't be right! Us Brightdale Delphins deserve a visit from old Phul, but he's never come! No, he's long gone – someone must be playing a trick on these Delphins!'

Fin sighed. 'We'll never know.'

Leaving the shrine, they climbed back up the steps and re-joined the others.

Telling Sandy and Kenji about it, Lark complained again about Phul never being seen in Brightdale.

Kenji grinned. 'Perhaps Phul is too busy here in Africa!'

They all laughed.

Lark snorted in disgust. 'No! He's long gone – swimming in a warm sea, far away!'

Guppy and Blenny set off along the tree trunk. Grilla skipped across after them, gripping the trunk with his feet; he had Mick under one arm, Crow and bible bag, loudly complaining, under the other. The others edged their way along, swinging on the rope, trying not to look down at the river tumbling over rocks far below.

All safely across they continued along the riverbank on the north side, with the river now on their right. Soon, the terrain started to climb steeply. The jungle denser, they battled on, slashing with their machetes at the undergrowth. The humidity draining their energy, clouds of insects biting their faces, went up their noses as all around them came the unending cacophony of jungle noise. Once they were alarmed by a crashing in the trees ahead, but it proved to be a troop of colobus monkeys disturbed by their advance. Ever alert for snakes, thankfully there were no encounters with any of the dangerous species Suki had listed.

At mid-day, they stopped to rest and drink from their water bottles. Grilla crashed off into the jungle, returning a few moments later with a couple of melon-like fruits. Lark sliced one open with his boning knife, revealing a juicy flesh surrounding numerous round black seeds.

'Is this fruit safe?' he asked Suki, sniffing the fragrant orange coloured flesh.

'Sure are! They're paw paws – my favourite fruit. Come on, Lark, slice them up and pass around the pieces.'

Flicking out the seeds and cutting up the fruit, Lark handed the slices around, saving a small slice for Mick, who carefully buried it under a bush.

Munching his fruit, Fin sighted Quilla perched above them on the topmost branch of a kapok tree. He climbed onto a tree stump and waved his arms to attract Bird's attention. The powerful bird swooped down and landed on the stump beside him. With cries of fright, Blenny and Guppy dived behind Sandy, and rattled their spears threateningly.

As Fin stroked Quilla's magnificent golden head, Bird waved at him from her pod in his eye. 'Everything O.K. love? Did you see the Delphins?' he called softly.

'Yep! Weren't they great! Where're we going now?'

'To M'Bopo's lair. Two Banto Delphins are guiding us.'

He pointed to Blenny and Guppy who were staring at him and Quilla in astonishment.

Suki could stand it no longer. Slamming her machete into a log, she hissed to Kenji: 'What nonsense is this? I have seen him talk to the bird before. Is he mad?'

Kenji pushed her forward. 'No! Go on Suki! It's about time you met Bird!'

Glowering with suspicion, Suki reluctantly approached Fin and Quilla and peered into what she thought looked like a large fish egg jammed in the eagle's eye socket.

Seeing Bird's tiny figure waving inside, she gasped. 'Oh my word – it's a person! Fin, she's minute!'

His eyes glittering with tears, Fin nodded dumbly.

Taking pity on Fin, Sandy led Suki away and sitting beside her on a nearby rock told the tale of Bird: how her soul was stolen at Birdoswald, and how she came to be inside the pod in Quilla's eye.

'That is why we are here: to rescue the holy cross and use it to save Bird before her body dies.'

Listening to the story, Suki became ever more distressed. When Sandy had finished, she ran to Fin and clasped him in a tearful hug.

'I'm so sorry Fin! It must be very hard, seeing your girl like this.'

Peering again into the bubble, she saw Bird's tiny face pressed against the transparent skin. 'Can she talk?' she asked in a whisper.

'Yes, she can talk, but nobody but me seems to be able to hear her.'

Lark interrupted. 'Well, I think I heard her the other day, when Quilla stole that leg from the lions – she sounded dead chuffed!'

Hearing this, Bird waved and called as loudly as she could. 'SUKI! LARK!'

But they didn't hear. She gave a sharp command to Quilla, who spread his wings, and soared up into the air, turning to a dot against the blue roof of sky.

Once more they set off, hacking through the undergrowth, their way becoming ever steeper. The sound of the river quieter, now and then they glimpsed high cliffs rising above the trees. Suki explained that they were nearing the Futa Jallon plateau and the Sacred Source of the River Gambia.

'The plateau is known as the Water Tower because its height draws heavy rainfall. There lies the derelict garden of Florain where there are rumours that in the ruined temples live fallen Gaiakins possessed by demons, and they practice loathsome rituals. Below is a cave system into which the source of the river falls from the Plateau above, flowing out at the base of the cliffs to eventually become the mighty Gambia. It is in the caves that M'Bopo has his lair where he stores his treasures.'

Suki shuddered. 'In the past few days there have been sightings of creatures of horror known as Phraggs, flying to the Plateau!'

'They will have come from Contagion!' Fin exclaimed.

'Aye, I know all about those devils – I've come too close to one!' Kenji muttered bitterly, massaging the scars on his sword hand.

As they neared the plateau, Blenny and Guppy slowed, then stopped, refusing to go further, agitatedly flapping their arms in attempted explanation.

Suki frowned as understanding dawned. 'It's M'Bopo's cave. We're getting close. They are very frightened of the Batfrits.'

'Can't turn back now,' Fin muttered, angrily fishing out his sketch of Queen Mab, and thrusting it at the cowering Bantos. 'Butterfly! Must find butterfly with jewel!' He stabbed at the cross drawn on Mab's chest.

Staring at the sketch in horror, Blenny and Guppy backed away from him as if he were mad. Waving a brief frantic goodbye, they scuttled off through the bush, disappearing in moments.

'That went well, didn't it!' laughed Kenji.

'Drat it Fin! You know you shouldn't have shown them your sketch.' Lark grumbled.

'Never mind,' Sandy said. 'We don't need guides now – we know where M'Bopo's lair is!'

They climbed on, ever closer to the source of evil that was their goal; it took all their courage not to turn and run after Blenny and Guppy.

An hour later, they reached the foot of the cliffs topped by dense jungle. At the cliffs' base the river flowed out from the high mouth of a dark cave, passing through large steppingstones before coursing on downstream. Stained white with bat guano and looking like the bottom row of dentures, the stones formed a crossing to the other side of the river, to where half-hidden by ferns, a steep stairway dug in the sandstone led up to the plateau above. Even from a distance, the cave seemed to exude an aura of such menace that, even in the stifling heat, they all shivered. The only way to it was along the stony edge of the river several feet below them.

Before they could stop him, Crow started scrambling down the bank. 'Get a move on Delphs! What yer waiting for? We must get jool from flutterby, afore she's off again!' he yelled shrilly.

As Fin made to follow him, Suki dragged him back.

'Batfrits!' she cried, pointing wildly downstream. Just above the tree line, dark silhouettes had appeared against the orange glow of the setting sun.

Lark leaned over and yelled to Crow: 'CROW, FRITS ARE COMING!'

Reaching out he just managed to grab the straps of Crow's pack and dragging him back up, hissed angrily: 'Yer daft bum boil! What do yer think yer doing?'

Struggling fiercely, Crow shrieked: 'Want jool! Want—' Sandy quickly clamped his over Crow's mouth.

The swarm of Batfrits streamed towards them. 'Eeekkk! Eeekkk! Eeekkk!' The shrieking of hundreds of mechanical voice boxes echoed off the cliff face. Whimpering, Mick scrabbled into Lark's jacket.

Pressing back deep into the undergrowth, they watched in fascinated horror as, like swallows returning to their roost, the flock headed for the dark cavern, spinning, and rolling on the air, leathery wings flapping, skimming the river.

Below them and a little behind, flew a bat much larger than the rest, the bulk of its mangy body festooned with sparkling jewelled regalia. His leathery wing tips splashing the water, M'Bopo's batteries were running low, and he needed to recharge. Flopping up and down, he disappeared into the cavern.

For a long while they waited as night gathered around them, not daring to move, dreading the return of any late coming Batfrits. From the plateau above raucous singing and harsh laughter could be faintly heard as sudden firelight blazed, sending sparks shooting into the night sky.

'Rogue Gaiakins!' Suki muttered grimly.

Above the trees the moon rose huge and red to shine on the river. Dozing fitfully, they waited for dawn and for the Batfrits to emerge from the cave. Once, when the moon had set and all was completely dark, a fiery light shot up from the plateau and streaking over their heads, zoomed northwards, and disappeared, leaving a stink of sulphur: they knew it was a Phragg.

# 6
# M'BOPO'S TREASURE

At last, after what seemed an endless night, dawn came. The first pale rays of sun glittering on the river, a nerve-shredding screeching jolted them alert. As if at a signal, the Batfrits streamed from the cave's mouth and flew off down the river. M'Bopo, heaving and huffing behind, was the last to disappear. Seeing them in daylight, Fin was reminded of flying foxes he'd seen when they sailed along the river, only these creatures were larger, with tattered chicken-leather wings, pointed snouts, and snapping jaws showing long sharp teeth. He glimpsed metal through their rust-red mangy fur.

Suki stirred. 'I think they've all gone! But I'll get out the shockers, just in case.'

She took out three from her pack and aiming one at a nearby rock, pressed the trigger: Spiff! A crackling line of blinding light smashed into the rock, leaving a dark stain.

She handed the other two to Sandy and Kenji. 'Be careful – they're primed: don't accidentally shoot yourself! When you fire, aim for the bat's head, it's where their electronic processors are. And remember – the shockers are charged with six shots only. When those are fired throw it away and use your own weapons.'

Kenji gingerly aimed his shocker at the mark Suki's shot had made. His hit a fraction to the right.

Sandy had a go next. Aiming as if he were firing his crossbow, he hit the mark dead centre.

He grinned boyishly. 'Right, we have only five shots each left, so we must be careful how we deploy them.'

Turning his shocker to neutral, and carefully stowing it in his belt, he stood at the edge of the high riverbank and looked thoughtfully to the cave.

'We must decide who shall go in, and who shall stay outside on watch. Kenji and Suki, it is best if you stay at the entrance to keep a look out, whilst Fin, Lark and myself go inside. Crow, Grilla and Mick must stay up here—'

Crow squealed indignantly. 'I mus' go inside: I wore Jool too! 'sides I best at creepin'.'

Frowning, Sandy looked doubtful, but Fin came to Crow's defence. 'It's only fair that Crow should come with us. As he said, he wore the cross and has every right.'

Sandy sighed. 'You are a bad lad Crow, and if you come with us, you must behave yourself!'

'Don't worry Sandy, I'll keep a close eye on him,' Lark growled as he scooped up Mick. Shoving him at Grilla, he gave them both a stern command. 'Stay! Do yer understand? Stay!'

Clutching Mick under his arm, Grilla grunted unhappily. Crow firmly pressed his bible bag into the gorilla's big soft hand. 'Monkey, keep Sparkie safe!'

Slinging the bag over his shoulder, Grilla turned and disappeared into the bush.

Searching the treetops, Fin saw Quilla soaring away. He hoped Bird would order him to fly down, but the great eagle rose higher and disappeared into the blue, so he reluctantly followed the others as they scrambled down the steep bank to the stony ledge beside the river. Remembering old Kisho's words: that Gressil now inhabited an underwater bobbitworm, he eyed the water uneasily.

Picking their way to the cave and peering in, they saw at the back the entrance to a high roofed tunnel from where the river came flowing out. Daylight, filtering through cracks in the tunnel roof, created pools of warm light and from within could be heard the distant sound of a waterfall.

Anxious and alert for any stray Batfrits, they entered the cave. On ledges in the high rocky walls was evidence of Batfrit roosts: oily white bat guano droppings and parts of Batfrits: metal, wires and a few bat limbs. Along the river's narrow gravel banks, clouds of black flies hovered over mounds of rotting food. Suddenly with a piercing screech, a Batfrit plunged out of the dark shadows. Suki's shocker flashed. Squealing tinnily, it bounced on the gravel bank and rolling into the river. Sparking and fizzing, it sank beneath the water, leaving a circle of ripples.

Leaving Kenji and Suki keeping watch at the entrance, Sandy, Fin, Lark and Crow warily edged along the riverbank and into the tunnel. Their feet disturbing insects and lizards, sending them scuttling away, they saw a ghostly white albino snake coiling down into the deep water. Thinking he spotted a long dark shape moving beneath the surface, a shiver ran down Fin's spine; he had a feeling something was watching them.

A few paces ahead, Sandy stopped and peering into a chamber dug deep in the rock, murmured: 'This must be some of M'Bopo's hoard of stolen treasure.'

Producing his stub of candle from a pocket, Lark lit it with his flint. Holding it up, sending moths fluttering in all directions, the flickering flame revealed a menagerie of stuffed animals, glass eyes catching the light: an elephant's head, a hyena, a male lion with a shaggy mane, poised mid-leap, teeth set in a snarl and several exotic birds, their plumage tattered and faded.

Crow, squeezing his small frame between the lion and a moth-eaten ostrich, couldn't go any deeper. Backing out as Lark snuffed the candle, he muttered glumly: 'No jool there!'

A little farther on was another chamber, much larger and jammed from floor to roof with ornamental brightly painted furniture; thrones, beds, tables, all decorated with jewels and precious metals, along with marble statues of human and animal figures. Fin was reminded of pictures he'd seen in Mossy's books of ancient Egyptian tombs.

Again, Crow squeezed inside to search, but soon came out shaking his head to announce: 'No room for flutterby wearing jool!'

Reaching an area where the roof of the tunnel had caved in leaving mounds of rubble littering the path, sunlight streamed in through a wide hole fringed by ferns and dangling roots. From ahead, the roar of the waterfall grew ever louder, but above the sound, they became aware of a low vibrating hum close by, reminding them of the turbine at the Barraconda Motherhome. The noise led them to a large cave, and within they saw rows of machines. Scattered on benches lay Batfrits in various stages of construction, some just metal frames, others almost complete, awaiting heads or limbs, flesh and fur. Along two walls were shelves stacked with spare parts: bundles of chicken skin leather, metal rods, coils of copper wire, rolls of red fur. Against another wall were rows of boxes, lights blinking above them. Behind their glass fronts were Batfrit heads with variously coloured wires attached to their skulls. It all reminded Fin and Lark horribly of the Frit factory beneath Gressil's Fortress in Contagion.

'I think they are being what is called programmed,' murmured Sandy.

As he spoke, a screech of rage rent the air: in a flurry of leathery wings a Batfrit swooped down. Sandy's shocker flashed and crackled. Howling in agony, the Batfrit fell to the floor, juddered, and was still. 'Hurry!' hissed Sandy, 'the noise may have alerted more Frits.'

They crept from the Batfrit factory and, the tunnel now open to the sky, keeping to the cover of the ferns hanging down from the roof, they continued alongside the river.

A little further on, the river widened to become a dark deep pool. Bubbles rising to the surface gave it a sinister air, and for a fleeting moment, Fin thought he glimpsed just below the surface a flash of teeth, and something that could have been a mouth. Not sure if his eyes were playing tricks, he didn't say anything.

'Hopefully, our search ends here!' Sandy whispered, indicating the opening to another cave beyond the pool. 'Such a hidden place must surely be where M'Bopo keeps his most treasured possessions!'

Edging past the pool, at the cave threshold, they stood in wonder. Through holes in the roof, sunbeams danced on a glittering mountain of treasure. Gold and silver coins, crowns, tiaras, huge rubies, diamond carbuncles, strings of pearls, sapphires, spilling out of boxes, caskets and bags, and spreading over the floor.

'Teg's knackers!' Lark squeaked, 'there couldn't be a single jewel left in all Africa!'

Sandy gasped. 'Look lads! Look up there!'

Above the mound hung Queen Mab. Suspended by her arms from a chain in the roof, her dainty toes brushed the top of the treasure. Head bowed, tattered wings drooping, she wasn't moving. Seeing the deep wound in her side weeping blood and pus, they wondered if she was dead. On her furred breast lay the Chi Rho, the jewels blazing brighter than all the rich treasury below.

His eyes fixed on the cross, unable to stop himself, Fin started scrambling up the mound sending the rich hoard beneath his boots cascading to the floor. As Sandy lunged after him Lark let out a strangled squeak: he'd spotted Crow in the shadows on the other side creeping up the mound.

'Sandy, Crow's going to climb too!'

'Quick, stop him!' Sandy hissed, grabbing Fin's boot.

Lark had started after Crow, when from the roof sped three Batfrits. Letting go of Fin's boot, Sandy drew his shocker and fired. Spiff. He hit one in the head. Then firing his last two shots, spiff, spiff, sparks pouring out of them, the Batfrits plummeted to the chamber floor. Throwing his empty shocker away, Sandy started up the mound after Fin who, reaching the top, even as he stretched up to grab the cross, Mab came to life. Spinning on her chain and screeching, she kicked out at him, sending him tumbling back among the treasure, triggering an avalanche of crowns, strings of pearls, and caskets of sapphires. As he tumbled a harsh cry echoed around the chamber.

'BOY! THE CROSS IS MINE!'

A figure rose from the jewels. At first sight it could have been a Gaiakin – Fescue or Mullein. But the light revealed a ghastly mockery of those graceful, slender limbed warriors: the face, almost dog-like, cruel mouth set in a yellow-fanged snarl. Chest and thighs swelling beneath tight fitting, greasy leather clothing, a mat of rusty-grey hair covered the thick neck and down the heavily muscled back.

The beast shook himself free of jewels, climbed out and with measured menacing tread, descended the mound. At his waist, he wore a belt with a row of razor-sharp edged throwing discs known as chakrams. Plucking one, he made ready to throw.

Sandy, jumping back to the ground, aimed his crossbow. 'GAIAKIN! Move a step more and you will die!'

With a defiant yowl, the monster sent a chakram spinning towards him. Swiftly ducking, the deadly blade skimmed close to the top of Sandy's head and clattered against the cave wall. His arrow went wide. His own true Gaiakin blood giving power to his human form, as two more chakrams flew past his face, Sandy drew his sword and with a mighty war cry leapt back up the mound towards his snarling opponent. As he sprang, from out of the jewels a second beast emerged, followed by a third, both hurling chakrams as they slid down the treasure mountain.

Outnumbered, even Sandy's almost superhuman fury could not save him. As he dodged a flying chakram, another of the murderous discs bit deep into his neck. With a roar of rage and pain, he tumbled down the mound and lay still and bleeding amid the sea of coins and precious stones, his sword fallen from his lifeless hand.

Desperate to reach him, Fin abandoned Mab, still frantically kicking and spinning on her chain. But as he scrambled down the stack, he was caught in a steel grip by the first devil Gaiakin. Helpless, he could only watch in horror as the two other Gaiakin monsters stood over their captive, the jagged tips of their swords inches from Sandy's heart, ready to deal their death thrusts.

Even as they raised their swords, from the pool outside came a loud splash as something huge broke the surface. Cringing in terror the Gaiakins backed away from Sandy's inert form, swords clattering to the ground, as an enormous worm slithered into the cave. Snaking across the floor the long, segmented body coiled into a circle, and raising its head, swaying from side to side, from between its teeth filled jaws a thin tongue darted in and out as the implacably evil eyes examined each of them. Its victim chosen, before the Gaiakin could cry out, the worm uncoiled and sprung, latching its jaws onto the Gaiakin's foul mouth in the mockery of an obscene kiss.

An instant later, released from the sucking embrace, his victim slumped to the floor. The huge worm, twisting its body back into a coil, raised its head and waited. Back arched, heels drumming the ground, battered mouth gaping, with one violent convulsion, the Gaiakin disgorged the fiery rags of a Phragg. Dripping sparks, the Phragg hovered for a moment, angry red eyes blazing, then shrieking like a lit firework shot out through the roof.

As the Phragg disappeared, the worm, its body twisting and corkscrewing in agony, with a violent heave, from out its gaping mouth spewed a thick black cloud. Drifting over the Gaiakin's contorted body, dark misty fingers probing and stroking, the cloud slipped into the Gaiakin's gaping mouth and with a satisfied hiss the mouth snapped shut. Abandoned by the foul dweller within it, the worm slid out of the cavern and plunged back into the pool. His companions gaping uncomprehending, the dead Gaiakin transformed, swaying and stretching, his body grew shapely and slender, the face, once pock-marked and scabby, smoothed into a cold beauty, the coarse matted hair turning to flowing silvery locks. Beneath the skin shimmered an ethereal green-blue light.

Still held in the third Gaiakin's steel strong arms, Fin moaned in despair as he realised what he had seen: Lord Gressil had escaped from the bobbitworm to enter a new more vibrant and versatile body.

Gressil lifted his head and opened his eyes: out of them blazed a fierce red light. Running his hands tenderly over his new body, from his mouth came a triumphant cry, depraved and yet so achingly beautiful:

'At last! At last! I have a body befitting me as a prince in Lucifer's kingdom!'

Looking up at his Queen hanging from her chain, head bowed, her wings drooping in exhaustion, her dark spirit almost spent, he called: 'I am coming my love! I shall save you!'

Seizing up a Gaiakin sword, with one great leap, almost flying, he was by her side. With two blows of the steel-edged sword, he severed her chains. As she slumped forward, he gathered her into his arms, and tenderly kissed her on the mouth. Gently wrapping her tattered wings around her, he carried her drooping body down the treasure mound.

'You – bring the Delphin runt!' he barked to the Gaiakin holding Fin. To the other, cringing uncertainly by Sandy's motionless body, he snarled: 'You – bring the human, even if it is dead: I have need of both.'

The creature heaved Sandy over his shoulder, and with Fin's captor roughly bundling him forward, they stumbled after Gressil and his precious burden as he strode out of the cavern.

In the deep shadows, ducking low, as swiftly as he dared Lark climbed the treasure mound behind Crow's small figure. About to catch him by the ankle several things happened: a scream filled the cavern and glancing up he saw Fin wobbling at the top of the mound as he dodged Queen Mab's flailing legs. At the same time, three Batfrits hurtled down from the roof. Three times Sandy's shocker spat and crackled, and they fell from sight.

Then from close above him a harsh voice rang round the cavern: 'THE CROSS IS MINE!'

A monster rose out of the jewels. With a terrified squeak Crow collapsed into Lark's arms.

A war cry from Sandy followed by despairing shout, moved Lark to action. As he started up, Crow hung onto him desperately.

'No! No!' he squeaked in a hoarse whisper, 'how we get to rescue Mr Sandy if the monster ketches us too?'

Reluctantly, Lark pressed back into the shadows, hand on the hilt of his boning knife. He gave a start as a spinning metal disk ricocheted off the wall above him and landed at his feet. Astonished, he grabbed the disc. His hand trembling, he gingerly ran his finger around the razor-sharp edge: the weapon could prove useful. As he tucked it inside his belt, from outside the cavern came a new sound: an ominous crash of water as if something huge was rising out of the dark pool. Desperate to know what was going on, Crow clutching his arm, dreading they might set off a landslide of treasure, they started crawling from the shadows, but an ear-splitting shriek sent them ducking back. The cave filled with a choking sulphurous stink. Flames flashed across the roof. Surely there wasn't a Phragg out there? Terrified, Lark and Crow clung to each other as a powerful voice, at once beautiful yet cruel, cried out something. A moment later, jewels, coins, and cups, tumbled all around them: someone was climbing the treasure mound. As they peeped up, a sword blade flashed. The chain holding Mab rattled loose, more jewels cascaded down. The cruel voice barked twice more, and a moment later silence fell in the cavern.

When they dared to creep into the open, it took a few moments to take in what they saw: pools of blood and water, Fin's pack half-buried under jewels, Sandy's crossbow, the shaft broken, his sword without its scabbard. Lark picked up the sword, then decided it was too long for him to carry as well as his and Fin's rucksacks, reluctantly dropped it.

As he shouldered Fin's pack, his eye fell on the Gaiakins' murderous throwing discs scattered on the ground.

'Crow! Wait!' he called. 'Let's take these, they're handy weapons!'

'OK, but quick! Quick!' Crow hissed agitatedly, 'we follow blood!' He pointed to a trail of dark splashes leading out of the cavern.

As they grabbed up the discs, tucking them in their packs, from far down the tunnel could be heard a confused din of shouting and screeching. Dreading what might lie ahead, they crept out of the treasure cave, following the trail of blood along the pool's edge: the uproar continued, getting louder as they pressed on.

They'd reached the Frit factory cave, its machines still humming, when Kenji and Suki appeared, running towards them. Suki was limping heavily.

'Thank goodness! Thank goodness! You're safe!' she panted, collapsing on a boulder by the wall.

'M-M-Monsters taken Fin and Mr Sandy!' squealed Crow. 'Quick after 'em!'

'Did you see them and the monsters? They left a trail of blood!' Lark pointed to the line of blood spots.

Kenji nodded as he slumped beside Suki. They were bleeding from several cuts on their arms and legs. 'Yes, we tried to rescue Sandy and Fin, but four more of the hellish Gaiakins came from outside – used all our shocker charges – just bounced off their thick hides! But I had my crossbow! Managed to hit one – as it fell, a Phragg shot out of it.'

'One of the beasts had Sandy slung over his shoulder, and another had Fin under his arm,' Suki choked. 'Sandy wasn't moving. Blood was dripping from a wound in his neck —' Tears flooding her eyes, she couldn't say any more.

'While we were distracted, fighting the other beasts, Sandy and Fin's captors sneaked off,' groaned Kenji. 'What looked a true Gaiakin was leading them – beautiful, shining silver hair – he carried the butterfly woman in his arms!

'The Gaiakin devils had a weapon of their own – chakrams – spinning wheels!' gasped Suki. 'Sliced through my trouser!' She showed them her bloodstained left trouser leg.

'We were on the point of defeat, when M'Bopo and his gang arrived!'

'Must have been alerted by the fleeing Phragg!' Kenji added. 'We were forgotten as a fierce battle started between the Gaiakin monsters and the Batfrits. Torn between going after the Gaiakins who'd captured Sandy and Fin or looking for you, we decided we should first look for you. We crept into the tunnel, dreading you were dead—'

He paused, realising the noise of battle back in the entrance cave had died away. 'Hurry! we must find out what's going on – see if the Batfrits are defeated, so we can go after the Gaiakin devils who have Sandy and Fin.'

'Yes!' Suki staggering to her feet. 'I know the way to their Garden lair – I went there once, out hunting with the Banto folk – but we must be careful – defeated or not, M'Bopo and his gang could still be about.'

As she and Kenji made to set off, Lark called them back. 'Wait! Sandy's sword is still in the jewel cave! I couldn't carry it, what with Fin's pack – we can't just leave it!

'Aye,' Kenji said, 'it would break Sandy's heart if his precious sword was lost!'

Running back to the cave, Suki and Kenji stood amazed at the sight of the treasure. Lark pointed out the chain Mab had hung from, and briefly told of what he'd seen and heard from his and Crow's hiding place. Kenji looked grimly at the pool of Sandy's blood and his sword lying on the ground but didn't speak. Picking up the sword, he tucked it firmly into his belt. Suki gathered up Sandy's shot arrows into her quiver. As they left the cave, she flung his broken crossbow into the lake.

Swiftly they ran to the cavern entrance where, amid the piles of rotting food and guano-caked rocks, were signs of a brief but fierce battle. Nearby lay a couple of dead Gaiakins, seeming strangely innocent now their demons had fled them. Several Batfrits lay lifeless, but there was no sign of M'Bopo and his gang.

Lark picked up more chakrams. 'These'll prove useful,' he told Suki and Kenji, sliding the lethal discs into his pack. 'Crow and I collected more in the treasure cave. Chuckums, did you call them?'

Suki couldn't help a chuckle. 'No, chakrams! You need skill at throwing for them to be of use!'

'Aye, I'm good at that!' Lark growled. 'Blew up an oil well once by chucking a stone – hit it dead centre. Made a huge explosion – t'was when we were in Contagion.'

'Yep! Yep! Lark expert at ducks 'n drakes! I got chuckers too,' squeaked Crow, showing them two he'd tucked in his belt.

Whilst Lark collected the chakrams, Kenji gathered up the few of his undamaged arrows he could find.

'Enough delay!' urged Suki. 'We must follow the blood trail while it's still fresh.'

Following the trail of blood out of the cave they saw several more splashes of blood on the white guano crusted stepping stones crossing the river.

'For certain the monsters have taken their captives above to the ruined garden!' exclaimed Suki pointing to the steps leading up to the plateau. 'Come we must cross! Take care, they could be slippery.'

Suki leading the way, leaping from stone to stone, the others followed. All safely across, they climbed the stairway and stepping onto the plateau, found themselves in an intensely humid, green world. No birds called. Sensing unseen eyes watching from the dense vegetation, the only visible life, a snake slithering back into a clump of macaranga plants. They saw before them, almost obscured by thick twisting roots, a cracked pavement of orange and black marble leading into the jungle. Among the thick forest of tree trunks could be glimpsed tumbled down walls and elaborately carved sandstone pillars from which heavily weathered sculpted faces stared through the undergrowth of liana, macaranga, ferns and palms.

Seeing spots of blood, fewer now, on the marble slabs, they started along the pavement. Using all their tracking skills, Kenji, and Suki searched for tell-tale signs of recent activity; Lark and Crow chafing at the slow progress. They came to a wide lake. Fed at the far end by the river spilling over a massive slime-covered wall, whilst in front of them across the lake's edge ran a dam of huge moss-covered stone gargoyles: dragons, serpents, sabre-toothed tigers. Through their gaping mouths the waters cascaded as a waterfall into a narrow chasm.

'I guess that must be the waterfall we could hear in the tunnel,' mused Lark.

'Yes,' agreed Suki, 'then it becomes the river again, running through M'Bopo's cavern, flowing out into the jungle, on to Barraconda and eventually to the sea.'

Across the top of the dam a balustraded causeway of broken marble led to the ruins of a red sandstone temple, its few remaining unbroken colonnaded pillars reflected in the waters of the lake, with tall tree trunks thrusting through what had been an elaborate roof of pineapple shaped domes. Out of the jungle beyond rose more towers and domes. A pall of dusty yellow light hung over the scene and a stink of burning rubber hung in the air.

In the pale distance, misty mountains could be glimpsed, where foaming white waterfalls, cascading down their cliffs, shimmered in the bright, clean sunlight. That outside world seemed far away: they were nearing the ruined garden of Florain.

Lark and Crow close behind Suki and Kenji, swords drawn, they set out across the causeway.

After a few paces, a scrap of white caught Lark's keen eye. 'Fin's sketch paper!' He gasped, snatching up the piece of torn parchment caught in a bramble.

He spotted more pieces in brambles further ahead. 'Look! Fin's left us a trail. We must be on the right track!'

Greatly encouraged, they moved on, led by the tell-tale parchment scraps. Noticing tendrils of purple flowered orchids twisting among the balustrade pillars, Lark was reminded of the breakfast courtyard in the castle at Florain, where similar orchids tumbled from silver urns around the exotic dolphin fountain. With a pang of sadness, he remembered Fin had promised to sketch him standing by the fountain, to send to Tissy. But that same day, Dancer had brought the shocking news that Skyhook had crashed, and Mossy was believed dead.

The parchment trail continued to the end of the causeway, and on into the temple, pieces of white fluttering tantalisingly among the ferns and palms. The temple was vast: weathered statuary among the remains of marvellously decorated walls and pillars all overrun by the choking jungle. Fear of falling through dark holes in the broken pavement, they made their way carefully knowing that below them lay M'Bopo's cave system. Peering into one wide, fern fringed hole they saw below them the Batfrit factory.

As they edged around it, a familiar cry came from above.

'Skeew! Skeew!'

'It's Quilla!' Lark exclaimed as the great eagle glided down and landed in the topmost branch of a nearby baobab tree.

Then from ahead a large, extra-furry rat bounced into view.

Crow screeched. 'Sparkie! Sparkie! Where you been? Has monkey lost you?' Tenderly he scooped the rat up into his arms.

Hooting a greeting, Grilla emerged from the undergrowth. Three more gorillas then appeared: a half-grown male, silver-back like Grilla, and a female leading a toddling infant. The half-grown one had Crow's bible bag slung on his back, from where there came muffled yowls and barks.

'Grilla, yer great lumbering twit!' Lark yelled. 'Tell yer friend to give us that bag, right now!'

The ape handed it to Grilla, who passed it to Lark with apologetic grunts. As Lark released the straps, Mick scrabbled out panting and whimpering.

Indignantly snatching the bag, Crow tipped it up: Grilla's squashed football tumbled out and was snatched up by the infant gorilla.

Disgustedly shaking the bag, Crow peered inside. Satisfied, he tenderly dropped Sparkie in.

Alarmed by the noise everyone was making, Kenji and Suki looked down into the factory cave. Rusty squeaks warned them at least one Batfrit was stirring.

'We must get away from here!' Suki hissed.

'What about Grilla's mates?' Lark asked, eyeing the peacefully squatting trio.

Suki grinned. 'They might as well join the party – some extra muscle power could be handy!'

'Watch out for more parchment!' Kenji called softly.

As he set off along the path, Grilla agitatedly pulled at his arm, signalling that he knew where they should go.

'Let him be our guide, Kenji! Grilla's a good tracker,' Lark suggested.

Grilla disappeared into the dense undergrowth, reappearing a moment later and handed Lark the stub of one of Fin's charcoal sketching sticks.

With their new gorilla friends leading and Mick keeping anxiously close to Lark's heels, they set off again. Seeing Quilla wheeling above them, Lark wished he could call him down and talk to him – tell Bird to search from the sky for Fin and Sandy.

A little way on Kenji stopped suddenly, uttering a soft cry. From a low branch, he unhooked a bright object hanging on a gold chain. He held up Sandy's pendant: a yellow enamel flower in the shape of a letter B.

'B for Betony –' Lark murmured sadly.

More anxious than ever, searching intently for clues, they pressed on. As dusk began to fall, they realised they were in the remains of the old formal Garden of Florain; where there had once been magnificent flower beds, sickly lupins, marigolds, delphiniums, struggled up through thorns and nettles. Making their way along the muddy paths, past elegant statuary, many smashed, they came upon pools containing stinking stagnant water and covered in slimy green blanket weed; others long dry, the skeletons of huge goldfish baked into the lifeless mud.

At one pool, Lark stopped and stared in dismay at the fountain in its centre, the figures so rusted away it was hard to tell what kind of creatures they had been. Thinking of the fountain in Florain he thought they could have been dolphins. At intervals, clearings had been cut in the jungle in which stood large cages. Lark guessed they were, or had been, used to keep animals. He wondered unhappily for what use the animals had been kept. In the corner of one lay a bleached skeleton which Lark thought looked horribly like the remains of a gorilla.

'This horror would break Queen Fleur and King Guelder's hearts,' he growled bitterly as he lashed out with his boning knife at a stinking corpse flower, sending a cloud of biting black flies into his face.

As the tropical night settled about them, clambering through a tumbled wall they entered a long-neglected rose garden, now a sinister tangle of stems blackened with blight, unnaturally long thorns tearing at their clothes as they struggled on. Ahead they saw a glow. Their footsteps crunching on the dry stony path snaking through slime covered rocks that had once been an alpine garden, the glow grew ever brighter. The stench of burning rubber that had been with them since they reached the gargoyle dam now hung heavy in the night air. Distant animal cries were making Grilla and his young companions ever more agitated.

As the cries became more insistent, Grilla, anguished now, pulled at Suki's sleeve. She shrugged him off, but wondering what he'd sensed, they slowed their pace. The four apes stopped, listened for a few moments, then slipped away and disappeared into the thick undergrowth. Mystified, the others pressed on towards the red glow.

Rounding a huge boulder, they saw ahead a low circular wall: from it rose a baleful red light. Creeping to the edge, they peered down. Far below, at the bottom of a deep pit, a molten fire bubbled and sparked. On shadowy ledges around the wall, dark forms glowed and pulsed.

Cringing back, Kenji hissed: 'Phraggs!'

Creeping away as swiftly as they could, from ahead the animal cries that had so agitated the gorillas were growing ever louder. Then came a sudden cry of agony.

'The Gaiakins fiends are torturing someone!' cried Suki.

Terrified for Sandy and Fin, casting caution aside, they sped on.

# 7
# BLOOD SACRIFICE

The barred door crashed shut and the harsh growls of their captors died away. Sandy lay shivering on the grimy stone floor, drifting in and out of feverish delirium. The deep cut in his neck was bleeding heavily. Kneeling by him, Fin thought he must be dying. Pressing his hand over the wound, blood welled up between his fingers. How he wished he hadn't lost his rucksack in the treasure cave – he could have torn up his spare vest for bandaging. He'd tried to tear a piece from his shirt sleeve, but the linen fabric was too tough.

He looked about, desperately searching for anything that might serve as a binding. The crumbling, seashell covered walls were covered in thick, sticky cobwebs. From outside came high pitched yowls mingled with cruel raucous laughter. Through the cell bars he saw a paved arena encircled by stone terraces rising up to jungle covered cliffs. In the arena's centre stood a gigantic statue: a snarling wolf-like animal; at its base stood a stone altar, stained dark with what he guessed was blood. Beside the altar a stone basin full of blood had overflowed and was oozing across the pavement onto a fire blackened area scattered with burnt bones. The statue and the altar reminded Fin of a picture in one of Mossy's books, depicting human sacrificial rites of the ancient Mayan people.

At the arena's edge, a large cage hung from a baobab tree. Imprisoned in it were several doglike creatures. Shaggy ginger and black fur covered their thick necks and shoulders, their bodies tapering to narrow hind quarters, ending in short bushy tails. They were being tormented by a group of Gaiakins poking sharp sticks through the bars, teasing the animals into hysterical fury. To Fin, these sadistic Gaiakins were even more horrible than those who'd captured him and Sandy. Over their greasy leather garments, they wore fur aprons, seemingly made of the same skins as the animals they were persecuting. At their backs swung black bushy tails, funny if the sight had not been so dreadful.

Sandy groaned. Turning back to press his hand once more on the wound, Fin started in surprise: a tall figure had appeared from the dark recesses of the prison. Seeing his inky blue robe and ebony skin, Fin gave a cry: for a crazy moment he thought Mossy had come to rescue them. But as the man moved into the light the illusion faded: he was a man in the prime of life, his tightly curled deep brown hair lightly peppered silver and not grey like Mossy's, and his ebony face bore few lines.

'Leave! I fix,' the man muttered, pushing Fin aside.

Delving into his robe, he brought out a pad of grey moss, and pressed it firmly onto the wound. Signing to Fin to take over, he prowled round the cell gathering cobwebs from the walls. Then pulling Fin's hand away, he skilfully wound the strong sticky threads around Sandy's shoulder, binding the moss firmly in place.

Fin looked at the man uneasily. 'Who—who are you?'

The man's eyes widened in surprise. 'You speak the Common Tongue! I know of no Bantos that do so.'

Fin smiled bleakly. 'I'm not a Banto – but like them, I am of Delphin race. Well, half Delphin – my father was a Delphin, but my mother's a Rom. And you? You remind me of a dear friend! Of what tribe are you?'

'I'm of the Dogons – my name is Malang.'

Fin shook the outstretched hand. 'My name's Fin – Fin Dandrum. I've never heard of your tribe. The Dogons, did you say?'

The man nodded. 'My homeland is to the north – several days trek from this evil place.' He gesticulated through the prison bars.

'How did you come to be there? Why are you locked up in this prison?'

'The evil creatures who captured you, also captured me. I was hunting for a rare fungus, prized for its healing of the deadly Ebola disease, and known to grow on the rotting trees in this now putrid land – where once the mighty Gaiakins had their garden. Collecting a thick patch from a dying cedar, I became careless—'

He stopped to frown at Fin. 'But you said I reminded you of a dear friend?'

'Yes, he lives in my homeland, but he is not of Delphin kind. We call him Mossy because his grey hair resembles moss growing on our forest trees. He's very special to us – his real name is Zagzagel.'

Drawing a sharp breath, Malang peered into Fin's face. 'Surely you are mistaken! The holy Zagzagel is too mighty to consort with an insignificant race such as yours!'

Indignant, Fin glowered at him. 'We Delphins are a proud and ancient race! And I'm not mistaken – Zagzagel has lived among us for as long as we can remember. Anyway, I know how special Mossy, er Zagzagel, is – I'm apprenticed to him!'

Malang bowed his head. 'Forgive me! I should not have spoken so, but you and your friend's presence is a wonder to me! Why are you here?'

Hesitantly, Fin pulled out his sketch of Mab. 'It's a long tale… We're chasing after this – this woman with a butterfly's body.'

He passed the sketch to Malang. 'She's – she's a demon. She stole a precious, very holy jewel from me, and – and I must get it back. It's the only way to save my friend!'

He pointed at the Chi Rho on Mab's breast.

Leaning towards the light from outside Malang peered at the sketch. 'A woman who is half butterfly! I have never heard of, or seen, such a strange woman!'

Handing back the sketch, he frowned at Sandy lying slumped on the ground. 'Your friend is badly wounded, but he is strong – the fever will break presently, he has no need of such a jewel!'

'It's not Sandy here, I'm talking about—'

Sandy groaned as another feverish shudder wracked his body, loosening Malang's binding.

Applying more cobweb, Malang sat back on his heels. 'Your companion is not Delphin – tall, with pale skin and red hair, he looks to be from a northern race.'

'He's of a royal line. On his father's side, he's descended from King Flaithri of the Cyning Clan, and is part Gaiakin from his mother's side. We call him Sandy, but his real name is Iskander. He too, is a close friend of Zagzagel.'

Just then Sandy's eyelids flickered and opened. 'Fin?' he croaked, trying to focus on Fin's face.

With Malang's help, Fin eased him to a sitting position. Pressing his water bottle to Sandy's mouth, Malang commanded him to drink.

After several long gulps, Sandy pushed away the bottle, and looked blearily at Malang.

'This is Malang. He's a prisoner like us!' Fin explained. 'He's saved you from bleeding to death. He's bandaged your cut with moss and cobwebs. One of those Gaiakin monstrosities threw a spinning disc at you.' He gestured through the prison bars. 'There's more of them out there – taunting some creatures in a cage.'

Sandy smiled gratefully at Malang. Wincing, he felt his shoulder. 'Is the wound deep? The blade flew at me from nowhere.'

'Yes, it is deep, but clean,' Malang said, adjusting the moss, 'you have lost a good deal of blood, so drink as much water as you can!'

Studying Malang, Sandy frowned. 'You remind me of someone—'

Fin grinned. 'You're thinking of Mossy! He wears the same dark blue clothes!'

Malang gave a deep chuckle. 'I am of the Dogons. I was surprised to learn that Zagzagel lives in your land! To us he is an angel, and we have longed for his return.'

An extra loud howl of pain from one of the caged animals made them shiver.

Sandy looked out anxiously. 'Where are the others?'

'They're not with us. Only you and I were captured. We were attacked by three horrible Gaiakins.' He shuddered. 'You were unconscious and didn't see the huge sea worm. It came out of the dark pool and slithered into the cave. Gressil was inside it! Picking one of the evil Gaiakins, and – and driving out the Phragg lurking inside, he entered the body himself. The Gaiakin was transformed – becoming beautiful and evil at the same time. He climbed the mound and carried down Mab in his arms. Then – then, he commanded the other two Gaiakins to take you and me with them – what happened to the others, I don't know.'

He turned to Malang. 'We were in M'Bopo's treasure cave. That was where the Batfrits had taken the butterfly woman – Queen Mab, she's called. They'd hung her above a great pile of treasure. Why are the Gaiakins here so horrible?'

'They are the ones who did not flee when their jungle home became diseased, and the trees and plants blighted. They are possessed by demons – you call them Phraggs. Even before the demons came, these Gaiakins were prone to evil. My people have long been plagued by them! They are known as Aardwolves – or Aards. They worship Agwang, the demon hyena god. Now that they are possessed, they are changing into hyenas too! The blood-stained altar beneath the statue of Agwang is where they perform their blood sacrifices.'

Tears glittered in Malang's dark eyes. 'Many of my people have met their deaths on that altar and I am to be next. The poor creatures in the cage are also to be sacrificed, even though they are natural Aardwolves!'

Falling silent, he stared long and hard at Fin. 'You said you are a servant of Zagzagel. We Dogons have a prophesy: that one day a servant of Zagzagel will come and aid us to overcome these monsters!'

Dismayed, Fin wondered how on earth could he and the others help the Dogons. It must be a terrible mistake – Mossy had never mentioned Dogons or their prophesy! He gazed miserably through the bars. The strange howling from the cage didn't sound like wolves, more like hysterical laughter.

It was turning dark, and on the blackened ground before the blood-filled basin a group of the Gaiakins, Malang called Aards, were piling wood for a fire. Others were busy at the altar, laying out goblets and platters. One, more ornately robed in the scarlet and gold of bird-of-paradise plumage, produced a ceremonial knife with a long blade and jewelled handle, which he reverently honed on a whetstone before placing it on the altar. From the way the other Aards cringingly obeyed him, Fin guessed he must be a High Priest.

As a full moon rose above the trees, the fire was lit. Flames and moonlight illuminating the nightmarish scene, Fin, Sandy and Malang watched in revulsion as a hyena was dragged from the cage, writhing and snarling, and tied down on the altar with its head above the blood-filled basin.

A rhythmic guttural chant rose from the assembled Aards, all gazing expectantly to the top of the steps leading down into the arena. After a few moments Gressil appeared, proudly holding the Chi Rho before him. Mab was leaning on his arm, her butterfly wings fluttering feebly. Pausing for dramatic effect, Gressil slowly lifted the cross above his head, its jewels sparkling in the firelight, an aura of unearthly blue-green light shimmering around his long silvery robe. The watching Aards gave a great growl of awed wonder.

Slowly Gressil and Mab descended the steps. At the altar, they halted. Seeing the hyena tied to the stone, Mab let out a shriek that silenced the Aards' chant.

'Where is the boy who tore my wing? Gressil, my love, I must be avenged – the boy's blood shall be spilt into the basin to give more power to the cross. Then I shall be healed, my beautiful dark spirit shall live for eternity by your side. Hurry, hurry my Lord, before I die! Bring the boy to the altar!'

Gressil glared at the trembling Aards. His voice, at once melodious but cruel, echoed around the arena: 'Fetch the boy! Now!'

Cackling hysterically, two Aards more animal than Gaiakin scrambled over each other in their rush to the prison. Other Aards untied the hyena, intending to throw the animal on the fire, but it struggled free, and disappeared yowling into the dark.

As the Aards entered the cell Malang launched himself at them, lashing out with fists and feet, but the snarling Aards were too much and he fell back, blood flowing from many bites and deep scratches to his arms and legs.

The two Aards fell upon Fin. Their rough rope bindings cutting into his wrists and ankles, they dragged him from the cell. Flung on his back on the altar, head hanging awkwardly over the stone basin, the stink of blood from the overflowing bowl inches below made him feel sick. Desperately he tried not to vomit. From close to his ear came the ominous sound of metal scraping on stone. Craning his neck, he saw the High Priest, again honing his jewel-encrusted ritual knife. Around the arena, the Aards had resumed their chanting, the monotonous growling din louder and louder, making his head swim.

Powerless in the prison cell, Malang helped Sandy crawl to the bars. Searching the dark sky, Malang groaned: 'Holy Zagzagel, where are you!' Collapsing beside Sandy, he took out a moss pad to staunch his bleeding bite wounds.

At the altar, Gressil gently laid Mab on the ground by the basin of blood. Proud and triumphant, he raised the Chi Rho high and in a mysterious tongue began calling on devilish spirits. The High Priest's deep menacing tones joined the chant as he laid the jewelled ritual knife across Fin's throat.

Gressil swung the Chi Rho over the basin, ready to catch the gush of fresh blood.

'Cut deep! Cut deep!' screeched Mab to the High Priest.

Even as he raised knife for the death cut, from out of the jungle night came a shriek of fury. 'SKEEW! SKEEW!'

Powerful eagle wings smashed the knife from the High Priest's grasp sending it skittering across the blood-drenched pavement.

'It's O.K. Fin! It's O.K.! The others are coming!' Bird called.

Quilla's outstretched talons ripped the cross from Gressil's grasp and with a deft flick of his beak, looped the heavy gold chain over his neck. Jewels flashing, he soared away. Howling with rage, Gressil leapt up after him, only to crash back to the ground. Screaming curses, Mab staggered to her feet and snatching up the knife, desperate fury giving her strength, tattered wings flapping, she lumbered into the air, up towards the eagle's dark form silhouetted against the golden moon.

'SKEEW! SKEEW!'

On the altar, fighting with his bonds, Fin could hear Bird's frantic instructions as Quilla plunged to meet Mab: 'Left! Right! Left again!'

Dodging Mab's flailing knife, the great bird tore at her wings with his talons. In her weakened state it was over in moments, and she plummeted to the ground. Gressil rushed to her. Wrenching the knife from her grip, his beautiful Gaiakin face distorted in rage, he turned on the High Priest. With a single slash, he severed the Aard's head from its body. Raising the knife to slice into Fin's throat: Thwack! Thwack! Two crossbow arrows pierced his arm. Squealing in agony, the knife clattered to the altar.

With a triumphant: 'SKEEW! SKEEW!' Quilla sped away into the dark trees of the jungle.

Enraged by the slaughter of their High Priest, the Aard pack fell on Gressil. The scene lit by the blazing bonfire, Sandy and Malang watched sickened as the Gaiakin body was savagely torn to pieces, strings of intestines pulled and stretched in a hideous tug of war, chunks of flesh, silky hair attached to scalp flung in the air. The melon sized Gaiakin heart – still pumping – rolled out of the melee and was pounced on by a quick-witted Aard.

As an arm, still in the silver robe's sleeve, rolled across the arena to come to rest against the prison bars, Sandy became aware of a low urgent call from the darkness outside. Kenji and Suki slid out of the shadows, crossbows still in their hands.

'Boss! Boss! We're here!' whispered Kenji, tugging vainly at the locked door.

Mick at his heel, Lark appeared, boning knife in hand.

'Out the way, Kenji!' he muttered, inserting the tip of his blade in the lock. After a few moments of gentle twisting, pushing, and pulling, the lock mechanism clicked. The door swung open and as they were about to enter Malang appeared. Supporting Sandy under the arms, he helped him from the prison and settled him on the ground. There was no time for introductions or explanations: whooping howls from the arena warned them they'd been spotted.

'Hurry! We must save Fin on the altar!' Malang cried to Kenji. 'Have you a spare weapon?'

Kenji immediately handed him Sandy's sword, then quickly drawing his own sword, he and Malang faced the slavering jaws of the oncoming Aards. Boning knife in hand, Lark took his place by their side, Mick at his feet growling. At the same time Suki re-armed her crossbow and crouched protectively in front of Sandy lying half-conscious on the ground.

The Aards upon them, they slashed and stabbed, severing arms, slicing into thick necks. From in front of Sandy's slumped form, Suki shot arrow after arrow, each time bringing down an Aard. But there were too many: for every Aard that fell from out of the jungle more appeared. Towering above Lark, one of the monsters, baring its yellow fangs, made ready to tear out Lark's throat.

With a cry of: 'TISSY!' he drove his knife deep into the monster's heart. But as the dying monster crumpled to the ground, the night was sundered by a screeching, so ear-piercing Lark thought his head would burst. Over the trees streamed wave after wave of Batfrits, flickering shapes darkening the moonlight. Their high-pitched shrieks reverberating around the arena, the dog-like Aard's sank to their knees in agony, their paw-like hands pressed over their ears. With a howl, Mick scrambled into Lark's jerkin.

At the prison door the embattled group were forgotten as the Batfrits swooped on the Aards, razor-sharp claws stabbing out eyes, raking deep grooves in muscled backs, tearing out tufts of rusty-grey hair.

'I'M GOING TO FREE FIN!' Lark yelled to Kenji. 'Give me covering fire!'

Kenji nodded and loaded his crossbow.

Setting off at a crouching run, Lark was surprised to find the dark stranger beside him: not sure if the man knew Common Language, he gave him a thumbs-up. Keeping to the shadows clear of the fighting, they sped around the arena towards the altar where Fin still struggled to escape his bonds.

Almost at the altar, Lark spotted Grilla and Crow creeping down the arena steps. Dashing forward, Crow scrambled on to the altar and pulling a chakram from his belt, cut through Fin's bindings.

'Quick, Monkey, help him down, or we'll be deaded!' Lark heard him squeal.

Lark and Malang ran up. 'Good work, young Crow!' Lark cried. 'You O.K. Fin?' he asked anxiously.

Fin groaned. 'Think so – my head's spinning, and I don't think my legs work!'

'Come! We must return to your friends!' Malang said urgently.

Grilla, scooping up Fin into his arms, headed back to the prison. As they ran a couple of Batfrits dived at them. Kenji's and Suki's arrows sang and the Batfrits crashed to the ground in a shower of sparks and flashes of flame.

'Phew that was close!' gasped Lark helping Fin sink down beside Sandy.

Fin grinned weakly. 'Nearly lost my head again!'

Leaving Suki and Grilla guarding Sandy and Fin, the others stepped forward, bracing themselves for the outcome of the battle between Aards and Batfrits: whoever won, they would have to face the victor's onslaught.

Malang turned to them. 'Do not let yourselves be taken alive. Batfrit or Aard, better death than to fall into the hands of either.'

Lark counted his remaining chakrams and handed three to Crow. 'If this is the end, we'll take down at least one each of those Bats or Aards!'

He saw tears rolling down the little Scav's scarred face.

'Th – Thank you for being my friend,' Crow mumbled.

'Come on, little bum boil, it's not over yet, we've seen worse!' Lark forced a grin and squeezed Crow's scrawny shoulder. Then, patting his jerkin front, he growled: 'Keep hidden, Mick. This fight's not for small dogs.'

Crouched on the ground beside Sandy, Fin saw Grilla had left them, his shadowy bulk gliding up the arena steps towards the jungle and wondered vaguely what the ape was up to. Feeling wet on his hand pressed on the moss and cobweb bandage covering Sandy's wound, he saw by the flickering light from the dying bonfire, blood seeping through his fingers. He called to urgently to Malang, his voice almost drowned by the howling: 'Have you more moss pads?'

Diving his hand into his robe, Malang threw him another pad.

Pressing it on the wound, Sandy stirred and plucked at Fin's arm. 'Fin, the cross – Quilla – Bird – must go to Jerusalem…'

Nodding dumbly and looking up through streaming tears, Fin saw Quilla perched on the topmost branch of a great kapok tree, his dark form outlined against the moon. 'Don't go just yet, Bird,' he whispered.

Again, and again the Batfrits swooped, razor claws slicing and slashing at the deafened and bewildered Aards. On a branch in the baobab tree above the cage of captive hyenas, M'Bopo roared instructions. Sensing victory, in his enthusiasm he jumped up and down once too often: his perch snapped. Falling through the branches, he landed on top of the cage of hyenas. The door flew open. Thirsty for revenge, howling and snarling, the freed hyenas fell on the Aards. Gibbering with excitement, leathery wings clattering, gleefully M'Bopo joined in, burying his snout into the thick neck of a wounded Aard.

His triumph was short lived. From out of the jungle a hail of lead slingshot tore through the Batfrits. Shredding fur and chicken wings, the mechanical creatures plunged to the ground, several landing on the bonfire's dying embers, bringing it back to life, spitting Frit shards in all directions. With a terrifying war cry, down the arena steps leapt six tall figures, fearsome snarling masks over their faces, semi-naked dark-skinned bodies covered in white war paint. Swiftly winding their slings about their waists and drawing their swords from the scabbards at their backs, they fell on the Aards.

'MY BOYS HAVE COME! MY DOGON WARRIORS HAVE COME!' cried Malang, striding to take his place with them. Scything and slashing, Iskander's sword in his hand sang as he chopped off heads and limbs. Close behind him came Lark and Crow, their chakras flying, biting into bat wings and Aard legs. At the same time, Kenji and Sukie, protecting Sandy and Fin, with their last remaining arrows picked off any Batfrit or Aard that came close.

The onslaught of the combined forces quickly began to tell and in moments the fight was over. Any Aards still standing stumbled into the jungle, whilst the few remaining Batfrits screeched away over the trees. As M'Bopo flapped after them, raging and cursing, from the top of the arena steps a Dogon warrior brought him down with a slingshot between the eyes. The King of the Batfrits tumbled slowly to the ground, twitched, and lay still.

As dawn came, they wandered the battlefield. Pausing by the altar Fin looked in disgust at Queen Mab, a dense cloud of flies around the seeping wound in her side, her hand stretched imploringly towards the sightlessly staring head – all that remained of the Gaiakin body that had housed Gressil.

Malang joined Fin and gazing at the strange creature, half butterfly, half beautiful young woman, pointed to the burnt scar in her furred breast. 'Was that mark left by the fabulous cross?'

Fin nodded: 'Yes, all those who wear the Chi Rho bear that wound – Crow has the mark, and so did my father. Now the eagle wears the cross, he too will have the mark.'

Watching Fin search the dawn sky for Quilla, Malang noticed his eyes: one nut brown, the other cold sea green. Seeing the anguish in them, his heart went out to him.

He laid a hand on Fin's shoulder 'Come, there's nothing to be done here. I see Iskander is watching us – he must be anxious for the return of his sword!'

Making their way back to Sandy, a laugh from Kenji drew their attention to where he and Suki had joined Malang's young warriors, searching among the scattered bodies to see if any were still alive. The warriors had removed their fearsome snarling war masks, revealing young faces painted with white whirls and stripes.

Kenji and Suki were talking to one of them, a tall, long-limbed young man, his lithe body not only decorated with white paint but also blue and yellow. Kenji had allowed him to hold his sword, and the young warrior was testing its feel by thrusts and feints.

Malang smiled fondly. 'Your Kenji is talking to my eldest son, Akpan. Now I am old, he is leader of the warriors. Over there are his brothers, Ayo and Albaba.' He indicated two youths arguing over a piece of jewellery taken from the pile his warriors had stripped from M'Bopo's body and shook his head resignedly. 'Akpan's brothers are already a trial to him! He has much to learn about how to discipline his troops. But come, we will leave my sons to fight over a necklace!'

They headed to where Lark and Crow were resting against a tree trunk talking to Sandy who had recovered a little.

Lark grinned. 'Fin, did you see Crow with his chuckers – getting to be a proper fighter!'

Looking smug, Crow fished out his last chakram to demonstrate his new found skill by skimming it towards the baobab tree, embedding it in the trunk.

Sandy smiled up at Fin. 'Nearly being executed is getting to be a habit with you, lad. Yet again Quilla and Bird had to come to your rescue!'

Fin grimaced, and avoiding Malang's questioning look, rummaged in his rucksack for a fresh sketch pad and charcoal sticks. He knew he should explain to Malang about Bird and Quilla, but at present couldn't face it. Settling down on a boulder, he began a sketch of the arena, the altar and the statue of Agwang, the Aards' god.

As he drew, Grilla, reappeared out of the undergrowth. Malang backed away in alarm.

'Well, young Grilla, have you been looking for your chums?' Lark called.

'Monkey needs us rescue his family,' Crow announced. All eyes turned to him in surprise. 'Yep! Monkey told me – they been takin' care of bible bag and Sparkie for me, whilst I went fightin'.'

Crow gestured vaguely towards the jungle, from where mournful gorilla hoots could be heard.

Grunting anxiously, Grilla tugged at Lark's arm. With a fizz of fear, Lark remembered the animal cages in the ruined gardens. 'Come on, Grilla! Show me!'

Mick at his heel, he and Crow followed Grilla as he plunged back into the undergrowth.

After a few hundred yards, they emerged into what was once a herb garden, now overgrown, the herbs choked by brambles. In the middle of the garden stood a cage. Inside cowered two mother gorillas, one with a trembling youngster clinging to her neck and the other hugging a small baby. Outside the cage sat the three gorillas Grilla had befriended in the ruined garden. One clutched the bible bag, from where there came a fearful squeaking. Another held Grilla's squashed and battered football. At the sight of Lark and Crow, they broke into frenzied chattering.

Lark studied the cage door lock. 'Another job for my boning knife!' he muttered. Just as at the prison cell, he inserted his knife blade into the lock and gently probed and twisted until, with a satisfying clunk, the door swung open. Encouraged by soothing noises from Grilla and his friends, the females with their little ones trooped out and clustered round them.

Come on, we must get back to the others,' Lark urged, fearing that some stray Aards or Batfrits might be lurking in the dense bush.

Feeling self-conscious Lark led Grilla and his newfound troop back into the arena. Crow, reunited with Sparkie, sitting proudly on his shoulder preening its whiskers, brought up the rear. At the sight of the strange party, the Dogons murmured uneasily.

'It's a family!' gasped Fin.

With elaborate gestures, Grilla pointed to each of the apes, then to himself, and finally towards the jungle. Grunting tenderly, he stepped forward to hug everyone in turn, finally folding Lark into a long embrace. Abruptly, with a snuffle that sounded very like weeping, he turned away. The family falling into line behind him, they loped into the jungle and were lost from view.

Lark, watching them disappear, muffled a sob. 'I got to love that big gentle gorilla!'

Fin sighed. 'It's for the best, Lark. He's found a family and couldn't have come where we have to go.' He went to sit by Sandy. 'We must make plans Sandy. Now Quilla has the cross, everything's changed.'

He looked anxiously towards the trees. 'I wonder where he is—'

As if having heard, Quilla appeared above the treetops. Lazily swooping down, he perched on a nearby fallen tree trunk.

Exclaiming excitedly, the Dogon warriors crept close to stare at the Chi Rho glittering on Quilla's russet gold chest.

At the sight of the Chi Rho so close, the familiar longing gripped Fin: to wear it once more, to feel its weight, to touch the smooth clear crystal where the splinter lay. He couldn't stop himself. Pushing through the group, he lunged at Quilla. Angrily shrieking Quilla leapt into the air with a flurry of wings.

Desperately reaching up, Fin heard Bird's cry from inside Quilla's eye: 'No! No! Fin, the cross is mine and Quilla's now!'

Ignoring her plea, Fin leapt up again, only to fall face down, sobbing with frustration. Quilla retreated to the top of the baobab tree.

Sandy called urgently to Lark. 'Help Fin, Lark! He must understand: the cross has gone beyond his care! It is the eagle who is the bearer now!'

Murmuring gently Lark helped Fin up. Stooped in dejection, Fin slumped down beside Sandy, who leaned over and put his arm around him.

Hearing Dogons murmuring of Bad Magic, Sandy beckoned Malang to his side. Yet again he explained about Bird's soul being trapped inside the eagle's eye, and how the Chi Rho would save her.

'The cross will reunite her soul to her body. But to do that we must go to Jerusalem where the Pool of Siloam will heal her – it is Zagzagel who has told us this!'

Malang gazed long and thoughtfully at the great eagle crouched in the baobab tree. 'It is a strange tale you tell, Iskander. But I understand now about our prophesy: it has happened as foretold! My people have been saved by the servants of Zagzagel! But Jerusalem is far from here!' He pointed to the rising sun. 'You will have to cross the Great Desert, and in your weak state that will be impossible! So, first you must come to my land of Dogon to gain your strength. My warriors will carry you there and you and your companions shall celebrate the victory with us!'

Then falling to his knees, with great reverence he handed Sandy his sword: 'Lord Iskander, I return your sword – greatly honoured I was to have used such an ancient and precious weapon, which even the Gaiakins of olden times would have been proud to own!'

A sparkle flickered in Sandy's midnight eyes. He gave a lopsided smile. 'You are right about the Gaiakins! This sword was forged by two Gaiakin brothers in their new garden of Florain!'

Malang's warriors hearing this, hissing through their teeth, stared at Sandy in awe.

'So, Fin told the truth – you are part Gaiakin!' gasped Malang.

Sandy bowed his head in acknowledgement.

Lark, unable to contain himself, exclaimed: 'The two Gaiakin brothers who made Sandy's sword, also made the Chi Rho – in this very garden! Mullein and Fescue are their names!' His face puckered in sadness. 'But Fescue died, saving us in Contagion!'

Once more Malang looked amazed. 'Even now there are yet more wonders to learn about you all! As we journey to my land, you shall tell me about the new garden of Florain, and the death of Fescue the Gaiakin!'

Kenji cleared his throat noisily. 'Er, Boss, talking of going to Dogon…'

Everyone turned to find Kenji and Suki standing holding hands, grinning self-consciously. Kenji ploughed on. 'I, er that is, we – I mean Suki and me, we want to be together with the Sanyo family at Barraconda Motherhome. I've a mind to be a Geek like my ancestors…' His voice trailed off.

Sandy smiled ruefully and raised an eyebrow. 'Yes Kenji, I have been thinking about this! I agree. You and Suki should return to the Barraconda Motherhome, to send a radio message to Zagzagel. He must know of these developments as soon as possible – so that Wings, Dancer and Thetis can set off on their flight with Bird's body!

Kenji nodded, 'You can count on us, Boss!' He rummaged in a pocket. 'Er, whilst I remember. I found this in the gardens when we were tracking you.' He held out the yellow enamel flower pendant.

Sandy took it from him, and carefully hung it about his neck.

Then, slowly, as a grin spread across his face, he held out his hands. Kenji and Suki stepped forward and grasped them. 'Kenji, I discharge you from my service and I wish peace and happiness to you both! And your grandmother will be pleased you have not married a Round-eye!'

As the laughter died away, Fin spoke. 'It has been an honour to be with you, Kenji – and you Suki. Without you we could never have got this far. May Phul's blessings go with you.'

Lark grasped Kenji's hand. 'That goes for me too. It's been an honour to fight alongside you. And I sure will miss your cooking.'

Suki, cheeks wet with tears, giving Fin a fierce hug, whispered in his ear. 'One day, I hope to meet your Bird.'

Then turning to Lark, she ruffled his thatch of pale green hair. 'Dear Lark, I will always remember you – the bravest Delphin I have known.'

Silently gathering up their weapons, the couple turned away and with a last wave set off down the trail for Barraconda.

Breaking the silence, Lark, his voice thick with emotion, exclaimed, 'Well then, let's stop hanging about and get away from this hellhole!'

Malang's son Akpan issued brief orders to his brothers and the other warriors. They ran to the jungle edge, returning with branches and palm fronds, which Ayo and Albaba quickly wove into a simple but strong stretcher. Laying it on the ground for Sandy to sink onto, with two of their comrades they lifted it to their shoulders. With Malang at its head the little procession trooped out of the arena.

Above them, Quilla glided on the morning air, and in the distance behind them could be heard the thump, thump of a great silverback gorilla beating his chest.

In the deserted arena, Queen Mab stirred and moaned. For a little while, her sobs were the only sound. Suddenly, she sat up with a gasp of joy: from Gressil's severed Gaiakin head rose a dark cloud. Seeping along the ground to the lifeless body of M'Bopo, forming a swirling vortex, the cloud spiralled down into the gaping bat mouth. The corpse twitched and convulsed, sparks crackled about the metal joints, the chicken leather wings began to flap, weakly at first, then more strongly.

Watching in anticipation, Mab drew strength from her Lord. Flexing her velvet limbs, her tattered wings fluttered. With strengthening beats, she rose a few feet from the ground.

Ponderously at first, Batfrit and Butterfly flew low round the arena. Then, at first just skimming the treetops, they climbed higher and higher, until with a scream of triumph from Mab, they set off in pursuit of the great eagle.

# 8
# DOGON CITY

The march to the city of Dogon took four days. Descending from the Futa Jallon plateau by a steep, overgrown path was particularly difficult, especially for Malang's sons and the other stretcher bearers carrying Sandy, who often had to get off and walk with their support. After two days of struggle through thick jungle, they reached a grassland plain where herds of zebra, antelope and water buffalo grazed, reminding them of the plain Suki had shown them on their journey to the Banto village.

Following the course of a wide river, they headed north-eastwards, the path wide enough for Fin, Lark and Malang to walk beside Sandy on his stretcher. Crow, with Sparkie on his lap, and Mick, were given permission to sit at Sandy's feet, and enjoy a comfortable ride.

Warned by Malang of the danger of Quilla being shot by hunters skilled with bow and arrow, Fin had persuaded Bird not to let the eagle fly high searching for prey. So after quick forays in the long grass for small game, he perched on the stretcher too, and Fin was able to talk softly to Bird.

As they marched, at Malang's insistence, Sandy told the Dogons about the northern world of Britannia, of how the Gaiakins settled there and made their garden of Florain. He also told them the story of Gressil, with his Queen Mab, bringing horror to Contagion. To Fin's discomfiture and Lark's glee, Sandy described the part they had played in the drowning of Gressil's Compound, gaining the two diminutive Delphins greater respect from the young Dogons.

When Malang, still puzzled by Sandy's parting instructions to Kenji and Suki, asked how they could get a message to Zagzagel on their return to Barraconda, Sandy explained about the worldwide network of Motherhomes and how their Geeks guardians communicated by radio. The Dogons, never having heard of Motherhomes and mystified by the idea of radio, were astonished to learn there was one hidden so close to their homeland of Mali.

Akpan exclaimed: 'Several times my brothers and I have passed Barraconda on our way to Banjul, to buy lead shot for our slings from the ships trading in metals – we never knew such a hideout was there!'

'Do the small people at Banto know of this strange place?' Ayo asked indignantly.

Lark, frowning in thought, answered warily: 'As the Bantos know Suki, I reckon they must do. Even so, the Motherhome is so well hidden, nobody would ever find it without being taken there. It's a snug place, deep under water, and has a radio mast poking out into the sky that sends invisible messages through the air! But I won't tell you how to find it – that's best kept very secret. So, don't go nosing around there, or you'll have to answer to Suki and her shocker gun!'

The brothers scowled but made no reply.

They came to Dogon just after dusk. Earlier, a couple of the warriors had sprinted ahead to announce the return of Malang with his rescuers.

Waving flaming torches, cow horns blowing and drums beating, the people came out to greet them, men, women and children joyfully shouting: 'MALANG IS ALIVE! MALANG IS HOME! ALL PRAISE BE TO HIS SAVIOURS!'

Hoisted between Ayo and Albaba on their strong shoulders Malang was carried into the city. As they were swept through the narrow streets dazed by the clamour and in danger of being crushed by the chanting throng, Fin, Lark with Mick clutched to his chest, and Crow tightly gripping his bible bag, clung onto Sandy's stretcher, whilst Quilla flew to the safety of the shadowy rooftops. The buildings of dried mud seemed to crowd in on them, the light from the swaying torches illuminating grotesquely carved creatures looming threateningly from beneath the pointed thatched roofs.

The procession surged into a wide square where an ox carcass was being turned on a spit over a roaring fire. The crowd hustled them to a circle of benches surrounding the fire and Sandy was helped from his stretcher with great ceremony. Then when they were all seated, Ayo and Albaba setting Malang down from their shoulders onto a hastily built dais of wooden crates, silence fell. Light from the flames flickered over the eager faces gazing expectantly up at him. Sweeping the sleeves of his blue robe aside, Malang raised his arms above his head.

'GREETINGS MY PEOPLE!' he cried.

Whistling and hooting, the crowd shouted: 'GREETINGS HOGON, OUR HOLY HEALER!'

Malang bowed and raised his arms again for silence. 'People of Dogon, I bring you astonishing news! It has happened as was foretold! The Aards of the evil garden of Florain have been destroyed. We have been saved by the servants of Zagzagel! By Lord Iskander here, and his small companions!'

He waved his arm to indicate Sandy, Fin, Lark and Crow who sat looking self-conscious.

The crowd roared its approval. 'PRAISE BE TO THE SEVANTS OF ZAGZAGEL!'

Akpan and his band of warriors now leapt onto benches. 'BY OUR SLINGS WE HAVE SLAIN THE BATFRITS. REJOICE PEOPLE, REJOICE. THE BATFRITS ARE NO MORE!' they chorused.

The crowd, whistling and hooting, shouted: 'PRAISE BE TO AKPAN AND HIS WARRIORS!'

A chant started: LET THE FEASTING BEGIN! LET THE FEASTING BEGIN!

The crowd parted to make way for men carrying trestle tables, followed by children carrying stacks of wooden platters and baskets of drinking gourds. Tables set up, platters laid out, a procession of women and girls entered with steaming tureens filled with savoury smelling vegetable stew. The tureens set at intervals along the tables, the cooks began carving the ox. The most tender and succulent slices were added to platters piled high with vegetable stew and then served reverently to the honoured guests.

That done, with much friendly jostling the crowd helped themselves to food.

Then a new chant arose: 'WHERE'S THE PALM WINE? BRING IN THE PALM WINE!'

A line of men entered the square bent under the weight of giant calabashes filled with palm wine, and enthusiastically passed around, feasting began.

A long time later, the last vestiges of gravy wiped from platters, tables cleared and spirited away, there came from a corner of the square tentative notes on pipes, the sound of softly thumping bongo drums and the gentle rattle of shaking calabashes: a group of musicians were tuning their instruments. Gradually the square filled with a pulsating rhythm, growing louder and louder, rising above the chatter and laughter. Palm wine coursing through veins, the dancing began: young and old gyrated around the square, stamping their feet to the thump, thump of the insistent music. Bead and bangle-bedecked bodies gleaming in the firelight, the hooting and whooping grew ever more frenetic.

As the stamping procession encircled their bemused guests, a girl scantily clothed in feathers, grabbed Fin by the hand and dragged him from the bench. Confused from the palm wine and tired from the journey, he was unable to resist. Guessing they too might be drawn in, Lark and Crow, still clutching his bible bag, ducked down beneath their bench, where Mick was happily engrossed in a meaty ox bone.

From Quilla's perch on a nearby thatched roof, Bird watched the scene in the square below. By the light of the bonfire, she could see just below her the carved wooden creatures jutting out from the roof: a snapping crocodile, a rearing jackass clawing the empty air, and a coiling snake leaping mid-strike. Above her the stars had come out, countless pinpricks of light in the velvet sky. Beyond the city roofs she made out the shadowy forms of trees outlined against silvery sand dunes.

Tired after the journey, she had been startled from sleep by the thumping music. For the third time since Quilla had seized the cross from Gressil she'd had the horrid nightmare again: a man pinned by his hands and feet to a wooden cross, his face covered in blood flowing from wounds made by a coronet of tangled thorns about his brow.

'Quilla, are you awake?' she called. 'I've had that nightmare again – the poor man on the cross groaning in dreadful pain and gasping for air.'

The liquid in her bubble wobbled as Quilla shook his feathers irritably. 'Dear me child, I can't understand how a young, innocent lass like you could conjure up such dreadfulness. As I have said – before you fall asleep, you must think of something beautiful, such as the cooing of a plump dove, succulent and ready to be snatched from the tree branch.'

Bird giggled. 'Rather not! I'd prefer dreaming of a lovely red rose coming into bloom. Or – or when Fin kissed me under …' To hide the sob rising in her throat, she looked out again, down into the square. At once she spotted Fin drunkenly hopping and jumping with the dancers.

'Just look at him, Quilla! Silly fool. Why on earth is he behaving like that?'

'I can't look!' Quilla snapped. 'I've no eyes!'

'I'm sorry – I forgot. It's Fin – a half-naked girl has dragged him into the dancing ring, and he's making an exhibition of himself – I bet he's drunk! Oh no! He's tripped over one of those calabash thingies. He's going to regret this in the morning! I'll make sure he's ashamed—'

Quilla shook his feathers tetchily. 'Hush child! If you don't stop grumbling, I'll close my eyelids so you can't see out.'

Grudgingly Bird fell silent.

The moon rose huge and silver, revealing beyond the dunes a vast desert stretching to the horizon. The moonlight caught the cross lying on Quilla's feathered breast, turning the central crystal to icy fire.

'Quilla! The moon's shining on the cross! Bend your head, so I can see it better.'

Pressing her face against the surface of the bubble, she saw the gold arms inlaid with their filigree of twisted fine wires and edged with pearls, the sapphires, emeralds and rubies gleaming blue, green and dark red. She could see right into the crystal, as flawlessly clear as spring water.

'Quilla, is the cross heavy? Can you feel it through your feathers?'

'Yes! It's beautiful and warm.'

She knew that beneath the crystal, embedded in the blue enamel was the splinter of wood, blood soaked and full of healing power – the power to escape her bubble prison, to have her body back, to be whole. Desperation overwhelmed her, she hated this delay: they must get to the Pool of Siloam, not be getting drunk and dancing with silly girls! Then she remembered why they were here in this strange city: so Sandy could recover from his wound. He'd come on this journey to rescue her, and she knew she could never repay him for his love and bravery.

She thought about her body back home in Brightdale. Kenji had told Fin that he had seen her body, safe in a box of straw by the kitchen fire, devotedly cared for by Tissy and Dancer. Kenji had also told Fin about Bee's funeral: that her mum and dad had scattered her ashes in the river, down by the sandy beach where young Delphins go skinny dipping at Highsun.

Sometimes she felt as if part of her soul was still inside her body, giving her glimpses of her surroundings and feeling for things, the soft touch of a hand on her head, a wooden spoon against her lips. Lately she'd had the sensation of straw tickling her face and the rough wickerwork of a basket pressed against her cheek, giving her hope that Tissy and Dancer had packed her body in a basket ready for going with Wings in his flying machine.

Becoming aware of Quilla's shoulders drooping, a wave of affection for her lovely friend washed over her. Over the days she'd been in his eye she'd got to know his thoughts and feelings, almost as if she and the bubble were growing into his body.

'Quilla, perhaps when I'm healed by the cross, you too will be healed – have new eyes —'

Shaking his feathers, Quilla said quietly: 'No child, you are my destiny – my nemesis – the reason why I was hatched from my egg, those fifteen years ago. When you are healed, my task will be over, and it might be that my life will be forfeited—'

'Don't! Don't!' Bird wailed. 'Quilla you mustn't talk like that! The cross will heal you too, I'm sure!'

Sobbing quietly to herself, she swam to float in the darkness at the back of the bubble. She knew now the cross had the power to make people good, so good they'd be willing to sacrifice their life for someone.

A chuckle from Quilla brought her out of her gloom. 'Come, look again. What are the lads up to? The drums and singing are much louder. Is Fin still dancing? What's Lark doing?'

Bird swam to look down. 'They're both lying on the ground near where Sandy is sat on a bench. Oh, how funny! Crow's chucked a bucket of water in their faces! They're sitting up, spluttering. They ought to get some sleep. Fin said that in the morning they'll be making plans for the journey across the desert. The man Malang told him a camel train will be arriving soon from the Red Sea, and that we could join it on its return trip.'

Bird felt Quilla stretch his wings. 'Perhaps the desert will have some tasty prey: fat rats or desert hares.'

Bird giggled. 'Hope you've not been tempted again to pinch Crow's rat! Anyway, I'm tired, I need to get some sleep too. But this time I'll do my best think of something beautiful to stop me having that nightmare.'

Stretching, she relaxed into the bubble's soft liquid. Drifting off to sleep, she willed herself to think about finding food for Quilla's voracious appetite. She'd become expert at spotting creatures she could guide him to catch on the ground and in the air.

Fin was woken by Crow thumping his chest. Groaning he sat up and pushing him away, squinted at his surroundings. He was lying on a zebra skin mat on the floor of a long windowless room. The harsh daylight streaming in through tall wide doors made his head ache. Around him under blankets were the sleeping forms of the young Dogon warriors. Along each side of the room, rows of wooden pillars carved into grotesque, life-sized, naked human figures supported the thatched roof. Leering down on him from the surrounding mud-walls, were hundreds of blank-eyed, painted masks.

With only a vague memory of how he'd got here, he recalled that one of Malang's warriors had called the place the Great Hall. He felt a pang of sadness: how different this hall was to the Great Hall at home, with its high windows covered in thin horn, the stone walls hung with hunting swords and spears, the cold slate floor spread with rush.

Beside him, Lark was stretched out, snoring loudly. Mick, half out of Lark's jerkin, stretched and yawned.

Fin scowled at Crow's face peering at him. 'What do you want, Crow?'

'Tiny voice inside eagle's eye wants to tell you off!'

He got up with a sigh and followed Crow outside. The square was littered with discarded calabashes, the fire just a mound of ashes. Quilla, shoulders hunched, perched on a wooden post; the cross, shining in the bright sun, seemed to hang heavy from his neck. Fighting a pang of jealousy, he approached and gently stroked the russet feathered head. Leaning close, he peered into the bubble in his eye. Bird's tiny figure swam into view.

'Hi, love. You O.K? Crow said you wanted to tell me off.'

'Yep! Last night, you looked ridiculous! If that was your effort at African dancing, you weren't any good!'

He heard a faint sob. 'Fin, I had the most dreadful dream last night – there was this poor man – he'd been pinned to a wooden beam. It makes me so frightened.'

Shocked, Fin's memory of his nightmare dreams came rushing back. Bird was having them too! 'It's the cross,' he choked 'Quilla wearing the cross is giving you these dreams. The sooner he stops wearing it the better!'

'Oh Fin, sometimes I think I'll be inside this horrid bubble for ever! Why are we hanging around here? We should be getting on our way!'

Desperate to comfort Bird, Fin pressed his face to Quilla's side, smelling his musty feathers.

'Don't cry, Bird! It won't be long. With Malang's healing skills, and his own strength of will Sandy is getting better all the time. We'll soon be on our way to Jerusalem. Like I told you, we're waiting for a camel train from the east. We'll return with it to the Red Sea, and then on to Jerusalem.'

Peering even closer into the bubble, he saw Bird's tiny hand pressed against the skin, and longed to be able to take her in his arms, to hold her close.

'Fin, I keep wondering how it will happen, how my soul and body will be together again. Will I be the same person?'

'I don't know, Bird – I don't know. But we must trust Mossy. He – he promised you'll be healed in the water of the Pool of Siloam.'

'But there's Quilla – he thinks he might have to die to make me whole again!' Bird's tiny voice wailed.

Quilla shook his feathers angrily. 'Quilla's telling me off! Threatening to peck you if you don't go away. Look, there's Lark. He's finally woken.'

Fin saw Lark standing at the entrance to the Great Hall, looking around blearily and yawning. Mick, by his side, pottered off to cock his leg.

'Go and tell him I'll be reporting him getting drunk to Tissy …' Bird's voice faded as Quilla flew off to a rooftop.

Sitting with Lark on a bench near the cold bonfire, they studied their surroundings. Last night it had been too dark to see much of what Malang had proudly called his city.

Set against a backdrop of high sandstone cliffs, Dogon was beautiful, a city of mud-built dwellings, with narrow streets running between them, more buildings rising higgledy-piggledy towards the foot of the cliffs. The architecture amazed them, tall narrow buildings tapering to conical thatched roofs, their windowless facades set with a series of doors. Too bewildered last night to understand, they now admired the elaborately carved wooden creatures rearing out of the eaves beneath the roofs: crocodiles, jackasses, snakes, the sunlight casting their long shadows down the mud walls.

Across the square Malang and Sandy sat beneath a canopy of interwoven branches, on a veranda fronting a low roofed building. Inside the building's dark entrance candlelight flickered. Crow was sitting on the veranda steps, Sparkie on his lap being petted by a group of admiring children.

A young woman with long dark hair and dressed in blue robes was kneeling beside Sandy gently sponging his wound with liquid from a bowl; enjoying the attention, he looked considerably better. He said something to the young woman that made her laugh, the pretty sound carrying across the square.

Lark stood and stretched. 'Let's go and talk to them. There might be the chance of a spot of breakfast.'

Malang introduced the young woman as his daughter: 'I am teaching Miryam the healing arts.'

Fin gasped. 'Miryam! That's my mother's name! She's a Rom!'

'My mother was also a Rom!' exclaimed Miryam. 'Rebecca – Rebecca Smith.' She studied Fin keenly. 'Father, can't you see Fin has the Rom blood too! Look at his skin and his dark hair!'

'Indeed, you are right, daughter!'

He smiled at Fin. 'I had forgotten when we first met in the Aard prison, you said your mother was a Rom.' Sadly, he added: 'My Rebecca died of Ebola. That was why I risked searching for the healing fungus in that evil place – to save others from the horror of that disease.'

'How did you meet your Rebecca?' Fin asked. So far, he hadn't seen any Roms among the people in the city.

'Sometimes caravans of Roms from the north come to Dogon to sell their wares – fine silks, metal ware and hunting dogs.' Malang sighed. 'It was love at first sight. I could not resist her beauty!'

Tears glittered in Fin's eyes. 'It was the same with my father. It caused a lot of trouble, my father marrying my mother – our people didn't approve of their Head's eldest son marrying a Rom girl.'

Miryam, noticing the contrast of icy fire and smouldering brown in Fin's mis-matched eyes, gazed at him in silent wonder.

Struggling to speak, Fin added: 'My father's dead now, murdered for the cross the eagle wears.'

Malang put a comforting hand on his shoulder. 'You have had much sadness in your young life, Fin.'

Fin smiled bleakly. 'My dad suffered much because of the cross, but he's happy now. I saw him, you know – swimming in the sea with the dolphins.

Lark couldn't contain himself any longer. 'You should know too that Fin's ma is someone very special! She's a holy woman – an Anchorite.'

'Yep, Aunty Krite my ma too!' came a croak from the steps below them: Crow had been listening. 'Hope she members me still – I miss her really bad!'

''course she remembers you, Crow,' Lark snorted. 'Didn't she promise you were always in her beating heart?'

Crow gave a loud sniff, and opening his bible bag, buried his face inside.

'There is much more I would like to know about you all!' Miryam exclaimed. 'But first, Iskander, I must bandage your wound.'

Gingerly feeling his neck, Sandy said: 'Thank you, but I am not sure I need a bandage: the skin is almost healed over!'

Malang studied the injury. 'You are right: air will help the healing now. But take care not to move too vigorously and open the cut again!'

As Miryam cleared away her sponge and bowl, Lark moved closer and sniffed the liquid in the bowl. He smelt a strong musty odour.

'My grandmother is teaching me a bit of healing art,' he explained. 'She'd be interested to know about this stuff. What's it made from?'

Miryam smiled delightedly. 'It is a distillation from the leaves of a shrub that grows in the fields around here: an evergreen with small yellow flowers. If you like, we will gather some, and I will show you how to prepare the balm.'

'That would be great—'

Fin interrupted. 'I don't think there'll be time, Lark. Now Sandy's so much better, we must be on our way – Bird's getting desperate!' He turned to Malang. 'When will the camel train arrive?'

'If all is well it will arrive very soon.' He looked at Fin, Lark and Sandy up and down critically. 'We must find suitable clothing for you: the desert sands are fiercely hot and jungle clothes won't do—'

He was interrupted by the clanging of a bell. Across the square, three women entered bearing platters piled high with fruit: slices of melon, mangoes, pineapples and bananas, followed by two others carrying a large tea urn. Behind them came the girl who'd danced with Fin at last night's feast, carrying a tray laden with small teacups. Her head bowed demurely, gone was her scanty covering of feathers: she was dressed from head to foot in a dark blue long-sleeved robe. After setting out the breakfast on the veranda, the women hurried away.

'Come, eat.' Miryam said, gesturing to the fruit before picking a selection and taking it to Sandy.

As she handed around the teacups, Malang's sons and the other warriors emerged bleary-eyed from the Great Hall. Helping themselves to fruit, they crouched in a circle silently munching.

The tea smelling of strong mint with a hint of liquorice, Lark was reminded of the brew old Llinos had given them when they had woken thick headed after the feast in the Boskie village. He thought fondly of the toothsome honeycomb she had served. Feeling Mick scratching his leg for attention, he gave him a piece of mango, which Mick pointedly dropped in the dust. Lark sighed, and silently told himself, he'd have to find his little dog some meat. Hoping there might be something left over from the ox roast, he sent him off there to scavenge.

Crow, his plate piled high, lovingly feeding his large rat a piece of mango, announced to the world in general: 'Sparkie keen on mangoes! But, better still, I knowed he'd like the juicy-sweet strawbs growed in gardens back home.'

'I'm sure he would, Crow,' Fin agreed.

'Bet your ma has good ones, Sandy, in her garden in Florain!' Lark said. He turned to Malang and Miryam to explain. 'Sandy's mother, Queen Ailis, has a proper cottage garden, the fruit and flowers all growing higgledy-piggledy together, along with scratching chickens to add fresh manure.'

Miryam sighed. 'Perhaps one day I will be able to see the garden of Florain.'

'You could meet Betony!' Lark exclaimed, 'she's keen on healing herbs—' Seeing the sadness on Sandy's face, he let his sentence die.

Quickly changing the subject, Fin pointed to the strangely carved wooden creatures jutting out from the roofs of the buildings around the square. Quilla was perched on one: a long-snouted crocodile.

'Those carvings remind me of the stone gargoyles on the roofs of Durholm Cathedral. They were carved thousands of years ago, are these as old?'

Malang nodded. 'Yes, some are at least two thousand years old. Us Dogons are proud of our carvings: jackals, snakes and crocodiles are mostly favoured. We reverence the ability of a jackal to run fast, a snake to strike quickly, and a crocodile to kill swiftly!

'But come, Fin and Lark, now you have eaten, you must see inside our Worshipping House.'

Malang led Fin and Lark through the arch into the building behind them. In the gloom they saw rows of benches facing an altar lit by banks of candles and arrayed with vases of flowers. Behind hung a backcloth of shining gold material.

'This is where we worship Amma, the Lord of life and death, the all-knowing Being. He has many names. Iskander tells me that in your land, he is called The Creator—but follow me! There is something I wish show you!'

Leading them through a side curtain, they entered a chamber lit by lamps hanging from the roof. Against one wall stood a wood statue: the figure of a tall, beautifully carved, black-faced angel wearing long flowing inky blue robe, arms outstretched in welcome. Enormous wings, covered in gold leaf, spread out behind him completely taking up the wall behind. On the old face was a lovely gentle smile.

Fin burst out: 'It's Zagzagel!'

Malang laughed. 'Indeed, it is! Legend says that the Gaiakin who carved the statue, carved it from life!'

Falling on his knees, Fin couldn't stop the tears. 'Oh, how I wish Mossy were with us now!'

Lark gave his shoulder a comforting squeeze. 'Knowing Mossy, I bet he can see us here.'

Turning to see if Malang agreed, he found he had left them. Kneeling beside Fin, Lark closed his eyes. 'Mossy? Can you hear me? Keep my Tissy safe!'

During the day news spread that the camel train had been spotted and would be arriving the next day. Traders appeared from the jungle lands to the west, setting up camp on the edge of the dunes outside the city, intending to barter their goods for the precious, much prized salt brought on camels' backs from the salt pans in the east. Restless, impatient to be leaving, to fill some time Fin and Lark wandered through the makeshift tented town, amazed by the variety of goods: sticky caramel-coloured cones of cane sugar, sacks of coffee beans, cured and brightly dyed leathers, zebra and leopard skins.

After the evening meal, Miryam helped them prepare for the desert, providing them with clothing worn by the cameleers, striped ankle-length robes called djellabas and head coverings called howlis.

'The howlis will keep sand out of your mouths and noses and protect you from the glare of the sun,' she said, demonstrating how to wrap the long strip of linen cloth around their heads, necks and over their faces, so that only their eyes showed.

At dawn the next day, out of the desert appeared some thirty camels loaded with rectangular blocks of sparkling grey salt. Breakfasting on the veranda, they watched fascinated as the train assembled in the square and the camels, coerced by their masters tugging at their metal nose rings, folded their legs with many complaining grunts, sinking to the ground for their burdens to be unloaded. The square soon crowded with traders, the business of bargaining and bartering quickly become heated. By late afternoon, all the haggling finally done, the traders from the west left with their mules laden with salt blocks.

Malang introduced the four to Omar, leader of the camel train, explaining that they hoped to join his train on its return trip across the desert to the Red Sea.

Of the Tuareg people, Omar was a bad-tempered stocky man whose thin black moustache twitched critically as he sized them up. First taking in the sword on Sandy's back, his tall powerful build and his unflinching blue-eyed gaze, he turned a scornful eye on the diminutive figures of Fin, Lark with Mick tucked in the crook of his arm, and Crow with Sparkie II sitting on his shoulder.

He turned back to Sandy: 'You warrior, with your sword, can go cheap, but the midgets with their menagerie must pay much Impshi—'

Malang interrupted angrily. 'Omar! These are good brave people! They saved my life and freed my people by destroying the evil in Futa Jallon. If you want payment, I will give you what you want. But in exchange you will take them to Red Sea – and make sure they get there safely, or you'll have me and my warriors to deal with!'

'No Malang!' Fin exclaimed. 'You mustn't pay. We've plenty Impshi!' Delving deep in his rucksack he brought out the Dandrum Sword scabbard and prising off one of the last two large pearls showed it to Omar: 'Will this do?'

About to take the pearl, Omar started back in alarm when Quilla flew down from the veranda roof and landed on Fin's shoulder, his wings half spread threateningly. Omar's cameleers spotted the cross among his breast feathers and gathering at a safe distance greedily eyed the magnificent jewels.

Malang grabbed Omar by the front of his djellaba and hissed fiercely. 'You must know, Omar: that cross is sacred. It brings death to any who try to steal it. Take the pearl and do as I have said, make sure Fin and his companions get safely across the desert!'

Pushing Malang away Omar gazed at Fin with new respect. 'Alright, I will take them. But they must be ready early: we leave next day before dawn, and I will not wait!'

It was still dark when they made ready to set out, backpacks over their djellabas, heads covered by howlis. They watched Omar, torch in hand, move quietly amongst the kneeling camels, inspecting a harness here, checking a strap there as his team heaved sacks of coffee beans, rolls of leather, bags of sugar cones and other bartered goods aboard the camels – bedding, food and water for the journey were loaded on the smaller beasts. The camels endured all this with expressions of weary disdain.

Now it was Fin, Lark, and Crow's turn to mount. Mick inside Lark's jerkin and Sparkie safe in Crow's bible bag, Omar unceremoniously lifted them on to the saddled humps of three camels carrying animal fodder, warning them to hold on tight to the pommel.

'Zzt! Zzt! Zzt!' Giving each camel a sharp whack on the backside with his stick, the camels lurched to standing, hind legs first then front legs. Swaying violently forwards then backwards, Fin and Lark just managed to save themselves from tumbling to the ground, but Crow fell off. Tut-tutting, Omar picked him up and threw his small frame into the saddle, followed by the bible bag from where indignant squeals could be heard.

Omar now turned to Sandy. 'You wish to ride?'

Eyeing the bad-tempered camels with dislike, Sandy shook his head vigorously.

'No, I'm strong enough to walk! My wound is healed.'

Having watched the loading, Malang and Miryam reached up in turn to Fin, Lark and Crow to squeeze their hands, calling thanks and goodbyes.

Handing Sandy a tall walking stick, Malang said: 'Iskander, I lend to you my trusty stick – it has supported me on journeys across desert and through jungle! Though ancient, it is still strong. Legend has it that it was carved by Zagzagel himself! When you reach your destination, give it to Omar who will return it to me.'

Bowing respectfully, Sandy accepted the walking stick. Made of hard black ebony, it had a thumb notch and was engraved with crocodiles in the style of the Dogon roof carvings. Looking down from his camel, Fin remembered the ebony walking stick Mossy kept by the door in the lobby of the Bookshop.

Malang gazed wistfully towards the north. 'Who knows? Perhaps one day, I may need the stick on a journey to your Northern lands, when perhaps Zazagel will permit me to learn how you all fared in your dangerous quest!'

Waiting at the train's head, his camel's bridle rope in hand Omar hissed impatiently. Giving Malang's hand a last shake and Miryam a brief hug, Sandy strode to join him, new stick in hand. Prodded by the cameleers the line of camels moved off, snapping and snarling, complaining about their heavy loads.

Getting used to the rhythm of his camel's stride, Fin glanced skywards. His eye caught by a flash of gold in the rising sun, he saw Quilla swooping and gliding as he hunted for food. The sight suddenly smote his heart: Bird's pearly soul was up there, but her burnt body was far, far away in Brightdale. Would they ever be reunited? Would Wings, Tissy and Dancer make it to Jerusalem?

He thought again about the chapel where the Dogons worshipped and the carved black angel with flowing ink blue robes.

'Please Mossy, make it all happen as you said!' he whispered.

For a moment he thought he heard a gentle laughing reply: 'Fin! Fin! Surely you know by now that I always keep my promises?'

But it could have just been the whisper of the soft dry sand running between his camel's broad toes as it padded on.

# 9
# SAHARA

Dawn in the Sahara. Already cruelly hot, the sun's rays crept across the baked sand, chasing away shadows, sucking up last night's dew. Rusty-red dunes rolled away to a shimmering horizon broken by jagged hills, stripped bare by the relentless wind.

Gressil and Mab crouched in a patch of shade beneath overhanging rocks in a long-dry riverbed. From a crack in the rocks nearby a Deathstalker scorpion observed the bedraggled couple. Mangy fur hung off the body that had been the Batfrit King, M'Bopo. On one cheek an eye lens dangled by a wire, which Gressil had to repeatedly shove back in its socket. Mab was in an even worse state. The wound left by Quilla tearing the cross from her breast had turned septic. The gash in her side was also infected and weeping pus. Worst of all was her thirst. Unlike M'Bopo, whose body was mainly machine and required little liquid, her butterfly body needed water.

The Deathstalker scorpion's sting pumping with powerful venom, it pounced. Thud. Landing on M'Bopo's leathery wing, it stabbed. Crackle! Fizz! A halo of electricity sparked around its carapace. M'Bopo's metal fingers snapped: squish! Creamy insect juice squirted across a flat stone.

'Mab, my darling, eat!' Gressil cooed sweetly from inside M'Bopo's body. Holding the stone to Mab's mouth, he grimaced as he watched her parched tongue lick avidly. Once he too had a scorpion's body, but so, so much bigger: Mab would have found all the thirst-quenching juice she needed from that huge body!

Descending from the Futa Jallon plateau then flying low, they had rested on the ground or in treetops, conserving energy as best they could. It hadn't been easy for the dilapidated Batfrit and weakened butterfly woman to keep up with their quarry but keep up they did, as far as Dogon. Hiding in an uninhabited cave on the town's outskirts, they had waited and rested, knowing that the eagle and his companions must soon cross the desert. Leaving Dogon city, it had taken Gressil and Mab twelve days to reach where they now sheltered: in the hinterlands of the massif once known as De l'Air, half-way across the Sahara.

For the first week, they had managed to keep the camel train within sight. Guided by the eagle as it flew high searching the ground for prey, the glimpses of the gold jewelled cross flashing in the sun had been a torture. But gradually the camel train left them behind.

Now, as Gressil listlessly searched the sky, he could see nothing in the cloudless blue. Suddenly he sat up: his good lens eye had spotted movement beneath the sand of a close by dune. Lurching out of the shade and sifting through the soft dry sand with his Batfrit claws, he drew out the writhing body of a sand viper. Its long body coiling around his claw, he lumbered back to the shade and savagely twisting off the head, held the blood dripping body to Mab. Sucking deep, rivulets of blood running down her chin, the liquid gave her renewed strength. Once more the ragged winged butterfly and bedraggled Batfrit struggled on, half-flying half crawling across the desert.

The next day, when the sun was at its highest, they sought shelter once again. Finding a few inches of shadow beneath a baking cliff face, they rested. Becoming aware of a humming sound on the boiling air, Gressil sat up sharply and listened intently. The insistent thrum grew louder. Speeding out of the north six large hornet shapes appeared. The shapes became Snoopers.

Papery wings whirring, long legs dangling, a vinegary stink hanging in the furnace-like air, they hovered above the couple. Dipping their black and yellow striped bodies they bowed in reverence to their Lord. Thud! Thud! Thud! Thud! Thud! Thud! One by one they landed, raising clouds of sand. As the last Snooper landed it dropped a heavy metal water canteen that hit the ground with a clunk. Staggering onto his clawed feet, Gressil glowered at the pitiless armoured faces surrounding him – each multi-faceted eye reflected back at him row upon row of mangy Batfrits.

'About time!' he snarled. 'I called you days ago! If my Queen had died, the agony you would have suffered would be beyond imagining.'

Bobbing and swaying, fanged jaws working agitatedly, the huge insects set up a shrill chorus of excuses.

I am not interested! No more delay!' Gressil raged. 'We set off immediately! The cross is already far ahead of us!' Stabbing his claw at a Snooper, he rapped out a harsh command. 'You – go on ahead – search for the eagle wearing the cross!' He motioned to two other Snoopers. 'You two as well: the eagle will be no match for three of you.'

Full of relief at their escape, the insects sped off into the horizon.

M'Bopo grabbed the water canteen. 'Here my love,' he said tenderly to Mab. 'Before we fly you must drink.'

'Yes! Yes! Water – give me water!'

Taking big gulps until her thirst was satisfied, Mab lurched to her feet. Opening out her wings, once shining peacock-blue, icy turquoise, pansy-brown, mustard, scarlet and silver, now dulled and frayed, she tentatively flapped them before ponderously rising into the air.

Stretching out his chicken skin wings, Gressil rose beside her. 'Hold on to me, my sweet one,' he cooed, taking her small hand in his claw. 'Together we shall search out the eagle and take back your precious cross.'

'Then, I will not die, will I Gressil?' Mab asked anxiously. 'The cross will heal me?'

'Yes! Yes! It shall give you healing life!'

'And I shall have my revenge on the boy: he shall suffer before he dies!' Her vengeful shriek cut through the searing heat.

'Yes! Yes!' howled Gressil's beautiful voice.

Hand in claw, the strange couple flew off, low above the ground.

Humming encouragement, the three remaining Snoopers kept a protective pace around them.

For Fin, Lark, Crow and Sandy the first stage of their journey across the Sahara came as a surprise. Not an ocean of lifeless sand but clumps of tough grass, acacia, and other thorny shrubs dotted the landscape. There was wildlife too: snakes and scorpions, jackals and rat-like animals Omar called jerboa. Once they came across a herd of antelope with long twisted horns. Fin, recalling Mossy's wildlife books thought they could be screwhorn antelopes.

The days settled into a routine: walking for fourteen or fifteen hours during the night and morning, stopping when the sun was at its highest, the camels brought to their knees, their water and fodder unloaded. The noonday meal was a stew of millet and dried meat, soaked in camel milk and cooked over a fire of camel dung. After eating they slept until late afternoon when the animals were brought to their feet, provoking a tumult of braying and grunting, and they set off once more.

After a week, they reached the oasis at Bilma. The sight of water welling out of grassy sedge and spilling over the damp sand, was like a miracle. Omar warned them to fill their flasks here, as after this two they would be crossing true desert: a land so arid that not even krim-krim grass (as he called it) could grow.

Flasks filled and the camels watered, they took off their boots, and for a few glorious moments dug their toes into the wet sand. After their meal Lark rested in a scrap of shade beneath the thorny branches of an acacia tree, idly watching the camels hunkered down in the baking heat munching on their lunch of hay, indifferent to the clouds of black flies plaguing their lips and eyes. He was reminded of the dairy cows chewing the cud, knee deep in Brightdale's lush meadow grass. Beside him, Mick sleeping soundly, yipped as he dreamed, his short legs twitching. Lark smiled at him fondly. What was his little dog dreaming about? Catching rabbits in the woods down by the meadows?

In Brightdale Highsun was approaching. It would soon be haymaking, and he wasn't there to help. Longing almost overwhelmed him: to see Tissy's sparkling lavender-green eyes smiling up at him as together they forked hay onto the waggons. It was at haymaking time that he'd first told her he loved her. What was she doing now, he wondered? Where was she? Had Wings built his new flying machine? Had they set out with Bird's body?

He squeezed his eyes shut, knowing he shouldn't be thinking of Tissy but trying to snatch some sleep before sundown, when they would set off once more in the cool of the evening.

A loud laugh made him open his eyes. Beneath the shade of a nearby acacia the camel drivers had gathered around Crow who was showing them a trick he'd taught Sparkie II: throwing up a date for the rat to catch in its almost hand-like front paws. Even though Crow couldn't speak their language, with signs and gestures he'd become firm friends with the camel men who'd adopted the skinny little Scav as a mascot. Lark was amazed how much fitter Crow had become: his pale face now nut brown, his once sparse grey hair nearly as thick as his rat's.

Under a third tree, Omar and Sandy were chatting quietly. Fin dozed beside them with Quilla who crouched, shoulders hunched, at his side, the feathery remains of a pigeon littering the sand. Seeing the cross gleaming on the great eagle's chest, again Lark felt a niggling worry: the eagle was attracting greedy glances from the camel drivers. Could they be trusted? Would one of them try to steal the cross? Try to kill Quilla? He shivered: the sooner they travelled alone, free of prying eyes, the better.

Looking at Fin, Sandy and Crow, like him now completely at home in their howlis and djellabas, their hands and faces almost mahogany, he still found it hard to take in how they'd all changed, and how far they'd travelled – and still had to travel. Back at Dogon Malang had told them that the journey to the Red Sea was over two thousand miles! He smiled to think that, back home, when they'd first arrived in Holy Island he'd been amazed by the eighty miles he'd travelled from Brightdale.

Afternoon turned to early evening. Goading the grumpy camels to their feet, they set off once more.

Another week passed. Hotter than ever, now dunes rolled to an unreachable horizon: a barren land purged of every living thing, with not even a wisp of cloud to relieve the unrelenting glare. The scorching wind blew gritty sand into their faces, searching out gaps in their howlis, making their lips cracked and dry. Every now and then they came across the half-buried skeleton of a camel.

It was at the end of another long hot day, evening was falling, and they just had set off once more, when Lark, swaying on his camel, felt a low growl from Mick inside his djellaba. With a clutch of fear, he heard a steady hum, an all too familiar angry buzzing. Sitting up sharply, he twisted around to Fin on the camel behind.

'Can you hear—'

Fin didn't let him finish.

'SNOOPERS!' Fin yelled to Sandy trudging beside Omar at the head of the train, 'I can hear Snoopers!'

Sandy and Omar spun round in surprise. The camel train shuffled to a ragged halt. From behind them, out of the west flew two dark shapes: Snoopers.

Ping! Ping! Needle-like stings hit the rumps of two camels carrying bags of coffee bean: the pain making them buck wildly, they careered off into the desert. Ping! Ping! The Snoopers discharged more stings. Maddened by fear, the rest of the camels bolted, loads of sugar and coffee beans scattering behind them, their masters haring after them.

As they disappeared, Sandy, Omar and a remaining cameleer rushed to grab the bridles of Lark's, Fin's and Crow's camels. Dragging them to a slow halt and whacking their flanks, they forced them to the ground. Tumbling from their saddles, Lark, Fin and Crow quickly ducked down behind their trembling animals, but Mick, oblivious of the danger, leapt up, snapping savagely at the dangling legs. Ping! Thud! Ping! Thud! The Snoopers discharged two more stings into the sand, grazing the fur on his back. Then hovering for a moment buzzing excitedly, swinging around, they headed back from where they came.

Shh! Shh!' Omar covered Fin's camel's eyes with his hand, slowly calming the trembling beast. Taking his lead, Sandy and the cameleer treated Lark and Crow's animals the same way.

Fin anxiously searched the sky for Quilla and was relieved to see a distant speck in the deep blue. The great eagle was far too high for the Snoopers to have seen him. Soaring on a thermal up current, Quilla swooped back and forth. Suddenly, wings folded, he dived into a stoop, speeding like an arrow towards Fin. With a gliding curve he hovered just above his head. From his eye came Bird's frantic call: 'Fin! The Snoopers are coming back! And there's one more! Tell everyone – get away as fast as you can!'

It was too late – three Snoopers raced towards Quilla as he soared away. Attempting to snatch the cross, the leading Snooper scraped its sabre-like fangs across Quilla's side. With a squawk of pain Quilla twisted back, his talons raking open the insect's soft underbelly. Entrails flying, the Snooper crashed to the sand.

From inside her bubble, Bird yelled frantic instructions: 'Look out Quilla! One's coming from the left! Twist right! No, no, don't – another below us! Go up! Go up!'

Weakened from his injury and losing feathers, Quilla struggled to fly but the two remaining Snoopers were closing in on him, one snapping at his long tail feathers. He spun about and gouged his talons into the insect's face. Twisting and whirling, it was as if giant insect and eagle were engaged in a macabre flying dance. Hampered by his blindness, Quilla was lost to sight amongst the whirring wings and jumble of insects' bodies. Groaning, Fin fell to his knees as golden feathers fluttered down around him: how he wished Sandy had his cross-bow – left broken in M'Bopo's cave!

Suddenly, with a shout Lark pointed upwards: 'LOOK! LOOK! MORE EAGLES!'

In the deepening blue of the evening sky two large birds raced towards the fight. 'NO!' Omar gasped. 'Not eagles – buzzards! The White Riders are coming!'

Skeew! Skeew! Their shrieks were shriller than Quilla's. Their talons tore into the Snoopers: ripping, slashing, tearing open the brittle bodies, shredding fragile wings, shards of carapace fluttered to the ground. Taken by surprise, the Snoopers were soon overcome by the birds. Only one escaped: a wing hanging, guts trailing, wobbling in flight, it disappeared into the horizon.

Quilla fell drunkenly to the ground, closely followed by the protective buzzards. Leaping up, Fin rushed to him and ducking down beneath the hovering buzzards' powerful wings, heaved Quilla on to his lap.

'Bird! Bird! Are you O.K.?' he called frantically.

Behind Quilla's closed eyelid he could only just hear her faint sobbing voice. 'I can't see! Quilla's eyes are shut! I was so scared! Is he hurt badly?'

'Yes – he's bleeding dreadfully!' groaned Fin. Whipping off his howli, he tried to stem the flow of blood. The cross on its heavy gold chain was twisted under a wing. Gently loosening the chain and setting the cross straight, he saw a raw cross-shaped sore on the skin where the feathers had been lost. A chill ran down his spine: as with all who wore the Chi Rho, the cross had started to embed into Quilla's breast.

From behind him, Omar called out. 'At last! Ruzanna and her White Riders are here!'

Out of the east galloped four magnificent white camels, their long-legged pace so effortless they seemed almost to glide over the dunes; three carried riders, the fourth supplies. As the riders circled, the group on the ground gazed in wonder at their harnesses: scarlet fringed bridles adorned the camels' foreheads, bronze chains decorated their throats and swung down their curved necks, each chain ending in a tinkling silver bell; their saddles were similarly decorated. Faces half-hidden beneath scarlet howlis, the riders wore dark blue djellabas and on their backs they carried curved swords set in jewelled scabbards.

Bringing their camels to a halt, the riders gracefully dismounted, sliding to the ground without their mounts needing to bend their long legs. Two of the riders, with shrill whistles called the buzzards circling above, and both birds immediately swooped to settle on the thick leather pads on their masters' shoulders.

Omar stumbled to the one without a bird, who appeared their leader. Trembling, took her outstretched hand. 'Lady Ruzanna! Praise be to Allah! You arrived just in time!'

Ruzanna nodded curtly. Loosening her howli, two dark plaits to dropped to her waist. 'Good Omar, it was fortunate that we were riding in the vicinity! Never before have we seen such evil creatures!' She turned to look at Fin with Quilla, Lark and Sandy crouched beside him. 'Introduce me to your unusual friends, Omar.'

But as Sandy got to his feet, she didn't wait for an answer. Her dark eyes narrowing, she studied at him. Taking in his height and bearing, she said: 'I recognise, you sir, with your blue eyes and mighty sword, as a warrior from the North.'

Sandy bowed. 'My name is Iskander. My ancestors were Kings of the Northern Isles.' He then nodded to Fin and Lark. 'These are my friends Fin Dandrum and his servant Lark Annunder.'

'And why, Lord Iskander, were those flying monsters attacking you? Where do they come from?'

'They come from our Northern land and are servants of the devil known as Gressil – Snoopers they are called. They covet the jewelled cross the eagle wears.' He gestured to Quilla lying in Fin's lap.

Ruzanna studied Fin and Lark crouched by him with Mick in his arms. 'You have the look of the Banto, but your skin is paler. Do you too come from the northern lands?'

Shoving Mick away, Lark stood up, his back straight as he announced proudly: 'We are of Delphin kind! And yes, like Iskander, our home is in the North. Though legend has it, like the Bantos our race originated in jungle lands.'

'It is a wonder to meet you, Fin and Lark of the Delphins!' Ruzanna exclaimed. 'We of the Sahara have never heard of your race before!' She turned to her two companions. 'Is that not so?'

The two men nodded in agreement. Their faces, like their buzzards, were fiercely hawk-like, their keenly intelligent eyes as black as night. One, clean shaven, appeared the younger and the older had a grey beard.

'I am Wazim,' said the younger man. 'And this is Zaki. We are known as the White Riders – we are called so because of our white camels.'

Ruzanna knelt beside Fin. 'Is your bird badly injured?'

Pulling open the howli, seeing the Chi Rho gleaming on Quilla's breast she drew a sharp breath.

Looking over her shoulder, Wazim and Zaki whistled in amazement

'This is a wonder indeed!' Zaki exclaimed. 'A bird of prey wearing a jewel, and of such richness!'

Gently lifting Quilla from Fin's lap, Ruzanna laid him on the sand, and looked with concern at the deep wounds gouged into his side. 'Wasim, fetch the potion!' she hissed.

Wazim hurried to Ruzanna's camel and brought her a glass flask from a saddle bag. Ruzanna pulled out the stopper with her teeth to pour sticky black liquid onto the wounds. Quilla's powerful wings flapped so violently she struggled to keep hold of him. Lark immediately took over. Firmly folding Quilla's his wings and putting his mouth close to the bird's head, he whispered softly. Gradually Quilla relaxed. Letting go his wings Lark held out a hand to Ruzanna.

'Here, Mistress, give me the bottle.' Tenderly he smoothed more of the liquid onto the torn flesh. 'There, there lad, let Lark make you all better.' As he softly cooed, he became aware of Ruzanna and her companions gazing at him in wonder.

'I thought I knew all there was to know about caring for injured birds!' exclaimed Wazim. 'But you, small man, have a touch of witchcraft!'

Blushing hotly beneath his suntan, Lark muttered. 'Being a ghillie by profession, I know that an injured bird, whatever its size, has to be treated like a chick again.'

Before handing back the flask to Ruzanna, he sniffed the dark liquid inside. 'Is it tar?' he asked. 'In my land, tar's expensive stuff and can only be got in small quantities from the Roms who come on market days.'

Taking the flask, Ruzanna said. 'This is a mixture of tar with special salts from the pans at Merga: nowhere in the world is there such healing power as that of the Sahara's salts.'

Wrapping Quilla once more in the howli Ruzanna lifted him back onto Fin's lap.

Fin smiled gratefully. 'Thank you for helping us! The eagle is very precious to me!'

Ruzanna turned to Sandy. 'Tell me, why are you here – so far from your Northern land?'

'We are travelling to Jerusalem to find healing for the eagle at the Pool of Siloam – we hope to restore his sight.'

Ruzanna frowned. 'The Pool of Siloam! Rumour has it the pool is closed, no one is allowed to go there, the garden around the pool overgrown, the entrance gate locked and guarded. Who told you that you could go there?'

'A friend told us!' Fin cried in dismay.

Zaki snorted. 'Then your friend doesn't know Jerusalem now!'

'Our friend knows everything!' Lark exclaimed indignantly. 'He's an angel – and—'

Sandy put a hand on Lark's shoulder to silence him. 'It was Zagzagel who told us to go there. You know of him?'

Ruzanna opened her eyes wide in surprise. 'The mighty Zagzagel! It is long since the desert people have heard of him. We believed he turned his back on the world and us humans!'

Fin gave Ruzanna a wintery smile. 'You're wrong! He never left the world but came north to live with us Delphins. I know him well and I know that he would never have sent us on this journey if —' Tears sparkling in his eyes, he turned away.

'Rumours or no about the Pool, we have come all this way and we shall go there – and overcome whatever we might find,' Sandy said, his face grim.

'Besides, we've planned to meet our friends there! And we mustn't let them down!' Lark chipped in.

Ruzanna sighed. 'Well, since you are determined, I and my companions will help you on your way across the desert. First, you will come with us to our home, the Oasis at Merga. Then we shall make for Port Sudan on the Red Sea where you can find a passage on one of the ships that go through the Gulf of Aqaba to Eilat. From there you will have to make your own way to Jerusalem.'

Sandy smiled his thanks. 'Mistress Ruzanna I am indeed grateful for your kindly assistance!'

'Assistance?' Wazim growled. 'If the rumours are true, we will be assisting you to your deaths!'

Sandy, Fin and Lark looked at him in dismay.

Ruzanna nodded ruefully. 'Wazim is right. Jerusalem is in a dangerous place: a tyrant king is the ruler there and the land about has long been blighted by the plague of rabies.'

The darkness of Saharan night was almost upon them. She gestured to the east. 'We will set out immediately and travel all night. Omar, we must leave you to gather the camel train together on your own!'

Omar grinned. 'That will be easy – I have a feeling that once you have gone you will take any danger with you!'

Lark suddenly remembered Crow. 'By the way, there's a fourth member of our party!' He gestured to Crow peeping over one of the resting camels. 'His name is Crow: he is of the Scav race.'

Crow edged round the camel; bible bag clutched to his chest. 'Yup, I'm Crow 'cause of my eye being pecked out by a crow. Scaving were my prefession, but I retired now because of my jool being stolen—' Hiccupping a sob he buried his face into his bible bag from where came indignant squeaks.

Sandy hastily intervened. 'He refers to the cross the eagle wears. He too wore it once.'

Lark eagerly explained: 'You see it's a sacred cross. The eagle is its present guardian and, and we're his companions—'

Again putting a warning hand on Lark's shoulder, Sandy continued the explanation. 'The cross has much power. That is why it is desired by the demons who are following us.'

Shaking their heads in disbelief, Wazim and Zaki went to tend to their camels.

Ruzanna now issued instructions. 'Iskander, you will ride Laith, the camel that usually carries our water and fodder – we will leave the supplies for you, Omar. Laith means powerful lion and will easily bear your magnificent frame! Lark, you will ride with Wazim on his Shaheen, which means falcon. Zaki you will take the Scav up on your camel.' She smiled encouragingly at Crow who looked alarmed. 'Do not fear little Crow! Zaki will take care of you, and whatever creature you are hiding in your large bag. His camel is called Uqab, which means mighty flyer.'

Finally, she turned to Fin. 'Fin Dandrum you and your precious eagle will ride with me on my sweet tempered Rasha– but no more delay, we must reach Merga by dawn.'

She turned to Omar. 'Omar, hold Laith so Iskander can mount him!'

'No need!' Sandy said, 'Laith and I have already become friends.' Prodding the camel to its knees, he handed Malang's walking stick to Omar. 'Thank Malang for me, Omar, for the use of his fine stick. Tell him, one day I hope he and Miryam will come to our northern lands and stay a while!'

Taking the stick, Omar stood back as Sandy mounted his camel and expertly brought the animal to standing. Watching in admiration, Zaki asked: 'You have ridden camels before?'

Sandy grinned. 'No! But I know how to ride a horse – also I have skills in sailing a boat! I reckon handling a camel is little different to either!'

Shrugging in puzzlement, the White Riders helped Lark, Mick tucked in his jerkin, scramble onto a cushioned perch at the front of the camel's saddle. Zaki did the same for Crow and his bible bag. Their now hooded buzzards perched on their shoulders, Wazim and Zak mounted behind their passengers. At the same time Fin, struggling under the weight of Quilla cradled in his arms, Ruzanna quickly brought her camel to kneeling, and helped him onto the saddle perch of her camel. As he settled, he asked Ruzanna about the camel's name, what Rasha meant.

Ruzanna smiled. 'Rasha means gazelle – her gait is steady so you will find the ride smooth for your injured eagle.'

Climbing up behind him, she brought her camel to standing and the party set off at a swift pace, leaving Omar and his cameleer watching them disappear into the night.

Fighting drowsiness as he rocked to the rhythm of Rasha's gait, Fin gazed up at the stars in the velvet sky. The only sounds were the soft tinkling of the camels' harness bells and the whispering thump of hooves in the dry sand. Quilla, heavy in his lap, every now and then twitched in pain. Fin could just make out in the dim starlight, a dark stain spreading on his howli wrapped around Quilla's body and hoped desperately for the nightmare journey to end. What would happen to Bird's soul if Quilla died? He recalled when he was in the Treatment Shed in Gressil's Compound, Bird's cry from inside Quilla's eye, "You mustn't take the pod from his eye, you'll kill me!" The memory was like a hot knife twisted in his heart. Should he asked Ruzanna to stop so he could have a closer look at Quilla's wounds? No, the sooner they reached their destination the better.

The nightmare journey dragged on.

Just when he began to think his stiff knees could no longer grip the camel's neck, or his aching arms keep hold of Quilla, dawn came, spreading golden light over the dunes. Out of the bleached landscape the oasis of Merga appeared as a green vision.

Soon the vision became real. Entering a grove of date palms, all around them came the sounds of gurgling streams and bird song. A wide rush-filled lake came into view. At its edge stood a cluster of carpet tents from where drifted the rich aromas of hot coffee and baking bread.

The villagers, emerging from the tents with cries of welcome, eagerly gathered around as the travellers brought their camels to their knees. Tumbling from the saddle Fin laid Quilla on the sand and Sandy and Lark, slipping from their camels, ran to join him. Unwrapping Quilla from his blood-stained howli Fin called urgently to Bird. 'Can you hear me Bird? Are you O.K.?'

For a few agonizing moments, Quilla's eyelids remained closed, then a shudder went through his body and they slowly opened. Fin heard Bird's voice, so soft he struggled to hear.

'Quilla says he's in terrible pain. He thinks he's got a Snooper's sting in his thigh.'

With trembling hands, Fin gently parted Quilla's feathers to find a sting sticking out.

Again, Lark took command. Pushing Fin's hand away, without hesitating he grasped the sting and pulled. As it slid out, Quilla gave a screech of agony. A strong stink of vinegar caught their throats.

Pressing his hand over the wound, Lark hissed urgently to Ruzanna. 'Quick, get your lotion to clean away the poison.'

Pouring the black ointment into her palm, as she applied it, the blood oozing from the puncture wound frothed fiercely.

'Skeew, Skeew.' Quilla struggled weakly, then went limp.

'Quilla! Quilla! Wake up!' Fin could hear Bird's terrified voice.

Searching beneath the feathers to find Quilla's heart, Lark began pumping gently.

Everyone held their breath. Moments later, Quilla gave a squawk. From around them came a loud collective sigh and they looked up to realise an audience of village children had gathered to watch.

Old Zaki bustled up waving his arms, scattering the children like a flock of starlings.

'Food is ready!' he called. 'Come and eat, otherwise the Scav and his fine rat will eat everything!' He gestured to where carpets had been laid before one of the larger tents facing the lake, and laden with baskets of flatbread, bowls of yoghurt, coffee pots and cups. Crow, surrounded by an admiring audience, was demonstrating Sparkie's trick with the dates. Quilla once more wrapped in his howli, Fin helped by Sandy, got to his feet, and they all joined Crow on the carpet.

When they had eaten, they rested in the shade beneath the palm trees, sipping strong sweet coffee and enjoying the damp green and sparkling water of the oasis.

The poisonous sting removed, although struggling to stand, Quilla managed to take a few morsels of pigeon meat from Lark's hand and was soon regaining some of his strength.

Reassured, Lark relaxed and watched the bustle of activity as the villagers went about their morning chores. He turned to Ruzanna: 'I see a lot of old people and children, but few young men and women. Are you, Wazim and Zaki the only White Riders, or are there more?'

Ruzanna gave a gurgling laugh. 'Indeed, there are! We are some twenty in number, but the others are out patrolling the desert, dealing with the bandits who plague the camel trains.'

Sandy put down his coffee cup and got up. 'I promised Laith a massage where he has a saddle sore. If he and I are continuing to journey together, I must keep on the right side of his temper!'

Watching Sandy heading off to where the camels sat legs folded, Wazim shook his head in admiration. 'Never before has anyone been able to handle Laith like him!'

Zaki nodded agreement. 'It is said that only a mighty Gaiakin could train a stubborn camel as Laith into a riding camel!'

Lark grinned delightedly. 'Well, you've got your answer there! Sandy has Gaiakin blood.'

Zaki and Wazim turned to Lark in astonishment.

'Yep, his mother, Queen Ailis is part Gaiakin. She lives in the garden of Florain – not the evil Futa Jallon garden that you know of – but the one in our northern land, to where the Gaiakins fled. Fin and I've been there and met the Gaiakin King and Queen. And it's the home of the Gaiakin brothers, Mullein and Fescue, who made the cross Quilla is wearing!'

Zaki and Wazim looked speculatively at Quilla. Seeing the gleaming jewels among the bloodied feathers on his breast, they were beginning to have a suspicion that there was more to the blind eagle than they'd first thought. Could he be the Egyptian bird-god Horus? Exchanging looks, they shook their heads in wonder.

Later that evening, sitting watching the glowing dying embers of their charcoal fire before going to bed, Fin turned to Sandy.

'I was thinking about what Ruzanna said about the Pool of Siloam. Could Mossy have got it wrong – that the water has lost healing power, which is why no one goes there?'

'Zagzagel does not get things like that wrong,' Sandy replied. 'She did not say the Pool had lost its power: only that it is guarded, and no one allowed to bathe there. It could be that the evil king who rules Jerusalem keeps it for his own private use!'

'Well, come what may, we must go there!' Lark said, a determined look on his face, 'It's our only hope to save Bird! And – and Tissy will be waiting for us. I'm not going to let her down!'

Fin gave a quivering sigh. 'Sandy, it's all being so difficult! What with the Snoopers too. How did they find us? Could Gressil have sent them? Do you think he's gone into yet another body?'

Looking grim, Sandy nodded. 'I fear so, Fin. What kind of body, I can only speculate – probably another Aard.'

Lark shivered. 'Would Gressil need a body? I thought demons could get about without them. Could he be lurking somewhere around here?' He searched the shadows beyond the firelight, dreading he might spot the green glow of a demon's eyes.

Sandy shook his head. 'No, we need not fear Gressil without a body. Both he and Mab are cursed – cursed by Zagzagel. If they drift too long without a sentient body as a housing, their dark spirits will dissolve, and they will exist no more.'

'Well, I hope it's a slow, lumbering body our camels can outrun,' Lark growled. 'When that injured Snooper gets back to him without the cross, Gressil won't be best pleased!'

He gave a great yawn. 'Anyway, nothing we can do about that now. I'm off to my bed! The lady Ruzanna said we'll be setting off very early, and I need some shuteye.'

A hundred miles to the west, in the cold desert moonlight, dark shadows glided over the rolling dunes. Gressil and his Queen were making steady progress in their relentless pursuit supported by their three Snoopers, almost the last of their evil kind. Most had drowned in Contagion, along with the Snooper nursery. Of those that escaped, more were burnt alive by Tissy, Dancer and their companions. Of the last six that Gressil had summoned from the North, he had sent three to attack Quilla and regain the cross. Two were killed by the White Riders' buzzards. The third, escaping but badly injured by the buzzards, returned to Gressil bringing news of the failed mission. Fury gave Gressil renewed energy: using M'Bopo's weaponry of claw and teeth, he destroyed that Snooper, leaving the broken body for vultures to pick over.

Stopping to rest on the top of a high dune, stretching tall, Gressil stared fixedly to the southwest beyond the dark horizon. Opening M'Bopo's leathery wings wide as a sounding board, from his chest started a low hum. Growing louder, suddenly an ear shattering shriek exploded out of his Batfrit mouth, sending shockwaves pulsing through the sand. Mab covered her ears as wave upon wave of shimmering sound rippled southwestwardly through the night air. Buzzing agitatedly, wings quivering, the Snoopers reeled around her.

Far away on the Futa Jallon plateau, in the derelict garden of the Gaiakins, the waves of sound arrived, weaker now but still with the power to shake the trees. Deep in a well something stirred. On shadowy ledges around the wall glowing forms pulsed and took shape like dusty rags. Demonic eyes glared angrily up to the velvet dome of night. One after another, flapping their fiery rags, the Phraggs shot, up, up, out of the well. Whoosh! Whoosh! Whoosh! Leaving a trail of sparks, they sped north-eastwards. For any watcher on the ground who happened to look up, they might have thought they had seen shooting stars streaking across the sky – the only clue to the truth was the reek of burning rubber in the air.

Restlessly stirring as he laid under his blanket, his thoughts troubled, Fin found it hard to settle for the night. Turning to Quilla crouched beside him he saw in the moonlight streaming in through the door of the tent, the eagle's eyelids were closed, so knew he couldn't talk to Bird. Glimpsing the cross on Quilla's chest, he wondered if Bird was having what he thought of as his Cross Dream. Overcome by a longing, so strong it made his fingers itch, to grab the chain, as he reached out, a high, drawn out howl froze his hand. Sitting up and looking out of the tent, he saw Sandy's tall figure silhouetted against the moon, staring towards the west.

Getting up and standing beside him he whispered 'Was that an Aardwolf? Could there be packs roaming the desert?'

The howl came again, ending in a long blood-chilling shriek that could have been laughter.

Sandy shook his head. 'No Fin. Did you not recognize the voice of Gressil? I have a feeling he is summoning his Phraggs from the putrid garden on Futa Jallon!'

'Surely Futa Jallon is too far away?'

'I hope that is so. It could be just a cry – a cry of desperation from Gressil. But we must be ready to face the Phraggs, in whatever form they may appear.'

Remembering the vile Phragg that had invaded Hardwick, a shiver ran down Fin's spine. He looked back into the tent, at the sleeping forms beneath their blankets. He and Sandy appeared to be the only ones to have heard the howl. 'Should we wake everybody – set off immediately for the Red Sea?'

'No, the camels need more rest, as do we all. From the force of the sound, I think Gressil and Mab may still be a long way behind us. Try to get some sleep. You will need all your strength in the days ahead!'

Reluctantly Fin returned to his blanket, leaving Sandy immobile as a statue, still staring into the west.

Lying gazing out at the myriad galaxies in the night sky, he recalled Mossy naming some of them as they sat beneath the apple tree in the bookshop garden: that seemed like a lifetime ago. Then distant hissing shrieks like fireworks made him sit up: he saw fiery arrows streaking across the horizon.

He heard Sandy groan out one word: 'Phraggs!'

# 10
# SKYHOOK II

On the heather moorland above Dandrum Den, Tissy and Dancer were sitting on a flat lichen-covered rock near the Delphin funeral ground of Kirion. At their feet lay a bundle of home-made flags: squares of white sheeting tied to sticks. Nearby, Mossy stood watching the horizon, his dark form silhouetted against the orange glow of the setting sun. Lass crouched by his side, head turning, ears pricked for faint sounds of unseen creatures settling down for the night. This morning, Mossy had revealed one of his mysterious insights about the outside world, announcing that today Wings would arrive in his flying machine.

Two months ago, when Kenji had left to join the others on Orca, Mossy had carefully searched for a landing spot. After several days he found a narrow flat strip, roughly two hundred yards long, said to be part of an ancient military road. Here, helped by Dandrum farmhands, clearing away stones and dead branches, they had created a makeshift runway.

Eyes squinting against the setting sun, Tissy gazed lovingly at Mossy. He was so still he could have been made of stone. 'He's like a statue of Phul, set to guard the borders of the Dale,' she whispered to Dancer.

Suddenly Mossy gestured to the horizon. Faintly at first, a low droning could be heard. Snatching up two flags Dancer sprinted down the runway. Tissy grabbed another two and standing on the flat rock, began waving them above her head.

The droning grew louder. What could have been a huge bird came into view. Then the machine was overhead, the engine roar deafening. Barking hysterically, Lass dived behind the rock. Mossy raised his arms in salute. Skimming the fir trees surrounding Kirion, the machine dipped below the hillside to reappear heading towards them. Jumping up and down on her vantage point, Tissy frantically waved her flags, whilst Dancer ran up and down, her flags flashing white in the twilight. Had Wings seen them Tissy wondered?

Flying low the aircraft circled around then, first brushing the heather tops, its wheels touched the far end of the runway. They watched hearts in mouth, fearful they might have missed a hole or boulder, as it bounced twice before rolling steadily towards them. Finally, it halted a few yards from the base of their rock. The blur of the propeller slowed and stopped. With a last wheezing sigh, the engine fell silent. Lass crept back and stood close to Mossy once more.

From behind the windscreen, Wings' face grinned out at them. A side door opened and a metal foot strapped to a leg appeared, followed by a more ordinary booted leg. The machine swayed as Wings clambered out and grunting and cursing, dropped clumsily to the ground.

'Tad of a squeeze, chaps!' he exclaimed. 'I'll need a bit more practise getting in and out.'

They crowded around him, laughing delightedly. Dancer gave him a hug, whilst Lass sniffed his metal foot suspiciously.

Standing back, Mossy studied the new Skyhook, running his eye appreciatively over the broad wings, supported by metal struts, extending out from the sleek canvas-covered body.

'Isn't she a beauty,' Wings said proudly, using his long scarf to wipe of an oil stain from one of the shining new wing struts.

Dancer ran her hand over the propeller's smooth surface.

'You and your engineering friends must have worked non-stop to get this amazing machine finished!' she exclaimed, squinting at a neat row of copper pipes protruding from the engine housing, still shimmering with latent heat from the cooling engine.

Tissy looked on fearfully, remembering the night Wings had come to take Mossy away in his flying machine. Although this machine bore little resemblance to that flimsy contraption it would take a lot of her courage to fly in it.

She could never know the valiant effort that had gone into the design and construction of the machine that stood before them. Driven by the urgency of Bird's plight, Wings and Boff Spanner had spent many days designing, abandoning designs, then redesigning until they were satisfied they had planned an aircraft that could take off and land using the smallest possible area of open ground – as well as having a tank large enough to fly many hundreds of miles before refuelling. Helped by their resourceful friends at the Engineering Works there followed hours of labour turning their plans into reality.

Days turned into weeks. At last came the day of the first test flight. Watched by a tense crowd, Wings took off from a hastily cleared runway behind the engineering works, to roar away towards the horizon, returning an hour later bringing a long list of modifications and adjustments that took more days of frantic activity. After that, more test flights, more adjustments, fewer each time, until finally Wings pronounced himself satisfied.

They had produced Skyhook II. A purposeful looking monoplane, its wings attached by V-struts to a steel-framed canvas-covered fuselage standing on two wheels with another smaller wheel beneath the tailfin. The cockpit enjoyed the luxury of rigid clear plustic windows. Although cramped, as well as the pilot she could carry two passengers, with room in the tail for a small amount of light cargo as well as the large fuel tank. Behind the shiny metal propeller was a powerful six-cylinder engine, discovered beneath a tarpaulin in a corner of the Engineering Works, and lovingly restored in record time by the older Engineers.

Sensing Tissy's anxiety, Wings limped over to take her hand.

'Come Tissy – look inside!'

He lifted her up to see in. 'Observe: two strong but comfortable passenger seats, so you won't hurt yourself. Go on, sit in one!'

Clambering in, Tissy gingerly sat behind the pilot's seat, running her hand over the new leather armrests stuffed with horsehair. Craning her neck, she could just see out through the windows on either side. If she didn't want to, she wouldn't have to look down at the ground far below.

She smiled shyly at Wings leaning in through the door. 'It all seems very luxurious – I bet Lark didn't find the other Skyhook so comfortable.'

'You could say that!' laughed Wings. 'He spent most of his flying time with his eyes shut – but Mick loved it!'

'Come out now, Thetis,' Mossy called, 'night is drawing on, and we must make plans.'

As Tissy eased herself out, Wings sniffed the air. 'I don't think there'll be a wind, but before we go, I'd better tie Sky down for night. And set up my anti-theft alarm too!'

From the cargo space, he brought out a small box which he strapped to a wing strut. Producing a key from inside his leather flying jacket, he opened the box to turn a dial and flick a switch. As he relocked it, a red light on the lid started winking.

'Anyone who comes too near, will get a surprise!' he said with a grin. To demonstrate, he waved his hand in front of the red light and a shrieking squeal almost deafened them. Quickly reinserting the key, he shut off the noise. 'Good, that's tested. Now how about some grub? Haven't eaten since early this morning!'

They headed down the hill past Dandrum Den, for Watersmeet and Mossy's shop, where there was a hearty lentil stew keeping warm on the hob.

Whilst they ate, Wings told them about Orca, how Fin paid for her by bartering pearls from the Dandrum Sword. 'Worth every precious pearl! She's a beauty! Even broke off building Skyhook II to see her off – sails billowing, she skimmed the waves like a porpoise! Sandy's sailing skills were tested to the limit!'

Listening to him, worry gnawed at Tissy. Was Lark being sensible, and not showing off? Did they think to take plenty of warm waterproofs?

Their meal over, the table cleared, Wings brought out a thickly folded map from his rucksack. He spread it out as beer mugs in hand, they gathered round.

'This is the Gaiakins' map we studied on the Isle of Man. After a lot of humming and hawing, Boff and his chums allowed me to have it.'

Leaning close, Tissy and Dancer studied the worn and stained parchment: the miniature drawings of settlements, the rivers, mountains and deserts. The African continent was embellished with lions, elephants, and monkeys among trees. Mossy pointed to a spot illustrated by gardens and temples.

'The Gaiakins made their jungle garden home here, at the source of the River Gambia where it rises from the Fouta Djallon plateau. That is where Fin and the others are headed. Iskander believes it is where Queen Mab will go, as it is rumoured that the Evils lurk there – the Phraggmorgia and their servants: a place of death and misery, like Contagion!'

Tissy was filled with dismay: were Lark and Fin in great danger?

Mossy's finger now swung to the East, across a huge stretch of desert, to a city, illustrated by a cluster of buildings with domed roofs and tall towers.

'Jerusalem! That is where the Pool of Siloam is – the place to which you must take Bird's body and where all must come together: you bringing Bird's body, Fin and Lark with the Chi Rho, and the eagle carrying Bird's soul in its eye!'

Wings leaned in and ran his finger along a wavy red line he'd drawn on the map, showing a route south from Brightdale, across a short stretch of sea, over the vast forests covering the landmass of Europe, across another stretch of sea, and finishing at Jerusalem.

'I reckon from here to there is close on two thousand miles – so, we're in for a long haul!'

For a few moments there was silence, all overwhelmed by the sheer distance they would have to travel.

Wings continued: 'As you see, along the route I've marked a couple of Motherhomes where they make the biofuel Sky flies on. The stuff's distilled from rapeseed oil – needed by the Motherhomes for their generators. I found out their location from a grain trader who sails the European rivers.'

He pointed to what looked to be two new drawings, double underlined: tiny bunkers surrounded by fields of golden rapeseed, one at the mouth of a river called the Rhine and another alongside the banks of another river marked as the Danube.

'With an average cruising speed of 145 miles per hour, Skyhook can travel roughly 450 miles on a tank of fuel. After flying from the Isle of Mann, she's about half-full and I reckon we'll have sufficient to get us to the Motherhome at Felixstowe on the coast here.' He pointed to the south. 'The tank full again, we'll cross the sea to Rotterdam and follow the rivers Rhine and Danube, where we can refuel for a second time. Beyond Vienna, we'll have to take our chances, as the grain trader hadn't been any farther east.'

'What are Motherhomes?' Tissy asked. 'They sound very mysterious.'

'I was intending to teach you the technology,' Mossy said. 'But events have intervened! Dancer knows of them, do you not?'

Dancer nodded. 'Yes, Yrvik. When I became a member of Iskander's squad, we were stationed there before we were seconded north to Durholm. But I've never tried to understand radio technology! When we get to Felixstowe, Tissy, you'll have a chance to see for yourself the amazing way they talk to each other through the air, sometimes for thousands of miles!'

Wings grinned and said teasingly: 'Dancer old girl, you're going to have to learn!'

'What need do I have of knowing that tech? Fighting's my profession!' Dancer said defensively.

Mossy frowned and quickly changed the subject. 'Thetis and Dancer, have you completed your preparations for Bird? Have you planned how she will travel? Now she has grown so small and weak, she is very vulnerable.'

Dancer nodded. 'Yes, we found a food hamper in the kitchen cellars, a lidded basket with straps, so she'll be safe. That's all she'll need, apart from a blanket and straw.'

'Poor little mite,' Wings muttered. 'What people will make of her, goodness knows!'

Mossy gave him a sharp look. 'If possible, when others are around, you must keep the little lass hidden in her basket. If you do have to take her out, and people show curiosity, explain that she's ill and you are taking her to the Pool of Siloam for a cure – in a way that is true. But remember, no one must know that her soul is stolen!'

He turned to Tissy and Dancer. 'Go now! The hour is late: it is time you returned to Spinner Hall.'

They hurried down the stairs, leaving Mossy and Wings discussing the route.

To their frustration, the weather turned stormy. It was nine days before Wings decided it was safe to fly. At mid-day, Skyhook finally loaded and everyone in their seats, Wings pressed the starter button. The engine coughed and died. He pressed again, and Skyhook growled into life. The metal and canvas body shuddering, he swung her round into the wind, and she crept forward, her wheels spinning on the make-shift heather-grown runway. Gaining traction, her engine note turned to a roar. Bouncing over the rough ground, she increased speed. Tissy gripped the arm rests of her leather seat and squeezing her eyes tight shut held her breath. Two more bounces, and Skyhook left the safety of the ground. Tissy felt as if her head was being pressed into her shoulders as her stomach lurched towards the vibrating floor beneath her feet. Terror seized her: surely this heavy machine couldn't stay in the air! It was simply all there was between her and a drop of hundreds of feet.

Desperately fighting panic, she whispered: 'Kassabel, keep us safe. Please, please, don't let us crash.'

Calm flowed through her: Lark had flown in old Skyhook and had survived. She must be as brave as him! She forced her eyes open. In front of her, Wings pushed the joystick to the left, taking Skyhook in a tight circle. Now she must make herself look out before they lost sight of Kirion. Stretching up in her seat, she peered through the scratched plastic window. On the ground, Mossy, Nutmeg and her brother Kelp were waving, their upturned faces growing ever smaller. Tears smarted in her eyes: would she ever see them again?

Watersmeet and Spinner Hall came into view, then the high fells rose before them and all too soon her home was lost to sight. Wings was heading for the coast, hoping to make Felixstowe before nightfall. There, as well as refuelling, they could send a radio message to the next Motherhome. Also, Mossy had asked them to radio Barraconda on the River Gambia, to where Fin, Lark and the others were heading.

She thought about Lark's letter: when he, Fin and Wings were flying to Holy Island a squadron of Snoopers had attacked the old Skyhook, and they'd crashed into the mud. She hoped fervently that none of those monsters would appear now, intent on revenge for the burning of their nest on Donkey Crags. She searched the sky outside the window: apart from a few puffy clouds, the sky was empty. Remembering what Wings had said: this Skyhook with her powerful engine could easily outfly a Snooper, she hoped he was right. Settling back into her seat and twisting around, she saw Dancer had her eyes tight shut. On her knee Bird was wrapped in a blanket, her face buried in its soft folds. Turning to the front again, she thought back to their packing and loading, fraught with arguments. Grammer Nutmeg trying to persuade them to take hundreds of items she was sure they couldn't do without – last season's hazel nuts and dried fruit, flasks of water, changes of clothing, blankets, spare silk vests and knickers she'd made for Bird from her old underclothes, and extra straw for her basket, Tissy was constantly making peace between Nutmeg and Wings, who grumbled that it was all too heavy and bulky.

Last night, in Mossy's room, for the umpteenth time, they'd adjusted their packing list. Mossy declared that they must have a more advanced navigational aid than relying on the sun's position and a battered old compass Wings had dangling from a knob on Skyhook's instrument panel. He insisted they take his brass compass reputed to have been made by a Chinese watchmaker, large and ancient though it was.

Just when they were congratulating themselves on having thought of everything, Nutmeg announced they would need money, or something valuable to barter with, and proudly produced her dowry box – kept under her bed since the death of her sweetheart Ged Spinner, killed by a boar many decades before.

'Eee!' she'd giggled as she brought out a string of amber beads and a silver peacock brooch set with rubies, emeralds, sapphires, and other small gems. 'I can't think anyone would want to marry me now, at my age! I was going to pass these on to you, Tiss, when you and Lark are wed.'

Deeply touched by the old lady's generosity, Tissy had fought back tears as she wrapped them in the blue cloth in which the Chi Rho had been kept. Mossy said the cloth would be protection as the cross was so holy. The cloth packet now hung about her neck in a purse Mossy had made, just like the one he'd made for Fin. Lark's letters she left with Mossy in the Chi Rho's ornate box, except for one: the sepia picture of him with a startled expression and hair standing on end. Most precious of all was the battered ring that had belonged to Lark's mother. While she lived, she would never remove it: the only way would be if her finger were chopped off.

Her brother Kelp, whose initial scorn at her warrior ambitions had turned to admiration, had nagged her to take the crossbow he'd made for her, but Dancer thought it too cumbersome, so she took a small but viciously sharp dagger Kelp had used for gutting fish.

Thinking of Kelp reminded Tissy of this morning when she'd goodbye to everyone at Dandrum Den. Putting her head around the door of the bedroom where her mother and sister were in bed sobbing into handkerchiefs, her farewell had passed unnoticed, so she'd gone downstairs to kiss her father's shrivelled cheek where his body lay, crumbling and inert on the table in the Great Hall. Mossy had driven out Raaum the demon, but Roach's soul had never returned to his body – Mossy believed his soul had drowned in the destruction of the Treatment Shed in Gressil's Compound in Contagion.

Relieved to get away from Dandrum Den, she went with Dancer to collect Bird from Spinner Hall. The farewell from the Spinners was more painful: Bird's mother wept unconsolably before finally parting with her daughter.

She was startled out of her reverie by a call from Wings as he pointed downwards: 'Tissy, lass. Look! There's the sea.'

A tingle of excitement ran down her spine. Below her lay a glittering grey-green sheet of water, and she remembered Lark's first letter saying how amazed he'd been at his first sight of the sea.

Banking away, Wings headed south following the sand dunes along a golden shore.

Half an hour slowly passed. Massaging her stiff knees, she longed to stand and stretch. She was getting to hate the vibration and relentless drone of the engine but knew that if it stopped, they would crash, and the ground was so far down.

Yet again, she whispered. 'Kassabel, keep us safe.'

Another half hour passed. Skyhook droned on. The sun would soon be setting and there was no sign of Felixstowe. Far below, shadows from the sand dunes fringing the beaches were lengthening, and the glittering green blue of the sea was turning to navy.

Tissy could sense Wings was getting increasingly anxious as he peered through his windscreen, searching the horizon: his repeated tapping of a gauge on the instrument panel told her they were getting low on fuel. She turned to look at Dancer, her reptilian head slumped forward in sleep. On her lap, Bird, her little body lost in the folds of a blanket, also appeared to be asleep. Tissy frowned in worried thought. They were finding it ever harder to persuade Bird to eat anything nourishing; all she would eat now were Grammer Nutmeg's blackberry fruit leathers. She hoped their supply, stored in the cargo hold with the rest of the supplies, would be enough.

An hour later, Tissy was woken from an uneasy doze by a change in the engine note. The sun had set and shadows filled the cabin. Wings was banking away from coastal dunes. Below them a settlement straddled an estuary, with an assortment of boats bobbing inside a stone breakwater. Through the opposite window, she saw a haze of grey cloud over the distant horizon. Could that be the great metropolis of London? Wings had said he hoped to avoid the place. Last night up in Mossy's room, pointing to it on the map, he'd muttered: 'The place is teeming with Scav scum!'

'Felixstowe!' Wings called, gesticulating ahead to where a column of black smoke rose into the sky.

As they drew near, they saw a row of brick buildings. Some were on fire, flames and smoke pouring out of windows. A horde of small figures could be seen scurrying in and out of those not alight, carrying out boxes.

'ROGUE SCAVS!' Wings yelled. 'Felixstowe's being attacked!'

Hearing Skyhook's engine, many of the Scavs looked up, some dropping their boxes and scuttling off to hide in the surrounding scrubland. Several of the braver Scavs armed with crossbows, setting their arrow tips alight, began firing up a Skyhook sending up a fusillade of flaming arrows. Thud. One glanced off Skyhook's undercarriage, filling the cabin with a smell of scorched canvas.

'HOLD ON CHAPS!' Wings shouted, swinging Skyhook round into a tight quarter turn. 'No good landing here – we'll have to cross the Channel and make for Rotterdam!' Increasing speed, engine roaring, he flew over the harbour and estuary and headed out to sea.

Searching the stretch of shadowy sea fading away into the dark horizon, Tissy wondered how far it was to Rotterdam. Would they have enough fuel? Would they get there before dark?

For a miserable, nerve-racking hour they flew on. Bird, woken by Skyhook's violent acrobatics over Felixstowe, alternately whimpered and shrieked, despite all Dancer's efforts to soothe her. All Tissy could do was watch the seemingly endless sea rolling beneath them, wretchedly aware of Wings' increasing anxiety.

At last a wide estuary surrounded by marshland came into view. The engine stuttered. Skyhook dipped and swayed. Holding her breath, she hoped if they did come down, Skyhook might float. Stretching to peer over Wings' shoulder, she could see a line of sand dunes, then beyond a stretch of flat land with a settlement of low buildings where lights twinkled. Was this Rotterdam?

Wings headed towards dark figures waving bright electric torches. Spluttering and coughing, Skyhook's engine died: the fuel gauge was on empty. The ground rushed up to meet them. Bouncing and wobbling on soft turf, rattling and creaking they rolled to a jarring halt that jerked them forward in their seats. With a final cough from Skyhook's engine, silence fell.

Massaging sore muscles, they waited as the bobbing torches approached.

Wings turned in his seat: 'Better be wary, chaps. Not sure what sort of welcome we'll get here. Was hoping to radio them from Felixstowe, warning of our arrival.'

Unfastening Skyhook's door, he jumped to the ground, followed by Tissy. Dancer hid Bird in her basket and strapping her sword to her back jumped down after them. As the group drew near, they saw them to be youths dressed head to foot in skin tight black clothes with painted white skulls blazoned on their chests. As well as electric torches, the leading youth carried what looked to Tissy like a long metal tube.

Wings gasped in amazement. 'He's got a shotgun! Where on earth did he get that fro— NO, Dancer!' he cried as Dancer leapt towards them, sword in hand. The youth raised the shotgun, aimed just above her and fired.

With a bang louder than Tissy had ever heard, a spray of hot metal slammed into Skyhook's body, peppering the canvas with small holes. Wings rushed to the engine where the last dregs of Skyhook's fuel dripped onto the tarmac – the fuel tank was punctured. 'LOOK WHAT YOU'VE DONE,' he roared turning angrily towards the youth, who appeared to be the leader.

The youth pointed his weapon at them. 'None of you move!' he barked in a nervous growl. Stepping forward, he pressed his barrel against Dancer's chest. 'Drop your weapon, Skwid!'

Seeing Dancer about to raise her blade, Wings cried: 'Do as he says, Dancer! He'll kill you with that gun!'

Miserably, Dancer let her sword clatter to the ground.

Snatching it up, the youth stepped back. 'Where've you come from?' he asked Wings, gesticulated to Skyhook.

'We've flown from Britain. We were going to land at Felixstowe, but the place is in flames – overrun with Plague Scavs.'

'Aye, we know!' another youth exclaimed. 'Some of the Felixstowe people have escaped here to Rotterdam. Managed to cross the sea in boats.'

Another, spotting Tissy peeping out from behind Dancer, gave a hoarse cry.

'Look, Ged, that scum Skwid's brought one of 'em Scavs with it! The Boss'll want to know!'

'Right! You're coming with us,' said Ged, the leader. 'Hands in air Skwid and no funny business, or I'll blast a hole through you!'

Two of the youths pushed Wings and Dancer before them whilst another grabbed Tissy by the collar.

Panicking about Bird, still hidden in her basket in Skyhook, Tissy was about to explain to her captor, when she stopped herself. Whatever would they make of Bird? They seemed deeply suspicious of everyone: they'd mistaken her for a Scav as it was. No, these people weren't friendly; better keep quiet about Bird and hope she would be safe.

Prodded along, stumbling towards a cluster of buildings, they headed for a long half-cylindrical corrugated metal hut standing beside a larger brick built shed from which came a loud mechanical humming. They entered a room packed with men, women, and children all pale faced with exhaustion, huddled on benches at a long table littered with plates and mugs. The smell of fatigue and anxiety hung in the air. Few people paid attention to the new arrivals.

Roughly pushed through a side door, the three found themselves in a small, crowded room. Men and women in overalls stood beneath a bright electric strip light, poring over a large map spread on a table. They turned to look at the newcomers enquiringly.

Ged spoke respectfully to a short, broad shouldered man with thick grey hair, standing at the head of the table.

'Boss! The engine roar we heard was a flying machine! We've captured the scoundrels!' He shoved Wings forward. 'This is the pilot, and these are his passengers. Look, one's a filthy Skwid and they've brought one of them Plague Scavs with them!' He gesticulated to where Dancer and Tissy were being held by two other youths.

The Boss scowled. 'Not now, Ged, deal with them yourself! We've got more pressing problems than a stray flying machine!'

'But the pilot said they're from Felixstowe.'

Dancer, getting increasingly angry, struggled fiercely. Kicking out at the youth pinning her arms, she sent him crashing into the group around the table. Outnumbered by the young guards she was wrestled to floor. At the same time, Wings, clumsily trying to lash out with his metal foot, lost his balance and fell heavily.

Tissy, still firmly gripped by her arms, screamed: 'Wings! Dancer! Don't! Please don't fight them!'

Struggling to loosen her captor's grip, she addressed the man called Boss. 'I'm not a Scav! Can't you see? I'm a Delphin!'

The man didn't appear to be listening. He was staring hard at Wings, still struggling to his feet. Suspicion in his dark eyes changed to disbelief, then joy transformed his fierce expression.

'Joe Lisle!' he cried. 'Is it you?'

Rushing to grab Wings by the shoulders, he lifted him up in a fierce hug.

Alarmed and bewildered Wings struggled to free himself then, recognition dawning, a grin spread across his face.

'Well, I'll be—' he choked. 'Rick? Rick Myers? It is you, old chum?'

'Yep, it's me!' The man called Boss nodded delightedly.

Everyone in the room stared open-mouthed, as alternately hugging then pushing away to have a good look, the two men laughed and cried, tears streaming down their faces. After a few moments they managed to contain themselves.

Rick barked at the two youths holding Tissy and Dancer. 'Let them go! Joe here is my oldest and best friend!'

He frowned at Wings. 'What did your small friend call you? Wings?'

'Yep! Because of me and my flying machines! Haven't been called Joe since we were Apprentices!'

Dancer and Tissy exchanged uncertain glances, bewildered by the sudden change in their fortunes. Wings grinned at them, 'Rick and I were apprentice Engineers in the Met. Shared an attic room together. But more of that later.'

He turned to Rick. 'Must explain why we've ended up here: took a flaming arrow at Felixstowe. And now our fuel tank's peppered with shot by one of these guys! How the blazes does he come to have a shotgun? They haven't been seen or used for centuries.' He scowled at the black-clad youths.

'Sorry about that!' Rick said apologetically. 'It was handed down to the lad through his family – I'll have a stern word with him later. We'll fix your flying machine in the morning.'

Tissy broke in. 'But Wings, we must get back to Skyhook now! Bird's still there!'

Wings groaned. 'Heck, I'd forgotten!'

Surprised, Rick said: 'Alright, go and get your pet bird. Then come and have some food. Having to feed the refugees from Felixstowe, supplies are low, but I'm sure our cookhouse chaps can find you something. You must spend the night here too – pitch dark outside.' He addressed the youths, hanging around by the door now looking embarrassed. 'You lot – guide them with your torches and help make the aircraft secure! Ged, give the Skwid back her sword. And give me that shotgun before you do any more damage!'

Reluctantly Ged handed them over.

As they followed their former guards through the door, Tissy hesitated. Should she explain about Bird? Hurrying after the others, she decided it would be too complicated.

They found Bird still in her basket buried deep in her straw. She whimpered as Dancer tenderly lifted her out. Once again Tissy felt a stab of fear. Would they be able to keep Bird alive long enough? She was getting smaller by the day, her body more like a blind, newly hatched starling than a Delphin girl.

By the youths' torch light, frowning crossly, Wings examined the holes peppering Skyhook's canvas. Ged, now keen to make amends, eagerly offered to organize a rota among his team to guard the plane through the night. Grumpily satisfied they'd learned their lesson, Wings tied Skyhook down, and they returned to the hut.

At the long table, Bird, wrapped in her blanket on Dancer's knee, attracted suspicious stares from their fellow diners, some of whom had pointedly moved away at the sight of a Skwid, but Dancer's fierce scowl stopped any questions. After locking his office, Rick sat with them, and whilst they ate – left-over soup served with hunks of dark dry bread and slabs of cheese – Wings and Rick exchanged accounts of their lives.

Rick started first. Specialising in electrical engineering, he'd become famous for his skills in making electrical machines and radios but had been driven out of the London Metropolis by the Scav plague.

'I've worked in several Motherhomes since those days, building radios, before ending up here, at Rotterdam. Been here quite a few years now – got to like the Dutch, as they are called. I've a wife in the village and my boy, Matt is grown now. Very brainy – radio expert. Stationed at Vienna. How about you? Did you marry?'

Rick listened in dismay as Wings told the story of how his Engineering Works was destroyed and his family killed. He quickly went on to explain that he'd found a home in the North. 'Been on some pretty hairy adventures since then,' he grinned as he told Rick about Skyhook I and losing his leg when she crashed. 'Made some good friends too – including Dancer there!'

Rick frowned across at Dancer coaxing Bird to eat a piece of bread.

'Never thought you'd be one to befriend a scum Skwid,' he muttered, nervously taking in the fearsome sword in its sheath on her back.

'Not so much of the 'scum', old friend. Having seen her use her sword, I wouldn't want to make an enemy of her,' Wings said levelly. Rick glimpsed an amused twinkle in his eye.
'She's part of a warrior squad that roam the North, defending the Motherhomes. Her leader, Lord Iskander, is a particular friend of mine.'

Rick shook his head in wonder. 'The North sounds a wild place to me! What's the progress on tech? We're hoping to develop a better system for storing Knowledge Discs, which are deteriorating fast.'

The two engineers fell into a deep discussion of something called electromagnetism.

Across the table listening, Tissy found their jargon frustratingly difficult to understand. She promised herself that one day, when they were all safely home, she would ask Mossy to teach her about radios and other things, like blast furnaces. What would Lark think, she wondered? Would he expect her to be a dutiful wife, and rear a brood of children? She sighed: with the horrors that had happened, and if they all survived the unknown adventures still to come, she'd be perfectly happy to settle down as wife and mother – for the moment it was enough to stay alive.

Coming out of her reverie, she realised Wings and Rick were once more discussing the Scavs.

'It was Plague Scavs that destroyed the Engineering Works at Southampton,' Rick was saying. 'That's how I ended up here. It's getting worse – it won't be long before they start travelling north. Like swarms of locusts, they descend on likely targets, overrunning Engineering Works and Motherhomes, burning the rape fields, destroying the seed for making biofuel. Felixstowe's the latest.' He nodded to the far end of the table where a group huddled together looking lost. 'They're Geeks from the Felixstowe Motherhome. When you've eaten, I'll take you to meet them.'

Wings looked across at the group. 'Yep, I must have a word with them. Had we landed at Felixstowe I was hoping they'd send a radio message to the next Motherhome. But talking of flying, before we continue our journey, I'll be needing more biofuel.'

Rick nodded. 'Yes, we can spare you a few gallons and still have enough for our generators.' He frowned at Dancer still struggling to get Bird to eat. 'But tell me, what are you doing with that pathetic little Delphin? Bird, did you call her?'

'That's tricky! It'll be hard to explain.'

Tissy intervened angrily. 'Bird's not pathetic! She's – she's ill. We're making for a place called Siloam, to get a cure for her.'

Rick studied Bird frowningly, her small face just showing in the folds of her blanket, her blind eyes searching the room as she sniffed the air.

'Is her illness contagious?' He asked uneasily.

'No!' Tissy said fiercely. 'It's a sickness of the soul.'

Wings struggled to his feet. 'We must be off tomorrow as soon as Skyhook is fixed up. We've got a long way to go yet – Siloam is away in the east. Is there somewhere we can sleep?'

'I was hoping you could stay a while,' Rick said disappointedly. 'Meet the family. But if you're in a hurry you'd better get going. You can sleep in my office – I'll get them to set up camp beds before I go home.'

Wings laid a hand on Rick's shoulder. 'Sorry Rick. Would've liked to get to know your family. Anyway, I'd better have a word with those Felixstowe Geeks…'

Leaving Wings talking intently with the Felixstowe Geeks, Rick opened his office for Tissy and Dancer, then ordered someone from the kitchen to bring a couple of camp beds and a mattress for Tissy and Bird.

Wings joined them an hour later.

'Those Felixstowe chaps have had a dashed rough time. Had a bit of trouble making them understand my plan to fly to Jerusalem. It seemed to amaze them! I managed to get across that Sky could easily do the trip in a couple of days or so, but I would need at least three stops for fuel. Rick said we can send a message to the Vienna Motherhome, where we're to head for next. His son is stationed there, so we should get all the help we need. Warned me not to stray from the Rivers Rhine and Danube and to keep away from the Alps: ten thousand feet high, tops covered in everlasting snow – flying machines have been known to crash into them. He told me a story of an air balloon attempting to fly over them and they were overcome by lack of oxygen and crashed into a mountain called the Mont Blanc! Also warned me to keep clear of the mountains near the Black Sea – the Carpathians. Something about vampire Phraggs. A lot of rot, I reckon!'

A while later, lying on the hard-straw mattress, Tissy held tight to Bird's hand. In the candle light she watched Dancer sitting on her camp bed, polishing her sword. Wings in the camp bed on her other side, was already asleep and gently snoring.

'Dancer,' she whispered. 'I've been thinking about what lies ahead – about what Rick said about crashing into high mountains, and – and the Phraggs lurking in that other place.'

'There's no need to fear, Tissy! Don't forget, we have angels of light who take care of us – Zagzagel and Kassabel. They have far more power than any of Lord Lucifer's servants! Come now, you need some sleep – we don't know what tomorrow will bring!'

Leaning from her camp bed, she gently covered Tissy and Bird with their blanket, and blew out the candle.

Squeezing her eyes tight shut, Tissy couldn't stop the frightening thoughts still churning. Once more she prayed to Kassabel. 'Kassabel, keep the demons from us!'

Peace washed over her, reminding her of Grammer Nutmeg's soothing balm on her hand after she'd scalded it. Listening to Wings snoring, she smiled beneath her blanket. How amused Lark would be when she told him Wings' real name is Joe Lisle! She just couldn't picture Wings as a small boy called Joe.

Back in Brightdale, sitting on the sofa in Mossy's room stirring her mug of tea, Nutmeg stared into the fire. It was evening, the curtains drawn, Lass dozed on her sheepskin rug, Mossy sat in his rocking chair, his rosary beads slipping through his fingers.

They had just returned from a visit to the Spinner Hall kitchen where they'd found the family in a distraught state; even Wolfie looked mournful as he crouched by the fire, guarding the empty box where Bird had slept. There was nothing Nutmeg could do to comfort them; even Mossy with his reassuring words was of little solace.

Nutmeg thought about the events of the past weeks. It was so hard to take in: Fin and Lark hundreds n' hundreds of miles from home. Strangers from outside coming to the Dale, warriors with swords, one a Skwid. Little Bee dead. Bird not dead but her body all burnt and shrivelled up, and something happened to her soul which even now Nutmeg couldn't quite understand. And – and then the tall man called Wings, dressed all in leather, arriving in a flying machine, taking Tissy away – high up in the sky in that dratted roaring machine!

'It's not natural, Mr Mossy! It's not natural! They'll crash somewhere in the wilds and we'll never ——'Tears welling up, she searched for her handkerchief. 'How am I going to cope up at Dandrum Den!' she wailed. 'The poor blind, sick and frightened creatures me, Hollin and Kelp are caring for – Brewdy, Almeria, and Alaria a fat lot of use.' A knock on the front door below interrupted her flow.

Mossy hurried downstairs. Lass, claws clicking on the wooden stairs, scrabbled anxiously after him. Expecting it to be no one special, Nutmeg continued sipping her tea. Hearing the sound of footsteps on the stairs and a rumble of voices, she hurriedly put her mug down by her feet. As Mossy entered two Beings stepped from behind him, flooding the room with glimmering light: one a male figure radiating silver moonlight, the other a female of astonishing beauty, projecting a soft comforting glow like the setting sun shining on a golden patch of marigolds. Nutmeg could only gaze stupefied at the awesome figures, as Lass, all dignity lost, danced around them tail wagging furiously.

'Mrs Annunder, this is Mullein, and this is Betony!'

All of a twitter, Nutmeg struggled to her feet, knocking over her mug.

Betony came and gently sat her back on the sofa.

'It is so good to meet you, dear Nutmeg,' she smiled, sitting next to her. 'I learned from your grandson Lark that like me you are a Healer. That is why I have come, to help you with the creatures escaped from Gressil's terrible Compound.'

'Eee, Miss Betony, I'm so thankful – I were getting desperate!' Nutmeg moaned. 'Never were there such pathetic, blind, injured creatures——' She trailed off, burying her face in her handkerchief.

'There, there, Mrs Annunder, you have Betony now!' Mossy said soothingly.

Nutmeg turned up her tear-stained face at Mullein. 'And, you sir, will you be able to help our Kelp and Hollin deal with the more fearsome creatures? There's a tigger with no eyes, no teeth, no claws, and, and a great bird with a bald head, a vicious beak and one leg – Hollin reckons it's a vulture.'

Mullein came and knelt by her. 'I am sorry, Mistress Nutmeg, I will not be staying; I have come to take Zagzagel from you. We are going on a long journey—'

Nutmeg, gazing spellbound into his shining silvery eyes, fell silent, then started to cry. 'Oh no! Why? Where are you going? You and Mr Mossy can't leave us in the Dale to fend for ourselves, what with all the evil that is happening!'

'Have no fear, the evil that lurked in your land has gone – far away to the land of Africa. That is why Zagzagel and I must go there.'

'Take heart Mrs Annunder,' Mossy said, busily going about filling his pack. 'If all goes well, by the end of Highsun the lasses and lads should be home – just in time for the harvest!' he added as he slung his pack over his shoulder. 'Come now and see us off! And then after you have locked up here, take Betony up to Dandrum Den and show her the sterling work you are doing for the creatures in the Great Hall. Don't forget to take Lass with you!'

Downstairs, as Mossy collected his carved stick from by the door Nutmeg asked anxiously: 'You will bring them all safely back?'

For a moment Mossy remained silent and then, first bending to hug Lass, stood again: 'If it be the will of the Creator, yes, they will all come home: Fin, Lark, Thetis and Bird. But do not look for me – it may be a while before you see me again.' Nutmeg saw tears glittering in his deep, fathomless eyes.

Laying a hand on her head in blessing, he and Mullein turned and walked away, their glimmering silvery figures fading into the night.

Her handkerchief covering her sobs, Betony by her side, Meg stood listening until the sound of Mossy's stick tap, tapping on the paving could be heard no more. Led gently by Betony, they returned upstairs to put out the fire and tidy the room. Then locking up the shop, they set off for Dandrum Den, Lass dejectedly trailing behind them.

# 11
# FLYING EUROPE

Shortly after dawn, anxious to be on their way, they returned to Skyhook. Bird settled asleep in her basket, they started work on the repairs. Rick had come with the youths who had confronted them last night, bringing metal filler, strong adhesive tape, and cans of tar. Rick helped Wings work on the punctured fuel tank whilst the youths helped Tissy and Dancer patch and tar the shotgun holes in Skyhook's bodywork. An hour later, with every hole patched, hoping the repairs would withstand the vibration and buffeting of flight, Wings refilled the tank from the stash of barrels kept in a secure lockup near the generator building. After watching intently for any leaks, he appeared satisfied.

When they had cleaned themselves up in washroom of the main building, Rick took them to the radio shed: a windowless brick building with a tall radio mast poking skywards through its corrugated iron roof. Lit by a single electric light hanging from the rafters, an expectant hush filled the room. A young woman sat at a radio twiddling dials. Watching over her shoulder were two of the men who'd escaped from Felixstowe.

Wings muttered to Tissy and Dancer: 'The radio operator is calling up another station—'

About to explain how it worked, he was interrupted by the radio bursting into life. Over background hissing and crackling a tinny voice barked out: 'Barraconda calling. Barraconda calling – your message received re Skyhook. Kenji wants to talk to Wings. Is he there? Over…'

The radio operator turned around with an enquiring look. Wings lurched forward, his metal foot banging against her chair leg and took the microphone.

'Yep! I'm here! Put Kenji on … er, over…' he called excitedly.

After more hissing, Kenji's unmistakable voice crackled around the room: 'Hello Wings! Relieved to know you escaped the invasion at Felixstowe. Your passengers O.K.? Over…'

'Yep! Got here last night. Off to Vienna today. If all well, we'll reach Jerusalem in a couple of days. Are the others with you? Over …'

'Nope! Left them more than ten days ago. They were heading for Dogon City and intended crossing the Sahara. Big, big news! They've got the cross back! The eagle fought Mab for it. Fin and Lar —' an ear-splitting screech from the radio interrupted Kenji. Tissy held her breath as the operator adjusted dials.

Kenji's voice came back. 'Sorry, Wings. Trouble with generator here. Power running low! Try calling us from Vienna—'

After a few more seconds screeching, the radio fell silent.

Hot tears burned Tissy's eyes. Why did the machine have to stop just then – when Kenji was going to tell them about Lark? Now she'd have to wait until Vienna and hope the radio box there worked better than this hopeless machine.

'Right, Rick,' Wings muttered, 'no more delay! We must be off. Must find out more: get to Vienna a.s.a.p. Can your chaps radio them we're on our way?' Leaving Rick instructing the radio operator, swinging about on his metal foot he headed for the door, Tissy and Dancer hurrying after him.

As she trotted beside Dancer, Tissy asked anxiously: 'They'll be alright now, Dancer, won't they – now Quilla and Bird have the Chi Rho?'

Dancer squeezed her shoulder. 'Yes, they'll be alright – they've got Sandy with them! When we hear from Kenji at Vienna, we'll know more.'

Gudrun, Rick's wife, a dumpy, motherly woman, joined him to see them off. Rick had told her husband about Bird's condition, so she insisted Bird had a jar of her calf's foot jelly, claiming it had wonderful nourishing properties.

Not done with that, she handed a round cake tin to Wings. 'Stollen cake for your journey – you cannot travel without stollen!'

Opening the lid, Wings found a dark fruit cake inside.

Finally, to Rick's agonized embarrassment, she produced a greasy parcel tied with string, containing bratwurst and pumpernickel, for their son at Vienna.

Before climbing into Skyhook, Tissy pressed a small sparkling emerald into Rick's hand. To pass the time on their flight yesterday, she'd prised out some smaller gems from Nutmeg's jewelled peacock to be ready for bartering.

'To pay for the biofuel and things,' she explained shyly. 'My Grammer Nutmeg wouldn't want me owing anything.'

Murmuring thanks, Rick solemnly wrapped the gem in his handkerchief and put it in an inside pocket. He didn't tell her he'd no intention of adding the jewel to the general Motherhome funds but would keep it as a memento of the first Delphin he'd known.

Once airborne, they headed east, following the winding course of the great river Rhine. Below them spread vast tracts of forest, broken by wide blue lakes teeming with wildlife. There was little human habitation; every now and then a ruined building rose out of the green: a cathedral or a castle, with cottages huddled about the walls, their turrets and towers looking like pictures from one of Grammer Nutmeg's fairy story books.

At mid-day they located the river Danube and after following its course for half-an hour, Vienna Motherhome came into view. Circling before landing, they saw that Vienna was much like Rotterdam: lying on flat land close to the river, the same collection of huts, including a brick shed topped by a radio mast and surrounded by barbed wire. In the distance could be seen the roofs of a small town.

As Wings brought Skyhook down her engine coughed ominously. Coming to a halt beside an aircraft hangar, he clambered out of the cockpit, followed by Tissy and Dancer, and limped to the engine, lifting the cowling to inspect the fuel tank.

A young man strode out of the hanger. 'Hi, I'm Matt, Rick's son. I've been looking out for you!' He took after his mother, short and round. 'Is everything alright?' he asked, seeing Wings looking in at the engine.

'Hope so,' Wings said, wiping oily hands on his long scarf before shaking Matt's hand. 'I thought there might be a problem with the mended fuel tank, but my patching seems to have held.'

Matt said: 'Let's go to the mess hut. I know you'll want to be on your way if you're trying to get to Jerusalem. Whilst we eat, we'll decide where you should land next. Jerusalem is much too far from here on one tank.'

'Yep, it's worrying me, that,' Wings said. 'Do you know of any more Motherhomes on the way that can supply us with biofuel?'

Matt frowned in thought. 'There aren't many Motherhomes farther east – Budapest and Belgrade used to be enormous cities before the Great Dying, but are now just settlements with little tech. I doubt they would be willing to spare any fuel – it's too precious and is needed for their old-fashioned generators. There was Bucharest farther east, which could have supplied you, but it's been destroyed. Dodgy situation in that part of the world – Vampires.

'But what am I thinking!' The young man suddenly exclaimed. 'We'll get in touch with the garrison at Transylvania Fort. They're your people – Skwids,' he added addressing Dancer. 'I'll put you in the picture whilst we eat. Come and meet my girl, Ruby – she's in the kitchen baking bread for the workers' evening meal. She'll rustle us up a brew of tea.'

Climbing back into Skyhook, Dancer lifted Bird out of her basket and wrapping her in a blanket, passed her down to Tissy.

Back on the ground, she handed Matt his mother's parcel. He groaned with embarrassment.

'Mum's convinced I'm not getting enough to eat. As you see,' he patted his round stomach, 'I need to eat less! Thanks, anyway. Kind of you to spare the room. I know weight and space are at a premium in an aircraft.'

He looked admiringly at Skyhook. 'That's a pretty piece of engineering. Sadly, Frank, our flight engineer, was killed a couple of years ago, and there's no one here interested in carrying on.'

He gestured to the nearby hangar where several battered aircraft stood lopsided or tilted on their noses, propellers bent or broken, their canvas torn. One reminded Wings of his old Skyhook. He shook his head gloomily. 'Seems nobody's interested in aircraft other than me. Wish I had time to have a look – some of those craft could be salvageable.'

They found the mess deserted, it being mid-day and the workers either in the rape fields or the oil refinery.

'Hi, Rube!' Matt called.

A pretty, plump young woman with blond hair appeared from the kitchen.

'These are the chaps Dad warned us to expect. They've come for a quick lunch.'

'Welcome,' Ruby said. 'I'll make a brew of tea! What would you like to eat? There's soup– –'

Wings hastily intervened. 'We're O.K. thanks. We've brought Gudrun's bratwurst, pumpernickel and stollen cake.'

Ruby laughed and went to make the tea.

Wings spread out his map on a mess table, and whilst munching sausages he and Matt studied it. Across the table Tissy and Dancer settled with Bird on Dancer's knee. Opening Gudrun's jar of calf's foot jelly, to Tissy's delight Bird started lapping eagerly from the proffered teaspoon.

Matt pointed to the small picture of the city of Jerusalem. 'Dad said you were trying to get to the sacred pool there, to heal your poor little mite.'

Swallowing a mouthful of sausage, Wings nodded. 'I hoped to find somewhere on the Aegean coast to refuel, then hop across to Jerusalem. But I'll need to stop off at least twice before then.'

Matt searched for the Carpathian mountain range. Triumphantly he pointed the end of his sausage at the sketch of a castle standing above a river running through a deep gorge. 'There it is: the Transylvania Fort. It's garrisoned by Skwids who fight the Vampire Phraggs. They'll have fuel there. Look, whoever drew this map knew about the Phraggs that lurk there – they've drawn some floating above it.'

Hearing what he said, Tissy dropped her spoon into the calf's foot jelly jar and peered over at the map. She saw three small white outlines that looked like sheets with black holes for eyes. Surely, they wouldn't be like the evil Phragg who stole Bird's soul?

'I don't suppose you know about the Phraggs?' Matt asked. 'Legend has it that they're descendants of Hellion and Grimalkin who fell into a fiery volcano when Queen Maligne came to Gaia. But it's said that the Phraggs lurking in the Carpathians were born of ice not fire.'

'Oh, we know about Phraggs right enough,' Wings growled. 'We were infested by them in the North – when that devil, Gressil took over the Doomstone Mines.' Wings sighed. 'But that's a long story. Little Bird here: they stole her—'

'Wings!' cried Dancer. 'You've forgotten Zagzagel's warning!'

Suddenly looking very tired, Wings rubbed his eyes. 'Sorry Dancer. Don't take any notice of my ramblings, young Matt!'

Matt frowned. 'The Skwids at Trans, more fighters than Tech Geeks, defend us here in Europe from that ancient Phragg evil: their Skwid eyes offer a degree of protection. They have a radio at Trans, so as soon as we've eaten, we'll go to the radio hut here, and get in touch.'

He smiled at Dancer. 'Interestingly, the group at Trans come from Cyprus. But of course, you'll know. The island of Cyprus is where the Skwids first settled, a thousand years ago, after the Great Dying – some important shrine there.'

Rainbow colours rippled over Dancer's head and face. Tissy stared at her in surprise.

Momentarily too overcome to speak, Dancer managed to say in a voice thick with emotion: 'It's my dearest wish, to go to Cyprus, where Kassabel has her shrine! And you say Skwids still live there? I always thought that after the Skwid persecution when we were dispersed to the four corners of the world, the shrine in Cyprus lay in ruins.'

Handing Bird to Tissy, she leaned over the map, eyes swivelling as she searched for Cyprus. 'Look, Wings! It's on our way to Jerusalem! Surely, we can land there. Will they have fuel?' she asked Matt.

'Sure do!' Matt said with a grin. 'They're the biggest suppliers on the Mediterranean. The Island has several refineries. In the spring, the Island turns chrome yellow from the acres of rape. They need the biofuel for their amazing fighting copters which are armed with flame throwers to fight off the Vampire Phraggs. Horizontal rotors keep them in the air, and they're expert pilots: whizz about like bluebottles—' He was interrupted by Wings.

'My old Sky was a VOTOL! I wonder how they've developed theirs – copter technology is very specialised. Dancer old girl, we'll certainly have to pay a visit to Cyprus.'

Wings studied the map again. 'Can you tell me how to locate this Trans place?'

'Keep to the Danube.' Matt pointed to the long river winding east. 'When we radio Trans, we'll ask them to meet you in their copters and guide you to their Fort. Come on! We'll go to the radio hut – Salamander, Trans' radio operator, is usually at her machine at this time of day.'

'Can you get in touch with Barraconda, too?' Tissy asked anxiously. 'This morning in Rotterdam, Kenji at Barraconda was going to tell us about our friends, but the radio stopped working.'

'I'll try, but Barraconda's generator is very unreliable.'

In the radio hut they gathered around Matt as he adjusted dials. He spoke into the microphone: 'Vienna calling. Vienna calling. Come in Transylvania … over …'

After a short interval of crackling and hissing, a husky voice from the radio echoed round the room: 'Trans calling. Trans calling. Hi Matt! Sally here. What can we do for you? Over …'

'Hi Sally. Got some friends wanting to visit the Fort! Flying to Jerusalem and their machine will need a stopover and refuel. Can you accommodate? Over …'

After a few moments of rustling and the sound of jumbled voices, a male voice came on: 'Flight engineer, Skink here. Biofuel not a prob. What type of VTOL? Over ...'

'Not a VTOL, Skink. Winged aircraft… will need a short runway. Over …'

'Great! Keen to see the craft! Runway not a prob. Landing strip in front of Fort —'

Skink was interrupted by another, more growly voice: 'Hi Matt. Dragon here. I'll send Gecko and Iguan to meet them at the Danube. Tell the pilot to look out for two copters! Over …'

'Thanks Dragon! Will do ... over and out.' Flicking a switch, he turned to Wings, Tissy and Dancer.

'Right that's organized! You'd better get going straight away. You must meet up with Gecko and Iguan before it goes dark.'

'But what about Barraconda?' wailed Tissy.

Wings squeezed her shoulder. 'No time, lass! We can do that when we get to Trans Fort. Don't want to be flying in the dark, especially when there's mountains around!'

Fuel tank filled they were ready to take off.

Tissy pressed a small ruby into Matt's hand. 'A ruby for your girl, Ruby,' she said, and without giving him a chance to refuse the gift, scrambled up into her seat.

Flying east, they continued to follow the silvery vein of the Danube. Below them the terrain resembled the flight from Rotterdam: forests spreading to the horizons, the monotonous landscape occasionally broken by lakes and castles with their surrounding settlements.

For three hours Skyhook droned on. Then a range of snow-capped mountains came into view. Wings turned and made a thumbs-up sign.

'Carpathians!' he called.

Gazing out of her window, Tissy watched the setting sun light up their snowy caps, turning them pink before it dropped down below the horizon. Thinking about what Matt had said, about vampire Phraggs lurking in those mountains, she shivered. In the evening light the mountains looked very beautiful. Surely evil couldn't lurk there.

An hour later, she noticed Wings twisting about in his seat, agitatedly searching ahead; she realised they were once again getting low on fuel.

Suddenly a tapping on the window startled her; ragged shapes sparkling with white frost floated past. For a moment she wondered if they were clouds.

Tap! Tap! She cowered down as long claw-like icicles again tapped the window. A face leered in, pale beneath a deep hood, runnels of blood dripping from the corners of a grinning, fang-toothed mouth. Terror paralyzed her. The roar of Skyhook's engine faded. She felt as if Skyhook were suspended in another dimension where time had stopped.

From seemingly thousands of miles away, Dancer's voice screamed: 'Don't look! Don't look! Shut your eyes!'

Beneath the hood the pale face's black empty eye sockets penetrated deep into her mind; the wailing sapped her will, draining her of all energy, filling her with utter despair.

Tap! Tap! Again, urgent icicle fingers tapped on the window. 'Little creature let us in! Let us in!' howled voices. 'Give us your life blood, give us your soul!'

Whoosh! Red tongues of fire shot across the window.

Whoosh! More flames lit the sky. The howls and wails faded: the icy shadows dissolved to dusty snow and vanished.

Dark against the setting sun, props whirring, two copters flew alongside. Gecko and Iguan had found them! The pilots waved from the glass covered cockpits and dipped their machines from side to side. Wings returned the greeting. One pilot gestured with his leather clad arm, indicating Skyhook was to follow. The copters spun about and headed fast for the mountains rising craggy black against the deep blue of the evening sky.

Half an hour's flying over rock strewn lower slopes then weaving between the highest crags brought into view the grey shape of a castle, standing on a small plateau separated from majestic cliffs by a deep gorge in which the white torrent of a mountain river gleamed in the misty twilight. Spanning the gorge was a bridge just long and wide enough to form a runway for Skyhook, ending at narrow steep steps leading to the wooden gates of the castle.

Badly shaken by the icy Phraggs' attack, his hand trembling as he gripped the joystick, Wings followed the two copters down and bouncing twice, Skyhook landed between the stone parapets of the bridge with only inches to spare. Joystick clamped between his knees he hauled on the brake lever, bringing her slithering to a halt just behind the two copters. The engine spluttered and died as once more she ran out of fuel. For a few moments nobody moved or spoke.

Then Wings struggled out of the cockpit, his metal foot ringing as it hit the ground.

The two Skwid copter pilots stood grinning at him in admiration; goggles perched on top of leather helmets, their leather flying suits were elaborately decorated with shining metal studs and chains.

'Hi! Brilliant landing, that was! Gecko and Iguan at your service,' they rasped in unison. 'Everything OK? We found you just in time!'

'Hello chaps, good to meet you! I'm Wings. Close shave that! Nearly lost control!' His hand still shaking, he wiped beads of sweat from his brow with his scarf. 'What were those fiends? Never come across 'em before! Young Matt did warn us, though – said something about Vampire Phraggs. Didn't realise how horrendous they were!'

'Yep,' Gecko nodded gravely. 'They have a terrible effect, especially on humans – known to send people mad. Us Skwids with our different eyes, can cope better. As you saw, our flame throwers knocked 'em out pretty effectively!'

'Is there anyone with you? Are they hurt?' asked Iguan. Seeing Dancer scrambling from her seat, excited colours rippled up and down his bare, rough scaled arms.

'Well, I'll be— you're a female Skwid!'

Dancer jumped unsteadily to the ground still weak from shock. She giggled 'Yep – well I'm pretty sure I was female when I last looked in a mirror. Shadow Dancer's the name but call me Dancer.'

Gazing in awe at the sword on her back, the two young Skwids shook her hand.

Hearing mouse-like squeaks, Dancer remembered Bird and turned to see Tissy holding Bird tightly wrapped in her blanket, struggling to get out of Skyhook. Helping her to the ground, the young Skwids eyed Bird uncertainly as Dancer introduced them.

Wings nodded to the two copters standing nearby, rotors drooping at a standstill. 'Pretty piece of flying you did,' he said admiringly. 'Used to fly a VTOL myself. Sadly, she crashed! That's how I lost my leg!' He shook his metal foot.

A croaking shout drew their attention to a figure emerging from a brightly lit cave in the cliff beneath the castle. Inside they could see machinery, tools, and rotor blades scattered on benches, with larger copter parts lying on the rock floor. The approaching figure was another Skwid, hoary scaled, getting on in years, his face disfigured on one side by a deep scar. Wiping his oily hands on a rag, he introduced himself.

'Skink's the name. I'm the maintenance engineer. I've come to look at your awesome machine.' He gazed appreciatively at Skyhook. 'What engine does she have? Can I see? Do you need any repairs?'

'Glad you mentioned repairs,' Wings said as, bristling with pride, he took Skink around to Sky's nose and released the engine cover latches. 'Bit concerned about the fuel lead. Landed at Rotterdam Motherhome and was shot at by some over excited guards: punctured the tank. So far the mends seemed to be holding, but until we refill the tank, we can't be sure.'

Skink peered in at the fuel pipe. 'Looks OK to me. The lights too poor now to see how the repairs are holding, but in the morning when we fill her up, we'll see if we can spot any leaks—'

They were interrupted as, hinges groaning, the castle doors opened. Three Skwids came down the steps: a mature male, broad shouldered, rough scaled, and wearing the same stud and chain decorated leather gear as Gecko and Iguan. He was followed by two females wearing crisply laundered white linen aprons over skin-tight suede leather garments. Glittering delicate silver and gold chain necklaces, ankle and wrist bracelets jangled as they moved.

The male Skwid halted before them and saluted: 'Commander Dragon, at your service.' He gestured to his companions. 'And my colleagues, Salamander and Lizard.'

Wings shook his hand. 'Name's Wings. Very grateful for your offer of hospitality, Commander – couldn't make it to Jerusalem without stopping off here!' He looked up at the castle's forbidding walls. 'Amazing place for a Motherhome!'

Dragon nodded. 'It's ancient. Its original name was Castle Drak. The legend says that Dracul, king of the Vampires lived here.'

Staring up at the sinister looking place, Tissy hoped there weren't any Vampires, like those who'd attacked them, lurking in its dungeons.

Wings introduced the others: 'This is Dancer, and this is Thetis with little Bird. Bird's poorly at present, so can't talk. That's why we're on this journey – taking her for healing at the Pool of Siloam.'

The two female Skwids surged forward. Taking in Dancer's sword and her simple warrior clothing, Salamander gripped Dancer's hand. 'Great to meet you Dancer! Whilst we have supper, you must tell us how you became a warrior.'

'Yes, come on everyone!' exclaimed Lizard. 'Skink, Gecko and Iguan, after you've tied down the flying machines, show our guests the beds prepared for them in the Great Hall and where they can stow their kit. Then bring them to the kitchen – supper's in the pot and will be ready soon!'

Salamander and Lizard bustled back up the steps, followed by Dragon at a more dignified pace. After drawing a heavy metal door on rollers across his hangar cave, Skink helped Wings tie Skyhook down for the night, all the while deep in discussion of aircraft tech. Then collecting their packs, Wings and Tissy, with Dancer carrying Bird, they followed Gecko, Iguan and Skink up the steps into the castle.

Crossing a courtyard surrounded by high grey stone walls topped with towers, they passed through wooden doors into a lofty chamber softly lit by solar powered wall lights. A log fire crackled and flickered in a huge stone fireplace, sending comforting warmth out to a semicircle of benches. Rush mats muffling their footsteps, Gecko and Iguan took them to where a heavy leather curtain separated two rows of straw mattresses covered with sheepskins.

'Pick a mattress,' Gecko said. 'The male quarters are this side. Ours are the ones with stuff on.' He gestured to mattresses covered with a motley collection of bits and pieces: leather clothing, weaponry and mechanical parts. On the curtain's other side, the mattresses were covered in brightly patterned eiderdowns and had plump pillows, two with neat piles of clothing at their foot, indicating Lizard and Salamander's beds.

Sleeping places claimed, Skink took Wings across the courtyard to show him the cellar where the barrels of biofuel were stored. Gecko and Iguan shepherded Tissy and Dancer carrying Bird down a flight of stone steps to the kitchen: a large cellar-like room with a blackened cauldron bubbling merrily on a cooking range. Salamander and Lizard were at a long table skilfully chopping strong-smelling garlic, huge bunches of parsley and what, to Tissy's concern, looked like raw liver. Dragon was pouring jugs of beer from wooden barrels standing along one wall.

'Yum!' exclaimed Dancer, watching the chopping, 'it's ages since I've had proper Skwid food!'

Salamander and Lizard, who insisted on being called Sally and Liz, eagerly quizzed Dancer as to how a female Skwid could become a warrior. Helping herself to a piece of raw liver, Dancer told them the story of Sandy's Trekker squad and how she trained to be a warrior. Their amazement made Dancer grin proudly, sunset yellow and pink rippling over her face.

Just then Skink and Wings clattered down the steps, still talking tech. Everyone took their places at the table. Tissy, feeding Bird her calf's foot jelly, tried not to look at Dancer's blood stained fingers. She hoped the stew didn't contain anything unpleasant as she was very hungry. To her relief, Liz served her and Wings extra-large helpings of the rich garlicky stew of field mushrooms from the cauldron.

As they ate, Wings asked if they knew of another refuelling point between Trans and Cyprus. 'Young Matt in Vienna said Cyprus has supplies, but it's too far to do in one hop.'

Dragon nodded. 'Yep, you'll certainly need to refuel before Cyprus. There's our base at Thessaloniki – I'll show you where it is on your map. It's about four hundred miles south-west of here – you'll need a reliable compass to find it!'

Wings grinned triumphantly. 'I've a Chinese-made compass hanging on Sky's control panel. A magnificent piece of engineering – given to me by old Zaggy back in Brightdale. So far I've navigated using the great European rivers. Even so, I've kept an eye on the needle, and found it far more precise than my old, battered compass.'

The meal over, as they relaxed sipping beer, Wings spread out his map.

Leaning in Dragon looked at the map admiringly. 'It's as beautiful as any in our archive cellars in Cyprus!'

He pointed to a stylised drawing of a mountain with a pointed summit. 'That's what you should look out for: Mount Olympus. Said to be the home of the ancient Greek gods. How true that is, I don't know: never seen any gods there! You'll find Thessaloniki nearby on the coast of the Aegean Sea. But don't stray east into Turkey!' He stabbed his scaled finger at a landmass on the other side of the Aegean. 'Rumours of rabies!'

Wings studied the area. 'Thanks for the warning. Years since I've encountered rabies!'

Dragon now sat back and frowned over his beer mug. 'And your destination is Jerusalem?'

Wings nodded. 'Yep, as I've explained, we're hoping to heal Bird with the sacred waters there.'

'Us Skwids have little knowledge of the Pool of Siloam in Jerusalem. We do know the city is where the tyrant King Fakhir has his palace. Few of us Skwids dare go there! The surrounding land is known as Dogland and teems with packs of feral dogs: the king and his soldiers hunt them for sport!' Eyes swivelling, he searched the deep shadows in the corners of the kitchen, and lowering his voice so only Wings could hear, hissed: 'There's rumour too of Sneaksouls – demons that possess people. Do you know what they are?'

'Oh, we know about them alright,' Wings muttered. 'We've been plagued in the north for years by those devils!' He noticed Tissy across the table watching him and Dragon anxiously. 'Tissy, come and have a look,' he said trying to sound reassuring. 'See if we can find Dogon, that's where Kenji said the others were heading.'

Searching the Gambia River, first they located the Barraconda Rapids, represented by a sketch of water tumbling over rocks. To the north east they found Dogon, marked by a cluster of tiny grass roofed buildings. From there Wings ran his finger east across a vast desert towards Jerusalem. 'They have a very long way to go. I wonder where they are now – Kenji said they were heading for Dogon over ten days ago.' He sighed gloomily.

Tears welled up in Tissy's eyes. How would Fin, Lark and Sandy manage to cross that huge desert? Would they be in danger? Then there was Bird's soul in the eagle's eye... She wished Kenji could have told them how Quilla had got the cross.

Sally, noticing Tissy's distress, jumped up from the table. 'Come on. It's time we went to the radio room! First, we'll call Thessy, warning them to look out for your machine. Then we'll try radioing Barraconda. Matt told me you're anxious to get in touch, so I'll have a go, but I can't promise much – it's always been difficult to communicate with Barraconda.'

'Tissy and Wings, you go,' Dancer said. 'I'll stay with Bird, and have a good long chat with Liz, Skink and the lads.'

Taking electric torches from a shelf by the kitchen door, Sally and Dragon led Wings and Tissy across the courtyard to where a shadowy tower loomed above the gates. What seemed to Tissy an endless narrow winding staircase brought them to the radio room. Seating herself at the radio and flicking a switch, Sally began carefully turning knobs to tune out the now familiar hissing and crackling.

Communication was good, and the operator from Thessaloniki quickly came on air. Sally passed on her message to look out for the arrival of a winged aircraft, then patiently turning the dials, she called into the microphone: 'Trans calling Barraconda. Trans calling Barraconda. Over…'

After a lot more hissing and crackling, a faint voice could be heard: 'Barraconda here. Hallo Trans. Over…'

Excited, Tissy gave a little skip. It was Kenji's voice! Sally turned to Wings. 'Quick! Come and speak before the radio signal fades!'

Wings stepped forward and grabbed the microphone. 'Hello Kenji. Wings here. Any news? Over …'

'Hi, Wings! Sorry no more news. When I left them ten days ago Fin and Lark were fine, but Sandy was badly injured—' Kenji's voice disappeared into the ether.

After a couple of minutes of fruitless dial twiddling, Sally sighed and gave up. She turned to Tissy. 'It's no use – the signal's faded.'

'Never mind. You did your best,' Tissy said, trying not to show how worried and miserable she was.

That night tucked up beneath her flowery eiderdown, she again went over in her mind what Kenji had said about Fin and Lark being fine. But that was days ago! Had they got safely to the place called Dogon? And then there was Sandy, badly injured. Was he able to look after them? She'd never met him, but from the way Dancer talked about her Squad leader, he sounded such a wonderful brave person.

'Kassabel, keep them safe!' she whispered.

Drifting into sleep, she thought she heard soft laughter from the rafters high above, but she wasn't sure.


To their relief, Wings and Skink found no leaks from the refilled tank and fuel pipe. With the aid of Mossy's Chinese compass, they reached Thessaloniki by late morning. They flew over a harbour lying in the sweep of a bay where numerous boats were moored to wooden piers. Above the harbour stood a cluster of tile roofed dwellings surrounded by fields of chrome-yellow rape. Beyond, lines of grapevines grew on the brown hillsides and to the south Mt. Olympus rose out of the blue haze.

The airfield occupied flat ground skirting the bay. Outside a row of hangars figures worked on copters, whilst other copters stood parked along the runway ready for take-off. At the end of the runway stood a tall brick observation tower with the usual radio mast projecting from its corrugated roof.

Escorted by two copters, Wings took Skyhook down to the runway, making an expertly smooth landing. Guided by a Skwid clad in a yellow overall waving two dayglo orange bats he taxied to a halt on the apron in front of the observation tower. He was pleased to see nearby a stack of drums containing biofuel. Climbing out, they were mobbed by excited copter pilots and mechanics who had abandoned their work to admire Skyhook. Besieged by keen questioning, Wings was soon lost in the world of aircraft technology. Knowing they were only stopping briefly they had kept Bird hidden in her basket.

From a door at the top of the nearby observation tower two Skwids clattered down a flight of metal steps. As they strode over Tissy saw the first Skwid had a commanding air, his skin crocodile rough. Like Dragon at Trans, his leather jacket and trousers were decorated with chains and studs. The second Skwid, a female, wore matching powder blue kid leather jacket and trousers with rows of amber beads around her neck and wrists.

'Back to work lads!' growled the male Skwid. 'Don't delay our guests who are in a hurry to reach Paphos before nightfall.'

But before the mechanics could leave, Wings hurriedly addressed the Skwid, 'I'd be really grateful if a couple of your chaps could help me with my fuel lead – I'm worried about leaks.'

'No problem,' growled the Skwid. He turned to his men, all grinning hopefully. 'You and you,' he gestured, 'check over the aircraft right away and deal with any repairs needed.'

The two mechanics sprang into action.

The Skwid introduced himself. 'Commander Gator at your service. Trans Fort warned us of your arrival.'

'Good to meet you Commander. Name's Wings, and this is Dancer, a Skwid warrior from our northern lands, and this is Thetis, also from the north.'

Gator introduced his companion. 'This is Iris, my second-in-command and radio officer.'

Iris looked admiringly at Skyhook. 'Pleasure to meet you, pilot Wings! I spoke on the radio to Engineer Skink today at Trans who told me all about your amazing machine.' She glanced quizzically at Commander Gator.

'Commander, may I show Pilot Wings the, er, the project?'

Gator chuckled throatily. 'I don't see why not; his knowledge might prove useful.'

Iris grinned at Wings. 'Come with me.' She marched towards the biggest hangar set apart from the rest. As they approached, she signalled to two mechanics to roll back the massive doors. Wings hobbled up to stop with a gasp of amazement. Before him in the hangar were two enormous copters. Standing on sturdy tricycle-wheeled undercarriages, their long metal rotors rose above fat fuselages painted with silvery blue scales to resemble Skwid skin. To the rear a pair of pusher rotors sat between twin booms, with endplates forming rudders. Slowly walking round the machines, their large eyes, painted on each side of their bulbous noses and uncannily like a Skwid's eyes, stared down at Wings imperiously.

'Who on earth designed...how long have these...what are the engines?' he blurted out as he reverently ran his hand over their silvery metal bodies.

'We've been developing these for five years,' Iris said proudly. 'We saw the need for transporter flying machines able to carry several passengers. Our people found a couple of old six-cylinder engines of about 450 horsepower that they've tuned to run on biofuel, just like your Skyhook. But come, no more delay – I know you want to reach Paphos before dark.'

Reluctantly tearing himself away, Wings followed Iris to a nearby hangar where Tissy, Dancer and Commander Gator were enjoying a morning snack of coffee and fruit with the pilots and mechanics. Drinking his coffee, Wings could have talked all day about the extraordinary machines he had just seen, but as soon as he'd finished, Gator and Iris, anxious that they wouldn't be flying in the dark, took them up to the radio room at the top of the observation tower to send a message to Commander Croc at Paphos in Cyprus, their next landing. That done, they discussed the route, and much to Wings relief, Gator offered an escort of two of his copters. They all then returned to where Skyhook waited on the tarmac. Her fuel tank full, Wings gratefully thanked Commander Gator, Iris and the mechanics who had checked her over and were able to report no faults found.

Shaking Commander Gator's hand warmly, Wing climbed his pilot's seat. Dancer followed and first checking that Bird was safe in her basket, settled in her seat. Before joining them, Tissy furtively fished out her neck purse. Pressing Nutmeg's amber necklace into Iris' hand, she whispered. 'To add to your beads – in payment for the fuel.' Before Iris could thank her, she scrambled into her seat, and watched with pleasure as Iris, rainbow colours of delight rippling over her scaly skin, hung the necklace around her neck.

Skyhook's engine roared into life and Wings taxied out on to the runway. Lining up behind two copters standing with their rotors spinning, all three aircraft took to the air and, forming an aerial convoy, set a steady course, south-east towards the Mediterranean Sea.

# 12
# RED SEA

Sitting with Ruzanna and Wazim beneath palm trees overlooking a beach, Fin, Lark and Crow heard Quilla's calling. Looking up, they saw him lazily circling high in the cloudless sky, wings spread wide as he rode the thermal air currents. Below him, spread along a sandy shore, lay the tented town of Port Sudan. At a wooden pier jutting out into the jewel-blue sea a line of boats tugged at their moorings in the salty breeze, whilst out at sea more boats bobbed at anchor. Farther along the strand, fishermen were hauling in a net bulging with glittering fish. Above them a flock of gulls screeched and plunged.

Hunkered nearby in rough shore grass, where the hooded buzzards dozed on their saddle perches, the white camels munched on their fodder. From the tent town came sounds of camel trains coming and going, wares being unloaded and loaded. On the pier Sandy and Zaki, looking to book a passage on a barge sailing for the Gulf of Aqaba, could be seen haggling with a mariner.

It had taken them a week to reach Port Sudan. Travelling during the cool hours between sunset and dawn, they followed the Camel Road from the Merga oasis to the Red Sea and Port Sudan, which being on the trade route between the Gulf of Aden in the south and the Gulf of Aqaba in the north, was where cargo vessels stopped to take on goods, supplies and some passengers.

Before they had left Dogon, Malang had told them that they must find berths on a boat bound for the trading city of Eilat through the Gulf of Aqaba. 'When you reach Eilat, you have no choice: you must risk travelling the King's Highway to Jerusalem: a desert land, full of robbers and wild beasts!' he explained grimly. 'With good fortune you will be able to join the safety of one of the mule trains – it is not possible to go by way of the Suez Canal into the Mediterranean as that way is blocked with plastic.'

On the journey from Merga, their pace swift on the white camels, they covered ninety miles a day, sometime meeting lines of camels laden with grey blocks of salt travelling west from the coastal salt pans, or overtaking camel trains east bound with coffee, animal skins and sugar.

During the first part of their journey, they were plagued by frequent sandstorms. The sky deepening to a muddy blue, bruised yellow clouds would rise on the horizon, forerunners of the rapidly approaching storm. Whirling sand invaded everything: blocking noses, filling their clothes, the grit making their lips sore and eyes raw. All they could do was hunker down in what shelter of their kneeling camels offered until the squall passed. Several times Wazim and Zaki had to dig them out from the windblown sand.

The fifth night saw them at the edge of a high escarpment looking out onto a wide flood plain. Moonlit fields spread before them, cut by glittering water courses and lush with growth. In the distance they glimpsed a gleaming body of water: the River Nile. Waiting for first light to descend a steep but well-trodden path zigzagging down the cliffside, they were joined by several camel trains. As the sun rose, they passed through fields and orchards, which after the relentless sand and heat, their eyes drank in the lush growth of salad crops, cabbages, tomatoes, cucumbers, and trees hanging heavy with lemons, oranges, peaches and apples.

At midday they reached the west bank of the Nile and a small town which Ruzanna announced was the trading town of Donga. Here they rested, enjoying hot coffee and freshly baked bread, before taking the flat-bottomed ferry boat across the wide river, joining the camel trains and market gardeners' with their donkeys and mules laden with vegetables and fruits, all on their way Port Sudan. Reaching there as night fell, they found a place to camp by the shore outside the tented town. The next day, whilst they waited with the camels, Sandy and Zaki went to search for a boat that would take them to Port Eilat.

From the bubble in Quilla's eye socket, Bird watched the fishermen on the strand hauling in their catch. 'Tilt your head more so I can see better!' she called.

Quilla didn't respond: the smell of tuna had all his attention.

'Did you hear me Quilla? Go lower so I can see the fishes. Yes! That's better – yum, what a feast!'

Quilla began a lazy descent.

'Hurry!' Bird called impatiently. 'The greedy gulls will get the biggest and best!'

'Hush your squeaking, child! It's hard enough to hear the wails of the fish above the screeching of the gulls! Yes, I smell tuna!'

Skeew! Skeew! Talons extended, he plunged gleefully through the cloud of seabirds to snatch a well fleshed tuna from the arms of a furious fisherman.

Bird's bubble filled with a smell of salt sea fishiness: over the weeks she'd bonded so closely with Quilla she now shared his powerful senses of smell and hearing, both heightened by his blindness.

'Skeew! Skeew!' Quilla cried as he carried off his wildly thrashing prize.

Landing at the water's edge below where the others sat with the camels.

Crow jumped to his feet. 'I goes 'n look at that fish,' he exclaimed excitedly. 'P'raps filch a piece of nice oily flesh for Sparkie.'

Hopping off down the beach, his rat on his shoulder, Mick would have followed if Lark had not commanded: 'Stay!'

'That eagle will bring us much trouble!' Ruzanna exclaimed. 'Fin, you must look after him better! Have you seen the many greedy eyes on the jewels glittering on his breast?'

'The cross should be taken off the bird – even if it kills him!' Wazim growled.

Worried by what Ruzanna and Wazim had said, Fin frowned in thought as he watched Quilla crouched over his tuna tearing at the thick flesh.

Would it kill Quilla if he took the cross from him? Surely the cross would be safer if he took charge of it – hide it again in the drawstring purse, still hung around his neck along with his mother's gold coin and Fescue's ring? But if Quilla was dead, what would happen to Bird?

Since they left Merga, Quilla had grown in strength, his injuries from the attack by the Snoopers healed, his feathers grown back. Now fully recovered, he and Bird were becoming restless, and they'd taken to flying off on long forays for food. These flights had caused both Zaki and Wazim concern.

'Control your eagle or you will lose it! You need a long tether to keep it from flying too far!' Wazim had exclaimed to Fin.

'Aye, and you should tie jesses to its legs!' Zaki added.

He'd turned to Lark scornfully. 'You said you are Fin's ghillie. It is your job to train the eagle!'

Mortified, Lark explained indignantly: 'We don't use eagles for hawking where we come from – they're too rare. When necessary Quilla will do what Fin says alright,' he added. 'So, don't you go interfering! Mind you, if we were back home, I'd have made Fin some kind of shoulder protection – the bird's too big and heavy to carry on the arm pads we use for our falcons and harriers.'

Fin rubbing his shoulder ruefully, said: 'I must admit I'm getting fed up with being punctured by Quilla's talons!'

'That is no problem,' Wazim exclaimed. 'I have a spare leather shoulder guard in my pack.'

From his camel's saddlebag he brought a thick leather pad, and adjusting the straps, fixed it to Fin's shoulder. 'There! You will be able to keep your mighty bird under better control. Also, when we have an opportunity, I will teach you how to hold him to lure.'

Fin had thanked him gratefully and wore the padded guard on the rare occasions Quilla settle on his shoulder. But Wazim's efforts training the eagle proved hopeless; Fin gave the bird's blindness as an excuse.

'Hurry everyone! I have found us passage on a boat,' called Sandy, startling Fin out of his reverie.

He saw Sandy and Zaki striding towards them along the beach.

'A barge is headed for Eilat with silks and carpets, but there is room in the hold for all of us. I have done a deal with Mr Silver, the ship's quartermaster. Goose is leaving as soon as Captain Erikson returns from business in the tent town and would not be pleased if there's any delay. Fin, I'm sorry, but you will have to sacrifice more pearls.'

Ruzanna looked worried. 'Zaki, is this Captain to be trusted? You know too well that some of these mariners are on the look-out for slaves. If not the Delphins, Sandy would fetch a handsome price in the King's Market at Jerusalem.'

'Do not fear Ruzanna. I questioned the quartermaster closely. Captain Erikson is a trader in plustic. He does not go anywhere near Jerusalem. He trades with the rich merchants in Eilat, slave owners who work the Scavs that gather plustic from the Suez Canal, which they barter for jewels, spices, silks and other treasures the Captain brings from the Orient. This time his vessel is far from full, so he will be glad to take paying passengers up the Gulf of Aqaba to Eilat.'

Sandy turned to Fin, Lark and Crow, who'd returned from the beach, Sparkie on his shoulder with a chunk of tuna flesh in his little paws.

'Collect your packs lads and we'll be on our way!'

Crow looked excited. 'I'll be 'trested in this boat. Could be plustic not seen before.'

Lark clipped the top of his head. 'Don't cause trouble, Crow – forget your Scaving days!'

Sniffing indignantly, Crow stuffed Sparkie into his bible bag and shouldering both the bag and his canvas pack, without waiting for the others, set off eagerly for the harbour.

Fin delved into his pack for the Dandrum Sword's scabbard, now almost bare of pearls. He carefully prised off one of the large ones and a handful of smaller ones and put them in a pocket.

'I hope Captain Erikson will only want a few small pearls,' he muttered worriedly, his conscience still pricking at the thought of his family treasure being so used.

'Before you go, you should make plans for the eagle,' Ruzanna said anxiously. 'Should the cross he wears be hidden?'

'As I've said so many times,' Wazim growled, 'the jewel should be taken from the eagle. If it causes injury, you can leave the bird with us – we'll take care of it.'

He looked nervously at Quilla crouched nearby, his crop full after his feast of tuna. Wazim had an uneasy feeling the bird understood what he'd said.

Fin stared aghast at Wazim. 'No! No! It's not just the cross, it's my friend too. If the eagle dies, she'll die too!'

'Fin, what is this strange thing you are saying?' Zaki asked, his old face a picture of puzzlement. 'Where is this friend of yours?' He looked askance at Lark. 'Your only friend I see is Lark here, and I don't think he is dying – he is overflowing with health!'

Looking thoughtful, Ruzanna leaned closed to stare hard at Quilla. 'I can see something in one of the eagle's eye sockets!' she exclaimed. Her voice tense with suspicion she turned to Sandy. 'Iskander, you have not told us the complete truth about this strange blind bird!'

Sandy shot Fin a questioning glance. His expression tense, Fin nodded without speaking.

Once more, just as he'd explained to Suki on their way to M'Bopo's lair, Sandy told Bird's story: the horror of her soul being stolen and how she came to be in Quilla's eye.

'That is why we must get to the Pool of Siloam as soon as possible. It is there that Bird's body and her soul will be reunited and she will be saved from death.'

'But where is this body?' Wazim exclaimed.

'That's on its way too,' Lark snapped. 'My girl and our friends are bringing poor Bird's burnt body to Jerusalem in a special flying machine.' He gazed up searchingly through the palm leaves in the vain hope that a new Skyhook would magically appear with Wings, Tissy and Dancer.

Wazim and Zaki grinned scornfully but Ruzanna peered again into Quilla's eyes and gasped.

'I see her – a tiny figure moving inside the eye. She waved!'

'Yes, that's my Bird,' smiled Fin tears sparkling in his mis-matched eyes.

Sighing, Ruzanna said: 'Fin, I wish you had told me the truth sooner. I have been wondering why you often speak to the eagle! And now you are to leave us, and I cannot help!'

Deeply suspicious, Wazim and Zaki studied the small bubble in Quilla's eye socket.

'There is bad magic with this bird, and this Delphin,' Wazim muttered, looking coldly at Fin. 'Ruzanna, the sooner these people are on their way, the better!'

'Yes!' Zaki said sharply. 'They must not delay! Look, I can see the Goose making ready to raise her sails, she will soon be leaving. Captain Erikson will want his payment too before he allows you aboard.'

Ruzanna frowned angrily at her two companions. 'Wazim and Zaki go— tend to the camels and your buzzards. We must leave here before night falls! Fin, Lark and Sandy I will come to see you sail.'

Lark whistled to Mick. 'I'd better catch up with Crow before he gets into mischief,' he said, grabbing his pack and making for the harbour. As Ruzanna and the others followed, Quilla rose in the air and with lazy wing beats flew above them.

Hurrying along the pier, they could see Goose's crew hauling on ropes raising her two sails. Quilla, now perched on the pad on Fin's shoulder, attracted greedy glances from sailors loading and unloading their barges and one or two stopped work to stare. Roughly jostled by one, with a clutch of fear Fin thought he glimpsed a sickly green gleam in the sailor's eyes.

As they neared Goose, the quartermaster, Mr Silver, a stocky man with curly grey hair and wearing dangling glass earrings, was looking out for them.

Crow started hopping up gangplank.

'HEY, SCAV! Ask permission before you go aboard!' Bellowed a voice.

A stern looking, freckled faced man with greying blond hair tied in a ponytail strode toward them; he was carrying a string bag stuffed with ancient-looking parchment scrolls.

'It's O.K. Cap'n, these people have booked a passage!' called Mr Silver.

Captain Erikson's keen blue eyes narrowed speculatively as he took in Sandy's tall frame, and the sword at his back. He turned his gaze on Fin, Lark and Crow and snorted scornfully.

'What strange collection of bodies have you agreed to take on board this time, Silver? Hope they're not another bunch of escapees from a slave ship?' His lilting accent reminded Fin and Lark of Sandy's northern brogue but more pronounced. Then, at the sight of Ruzanna's dark blue djellaba and scarlet howli, the Captain's expression rapidly changed to respect.

'Yess, Captain!' Ruzanna hissed, her dark eyes flashing angrily. 'As you see I am a White Rider. These people are my friends and I have come to see them safely on their journey.'

The captain bowed politely. 'Well, if they are your friends, ma'am, they are welcome on board.'

He addressed Sandy. 'How will you pay?'

Fin stepped forward. Quilla, still perched on his shoulder, was leaning into his neck, wings drooping, doing his best to look small and bedraggled as instructed by Bird.

Opening his palm, Fin showed Captain Erikson his collection of pearls.

'Will these do as payment?' he asked coldly.

The mariner took the large pearl and held it up to the light. 'Aye, this one will do! Keep the smaller ones to buy food at Eilat.'

He studied Fin curiously. 'Thought at first you were a Scav – but I see now, despite your small stature, beneath your desert wear you could be Delphin.'

He looked at Lark standing glaring at him, ever ready to come to Fin's aid. Mick, tucked under his arm, was snarling. 'And you – small fierce Delphin with your angry dog! Years since I've come across your race – then two together! When we have set sail, I will want to learn how you have all ended up here, so far from home: a Delphin with a ratter, a battered Scav who owns a large leather bag that squeaks loudly, a warrior from the North, but most strange of all, a Delphin with a blind eagle who wears a jewelled cross, and who pays his passage with a rare and large pearl. Get aboard now, we must sail before we lose the wind!'

Grinning with amusement, he turned on his heel and strode up the gangplank. With rushed hugs, they said goodbye to Ruzanna and hurried after him. The gangplank drawn up behind them, Goose's crew cast off, pushing away from the pier with oars. As the barge drifted out into the tidal current, they stood waving to Ruzanna until her slender figure and scarlet howli were lost among the bustle on the pier.

Mr Silver, bare feet padding across the deck, horny toenails tapping a rhythm, came over. 'Come, I will show you to your hammocks!'

He led them down a ladder into the cavernous hold. Lit by sunlight filtering through wooden grids in the deck they saw rolls of carpets and brightly coloured cottons and silks, stacked in silos. The ribbed floor was strewn with scraps of plustic from a previous cargo.

'Your sleeping quarters are down there.' Mr Silver waved to a row of hammocks strung beneath beams in the prow. 'The crew sleep aft.' He gestured to the stern where more hammocks hung, festooned with clothing and other belongings. 'The Cap'n and me sleep in the cabin up on deck. As soon as you've settled, come up for supper – the Cap'n doesn't like waiting.'

He eyed Quilla curiously. 'You'd better keep that bird close. The jewel it wears could tempt some of the more scurvy crew.'

About to leave, he spotted Crow undoing the straps of his bible bag. 'What've you got in there, Scav?' he growled. 'If it's a rat, you'll have to chuck it overboard!'

Crow gave a shriek. 'Nope! Nope! Come look – see Sparkie Two special!' Opening the bag, Sparkie's whiskered face emerged, and Crow reverently lifted him onto his shoulder. Stroking the rat's luxurious thick fur, he took a deep breath and pompously announced: 'Sparkie Two's a West Africky Shaggy Rat, and 'n dangered speechies I'm protecting.'

Frowning, Mr Silver studied the magnificent rat and shrugged his shoulders. 'Well, make sure you keep it under control. If I find it in the sacks of the rice in the food hold, I'll slit its throat.' He turned to Lark. 'Is that ratter of yours any good? I might be needing it's services!'

Lark grinned but didn't say anything. Mr Silver climbed the ladder to the deck.

Sandy looked to where the ship's crew's hammocks were hung. 'Mr Silver is right, some of those sailors look to be scoundrelly thieves. As we shan't be needing our howlis and djellabas whilst we sail best cover your packs with them.'

Unslinging his sword, he laid it down inside the hammock he'd chosen with his pack on top, then spread his howli and djellaba so they covered them. Each choosing a hammock, the others followed his example.

Lark glowered at his hammock. 'Never slept in a hammock before. Fin, if they're uncomfortable, you must ask for your pearl back!'

Fin smiled. 'We've slept on worse beds Lark. I'm thinking of Billy Rope's tarry sacks.'

'Worser still were the nook by Gressil's poo when we were in Contagion!' smirked Crow.

Whilst the others headed for the deck, Crow lingered searching through the scattered remnants of plustic on the floor. Most stuff was familiar to him from his days of scavenging the estuaries of his northern homeland: a faded yellow duck, a small hard green sheet with shredded edges, and what looked like a small plustic knife. But he was attracted by some small discs which reminded him of fish scales. Quickly stuffing the knife and a few discs into a pocket of his shorts, he hurried up the ladder.

Out on deck some of the crew were midship cooking lobsters over a charcoal brazier. Clouds of smoke smelling of garlicky fish billowed around them. Through the smoke Fin could see the men muttering to each other as they eyed Quilla, who had flown to the top of the main mast where he crouched, the cross, part visible through his feathers, glittering in the setting sun. Mick stationed himself in front of the brazier, attempting to ingratiate himself by tapping a sailor's leg with his paw.

In the stern Mr Silver stood at the helm on a high platform making constant adjustments, pulling with both arms as, sails billowing, Goose made sedate progress through the waves. The tents of Port Sudan soon lay behind them, low silhouettes against the setting sun. They were sailing east towards a dark landmass: finally, they had parted from Africa and were sailing for the coast of Arabia. It would take them all night to reach Gulf of Aqaba and Eilat.

On the upper deck the captain sat at a table outside the captain's cabin. He gestured to them, and they climbed a short ladder to join him. On the bench beside him lay his string bag bulging with scrolls and he had one unrolled on the table. Getting up, he held out his hand. 'My name is Leif Erikson.'

Shaking his hand, Sandy said, 'My name is Iskander, but friends call me Sandy. And these are my companions Fin Dandrum, Lark Annunder and Crow who is of the Scav people.'

Captain Erikson nodded to each of them in turn. 'Welcome to my ship. When we have eaten, we shall exchange our stories—' He stopped abruptly to glower indignantly at Sparkie who'd climbed on to Crow's shoulder. Then noticing the red spotted handkerchief tied around the rat's furry neck – the one Crow had worn on board Orca – the Captain's expression softened. Oblivious to being observed, Crow had fished out the plustic pieces he'd found in the hold and was busily setting them out on the table.

Reaching over, Captain Erikson picked up one of the discs and flicked it into the air. 'Once a Scav, always a Scav, eh?' he grinned. 'In the morning you must come to the cabin to see Mr Silver's collection of plustic brushes.'

The Captain turned to the others. 'Over the years of trading plustic, Silver has accumulated a large collection of toothbrushes, hairbrushes and various other brushes which since the Great Dying, have never rotted down!'

Crow squeaked with excitement. 'Much honoured I'd be, Mr Captain to see this c'llection! Proud friends here don't understand about plustic – they scorns my Scaving days!'

Lark picked up the small plustic knife. Testing it's sharpness on his palm, it snapped in two. Grimacing, he said: 'In our northern land, the Scavs dig plustic out of the mud of the river estuaries. It's a filthy job! Ruzanna told us that around here they gather it from the Mediterranean Sea and the Suez Canal.'

Leif nodded. 'Aye, that's right. Plustic is much sought after in the Orient. People there have developed reprocessing machines, shredding, or melting it, converting it into fabrics and other useful products. Dealing in plustic is a lucrative trade. There are some who have become very rich, and not all of them good people! The worst is that despot, King Fakhir of Jerusalem, whose armies of Scav slaves gather the stuff from the Suez Canal. Cruelly treated, their lives are wretched. They bring it to Eilat where King's merchants trade with barge owners such as me. We transport it in bulk through the Red Sea to the port of Aden, where plustic dealers pay us in jewels and spices as well as carpets, silks, and cottons from the Orient. After taking our too small cut, we in turn pay the King's revenue collectors with these riches: they are greedy heartless men!'

Picking up the pieces of the plustic knife Lark had broken, he scowled. 'It is a trade I am not proud of, but I ease my conscience with the thought the Suez Canal is slowly becoming free of plustic. In a few years' time large ships will once more be able to sail through from the Mediterranean. Soon I will have enough money to buy another clipper. I lost my own clipper, Goose off the Cape of Good Hope—' Swiping his sleeve across his eyes, he fell silent for a moment.

Seeing Fin intently studying the rolled-out scroll, intrigued he asked: 'Are you able to read the writing, Fin Dandrum?'

Fin nodded. 'Yes, but I'm no expert.' He turned to Sandy and Lark. 'It's Nordic rune writing. There's a scroll like this in Mossy's shop which he started to teach me to read.' He explained to Lief. 'At home I was apprenticed for a short while to a keeper of books. Trying to read the criss-cross markings was a struggle, but I managed a bit. I would've learned more, but I had to leave my home in hurry—'

Lark squeezed his shoulder. 'Never mind, Fin. You'll get your chance when you're home again. Come on, have a go at reading this scroll.'

In the glow of the setting sun, Fin peered at the first row of small lines running horizontally, upright and at angles across the parchment. Following them with his finger, slowly, with effort, he began reading aloud: '"The Saga of – of – Leif Erikson, son of Erik the Red."' He looked up at Leif in wonder: 'That's your name!'

Captain Erikson hissed excitedly through his teeth. 'This is the scroll I have been searching for!' he gestured to his string bag, 'I bought these scrolls from a trader in Port Sudan. For years I have been looking for the lost diary of my ancient ancestor, Leif Erikson, who is said to have discovered Newfoundland.'

Sandy pointed at a small drawing in the scroll's margin: an eye inside a triangle. 'I have a map with that mark. We used the map to find our way up the River Gambia: I was told it came from the library at Tombouctou.' He got up eagerly. 'I will fetch it for you to see!'

Watching Sandy disappear into the hold Leif remarked thoughtfully: 'Your friend Sandy has remarkable eyes: they have a look of Gaiakin!'

Lark bristled with pride. 'You're right there! As I explained to Ruzanna and her White Riders, Sandy's real name is Lord Iskander. He's part Gaiakin and grew up in Florain!'

Lief whistled in amazement. 'Florain did you say? The Garden in the North? One night, long ago, when I was sailing that coast, I saw the rainbow lights of Florain!' They saw tears glittering in his bright blue eyes. 'Those were my young days: the days of adventuring in my Goose—'

He broke off as Sandy returned with his map.

Carefully spreading the tattered salt-stained map on the table Sandy pointed out the ancient library mark. Leaning in, Lief murmured appreciatively at the map's beautifully drawn illustrations.

'You travelled this river?' he asked, running his finger along the blue line of the Gambia river meandering eastwards.

Yes, we were making for the Fouta plateau, where the River Gambia rises. It is where the Gaiakins first made their enchanted garden – abandoned when the Great Dying struck, and now full of evil. We were pursuing a thief who had stolen a precious treasure from us.'

Eyes narrowed, Leif studied his guests. 'There is much to wonder about you all! But I shall tell you my story first, and then you must tell me yours, how you came to be chasing after a stolen treasure. We shall be talking well into the night—'

Seeing Mr Silver carrying a tray of mugs and plates from the stern, he broke off to exclaim. 'Ah, the food is ready!' Rolling up his scroll he stuffed it back in his string bag. 'The light is too poor now to read. We shall continue in daylight if you are willing?' He looked at Fin who nodded.

Mr Silver was followed by three crewmen: one with a large dish of roasted lobsters swimming in a fiery red sauce, another carrying a platter piled high with flatbread. The third shouldered a heavy-looking calabash which, after pouring mugs of palm wine, he left on the table. Trailing jauntily behind the cooks was Mick with a whole lobster in his jaws. Soon, from under the table came the sound of crunching shellfish.

Supper over, platters piled with empty lobster shells and splashes of red sauce on the table, they sat back replete. Crow, his head slumped against the ship's rail, overcome with palm wine, snored peacefully. Sparkie, who'd filched some lobster shells, had joined Mick under the table from where crunching noises grew ever louder.

Goose's sails gently billowing in the soft wind, her prow cutting a shallow wave through the starlit glittering sea, the helmsman had little work to keep her on course for the Arabian coast. Midships, Mr Silver sat on deck with the crew eating his lobster supper, a tall mug of palm wine by his bare feet.

Quilla suddenly flew down from the mast and perched on the prow rail, making everyone start. Glowering at the great eagle, Leif passed around the calabash. His face, lit by the soft glow of the oil lamp, looked older than they had first thought.

'It is time to tell you my story,' he announced.

'As I have said – I have not always been a plustic trader with this old barge. Once I was a spice trader and sailed the world. My homeland is Iceland, but it is many years since I have been there! So, I was interested to learn that you too are all Northerners.

'Of particular interest to me is that you, Fin and Lark, are of Delphinkind: in my youth I came across Delphins.'

Fin and Lark sat up eagerly, keen to hear his story.

'When I was a youth, I went adventuring with my uncle on the trail of our ancestor, Leif Erikson. We sailed across the wide Atlantic Ocean to the islands of Newfoundland, reputed to be where Erikson had landed. We hoped to learn of his history from the Inuit people, but their dialect was difficult to understand, and we gleaned little information. It was when we came to Fogo Island that we met a people, very different to the Inuits. Speaking fluent Common Language, they told us they were Delphin.

'Their leader Tunny Long Beak said their clan, Stenella, was named after the Atlantic dolphins. They were eager to learn if we knew of any Delphin clans in our part of the world, but we told them we had never come across the Delphin race. They made my uncle and myself welcome and we spent a month with them. Does your Delphin clan originate from these people?'

Excitedly Lark turned to Fin who shook his head.

'No, our clans in Brightdale are descended from river dolphins who originated in the Amazon jungle.'

They listened in admiration as, after some thought, his eyebrows in a deep V of concentration, he quoted a page about Delphins from the Polychronicon of Zagzagel.

'The cetacean superfamily Platanistoidea, have adaptations to facilitate fish catching: a long, forceps-like beak with numerous small teeth, broad flippers to allow tight turns, small eyes, and unfused neck vertebrae to allow the head to move in relation to the body.'

He smiled whimsically. 'But of course, those creatures lived millions of years before anything like us Delphins appeared.'

Lief looked at him curiously. 'Fin Dandrum, who are you? Now I have got to know you, I notice, as well as Delphin, you have a look of Rom about you.'

It was Lark who answered. 'Aye, our Fin's special alright! For a start, his dad was Head of our Delphin clans! And his mum's a Rom – a holy woman who lives on Cuthbert's Island not far from Holy Island on our north-eastern coast.

Lief hissed through his teeth. 'Your mother is the Anchorite of Cuthbert's Island? On my travels I often called at Holy Island to meet with my friend, a man who made flying machines—'

Lark interrupted with a whoop. 'You know Wings? He's our friend too! It's him we're hoping to meet at Jerusalem – he's bringing my girl Tissy and our friend Dancer in his new flying machine. They're taking Fin's girl to the Pool of Siloam – her poor burnt body has to be healed there.'

Lief frowned at his guests. 'This is a strange story. Surely you must know about the Pool of Siloam? About the rumour of the monster god that lurks there?'

'When we set out on our journey, we did not know,' Sandy replied, 'but we have learnt from Ruzanna that the Pool is now forbidden. She did not mention that there is a god that lurks there!'

Lief grinned. 'It is a foolish story. One thought up by King Fakhir the Great, the present King's grandfather, about the Pool which is hidden in a garden outside the City walls. The god M'Benga lurks there in its depths in the form of a giant squid. M'Benga is supposed to guard the sluice gate at the bottom of the Pool. This gate controls the flow of water to the underground streams that feed the City's wells. If anyone dares to swim there, M'Benga would be become so angry that he would close the gate and the City's wells would dry out, and Jerusalem would crumble into dust and be blown away by the wind.

'The King keeps M'Benga appeased by sacrificing a goat to him every new moon. M'Benga's hideous face is said to appear out of the dark waters, and snatching the unfortunate goat in its long tendrils, disappears back into the depths – or so the more stupid people of Jerusalem say, including some of my crew!' He nodded scornfully at his crew sitting around the brazier drinking. 'They will believe anything!'

'But I reckon the real reason the Pool and the gardens are forbidden is commercial! Once, any ill person was allowed to bathe in the water, and indeed many were healed! But by the time the present King, Fakhir the Proud, came to the throne the Pool had become so polluted there was a danger the sluice would become blocked. Then the Pool, which is fed by the Spring of Gihon, would overflow, flooding not only Fakhir's precious olive and date groves in the Kidron Valley, but more vital to the people, cut off the water supply to the City.

'But tell me, why you did not go with Wings and your friends directly to the Pool? Why instead have you gone so far out of your way, to Africa and across the Sahara?'

'It's because of the Chi Rho – the jewelled cross the eagle wears,' Fin replied. 'It has healing power. Once it belonged to me and I was going to use it to heal my girl—'

'But Queen Mab stole it!' Lark interrupted. 'Flew away with it to Africa! And, and Mr Mossy, who's an angel you know, told us that we must get it back from her and take it along with the eagle to the Pool of Siloam, so, so Bird could have her soul and body put back together—'

Sandy, watching Lief's surprised expression as Lark's garbled story tumbled out, intervened. Yet again he recounted what befell Bird, the flooding of Gressil's Compound, Mab taking the cross, their pursuit after her to Africa and then Quilla rescuing the cross from her, their adventures in the jungles of Africa and their journey to the Red Seat.

When tale was told, Leif turned his gaze on Quilla who had flown onto Fin's shoulder. Shaking his head in disbelief, he leaned across the table and peered into Quilla's eye. Putting out his hand to touch the cross gleaming amongst Quilla's feathers, Quilla rose clumsily into the air.

'Skeew! Skeew!' he shrieked, flapping back to perch on the prow in a threatening stance, wings wide, head thrust forward.

Lief got up from the table and began pacing the deck, muttering to himself as he cast nervous glances at the great bird. Minutes passed as the others watched him, perplexed.

Then he spoke, his face set in determination: 'My mind is made up! I shall abandon this clumsy old barge and the plustic trade and go with you to Jerusalem.'

Early next morning they reached the Straits of Tirana and entering the Gulf of Aqaba, they sailed for Eilat. Last night they had slept well their hammocks, despite the raucous snoring from the ship's crew at the far end of the hold.

Sandy, Lief and Mr Silver were at the table drinking sweet mint tea and deep in talk. A piece of parchment lay spread out in front of them, a pot of ink and some quills beside it. With advice from Sandy, Lief had drawn up a sale agreement for Mr Silver to purchase Goose. From under the table there came crunching. Mick, sent early that morning by Lark to the ship's stores on a ratting foray, had covered himself in glory by catching six rats, earning himself an extra meaty goat bone. Nearby, Quilla was hungrily gulping down a whole rat; several more lay on the deck before him. Crow had left Sparkie Two below in his hammock, safely strapped in the bible bag with a ripe mango.

Eating a breakfast of bananas, Fin, Lark and Crow stood in the prow watching the shipping go by, clippers, schooners and, the most numerous, the flat decked, lanteen-rigged barges laden with plustic. Watching a convoy sail past they were amazed by the skill of the wiry Scav crews controlling their clumsy boats, some of which looked to be perilously overloaded. The first barge carried what appeared to be balls of fishing net impenetrably tangled with skeins of nylon line, spiked with pieces of bleached wood, rusted metal and plustic of all shapes and sizes. The second, so overladen it was in danger of sinking, was piled high with heaps of greying plustic sheeting. On the third sat a mountain of empty plustic containers, several of which, plucked by gusts of wind from under loosely flapping tarpaulins, bobbed along in the barge's wake. The ballooning bags floating on the water reminded them of the giant jelly fish, known as Portuguese Men of War, they'd seen from Orca when sailing the Atlantic.

Fin shook his head sadly. 'There must still be a lot of clearing to be done before anything large can sail through Suez Canal.'

'Aye, it's disgusting the filth and rubbish they left us from a thousand years ago!' growled Lark.

Crow, his one eye roving excitedly as he studied the debris floating past, squeaked indignantly: 'No stupid Delph! This stuff good! Much fresher and cleaner'n the muddy tat in Scav Land back home!'

An urgent cry from the lookout aloft made them start.

'Mr Silver, sir! Eilat harbour fast approaching!' shouted a crewman.

Bent over the parchment, an ink-filled quill in his gnarled fingers, Mr Silver had just signed the sales agreement. Flinging down his quill and vaulting over the rail he strode down the deck to take the helm, at the same time shouting orders to the crew. As one, they leapt into action, some hauling down the sails, others putting out oars to begin rowing. Lief and Sandy joined the others in the prow to watch the approach to Eilat.

Set in a wide bay with a backdrop of bare rocky hills, to the west of the city the magnificent gold domed palaces of the rich merchants stood along a marbled waterfront, their arched windows staring imperiously out to sea, tops of cypress and cedar trees showing above the high walls enclosing their luxurious gardens. To the east lay a jumble of humbler dwellings, accessed by a warren of narrow streets, where the lesser traders, servants and Scav slaves lived.

In the harbour a row of wooden jetties lined with cranes jutted out into deep water. At the end of each jetty a wooden sign on a pole indicated to mariners at which pier they should unload their cargo. Two jetties were dedicated to unloading goods: salt, coffee, sugar, fresh vegetables and fruit from the Nile valley, and bales of silk and carpets from the Orient, including the carefully guarded metal-strapped strong boxes containing the precious perfumes, jewels, silver, gold and pearls destined for the King's court and the rich merchants.

The remaining two jetties were where the Scav crews unloaded their harvest of plustic from their barges onto waiting trollies, which once piled high, teams of other slave Scavs would trundle them to giant warehouses fronting the harbour, to be sorted before being bought by local merchants or stored until reloaded on to barges such as Goose for shipping to the port of Aden for bartering with traders in the Orient. Overseers armed with vicious-looking whips supervised the Scav slaves, any slave who stumbled receiving a savage lashing.

Seeing a little Scav being unmercifully whipped across his already scarred back when he'd upset his trolley load, filled Lark with fury.

'Warty wemmers – can't the man see the bag of bones is too small to control that great load! Given the chance, I'd give the devil a taste of his own whip!'

'Aye, it's grim,' agreed Leif, 'But such is the King's power, no one dare challenge the bully.'

Crow let out a howl. 'Want jool! Mr Sandy tell eagle give me my jool!'

Lark patted his patchy bald head. 'There, there Crow lad – you know you can't have it!'

Sniffing loudly, Crow sunk on the deck behind the gunwale. 'Better me not watch nasty men,' he muttered.

Expertly steering Goose through the crowded shipping, Mr Silver headed for a free mooring at the jetty signposted for Oriental goods. Tying up, the crew set about unloading Goose's cargo of carpets, cottons, and silks. Two of the fiercest looking sailors, armed with cutlasses, helped carry Leif's strong box ashore. Inside were the jewels, pearls and coins he had received in payment at Port Aden for his last load of plustic. Mr Silver, now the owner, intended to store the box in one of the strong rooms rented out by Eilat merchant bankers. Hidden in a money belt under Leif's clothes, were the diamonds and garnets Mr Silver had paid him for Goose.

Sandy, Fin, Lark and Crow went below to pack their gear. Warned by Lief that the journey along the King's Road would be hot and dusty, once more they donned desert clothes. Under his djellaba, Sandy secured his sword in its sheath to his back.

'Just hope I don't need this in a hurry,' he remarked wryly.

Fin strapped Quilla's leather perch to his shoulder, then pulled on his djellaba. They all watched intrigued as Crow got out the pirate outfit he'd worn when guarding Orca at Tangier: striped tee shirt, red spotted handkerchief around his neck and small cutlass proudly tucked into his belt. Putting on his small djellaba, slinging his pack over his shoulder and stuffing Sparkie II into his bible bag, he announced importantly he was ready.

On deck, Mr Silver and the crew were making an emotional farewell to their Captain. Leif wore a black howli and a dark blue djellaba covered his large frame and at his waist, a business-like axe hung from a leather belt. In his pack on his back, as well as his clothes, he'd also packed the precious roll of parchment telling the story of his ancestor, Leif Erikson.

Giving Mr Silver a last handshake, he turned to his charges and studied their desert gear critically. Observing Quilla on Fin's shoulder and Mick looking out from the front of Lark's djellaba, he smiled briefly but made no comment. Giving a farewell glance around Goose's deck, he turned firmly on his heel and descended the gangplank; the others hurried after him. Striding along the jetty, Leif had a spring in his step.

Passing the warehouses on the harbour front, they glimpsed inside food stuffs, fresh produce, bolts of silks and cottons, rolls of carpets and various ornamental objects, reminding Lark of the square at Tangier where Fin had nearly lost his head.

Coming to the last warehouse where slave Scavs were trolleying plustic inside, to their horror they saw Crow had drawn his small cutlass and was marching purposefully towards one of the whip-wielding overseers who, fortunately, had his back to them.

'Hoy Crow! Come back!' Lark called.

Sandy strode to the rescue, scooping up Crow and bringing him back struggling under his arm.

Dumping him down, his midnight eyes flashing, Sandy said icily: 'That Crow, was very stupid. Do you want to get us locked up or killed?'

Hanging his head, Crow muttered his apology. 'Sorry, Mr Sandy. Couldn' stop meself.'

Steering well clear of the overseer they entered the warehouse. Pushing their way through the throng, passing booth after booth, they were amazed by the huge amount of plustic on display. In one booth, piles of discoloured plustic sheeting almost reached the roof. In another, different shapes and colours of broken nuggets filled great hoppers. Crow fizzed with excitement, and Lark had to keep a firm hold of him.

'Not like the Scav's stalls at Watersmeet market,' Fin remarked to Lark with a smile.

Lark laughed, 'Yeah, these mountains of plustic makes our muddy Scav traders' piles of stuff look right povvy!'

A heady scent of perfume drew them to a booth crowded with chattering women. Young and old, plump and thin, they were all gaudily dressed in brightly coloured floaty garments, faces heavily made-up with garish lipstick, rouge and kohl painted around their eyes. As well as a profusion of jangling, glittering jewellery, they had decorated themselves with gaudy coloured plustic, strings of plustic necklaces, brooches, and bracelets.

A large sign above the booth announced: FRANGIPANI'S EMPORIUM – BESPOKE PLUSTIC FOR THE LADY OF FASHION.

Inside the booth, spread out on tables were baskets of plustics of all shapes: lozenges, discs, square shapes, stars, curly strips, small, coloured bricks. From a striped canopy hung plustic fashioned into garlands or long chains of flowers, animals, and birds. Behind the display tables, women seated on stools were working on more plustic: polishing, cutting, shaping, stringing.

Waiting impatiently, Lief was about to move on when a shout from the back of the booth stopped him. From behind a tottering mound of plustic bottles emerged a plump Scav. Wearing a floor length scarlet robe, its voluminous folds caught round his waist by a jewelled gold belt, on his head he sported a tall green plustic bottle festooned with numerous links of gold chain hanging from the stopper.

'Mr Erikson, sir! Mr Erikson, sir!' called the Scav, bottles bouncing on the floor after him. 'Surely, you not pass me by!'

Bowing obsequiously, his links of gold chains trembling, he looked up at Lief. 'Surely you did not forget our agreement. A bolt of wild silk in exchange for my best extra clear bottles – specially put aside for your Indian customer? I dreads what the Lady Azure will do to me if she don't have her silk!'

Lief smote his brow in apology. 'I'm sorry Lord Frangi – I'd forgotten!' He grinned. 'I have to tell you that my plustic dealing days are over now! I've sold my Goose and the business to Mr Silver. From now on he'll be dealing with you. I'm off to Jerusalem with my friends here.' Lief gestured to the others.

Looking at Lief sorrowfully, Frangipani shook his head. 'You be missed Mr Erikson.

Turning to Sandy, Fin, Lark and Crow, he studied them speculatively, first looking up in awe at Sandy towering above him then staring scornfully at Fin, Lark and Crow, their small forms hidden beneath desert clothing. Taking in Quilla perched on Fin's shoulder, and the cross gleaming among the golden feather on Quilla's breast, they saw a greedy glint in his narrowed eyes.

'An' what would you be doing being friends with the likes of these dodgy types hidin' under their howlis, Mr Erikson? Look like 'scaped slaves to me!'

Lark stepped forward angrily. 'We're not slaves! Sandy here is a King of the North, and Fin and I are of Delphin kind.'

'And I's a proper independent Scav dealer,' Crow added indignantly, 'an no miserable little slave!'

'You've been told alright, Mr Frangipani!' smiled Sandy, his midnight blue eyes twinkling beneath his howli. 'As Captain Erikson has explained, we are trying to get to Jerusalem to find the Pool of Siloam for – for the healing waters. Lief is guiding us.'

Stroking his chin thoughtfully, Frangipani said. 'So, headin for 'Rusalem are you? Wantin to go to Pool of Siloam? Surely you know that not allowed! Mr Sandy, best you find me sister – she'll help you! She head of our Palmer clan and mighty powerful in 'Rusalem. Go to The Warrens – ask for Mistress Bougainvillea.'

Furtively glancing around, he rummaged in a pocket. Bringing out a small gold painted plastic disc he pressed it into Sandy's hand. 'This be a pass into The Warren – don't lose it. Keep it safe and hidden.'

Looking at the disc Sandy saw, scratched in the gold paint, the one word: Palmer. First bowing to Frangipani, with elaborate care he tucked it in a shirt pocket beneath his djellaba.

Frangipani turned to Lief. 'Mr Erikson, you be wanting a Mule Train to take you to 'Rusalem? Go to Zakary the Mule Master – mention me name – he'll see you right.'

He gestured to tall archways at the far end of the warehouse leading into the town's main square. Beyond, high barren hills could be seen rising in the distance.

Thanking Frangipani profusely, out in the square they found a market crowded with traders. In a plaza at the market's centre, lines of mules waited patiently in the hot sun, some of their owners touting for custom, others, their team hired, supervising the loading of the animals with people and luggage.

Zakary the Mule Master was easily found. Above his line of mules, a sign proclaimed in big bold letters: ZAKARY'S MULES – STRONG AND RELIABLE.'

They took the squat, hook nosed, fierce eyed man standing below the sign to be Zakary. His complexion deep olive, his thick beard dark and curly, he was dressed in a black djellaba and a white howli. He was in animated discussion with a tall arrogant looking man in long white robes, wearing a red and white striped cloth on his head held by a silk cord; they were to find that these garments were common attire for the important men of Jerusalem. With much head shaking Zakary and the man were gesticulating to a group of four women huddled together by a stack of bags and boxes. Covered from head to foot by their garments with only a slit for their eyes, two of the women wore silk in soft shades and the other two, their maids, wore simple cream coloured cotton.

After more shrugging and grumbling a deal was struck and payment, a small, heavy cloth bag, handed over. The arrogant man shepherded his women down the line of mules, picking out animals that looked most docile, whilst muleteers loaded their bags and boxes on to two of the biggest mules.

Zakary turned to his new customers, first considering Lief and Sandy, it seemed approvingly, before eyeing Fin, Lark and Crow suspiciously. Once again, they realised that the man thought they could be escaped slaves hiding beneath their desert wear.

Noticing his fierce eyes greedily studying Quilla, Fin stepped forward, asking firmly: 'Are you Mr Zakary? Lord Frangipani told us to mention his name. My companions and I wish to travel to Jerusalem with your Mule Train.'

Zakary, hearing the name Frangipani, relaxed slightly, though it was obvious from the amused look he shot Lief and Sandy, that he was surprised it was Fin and not one of them who had approached him.

'And how will you pay, little man?'

Ignoring the sneer, Fin took out the last of his small pearls and held them in his open palm for the Mule Master to see. 'Will you accept payment in pearls?'

Taking one, Zakary gently squeezed it between his fingers. 'Aye, pearls will do.' Pulling his thick beard through his fingers, he looked calculatingly beneath lowered eyebrows at the five of them. 'Six pearls for three mules is the deal: two of my biggest mules for the men, with you and the other small man riding with them. One small mule for the Scav and your water, food and gear.'

Lief, looking down from his impressive height at Zakary, said coolly: 'Mr Zakary, my friend Frangipani with whom I have traded for many years said you were an honest dealer! These people are famous in their Northern lands and should be dealt with fairly. If we must bring our own supplies, I say six pearls to include two of your largest mules, as well as three small mules for my two Delphins friends and Mr Crow the famous Scav here!'

Realising he'd met his match Zakary gave a resigned sigh. 'It is agreed! But as you have not brought your own supplies, I will need another two pearls for food and water.'

Lief snorted. 'We'll buy our own food, thank you! Surely, you don't expect us to pay for feed for your mules, I know that is your responsibility!'

'Aye, go and buy food then – nothing heavy mind. We shall be leaving in an hour, so make sure you return by then.'

Picking out six of the rounder, smoother pearls from Fin's palm, he carefully deposited them in an inside pocket, before turning away to deal with his next customer.

After a quick discussion, Lief and Lark went off to buy food from the market stalls, leaving the others to choose suitable mules. Zakary, intending to dictate which mules they could choose, found himself outwitted again. He could only stand by, first with annoyance and then with respect as Sandy chose the animals, going along the line, gazing into mule eyes and gently opening mouths to inspect teeth. Fin and Crow watched in amazement. It was as if he was able to charm the notoriously obstinate animals.

Gesturing to the five mules he'd picked, Sandy said: 'These two big john mules will suit Lief and myself and these three small hinnies will be suitable for the Delphins and the Scav – they have indicated to me that their master treats them reasonably well.'

Sandy's beaming gaze turning little Zakary's knees to jelly, drawing the mules out of the line, he mutely handed over the leading ropes.

Lief and Lark soon returned, Lief carrying several canvas bags of dried food: sticky sweet dates, wrinkled salty olives, dark, leathery carob pods, a bag of coarse grain flour, and a plustic bottle of cloudy dark green olive oil. Lark carried in his arms a small metal barbeque stove on top of a sack of charcoal, with the straps of five water canteens slung over his shoulder. Mick trotted behind, jaws firmly gripping a chicken leg he'd found under a meat stall.

Water canteens filled from a nearby pump, food bags strapped to their saddles – Lark in charge of the charcoal and barbeque – they mounted the mules. Sandy and Lief leading, Fin behind with Quilla on his shoulder, then Lark with Mick inside his jerkin, lastly Crow and his bible bag with Sparkie II inside, they joined the mule train. Their travelling companions included two lone men, and a family: a father, a mother, several children and their servants.

The last to be ready was the man with his four women. With indignant screeches the women were heaved into their saddles by Zakary's assistants.

Finally, the mule train set off, Zakary at the head, holding a large parasol above his head and riding a tall grey mule. It was a little after noon and the heat of the day was at its height.

Gazing along the road winding away into the distant hills, Lark thought of Tissy. Had she, Wings and Dancer arrived in Jerusalem? Were they waiting for them at the Pool of Siloam? Was she safe? Whilst they shopped in the market, Leif had told him that Jerusalem lay over a hundred miles to the north: it was still so far!

# 13
# KING'S HIGHWAY

Above the Negev Desert Quilla rode the cloudless sky, wings spread wide, quartering the barren rock-strewn wastes. Looking down, Bird searched for something he could eat. Not even the smallest creature moved. They'd been flying for an hour and Quilla was very hungry.

'Quilla, fly lower – my eyesight isn't like an eagle's!'

Languidly Quilla circled downwards, trying to conserve precious energy.

'That's better! Tilt your head from side to side,' Bird commanded, peering keenly into a patch of stunted mallow trees where a small herd of gazelle were pulling off the purple blossom. The sun caught the jewelled cross swinging from Quilla's breast, temporarily blinding her. Suddenly she spotted a big Monitor lizard scuttling out of the undergrowth.

'A giant lizard – quick, quick, dive!' she called.

'Skeew! Yes! I can smell it.'

Quilla plunged and talons scraping the sandy rock scooped up the lizard. Its tail lashing against his legs, climbing steeply he headed to where the Dead Sea shimmered in the heat, and where the mule train was camped on its shores. Gliding above the sea, she saw Lark and Fin on their backs floating on the salty surface.

When Quilla had first flown over the Dead Sea, Bird had hoped to spot fish for him, but soon discovered to her dismay why it was called dead: the water was so salty, nothing could live in it.

Fin saw a momentary flash as the sun caught the cross. 'Quilla's back!' He called to Lark bobbing dreamily his eyes closed.

Rolling over, feet finding the sandy bottom, they waded through the thick viscous water and settled on the hot sand. They didn't bother drying themselves, the sun's heat soon turned the salty water into a crust coating their shorts and bodies.

Wings outstretched, Quilla flew low overhead, a large lizard squirming in his talons. With a heavy thud he landed close by and began attacking the still writhing lizard, tearing hungrily at its flesh. Looking away in disgust, Lark observed the agonised look on Fin's face as he watched Quilla eating.

Lark had noticed recently that the whispered talk between Fin and Bird had become heated disagreements as Bird argued that she and Quilla should leave them and fly on ahead to Jerusalem. And lately he'd spotted one or two of the muleteers showing sly interest in the cross, greedy looks in their eyes. One had foolishly sidled up to Quilla to stroke his head, only to be seen off by a lunge of the great bird's fearsome beak.

He thought about what Fin had confided in him: that Bird was becoming worriedly conscious of her body, that it was rapidly weakening. She feared she might be dying, sometimes having a sensation of desperate thirst, at other times sharp straw scratching her face or rough hands grabbing her.

Turning back to see Quilla gulping the last remnant of bloodied lizard, Lark scowled. Perhaps it would it be best if the eagle did fly off: he would get to this Pool of Siloam much quicker. And with any luck Tissy, Wings and Dancer might have already got there. Yet again, as he'd done so many times, he glanced up at the sky, hoping against hope, to see the outline of an aeroplane: as ever the sky was empty.

He gazed miserably at the arid land around him, bare of habitation apart from the occasional remnant of a crumbling building succumbed to the desert. The only sign of wildlife was a wheatear bird sitting mourning on a rock, its black and white plumage stark against the backdrop of the sea where crusty mounds of salt had accumulated. Squinting into the distance, he saw undulating hills curving away into the setting sun, their ochre shades dotted with patches of dusty green scrub. The only fresh water was from a river flowing into the sea farther along the shore, its mouth thickly fringed with reeds, and where presently Mick was causing trouble among the nesting water birds. He'd learned from Leif that the river was the Jordan, and that the King's Highway continued along its route northwards towards Jerusalem.

Sounds of laughter turned his gaze to where Crow was chatting to a muleteer stroking Sparkie's luxuriant fur. Sandy and Leif, lounging in the sun after their swim, looked on in amusement. Lark had noticed that the rat was slyly intelligent. Amongst other tricks, Crow had trained him to chew through the thick grass tying the bunches of bananas.

Higher up from the shore, where a camp had been set up for the night in the shade of a group of Acacia trees, Lark saw the arrogant man in the red and white headdress standing glowering as his wives shrieked at their maids who were rummaging in the luggage searching for some missing items. Nearby Zakary and his muleteers were tending to their animals in the shade of cliffs where a path zigzagged precariously up to the dark mouths of some caves.

Plodding on their mules, it had taken two days to reach this place. Several times their train was nearly driven off the road by armed soldiers on horseback galloping on urgent King's business. They soon came to dread the sound of iron shod hooves ringing on the road's flagstone surface. Last night they had camped at Ein Yahav, the only well along the King's Highway providing enough water for mule trains.

They were joined there by another mule train with twice as many mules as Zakary's. The mean faced owner, Levi the Tall, spoke with an irritating whistle through a gap in his top front teeth. Like Zakary, with whom there was fierce rivalry, his main business was providing safe transport for people travelling to and from Jerusalem. That evening mutual hostility had hung heavy in the hot air. This morning, determined to beat his rival to the Dead Sea and claim the best campsite for the night, Zakary had woken his customers early, and they were well on their way before Levi and his customers had even started reloading their many mules.

That evening in their camp by the Dead Sea, supper over, there was still no sign of Levi's train. Despite their bitter rivalry, Zakary stood for a while at the edge of camp gazing worriedly back down the road to Ein Yahav.

Yesterday ...

In the bay of Port Sudan, the schooner, Spice Girl proudly rode at anchor, her glamourous mermaid figurehead gazing disdainfully over the humbler barges and fishing boats bobbing around her. The pink beams from her riding lights rippling across the dark water, from her sleek, oyster-shell white hull wafted fragrances of cloves and cinnamon.

On the upper deck Captain Constanza and her three female officers were sipping tequilas after their fish supper; Constanza's cook Yousif – her treasure and the envy of the other spice traders – had excelled himself with his poached John Dory and spiced mango salsa. From the deck below came the rumble of male voices where the crew sat midship around a charcoal brazier. A calabash of palm wine passing around, the men were grumbling about their supper. To the sailors the fancy cooking lacked substance: they would rather have a hearty octopus stew with plenty of rice and chillies. Dark eyes flashing, Constanza frowned down at the circle of scowling faces; she saw trouble brewing. She would have to keep a close eye on her sailors: the men didn't like a woman bossing them. Ideally, she'd have preferred an all-woman crew, but good female sailors were hard to find.

A woman in her late forties, the years of being the captain of a large sailing vessel had taken their toll on Constanza. Still fiercely beautiful, grey streaked her glossy black hair and there were the lines around her dark eyes from constant squinting at distant horizons. The owner of the schooner, Spice Girl, she made a rich living trading nutmeg, mace, cinnamon and cloves from the Moluccas islands, selling the spices to the wealthy merchants of Eilat.

Turning back to pour herself another tequila, she realised her three companions were arguing. In the middle of the table stood a small blue enamelled pot. From it wafted the pungent odour of musk. The musk had been bought at a knock down price by plump faced, blond Ulrika, the ship's quartermaster. Ulrika's air of vagueness hid an ability to drive a keen bargain; she intended to sell the musk at a handsome profit to perfumiers at Eilat catering for merchants' fat wives and concubines.

'It's disgusting. I want nothing to do with it!' growled Bojka, the ship's carpenter, a big bony woman with untidy iron-grey hair, her callused hand pushing the jar toward the table's edge. Ulrika snatched it from her reach.

'Neither do I!' exclaimed Eniola, the ship's surgeon, her brown eyes filling with tears. 'It's dreadfully cruel, how they collect the musk by torturing the poor creatures!' Princess Eniola was descended from the royal family of an Ashanti tribe and knew about the practice of collecting musk from African civets. Once famed for her beauty she had turned down marriage offers from kings and princes to become a skilled doctor.

Constanza smiled. 'I think this time, Ulrika, you've lost your common sense – you let yourself be distracted by perfumier Mustafa's curling waxed moustache and his promise of marriage!'

'Aye!' grinned Bojka, pointing a thick finger in the direction of the cabin boy dozing by the gunwale, empty tequila glass beside him. 'Everyone knows Mustafa would be more interested in Harry there!'

Saved by Constanza from a slave market, and more mascot than a servant, he looked up in alarm, his big blue eyes wide. Embarrassed, he sidled away to hide behind a sack of cinnamon bark.

Lulled by the murmur of talk from the captain's table, the sweet smell of cinnamon filling his nostrils, his eyelids began to droop again.

He was startled awake by a throat pinching stench of strong vinegar and the sound of shrill buzzing. Wondering if he was dreaming, he blinked up at the night sky: an enormous flying insect had appeared above the ship. Its iridescent wings gleaming in the moonlight, its fat body striped yellow and black, it could have been a giant wasp, or perhaps a hornet.

It hovered for a moment then dived on the crew staring up in astonishment. Pressing into the shadows behind his sack, Harry watched in stunned horror as from its backside a volley of long needle stings shot down, ping, ping, ping, puncturing faces and arms. Howling in agony, as one the terrified crew leapt overboard, some frantically swimming for the distant shore, one or two others vanishing into the murky deep.

Flinging their tequila glasses aside, Constanza, Ulrika, Eniola and Bojka rushed to the cabin, and emerged whirling silver cutlasses above their heads. Leaping up, slashing at the dangling insect legs, the monster hovered just beyond their reach. Its drone a taunting hum: ping, ping, ping, ping, firing a deadly salvo of stings, the four women slumped to the deck.

Harry knew he should get away, leap overboard after the sailors, but shock rooted him to his hiding place. His eye was caught by movement nearby: in the cold white moonlight he made out the dark shape crawling up over the gunwale. Feebly flapping its leathery wings, a huge bat crouched on the deck gasping painfully for breath. Then came more thrumming. The bat's ugly face looked up expectantly. Out of the night two more huge hornets appeared. Flying side by side, a ragged bundle dangled from their legs. At first Harry couldn't make out the shape. Then it dawned on him: it was a butterfly, a giant butterfly! Bedraggled wings drooping, head lolling, the butterfly had the body of a woman, her slender form covered in velvety fur. The hornets gently lowered her to the deck. Her silken wings crumpling around her, moaning the butterfly woman clutched her side – Harry saw wet blood seeping through her fingers.

She spoke, her voice feeble: 'Gressil … Gressil … I cannot go on … I'm fading! Will we never get my … my… healing treasure …?'

Heaving itself up, the bat dragged its bulk to her side. Clearing its throat with a rough phlegmy cough, a soothing voice floated out from deep within.

'Courage, my beloved. Courage!' purred the voice. 'We make good progress! Drawing ever closer! This ship will take us: she is swift and will easily catch up with the lumbering barge! But first, a new body—' claws clattering on the deck, the bat swung around and lumbered to where the four dead women lay, glittering needle stings sticking from their bodies.

Afterwards, no matter how often in his mind he revisited the horror, Harry never fully comprehended what happened next.

From out of the bat's mouth curled a dark mist. Seeping along the deck towards Constanza, gathering speed, it swirled around her lifeless head and with a rush disappeared into her gaping mouth. Constanza's body writhed and squirmed, whimpered then groaned, the groan turning to a snarl of triumph as the shapely female that had been Constanza rose to its feet: Harry did not know it, but Lord Gressil had taken on a new body. M'Bopo's mangy hulk shuddered violently and lay still. Standing tall and graceful, out of the woman's mouth came a commanding call so forceful it shook the deck.

Whoosh, whoosh, whoosh. A stench of burning rubber filled the air as three ragged black forms swooped down out of the night sky. Dancing in the air showering hot sparks, Harry saw faces – red glowing eyes, yellow fangs, hideous grins dripping molten fire. Hovering above the bodies of Ulrika, Eniola and Bojka each made its choice. Lips pouting into grotesque parody of kisses, greedily they plunged on to their chosen victim. Harry could take no more. Dragging himself over the gunwale, every moment dreading the scorching burn of molten sparks on his back, he slid down into the safety of the dark sea.

Striking out for the shore, after an agony of time, his feet touched sand. Crawling up the beach first he lay gasping, then plucking up courage, he looked across the water to Spice Girl. From her came a loud splash as M'Bopo's body was thrown overboard. Scrambling to his feet he ran as fast as his trembling legs could carry him, desperate to reach the tented town and comforting presence of other humans.

So, he didn't see Spice Girl weigh anchor and head out to sea, the three Snoopers flying before her, heaving on chains attached to her prow. At the helm stood Constanza, her body filled with Gressil's simmering malevolence, silver-streaked strands of glossy black hair crackling about her fiercely beautiful face. Maabella lay drooped on the deck at her feet and grouped behind her were Gressil's servant Phraggs: outwardly the bodies of Ulrika, Eniola and Bojka but, like Constanza possessed by Lord Gressil, deep within their bodies festered the fiendish presence of Sneaksouls.

Unlike the cunning Sneaksouls Raaum and Beliaal who had infested Hardwick and Roach Dandrum – Phraggs descended from Grimalkin – these Sneaksouls were children of his twin, Hellion. Called by their Lord Gressil from the blighted garden of old Florain, these were unintelligent killing machines, existing only to destroy. Plump faced, blond Ulrika, Eniola famed for her beauty, and grey haired Bojka with her homely common sense, had become fiendish beasts, voices harsh, their human faces contorted by the foulness within.

All night Spice Girl ploughed through the Red Sea, the three Snoopers doggedly pulling her by their chains. At dawn she entered the Gulph of Aqaba. Her mermaid figurehead gazing imperiously as she approached Eilat the Snoopers began to succumb to exhaustion. First one, then a second plummeted into the sea, drained of the evil life force given them by Gressil. Goaded by Gressil's snarls, with a final effort of will the last of the huge insects towed Spice Girl into the bay, then with a resigned sigh was received by the waves. So, the last of

Gressil's Snoopers met its end; seen only by a sleepy Scav keeping watch on his barge laden with plustic bottles – but being a mere slave, nobody believed him when, still terrified, he babbled out his story.

Dropping anchor where the imposing Merchants' residences looked out to sea, the three infested women, their sailor's canvas garb now badly scorched by the Phraggs' pent-up fire within, lowered Spice Girl's jolly boat. Gressil in Constanza's body climbed down to receive Mab into his arms, and the little boat rocking wildly, the three Phragg women followed. Taking up the oars, Ulrika, rowed them to the waterfront and tying up at Merchant Farnese's private jetty the bizarre group climbed the wide steps to the balustraded marble balcony. The many-windowed Farnese mansion was in darkness, the household deep in slumber after the coming-of-age celebrations for the Farnese's only daughter, Fatima the Plumptious. The one watchman on duty was speedily silenced by Phragg Eniola's efficient use of a fish filleting knife.

Silently, swiftly they headed through the walled ornamental gardens, past pergolas, pools and flowerbeds to the stables behind the mansion. Setting his beloved on a mounting block, his wicked spirit gazing out from the depths of Constanza's sightless eyes, Gressil studied her condition. Mab was deteriorating fast, reverting to her original form of a giant slug, slimy flesh erupting through splits in her velvet covered skin, bedraggled wings shedding dandruff-like flakes of peacock, mustard, and orange. For all his enormous powers, he knew he could not help her – Zagzagel had made sure of that, when they had fought those aeons ago, at the dawn of creation, when, given the task of nurturing Gaia's emerging life, Zagzagel had defeated and imprisoned Gressil in the body of a sea scorpion.

Frustrated Gressil turned furiously on his three Phragg servants. 'Go! Go! Fetch a carriage from the stables for your Queen! Horses too. Steeds that will fly like the wind!'

For a moment the three female forms didn't move; spitting sparks, they glowered sullenly at Gressil. Then shrinking back at the overpowering evil of their master's gaze, they slunk across the yard. Impatiently pacing up and down, from inside the stables Gressil heard a human shout, cut short by the filleting knife. Moments later shrill whinnying and the clatter of hooves heralded Bojka and Eniola dragging four trembling, terrified horses by their reins, followed by Ulrika pulling Mrs Farnese's favourite carriage: a landau painted gold and pink, its deeply padded seats concealed by a canopy of scarlet leather. Whilst Bojka and Eniola saddled three of the horse, Ulrika harnessed the fourth, a glossy black stallion to the landau. Lifting Mab inside, Gressil settled her on the padded seat, then springing onto the driver's foot board took up the reins. The three women mounted their restive prancing horses and the group set off at speed, out into the city.

Dashing through still deserted streets, they reached the market square. Early stall owners, setting out their wares, stopped to stare in astonishment as three women in sailor's garb, cutlasses at their waists, careered past on wild eyed horses, followed by a swaying, elaborately decorated carriage furiously driven by another seafaring woman, her whip cracking, her face contorted with fury. Taking to the King's Highway, hooves thundering on the paved road, the landau rattling and bouncing over the stones, they disappeared into the distance.

They drove their horses mercilessly, stopping only at the well of Ein Yahav to water them and to give Mab a rest. Racing on, by late afternoon they caught up with Levi the Tall's mule train. Dragging on the reins, they drew their horses to a slow walk. Gressil, standing on the foot board, scanned the line of mules and the people riding them, searching for any small Delphin figure, or a bird of prey.

The strangers' menacing presence made the mules uneasy, sidling nervously, their loads wobbling, some of the less skilled of Levi's customers fell off. At the head of the train Levi irritably turned his mule around, trotting back to confront the woman standing on the carriage and the three riders. Drawing near, he called out angrily: 'What's your business with us, madam? Be gone with you! You're spooking—'

Constanza's malevolent stare seared his soul and the words died in his throat. 'I am seeking a youth with an eagle,' hissed the sinister voice.

Levi pointed with a trembling finger up the Highway. 'He's not here – he's with Zackary's mule train!'

Gressil's howl of rage was the last thing Levi heard. Constanza's cutlass flashed and Levi's head bounced on the ground: no more would he whistle through the gap in his teeth when he talked.

Braying in terror, shedding their loads and riders, the mules galloped away into the desert. The three women Phraggs, fired with blood lust, setting out to pursue them, their scything cutlasses taking three victims before they were called back by Gressil's furious command. Leaving the dead lying in pools of blood, night drawing on, the carriage and its outriders charged on up the Highway.

At the Dead Sea …

More and more puzzled as to the whereabouts of Levi's team, but anxious to get away before his rival finally arrived, once again Zakary roused his customers before dawn. Bleary-eyed and complaining, they rolled up their blankets and soon a haze of charcoal smoke hung over the camp as breakfasts were cooked. Meanwhile, the muleteers gulped down their food and, grumbling among themselves, untethered the mules to lead them down to the river mouth to drink.

His hasty breakfast finished, Fin went to a nearby acacia tree where Quilla, perched on a low branch was stretching his wings preparing to fly.

Leaning close, he saw Bird's tiny hand waving. 'You'll be quick when you go hunting, won't you Bird? We'll be setting off soon.'

'We'll try – this land has little food for Quilla and he's getting very hungry. The lizard is all he's eaten for two days! It's a shame there's no fish—'

Quilla gave her no time to say anymore. Impatiently flapping his wings, he leapt into the air, quickly becoming a dot in the sky. Disconsolately Fin rejoined the others to help clear away the cooking gear.

Their packing done, Crow, shovelling a handful of dates into a pocket and stuffing Sparkie II back into his bible bag, announced: 'Afore we go, I'se going to inspect caves up there.' He gestured to the zigzag path leading up the cliff face to the dark cave mouths. 'I'se told by one of them mule men, rogue robber Scavs sometimes hide special plustic up there.'

His small figure had just disappeared into a cave when the distant ringing of hooves on the road made everyone pause uneasily. Was it another contingent of the King's fierce soldiers, or had Levi finally caught up with them?

At first hidden below the brow of a low hill, three figures on horseback galloped into view, followed by a carriage swaying as it strove to keep up. Leif and Sandy paused from loading their mules to watch the approaching group. As the riders drew closer, they appeared to be women, swarthy complexioned, cutlasses tucked into the belts of their sailors' clothes. The carriage driver, also a sailor woman, would have been beautiful, her hair black and glossy, if her face hadn't been twisted in a snarling grimace that made Leif and Sandy look at each other questioningly. Riders and carriage slowed to a ragged halt, their snorting horses looming over Zakary, who had been supervising loading of the pack mules. The carriage driver jumped down and strode over to him. Whip still in hand, she growled questions in a voice startlingly harsh for a woman. Zakary pointed a shaking finger at Lark, emptying his cooking stove of charcoal embers. He was alone: Fin had gone to the water's edge to wash the tea cups.

'Yes, yes, they have an eagle! Please, don't hurt me…'

'What the devil!' Leif muttered. 'I know that woman! It's … it's … I'll remember her name in a minute. Yes! She's a fellow captain. That's it: Constanza! Captain of the schooner Spice Girl – trades in spices. Those other women are her officers. But her voice… I'd better find out why she and her crew are here!'

About to stride towards the newcomers when there came a shriek from the carriage. The brocade curtains parted, and a woman's face appeared, haggard and hideously covered with sores.

'Gressil – Look! Look! The boy! Down by the water!' screamed Mab lurching out onto the running board, dragging bedraggled wings behind her.

Lashing Zakary aside with her whip, Constanza charged down the sand towards Fin, still absorbed in washing the cups.

'LIEF, THAT IS NO WOMAN – IT IS THE DEMON, GRESSIL!' Sandy shouted drawing his sword and running after Constanza. Astonished, Lief unclipped his axe from his belt, and sprinted after him.

Dropping his cooking stove, Lark stared dumbfounded at Mab slumped on the carriage running board, slimy slug flesh erupting like boils from her velvet furred body. At the sight of her protruding thick swollen tongue, all the horror rushed back: the taste, the sound of when she had sucked the cross from between his teeth. Retching at the memory, a thought came to him: could he finish what he'd started that day in Contagion – kill her and bring this nightmare to an end? Stealthily his hand went to his boning knife. Then he came to his senses: what would Tissy do if he got himself killed? He saw the three riders had leapt from their horses and were charging after Leif and Sandy. Shouting a warning, Sandy and Leif spun round to meet them. Sword and axe clashing with cutlasses, steel on steel, a fierce fight ensued. Mick at his heel growling fiercely, Lark raced to join the fight, dodging about trying to get in a thrust of his knife.

The skirmish gave Gressil just enough time: as Fin struggled to run in the soft sand Gressil fell upon him. Holding Constanza's cutlass to his throat he dragged him, kicking and struggling, to the carriage. With a triumphant bellow he commanded Sandy, Lief and Lark to drop their weapons. The three Phragg women, pushing them to the ground, and stood over them, cutlasses held to their throats. Yelping and whimpering in distress, Mick ran around and around, just out of reach of any cutlass thrust.

'Where is the eagle?' Gressil barked. 'Call the eagle or the boy dies!'

Before they could answer: 'SKEEW! SKEEW!' Quilla dropped from the sky, talons extended. Raking the top of Constanza's head, he tore out a clump of her black hair. Circling to attack again, Gressil raised his arm in defence, allowing Fin to push Constanza's blade away from his throat.

'BIRD! GET AWAY! FLY TO JERUSALEM!' he yelled. Hearing her faint sobs. 'I can't leave …' Bird's voice was lost as Quilla rose high in the sky and swung away towards Jerusalem.

With a howl of rage Gressil flung Fin up into Mab's eagerly waiting arms and leaping up on to the standing board, savagely whipping the horse set the landau dashing off down the road after the eagle.

Bewildered, the Phragg women gaped after the disappearing carriage. Sandy, Lief and Lark instantly seized the opportunity. Scrabbling for sword, axe, and boning knife they fell on them. Taken off guard, the three women began to fall back.

'Don't stand there yer warty wemmers! Help us!' Lark yelled to the frightened huddle of muleteers.

Zakary and two of his braver muleteers, pulling fearsome daggers from within their desert robes, ran to join in lunging and stabbing.

The Phraggs outnumbered, it was soon over. With a wild swing of his axe Lief beheaded Eniola. The Phragg within her, shrieking out of the rolling head, streaked away in a shower of fiery cinders. At the same moment Sandy drove his sword deep into Ulrika, and another screaming Phragg fled. As Bojka turned to run, Lark, Zakary and the muleteers, attacked her, stabbing and slashing. Stepping back from the mutilated lifeless body, the last Phragg shot out of her mouth and sped away after its fellows.

'Quick Lief, we must catch the horses,' cried Sandy.

They ran to the Phragg women's three horses standing a little way off, heads drooped with exhaustion. Grabbing the bridles of two of them, Sandy threw Lark and Mick up into the saddle of one of them, whilst Lief caught the third and surprising ease for a seafaring man, swung up into the saddle. Shouting a word of thanks to Zakary and his brave muleteers who were trying to calm their bewildered customers whilst gathering together the scattered mule train, Sandy sprang on to his horse, and the three took to the King's Highway.

Up on the cliff, Crow had heard the commotion. Creeping out of a cave where he was searching for plustic, he saw Gressil hurl Fin into the carriage.

'Oh Sparkie, what must we do?' he whimpered in terror. 'You knows Crow not brave lad, don' you. But this time me will be.'

Throwing aside his rucksack packed with plustic, Sparkie in the bible bag on his back, taking a big breath, as the carriage swept past below him, he jumped. Landing on the carriage's baggage board, dragged back by Sparkie's hefty weight, he clung desperately to the luggage straps. Neither Gressil fighting to control the careering carriage, nor Mab triumphant at having Fin in her power, noticed him.

Summoning her dwindling energy, her long nails digging into his neck, Mab pulled Fin through the curtains to the seat of the carriage. Clutching him in her weak arms, she hissed in his ear: 'Boy! Summon the eagle, or I will gouge your eyes out!'

But in her weakness Fin was easily able to fight free of her. Trampling her powdery wings, he quickly scrambled back out through the curtains.

'Gressil, the boy's escaping!' shrieked Mab.

Clinging onto the side of the carriage ready to leap off, Fin laughed scornfully. 'Blinding me won't get you the cross, you foul creature!'

Twisting round, Gressil brought down the handle of his whip in a stunning blow to Fin's head. As everything faded, he heard Gressil's voice thunder: 'Catch him, Mab! Pull him back! Do not lose—'

He heard no more.

From Quilla's eye, her face pressed against the bubble's surface, Bird spotted in the distance a city standing on a hill, its white walls sparkling in the rising sun. Far below the road wound towards it through dry rugged hills. Turning round, her cheek hard against the bubble, she peered behind. To her alarm she saw Gressil's carriage bouncing along the Highway: he was catching up. Flying in vee formation above the carriage were three fiery clouds of black rags. Suddenly they sped up towards Quilla, angry red eyes and gaping mouths plain to see.

'Phraggs!' screamed Bird. 'They're after us – fly faster!'

Frantically scanning the hills on either side of the road, she saw the tumbled remains of a stone fortress. 'Dive! Dive!' she yelled. 'There's a tower ahead where we can hide. Not so low – higher! A bit to the left! No! No – too far! That's it, we're there!'

Guided more by changes of air pressure than Bird's frenzied instructions, Quilla plunged blindly, his talons locating the stone of a sheltering wall. Tumbling behind it, he landed in an untidy heap on an abandoned nest of sticks.

'Turn around so I can see!' Bird cried. Lumbering round, Quilla tilted his head so Bird could peer over the wall of their refuge. Heart in mouth, she saw the Phraggs speeding towards the tower. Black rags streaming behind them, they streaked overhead, so close their scorching heat made Quilla jump back in alarm. 'They've shot past – quick hop around so I can see where they are!' Bird ordered. Squinting down into a paved courtyard, she gasped in horror. 'There's a flock of vultures down there feeding on an ox's body! Oh, how disgusting! The Phraggs are attacking them – feathers, blood and guts everywhere!'

One of the larger vultures broke free and as it flapped into the air, a Phragg snatched it up in its fiery maw. Streaking away from the scene of slaughter, leaving a trail of smouldering feathers, the three Phraggs headed off back to the distant Highway and their Lord Gressil's galloping carriage.

'They've gone,' breathed Bird. 'Quick, we must get away from here.'

'Not until I've eaten!' snapped Quilla. Tormented by the smell of fresh meat, he swooped down to the mutilated carcass and greedily tore at what was left.

Given renewed strength by his unexpected feast, he rose once more into the sky, and keeping to the shadows of the rugged cliffs rising either side of the Highway, flying low, Bird guided him towards the city.

'Sparkie II, what've we gone 'en done!' squeaked Crow, clinging to the luggage straps as the carriage rocked and bucketed along the Highway.

Settling himself more safely on the boards, his feet braced against the uprights, he squinted through the eyelets threaded with cords holding down the carriage's leather canopy. The butterfly woman was leaning out through the curtains screeching; beyond her stood Gressil mercilessly whipping on his exhausted horse. Fin sat groaning, rubbing his head where Gressil had hit him.

Sizing up the situation, Crow fished Sparkie from the bible bag and held him up. 'Now Sparkie my love, you got work to do with your fine ratty teethies.' The thickly furred rat's face stared back at him with intelligent, beady black eyes. 'We got to rescue Master Fin – he Aunty Krite's chile' and I'se promise her to take care of him.' Turning back to the canopy Crow pressed the rat's nose to the cords. 'Bitie through them banana strings, just like I showed you afore, an' don't argue!'

Crow's training paid off. Sparkie's fat little paws gripping the cords, his sharp front incisors began gnawing. One by one the cords came away, releasing enough of the leather canopy for Crow to poke his head under and tap Fin's shoulder.

'Master Fin! Master Fin!' he hissed, 'Crow and Sparkie here!'

'What? What?' Fin spun round and stared at Crow in dazed surprise.

Crow heaved at the canopy to make the gap wider. 'Quick! Quick! Afore she sees!' he muttered, beckoning Fin to climb through.

'Well done Crow!' Fin exclaimed, struggling through the gap. As his feet landed on the baggage rack Mab gave a shriek. Thinking Mab had spotted him, Fin peered under the canopy back into the carriage. Through the gap in the curtain above Mab's head, he saw three fiery clouds streaking through the sky towards the carriage. One carried a bird's limp body in its maw.

'Gressil, the Phraggs have the eagle!' Mab screamed joyfully.

'Yes, my love!' Gressil cried triumphantly. 'Now you shall be healed…' But even as he cried out, his voice changed to a howl of fury.

Fin had to stop himself laughing out loud: the bird the Phragg held in its maw was a dead vulture. Gressil's rage exploded: in an instant the three Phraggs were turned to clouds of soot. Crow, whimpering with fright, tugged Fin from staring under the canopy. Not a moment too soon: Mab realised he was gone. Her wail of despair was a distraction too much for Gressil, he lost control. The carriage swerving wildly, Scav, Delphin and rat were thrown from the baggage rack. Rolling down a slope at the highway's edge, they landed bruised and gasping at the bottom of a ditch.

The carriage careered on down the Highway. A couple of miles later, coming to a bend, it crashed into a boulder, ripping off a wheel. Flipping over, Gressil was flung off and the horse, its traces broken, galloped away, back down the road to Eilat desperate for its stable and normality.

Staggering to the wrecked carriage to rescue Mab, Gressil found Fin had gone. His dark spirit was once more almost at boiling point when a light sports chariot drawn by a high-stepping horse trotted briskly into view.

The charioteer, Ptolemy, a dark eyed young man with luxuriantly curling ebony black hair and beard – much admired by the young ladies of the Court – was a member of the elite squad of King's Couriers. He was on his way to Eilat with a special assignment from Jerusalem. At his feet lay a red leather satchel bearing the House of Fakhir's double horn device tooled in gold. Inside was a prescription for ground hyena teeth, a vital ingredient in the anti-rabies powder made by the Royal Apothecary. When out hunting the King carried this precious powder in a small alabaster vial hung on a gold chain around his neck.

Seeing the broken carriage and a hapless woman with her injured companion, Ptolemy, against his orders to stop for no one when on the King's business, but being of gentlemanly persuasion, brought his horse to a halt, and leapt from his chariot. Disconcerted by his concerned greeting being received in silence by the wild looking woman dressed in sailor's garb, he went to her companion lying on the ground. Taking a closer look he stood back in horror: 'What manner of foul creature is this?' he gasped.

A blow from Constanza's whip butt to the back of his head felled him and he knew no more. The effort of the blow put the final strain on Constanza's woman's body: collapsing in a heap like a rag doll, a dark cloud drifted out of her across the ground, its misty fingers probing Ptolemy's slumped body. With a satisfied hiss, the shadow slipped into his gaping mouth, and Ptolemy's eyes snapped open. Once more Gressil looked out from a new human form.

Gently folding Mag's ragged wings against her rotting body he wrapped her in Ptolemy's red cloak, then contemptuously tossing away the leather satchel, tenderly lifted her into the chariot. Seizing his whip from the ground, he leapt in to take up the chariot's reins.

'Take heart my love, forget the boy! We shall pursue the eagle! The blind bird shall not elude me for long, now I have a strong new body and a swift chariot!'

Releasing the brake and cracking his whip over the horse's head, heedless of the wheels bouncing over the heap of Constanza's body, the chariot sped off down the road.

Terrified Gressil would return to hunt for them, Fin and Crow crouched trembling in the deep ditch below the road, not daring to climb out. They'd been there half an hour or so when they heard the distant sound of horses' hooves. As the sound grew, they realised they were coming from the direction of the Dead Sea.

Standing up, Crow said: 'Me go on road, see who it is – I pretend to be Scav traveller.'

He crawled up the top of the gully and hopping on to the road, saw three riders on exhausted horses trotting raggedly towards him. As they drew nearer, he recognised the keen midnight blue eyes of the first rider fixed on the road ahead.

'Mr Sand –' he could only croak, choking as the dust from the road caught his throat.

'Stop!' Lark yelled, heaving on his reins. 'It's Crow!'

Sandy and Leif, pulling their horses to a fumbling halt, dismounted. Seeing Fin scrambling up on to the road, Lark flung himself out of his saddle and rushed to him. 'Fin! Are you O.K.?'

'Fine! Just got a lump on my head where Gressil knocked me out. Crow here is a hero! He jumped on the back of Gressil's carriage to rescue me. His rat too! Chewed through the cords holding down the canopy so I could climb out the back. But before we could escape, some of Gressil's Phraggs appeared. One was carrying a dead vulture – mistook it for Quilla – funny if it hadn't been so scary! Gressil was so furious, he destroyed all three of the Phraggs, then as he and Mab careered off down the road, Crow and I were thrown off – there's no sign yet of him returning.'

'Having seen Mab's wretched state, I believe Gressil is getting desperate!' Sandy said. 'He will be heading for Jerusalem; his one aim is to capture Quilla and regain the cross. We must stop him – even though our horses are worn out, we must ride on: Fin with me! Crow and his rat with you Lief.'

Lark quickly caught the bridle of his horse which was about to set off back down the road. All back in the saddle, they urged their weary horses into a fast trot and continued along the Kings Highway. They had only gone a mile when a horse galloped past going in the opposite direction: they recognised it as the horse that pulled Gressil's carriage. A few minutes later they came to the wrecked carriage and Constanza's body lying in the road.

Leif dismounted, and staring at her mauled remains, groaned in horror. 'What evil creature would inflict such injuries, Iskander?'

'Gressil is no creature, but the powerful servant of Lucifer!' Sandy said grimly. 'I fear he has infested a new body – what kind, I dread to think!'

Fin nodded at wrecked carriage. 'Whatever body he's in, he still has Mab to carry. I wonder what he's found now – having been cooped up with her, I know she's getting weaker all the time. She smells dreadful too, like a rotting dead sheep!'

Lief, who was prowling around looking for a clue, spotted the red satchel. Picking it up, he showed it to the others. 'This is a courier's bag! Not any courier, but one of the King's Couriers: special messengers famous for their lightweight chariots pulled by swift horses. If, as I suspect, he has occupied the courier's body and is driving his chariot, he will be covering a lot of ground fast and will have widened the distance between us our poor animals.'

'Then we must get a move on – get to the Pool before he finds Quilla!' Lark cried.

Digging his heels into his horse's side, it jerked forward into a fast trot. Mick, perched on the pommel, almost fell off, and Lark just managed to catch his tail.

Before leaving, Leif gently gathered the remains of Constanza's body and reverently laid them in the gully by the roadside. Then remounting, he hastened after the others.

# 14
# DOGLAND

Her face pressed to the Perspex window, Dancer was fizzing with excitement as Paphos came into view.

'Cyprus at last!' she shouted to Tissy above the noise of Skyhook's engine. 'My dream has come true! Oh, if only I could visit Kassabel's shrine!'

Twice they'd been scared by brief spluttering from the engine, but each time Skyhook had recovered and flown smoothly on. Nearing the airfield their two escort copters swung away to begin the return journey back to their home base at Thessaloniki.

Paphos, situated on a promontory jutting out into the azure blue of the Mediterranean, the airfield was surrounded by fields of rape glowing yellow in the setting sun, the rape seeds vital for making engine fuel. The runway was flanked with the usual collection of hangars and workshops outside of which copters were being worked on by Skwid mechanics. At the runway's end stood the observation tower, a radio mast projecting from its red tiled roof.

As Skyhook rolled down the runway, two Skwid signallers flourishing brightly coloured batons guided Wings to a halt. Nearby another Skwid stood waiting. Like Dragon at Trans Fort and Gator at Thessaloniki, he wore a leather flying suit decorated with studs and chains. Wings guessed this was Commander Croc. He struggled stiffly from the cockpit, followed by Tissy and then Dancer with Bird in her basket.

'I trust you had a good journey?' Commander Croc asked shaking hands all round.

Wings nodded. 'Engine coughed once or twice, but on the whole O.K. Perhaps your chaps could take a look at her?'

'It'll be a pleasure for my engineers!' Commander Croc replied, looking admiringly at Skyhook. 'But as night will soon be falling, we'll look tomorrow. Come to our home where we can make you comfortable.'

The Commander led them across the airfield, to the top of cliffs and down steep steps into a series of caves. A wide high tunnel took them past several airy caverns with open arches overlooking the sea glittering in the rays of the setting sun. At the tunnel's end they entered a large communal chamber with rows of tables and benches. Outside, a balconied ledge looked towards a bay and a series of rocky islands which they learnt later were, according to legend, the birthplace of the goddess Aphrodite.

The whole Skwid community were waiting to make them welcome, the hundred or so adults and children crowding around, their chameleonlike skins rippling a kaleidoscope of pleasure. After a meal of grilled fish and seaweed stew, they were taken to the dormitory, a dark inner cave where the adults slept on thick rape-straw mattresses in curtained-off ledges cut in the walls.

Next morning, whilst the mechanics overhauled Skyhook, Commander Croc instructed a young copter pilot called Anemone to take them on a tour. Leaving Bird in the dark dormitory, tucked up asleep in the straw of her basket, Anemone first showed them around the cave system: the kitchens, The Nest, a nursery cave where the youngest Skwids lived, and the school for older Skwid children. Back above ground, she took them to the large, corrugated iron sheds situated by the rape fields. These were the factories where seeds were processed into biofuel.

From there, Anemone led them through the yellow fields, across to an imposing circular building with a red tiled domed roof, whitewashed walls and window shutters painted blue. She explained this was where the Skwids gathered once a week to sing praises to the angel Kassabel. Inside, the place was bare apart from a series of brightly painted wall murals depicting the story of the Skwid people: how they came from the Universe of White Light, 'hitching a ride' on the Gaiakin ships and taking on a reptilian appearance.

Anemone was keen to point out one painting in particular. It depicted a creature, its fiery black rags streaming out behind as it clung to a saucer shaped object shooting across a starry sky.

'That's NYX, the first of our race. Distantly related to the Phraggmorgia she didn't fall into evil like them but went her own way. Her descendants became worshippers of the angel Kassabel who took on the body of a Skwid. The ancient shrine to Kassabel stands among pine trees in the Troodos mountains. That is why we love this island of Cyprus!'

Silently, slowly, Dancer walked around the walls, carefully studying each picture in turn. Then she turned to Anemone. 'And Kassabel's shrine, is it far?' she choked in a husky voice, her face rippling sunrise pink and gold. 'I would dearly love to see it!'

Anemone put her arm around Dancer's shoulder. 'This afternoon I will fly you there! But come now everyone, I will be getting into trouble if we don't return to the Cave – our lunch will be on the table!'

After the meal, leaving Tissy looking after Bird and Wings going to check on the progress with Skyhook's maintenance, Anemone and Dancer hurried to the line of flight-ready copters and took off for Kassabel's shrine. It was evening when they returned from the mountains, Dancer so full of emotion, for a while she couldn't speak. Tissy and Wings had to wait patiently until she managed to describe the statue in the shrine.

'Her garments – like a mist of gold dust! The light in her eyes shining like the sun and her skin rippling like a thousand rainbows,' she breathed throatily. 'For a moment I thought she was alive! Her smile …' She couldn't say any more.

Next day, to their frustration, Commander Croc's mechanics discovered a problem with Skyhook's fuel pump which it would take them a day to fix, so Tissy decided to take Bird down to the beach for a paddle in the sea. Taking off her green dress and holding her above the waves, Bird gave excited squeaks of pleasure as she blindly splashed her toes in the water, but soon grew tired. Anxiously feeling the bones beneath her skinny frame, once again Tissy felt frightened. Bird was rapidly wasting away. The calf's foot jelly finished, apart from sips of water, all she had eaten was a few small grapes provided by the kitchen cooks. Carrying her back up the beach, Tissy set her down in the warm sand and put her green dress back on. Curling up, Bird immediately went to sleep. Sitting next to her gazing out to sea, Tissy remembered what Wings had told her, that beyond the horizon lay Africa.

Africa! That was where Lark and Fin were! Just across that stretch of water. And … and Bird – the real Bird. Not this pathetic creature asleep in the sun. In one of his precious letters Lark said that the real Bird was in an eagle's eye. Whatever could he mean? It was all so fantastical! She couldn't convince herself that it wasn't all a waste of time: carting poor Bird's little burnt body across Europe with some idea she could be healed at that pool called…what was it… Siloam?

Commander Croc's growling voice brought her back to her surroundings.

At the top of the beach, in the shade of a grass roofed veranda, he and Wings were seated at a table poring over Wings' map with a copter pilot called Turtle giving advice. Dancer sat with them. Still overcome by her visit to Kassabel's shrine, she was gazing mistily to the Troodos mountains rising in the distance.

'Wings, what you plan is so dangerous! Is the little scrap worth the risk?' Growled Croc, nodding to where Bird lay asleep in the sand.

Quickly gathering Bird into her arms, Tissy joined them. Carefully settling her under the table, she watched anxiously as they studied at the ancient map.

Turtle pointed with a scaly finger. 'That picture of Jerusalem with its golden domed mosque, is not accurate. It is now King Fakhir's vast palace.'

The pilot's left arm was in a sling, blue Skwid blood staining the bandages, the souvenir of a recce over the region they called Dogland. His copter had been shot at from the ground, crossbow darts peppering his copter, almost bringing him down. Injured, he had only just managed to nurse the aircraft home.

With his good arm Turtle rummaged awkwardly in a pocket for a piece of charcoal. 'A high wall surrounds Jerusalem.' He drew a wobbly black charcoal circle around the old drawing. 'Thirty-foot-high and ten feet thick, it was built to keep out the evil of Dogland to the north, where huge packs of feral dogs roam the plains and hills.' He stabbed his charcoal at stylized drawings showing hills and deep valleys. 'There's been several outbreaks of rabies!' he added with a shudder.

'Is there somewhere flat for Skyhook to land: the terrain looks very hilly?' Wings asked, ruefully rubbing at Turtle's charcoal marks in an attempt to clean his precious map.

'You need to make for Lod!' Turtle pointed to the drawing of a cluster of huts north west of Jerusalem. 'The area there is mainly flat scrubland; in ancient times there was an airport – called Ben Gurion or some such name. Where the old control tower stood there's a large brick-built hunting lodge. The King and his chums stay there when they're out hunting dogs. You'll need to keep away from that – there's a permanent guard of troops armed with crossbows. I landed nearby once on a recce – trying to locate one of our copter pilots who'd been shot down. Never found young Froggy – he shouldn't have gone on his own like that.'

Cold grey and icy green rippling his scarred face, he turned away for a moment to gaze out to sea. Shaking himself, he turned back and pointed out the terrain beyond Lod. 'There are areas of flat land there where you could land your machine.'

Dancer, who'd started to pay attention, leaned in, and traced her finger from Lod to Jerusalem. 'How far is it from there to Jerusalem? Will it take long on foot? We don't want to get caught by this King's soldiers or attacked by rabid dogs!'

'It's about a day's walk for someone fit, but with your problems—' Turtle looked down meaningfully at Wings' metal foot. 'It would be best if you went at night. There's tree cover you could use and as you get nearer to Jerusalem, there are high hills and deep valleys.'

'And the pool of Siloam?' Tissy asked worriedly. 'Do you know where it is?'

'Never landed in Jerusalem – Skwids are not welcome! Know nothing about a pool called Siloam.'

A silence fell as everyone looked gloomily at the map.

Then Croc spoke: 'As I have already said, what you plan is so dangerous, if not impossible!'

Wings squinted sideways at Tissy and Dancer. 'Well chaps, you've heard what they've said. Are you still willing to get to Siloam? I'd understand if—'

Tissy interrupted him, fiercely. 'Kassabel will help us! I trust in dear old Kassabel!'

Next day, Skyhook's fuel pump checked once more by the mechanics who gave her bodywork one last loving wipe, they took off late afternoon. Wings intended to reach Lod as dusk fell when, with luck, few inhabitants would be about; he reckoned it would take two hours. He'd firmly refused Commander Croc's offer of an escort of two of his copters.

'Too many machines would draw attention to us, and having heard Turtle's experiences, it wouldn't be fair on your pilots! They don't need to risk their lives for us! Besides, I've got my Chinese compass and I'm used to flying over strange terrain – spent most of my adult life doing that!'

High in the air, craning her neck to look out of the port window, Tissy saw far below shimmering greeny-blue sea stretching to the distant horizon with no sight of land. A shiver went down her spine: if Skyhook crashed, she knew they had no hope of rescue. She wondered if this would be their last flight into the unknown. Whilst waiting for Dancer to settle Bird in her basket, she'd given Anemone a small blue gemstone, prized from Nutmeg's jewelled peacock. She wished she had something to give Croc and Turtle, but Grammer Nutmeg didn't go in for chains. She turned away to watch Wings hunched over his instruments. Tapping at his compass and then peering at the clock on his instrument panel, every now and then he searched ahead through his windscreen. Will he find Lod? Would he find somewhere to land? Would they find the Pool of Siloam? Croc and Turtle didn't know where the pool was. She thought about what they'd said about the wicked King of Jerusalem. At all costs they mustn't be captured by his soldiers!

Two hours later they reached land. Below them floating islands of plustic, drifting along the margin of the sandy shoreline, glinted in the setting sun. Among the plustic islands small figures could be seen in rowing boats gathering in the debris; alerted by the engine noise, pale faces looked up.

They headed inland, flying high over a parched land scattered with small settlements of squat mud buildings; the noise of their engine once more attracting attention, little figures came out to stare up at the novelty. As they flew on, the terrain became increasingly deserted, low growing trees casting long shadows in the setting sun. Wondering if her eyes had deceived her Tissy saw what looked like a shadow moving swiftly over the ground like a wave. She realised it was a huge pack of dogs; dogs of all shapes and sizes, at least a hundred of them, some stubby in stature, short legged and trailing behind the larger, long legged hounds trotting purposefully over the ground. She shuddered fearfully: this must be Dogland.

Wings began searching the terrain, looking over one side then the other, before turning back to his instrument panel, tapping his compass, and peering at his clock. His back suddenly stiffened and turning to Tissy and Dancer he made his familiar thumbs-up sign. Stretching to see ahead over his shoulder, Tissy saw a large brick building surrounded by a high wooden fence: they'd found the King's hunting lodge at Lod. Banking away and giving the building a wide birth, Wings searched for a clear piece of land among the rocks and scrub where Skyhook could land.

Thud! Thud! Heart in mouth, Tissy gripped her arm rests as two arrows glanced off Skyhook's port wing. Thud! A silvery stream of oil flew past the window – the fuel pipe had been hit again! Skyhook's engine screamed, coughed, and fell silent. Hauling on the joystick, desperately Wings tried to keep her nose up as she glided.

Squeezing her eyes tight shut, Tissy held her breath. A yell from Dancer made her start: 'Wings! Don't land! Keep flying. There's horsemen below – chasing us with crossbows!'

Wings stabbed at the starter and Skyhook's engine spluttered back into life. Stopping and starting, nursing her along, he made for pine covered hills ahead. Tissy realised he hoped to fly over them and out of sight. Looking back, she saw the riders were being left behind, their figures growing smaller as they faded into the dusk. Nearing the first hill Skyhook's engine stuttered and finally died. Wheels skimming the rocky summit, Wings fought to keep her nose above the pine trees, but she was too low. With a graunch of tearing metal and a crash of splintering branches Skyhook hit the ground.

Harsh barking brought Tissy up from oblivion. For a moment she wondered if she'd fallen among the pack of dogs she'd seen from the air. Her head thumping with pain, she felt warm blood oozing down her neck. By flickering light, she made out a man crouching over her. His fierce bearded face close, she saw he only had one eye, his left a dark socket. Cringing away, sharp pain bit her wrists and ankles; she was lying on the ground, hands and feet bound with cord. Beyond the light of a wide circle of guttering torches planted in the soil, all was darkness. Growling in a strange language, sounding like an old sheepdog's rusty bark, the man left her to join his companions standing around a fire in the centre of the torch-lit circle.

Squat framed, with thickly muscled arms and legs, all heavily bearded, they wore a kind of military uniform, wide leather belts covering their bellies, emblazoned with large silver badges depicting a dog's snarling face. On their feet they wore opened toed sandals held by leather lattices criss-crossing up their legs. At their backs they carried double-stringed crossbows, and in pouched leather straps across their hairy chests, rows of crossbow bolts gleamed in the firelight. The one-eyed man appeared to be the leader, sporting an extra-large dog's head badge on his belt.

Movement beyond the fire caught her eye. She could just make out a tethered group of shaggy maned ponies munching on a pile of hay. She wondered if her captives were the riders she'd seen racing after Skyhook. Her mind flashed back to when they'd crashed: Wings slumped over his control panel and Dancer yelling as she leapt out of Skyhook wielding her sword.

Hearing barking laughter from close by she turned to see one of the men standing over a figure struggling on the ground: it was Dancer. Her arms and legs bound he was prodding her with the tip of her sword. Wings, also bound, lay nearby: he wasn't moving. Then she remembered Bird. Frantically searching the ring of torchlight, she couldn't see her or her basket anywhere! Where was she? Painfully wriggling over the few feet of rough ground to Wings she nudged him as best she could with her tightly bound hands. To her relief he stirred and opened his eyes.

'Wings where's Bird? I can't see her anywhere!' she whispered.

His voice faint, she leaned close as he muttered. 'I think they…they didn't see her basket. It was too…'

The man poking Dancer with her sword spotted Tissy. Snarling in his guttural language, he gave her a warning kick in the ribs. Slamming Dancer's sword back into its sheath, he took it off to show the others gathered around the fire. Each man handled it admiringly, drawing out the blade and running a finger along the edge then lunging with it in mock sword play.

Hearing sobs of frustrated anger from Dancer, Wings hissed a warning. 'Keep quiet old girl – mustn't draw attention to us!'

Tiring of their sword play, the men began cooking their supper, threading bloody-looking meat on to skewers. As it roasted, a rancid smell filled the air, turning Tissy's stomach. She wondered what kind of meat it was. Could it be dog? The men passed around flagons of liquor, their growling soon turning to raucous laughter. For a while, their high-spiritedness became more boisterous, prisoners forgotten until the leader, One-Eye as Tissy thought of him, called a halt. After checking their ponies' tethers, the men prepared for the night, wrapping themselves in sacking blankets and settling around the fire. Before joining them, One-Eye wandered over to the three, brandishing a flagon. Despite their struggles he forced each of their heads back, pouring drink down their throats. Choking on the fiery liquid, for a few moments Tissy's head spun crazily until she passed out.

Terrified whinnying, snarling and yelling brought her up from unconsciousness. In the glare of the men's waving torches, she saw dark forms leaping among the plunging and rearing ponies. Vaguely she realised that the camp was being attacked by a pack of dogs. Too exhausted and dazed to feel fear, she fell back into deep sleep.

The next time she woke the rising sun was on her face. Opening her eyes, she saw Wings and Dancer were already awake and had pushed themselves into a sitting position. Both looked battered, their faces blood caked. Dancer had a cut on her chin still oozing blue Skwid blood and Wings left eye was swollen. His metal foot was twisted out of place; hands tied he'd been unable to straighten the straps.

Seeing Tissy stirring, Dancer breathed a sigh of relief. 'Tissy! Thank Kassabel you've come to! Now you must drink.' Her bonds hampering her, awkwardly taking up a canteen of water their captors had left within reach she wriggled over and with an effort managed to flip off the stopper to hold the canteen to Tissy's parched lips. Tissy eagerly took several huge gulps. Tasting like pond sludge, she was so thirsty the water could have been morning dew.

Struggling to a sitting position, she saw the camp was almost deserted. Leaving two men to guard them, the rest had taken their ponies up the hillside to the wreckage of Skyhook among the pine trees. She looked a sorry sight: nose buried in the ground, tail pointing skywards, the cabin door hanging open. The ponies waited patiently to be loaded as the men swarmed excitedly over her and wriggled in and out of the cabin.

Half an hour later, ponies laden with what could be easily salvaged, the raiding party returned to unload their loot. Wings, Dancer and Tissy watched in misery as pieces of metal plating, a wheel and various other bits loosened from the bodywork were eagerly examined.

Skyhook's beautifully made propeller now bent and twisted, too big to load on a pony, had been carried back by two of the men. Groaning in despair, Wings watched them trying to straighten it: pushing and pulling, standing on it with sandaled feet. Another was triumphantly waving Mossy's Chinese compass above his head. The raiders had ransacked the hold and were eagerly delving in the food and clothes bags, bringing out packets of dried fruits, oat cakes, strips of fruit leather, blankets, and spare clothes; from their excitement, it was clear these were rare luxuries.

Part horrified, part relieved, Tissy saw a man carrying Bird's basket. After shaking it to feel the weight, thinking it empty he threw it down then strode to join another group going through Wings' toolbox, whistling in wonder as the sets of spanners, hacksaws, bolts and screws were brought out. Bird's basket lay ignored on the ground the straps firmly closed. Tears stung Tissy's eyes: why wasn't Bird screeching like she normally did when frightened? Could her poor little body be … be dead?

Barked commands from One-Eye made her start. She watched anxiously as his men reloaded their ponies: nobody had picked up Bird's basket. Drawing a knife from his belt, One-Eye ambled over and cut the ropes binding their wrists and ankles. Tracing his blade lightly across his throat as a warning sign, he gestured that they should stand. Stiff limbed, Dancer and Tissy clambered to their feet, but Wings, his fingers numb from lack of circulation, struggled with his twisted metal foot. Dancer helped him straighten the straps and at a second attempt he stood up.

Prodding them with his knife, One-Eye indicated they must line up behind the men leading their loaded ponies. Bringing up the rear with his own pony, he spotted Bird's abandoned basket. Undoing the straps, he brought out Bird struggling weakly and mewling. Holding her by a leg he examined her with curiosity then, with a shrug, dropped her back in and re-buckling the straps, tied the basket to his saddle. In response to his raucous shout the party moved off.

Stumbling over the dry, boulder strewn ground, feeling ever more wretched, every now and then they came upon droppings which Tissy knew must have been left by the dogs that had attacked the ponies during the night. The day growing ever hotter, at last they came to a road. Deeply rutted by years of cartwheels, it wound out of the heat haze from the north and headed south. Here they were made to sit down.

The sun beating down on their heads, Dancer, whose Trekker training had ensured she brought the water canteen, took a swig then passed it to Wings and Tissy.

Surreptitiously nodding in the direction of One-Eye leaning on his pony she muttered: 'Do you see, the vile man's got Bird's basket tied to his saddle.'

'Yes,' Tissy whispered. 'I saw him opening it and take Bird out. Thank goodness he didn't hurt her but put her back again; at least we know where she is.'

Wings shook his head sadly. 'Poor little mite, she's so shrunken, perhaps he didn't think she was of much value: not like my compass.'

'Nor my sword!' Dancer hissed angrily. 'Given the chance, the ruffians will find out the value of my sword alright – when I take their heads off!'

Hearing her raised voice, One-Eye drew his knife and waved it threateningly as he snarled an unmistakable warning in his language.

'Keep calm Dancer,' Wings murmured out of the side of his mouth. 'Until we know what plans they have for us, best do as we're told.'

The three of them lapsed into depressed silence.

Her hands now free, Tissy searched inside her jerkin, discovering her neck purse had been stolen whilst she was unconscious. A lump rose in her throat as she thought of Nutmeg's filigree silver peacock, lacking most of its gems but still precious to her. She'd kept it wrapped in the shimmering blue cloth Mossy had told her was where the holy cross had lain. The thought of those men handling the sacred cloth with their filthy, rough hands made her sick. Tears pricked her eyes: she'd lost the picture of Lark as well, of him with a startled expression and his hair standing on end. But she still had his ring. Twisting the small green stone out of sight inside her finger, she stared defiantly towards the group of men as they sat by their ponies growling to each other: if they wanted to steal her ring, they would have to cut her finger off.

After an hour, down the track a cloud of dust appeared, followed by a low rumbling like distant thunder. A huge cart drawn by a team of four oxen rolled slowly into view. Five more followed, all loaded with great blocks of creamy white limestone. Later they learned the stone, from quarries in the hills north of Lod, was destined for the king's palace which he was having made even grander. Lastly came a caged wagon drawn by two oxen. Inside the cage a dozen or so men slumped on benches, their backs against the bars. Wearing only loin cloths the men's bodies were caked head to toe in white limestone powder. The stillness of their exhaustion gave them the appearance of statues.

One-Eye shouted to the driver and as the wagon drew to a halt one or two weary faces turned to gaze out disinterestedly through the bars. Jumping down, the driver drew the bolts on the back of his wagon and flung open the door. Prodded by One-Eye Wings, Dancer and Tissy climbed inside. Untying Bird's basket from his saddle, he threw it in after them. The men, who bore a variety of injuries, heads, arms, legs bound with bandages, shuffled reluctantly along their benches to make room. The driver slammed the door shut, shot the bolts across, and climbed back on his driving seat. The wagon lurched forward, and Wings and Dancer watched miserably through the cage as their precious possessions were left behind, strapped on the backs of the soldiers' laden ponies.

The moment the men were out of sight, Tissy scrambled to Birds' basket. Gently lifting her out, she sat her on her lap. She felt so light; Tissy was reminded of the dried-up body of a jackdaw she'd found once, trapped in the chimney flue in the kitchen at Dandrum Den. More alarming was her mouth, her lips so dried and cracked, they were oozing blood.

'Dancer! Have you got that canteen of water?' she wailed.

Dancer shook her head. 'They took it from me!'

Leaning over to look at Bird, Wings tut-tutted. 'Chaps, this isn't good!' He turned to look challengingly at their fellow passengers. 'Any of you guys got water?' The prisoners' heads bowed in utter exhaustion, there was no response.

'Scuse me,' a voice squeaked. 'Them don't talk Common Tongue.'

Tissy, Wings and Dancer stared in surprise at the small figure who had appeared from beneath a large cylindrical drum strapped to the bars at the front of the wagon. He too was caked in limestone dust from his spiky hair down to his bare feet. He wore an old sack caught at his waist by a piece of string, his stick thin legs and arms poking out through holes made in the sacking.

He waved a dented cook's ladle at the drum. 'Me temporary W.B. – Water Boy,' he announced importantly. Going to the drum, he lifted the lid and dipped in his ladle. Carefully carrying it the length of the rocking cart, he gently held it to Bird's mouth.

'Thank you, oh thank you!' Tissy gasped as Bird sucked the water eagerly.

The little figure stood back and looked Tissy up and down, the expression on his thin weaselly face full of wonder. 'You'm Delph!' he exclaimed. 'Delphs special to us!' He reverently took her hand and shook it. 'How do, miss. My name Carob. Me from Scav people.'

Tissy smiled. 'Good to meet you Carob. My name is Thetis Dandrum – but you can call me Tissy.'

Carob bowed. 'Much honoured!' He turned his attention to Dancer and Wings, showing particular interest in Wings' metal foot. 'How come Miss Tissy, you with these dodgy types? Not good company for a Delph: a human with tin foot, let 'lone a pesky Skwid!'

Dancer chuckled. 'Skwids have a bad reputation here, do they? Name's Dancer – warrior from the North! I'm Tissy's bodyguard.'

Carob eyed her curiously. 'That's O.K. then. And you?' He turned to Wings.

'Wings' the name. In charge of the transport. Or was, until my flying machine was shot down by those blighters who captured us. But where are we heading?'

'Heading for 'Rusalem. These guys injured by falling stones in quarry and being sent back to H.Q. for R. 'n R.' Carob gestured to the men slumped on the benches. 'But 'spect you be taken to King's Vizier to be dealt with.' He shuddered. 'Boulos evil nasty – best keep in his good books!' He gave them a jaundiced look. 'Spect you Dancer, being Skwid, destined for fodder for King's lions! You, Wings more likely a slave for rich merchant. But Miss Tissy, you'm being exotic Delphin, bet you go to King's Menagerie to live with spider monkeys.'

They look at him in dismay.

'But what about Bird? Tissy wailed. 'Where will the Vizier send her?'

Carob shook his head. 'Likely her sent with you to Menagerie. What wrong with little creature? And how come you in this pickle?'

He listened as Tissy explained about getting Bird to the Pool of Siloam for healing, his pinched face becoming animated.

'I know'd Pool of Siloam! My ma washed from rabies there! It very special to us Palmers – that our family name. Pool garden is where we grow our extra sweet dates – that very secret, so don't you go tellin' anybody, 'He added sternly. Then his expression turned to hopelessness. 'But no humans allowed at Pool – King's Orders!'

'In that case,' Wings said firmly, 'we're going to have to escape from this wagon, and then you can show us the way.'

Carob looked at him terrified. 'No! No!' he squeaked. 'Too dangerous! 'sides, we locked in and no way out.'

Snorting in scorn, Dancer shifted over to the cage door, and tried to get her long fingers through the bars to reach the bolts, but the gaps were too narrow. 'Tissy, see if you can get your small fingers through.'

Wriggling past her, Tissy found she could get her fingers through but hadn't the strength to draw back the tight bolts.

Carob drooped his thin shoulders. 'It no good. You certain go to Boulos!' Then he brightened. 'But p'raps my ma will know what to do. Yes! Ma big boss of us Palmers. She very nifty with brain. She get one on Old Boulos' men for sure – they dim!' he added scornfully. 'We soon get you free and take you to Pool. Us Scavs knows the secret way. Bird creature soon made better.'

Tissy looked at Carob, full of doubt. How could such a pathetic little creature help them? She gave a little sob. 'Dancer, Wings, it's all going horribly wrong!'

420

Wings put his arm round her. 'Now, Tissy, you mustn't despair – don't forget old Zaggy's keeping his eye on us!

She brightened. 'Yes, and Kassabel, too!'

Mile after mile the wagon creaked on through a parched deserted plain. Jolting over the rough road, weary and hungry they wondered if their ordeal would ever end. By mid-afternoon, the ground began to rise, the wagon going ever slower as the oxen strained at their yoke. Peering through the bars, they saw ahead a range of rounded brown hills glowing ochre in the sun. An hour later, they entered a shadowed valley. On the highest hill towered a massive sandstone wall some thirty feet high. Within it rose the elaborate minarets and sparkling white limestone walls of a vast palace, where glimpses of green tops of trees hinted at pleasure gardens.

''Rusalem!' Carob announced importantly.

The valley narrowed and became a gorge leading towards tall iron gates set in the wall. From the ramparts high above a face appeared momentarily and shouted down. With a rattling of heavy chains, the gates ponderously swung open to allow the wagons to trundle into a courtyard. Enclosed by more high walls, the place was full of the commotion and echoing din of shouting as men, clad only in loincloths, bodies glistening with sweat, laboured with cranes unloading blocks of limestone from ox carts, the teams of oxen patiently waiting, chewing the cud.

Their prison wagon headed for the far end to a high platform on which stood a short fat man, his long beard covering the bulging paunch of his stomach, small piggy eyes gazing imperiously over the busy scene. Four helmeted guards in gleaming armour stood to attention behind him, scimitars drawn and held at the ready.

'Old Boulos – King's Vizier and his men,' croaked Carob. 'Mind manners, or they chop your heads off!'

Drawing his team of oxen to a halt in front of the platform, the driver jumped down and bellowed above the noise to the Vizier who gave him a cursory nod. Drawing back the bolts, the driver swung open the wagon door and stood aside whilst the quarry workers, roughly pushing past Wings, Dancer, Tissy and Carob, climbed stiffly to the ground. Some limping from their injuries, they headed for a dark torchlit tunnel. Wings, Dancer and Tissy were about to follow, when Carob called them back.

'You wait inside wagon!' he hissed. 'P'raps you be forgotten, and I come back for you later.'

Hearts thumping, they quickly sunk to the floor between the benches. Putting on a nonchalant air, the little Scav clambered down, and swinging the door shut, sauntered off after the quarry men.

But the driver wasn't fooled. Opening the door, shouting curses, he grabbed Tissy who was nearest. Tumbling out, she managed to snatch hold of Bird's basket. Falling to the ground, she clutched the basket to her chest.

Full of fury, Dancer leapt out after her. Knocking the driver down, she landed on his chest. 'Bully! Bully!' she yelled, pummelling him about the head.

Horrified, Wings stumbling on his metal foot, fell out through the door. 'Dancer! Dancer! Watch out, the Vizier's guards—'

With a roar, the four guards leapt from the platform and fell on Dancer. Ferociously she turned on them, kicking and biting, sending one of their helmets flying, but in her weakened state, they soon overcame her. One, whipping handcuffs from his belt, locked her wrists together, whilst the other two dealt with Wings and Tissy, one dragging Wings up off the ground where he'd fallen and the other lifted Tissy, still tightly clutching the straps of Bird's basket, over his shoulder.

From the platform above the Vizier leaned down. Speaking in Common Language, he shouted: 'Take the scum away! The Skwid and tin foot for the holding prison. The shrimp and her basket to the Menagerie!'

Two of the soldiers roughly pulling Dancer by her arms as she kicked wildly, another dragging Wings, groaning in pain, his metal foot hanging off, headed for the tunnel. The fourth soldier with Tissy over his shoulder, still clutching Bird's basket, made for a side door in the courtyard wall.

Slipping unnoticed out of the shadows by the door, Carob scurried in after the soldier and Tissy.

# 15
# KING FAKHIR THE PROUD

Hanging over the soldier's shoulder as he strode through a seemingly endless warren of passages, Tissy clung with grim determination to the straps of Bird's basket, terrified she might drop her.

Coming to a door, the soldier kicked it open and entering a wide courtyard, they were met by a racket of screeching and whooping. The commotion came from animal cages set among giant potted plants: palms, figs, bananas, ferns, almost reaching the glass roof and giving the appearance of a jungle garden. Twisting her painfully stiff neck and squinting under the soldier's arm, Tissy saw in one cage a lion pacing up and down roaring mournfully, in another, parakeets in gaudy plumage squawked shrilly, whilst in another a family of meerkats scurried about, their leader imperiously staring at her through the bars. Ahead, a burly cruel-faced keeper was hosing down the tiled walkway.

Stopping at a cage of chattering long-tailed monkeys leaping and swinging among branches and ropes, the soldier shouted to the keeper. Dropping his flowing hose, he selected a key from the heavy bunch hanging from his belt and unlocked the cage door. The monkeys swarmed towards him and snarling a curse he grabbed the hose and turned it to a fierce jet, driving them shrieking and gibbering to the top of the cage. Swinging Tissy off his shoulder, the soldier threw her in. Landing face down in the swamp of rotting fruit and dung covering the cage floor, Bird's basket flew from her grasp. The door clanged shut behind her and whooping excitedly the bedraggled monkeys swarmed down from the cage roof and crowded around her. Wiping the filth from her eyes and backing away in fright, before she could stop them two of the largest monkeys snatched the basket and swinging it between them, scampered off with it up a tree branch. The lid flew open and wailing in fear, Bird tumbled out, the basket tumbling after her in a shower of straw. Lunging to catch her Tissy just managed to break her fall, and they collapsed together onto the filthy floor. Bird, her thin little body bleeding from scratches made by the branches, the green velvet dress given her by Betony had torn, revealing the silk vest and knickers lovingly made by Nutmeg from her old underclothes.

The monkeys' shrieks rising to a crescendo, as the keeper again aimed his powerful jet into the cage, Tissy noticed across the walkway behind him a tall fig tree trembling violently in its pot as it moved slowly sideways on casters. A marble slab in the wall swung open and a group of small figures clad in dark clothing and balaclavas on their heads inched from behind. The leader, a business-like wooden club in hand, was followed by three companions carrying a big rope net. Stealthily creeping up behind the keeper, with an expert throw they flung the net over him, and the leader clubbed him with a heavy blow to the back of his head. Crashing to the ground, the hose, still on full blast, fell from the keeper's limp hand. Lashing around like an angry python, the leader dived for the hose's nozzle.

'FIG, HELP US!' Shouted a familiar voice: it was Carob!

One of his companions sprang to his aid, and after a frantic few moments chase, they grabbed the nozzle, but such was the jet's force they were instantly hurled towards the glass roof, then against the lion's cage, then the parakeet cage.

'Lill! Olly! Find tap!' Screeched Carob at the two other figures standing bewildered. Galvanised to action, they dashed back along the hose to the tap somewhere out of sight. The jet turned to a dribble, and the hose fell limply to the ground. Winded and bruised, shaking themselves, Carob and Fig stood up unsteadily. Limping to the motionless keeper, Carob unclipped the bunch of keys from his belt.

Frustratedly he tried key after key in the monkey cage lock, Fig, Lill and Olly peering over his shoulder, whilst the monkeys and Tissy looked on anxiously. After what seemed an age, a key slid into the lock and clicked. Triumphantly Carob flung back the door and brandishing his club to keep back the screeching monkeys, hurried to Tissy cowering in a corner with Bird in her arms. Leaning close he muttered in her ear: 'No be affrighted, me and my chums have come to rescue you.'

Helping Tissy and Bird out of the cage, Carob slammed the door shut – but not quick enough to stop one monkey escaping. Chattering with glee it swung off into the roof, lost its hold, and fell through the bars of the lion cage to quickly become an ex-monkey.

Lill supporting Tissy carrying Bird, they all ran for the opening behind the potted fig, Olly and Fig scooping up the net on the way, and Carob giving another hefty blow with his club to the keeper, now stirring and groaning. All safely through, Fig and Olly heaved on a sprung bar on the wall and the marble slab juddered back into place, closing with a thud.

'Phew!' puffed Lill, letting go of Tissy's arm and leaning heavily against the slab.

They were in a narrow, paved alleyway. Although deserted, from windows set high in the stone walls came sounds of voices and the smell of cooking. In the gap between the roofs Tissy saw the sky was turning pale as the sun set.

Yanking off his balaclava, Carob turned to his team. 'Men, this be Miss Thetis, who –as you can see – be of amazin' Delphin kind!'

Tissy noticed that in his rush to rescue her, he still had white stone dust in his hair and behind his ears.

Balaclavas removed, Lill and Olly revealed a mass of copper curls, whilst Fig sported short ginger spikes. Round faced and snub nosed, they looked younger than Carob. All three gazed at Tissy in awe.

Overcome with relief at her escape, Tissy couldn't help giggling. 'I'm nothing special! Call me Tissy! And this is my best friend, Bird.' Holding Bird against her shoulder, she gently straightened Betony's torn velvet dress as best she could. 'She's a Delphin too. But she's very poorly and you'll have to forgive her as at the moment she can't see or talk.'

'She so tiny!' exclaimed Lill, gently patting Bird's thin shoulder. Squeaking in fright, Bird buried her face in Tissy's neck.

''nough talk,' Carob exclaimed with a frown. 'Must get home quick now! Ma will be fussing!'

Scurrying through a bewildering network of narrow passageways, up and down stone steps, through arches, once diving through the door to a laundry, fighting their way through lines of wet washing where, enveloped in hot steam, female Scavs were pummelling clothes in wooden barrels of soapy water, and then out into another alley. Tissy was wondering how much farther she could carry Bird, when they entered some stables. The sweet smell of hay mixed with horse manure in the air, they hastened between the rows of stalls where horses stared down at them, whinnying and stamping heavy hooves, they came to a tack room, its walls hung with saddles and harnesses.

Carob headed for a low door. Putting his mouth to a crack in the wood he gave a soft, elaborately tuneful whistle. From within came the thud of drawing bolts, and the door swung open to reveal a small figure donned in armour made from a hotchpotch of saucepan lids and frying pans. The figure gulped nervously.

'Password!' he squeaked, brandishing a sharpened stick, his little hands shaking with fear.

Cuffing the figure about his sandy coloured head of hair, Carob scornfully pushed the stick aside.

'It us, the SWAT team, Cactus yer twit. Didn't I tell yer – yet again – to 'member me special whistle?'

Crestfallen, with a clank of pans the little Scav stood back, allowing everyone through before slamming the door and shooting home the bolts.

Peering about in the soft light of oil lamps hanging from the roof beams, Tissy saw she was in a long narrow room with a high roof and a stone floor. Across the room steps led up to a door which, she would soon find, led out into a street. Along the long wall above the door a row of small, barred windows let in the glow of sunset. To her right stood a cooking range, flanked by cupboards and storage shelves that reached to the roof. From the roof itself hung strings of onions and bunches of herbs. To her left the wall was occupied by three tiers of bunks, enough sleeping space for at least thirty Scavs. At the far end of the room shelves were filled with clothing and bedding.

The smell of garlic and herbs suggested it was almost mealtime. Chattering and laughing, twenty or so Scavs sat either side of a long table, whilst a cook and her helpers busily stirred pots and pans at a blackened cooking range.

An old Scav, queening in her rocking chair throne by the range, spotting the new arrivals, gave a shriek of joy. Tissy guessed this must be Carob's Ma.

'SWAT's are back!' cried Bougainvillea, heaving her small stout frame out of her chair, and waddling over to hug Carob.

The other Scavs jumped up from the table to gather round. Abandoning their bubbling pots and pans, the cook and her team hurried to join in the welcome. They all greeted their SWAT with cries of relief.

'An' be this your friends, Mistress Thetis and Mistress Bird, you'n told us of, Carob?' asked Bougainvillea, peering with small grey eyes at Bird's little body in Tissy's arms.

'Aye Ma! Of Delphin kind!' Carob said proudly.

The surrounding Scavs hissed with whistles of awe.

'Delphin kind!' chorused several of the younger Scavs, round eyed with wonder.

'Ne'er would have I in – in me long days…' croaked an old grizzled Scav called Cedar, his wrinkled face crumpling with emotion.

'So beautiful!' whispered Carobina the cook, putting out her work roughened hand to reverently stroke Bird's torn velvet dress.

Agitated, Bird started struggling. Feeling suddenly dizzy, Tissy's knees gave way and she collapsed to the floor. 'Oh dear, I don't feel well – crashing in the flying machine – being captured by the dog soldiers – and – not knowing what's happened to Dancer and Wings—' She burst into tears.

Stooping to sweep Bird out of Tissy's arms, Bougainvillea took charge: 'Lill and Olly, don' stand there like a useless pair of broken brooms – help Miss Tissy to the bench. An', Acacia, fetch red wine – not everyday stuff, the special wine Juniper filched from King's cellars.'

Immediately all was action. Helped by Lill and Olly to a bench at the long table, Tissy leant against Lill's comforting shoulder, whilst Acacia, a young male Scav, scurried to take down a dusty, crusted bottle from the shelves by the cooking range. Carefully pouring out dark liquid into a mug, he respectfully handed it to Tissy. Sipping the sweet wine, she gradually regained her composure and was reassured to see Bougainvillea had taken Bird to her rocking chair and was holding her close. Soothed by the rocking to and fro Bird soon fell asleep.

At a shout from Carobina of: 'Supper's ready!' there was a rush for the table as her cook helpers bustled up and down, their trays laden with steaming bowls of artichoke soup and baskets of pitta bread. Sitting next to Tissy, Carob pushed a bowl of soup in front of her and passed her a pitta bread.

'Come, eat, Miss Tissy! Need strength.'

After swiftly consuming two bowls of soup and several breads, Carob got to his feet and banging his spoon on the table, a hush fell.

Taking a gulp of wine, he cleared his throat. 'Palmers! I knows you agrees with me – we honoured indeed to have two Missy Delphins as our guests!' He bowed to Tissy.

'AGREES! AGREES!' Everyone shouted, banging their spoons on the table.

'Little Missy Bird need our help.' He waved to where Bird, on Bougainvillea's lap, was blindly sipping the soup being fed to her. 'She be very poorly. That why brave Miss Tissy brung her here – must get to Siloam Pool for her healing. But first, we needs to rescue Miss Tissy's friends, Miss Dancer the Skwid an—'

Drowned out by shouts of disgust, Carob banged his spoon on the table. 'I knows! I knows! Miss Dancer may be Skwid kind, but she mighty warrior an' – an' not like baby eatin' Skwids. She very brave – fights mightily for our little Missy Delphins. An' I's likes her,' he added defiantly glowering at his indignant audience.

'Also, we need rescue Miss Tissy's flying man who brung them all to Dogland in his machine that flies high – high up, up and crashed mightily. Wings, he be called, and he be as tall as flagpole – an' as thin! Oh, an' has a tin foot too, which makes him special, don't you think?'

Carob's words were met with nods and murmurs of agreement. A lively discussion followed, suggestions as how to rescue Dancer and Wings ranging from sensible to bizarre. Sipping her soup and nibbling at a pitta, amid the excited talk, Tissy tried to concentrate on what was being said. Someone stressed that Wings and Dancer must be freed before the slave auction at the Forum prison before they were bought by their new owners. There was talk too of the need for disguises. An older female Scav offered to pinch from the laundry room two burqas belonging to Queen Jazzmyn the Fragrant and her serving maids.

Soon, made drowsy by the wine, Tizzy longed to lie down. Plucking Lill's sleeve, she asked in a whisper if there was there somewhere for her to sleep. Lill helped her up from the table and guided her to one of the lower bunks. Gratefully Tissy sank onto the mattress with a sigh of relief.

'No fret, Missy Tissy,' Lill said, tenderly covering her with a blanket. 'Sleep now – you and Missy Bird safe with us in Palmer Den.'

Drifting off to sleep the last thing Tissy saw was Bougainvillea still sitting by the cooking range, crooning to Bird as she rocked her on her knee.

Tissy was woken by a cook Scav bringing her a mug of sweet mint tea; daylight filtered in through the barred windows overlooking the street. The Den loud with chatter, the Palmers bustled about making bunks, downing bowls of yoghurt and fresh figs. The palace workers were heading up the steps and out into the street: cleaners, cooks and the gardeners who tended the King's exotic gardens.

Bird was up, sitting on a rug by the cooking range. Dressed only in her underwear, she was being fed yoghurt by a young female called Myrtle; Bougainvillea, in her rocking chair, was mending her green velvet dress.

Hurriedly pulling on her boots, Tissy went to watch amazed as Bird, chirruping happily, slurped spoonful's of yoghurt.

'Thank you so much, Myrtle! I've had such trouble getting Bird to eat anything!' She turned to Bougainvillea. 'Thank you too – for mending her dress!'

Smiling, Bougainvillea stroked the soft green velvet, which seemed to gleam even in the gloom of the Den. 'Such beautiful material! You very rich in your land? Not even t' Queen has such cloth!'

Tissy shook her head. 'No, we only have plain woollens and linens – silk and velvet on special days. Bird's dress was given to her by a Gaiakin from Florain – when she was taken there for healing. Sadly, the Gaiakins couldn't cure her.'

She was interrupted by Carob calling her to the long table. 'Miss Tissy! Hurry now, come have breakfast! We must be off to Forum afore the viewing starts.'

Seating her at the long table, Carob brought her a bowl of thick creamy yoghurt. When Tissy tasted it, she understood why Bird was so happy to eat some. Munching a juicy fig, she noticed across the room hanging on the wall, a large banner in the form of a palm tree embroidered in colourful silks. Stitched on the trunk was a woman's face, her luminous brown eyes and lustrous dark hair done in the finest threads. Across the palm fronds in shining gold thread were the words: PALM OF TAMAR.

Perched on a ladder beside the banner, the old Scav called Cedar was using a long-handled feather duster to carefully dust a row of glittering cut-glass bottles on a high shelf, the clear liquid inside gleaming in the light of a lamp flickering above. Noticing her interest, Cedar, climbed down and beckoned her to join him.

He pointed lovingly with his duster up at the bottles on the shelf.

'That be Tamar's Palm Wine – brewed from extra sweet dates, specially c'llected by us Palmers – at high summer's full moon, from palm groves in forbidden Siloam Garden.'

Tissy felt a clutch of fear. In the wagon on the road to Jerusalem Carob had said something about humans being not allowed to bathe in the Pool.

Cedar interrupted her thoughts. Wafting his duster in the direction of the banner, he said: 'This be our Palmer Emblem – it be ancient!' He ran his duster over the face on the trunk. 'She be our Mother Tamar who brought our tribe out of Affric as servants of the most noble clan of Delphins, worshippers of holy Phul. One day, when we be free once more and not slaves, we go back to Affric, sail, sail over sea—'

'No time for stories now, ol' Cedar! We be gettin' ready to rescue Miss Tissy's friends,' Carob called from where he and his SWAT team, watched admiringly by the younger Scavs, were preparing their outfits. Tissy learned later that these costumes had been made by the Palmer clan's aunties and mums; the balaclavas knitted from unravelling a woollen cloak pilfered from the King's grandmother by a palace cleaner Scav, the trousers and tops originally a chocolate brown velvet robe, handily mislaid from the vast wardrobe of Queen Jazzmyn the Fragrant.

A young female called D'Vine was with them. Wearing a low-cut tight-fitting dress of scarlet satin, she sported a long blond wig. Teetering on bright red high-heeled shoes, she was applying make-up in front of a mirror: frantic-pink lipstick, blush cheek rouge and long curling false eyelashes. Leaving her and the SWAT team to finish preparing, Carob took Tissy up the steps and out in the street.

Plunging into the noise and bustle of the city they hurried through a bewildering labyrinth of alleyways and passages, every now and then crossing squares bounded on all sides by tall houses, their balconies draped with washing. Reaching the colonnaded walkway surrounding the Forum as they pushed their way through the crowd, the blare of trumpets told them they had only just arrived in time.

At the far end of the arena a flight of marble steps led up to a canopied podium in front of two huge mahogany doors. To a fanfare of trumpets, the doors were flung open with a crash and another fanfare announced the King and Queen with their entourage of rich Jerusalem merchants.

Straining to peer round a foul-smelling fat man in a greasy brown djellaba, Tissy gazed in astonishment at the King and Queen. The King, who Tissy judged to be no more than five feet tall, was dressed in a floor length purple velvet robe. Weighed down with gold and pearl necklaces and bracelets, he wore a silver crown encrusted with sparkling jewels and topped by two enormously long antelope horns curling out from either side of his head, making him look absurdly like a goat in fancy dress. Equally ridiculous was Queen Jazzmyn the Fragrant, her face a mask of heavy make-up, grey hair set on top of her head in a bun and decorated with brightly coloured plastic toothbrushes poking out at odd angles. Her peacock blue satin robe was covered in long garishly coloured strips of plastic reminding Tissy of the fly screen Grammer Nutmeg put up at her larder door in hot weather. The city merchants, robed in silks, satins, and velvets, were also decorated with plustics of all kinds, but in deference to their royal patrons, not so elaborately.

Taking their places on ornately carved seats beneath the purple and gold canopy, at a signal from the King, at the far end of the square a barred door clanged open. Led by Boulos the Vizier the sorry looking captives were marched out from the holding prison, escorted by guards bearing drawn swords. Tissy gave a sobbing groan when she spotted Wings and Dancer. Both looked in a terrible state. Supported by Dancer, Wings was limping heavily. Dancer, her face smeared with blue blood, had a gash on her forehead.

'No fear, Miss Tissy!' Carob said, squeezing her hand. 'Us SWATs will rescue Tin Foot and Miss Dancer.'

The guards' swords jabbed the prisoners into line and Boulos marched stiffly to the podium steps, bowing to the royal audience. The crowd fell silent and the King arose from his throne.

'ALL MIGHTY AND PROUD MAJESTY, MAY YOU LIVE FOR A MILLION YEARS!' shouted Boulos, 'Fresh captives await your inspection!'

Leaning on two servants, Fakhir the Proud descended the steps. With Boulos bowing and walking backwards before him, they made their way along the line of prisoners, the King stopping every now and then to disdainfully prod a prisoner with his gloved hand. Coming to Wings, Fakhir eyed him dismissively. Passing on to Dancer, standing arms folded, glaring fiercely down at him, her scaly skin rippling black and navy, he shuddered and quickly moved on.

The King's inspection finished, it was the merchants' turn. Prodding and poking the prisoners with a view to placing a bid for any they thought might be useful in their kitchens, gardens, or if of superior appearance, to tend to their robing, and wait at table. After a half hour of discussing among themselves, making notes on wax tablets, the merchants returned to the podium. The inspection had been so complicated, Tissy couldn't work out if Dancer and Wings had been bought by any merchant.

The ceremony over, the prisoners were led out of the Forum back to the prison, and with a last blare of trumpets, the King and entourage left.

'Quick Missy Tissy!' Carob grabbed Tissy's hand. 'We must get back to the Den now and alert the SWAT.'

Trying to hurry through the crowded streets Tissy desperately hoped the plan Carob and his team had hatched at supper last night would work.

Meanwhile back at the Den, whilst Tissy and Carob were in the Forum, Lill, Olly and Fig sprang into action. Business-like in their SWAT outfits, they left by the back entrance into the stables, leaving Cactus, armed with his pointed stick, to bolt the door behind them.

Reaching the Laundry, they were delighted to find that today one of the washerwomen was Fig's Aunty Apricot. Explaining their mission to her and her colleagues, the women were pleased to put one over the detested King and Queen. Taking them to the drying room, Aunty Apricot helped them search the burqas for the right size to fit Wings and Dancer's tall frames, eventually pulling down two dark blue burqas belonging to Queen Jazzmyn's tallest handmaid.

Rolling them into a tight bundle they said goodbye to the giggling washerwomen and scuttled back to the Den to find Tissy and Carob had returned and were helping D'Vine putting last touches to her glamorous finery. Lill, Olly and Fig performed a quick change from SWAT outfits to street clothes, and with the two folded burqas under Olly and Lill's arms, they set off for the Forum with Carob and Tissy.

A few moments later, high heels clacking, D'Vine teetered up the steps and out into the street, a hand basket covered with a checked cloth on her arm. Under the cloth were some of Carobina's iced fairy cakes and two bottles of strong syrupy-sweet sherry wine nabbed by Juniper from the King's cellars – Carob had laced the drink with several sleeping powders before carefully recorking the bottles. Hurrying through the familiar warren of alleyways and backstreets, her exotic outfit attracting curious looks and some coarse comments, D'Vine made her way to the Forum. Nearing the prison she spotted the others clustered in a doorway trying to look casual. She found the prison guarded by only two of Boulos's sentries, sitting on stools behind the gate gazing moodily through the bars. They were fed up: drawing lots, they had been left to guard the prisoners whilst the other guards sloped off to the nearest drinking den – Peachysweet's, the guards' favourite bar – for a mid-morning tipple.

First pretending to pass by, D'Vine came to a hesitant halt. Fluttering her false eyelashes prettily, she teetered up to them.

'Weeell, heeello lads!' she simpered, running her red nail-varnished fingers seductively through her long blonde wig. 'Seeing your gloomy faces, I couldn't help stopping! Not even a dry biscuit for your morning break? That'll never do!'

The two guards, first peering suspiciously at the small figure, then taking in the low-cut, tight fitting scarlet dress, and pouted mouth smeared thickly with frantic-pink lipstick, got to their feet and gave her a greedy leer.

'Two gorgeous strapping men like you need sustenance for your hard job!' cooed D'Vine. 'Guess what I've got in my basket?' She provocatively twitched aside a corner of the checked cloth to expose a glimpse of a sherry bottle.

At the sight, two men's eyes gleamed. 'Spare us a drop, little lady – me throat fair parched!' wheedled one guard.

The other picked up a couple of tin mugs from the floor and shoved them through the bars. 'Go on, draw the cork and give us a splash!' he drooled.

Suddenly swaying, D'Vine put out her hand to steady herself on one of the prison bars. 'Oh dear, I've sudden come over poorly. Need to sit down…'

The guard quickly unlocked the prison gate and guided her to a stool.

Sitting with her head bowed, after a few moments she appeared to recover.

'Feel better now – us silly females tend to faint! You kind lads must have a reward.' Whipping off the cloth from her basket, she took out a bottle of sherry and drew the cork. 'Hold out your mugs!' Splashing in a generous quantity, she held out her basket. 'Help yourself to cakes – my auntie's best fairy cakes.'

The guards dived in eagerly, then taking big gulps drained their mugs of sherry. D'Vine quickly topped up them up and as the bottle emptied, opened the next one. Grinning stupidly, the guards singing dissolved into helpless laughter. Their raucous antics could be seen and heard from inside the prison, attracting the attention of the miserable prisoners shackled to the walls. One or two, understanding what D'Vine was up to, began to look hopeful.

In the far shadows, where she and Wings were huddled, Dancer whispered: 'That strange little figure talking to the guards is a Scav. Do you think she might be a friend of Carob's?'

'Might be…don't know,' Wings said, peering uncertainly at D'Vine as she plied the guards with sherry.

The second bottle now almost empty, one of the guards, clutching a bar to steady himself, peered cross-eyed into his mug, shot D'Vine a suspicious look, then crumpled to the ground, followed a moment later by his colleague.

Snatching a heavy key hanging by the door, D'Vine slipped off her high heels and ran barefoot through the gate to where the others still lurked in their doorway.

'Both guards are down and out!' she chortled.

'Gran' job, D'Vine!' Carob grinned, grabbing the key from her. 'Now make yoursel' scarce, girl.'

Diving into the nearest alleyway, D'Vine stripped down to a leotard, dumping her outfit, including her long blonde wig, into a nearby bin and disappeared into the backstreets.

The rest of the team sprinted into the prison, jumping over the guards sleeping peacefully in the doorway. Whilst Fig kept a lookout for the other guards returning, Carob quickly unfastened the padlock to release the long chain that ran through the prisoners' shackles. Heaving together Olly and Lill pulled it free. The prisoners clambered to their feet and, massaging their numbed wrists, dashed for freedom.

Tissy ran to Wings and Dancer. 'It's O.K. we've come to get you!' Helping them to their feet, she called to the others. 'I've found them. Quick, bring the disguises!'

With Tissy, Carob and Lill's help, Wings and Dancer struggled into their burqas. Standing back Carob studied them critically: Dancer's almost covered her, and it was impossible to tell she was a Skwid, but Wings' metal foot showing beneath the hem of his burqa looked most peculiar. But there was no time for adjustments as Fig shouted a warning from the door.

'The other guards are coming back!'

Everyone dashed for the prison gate. Dancer, supporting Wings, momentarily stopped to grab a sword from one of the unconscious guards. Squeaking in terror, Carob dragged her away as she hastily hoisted her burqa to tuck it in her belt. Once safely outside, from the Forum behind them came loud shouts: the guards had discovered their sleeping colleagues and an empty prison. Terrified of their fate at the hands of Boulos the Vizier they spread out to hunt down the escaping prisoners, ignoring the little group of Scavs and two burqa clad figures strolling nonchalantly into an alleyway.

Once out of the guards' sight, Carob led the way through the streets; the only alarming incident was Wings' foot coming loose as they pushed their way through a wedding party. Attracting a few curious stares they all clustered round him whilst he propped himself on a mounting block to strap it back on.

Reaching the Den, as everyone hurried down the steps from the street, Wings tripped on the hem of his burqa, almost falling, but was saved by Dancer. Arriving at the bottom Dancer impatiently flung off her disguise, causing uproar among the Palmers. With howls of 'SKWID! SKWID!' they dived in all directions, some under the long table, others under blankets on the bunks.

'No feered, silly Palmers!' shouted Carob. 'This be Miss Dancer! As I tol' you, she be Misses Tissy and Bird's special friend. She be warrior who guards them – look she has a sword!'

Only partly reassured, one by one the Palmers crept warily out from their hiding places. Carob gesticulated to Wings, who, to the sound of ripping seams, had fought his way out of his burqa. 'And as I explained afore this be Tin Foot, who brung them all to Dogland in his flying machine – he called Mr Wings.'

Bougainvillea, pulling off the tea towel she'd draped over her head in an attempt to hide herself, rose from her rocking chair to greet them. 'You be most welcome, friends of Misses Delphins!'

Tut-tutting over Dancer and Wings injuries, she set about organising the comfort of their large guests, ordering mattresses to be dragged down from the loft, to be lined against the wall beneath the PALM OF TAMAR, so they could sit. Then ordering the cook's helpers to fetch bowls of warm water and cloths, she bustled to her medicine cupboard for various healing unctions. Wounds dressed, plied with wine and cakes, Wings and Dancer soon felt better.

Tissy brought Bird, in her newly mended velvet dress, to sit with them. Hearing Dancer's husky voice, by squeaks and chirrups Bird insisted on sitting on her lap where she settled down happily. Then Tissy recounted her adventure in the menagerie and Carob and his SWAT team's daring rescue.

By supper time, the Palmers and their guests were firm friends. Carobina and her cooks had prepared a special meal: falafel, challah, and gefilte fish with spicy sauces. As the wine flowed – courtesy of, but unknown to, King Fakhir – Carob and his SWAT team told the story of the prison rescue, including D'Vine's part which drew roars of laughter. The story became ever more exaggerated until the party broke up very late. Tired out, Carob, Tissy, Dancer and Wings agreed to leave planning their next steps until the morning.

But lying in her bunk Tissy's mind was full of troubled thoughts. What lay ahead? How would they get Bird to the Pool of Siloam? And when they got there, what then? Would Lark and Fin be waiting for them with Bird's soul inside the eagle's eye? Mossy never said anything about the Pool being forbidden. How could they escape being caught by the King's soldiers? She must ask Carob in the morning – it was all so frightening! So daunting!

Squeezing her eyes tight shut, desperate not to cry out loud, a soft laugh close to her ear made her jump. A hand gently brushed her cheek.

'Now, Thetis! Do not fret so! All will be well in the end.'

Opening her eyes, she peered around the Den lit only by a flickering nightlight in a holder on the table. There was no one up and about, everyone was sleeping. But she wasn't frightened any more. Turning over to face the wall, she drifted peacefully into deep sleep.

Far away to the West, from the top of a lighthouse two figures gazed over the moonlit waters of the Atlantic. Zagzagel and Mullein were watching two vessels approaching the ancient harbour of Cadiz. Sails billowing, Orca and Aurora rode the waves towards them. Like figureheads, in the bow of Orca stood Kassabel and in the bow of Aurora stood the diminutive figure of the angel, Phul.

Later that night, Zagzagel and Mullein safely aboard Orca, the vessels once more set sail. Passing through the Straits of Gibraltar, they entered the Mediterranean Sea.

# 16
# POOL OF SILOAM

Bird guided Quilla along the Highway, keeping him to the shadows cast by the rugged cliffs. Casting anxious glances back along the road, she couldn't see Gressil's carriage. Looking ahead, she saw the white walls of the city coming up fast. Moments later they were there.

'Fly higher now Quilla!' she called. 'And circle round so I can spot the Pool.'

Below lay a muddle of buildings; enclosed within massive battlements, the smaller dwellings huddled up against the gleaming white walls of a palace complex with courtyards, domed towers, gardens of tall cypress trees, flower borders, pools, and fountains; she doubted whether any of those might be the Pool. Hadn't Leif told Fin it was hidden in a garden outside the city walls?

Turning her gaze from the city to where roads from north, south, east, and west wound over rocky slopes and through ravines towards the city gates, she was about to call out to Quilla to fly lower when, dipping his wings and swinging about to face the north, he let out an excited squawk.

'Corvids! I can hear corvids!'

Bird saw a cloud of gulls wheeling and swooping over what looked like a vast rubbish dump. Among the gulls was a group of larger birds their plumage gleaming black.

'Yes, it's a flock of ravens – they're feeding at a rubbish dump and having a row with the gulls!'

'Ravens! That's good: they are the most intelligent of the corvids. We'll go down – I'll talk to them – ask about the Pool.'

At the sight of the great eagle descending on them the gulls scattered, but when Quilla landed amongst the rotting vegetables and meat, the ravens landed too. Gathering at a safe distance, cocking their heads from side to side, they studied him curiously.

Giving a series of small cheeps, Quilla bowed respectfully and two of the older, grizzled birds hopped over and began a low chattering.

Listening to their whispering squeaks Bird's heart gave a tug: she was reminded of home, when the jackdaws nested in the eaves outside her bedroom window – when Bee was alive.

'What are they saying, Quilla?'

'They know about the Pool and its healing properties. They wanted to know why I was looking for it, so I told them about you. It's not far, on a plateau above a valley of palm and olive trees, just south of the city walls. I explained that I am blind so their leader will show you the way.'

'They don't need to!' Bird exclaimed. 'Just ask them where it is.'

'No, we'd better let them – don't want to offend, ravens can turn nasty!'

A fierce looking bird's face appeared close outside her bubble and peered in with an intelligent glittering eye. Bird gave it a wave and the raven hopped into the air.

'Caw! Caw!' it called.

'Skeew! Skeew!' Quilla replied.

Guided by Bird's instructions, flying low, Quilla followed the raven as it headed south around the outside of the city to where a plateau jutted out from cliffs beneath the battlements. She saw below, in a deep narrow valley a garden of date palms and olive trees, all enclosed within a high wall. The plateau, valley, and garden, lush with trees, grasses, and ferns, were in stark contrast to the surrounding dry, dusty land. In the rock wall above the plateau, a waterfall spouted from a dark tunnel mouth. Sparkling in the sun, it cascaded down through ferns growing out of crevices in the cliff to where, in a rectangle of white marble pillars and half-hidden among the columns of cypress trees, Bird glimpsed the gleam of water. Was that the Pool of Siloam, she wondered?

Following Bird's instructions, Quilla landed clumsily on the top of a cypress tree, sending it swaying. The raven circled round, calling 'Caw! Caw!' Then flew off.

From their perch, Bird could see down into the Pool; the water deep and dark, the waterfall splashing into it sent out circles of ripples. Surrounded by pillars and cypress trees, the place looked little used, the paving on the walkway around the Pool moss covered and crumbling. Steps, cut into the fern-covered cliff-side, led up to a narrow ledge beside the tunnel from where the waterfall gushed.

'What now?' Quilla asked, the branch bending alarmingly as he shifted his weight.

'There's a broken pillar right below us, it'll be safer than this tree. The top's flat and wide, so you can easily hop down to it. Just do as I say. We'll wait there for the others – I hope they won't be long!'

Mighty wings clattering through the branches, he hovered for a moment before locating the top of the pillar with his talons and settling. Peering across the Pool, Bird spotted movement on the steps leading up to the ledge beside the waterfall: a little figure in dark clothes and wearing a balaclava had appeared out of the ferns. Scuttling up onto the ledge, the figure turned and for a long moment stared out from behind his balaclava across to where Quilla perched, before disappearing into the darkness of the tunnel.

From where she was, Bird could not see the winding track that led from the King's Highway down to the palm garden. Nor could she know that along it raced a chariot driven by a handsome young man with luxuriantly curling black hair.

The thunder of hooves approaching the gate to the garden woke the guard dozing in the sun. The chariot coming to a halt, the guard, recognised one of the King's special couriers, and sprang up in surprise. Leaning down, the young man smiled. Then, before the guard could react, the young man's sword flashed, and the guard's head fell spinning to the ground.

Jumping down from the chariot, Gressil lifted out Mab's drooping cloak-wrapped form, and kicking open the gate, carried her down the steep slope into the rows of trees where he gently laid her in the shade of a palm hung with fat bunches of luscious, sweet dates.

'Not long now, my love. We are nearly there,' Gressil said, softly brushing Ptolemy's ringed hand over her shrivelled, slug-slimed cheek.

Mab's eyelids fluttered but didn't open.

Outside the gate the exhausted horse, still harnessed to the chariot, its head hanging in the hot sun, swayed for a moment before its legs buckled beneath it and it fell to the ground, dead.

At the Palmer Den the door from the stables crashed open and Fig tumbled in, his balaclava askew.

'EAGLE! I'SE SEEN T'EAGLE,' he yelled.

Tissy, Lill, Olly and Dancer were sat at the table cluttered with the remains of their lunch. Across sat Bougainvillea, Cedar and those Palmers who were not on duty at the Palace, gardening, cooking, or cleaning. On the rug by the cooking range Bird was being fed yoghurt by Myrtle.

Cactus sat on the floor near Dancer. Using a honing stone, he was proudly sharpening the sword she had stolen from the prison guards. Earlier, watching Dancer testing the sword, lunging, slashing, wielding it above her head, Cactus had tried to imitate her with his pointed stick, causing great danger to those nearby.

Wings and Carob were not there: they had gone to the Eilat Gate to lookout for Fin, Sandy, Lark and Crow.

Earlier, at breakfast, Wings had told the assembled Palmers what he, Tissy and Dancer had learned: that their friends were crossing the Sahara Desert, heading for the Red Sea, intending to make their way from there north to meet up with them in Jerusalem. He explained they were accompanied by an eagle wearing an amazing, jewelled cross with wondrous healing powers, and that the cross and the eagle were vital to their mission to heal Bird at the Pool of Siloam. The Palmers immediately wanted to know more about the mysterious cross and the eagle. So, plucking up her courage, Tissy had tried to tell them about Bird, how her soul was stolen and had ended up in an eagle's eye, but unsure of the story, she got into a hopeless muddle and burst into tears. The Palmers, being kindly folk, quickly reassured her that as she was of the Delphin race, whatever she said, they would believe, and she must not fret.

But then Lill had brought up a problem which nearly made Tissy cry again.

'What about M'Benga, lurking in the Pool, waiting for something to eat? He'd snap up Missy Bird's tiny body pretty quick!'

'Aye, he'd spit out her bones in a trice before any eagle with a cross could come near!' Olly groaned in theatrical ghoulish horror.

Bougainvillea snorted. 'Soon sort M'Benga good and proper – give him a strong dose of Tamar's Elixir.' She waved to the glass bottles gleaming on the shelf beside the Tamar Banner. 'Get him so dizzy he'd get his tentacles all knotted!'

So, plans had been made. Carob and Wings, his tall frame hidden again beneath his stolen burqa, would go to the Eilat Gate to watch out for Fin, Lark, Sandy, and Crow, whilst Fig, in his SWAT outfit, would go to the Pool and watch for the eagle wearing the cross. Tissy and Dancer would stay behind, ready to bring Bird to the Pool.

'Eagle wearing the shiny jool, just as Missy Tissy says!' Fig gasped flinging off his balaclava.

As one, everyone jumped up from the table.

'Right, we'll be off,' Dancer said. 'Cactus, quick, give me my sword!'

Giving the blade a last wipe with his oily cloth, Cactus reluctantly handed it over and Dancer tucked it in her belt.

A thrill ran through Tissy as she hurried over to Bird: whether of excitement or dread, she couldn't quite tell. Would she at long last see Lark? Gathering Bird up from the rug and saying goodbye to her newfound friends, she couldn't help a few tears. As Bougainvillea hugged her she wished she could have given the old Scav the last of the jewels from Nutmeg's peacock brooch, stolen by the dog soldiers!

Obeying Carob's earlier commands, Lill, Olly and Fig– who were to guide Tissy, Bird and Dancer to the Pool – armed themselves with some of Carobina's wickedly sharp kitchen knives, whilst Old Cedar climbed his ladder to the shelf of Palm Elixir and handed down one of the bottles to Bougainvillea who carefully wrapped it in a cloth before putting it into a rucksack which she thrust into Cactus's trembling hands. To his immense pride not only had he been allowed to go with the others, but more importantly, be in charge of the Elixir.

Farewells over, Tissy and Dancer, who insisted that she should be the one to carry Bird, followed Lilly, Olly, and Fig out into the tack room. Cactus, pointed stick in hand and rucksack containing the Elixir on his shoulder, brought up the rear, leaving Cedar to close the door behind them with a rattle of bolts.

In the tack room everyone stood for a moment listening. All was quiet: being mid-day there was nobody about. They hurried past the stalls where horses munched on bales of hay, then on through the laundry; the Scav washerwomen had gone to their mid-day meal, tubs of steaming washing abandoned. Just before the door to the drying room, they stopped at the entrance to a dark cramped passage. Fig took a small clay oil lamp from a recess and lighting the wick with a spark from a flint, led them down the steep slope, his small flame flickering on the walls. From the darkness ahead came the soft gurgle of running water. Five minutes later the passage opened out onto a paved area. In the dim lamp light, they made out the gleam of water bubbling out of the rock below them.

They had come to the underground Spring of Gihon. Swirling around a dark pool, the water spilled over the edge to cascade down a dark tunnel. His lamp held high, they followed Fig along a narrow ledge beside the rushing stream, which every so often cascaded over a shelf to a lower level, forcing them to pick their way down treacherously slippery steps. Holding onto the rock wall to steady herself, twice, to Tissy's alarm, Dancer, Bird in her arms, stumbled on the steps. Thankfully, Bird seemed untroubled as she nestled peacefully against Dancer's shoulder.

About fifteen minutes later, daylight appeared ahead, and they stepped out onto a flat rocky ledge. All around them ferns grew, covering the cliff face that reached up to the very base of the City wall. To the left of the ledge, the stream raced out of the tunnel and plunged down into the deep Pool below.

Looking down, Tissy breathed a sigh of relief. 'At last! The Pool of Siloam! Come on Dancer, let's go down!'

Using the ferns as hand holds to steady herself, she eagerly started down the steep steps leading to the walkway surrounding the Pool. Behind her Dancer with Bird descended cautiously, followed by the others.

Once on the walkway gazing into the sinister depth of the Pool, Tissy recalled what Lill had said about a monster lurking there. For a second, she thought she glimpsed a large milky-white eye, its black elongated pupil regarding her intently. Quickly stepping back from the edge, she searched around the undergrowth growing amongst the cypress trees and pillars surrounding the Pool, hoping against hope that Lark would step out.

Cactus suddenly let out a screech. 'Look! T'eagle with the cross!'

A fleeting flash of gold and a rainbow of sparkling light dazzled them.

'SKEEW! SKEEW!' The cry echoing around the Pool had a joyful note.

'SKEEW… SKEEW …'

The eagle's call echoed faintly down the valley to where Ptolemy sat beneath the date-laden palm tree.

Lying in his arms, Mab's misted eyes flickered open. 'Did you hear, beloved?' she whispered in a wavering voice.

'Yes, my love. The eagle has arrived! Soon we shall have the cross! No one can stop us!' He plucked a date dripping with syrup from a bunch above. Lovingly he pressed it to her slime oozing lips.

'Come, eat another of these dates: they are the fruit of the Tamar Palm and will give you strength for our final victory!'

'Gressil, am I dying...?' Mab's voice faded, the date fell from her lips, and she lost consciousness.

Gressil leapt to his feet, demonic anger glittering in what had once been poor Ptolemy's gentle brown eyes. Wrapping her in the red cloak and cradling her in his arms, he strode purposefully through the palms and olive trees towards the beckoning white marble pillars surrounding the Pool on the plateau above.

From her vantage point in Quilla's eye on top of the pillar, Bird had seen the group appear out of the tunnel. As they descended the steps onto the walkway, her excitement grew. Could one be Dancer? Was that Tissy? Yes!

'They've come, Quilla! They've come – Tissy and Dancer! And – and—'

Filled with dismay, she peered at the small bundle in Dancer's arms, 'Oh, Quilla, my body's so thin, so wasted—' she choked.

Quilla interrupted impatiently: 'Tell me where to land!'

'Fly across the Pool – a little down and a short way ahead. Careful not to land in the water!' Swooping down from the pillar, talons almost brushing the Pool's surface, Quilla landed on the walkway in a flurry of wing beats.

Seeing the great eagle plunging towards them, squeaking in panic the four Palmers dived into the safety of the ferns growing in the wall, before cautiously creeping out, kitchen knives and pointed stick at the ready.

His wings drooping in submission, the huge bird twisted his head about, blindly searching, the jewels on the heavy cross around his neck sparkling in the sunshine. Warily Tissy approached and searched the blank eyes.

'I can see a tiny figure – no bigger than – than a tadpole! It's waving! Dancer come and look.'

Setting down Bird's body on a patch of soft moss, Dancer bent close. Her round Skwid eyes flickered in excitement. 'Yes – it's Bird! She can definitely see us. Call to her.'

Conscious of Quilla's fearsome beak, Tissy leaned near. 'Can you see me, Bird?' she called. 'It's Tissy!'

Turning her ear to the eye, she heard a voice too faint to understand. But it could have been her imagination. Hadn't Lark, in his letter from the Isle of Man, said only Fin could hear Bird's soul?

Desperately she called again. 'Bird, where are the others?'

Moving still closer, she saw the tiny figure dancing about gesticulating.

Suddenly, from Bird's body lying on the moss came an agitated shriek. Tissy and Dancer looked at her in surprise: she was trying to crawl toward Quilla.

Tissy gave a sob. 'Oh Dancer, she knows! Her poor little body knows her soul is near!'

A brusque shout gave them a start. Looking round they saw a man come striding up the steps from the valley below.

'What are you doing here? The Pool is forbidden!' the man barked imperiously. He was young, with dark curling hair, and wearing a uniform, with the device of a double goat's horn embroidered on his tunic. He carried someone in his arms wrapped in a red cloak. Gently laying the shrouded figure on the pavement a shrivelled arm poked out. Snatching at the cloak he quickly covered it.

Olly stepped nervously forward. 'It be O.K. sir,' he squeaked. 'We be gardeners – come to prune the date trees.' He waved his kitchen knife as evidence.

The young man nodded at Dancer and Tissy. 'And what about them? Don't look like gardeners to me.' His eyes slid towards Quilla crouched over Bird's wasted body. Dancer glimpsed in them a sickly green glitter.

'Tissy get Bird away from here!' she hissed. 'That's no man – it's a demon!'

Pulling her borrowed sword from her belt, she lunged at him. Ptolemy's hand flashed to his sword, but in that moment, Quilla flew at him. Talons sinking into Ptolemy's arm, beak stabbing at his eyes, the blow intended to slice off Dancer's head slashed instead deep into her shoulder, and she fell backwards, blue blood spurting from the wound.

Tissy screamed to Lill: 'Run! Get help!' Scooping up Bird's body, she threw her into Lill's arms.

Dashing to Dancer and pressing her trembling hand to the wound, trying to staunch the flow of blood, she saw Lill with Bird struggling wildly in her arms, stumbling up the steps to the tunnel. To her horror, halfway up Lill dropped Bird, and they both tumbled back down. Meanwhile the fight between the demon and Quilla raged on, the demon screaming curses as Quilla's hooked beak jabbed at Ptolemy's eyes and talons raked through his now shredded

436

uniform. Cactus, who had snatched up Dancer's sword, was prancing around his legs trying to stab him.

Olly, wielding his kitchen knife and rushing to help Cactus, shouted to Fig dithering uncertainly between joining the fight and helping Tissy and Dancer: 'Fig! Go get Carob and Mr Wings! Go by the Garden gate – NOW!'

Fig dashed away.

Desperately pressing her hand to Dancer's wound, Tissy noticed the wrapped figure lying on the ground was struggling to sit up. The cloak fell away to reveal a dreadful sight: what could once have been a woman – only she had butterfly wings trailing from her back, tattered nearly to shreds, the swirls and roundels of peacock-blue, icy turquoise, pansy-brown, mustard, silver and scarlet faded to powdery grey – her body, which must have once been beautiful was now a hideous mess of suppurating slime.

The woman pointed to the Pool and screeched: 'GRESSIL! M'Benga rises! He has come to our aid!'

Tissy spun her head round to the Pool. Just beneath the surface she glimpsed the shadow of a huge body. Its pulsing flesh ever changing colour, rippling silver green then dark orange, on the front of its face a ring of long tentacles coiled and twisted. Behind them two black elongated pupils in white rimmed eyes stared directly at her.

'Lark!' she sobbed. 'Where are you——' All around her went fuzzy grey and faded……

On the King's Highway, their horses stumbling with exhaustion, reluctantly Sandy decided to abandon them. 'Right lads,' he said, dismounting. 'Walking will be swifter than plodding on these poor animals. Unload your packs and take off their saddles and harness. We will leave the brave beasts to find their own way home, or wherever they wish to go.'

'Have courage everyone!' Lief said. 'Jerusalem is not far. Just beyond the next hill.' He pointed along the road winding through the valley towards a hill.

Leaving the horses grazing on dusty scrub beneath a drooping fig tree, they shouldered their packs and set off. At the crest of the hill, they stood for a moment in wonder. Across another valley, narrow and deep, on a far hillside stood a city. Within its surrounding high walls, white towers and red roofs gleamed in the glare of the midday sun. The Highway would lead them to a gated archway in the wall.

Moving close to Fin, Crow croaked in a low voice: 'So Fin, that be Rusalem!'

'Yep, here at last, Crow!'

'That be place where Sparkie and I will – find how we'll – end,' he whispered.

Fin frowned. 'Many have found an end here, Crow. Some happy endings. Some sad. I wonder what ours' will be—'

He thought about his dream. It was somewhere outside those city walls that the man on the cross had died. And where the blood had dripped on Fescue's hand when he'd taken his splinter of wood. Reaching beneath his djellaba, he clutched the purse still around his neck; inside was Fescue's ring, with his mother's gold coin. Should he leave the ring here, throw it in the Pool perhaps? He had planned to give it to Mullein – but that depended on getting home with Bird made whole again.

He searched the sky looking for Quilla; apart from a flock of circling ravens, the sky was empty.

'No sign of Skyhook,' Lark muttered, tears in his green-grey eyes as he squinted up. 'Hope Tissy's safe.'

'Come on everyone,' Sandy said, 'the sooner we find the Pool, the sooner we'll know if Quilla has got there.'

Hitching their rucksacks higher on their shoulders, Lark whistling urgently to Mick cocking his leg against the trunk of a fig tree, they moved off.

Plodding down the steep dusty road to the valley floor then climbing again, when they reached the gate, they found it crowded with traders and their mule trains as well as herders with cattle, goats, and sheep, all waiting for permission from officials to enter the city. The Eilat Gate was not only approached by the King's Highway from the south, but by another road from the east, which Leif explained was the road from the far-off trading city of Damascus.

Disconcerted by the unexpected hustle and bustle, they stood beside the road at a distance, uncertain what to do next. At Leif's suggestion, he and Sandy went to make enquiries. Taking off their howlis to wipe their hot faces, Fin, Lark and Crow thankfully sank down to wait in the shade of a fig tree.

As he watched Lief and Sandy talking to one of the officials, Fin was startled by a tap on his shoulder. He looked round in surprise. A tall figure covered in a burqa accompanied by a Scav were lurking by some dusty bushes.

'Fin – it's me, Wings!' hissed a low voice from beneath the burqa.

Jumping to his feet, Fin gave shout of joy. 'WINGS! Is it really you?'

Unbelief on their faces, Lark and Crow got up and gaped open mouthed at the figure, whilst Mick, with a yelp, threw himself at Wings' chest.

'Keep your voices down, chaps!' Wings muttered fiercely, pushing Mick to the ground. 'Don't want to attract attention. Me and Carob here have been watching out for you all morning.' Wings indicated the Scav standing by his side. 'He and his family have been looking after us!'

'Wings! Tissy and Bird – are they safe?' cried Lark.

'Yep, they're with Dancer, being looked after by the Palmers – Carob's family.'

Carob stepped forward and bowed. 'Honoured I be to meet Delph friends of Missy Tissy and poor little Missy Bird – never in all my life have I seen so many Delphs afore!'

He looked Crow up and down and asked imperiously. 'An' what you doin' with this Scav? Not a Palmer for sure!' Then regarding Sparkie on Crow's shoulder, observed: 'You got mighty fine rat, young Scav – where you get it? Not like filthy Rusalem rats.'

'Sparkie Two an' West Africky Shaggy – 'ndangered speechies I pick up on my travels,' Crow said, trying to look nonchalant.

At that moment Sandy and Leif strode up, spotting the tall burqa covered figure leaning over them.

'What's going on here?' demanded Sandy.

'It's Wings, Sandy!'

Sandy gasped in surprise. 'What the …?' Grabbing Wings by his shoulders he gave him a relieved shake. 'Why are you dressed like that?'

Seams tearing, Wings impatiently struggled out of his disguise. 'I'm a wanted man, Sandy. Dancer and I were taken prisoner by the King's vizier chappie. Young Carob here and the Palmers rescued us!'

Sandy turned to Carob. 'So, you are a Palmer!'

'Yep, I'se son of Bougainvillea.'

Sandy fished out the disc Frangipani had given him. 'I was told by Frangipani to search out your people and to show you this. He said you will show us the way to the Pool of Siloam.'

He explained to Wings. 'Quilla flew on ahead to find the Pool and also escape Gressil who is chasing after him. We have had several encounters with Gressil and Mab on our journey. Gressil has infested several unfortunate victims; at present he is in the body of a young soldier – one of the King's special couriers – he is racing along the Highway in the soldier's fast chariot.'

'We've been following on borrowed horses – but the poor beasts became so exhausted we had to leave them behind and continue on foot!' Fin added.

'Mab's in a horrendous state, too!' put in Lark. 'She's changing back into a slug – slimy flesh popping out of her silken furred skin.'

Fin grimaced. 'At one stage she and Gressil managed to capture me. I was up close to her in their carriage – she stinks of rotting death. Crow very bravely rescued me!' He gave Crow's shoulder a squeeze. 'He jumped onto the back of the carriage as it hurtled along!'

'Yep – Sparkie chewed through ropes holding down the canopy!' Crow said proudly.

Whilst Wings listened to their talk, he was eyeing Leif. 'I know you from somewhere,' he remarked, looking thoughtful. 'Yes, by Jove – it's Leif Erikson! Lief, old boy, what on earth are you doing here?'

The two men shook each other's hand's warmly.

'Last time we met was at Rosie's – years ago!' laughed Lief. 'Is she still going?'

'Yep! Carlos – you remember old Carlos – cooks for her customers now.'

Lark interrupted impatiently. 'Wings, shouldn't we be getting a move on? I want to see Tissy for myself!'

'Yes chaps! Must get going – they'll be waiting for news.'

'Yep, talk later at the Palmer Den – with good food an' wine,' Carob said, hopping from one foot to another, getting more and more agitated. He had noticed they were beginning to draw stares from the officials at the gate. 'Also, one of my Palmer men – Fig – has gone to t'Pool to look out for eagle with jewel – must see if he's back with news!'

'Very well, let's get going,' urged Sandy, but a shout halted them.

'CAROB! CAROB!'

From the track outside the city wall leading to the garden and the Pool, Fig appeared running. 'Come—come quick,' he cried, gasping for breath, 't'eagle has arrived at Pool and is fightin' a demon—' Panting, he stopped to look uncertainly at the people with Carob.

'It's O.K. Fig, these be friends,' Carob said. 'Eagle fightin' with a demon, did you say?'

'Yep!' wailed Fig. 'Missy Tissy, Bird and Dancer in dreadful danger! Olly and Lill are fightin' too – with kitchen knives!'

'Where do we go? Show us the way!' cried Lark.

'We go the outside way – it quicker!' Carob pointed down the track from where Fig had come.

Carob and Fig impatiently waited as they cast aside their packs to drag off their djellabas. Then packs back on their shoulders, Crow and Fig leading the way, Mick yapping at their heels, they set off at a run.

Halfway down, Wings bringing up the rear supported by Leif, hobbled to a halt. 'Drat it – my foot's gone astray! Hang on a sec everyone!'

'Wait!' Sandy called to the others. 'Wings is having trouble with his foot.'

'How did you come to lose your foot?' Lief asked as Wings tightened the straps.

'Crashed in my dear old Skyhook,' Wings replied, testing his walking. 'Right! That'll do for now. Sorry chaps!'

Dashing on down to the garden they found the gate open, the gatekeeper's body lying across the entrance, his head lying someway off. Ptolemy's chariot stood nearby, the horse, still harnessed, dead between the shafts.

Sandy bent to study the ground around the chariot, finding pieces of tattered butterfly wing with gobbets of yellow pus trailing off through the gate.

'The wound in Mab's side is oozing badly!' he exclaimed. 'She must be deteriorating fast. Come, we will follow her trail.'

Stepping over the dead gatekeeper, a narrow valley lay below them. Filled with palm trees laden with sweet juicy bunches of dates, among them grew ancient olive trees, their gnarled and bent trunks spreading over the rich carpet of grasses and ferns.

'That is where the Pool be!' cried Carob gesturing up to the head of the valley where beneath the city wall could be glimpsed the white gleam of a waterfall cascading down the cliff to a plateau where tall cypress trees grew and from where they heard distant shrieks.

They paused to draw their weapons – Sandy his sword, Lark, his boning knife, Lief his axe, and Crow his small cutlass. Only Fin remained unarmed, the broken Dandrum sword buried deep in his pack. Leaving Wings trailing behind, they sped through the palm and olive trees to where a flight of steep steps cut into the rocky hillside led up to the plateau. Sandy leading the charge, leaping up steps two at a time, Mick at his heels, at the top, they all came to an abrupt halt, horrified at what they saw.

Half in and half out of the Pool was a giant squid. Bulging eyes crazily spinning, viscous beak-like mouth snapping greedily, its tubular body rippling fiery red and angry orange, it loomed over an elf-sized person on the walkway bravely stabbing with what looked a cook's long carving knife at its eight wildly waving tentacles. Farther along, Quilla, one wing drooping, circling lopsidedly, was diving at a man flailing at him with a sword, whilst another small person with a rucksack on his back was slashing at the man's legs using a sword far too long for him. Close by was the hideous figure of Mab. Swaying on slime oozing legs, she was screaming curses as she frenziedly tried to leap into the air on what remained of her tattered wings.

Leaving Crow clutching his cutlass and shaking in terror at the top of the steps, Sandy and Lief, Carob and Fig immediately rushed to the aid of the figure fighting the huge squid and joined in slashing at the tentacles with sword, axe, and knives. Meanwhile Lark, seeing Tissy slumped over Dancer's body, dashed to her, wailing 'Tissy! Tissy!'

Howling, Mick raced after him.

Fin ran to Quilla. 'BIRD!' he shouted, 'WE'RE HERE!'

He could just hear her faint voice calling. 'Fin, keep away! Quilla will deal with the man – go to my body! The monster's after my body!'

Frantically looking around, Fin spotted one of the squid's long tentacles sneaking furtively over the walkway towards two more small figures: a female Scav desperately trying to keep hold of another figure struggling wildly in her arms. To his horror he realised the small wizened person in the Scav's arms was Bird's body.

'Oh no, oh no,' he sobbed, starting to run. He was too late: the tip of the tentacle curled around the little figures and snatching them up, dragged them down into the depths of the Pool.

Carob yelled to the figure with the sword and the rucksack: 'CACTUS, YER TWIT, THROW T'ELIXIR!'

Dropping Dancer's stolen sword to the ground, Cactus froze. As if in slow motion, like a wooden puppet, jerkily his little arms reached behind into his rucksack for the cloth wrapped bottle. This was his moment: holding it gave him new strength. Drawing his arm back he hurled the bottle towards M'Benga's snapping beak. His aim was true: the spinning bottle flew through the air and disappeared inside. But Carob's triumph had taken him too near: with a screech of alarm, he toppled in after the bottle. M'Benga gave a shuddering gulp. Staring eyes blinking in bewilderment, tentacles corkscrewing around his body, he slowly sank beneath the surface. A moment later, he resurfaced, the beak opened, and with a gurgling belch, Cactus shot out and landed on the walkway covered in foul smelling squid phlegm. M'Benga's body, now mud coloured, rolled onto its side and sank once more into the depths.

A mighty voice thundered out. Everyone started.

A tall warrior stood before Ptolemy, the familiar midnight blue eyes blazing with the searing white of another universe, the shining blade of his fearsome sword shimmering in the sun's glare.

'GRESSIL! ATTEND TO ME! It is I, Lord Iskander come to revenge my brother, Fescue.' The sword flashed, Ptolemy's head, with its luxuriantly curling black hair, spun in the air, hung there for a second, then smashing with a bloody thud on the stone paving, bounced into the Pool. With a howl of despair Mab lunged forward and slipping in the blood, fell headlong after it. As she disappeared, a black shadow, seeping out of Ptolemy's headless neck, slid across the walkway, and slipping over the edge of the Pool, sunk in after her.

Blood dripping from his torn wing, Quilla fluttered weakly for a moment above the ring of bubbles where the two demons had disappeared then sank into the dark water, carrying the Cross and its gold chain with him.

Fin staggered to the Pool's edge moaning. 'Bird, oh Bird my love…' Sobbing brokenly, half falling, half throwing himself, he too toppled in. From the ferns came a shrill cry. Crow burst out of the foliage from where he had gone to hide. 'Fin! I come too!' With a leap and a bound, he and Sparkie dived in.

At that moment Wings appeared at the top of the steps leaning on an olive tree branch as a makeshift crutch.

'I say chaps, what's all the shouting?' he called hopping awkwardly forward, his loose metal foot clattering on the paving. 'Where's …?' He looked around bewildered, taking in the group gazing down into the Pool: Sandy head bowed in weariness, his sword still softly gleaming, the unearthly light gone from his eyes. Carob, Cactus, Olly, and Fig were gathered around him.

Then Wings saw Lark slumped on the ground, Tissy in his arms, and Mick with his front paws on Lark's arm, gazing anxiously into Tissy's pale face. Next to Lark, Leif was leaning over Dancer lying motionless in a spreading pool of blue blood.

'Dancer, old girl!' he cried, hobbling over and collapsing beside her.

# 17
# DEMONS AND ANGELS

Sinking through the murky water, Fin wondered if he was drowning. Overcome by a strange peace he faded once more into his dream.

*He was in a garden of olive trees. In the distance on the round hill outside the city walls, the cross stood empty – the body had gone. Nearby was the dark opening to a tomb. Before it, smiling at Fin, stood a shining Being.*
*'Fin why are you seeking the living among the dead?' the Being asked.*

Fin tried to cry out: 'Mossy!' but water filled his mouth. The dream was broken. Someone touched his shoulder. He spun around. It was Bird! Her body perfect, her wheat-gold hair swirling about her lovely, familiar face. She was holding hands with the little Scav who had been dragged into the Pool with her. Bird pushed Fin and the Scav towards the surface where Sandy's strong arms hauled them out onto the walkway.

Gasping for breath, Fin turned back and wildly searched the dark depths: where was Bird? He saw a flash of pale skin and her smiling face appeared. Grabbing the Pool's edge, she leapt nimbly up onto the walkway beside him.

'I'm whole again! Oh Fin, I'm all back together!' she laughed.

Sobbing with joy, Fin pulled her into his arms.

After a few moments she pushed him away and chuckling with delight, ran her hands up and down her lovely Delphin body.

Then looking back into the Pool, she asked: 'Where's Quilla?' Then sadly, she remembered: 'Dear Quilla – he said he would have to die for me.'

Sandy shook off his jerkin and draped it over her shoulders. 'Come lass, cover yourself! What would your Grammer Magette say, Skinny Dipping in broad daylight?'

'Oh, blow that,' giggled Bird. Then, realising she had an awed audience of Lill and the other Palmers, wrapped the jerkin around her.

'Little Missy Bird, you be so beautiful,' they chorused.

'I SAY CHAPS, NEED YOUR HELP HERE! Dancer's bleeding dreadfully!' Wings shouted.

Everyone turned.

'Oh, no! Dancer!' Bird cried. 'And Tissy! What's wrong with Tissy?'

She and the others ran to where Lark cradled Tissy and Wings and Leif were kneeling beside Dancer's motionless form. Lief had his hand pressed on her wound, blue Skwid blood seeping through his fingers.

They turned to Lark with Tissy lying unmoving in his arms, Mick crouched miserably by his side. 'I think Tissy has only fainted,' Lark said, 'I can't find any injury. It's Dancer we're more worried about – Sandy, can you stop her bleeding?'

Stripping off his shirt to make into a bundle, Sandy pushed Leif's hand away and pressed the cloth to Dancer's wound. Supporting her head with his other hand, he called to her: 'Dancer! Dancer!'

Dancer opened her eyes, and looking up at him, murmured. 'Is that you, Boss? Glad you're here: I'm sorry, I think I might be done for—'

'Hush my dear, save your strength!' Sandy said softly.

Hearing a joyful yap from Mick, they turned back to Tissy. To their relief they saw her lavender-green eyes were open and sparkling. For a long moment she stared, puzzled into Lark's sun-browned face streaked with tears. Then puzzlement turned to joy.

'Lark is it really you?' she whispered.

'Yes, Tissy, it's me, your very own Lark!' breathed Lark. 'Whatever are you doing, fainting?' he chided helping her to her feet.

Fin and Bird looking on holding hands, laughed in relief. For a long moment, the four Delphins gazed lovingly at each other, then hearing gasps and ragged applause, they turned to find a circle of Scavs looking at them in awe.

'So many Delphs!' Lill, Carob, Fig, Olly, and Cactus sighed in chorus.

'But what about dear Missy Dancer!' whimpered Cactus, stumbling to where she lay. Wings was wiping her face with his long scarf.

'Mr Wings look at her Skwid skin – it all chalky grey!' he moaned, peering into her face. 'Missy Dancer, I get your sword for you, so you can fight!'

Dancer slowly turned her head and peered at him. Giving a weak throaty chuckle, she whispered: 'Hello Cactus. I put you in charge of it now—'

Her voice broke into convulsive coughing.

Suddenly shrieks of fear from Lill and Olly startled them. Everyone looked to where they were pointing. Watching in wonder they saw the Pool's surface was heaving and bubbling as if boiling. Hissing and fizzing, a column of shining gold rose out of the water. Growing taller and taller, the column took on the shape of a huge golden eagle. Its beak like polished amber, its delicate silvery gold feathers shimmered brightly in the sun. The majestic head turned about until its brilliant diamond eyes focused on Bird. With slow heavy wing beats, it rose into the air and flew towards her.

'SKEEW! SKEEW!' With a triumphant cry its gleaming talons gently brushed the top of Bird's head. Then it soared into the sky becoming a pinpoint of bright light against a bank of black thunder clouds.

'Goodbye, dear Quilla,' Bird called, holding up her arms in farewell. 'Goodbye!'

Just as Quilla finally disappeared, Carob gave a cry: 'LOOK!'

Now, in the centre of the Pool a violently spinning whirlpool was forming. Suddenly from its heart a spout of water shot into the air. They stared in astonishment: on the top sat the scrawny figure of Crow, a look of utter ecstasy on his wizened face. Against his thin chest lay the Chi Rho, on his shoulder sat Sparkie II, shaggy fur spiky with water, his rat's paws clutching the heavy gold chain hanging loosely around Crow's neck. As abruptly as it had risen the waterspout collapsed. As if a plug had been pulled, all water drained from the Pool. Too shocked to speak, the watchers stared down at the muddy grey bulk of M'Benga's body lying on the bottom. There was no sign of Crow. In the far wall they could see the sluice gate standing wide open. They fell back in alarm as out of the dark boomed a cackle of hysterical laughter.

'GRESSIL, MY LOVE – LOOK, MY WOUND IS HEALED!' echoed Mab's voice.

'YES, MY SWEET QUEEN! AND YOUR BODY IS ONCE MORE BEAUTIFUL!'

The triumphant cries were followed by a sinister rumbling gurgle: out through the sluice roared a huge tide of brown water. Crashing against the sides of the Pool, in moments it reached the walkway and flooded over.

'This is Gressil's work! Gressil and Mab still live!' Sandy cried lifting Dancer into his arms and clambering to his feet. 'Hurry, we must get away before we drown!'

Water sloshing around their feet, Lief again supporting Wings, they headed for the steps down to the garden.

Holding Lark's hand, as Tissy ran, she looked back to see the Palmers heading for the steps to the Gihon Tunnel.

Carob called to her: 'Goodbye Missy Tissy! Us Palmers must go back to Palmer Den. But you get to safety out through Garden – quick, quick!'

'Goodbye! Goodbye!' Tissy cried as Lark pulled her after him, Mick close at his heel.

As they ran down the steps the rushing water raced after them. Dragged beneath the surface, the deep tide swept them on into the garden.

Sandy, the tallest and strongest, was the first to emerge. Gasping for air he stood waist deep, just managing to keep his balance as he held Dancer above the flood. Looking around urgently, he saw the tall figures of Wings and Leif rise coughing and spluttering nearby. Then Mick's little head bobbed up, followed by Fin, Bird, Lark and Tissy.

'Make for the high ground by the garden wall!' he shouted as, swept along, all they could do was to snatch ineffectually at passing vegetation.

Half wading half, half swimming, Leif and Wings reached high ground first, followed by Sandy, struggling with the weight of Dancer's body. They scrambled up to the gate where a great ancient olive tree stood sentinel, its branches spreading out over the waters rushing beneath. Wings collapsed by the wall and Sandy laid Dancer next to him. Looking back they saw the Delphins, heads bobbing above the water, struggling to swim towards them.

'Leif, if we climb this olive tree,' Sandy called above the roar, 'we could reach out to them from its branches!'

Shinning up the tree's gnarled trunk they clambered along the lower, stronger branches spreading over the water. Leaning down just as the small Delphins were swept beneath him, Sandy grabbed Lark whose hand still firmly clasped Tissy's. At the same moment Lief caught Fin and Bird, also holding hands. Hauled to safety, one by one they all edged back along the branches and down the trunk. Collapsing next to Wings and Dancer, from below them came an indignant yelp as Mick, covered in mud, struggled up the bank. With his strong doggy sense of survival, he'd made his own way to safety.

For some moments they sat resting against the wall, too dazed and exhausted to speak. Then Sandy turned to look anxiously into Dancer's motionless grey face. Taking her limp hand, Wings began chafing it. 'Do you reckon the old girl's nearly done for?' he muttered to Sandy.

About to reply, Sandy's voice was drowned by a rolling crash of thunder that shook the ground beneath them. As if some mighty hand had thrown a switch in the sky, the world was plunged into darkness. Blinding flashes of lightning zigzagged across the black sky. From the Pool on the plateau above grew two shimmering clouds. The clouds formed two gigantic figures clothed in robes of swirling pink, green, and blue like some aurora borealis. In their cloudy hair diadems of fork lightning flashed and crackled. Their faces made of soft pink cumulus, although achingly beautiful, the gaze from their huge eyes was as icily cruel as the blue star Rigel.

'AT LAST! AT LAST!' boomed Gressil's voice above the roar of the thunder. 'I AM LORD OF THE UNIVERSE! BOW DOWN ALL YOU WORMS ON EARTH AND BEHOLD MY ALMIGHTY POWER!'

His cry of triumph struck the little group as a physical force, beating them back against the trembling stone wall.

Menacingly the figure of Mab leaned forward and searched out Fin.

'FIN DANDRUM, AM I NOT BEAUTIFUL?' she cackled, reaching down a shimmering cloud hand to pull him up. 'COME, I SHALL GIVE YOU A KISS!'

Even as Fin and Bird clung together, Mab's words died on the air, drowned by a voice the Delphins knew so well but amplified a hundredfold: 'BEGONE, FOUL BEINGS! YOU HAVE TORMENTED THIS WORLD ENOUGH! ZAGZAGEL COMMANDS!'

From out of the West howled a mighty wind, blasting through the shining cloud figures tearing them into a million fragments, their screams of terror dying away as the last remnants of lightning flickered out and the sun shone once more. In the blue sky a few scraps of black cloud drifted away into the horizon. Gressil and Mab were no more.

For a while, no one moved.

Then Lark spoke. 'Newt's knickers – as little Bee would say – that was awesome! Fin, have you got your sketch pad handy? You'll need to get a picture down before you forget what they looked like.'

Fin delved inside his sodden pack. Bringing out a mush of parchment, he held it up ruefully.

'Never mind,' laughed Bird, giving him a hug. 'When we get a chance, I'll help you remember!'

Looking down into the garden, Lark exclaimed. 'Well, that's amazing, the flood has already gone, and all the trees are still standing!'

The water had drained away through an opening in the far wall, sinking into the dry land beyond, leaving rivulets trickling between the battered olive and palm trees, sunshine making drops of water sparkle on the bunches of dates.

'Yes, gone – like Gressil's powers,' breathed Sandy thankfully.

'Oh look!' cried Tissy, pointing to the wall above the waterfall where she spotted a flash of gold. 'The Palmers are up there. They're waving their Palm of Tamar Banner!'

She went to kneel by Dancer, cradled in Sandy's arms. 'Did you hear, Dancer – Carob and the Palmers are all safe!'

Dancer's eyes flickered but didn't open. Tissy noticed the blue blood stain on Sandy's sodden shirt bound to her wound was still spreading. Miserably, she returned to sit against the wall's sun-warmed stones. Everyone was too shocked to talk or make plans.

They had been resting perhaps an hour when from the West came the Thump! Thump! Thump! of powerful engines. Over the brow of a rugged hill two large flying machines rumbled into view. Their rotor blades a blur above them, the machines could have been mistaken for flying reptiles, their bulbous fuselages painted silvery blue to resemble Skwid scales, they had round Skwid eyes painted on either side of their fat noses.

Struggling to his feet Wings clung to the wall behind him and grinned in excitement as he remembered the two giant machines standing in the hangar at Thessaloniki.

'Gator's copters!' he gasped. 'Wave, chaps, wave! Show them we're here.'

Overcome with elation, forgetting his loose metal foot, he tried to run into the open and would have fallen heavily if Leif hadn't hastily helped him sit back down. Leaving him with Sandy and Dancer, Leif and the Delphins ran out to jump up and down waving frantically. Mick adding to the excitement by running around in circles barking.

As the two copters grew closer, they saw the Skwid pilots, Commander Gator and Commander Croc, give a 'thumbs up' from behind the windscreens. Moments later the machines were hovering overhead, the downdraught from their rotors snatching at tree branches. Finding a big enough area of flat open ground nearby they landed side by side.

Landing gear settled, their rotors spinning slowly to a stop, the door of the nearest copter slid open and a tall Skwid climbed down.

'It's Kassabel!' Fin and Lark chorused joyfully.

'Hello lads!' she called, her face rippling with rainbow colours.

Fin turned to Bird. 'Do you remember her, Bird? Queen Rami who saved me from having my head chopped off in the square at Tunis?'

'Come on Tissy,' Lark said, taking Tissy's hand, 'Kassabel is no ordinary Skwid – you must meet her!'

About to set out to run and greet her, the four of them skidded to a halt in disbelief as from the other copter another figure climbed out, his lovely face full of laughter as he strode to meet them.

Fin fell into his open arms, his face pressed to the inky blue robe, the honey-sweet smell sending his mind spinning back to the sunlit fells above Watersmeet.

'Well, Delphins! Here we are, together again!' Mossy chuckled, releasing Fin, and surveying the circle of eager Delphin faces. 'My word Bird, how beautiful you are! Your Ma and Pa will wonder if you are really their dear daughter! And you Thetis and Lark – warriors both! Mrs Annunder will be so proud of you. I have a feeling you will have a few stories to tell her!' He picked up Mick who was leaping up at him yapping. 'I see Mick has not lost his fizz!' he laughed, giving him a gentle shake.

'And what about Iskander, Zagzagel? Does he not deserve admiration?' asked a low voice from behind them. Everyone turned to see Sandy smiling wryly.

Mossy gave a rich laugh. 'Greetings, Lord Iskander! From what I've learned from Kassabel, you are now a skilled sailor!'

Wings called to Mossy. 'I say Zaggy! Dancer's in a desperate state! Can you do something?'

He was with Commander Gator and Commander Croc by the wall where Kassabel sat with Dancer in her arms. Leif was crouched by her too, his hand pressed on the shirt binding her wound.

Hurrying over, they saw Dancer's eyes were open, faint colours rippling across her face as she gazed up at Kassabel.

Weakly lifting her hand, she touched Kassabel's face. 'My lady Kassabel is it truly you?' she whispered in wonder.

'Yes, it's me,' smiled Kassabel.

Dancer gave a long quivering sigh. Her eyes dimmed, her head fell back, and she went still. Tissy looked up at Mossy. 'Is she—?'

Mossy nodded. 'Yes, Dancer has gone to join her ancestors in the Universe of White Light.'

Gently taking Dancer's hand and squeezing it, Bird gave a tremulous sigh. 'She was the first Skwid I knew and the best!' She turned to Sandy. 'She loved you, you know. That's why she became a Trekker.'

His midnight blue eyes clouded by tears, Sandy knelt to kiss Dancer on the forehead.

Kassabel got to her feet, Dancer in her arms. 'Come my children! Your Orca is at Paphos waiting to take you home.'

They boarded the copters. In Gator's copter went Tissy and Lark, Mick tucked in his jerkin, Kassabel sitting by Dancer's body which lay under a blanket. To Wings' great delight Gator invited him to sit by him in the cockpit, where Leif helped him to settle in his seat. Fin, Bird and Sandy flew with Mossy in Croc's machine.

It was nearing sunset as they circled above Paphos. Gazing down, they saw Orca and Aurora moored together at anchor in the bay. Conscious of the waiting audience below, Croc and Gator brought down the copters to a perfect landing then taxied to a halt by the hangars where Turtle and Anemone stood with a group of Skwid mechanics and copter pilots.

As the passengers climbed down from the copters, Commander Croc ordered four of the mechanics to fetch a stretcher for Dancer's body, which, accompanied by Mossy and Kassabel, they then carried across the fields to lie before Kassabel's image in the worshipping place.

Back at the hangars, the chatter of introductions and reunions was stilled as, to the great surprise of Sandy, the Delphins and Wings, a tall figure, his long hair the colour of moonlight, eyes as silvery as sun on ice, walked up the beach accompanied by Captain Kamal and Zahhak, from where they had left Orca and Aurora's jolly boats.

'Mullein!' the Delphins chorused joyfully, Mick adding to their voices by barking shrilly from Lark's jerkin.

'Brother, how wonderful!' gasped Sandy, taking the Gaiakin in a long hug before pushing him away to look hungrily into his beautiful face. 'Why are you here? Did you come with Zagzagel?'

446

'Yes, I am on my way to the Fouta plateau. There I intend to work, healing and mending the old Garden, making it ready for some of our brothers and sisters to return there.'

Hearing talk of the old Garden of Florain, Fin remembered Fescue and that it was there that he made the Chi Rho.

Fishing out his purse, he cried: 'You can take Fescue's ring there!' He laid the ruby ring reverently in Mullein's open hand.

'I rescued it when Fescue died…' His voice trailed away as he remembered Fescue's fading body on the floor in Gressil's cave above the compound in Contagion; it seemed a lifetime ago.

After they had introduced Mullein and the others to Leif, Captain Kamal, observing their damp mud-stained clothes, said: 'Come now to Orca where we have put out fresh clothes!'

'Yes, go and make yourselves smart,' laughed Anemone, 'You are invited to a feast in the refectory! I will warn the cooks to delay the serving up. They have prepared a special meal to suit both Delphins and humans, so fear not – no chopped raw liver and parsley which dear Dancer so loved!'

At the mention of Dancer, Tissy turned to Sandy.

'Instead of feasting, shouldn't we have gone with Mossy and Kassabel to keep vigil by Dancer's body?'

Sandy squeezed her shoulder. 'No, Dancer would have been mortified. Ceremonial feasting is very important to Skwids.'

So, taking leave of their Skwid friends, they went down to the beach and crowding into the two jolly boats, Kamal and Zahhak rowed them out to Orca.

Once aboard, Sandy and Lark proudly showed Lief, Wings and Tissy around, whilst Bird, keen to get out of Sandy's jerkin, she and Fin went into the cabin to see what clothing Kamal and Zahhak had provided.

Rummaging among the piles of sailors' clothes on the bunks, they came upon a selection of Delphin-sized Skwid children's trousers and jackets made of soft kid leather and decorated with studs. Bird chose a pink set, and Fin went for brown. By this time the others had joined them. Tissy and Lark chose matching sets of Skwid trousers and jackets dyed dark green whilst Sandy, Leif and Wings went for sailor's clothes. All dressed, Kamal and Zahhak rowed them back to shore where they found Mossy and Kassabel had returned from laying out Dancer's body.

Anemone guided them through the underground tunnels of the Skwid living quarters to the great chamber with its arched windows overlooking the bay. To their embarrassment, they entered to the applause of what seemed to be the whole Skwid community seated at long tables on which a feast was spread.

About to sit with Mossy the four Delphins noticed, sitting a little apart at another table, a person Delphin-like in appearance. Gesturing to them to join him, they turned to Mossy for reassurance who, smiling softly, waved them towards the stranger. As he rose to greet them, revealing a white robe and a shadowy glimpse of silvery wings floating at his back, Fin's mind rushed back to the wall painting in the jungle shrine shown to them by their Banto guides Blenny and Guppy. Unable to speak he clutched Lark's arm.

Then he burst out: 'Is it – is it – Phul? Lark, Bird, Tissy, its Phul!'

The person opened his arms in welcome. 'Yes, my children! It is I. Come sit! We are holding up the feasting.' He gestured to empty spaces on the bench either side of him. Awestruck, they took their places. Hunger was forgotten as Phul talked to them, and they hardly noticed the food laid before them.

It was not until the meal was ended, and Commander Croc, on behalf of the Skwid community, stood to make a speech of welcome, then Sandy rising to thank them, that they realised how desperately tired they were. Kassabel, seeing the Delphins nodding over their cups of wine, came to their table. With a kindly parting blessing from Phul, they followed her as she briskly rousted Kamal and Zahhak where they sat, loudly enjoying jokes with a group of mechanics, and commanded them to row everyone back to the ships. A tent on the deck made ready, the Delphins tumbled in and fell instantly asleep, Mick settling happily on Lark's folded jerkin, whilst Mossy, Sandy, Wings and Leif settled on the four bunks in the cabin. Kassabel, Phul and Mullein slept on Aurora.

The following morning piloted again by Croc and Gator in the large copters, they flew with Dancer's body to Kassabel's shrine in the Troodos Mountains. After an ancient ritual led by two Skwid Elders they buried her in the cemetery, Sandy speaking at the graveside of Dancer's courage and kindness. On the return flight, their thoughts full of memories, they were glad the noise of the copters' engines made talk almost impossible. Back at Paphos, they spent the rest of the day on Orca quietly preparing for the journey home.

It was whilst looking through his ship's carpenter's toolbox that Lark found a little canvas bag among the few remaining brass screws and stainless-steel nuts. Loosening the drawstring, he found it full of faded bits and pieces of plustic left behind by Crow. Showing it to the others, everyone fell silent, their thoughts full of sad memories of the strange little Scav and the astonishing end to his life.

Remembering Crow's only consolations in his miserable life had been Sparkie and his 'Aunty Krite', Fin promised himself that when he took Bird to meet his mother on Cuthbert's Island, as he was determined to do, he would ask her to remember Crow when she prayed to her dear Lord.

That evening their spirits were lifted when they joined everyone on Aurora for a meal prepared by the cook, Mokele.

Back on Orca, at mid-night whilst Mossy, Sandy, Wings and Leif slept, Fin and Bird, Lark and Tissy crept out of their deck tent. Slipping overboard into Aphrodite's Bay, they went Skinny Dipping in the moonlight.

The next day, down on the shore with the Skwid community and Aurora's crew looking on, in an atmosphere of great joy, Mossy and Phul concelebrated the Delphin couples' marriages. In the late afternoon, escaping from an open-air party that looked set to continue well into the night, they all boarded Orca and Aurora, and watched by the cheering Skwids on the beach, raised anchors and set sail into the West.

A week later, Orca and Aurora sailed through the Straits of Gibraltar and dropped anchor in the bay of Tangier. Moored close together for the last time, they held a farewell banquet on Aurora, Mokele doing them proud with a superb lobster tagine.

But the evening was tinged with sadness; tomorrow would be their final parting. The Delphins, Sandy, Wings and Leif were to sail north in Orca, whilst Mossy, Phul and Mullein headed south with Kassabel on Aurora, bound for the Gambia river and Barraconda to visit Kenji, Suki, and the Sanyo family. From there Mullein would travel on to the old Garden of Florain, his mission, with the help of Banto villagers, to restore the gardens ready for Gaiakins to return.

Before they parted, Fin, Lark, Tissy and Bird implored Mossy to promise he would return one day to Brightdale. Solemnly he agreed, then to her delight asked Tissy if she would look after the Bookshop and keep the upstairs room ready for his home coming.

Next day, the southerly wind pushing Orca homeward, Leif was at the helm, running his eyes lovingly over the billowing sails above his head. At the farewell banquet, to his amazement and joy, Sandy had proposed that when they reached Peel harbour, Leif should become Orca's new owner.

He still couldn't believe his luck. Remembering the old barge, Goose and the day he took on board the motley collection of passengers – a battered looking Northern warrior, a couple of Delphins, and a Scav – the three of them with their pets, a dog, a fat rat, even an eagle, he smiled to himself. He was once more a true seafarer! And he had found his friend Wings! He'd promised to stay with Wings on the Isle of Mann for a while, to see him building his new flying machine.

On a starry night two weeks later, Orca was at anchor in a sheltered bay off the island of Ynys Mon. Tomorrow would see them reach the Isle of Mann. Whilst his friends slept, Sandy's tall figure stood in the prow. Gazing north, holding Betony's pendant, he was whispering in an alien language.

Mick, standing sentinel beside Sandy, glanced up at him for a moment before, nose twitching, he returned to sniffing the night air: he smelled Home … Home rats … Home rabbits …

In the courtyard of Dandrum Den, Betony and Nutmeg sat drinking chamomile tea, gazing up at the star filled sky. They had left Kelp and Alaria for a while in charge of the last few blind Scavs, refugees from Contagion, lying sick in the Great Hall. Kelp and Alaria were glad of the distraction: last night their father Roach, Brightdale's first victim of Gressil's Sneaksouls, had been sent to join his ancestors, his body burnt on a funeral pyre up at Kirion. Brewdy and Ramora, their mother and grandmother, weren't with them but had taken to their beds again.

'What a beautiful night,' smiled Betony. 'Nutmeg, I have a feeling, now that the evil that was Contagion is so more, this summer will be the best for many years.'

Nutmeg nodded distractedly. In the glow of light from the horn covered windows of the Great Hall she'd spotted a rat slinking down the steps to the kitchen.

'Heck, another one!' she grumbled, 'Lark's Mick is desperately needed!'

Suddenly Betony sat up straight as if listening, her large eyes pools of stars as she stared hard into the south.

'Have you heard something, Betony? The sound of an engine?' Nutmeg asked, full of hope, having come to know well her companion's Gaiakin powers.

'No, there is no need for a flying machine – Iskander is bringing them home overland from the sea – all your dear ones, safe and well!'

Nutmeg gave a long and happy sigh. 'That's good! Just in time for harvest – and Fin to take his rightful place as Dandrum Head.'

# EPILOGUE

The year is 3583 CE. In the city of Jerusalem, it has not rained for fifty years. The tiled domes of a palace gleam in the hot sun, its ruined walls half-buried in the dusty soil.

Beneath the city in a dark dried-up tunnel lies a small skeleton, no more than a bundle of bones. On the breastbone rests a richly jewelled cross, held about the neck by a gold chain; the cross has been there so long that the gold has eaten into the bleached bone.

Now, though they must always dig deeper and deeper wells, the inhabitants do not abandon the city, to search for water elsewhere, for they are guarding the skeleton, awaiting the day when an angel will claim the cross and in exchange bring rain.

In the end, an old man walked out of the desert, his skin ebony brown, his tight-curled hair grey as lichen on the trees of an ancient wood. Though he had sweat on his brow and his feet were caked in dust, they knew him to be the angel, for he had appeared from out of the wilderness where no earthly being could live.

In procession they led him down the steps to the tunnel, and silently watched him lift the heavy chain from around the skeleton's neck and prise the cross from where the gold had eaten into the bone. When he had hidden the cross deep in a pocket of his inky blue robes, the old man gathered up the bones and turned to the watchers.

'Take these bones to your burial ground,' he commanded, 'and when they are buried, you will have rain.'

Before returning to the desert the old man rested in the shade of a courtyard in the ruined city. Bringing him food and water the people begged him: 'Sir, tell us the story of the jewelled cross and of the small skeleton that wore it!'

Reluctantly, gathering his robes about his long legs, he settled once more and began his story: *'It all started with a crucifixion—'*

Excitement rippled through his listeners. Wrapping threadbare cloaks tighter around their thin shoulders, they sat down to listen.

When he had finished, without another word he stood and walked away, his tall figure melting into the shimmering heat.

Gazing up at the cruelly blue cloudless sky, the people became full of anger that they had been fooled, and that the man was only a thief who had stolen their treasure. Then, the wiser among them, remembering what the man had instructed, they took the bundle of bones to the burial ground, and buried them in a favoured spot beneath the dry branches of an ancient olive tree, placing at the grave's head the engraved wooden plaque the man had produced from within his robes.

It read: CROW. *One time bearer of the Chi Rho and who died wearing it.*

Even as they hammered the post into the mound, dark clouds filled the cruel blue sky. All around them tiny explosions of water drummed on the dusty ground, and the air filled with a strange smell. A forgotten smell: that of fresh rain on parched soil, and the people danced for joy.

Printed in Great Britain
by Amazon